THE
ALCHEMYST

THE GRAPHIC NOVEL

Also by Michael Scott

The Secrets of the Immortal Nicholas Flamel Series

The Alchemyst

The Magician

The Sorceress

The Necromancer

The Warlock

The Enchantress

The Secrets of the Immortal Nicholas Flamel: The Lost Stories Collection

Magic and Myth: Ireland's Fairy Tales

Legends and Lore: Ireland's Folk Tales

Saint Patrick: An Irish Tale

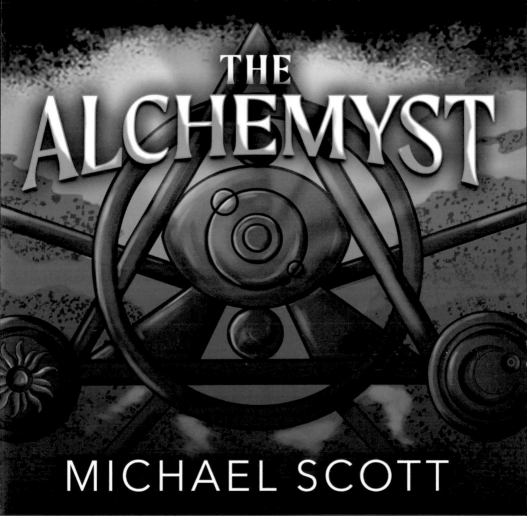

THE SECRETS OF THE IMMORTAL
NICHOLAS FLAMEL

THE GRAPHIC NOVEL

THE
ALCHEMYST

MICHAEL SCOTT

ADAPTED BY **NICOLE ANDELFINGER**
ILLUSTRATED BY **CHRIS CHALIK**

DELACORTE PRESS

This is a work of fiction.
All incidents and dialogue, and all characters with the exception of some well-known historical and public figures, are products of the author's imagination and are not to be construed as real. Where real-life historical or public figures appear, the situations, incidents, and dialogues concerning those persons are fictional and are not intended to depict actual events or to change the fictional nature of the work. In all other respects, any resemblance to persons living or dead is entirely coincidental.

 Published in the United States by Delacorte Press, an imprint of Random House Children's Books, a division of Penguin Random House LLC, New York.

Delacorte Press is a registered trademark and the colophon is a trademark of Penguin Random House LLC.

Visit us on the Web! GetUnderlined.com

Educators and librarians, for a variety of teaching tools, visit us at RHTeachersLibrarians.com

Library of Congress Cataloging-in-Publication Data
is available upon request.

ISBN 978-0-593-30467-9 (hardcover) — ISBN 978-0-593-30468-6 (paperback)
ISBN 978-0-593-30470-9 (ebook)

Interior design, word balloons, and typesetting by Bob Bianchini

MANUFACTURED IN CHINA

10 9 8 7 6 5 4 3 2 1

First Edition

For Claudette, of course

PROLOGUE

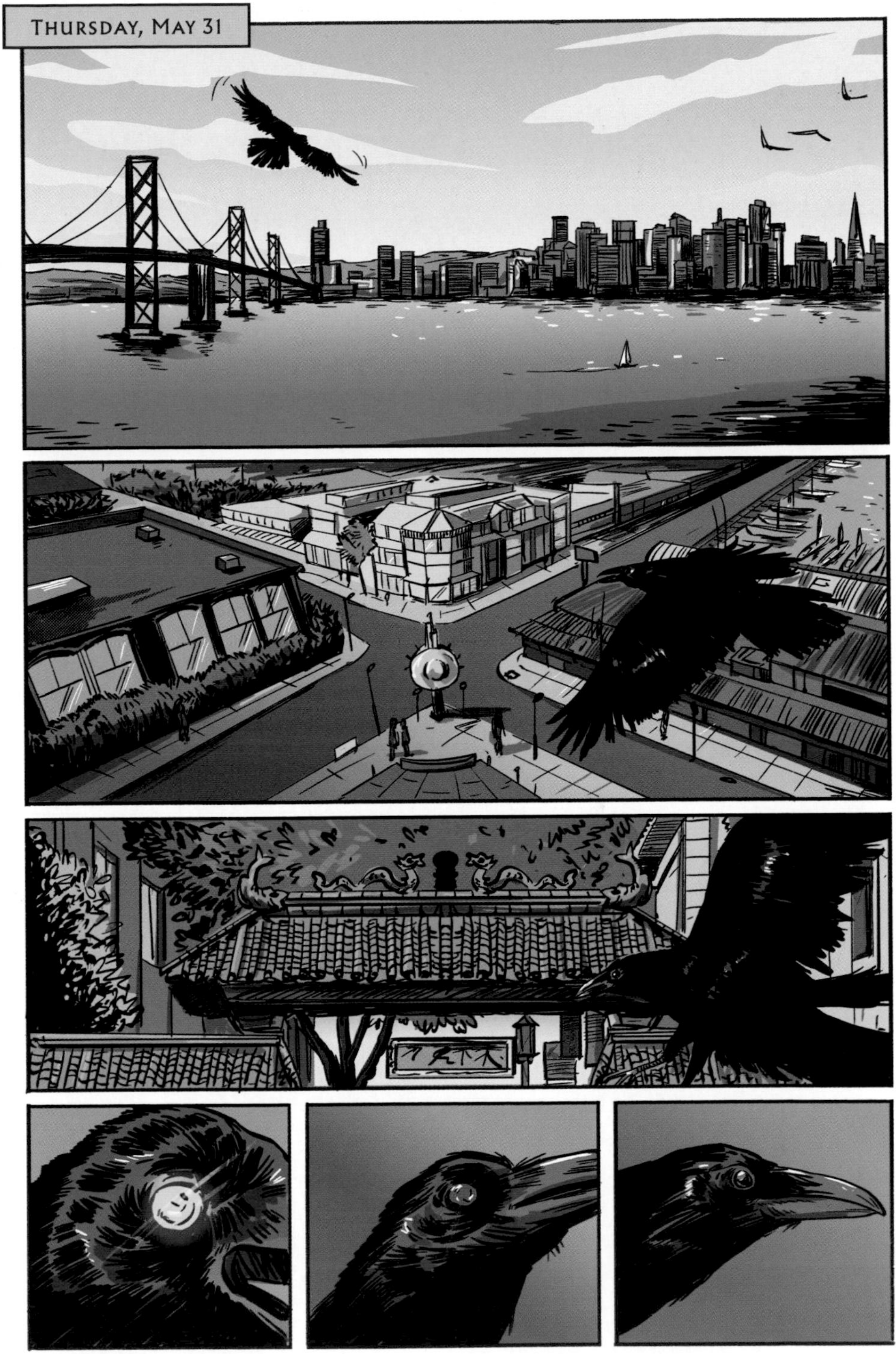
THURSDAY, MAY 31

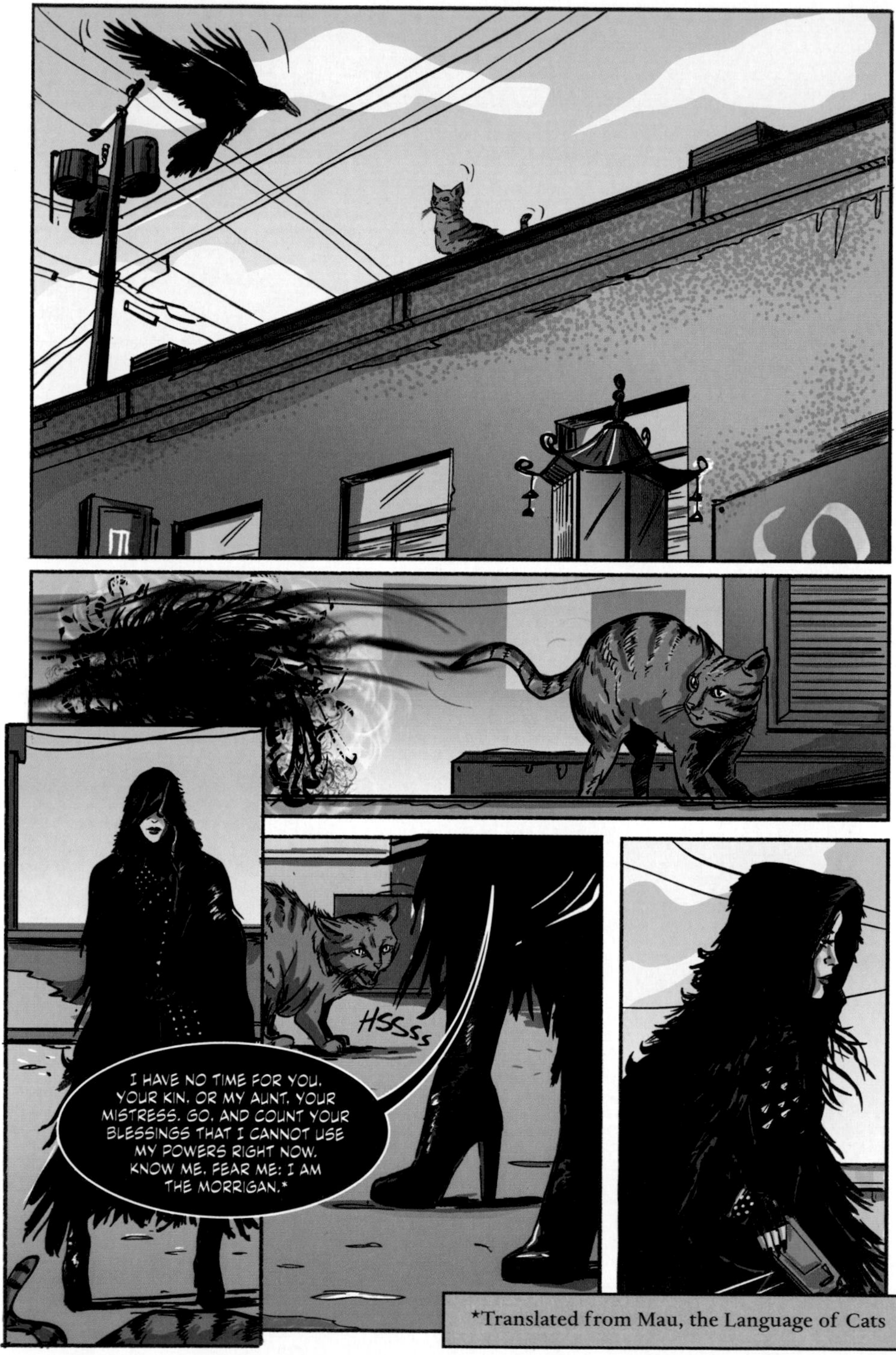
HSSSs
I HAVE NO TIME FOR YOU. YOUR KIN. OR MY AUNT. YOUR MISTRESS. GO. AND COUNT YOUR BLESSINGS THAT I CANNOT USE MY POWERS RIGHT NOW. KNOW ME. FEAR ME: I AM THE MORRIGAN.*
*Translated from Mau, the Language of Cats

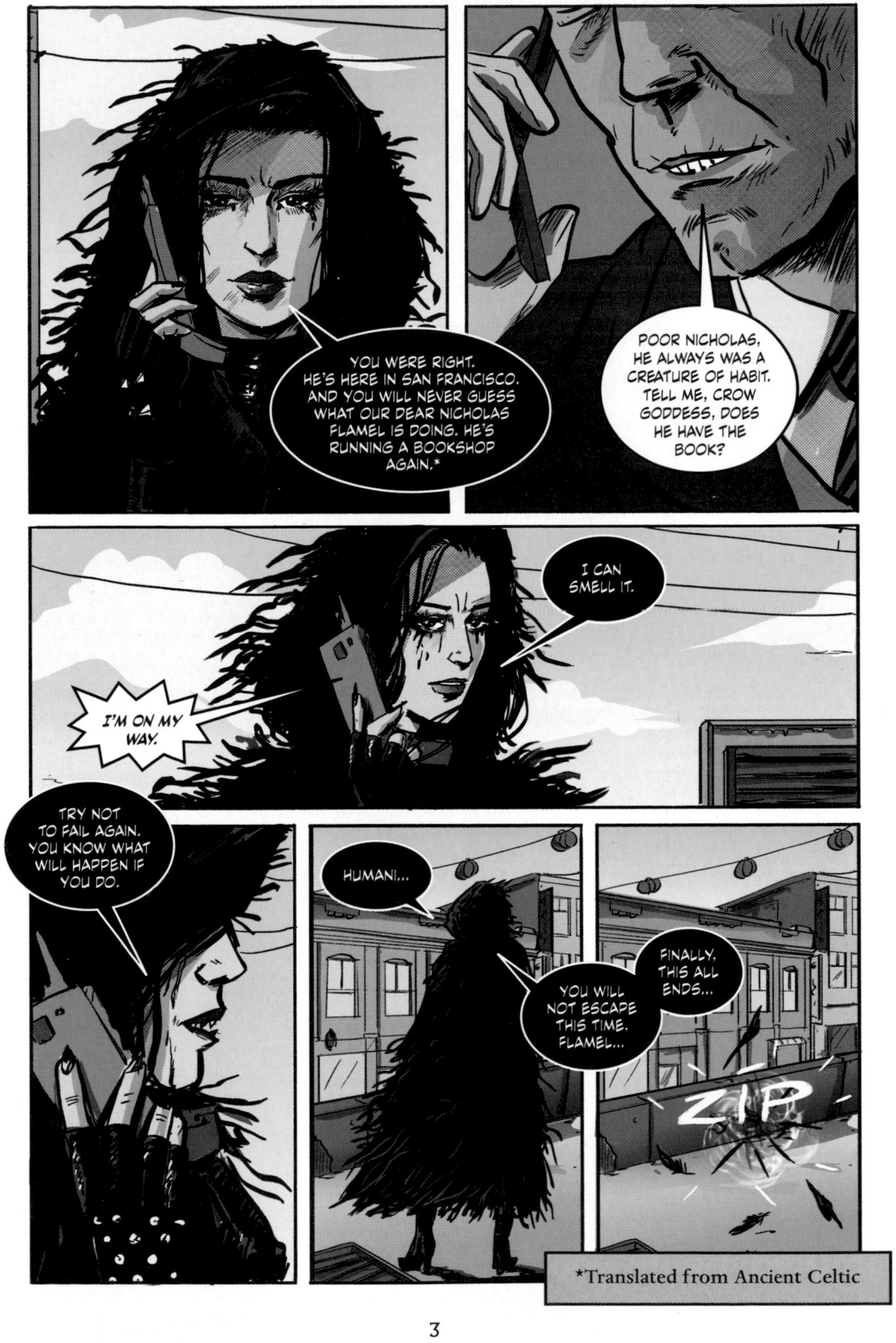
YOU WERE RIGHT. HE'S HERE IN SAN FRANCISCO. AND YOU WILL NEVER GUESS WHAT OUR DEAR NICHOLAS FLAMEL IS DOING. HE'S RUNNING A BOOKSHOP AGAIN.*
POOR NICHOLAS, HE ALWAYS WAS A CREATURE OF HABIT. TELL ME, CROW GODDESS, DOES HE HAVE THE BOOK?
I CAN SMELL IT.
I'M ON MY WAY.
TRY NOT TO FAIL AGAIN. YOU KNOW WHAT WILL HAPPEN IF YOU DO.
HUMANI...
YOU WILL NOT ESCAPE THIS TIME, FLAMEL...
FINALLY, THIS ALL ENDS...
ZIP

*Translated from Ancient Celtic

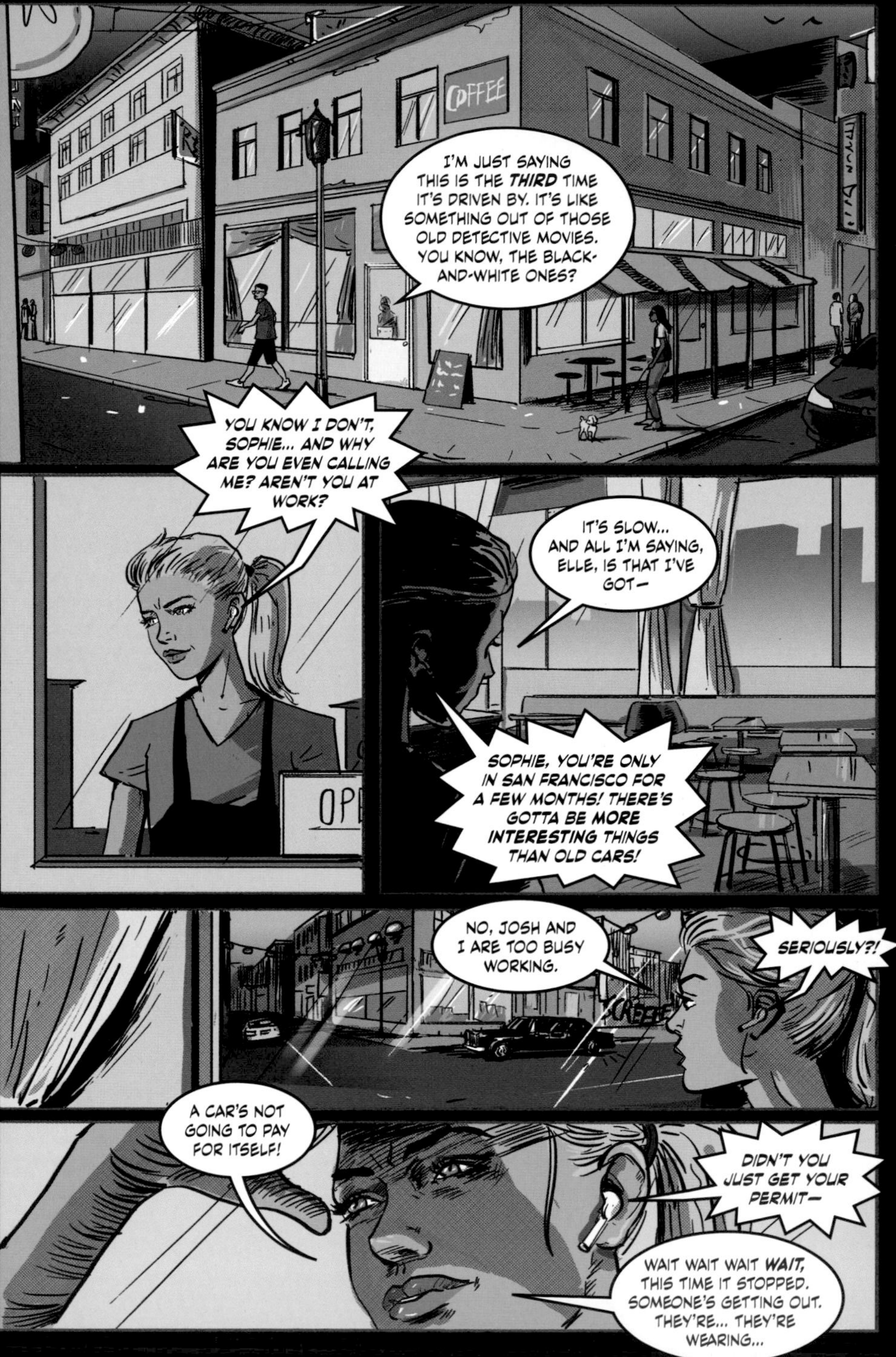
COFFEE
I'M JUST SAYING THIS IS THE ***THIRD*** TIME IT'S DRIVEN BY. IT'S LIKE SOMETHING OUT OF THOSE OLD DETECTIVE MOVIES. YOU KNOW, THE BLACK-AND-WHITE ONES?
YOU KNOW I DON'T, SOPHIE... AND WHY ARE YOU EVEN CALLING ME? AREN'T YOU AT WORK?
IT'S SLOW... AND ALL I'M SAYING, ELLE, IS THAT I'VE GOT—
SOPHIE, YOU'RE ONLY IN SAN FRANCISCO FOR A FEW MONTHS! THERE'S GOTTA BE **MORE INTERESTING** THINGS THAN OLD CARS!
NO, JOSH AND I ARE TOO BUSY WORKING.
SERIOUSLY?!
SCREEEE
A CAR'S NOT GOING TO PAY FOR ITSELF!
DIDN'T YOU JUST GET YOUR PERMIT—
WAIT WAIT WAIT ***WAIT,*** THIS TIME IT STOPPED. SOMEONE'S GETTING OUT. THEY'RE... THEY'RE WEARING...

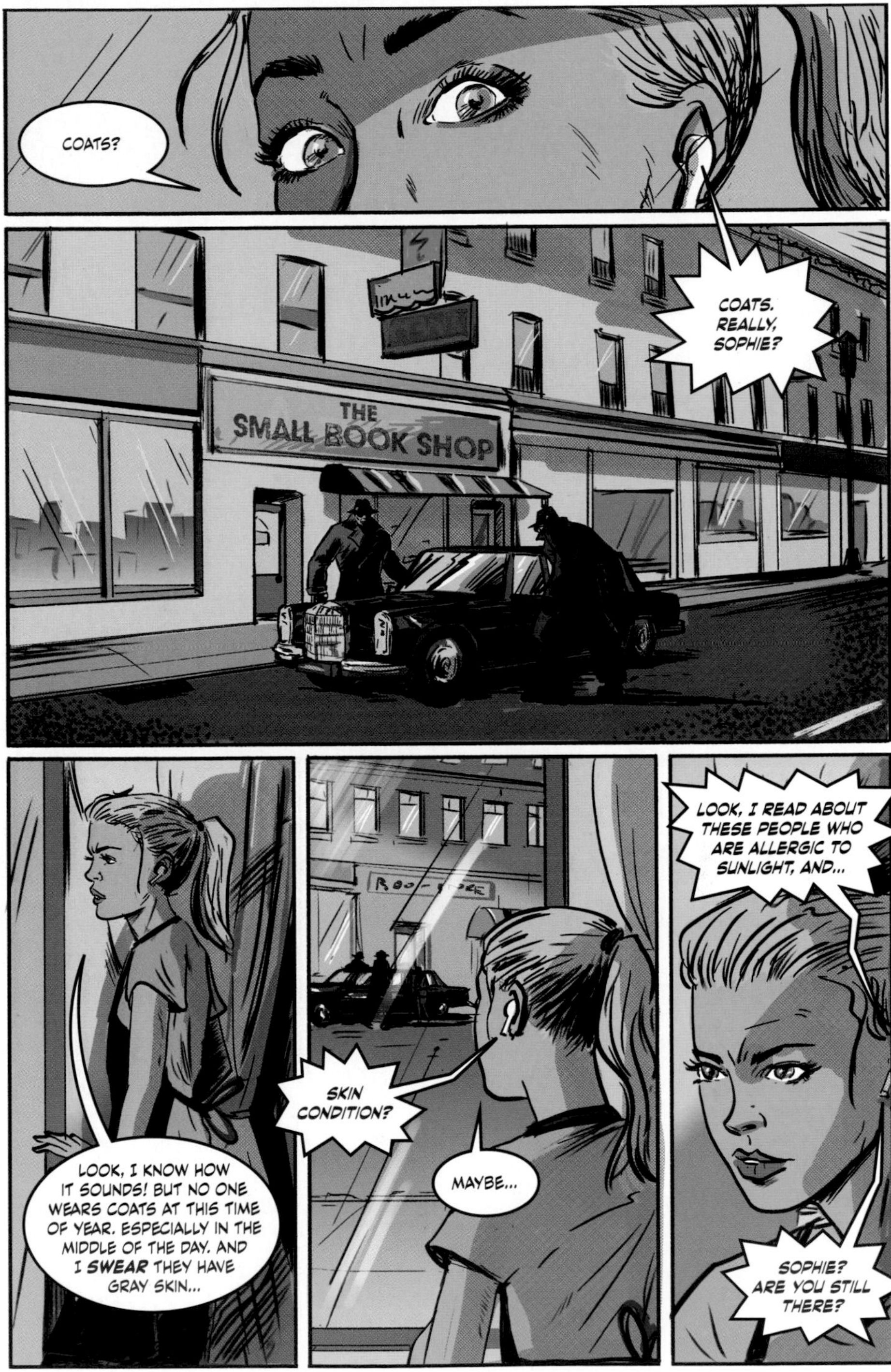
COATS?
COATS. REALLY, SOPHIE?
THE SMALL BOOK SHOP
LOOK, I KNOW HOW IT SOUNDS! BUT NO ONE WEARS COATS AT THIS TIME OF YEAR. ESPECIALLY IN THE MIDDLE OF THE DAY. AND I **SWEAR** THEY HAVE GRAY SKIN...
SKIN CONDITION?
MAYBE...
LOOK, I READ ABOUT THESE PEOPLE WHO ARE ALLERGIC TO SUNLIGHT, AND...
SOPHIE? ARE YOU STILL THERE?

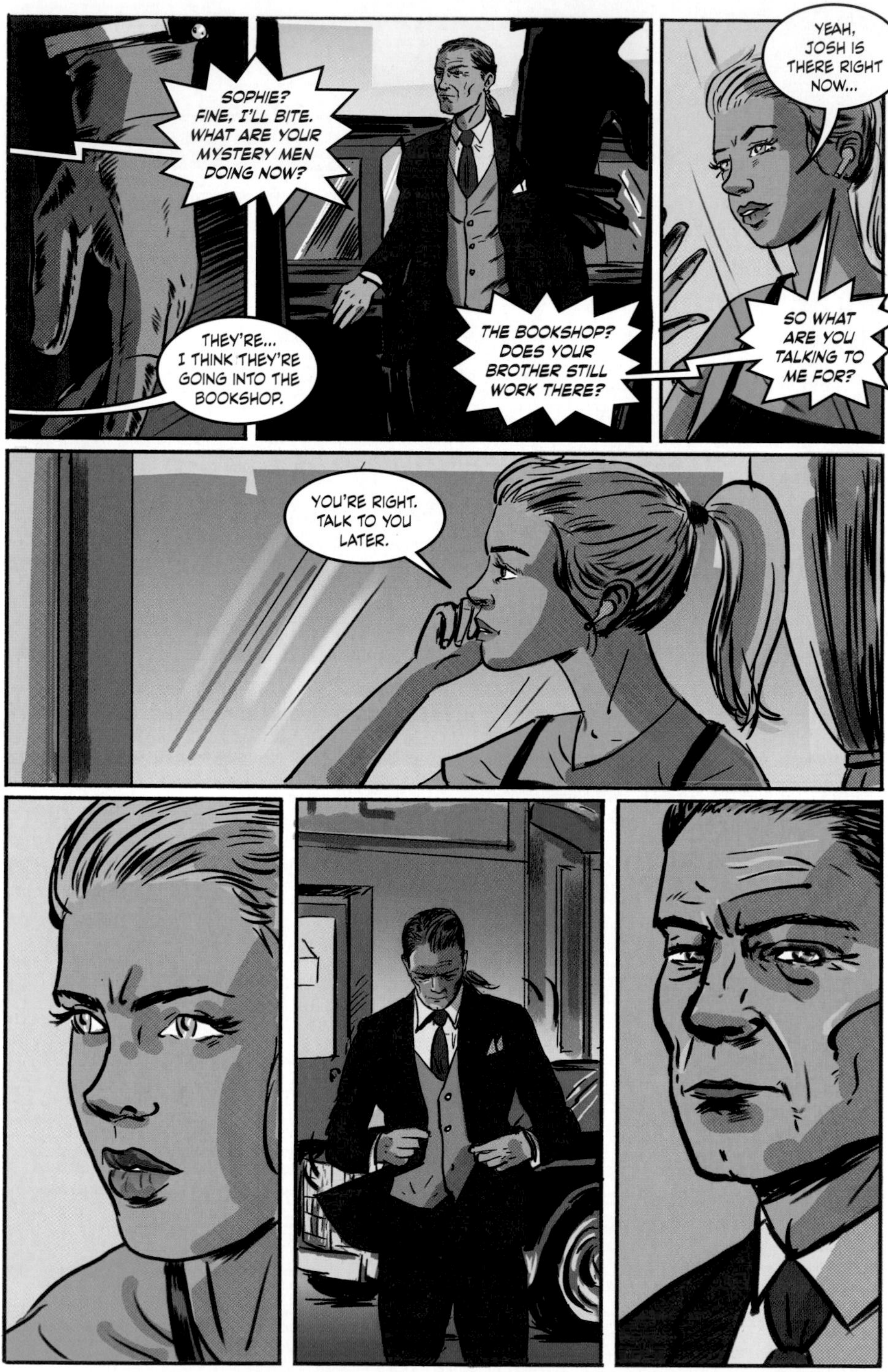
SOPHIE? FINE, I'LL BITE. WHAT ARE YOUR MYSTERY MEN DOING NOW?
THEY'RE... I THINK THEY'RE GOING INTO THE BOOKSHOP.
THE BOOKSHOP? DOES YOUR BROTHER STILL WORK THERE?
YEAH, JOSH IS THERE RIGHT NOW...
SO WHAT ARE YOU TALKING TO ME FOR?
YOU'RE RIGHT. TALK TO YOU LATER.

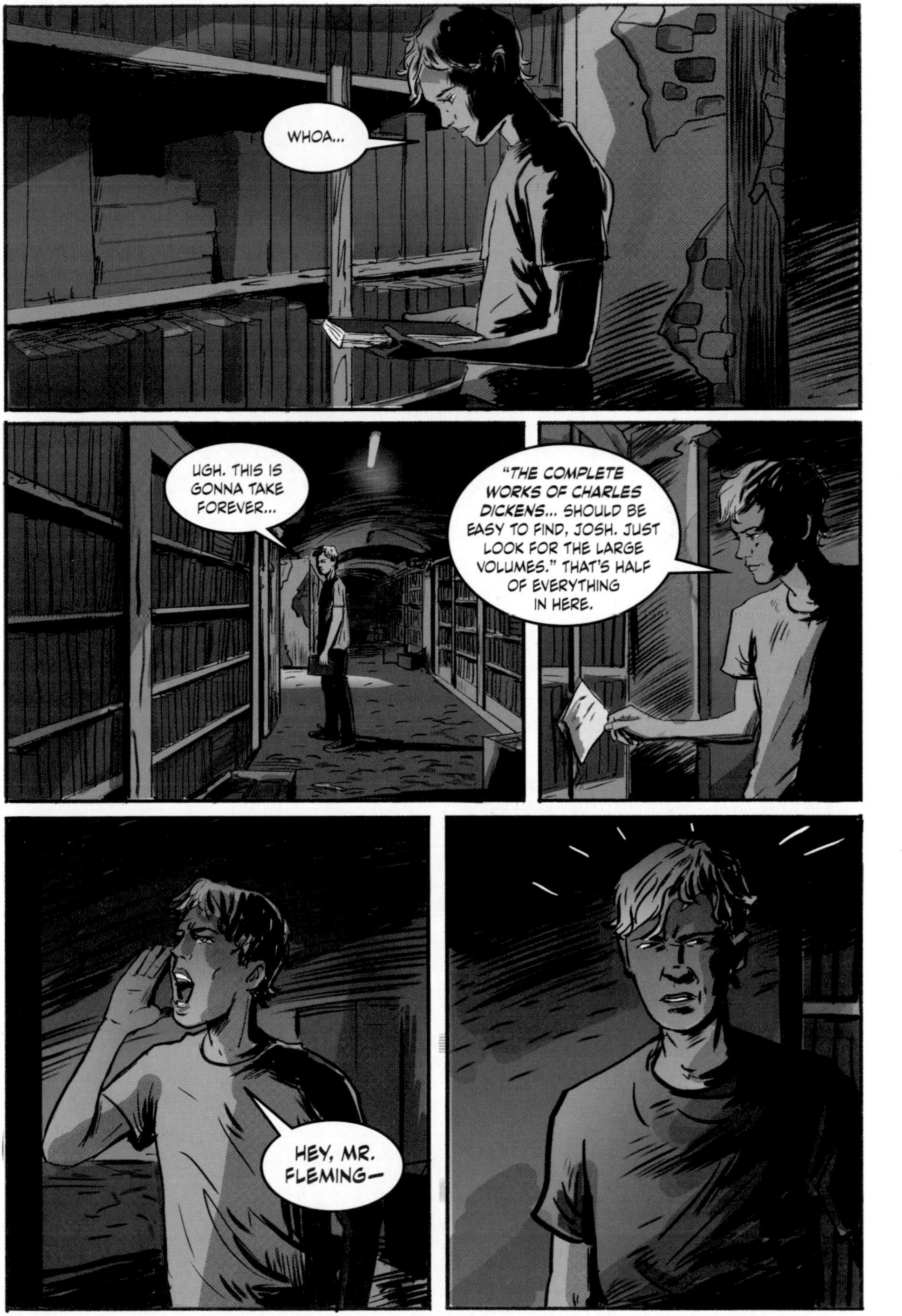
WHOA...
UGH. THIS IS GONNA TAKE FOREVER...
"THE COMPLETE WORKS OF CHARLES DICKENS... SHOULD BE EASY TO FIND, JOSH. JUST LOOK FOR THE LARGE VOLUMES." THAT'S HALF OF EVERYTHING IN HERE.
HEY, MR. FLEMING—

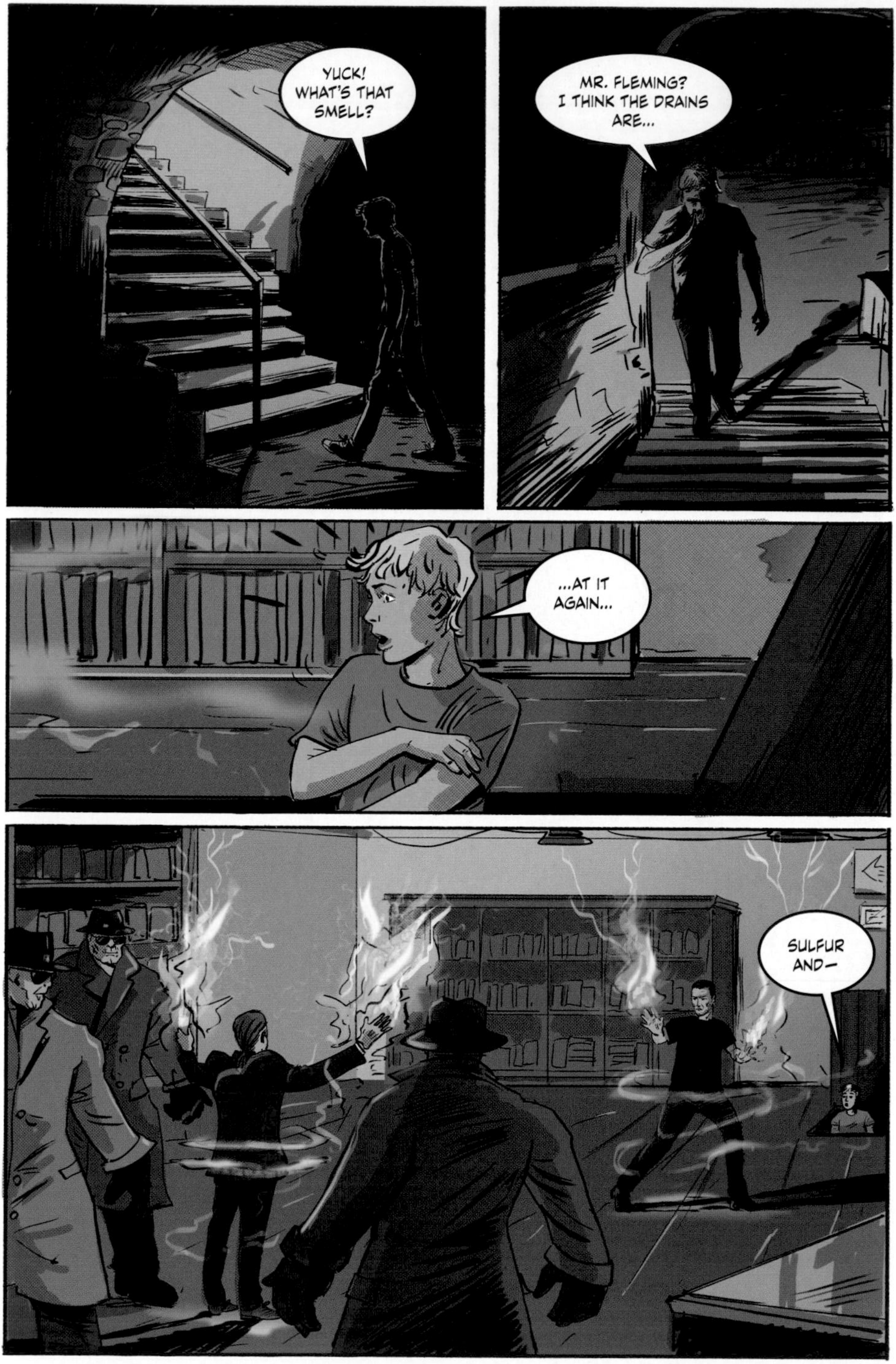
YUCK! WHAT'S THAT SMELL?
MR. FLEMING? I THINK THE DRAINS ARE...
...AT IT AGAIN...
SULFUR AND—

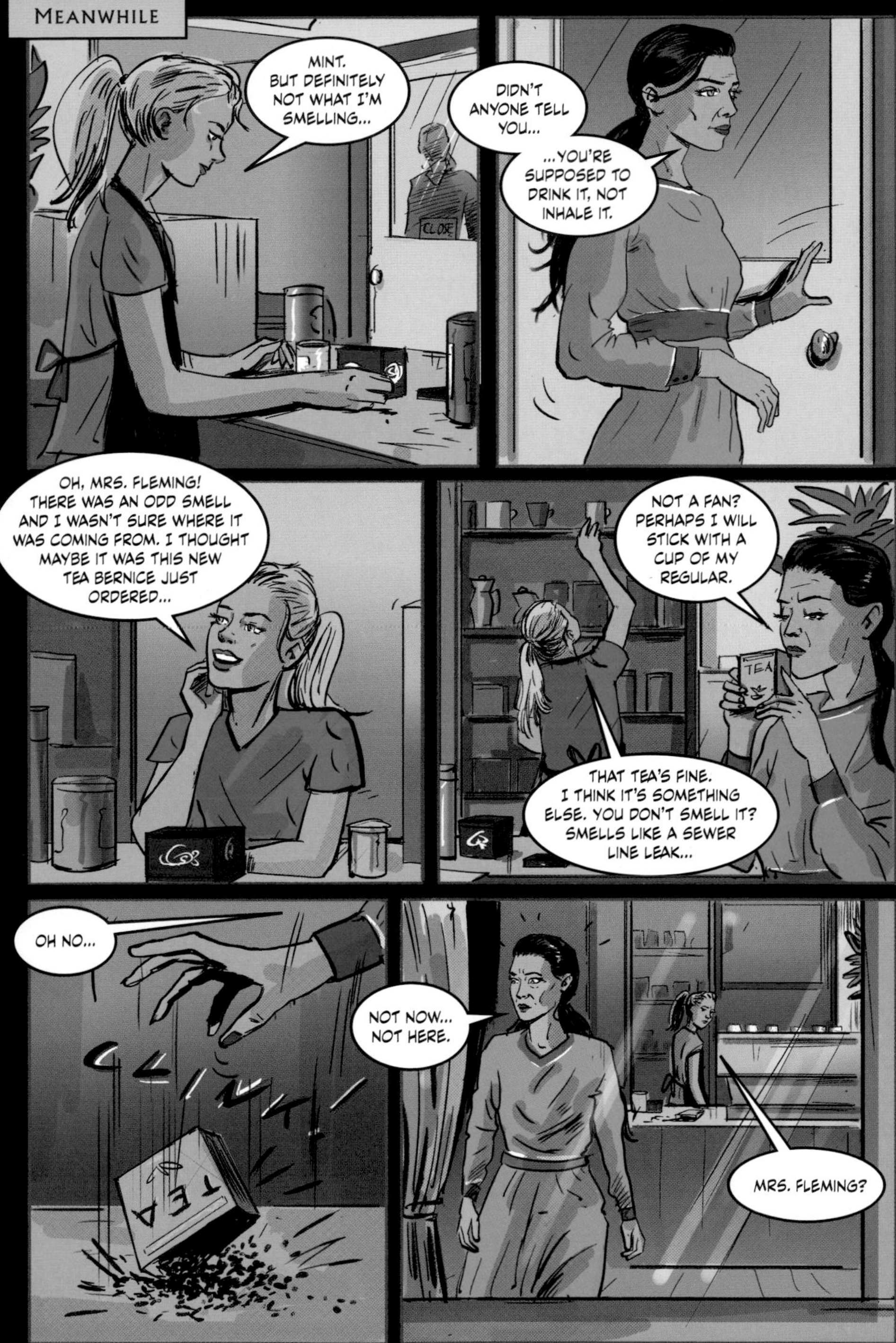
MEANWHILE
MINT. BUT DEFINITELY NOT WHAT I'M SMELLING...
CLOSE
DIDN'T ANYONE TELL YOU...
...YOU'RE SUPPOSED TO DRINK IT, NOT INHALE IT.
OH, MRS. FLEMING! THERE WAS AN ODD SMELL AND I WASN'T SURE WHERE IT WAS COMING FROM. I THOUGHT MAYBE IT WAS THIS NEW TEA BERNICE JUST ORDERED...
NOT A FAN? PERHAPS I WILL STICK WITH A CUP OF MY REGULAR.
TEA
THAT TEA'S FINE. I THINK IT'S SOMETHING ELSE. YOU DON'T SMELL IT? SMELLS LIKE A SEWER LINE LEAK...
OH NO...
CLINK!
TEA
NOT NOW... NOT HERE.
MRS. FLEMING?

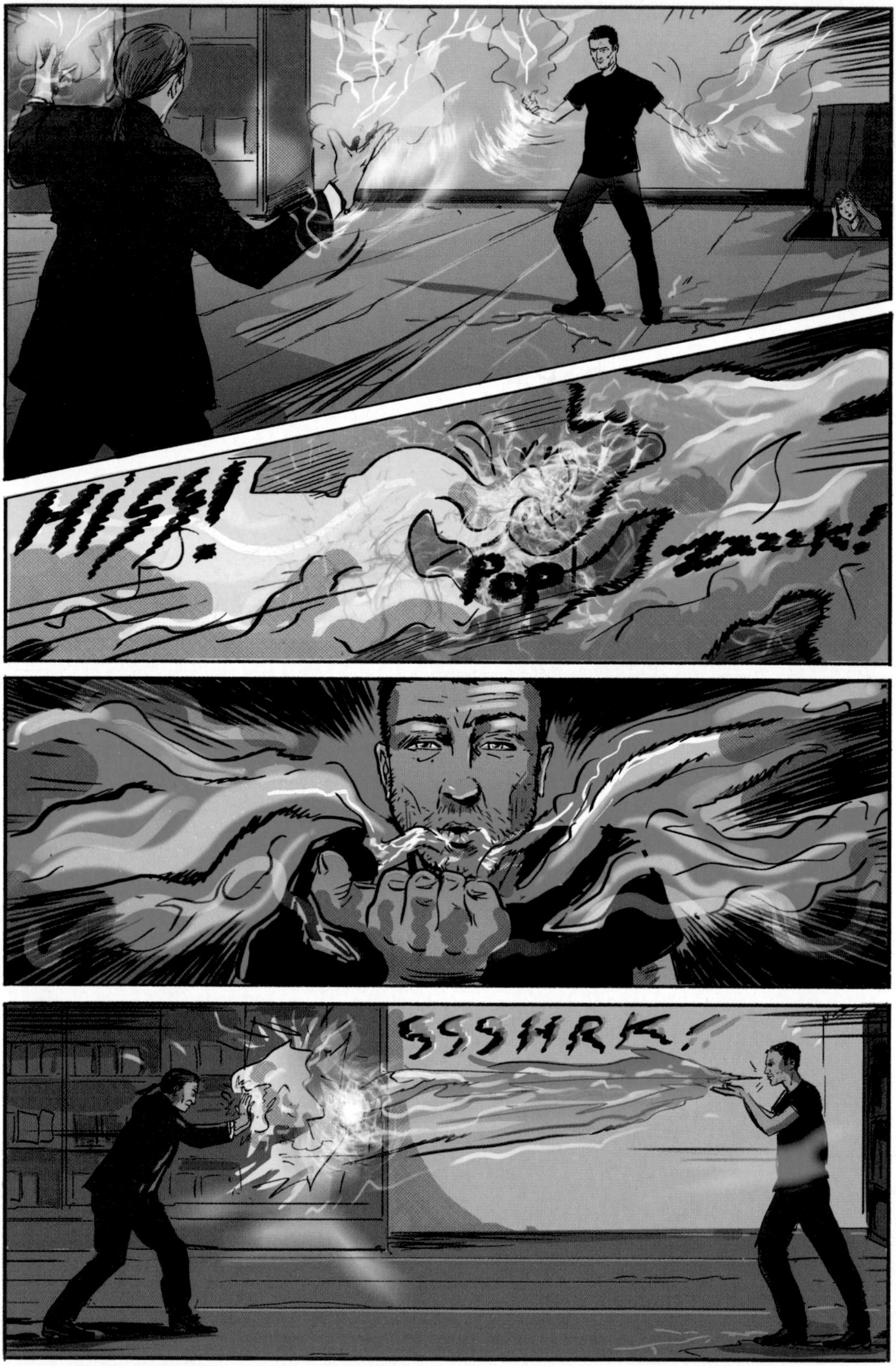
HISS!
POP!
ZZZZK!
SSSHRK!

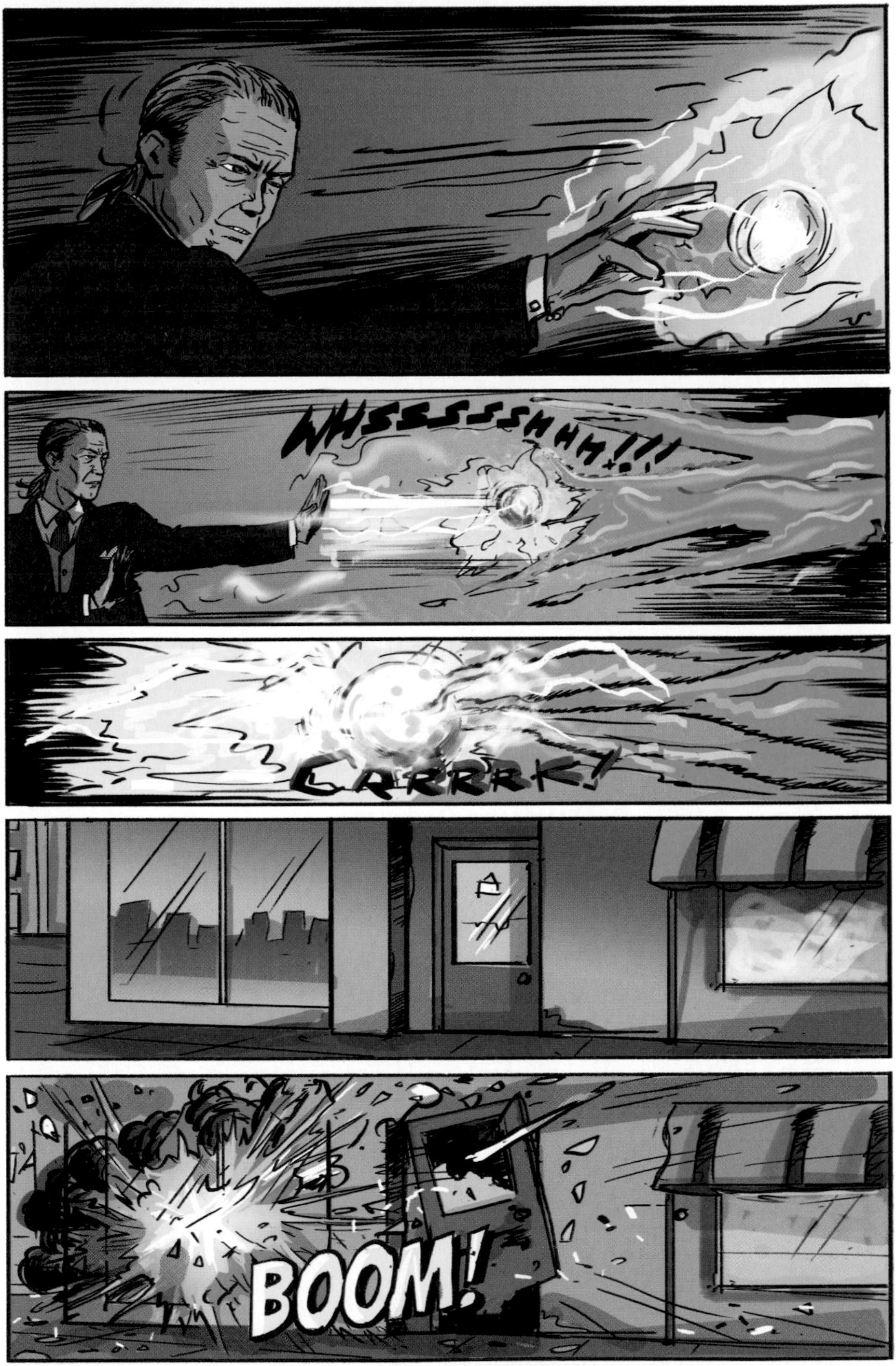
WHSSSSSHHM!!!
GRRRRK!
BOOM!

WAIT!!!

BUT JOSH!

JOSH?

WHAT WAS—

STAY DOWN. HE'S BROUGHT GOLEMS WITH HIM.

WHOOSH!

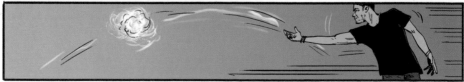

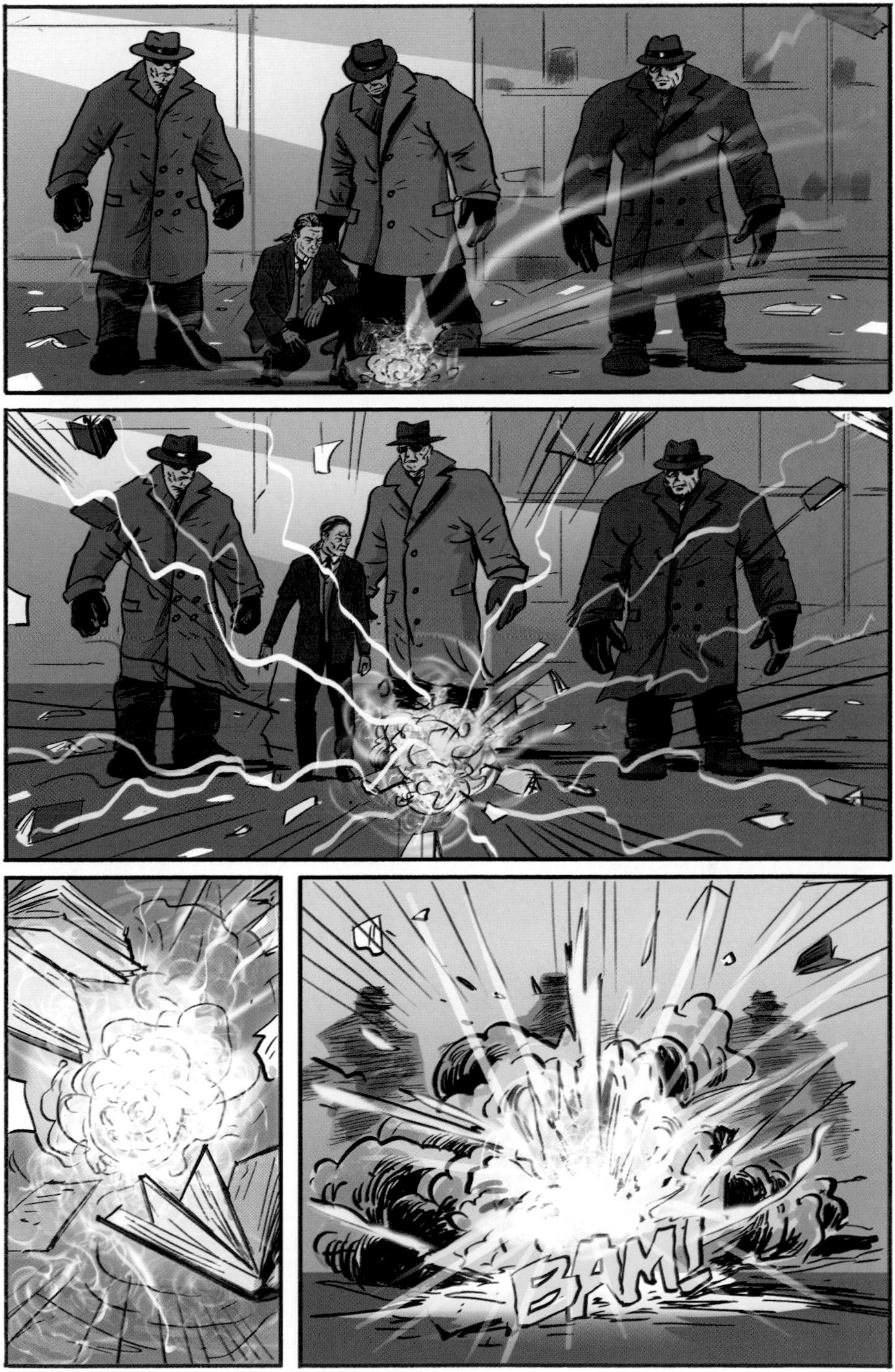
BAM!

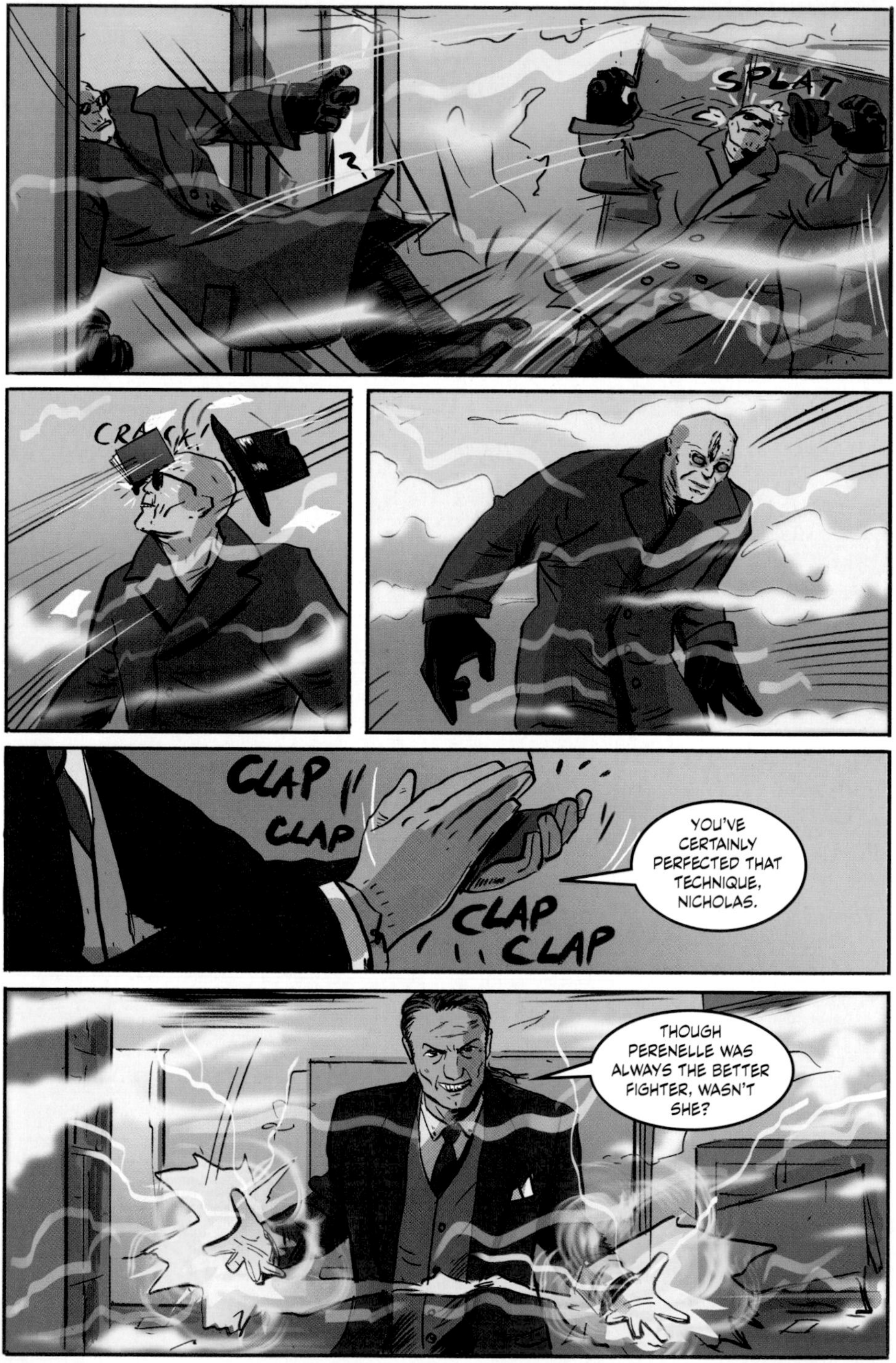
SPLAT
CRACK!
CLAP
CLAP
CLAP
CLAP
YOU'VE CERTAINLY PERFECTED THAT TECHNIQUE, NICHOLAS.
THOUGH PERENELLE WAS ALWAYS THE BETTER FIGHTER, WASN'T SHE?

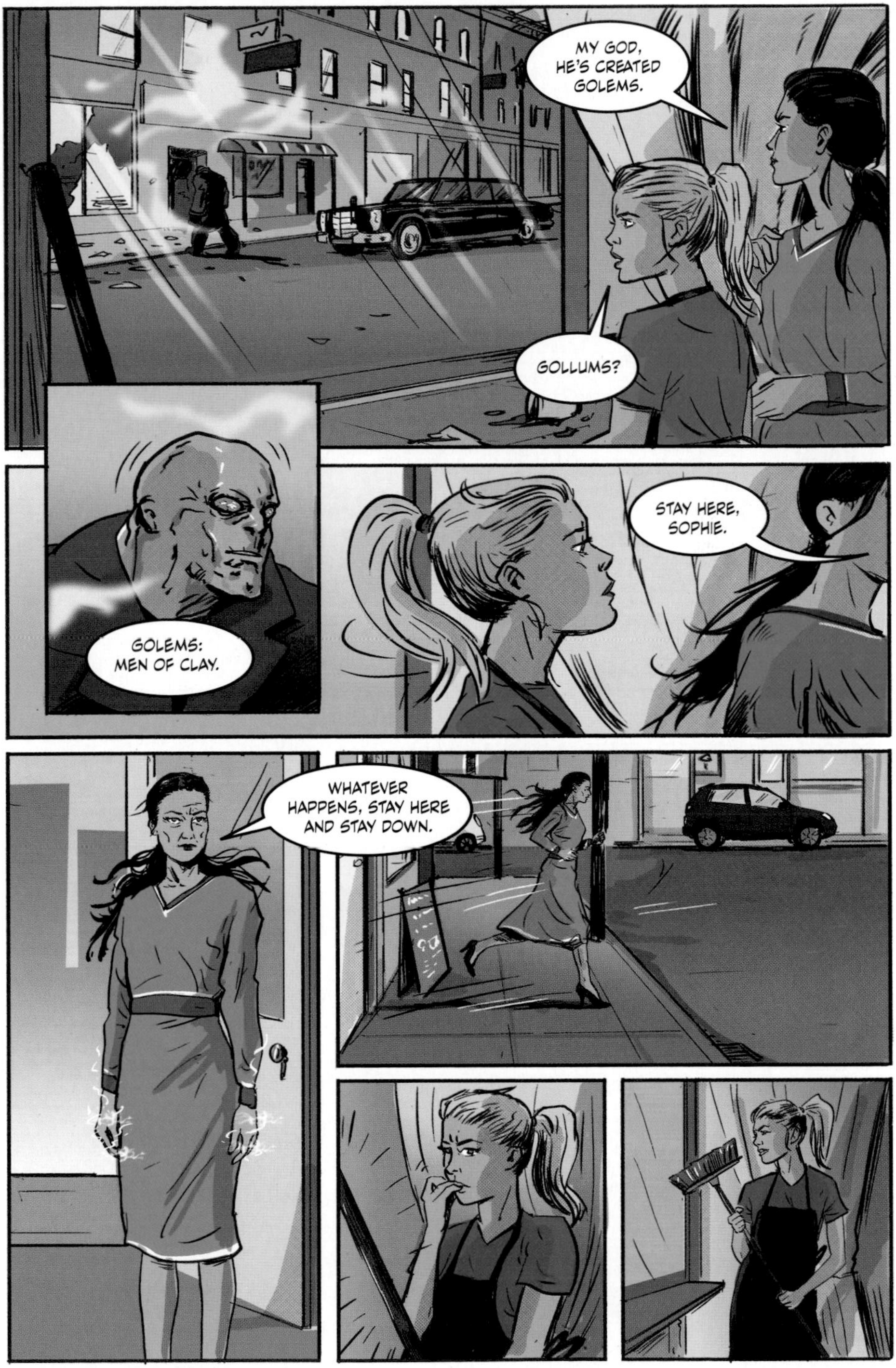
MY GOD, HE'S CREATED GOLEMS.
GOLLUMS?
GOLEMS: MEN OF CLAY.
STAY HERE, SOPHIE.
WHATEVER HAPPENS, STAY HERE AND STAY DOWN.

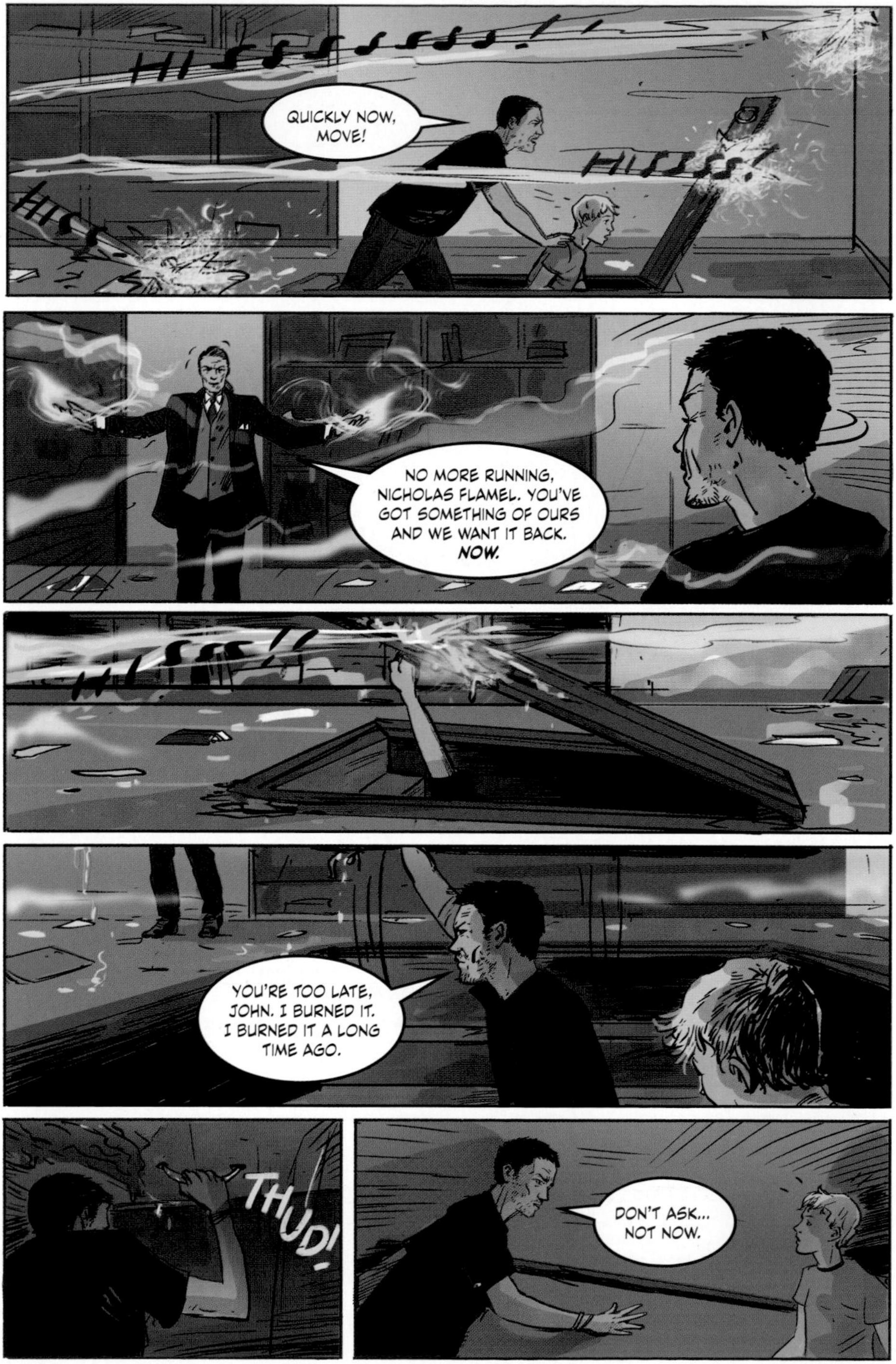
HISSSSSSSS!!
QUICKLY NOW, MOVE!
HISSSS!
NO MORE RUNNING, NICHOLAS FLAMEL. YOU'VE GOT SOMETHING OF OURS AND WE WANT IT BACK. ***NOW.***
HISSSS!!
YOU'RE TOO LATE, JOHN. I BURNED IT. I BURNED IT A LONG TIME AGO.
THUD!
DON'T ASK... NOT NOW.

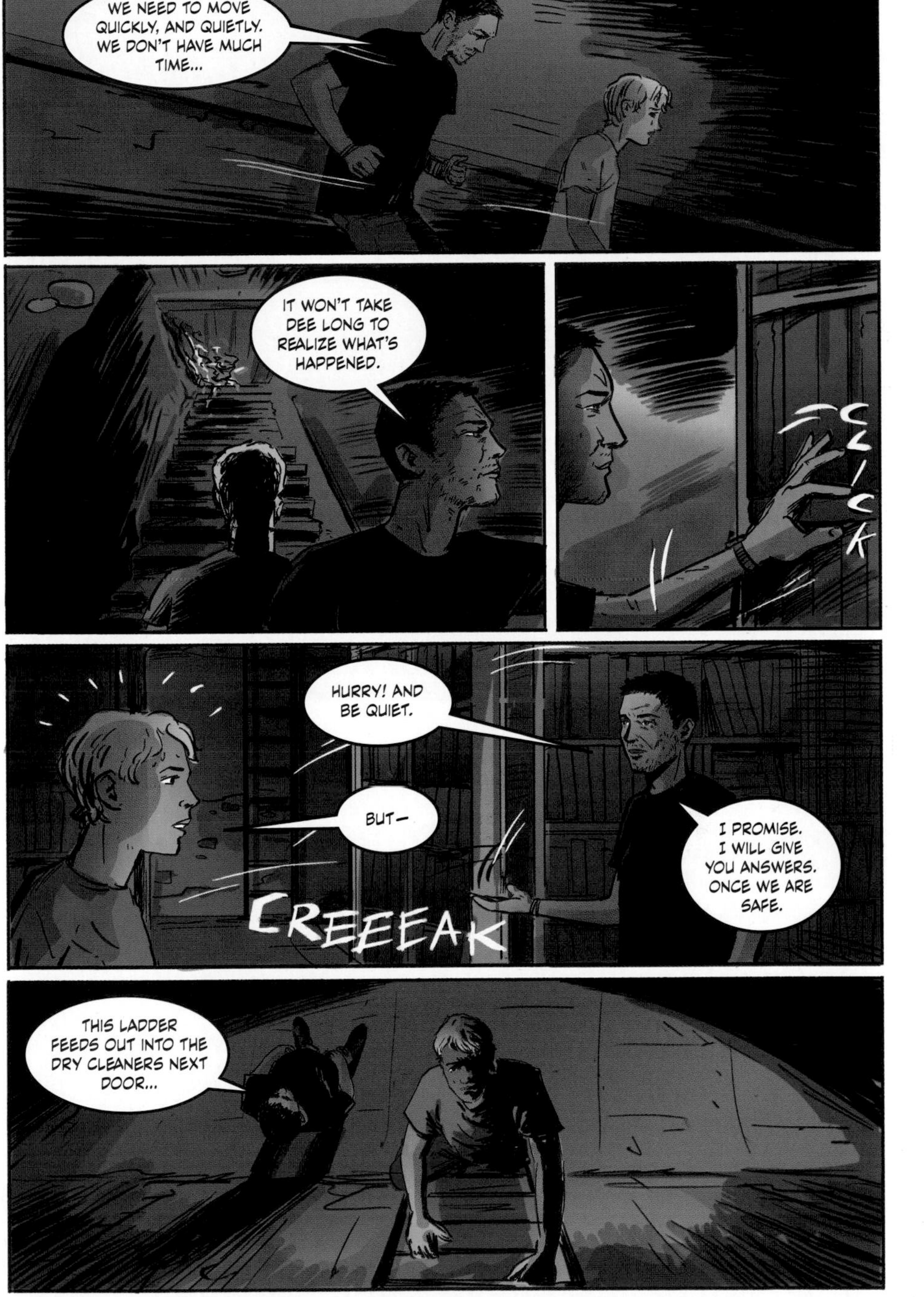
WE NEED TO MOVE QUICKLY, AND QUIETLY. WE DON'T HAVE MUCH TIME...
IT WON'T TAKE DEE LONG TO REALIZE WHAT'S HAPPENED.
CLICK
HURRY! AND BE QUIET.
BUT—
I PROMISE. I WILL GIVE YOU ANSWERS. ONCE WE ARE SAFE.
CREEEAK
THIS LADDER FEEDS OUT INTO THE DRY CLEANERS NEXT DOOR...

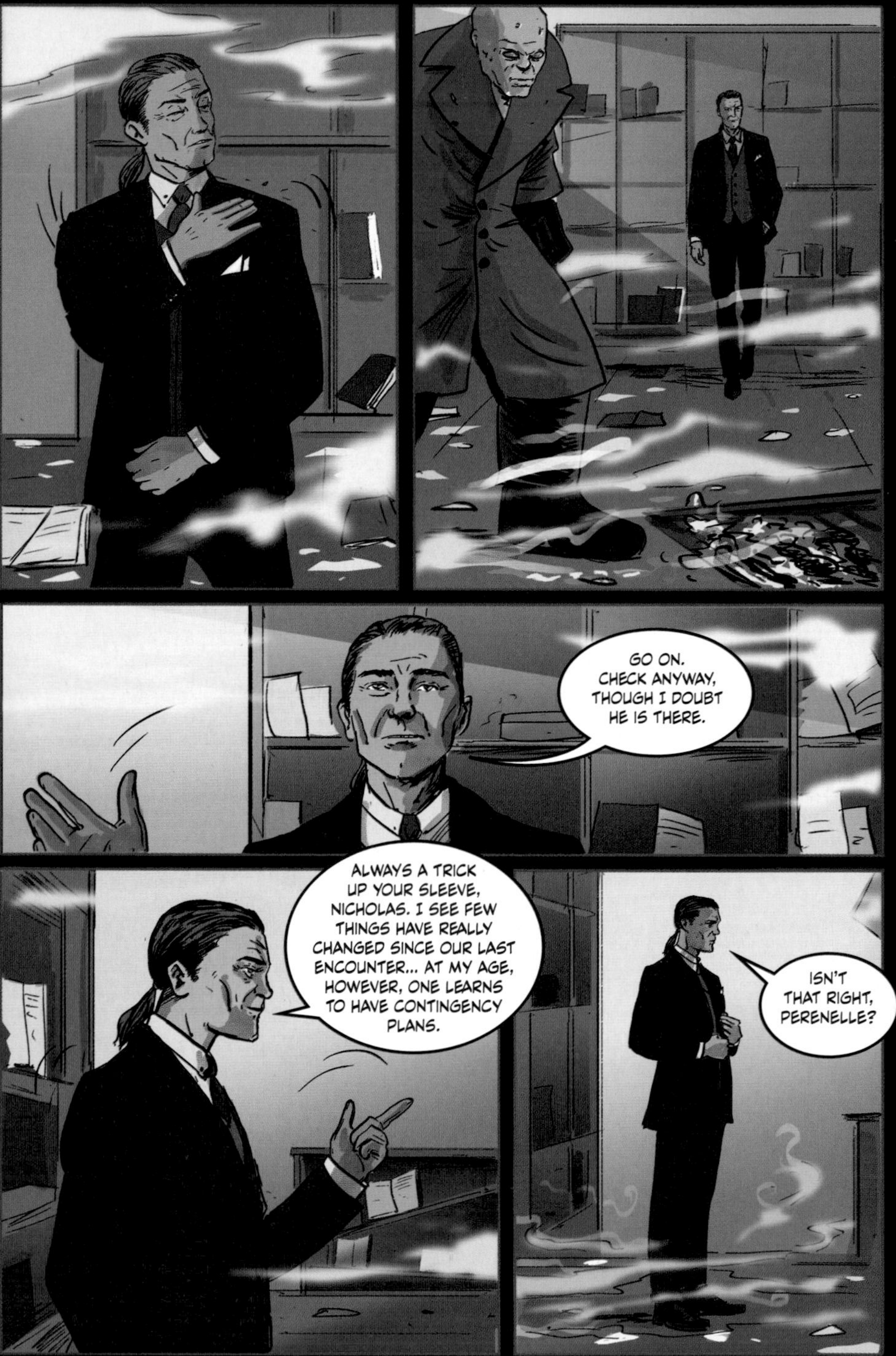
GO ON. CHECK ANYWAY, THOUGH I DOUBT HE IS THERE.
ALWAYS A TRICK UP YOUR SLEEVE, NICHOLAS. I SEE FEW THINGS HAVE REALLY CHANGED SINCE OUR LAST ENCOUNTER... AT MY AGE, HOWEVER, ONE LEARNS TO HAVE CONTINGENCY PLANS.
ISN'T THAT RIGHT, PERENELLE?

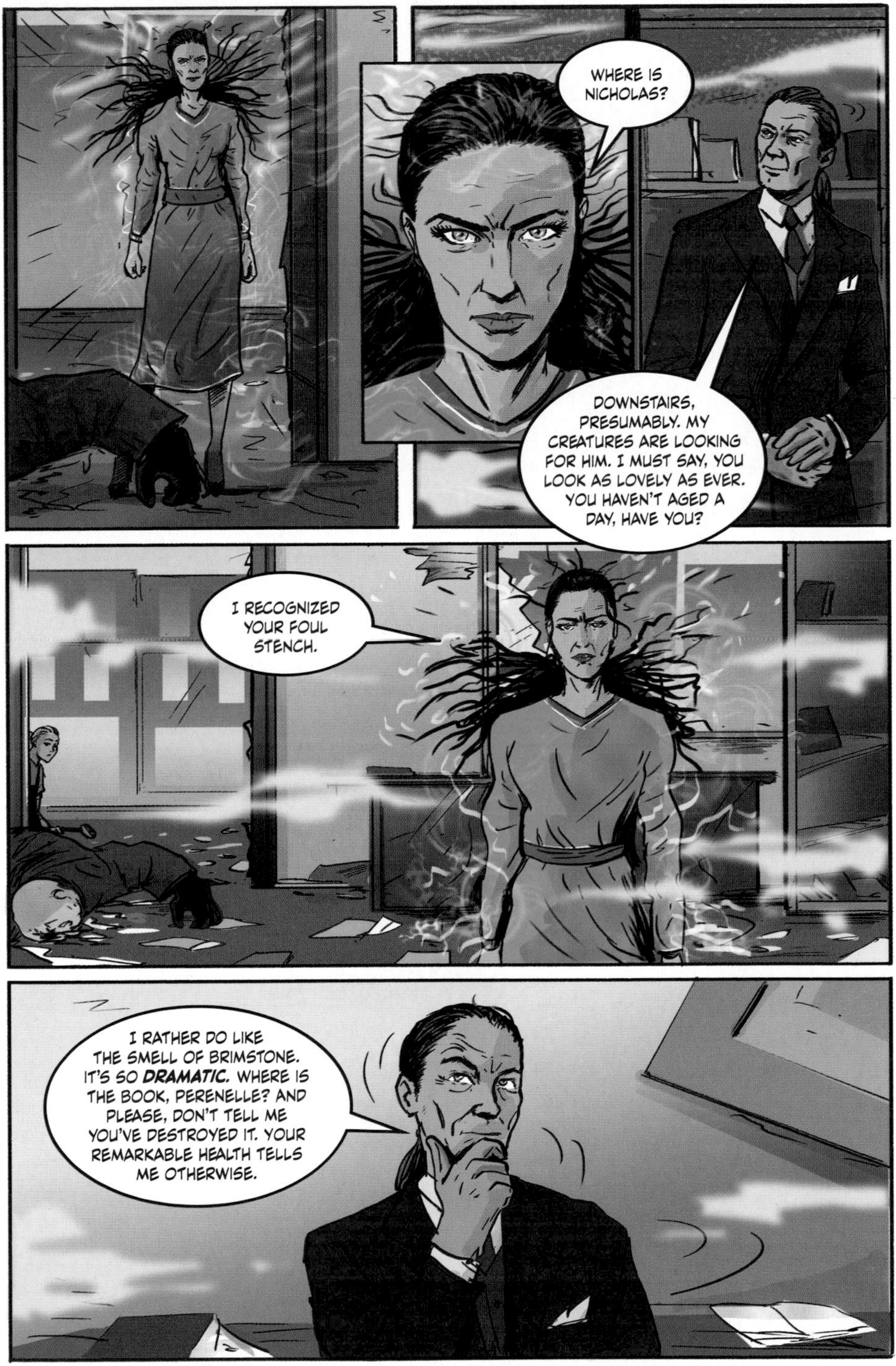
WHERE IS NICHOLAS?
DOWNSTAIRS, PRESUMABLY. MY CREATURES ARE LOOKING FOR HIM. I MUST SAY, YOU LOOK AS LOVELY AS EVER. YOU HAVEN'T AGED A DAY, HAVE YOU?
I RECOGNIZED YOUR FOUL STENCH.
I RATHER DO LIKE THE SMELL OF BRIMSTONE. IT'S SO ***DRAMATIC.*** WHERE IS THE BOOK, PERENELLE? AND PLEASE, DON'T TELL ME YOU'VE DESTROYED IT. YOUR REMARKABLE HEALTH TELLS ME OTHERWISE.

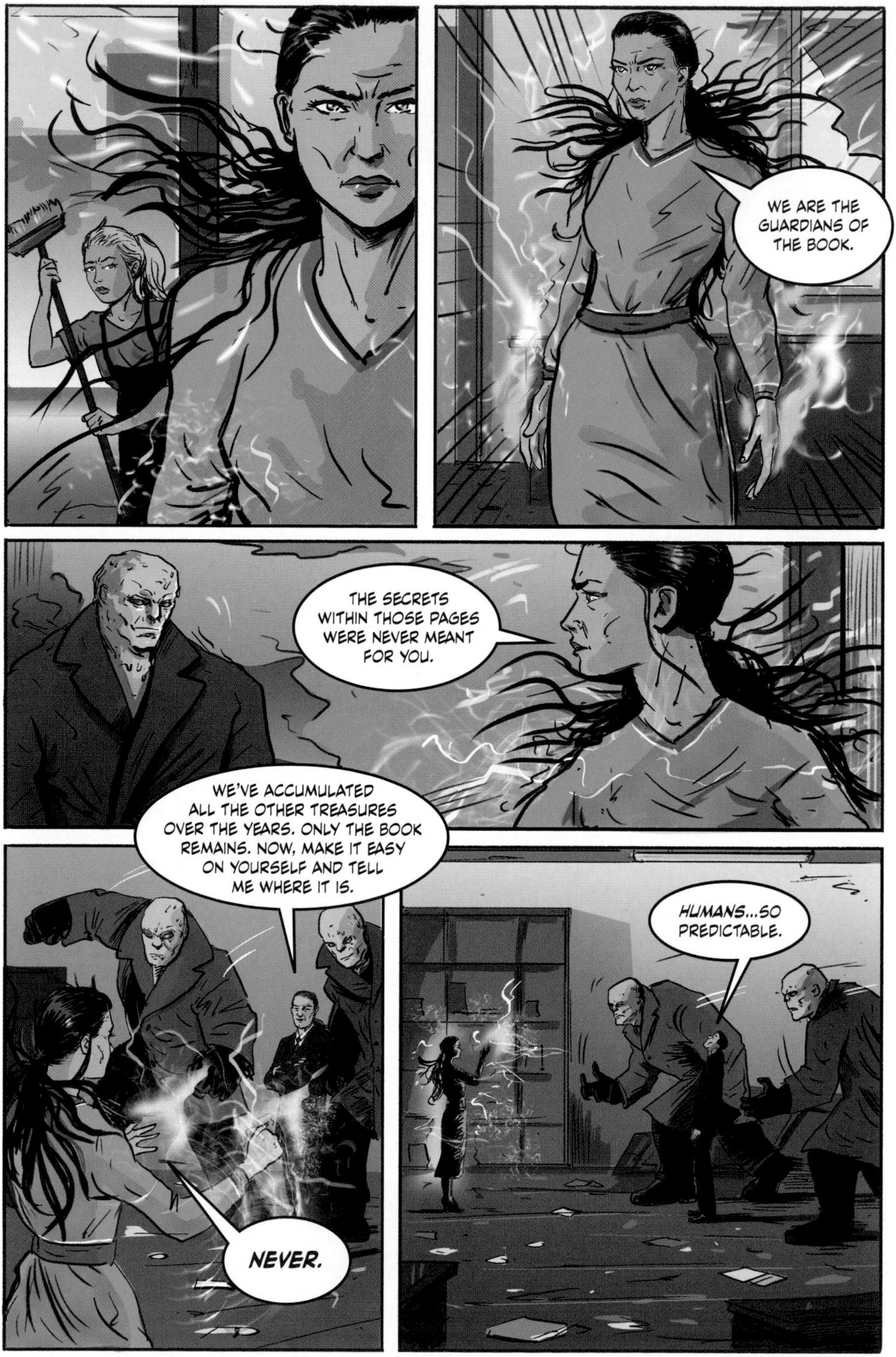
WE ARE THE GUARDIANS OF THE BOOK.
THE SECRETS WITHIN THOSE PAGES WERE NEVER MEANT FOR YOU.
WE'VE ACCUMULATED ALL THE OTHER TREASURES OVER THE YEARS. ONLY THE BOOK REMAINS. NOW, MAKE IT EASY ON YOURSELF AND TELL ME WHERE IT IS.
NEVER.
HUMANS...SO PREDICTABLE.

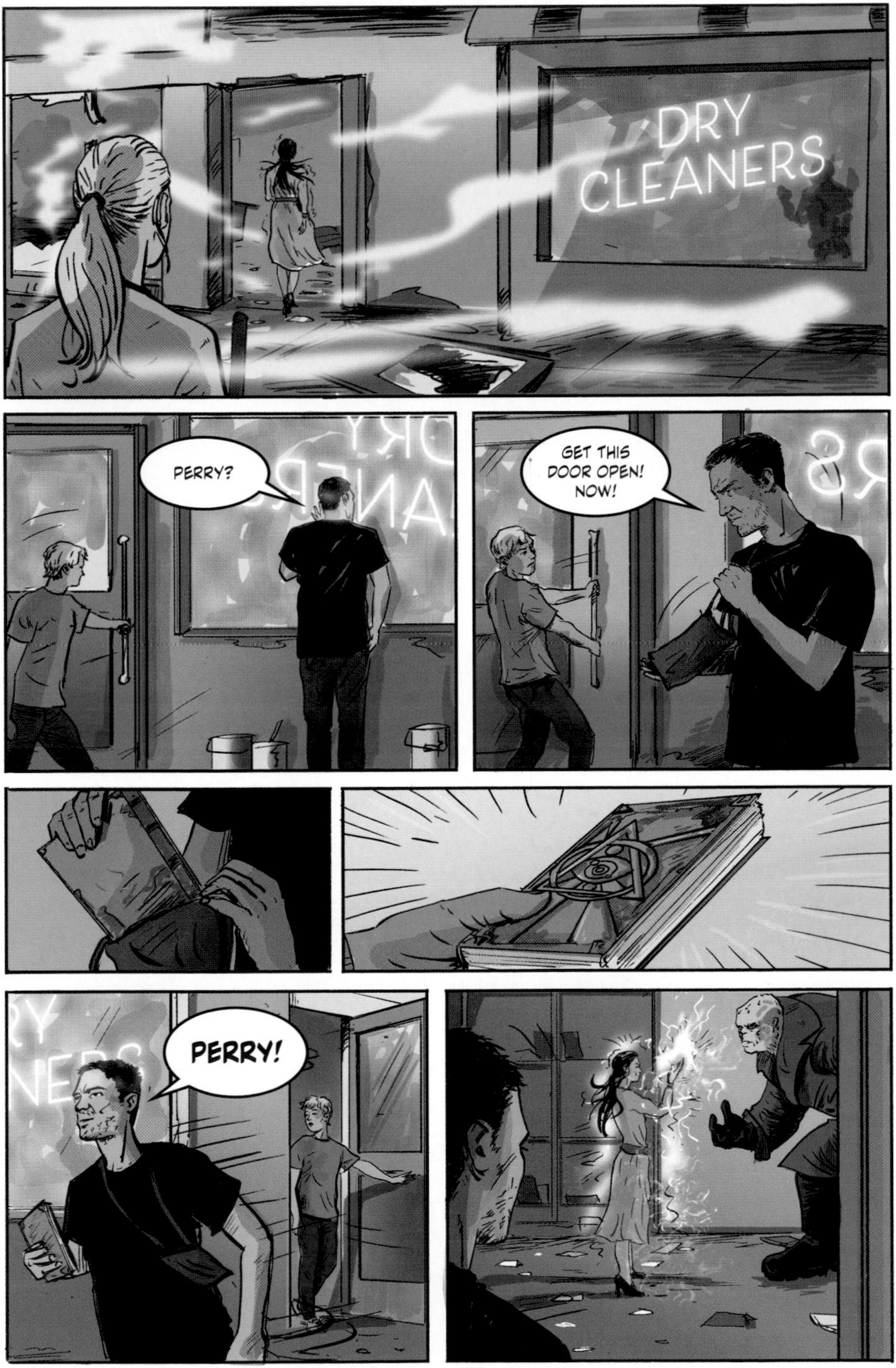
DRY
CLEANERS
PERRY?
GET THIS DOOR OPEN! NOW!
PERRY!

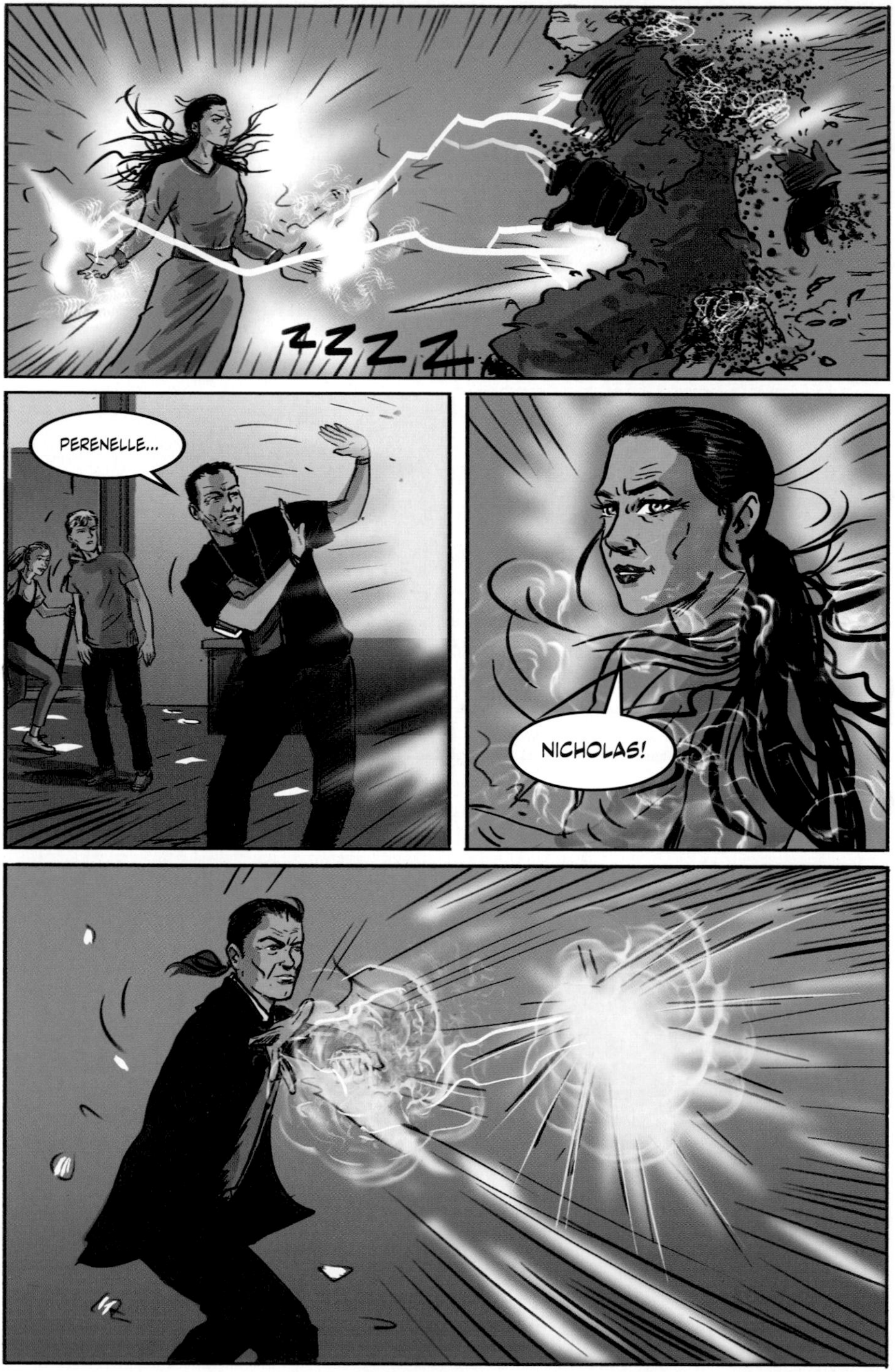
ZZZZ
PERENELLE...
NICHOLAS!

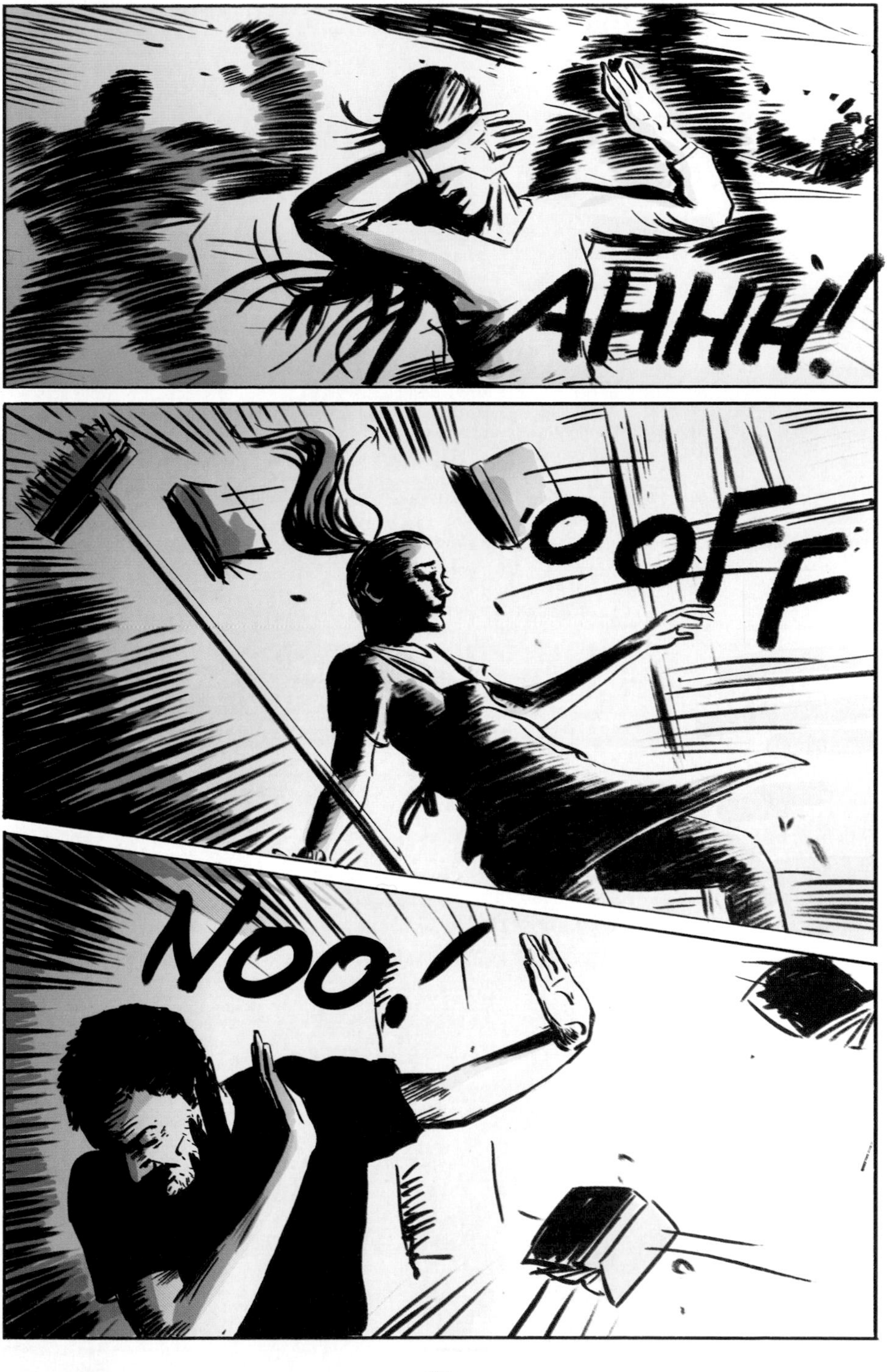
AHHH!
OOFF
NOO!

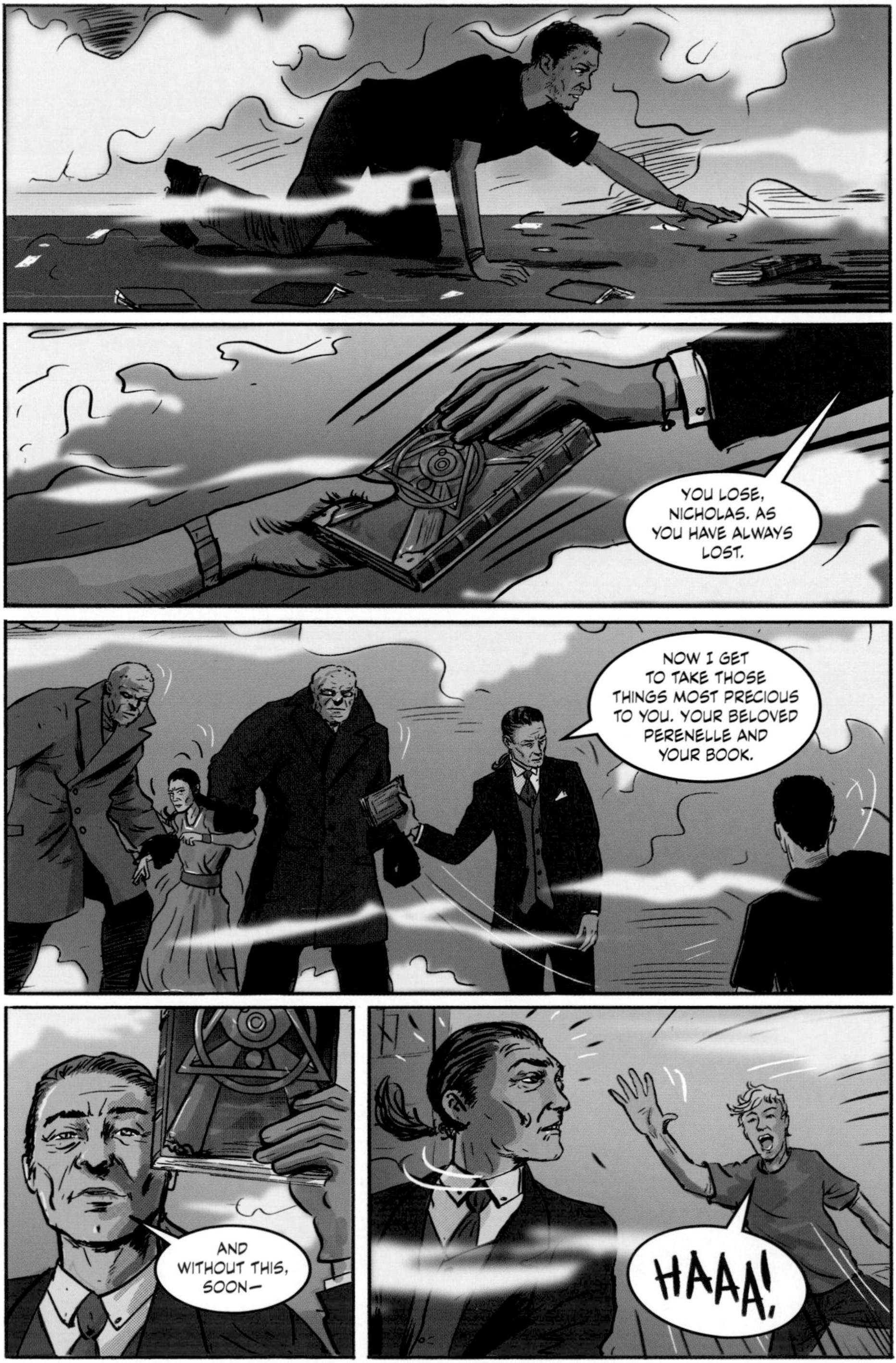
YOU LOSE, NICHOLAS. AS YOU HAVE ALWAYS LOST.
NOW I GET TO TAKE THOSE THINGS MOST PRECIOUS TO YOU. YOUR BELOVED PERENELLE AND YOUR BOOK.
AND WITHOUT THIS, SOON—
HAAA!

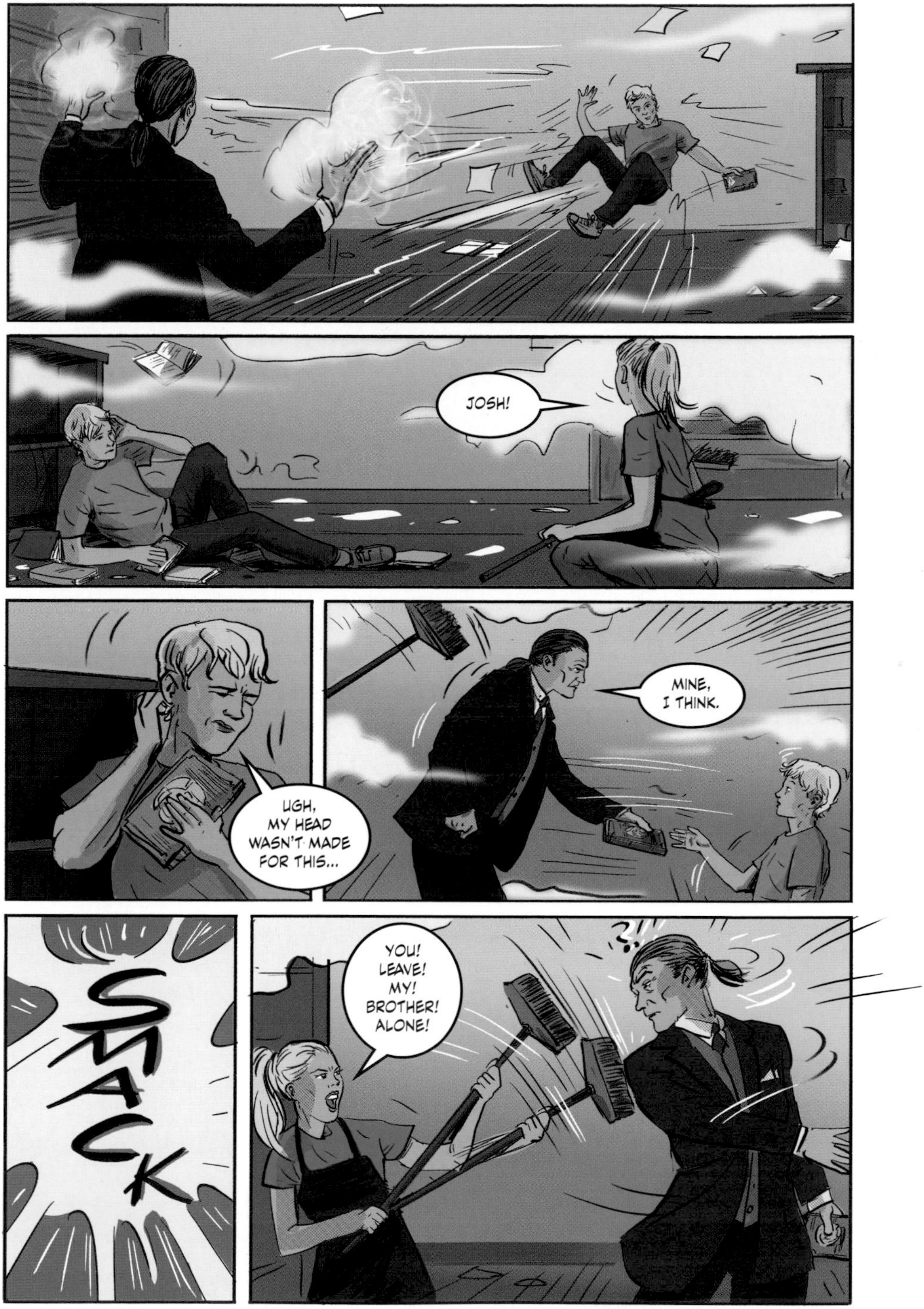
JOSH!
UGH, MY HEAD WASN'T MADE FOR THIS...
MINE, I THINK.
SMACK
?!
YOU! LEAVE! MY! BROTHER! ALONE!

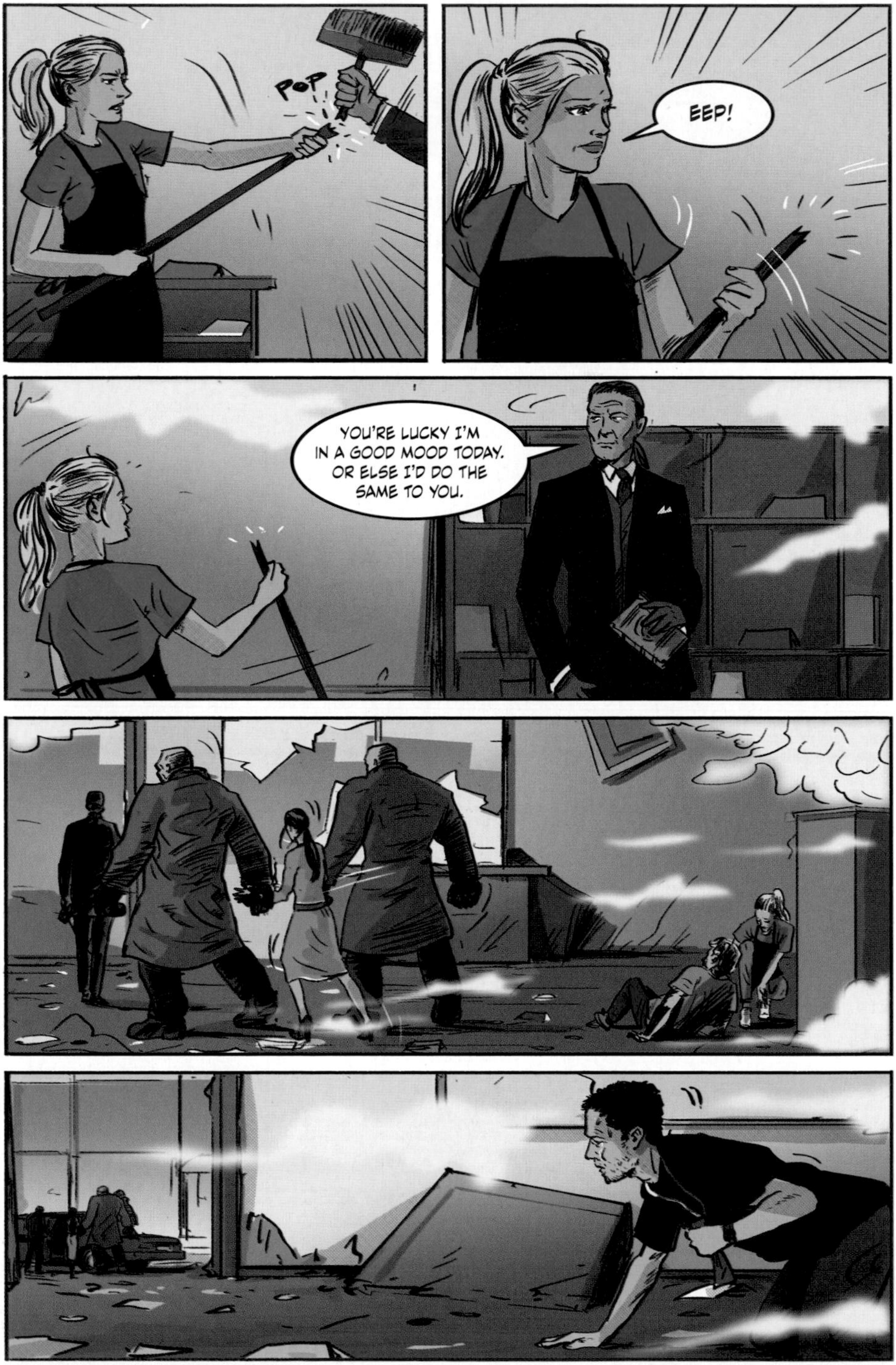
POP
EEP!
YOU'RE LUCKY I'M IN A GOOD MOOD TODAY. OR ELSE I'D DO THE SAME TO YOU.

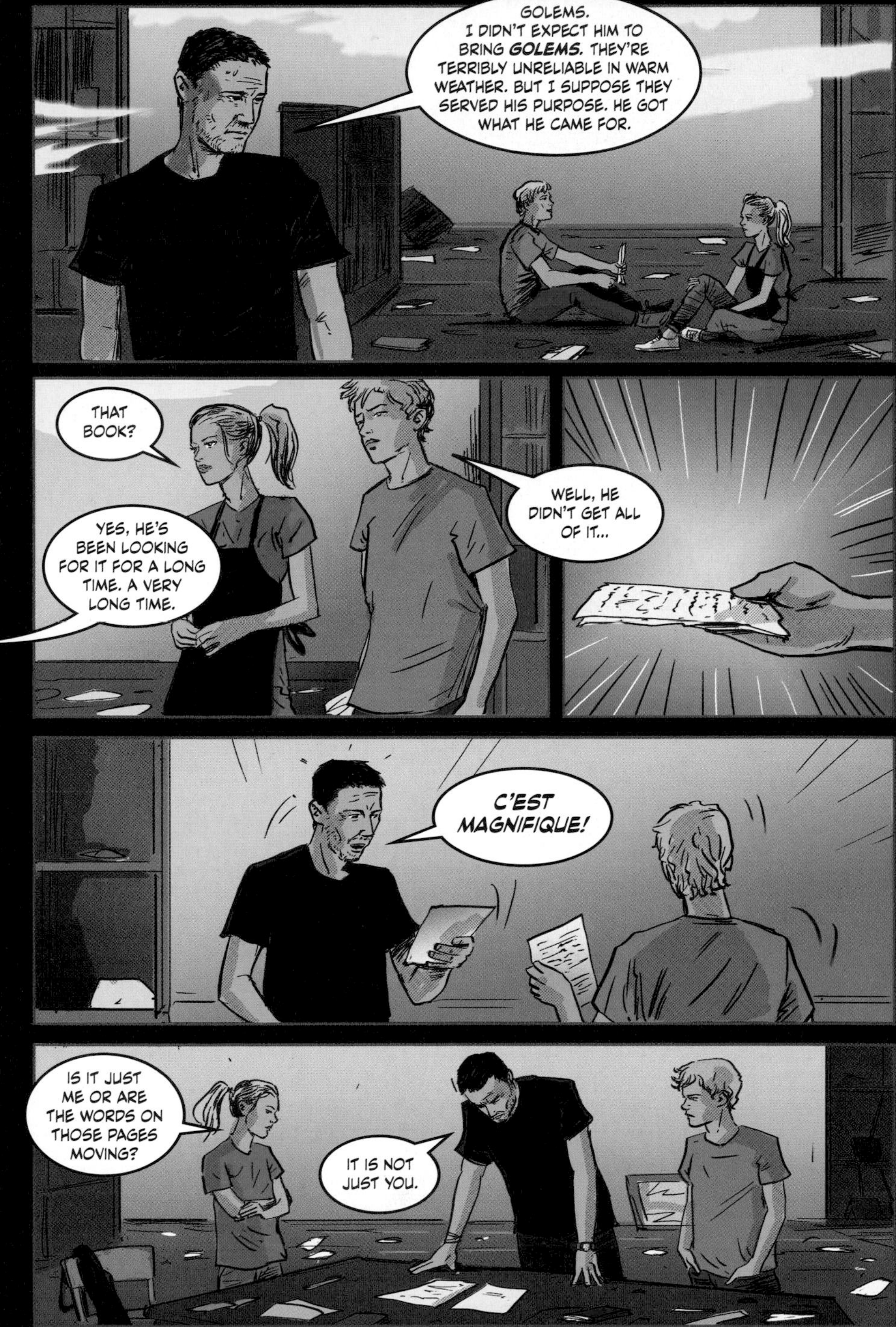
GOLEMS.
I DIDN'T EXPECT HIM TO BRING GOLEMS. THEY'RE TERRIBLY UNRELIABLE IN WARM WEATHER. BUT I SUPPOSE THEY SERVED HIS PURPOSE. HE GOT WHAT HE CAME FOR.
THAT BOOK?
YES, HE'S BEEN LOOKING FOR IT FOR A LONG TIME. A VERY LONG TIME.
WELL, HE DIDN'T GET ALL OF IT...
C'EST MAGNIFIQUE!
IS IT JUST ME OR ARE THE WORDS ON THOSE PAGES MOVING?
IT IS NOT JUST YOU.

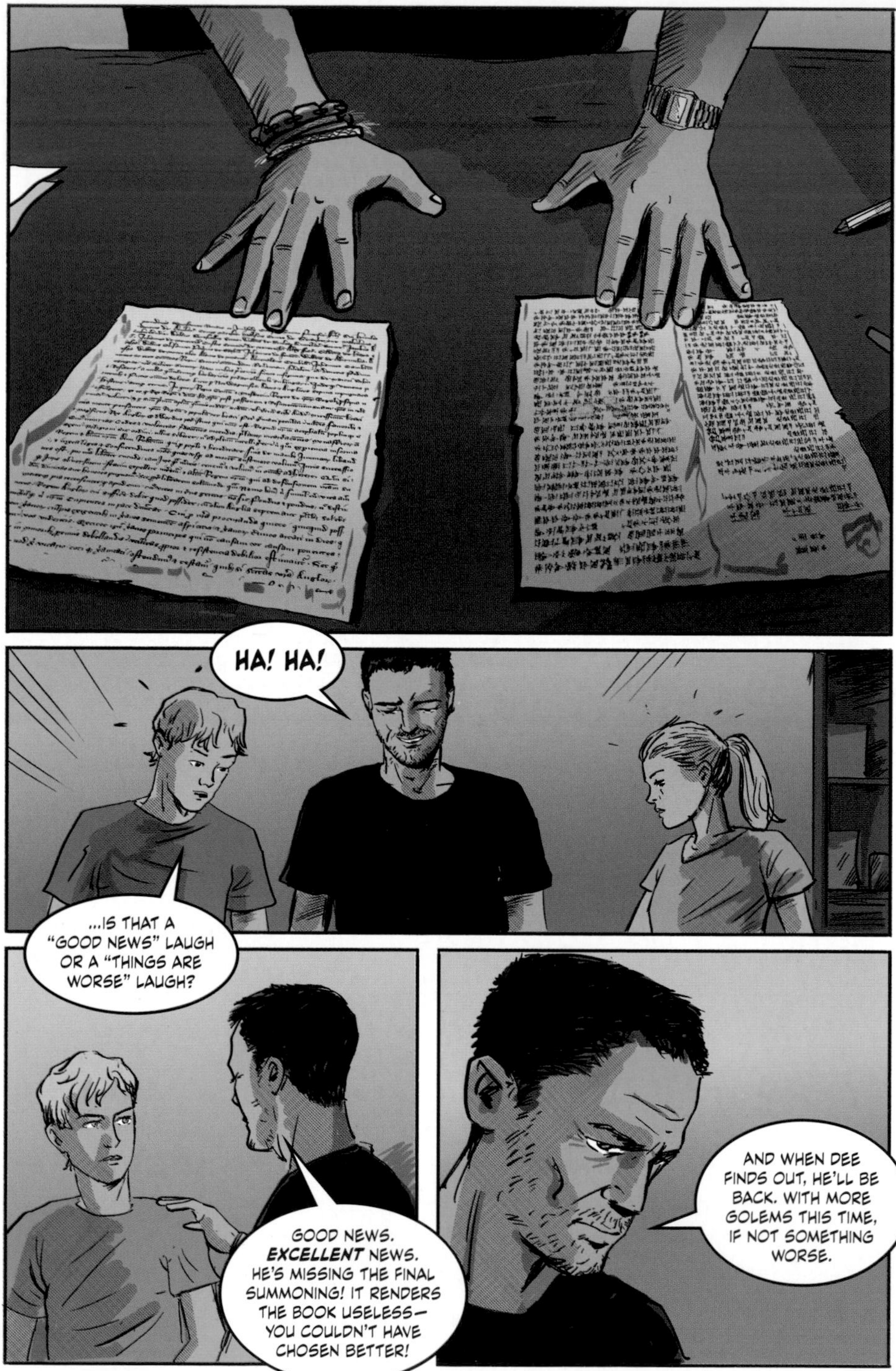
HA! HA!
...IS THAT A "GOOD NEWS" LAUGH OR A "THINGS ARE WORSE" LAUGH?
GOOD NEWS. ***EXCELLENT*** NEWS. HE'S MISSING THE FINAL SUMMONING! IT RENDERS THE BOOK USELESS— YOU COULDN'T HAVE CHOSEN BETTER!
AND WHEN DEE FINDS OUT, HE'LL BE BACK. WITH MORE GOLEMS THIS TIME, IF NOT SOMETHING WORSE.

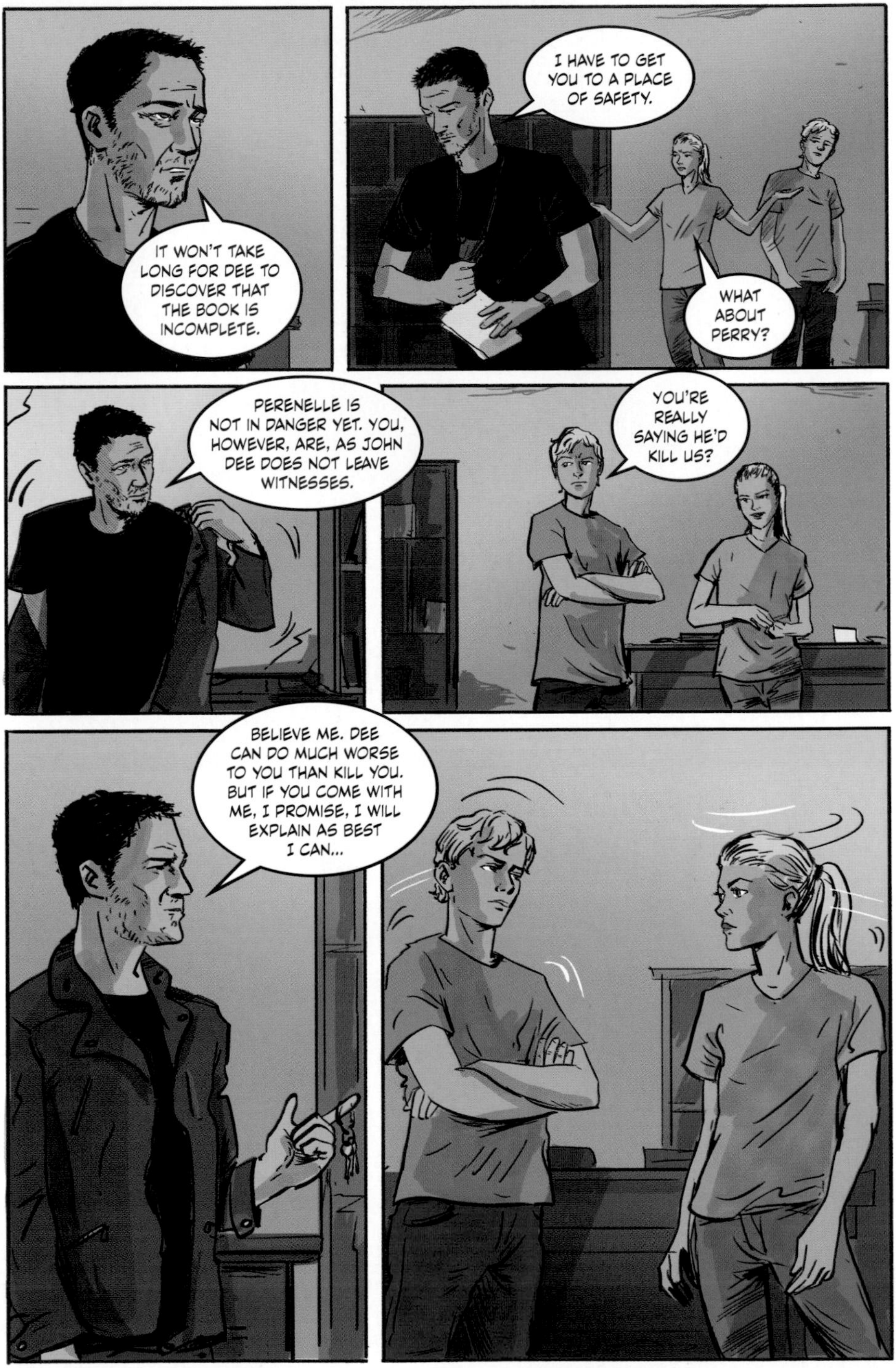
IT WON'T TAKE LONG FOR DEE TO DISCOVER THAT THE BOOK IS INCOMPLETE.
I HAVE TO GET YOU TO A PLACE OF SAFETY.
WHAT ABOUT PERRY?
PERENELLE IS NOT IN DANGER YET. YOU, HOWEVER, ARE, AS JOHN DEE DOES NOT LEAVE WITNESSES.
YOU'RE REALLY SAYING HE'D KILL US?
BELIEVE ME. DEE CAN DO MUCH WORSE TO YOU THAN KILL YOU. BUT IF YOU COME WITH ME, I PROMISE, I WILL EXPLAIN AS BEST I CAN...

CHAPTER 5

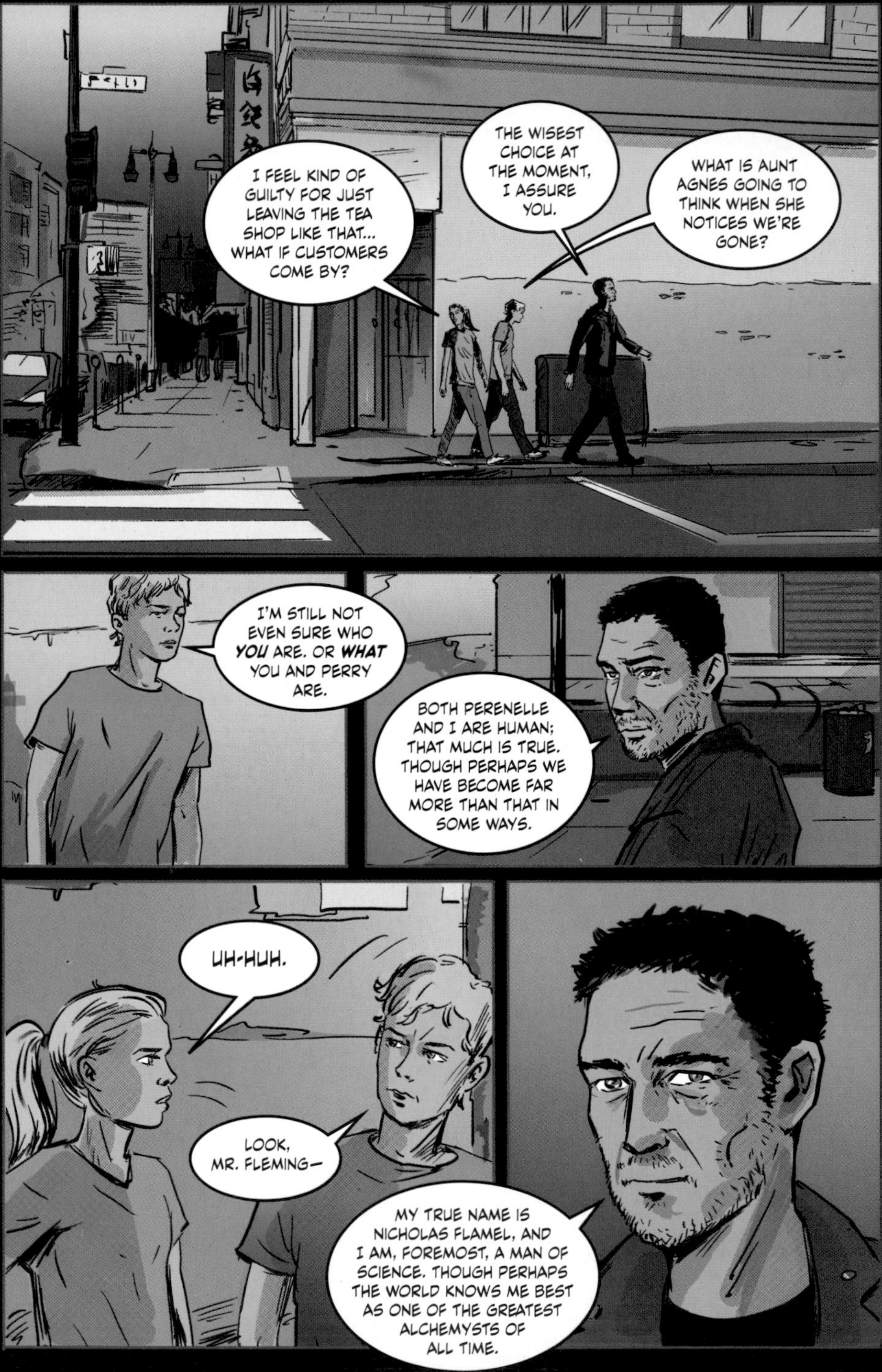
I FEEL KIND OF GUILTY FOR JUST LEAVING THE TEA SHOP LIKE THAT... WHAT IF CUSTOMERS COME BY?
THE WISEST CHOICE AT THE MOMENT, I ASSURE YOU.
WHAT IS AUNT AGNES GOING TO THINK WHEN SHE NOTICES WE'RE GONE?
I'M STILL NOT EVEN SURE WHO *YOU* ARE. OR *WHAT* YOU AND PERRY ARE.
BOTH PERENELLE AND I ARE HUMAN; THAT MUCH IS TRUE. THOUGH PERHAPS WE HAVE BECOME FAR MORE THAN THAT IN SOME WAYS.
UH-HUH.
LOOK, MR. FLEMING—
MY TRUE NAME IS NICHOLAS FLAMEL, AND I AM, FOREMOST, A MAN OF SCIENCE. THOUGH PERHAPS THE WORLD KNOWS ME BEST AS ONE OF THE GREATEST ALCHEMYSTS OF ALL TIME.

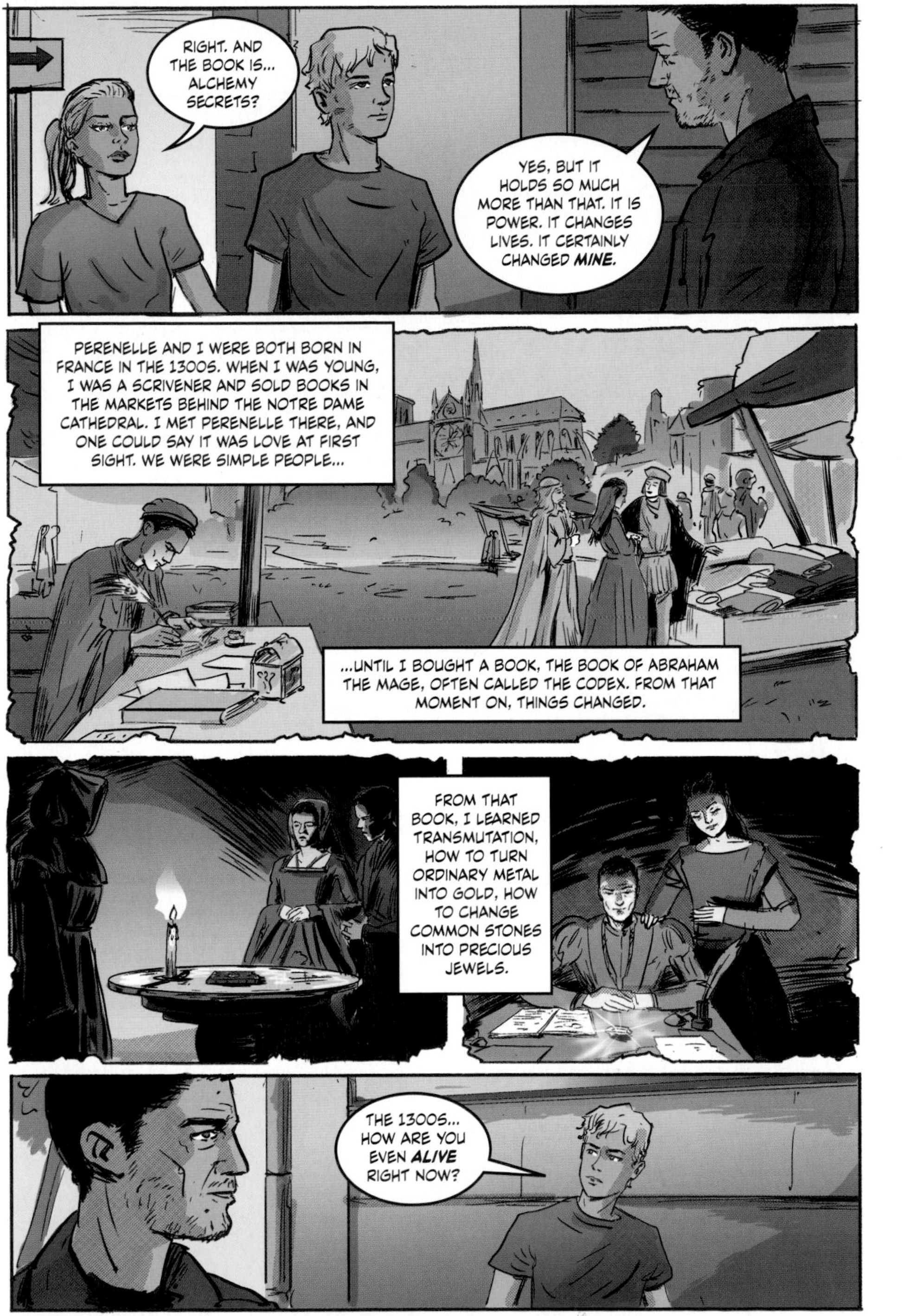
RIGHT. AND THE BOOK IS... ALCHEMY SECRETS?
YES, BUT IT HOLDS SO MUCH MORE THAN THAT. IT IS POWER. IT CHANGES LIVES. IT CERTAINLY CHANGED ***MINE.***
PERENELLE AND I WERE BOTH BORN IN FRANCE IN THE 1300S. WHEN I WAS YOUNG, I WAS A SCRIVENER AND SOLD BOOKS IN THE MARKETS BEHIND THE NOTRE DAME CATHEDRAL. I MET PERENELLE THERE, AND ONE COULD SAY IT WAS LOVE AT FIRST SIGHT. WE WERE SIMPLE PEOPLE...
...UNTIL I BOUGHT A BOOK, THE BOOK OF ABRAHAM THE MAGE, OFTEN CALLED THE CODEX. FROM THAT MOMENT ON, THINGS CHANGED.
FROM THAT BOOK, I LEARNED TRANSMUTATION, HOW TO TURN ORDINARY METAL INTO GOLD, HOW TO CHANGE COMMON STONES INTO PRECIOUS JEWELS.
THE 1300S... HOW ARE YOU EVEN ***ALIVE*** RIGHT NOW?

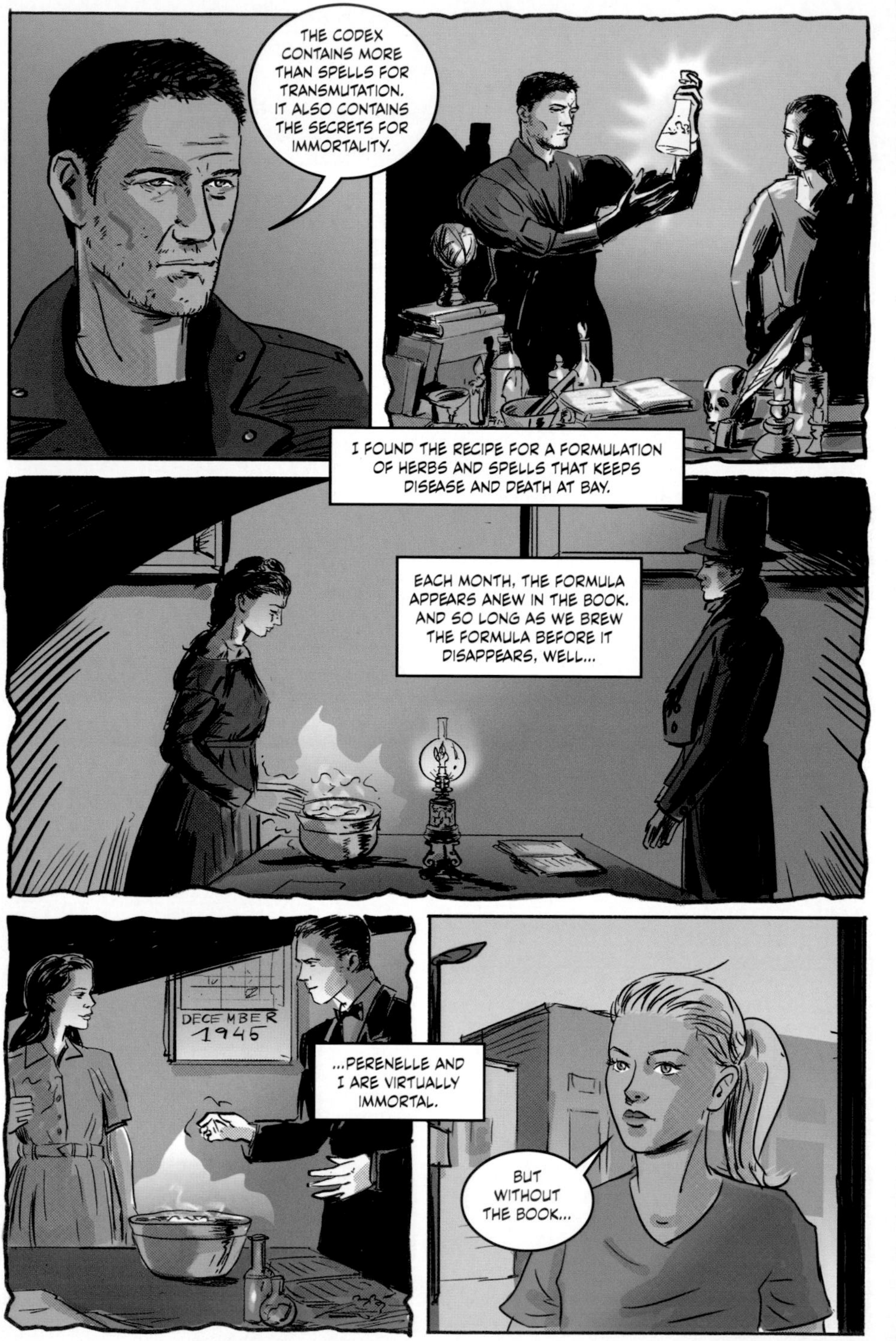
THE CODEX CONTAINS MORE THAN SPELLS FOR TRANSMUTATION. IT ALSO CONTAINS THE SECRETS FOR IMMORTALITY.
I FOUND THE RECIPE FOR A FORMULATION OF HERBS AND SPELLS THAT KEEPS DISEASE AND DEATH AT BAY.
EACH MONTH, THE FORMULA APPEARS ANEW IN THE BOOK. AND SO LONG AS WE BREW THE FORMULA BEFORE IT DISAPPEARS, WELL...
DECEMBER 1945
...PERENELLE AND I ARE VIRTUALLY IMMORTAL.
BUT WITHOUT THE BOOK...

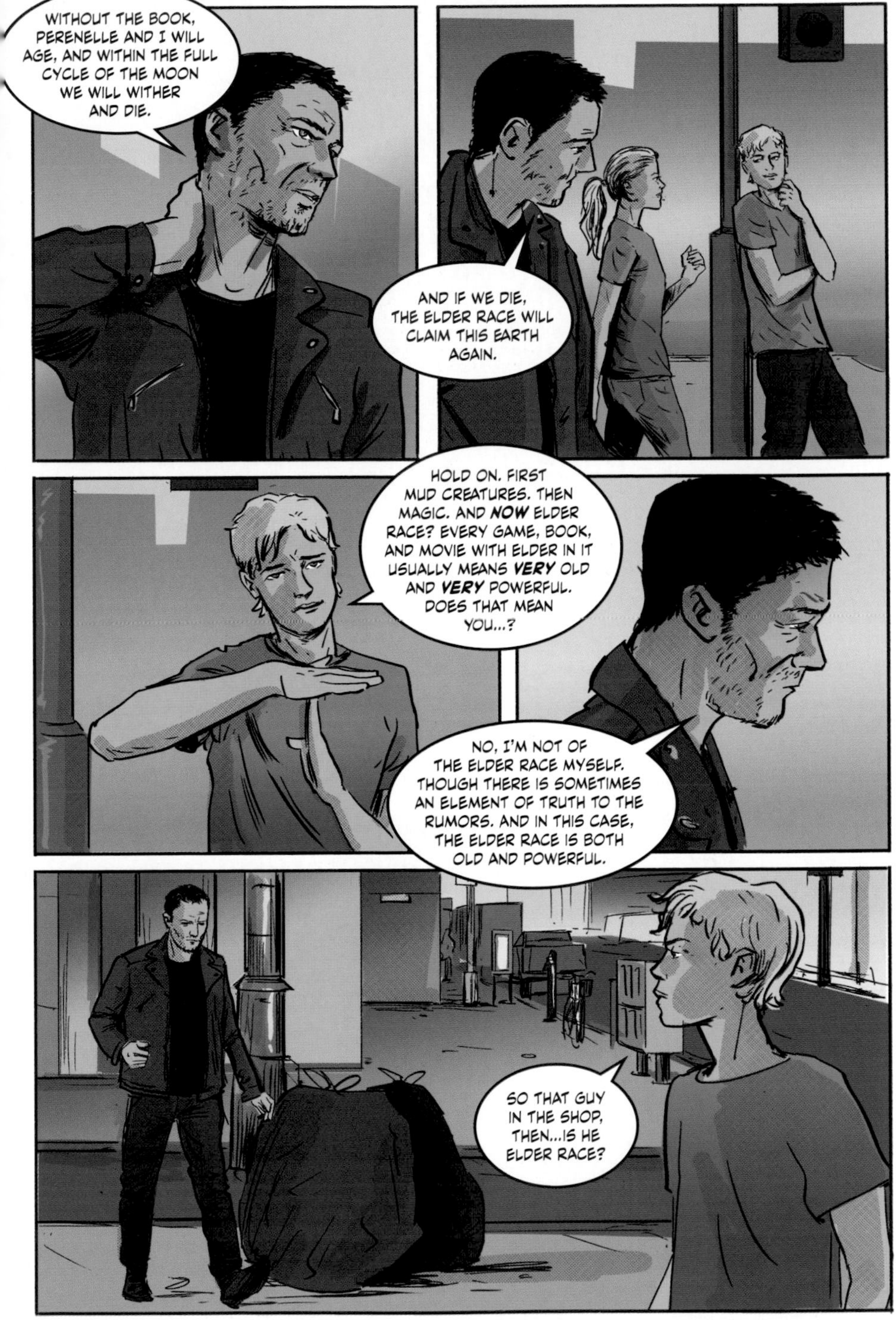
WITHOUT THE BOOK, PERENELLE AND I WILL AGE, AND WITHIN THE FULL CYCLE OF THE MOON WE WILL WITHER AND DIE.
AND IF WE DIE, THE ELDER RACE WILL CLAIM THIS EARTH AGAIN.
HOLD ON. FIRST MUD CREATURES. THEN MAGIC. AND *NOW* ELDER RACE? EVERY GAME, BOOK, AND MOVIE WITH ELDER IN IT USUALLY MEANS *VERY* OLD AND *VERY* POWERFUL. DOES THAT MEAN YOU...?
NO, I'M NOT OF THE ELDER RACE MYSELF. THOUGH THERE IS SOMETIMES AN ELEMENT OF TRUTH TO THE RUMORS. AND IN THIS CASE, THE ELDER RACE IS BOTH OLD AND POWERFUL.
SO THAT GUY IN THE SHOP, THEN...IS HE ELDER RACE?

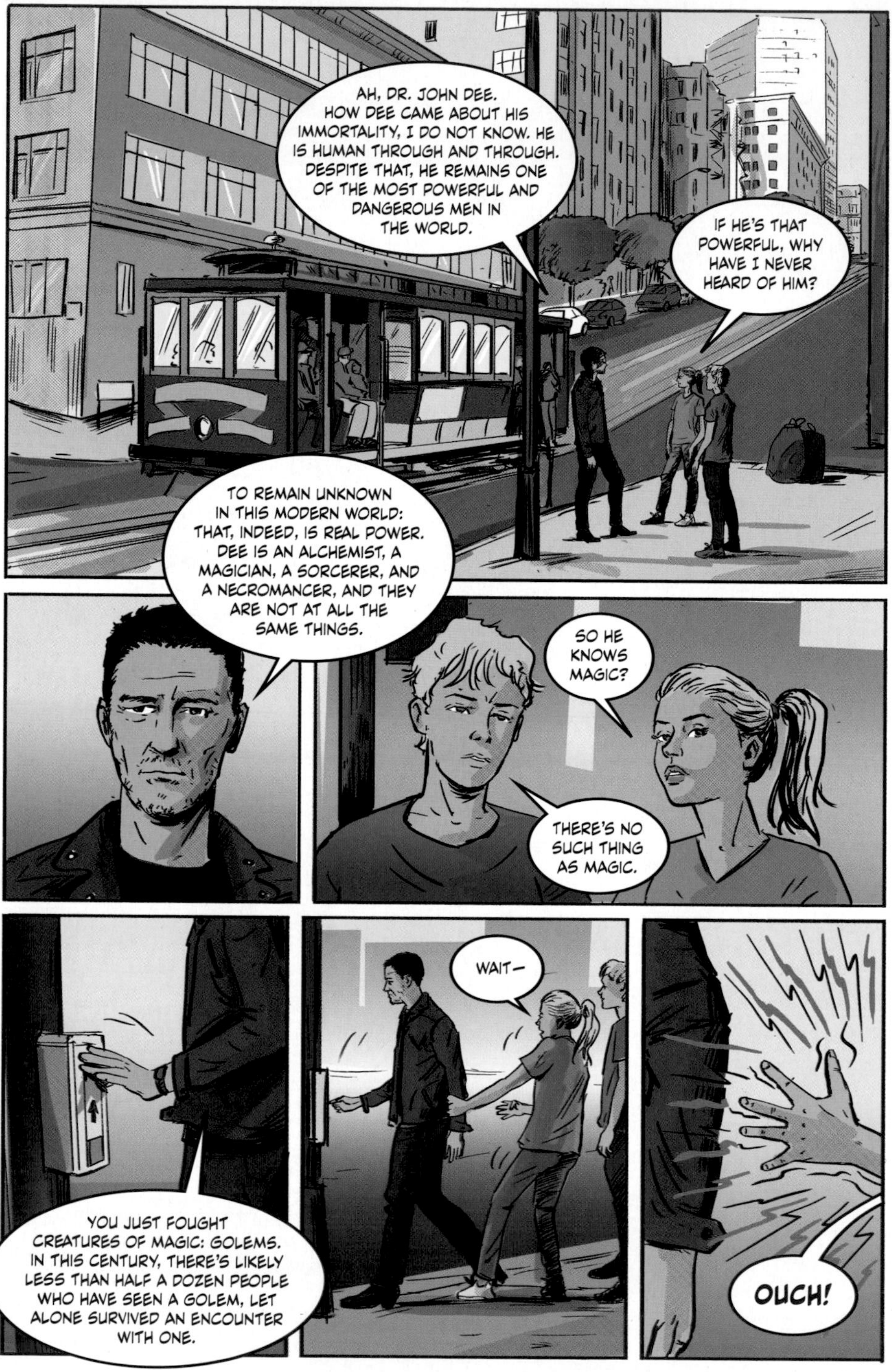
AH, DR. JOHN DEE. HOW DEE CAME ABOUT HIS IMMORTALITY, I DO NOT KNOW. HE IS HUMAN THROUGH AND THROUGH. DESPITE THAT, HE REMAINS ONE OF THE MOST POWERFUL AND DANGEROUS MEN IN THE WORLD.
IF HE'S THAT POWERFUL, WHY HAVE I NEVER HEARD OF HIM?
TO REMAIN UNKNOWN IN THIS MODERN WORLD: THAT, INDEED, IS REAL POWER. DEE IS AN ALCHEMIST, A MAGICIAN, A SORCERER, AND A NECROMANCER, AND THEY ARE NOT AT ALL THE SAME THINGS.
SO HE KNOWS MAGIC?
THERE'S NO SUCH THING AS MAGIC.
YOU JUST FOUGHT CREATURES OF MAGIC: GOLEMS. IN THIS CENTURY, THERE'S LIKELY LESS THAN HALF A DOZEN PEOPLE WHO HAVE SEEN A GOLEM, LET ALONE SURVIVED AN ENCOUNTER WITH ONE.
WAIT—
OUCH!

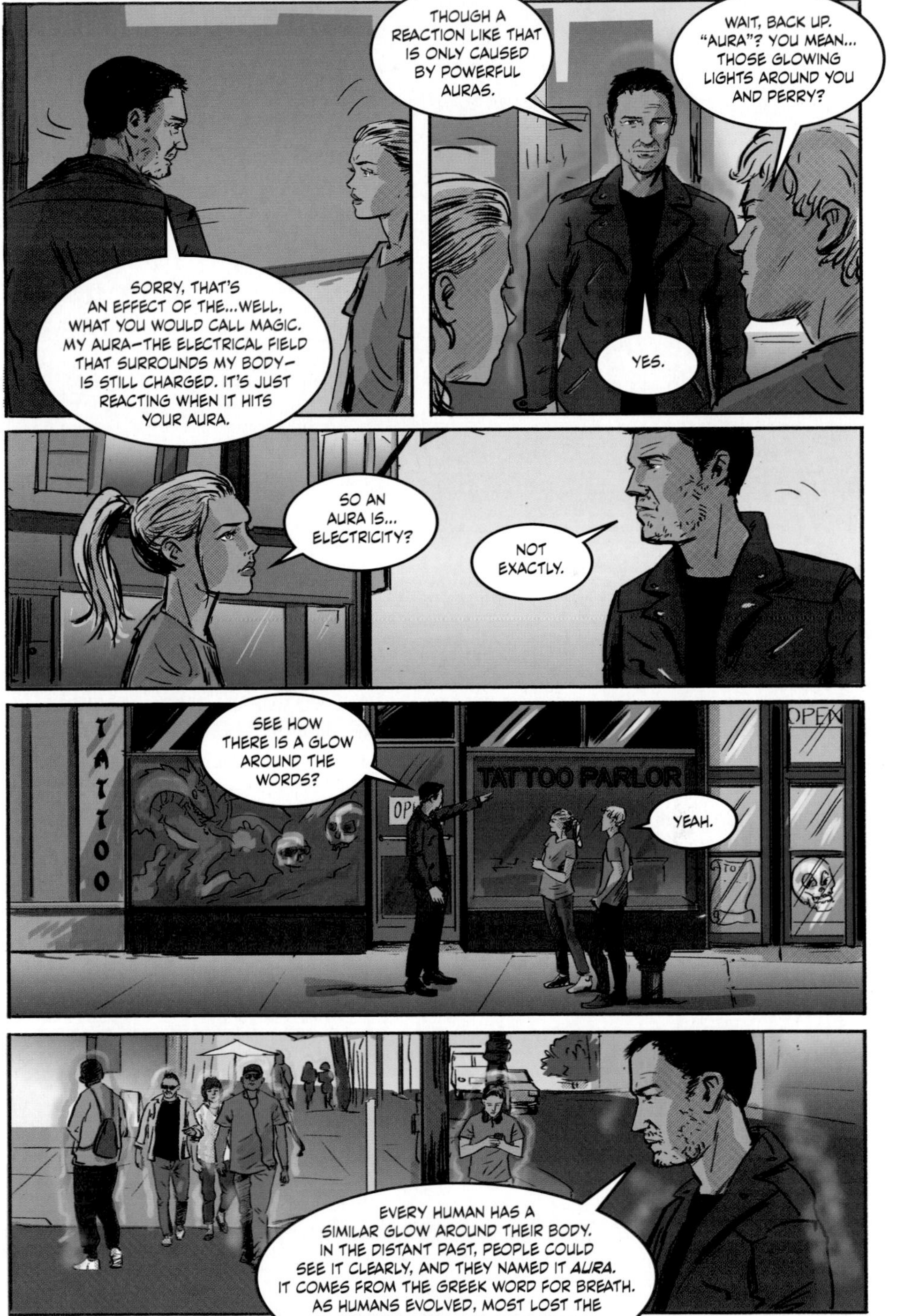
THOUGH A REACTION LIKE THAT IS ONLY CAUSED BY POWERFUL AURAS.
SORRY, THAT'S AN EFFECT OF THE...WELL, WHAT YOU WOULD CALL MAGIC. MY AURA—THE ELECTRICAL FIELD THAT SURROUNDS MY BODY—IS STILL CHARGED. IT'S JUST REACTING WHEN IT HITS YOUR AURA.
WAIT, BACK UP. "AURA"? YOU MEAN... THOSE GLOWING LIGHTS AROUND YOU AND PERRY?
YES.
SO AN AURA IS... ELECTRICITY?
NOT EXACTLY.
TATTOO
SEE HOW THERE IS A GLOW AROUND THE WORDS?
TATTOO PARLOR
OPEN
YEAH.
EVERY HUMAN HAS A SIMILAR GLOW AROUND THEIR BODY. IN THE DISTANT PAST, PEOPLE COULD SEE IT CLEARLY, AND THEY NAMED IT *AURA*. IT COMES FROM THE GREEK WORD FOR BREATH. AS HUMANS EVOLVED, MOST LOST THE ABILITY TO SEE THE AURA. ONLY SOME STILL CAN.

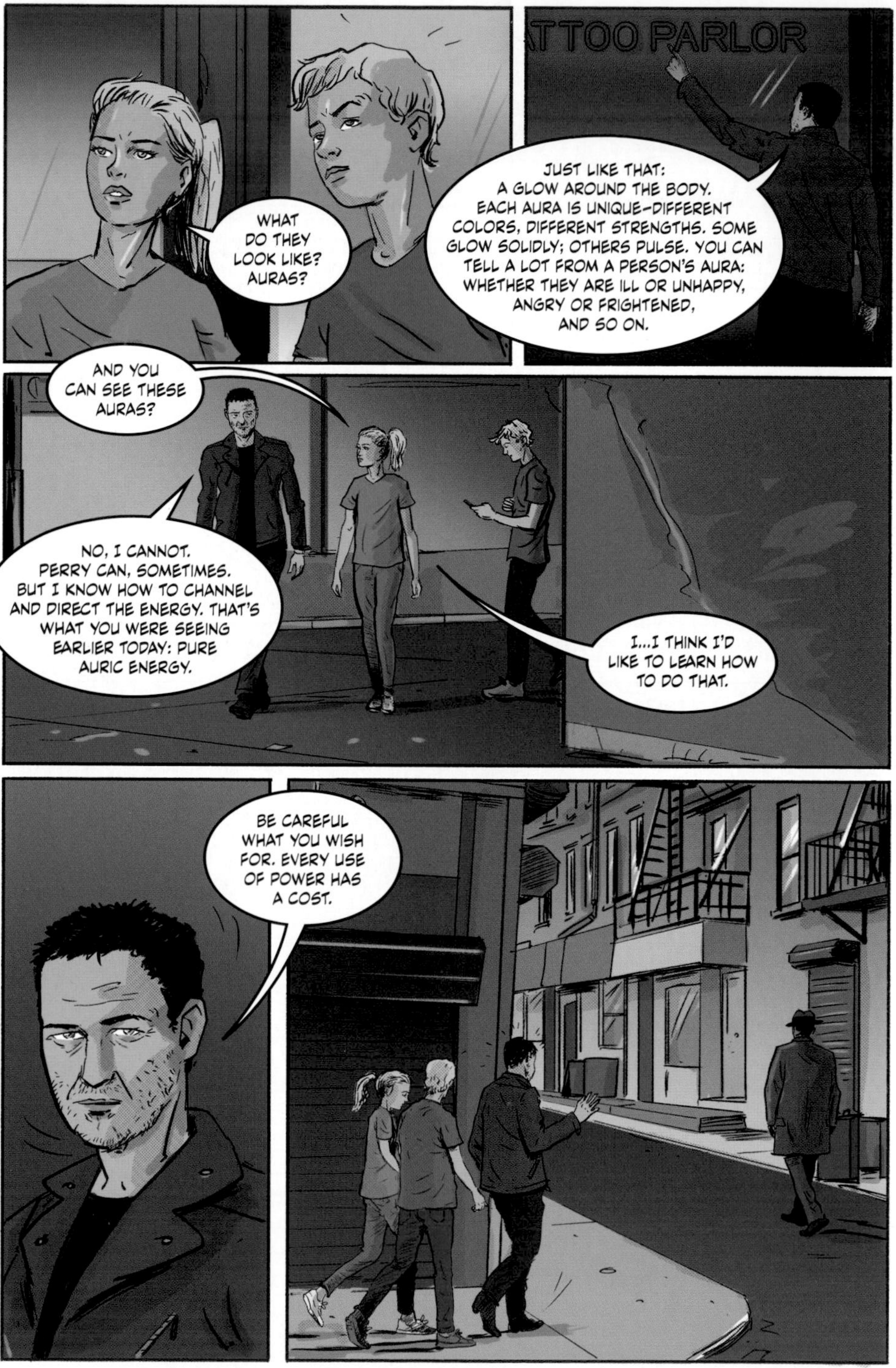
ATTOO PARLOR
WHAT DO THEY LOOK LIKE? AURAS?
JUST LIKE THAT: A GLOW AROUND THE BODY. EACH AURA IS UNIQUE—DIFFERENT COLORS, DIFFERENT STRENGTHS. SOME GLOW SOLIDLY; OTHERS PULSE. YOU CAN TELL A LOT FROM A PERSON'S AURA: WHETHER THEY ARE ILL OR UNHAPPY, ANGRY OR FRIGHTENED, AND SO ON.
AND YOU CAN SEE THESE AURAS?
NO, I CANNOT. PERRY CAN, SOMETIMES. BUT I KNOW HOW TO CHANNEL AND DIRECT THE ENERGY. THAT'S WHAT YOU WERE SEEING EARLIER TODAY: PURE AURIC ENERGY.
I...I THINK I'D LIKE TO LEARN HOW TO DO THAT.
BE CAREFUL WHAT YOU WISH FOR. EVERY USE OF POWER HAS A COST.

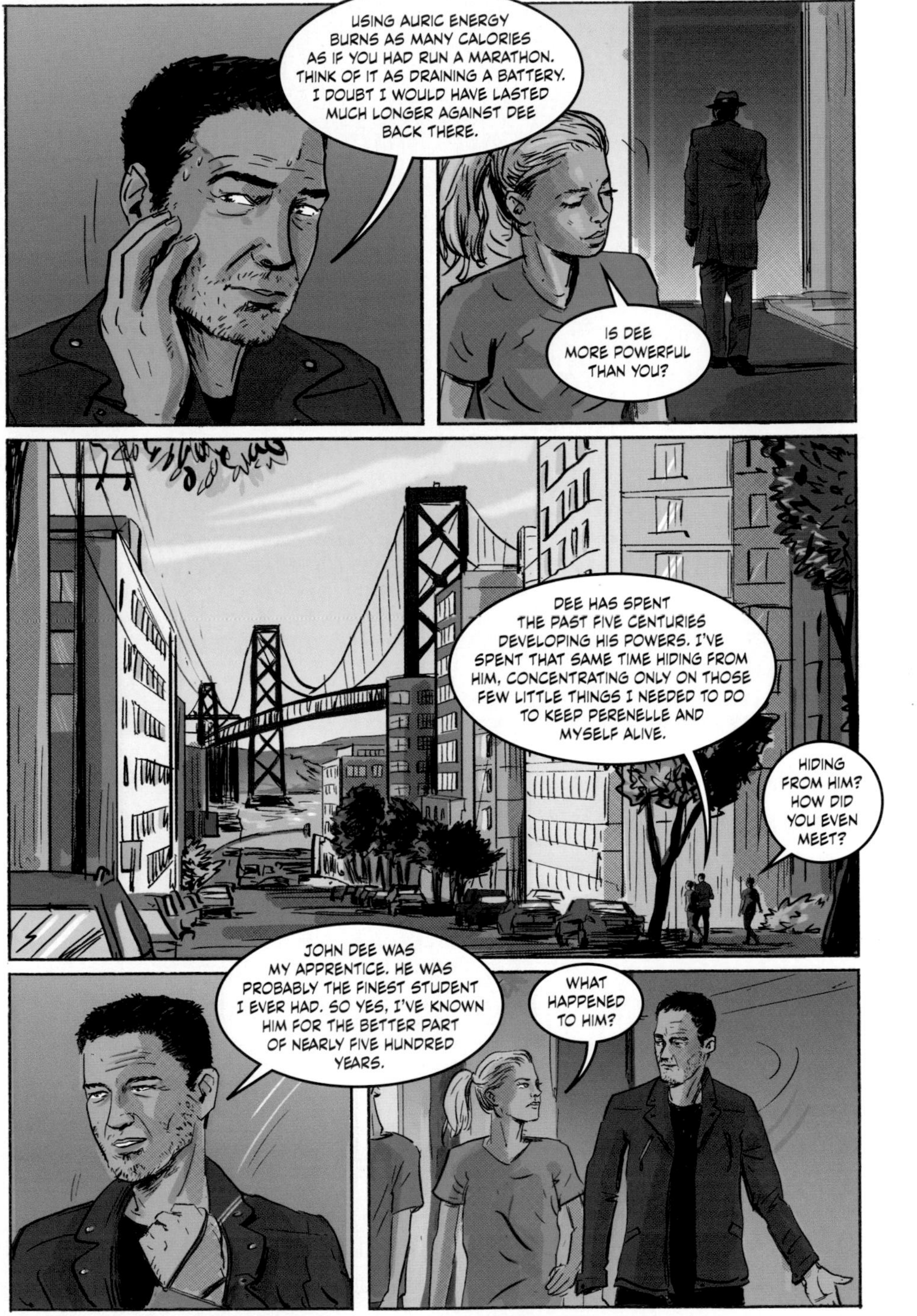
USING AURIC ENERGY BURNS AS MANY CALORIES AS IF YOU HAD RUN A MARATHON. THINK OF IT AS DRAINING A BATTERY. I DOUBT I WOULD HAVE LASTED MUCH LONGER AGAINST DEE BACK THERE.
IS DEE MORE POWERFUL THAN YOU?
DEE HAS SPENT THE PAST FIVE CENTURIES DEVELOPING HIS POWERS. I'VE SPENT THAT SAME TIME HIDING FROM HIM, CONCENTRATING ONLY ON THOSE FEW LITTLE THINGS I NEEDED TO DO TO KEEP PERENELLE AND MYSELF ALIVE.
HIDING FROM HIM? HOW DID YOU EVEN MEET?
JOHN DEE WAS MY APPRENTICE. HE WAS PROBABLY THE FINEST STUDENT I EVER HAD. SO YES, I'VE KNOWN HIM FOR THE BETTER PART OF NEARLY FIVE HUNDRED YEARS.
WHAT HAPPENED TO HIM?

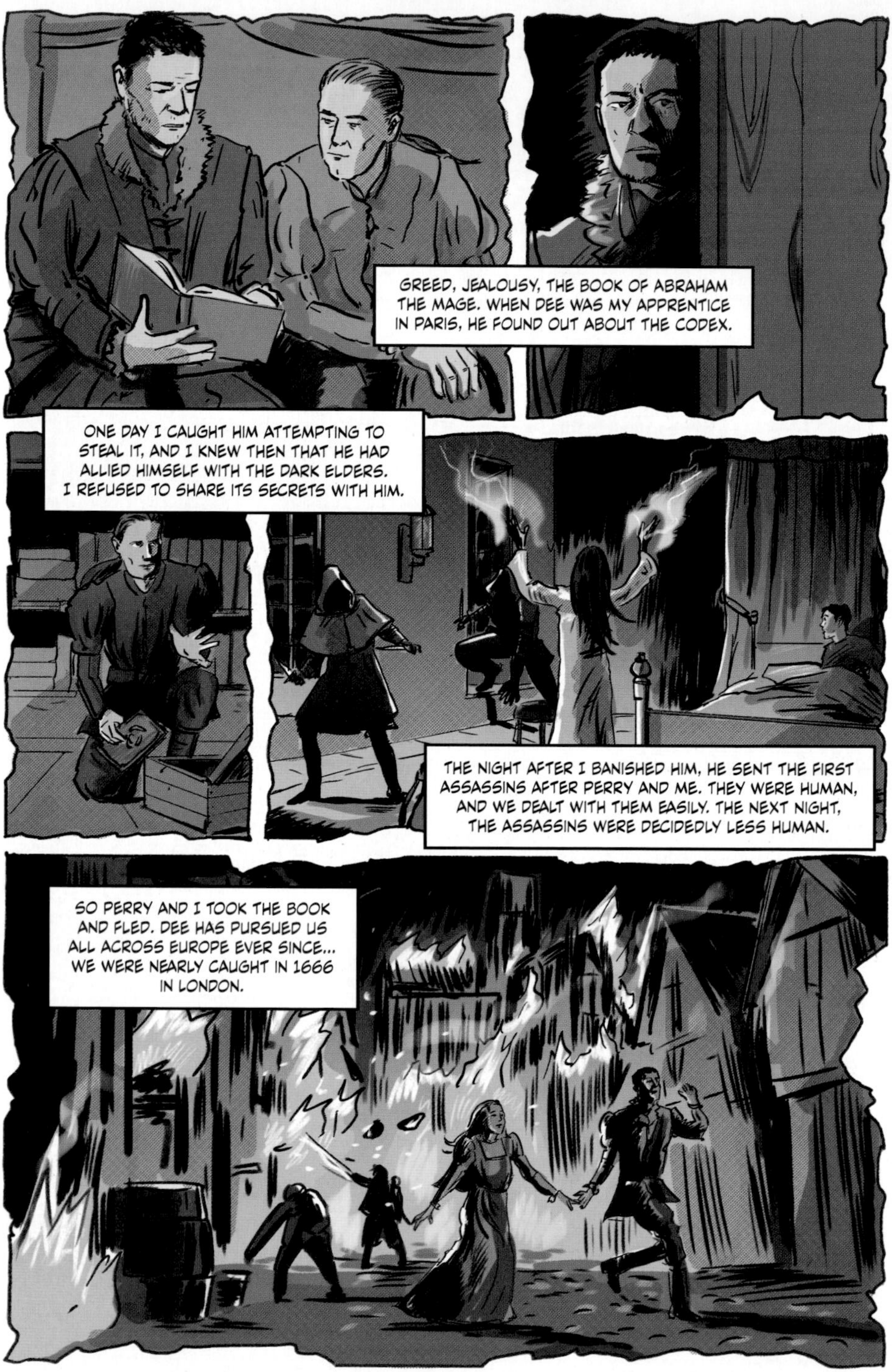
GREED, JEALOUSY, THE BOOK OF ABRAHAM THE MAGE. WHEN DEE WAS MY APPRENTICE IN PARIS, HE FOUND OUT ABOUT THE CODEX.
ONE DAY I CAUGHT HIM ATTEMPTING TO STEAL IT, AND I KNEW THEN THAT HE HAD ALLIED HIMSELF WITH THE DARK ELDERS. I REFUSED TO SHARE ITS SECRETS WITH HIM.
THE NIGHT AFTER I BANISHED HIM, HE SENT THE FIRST ASSASSINS AFTER PERRY AND ME. THEY WERE HUMAN, AND WE DEALT WITH THEM EASILY. THE NEXT NIGHT, THE ASSASSINS WERE DECIDEDLY LESS HUMAN.
SO PERRY AND I TOOK THE BOOK AND FLED. DEE HAS PURSUED US ALL ACROSS EUROPE EVER SINCE... WE WERE NEARLY CAUGHT IN 1666 IN LONDON.

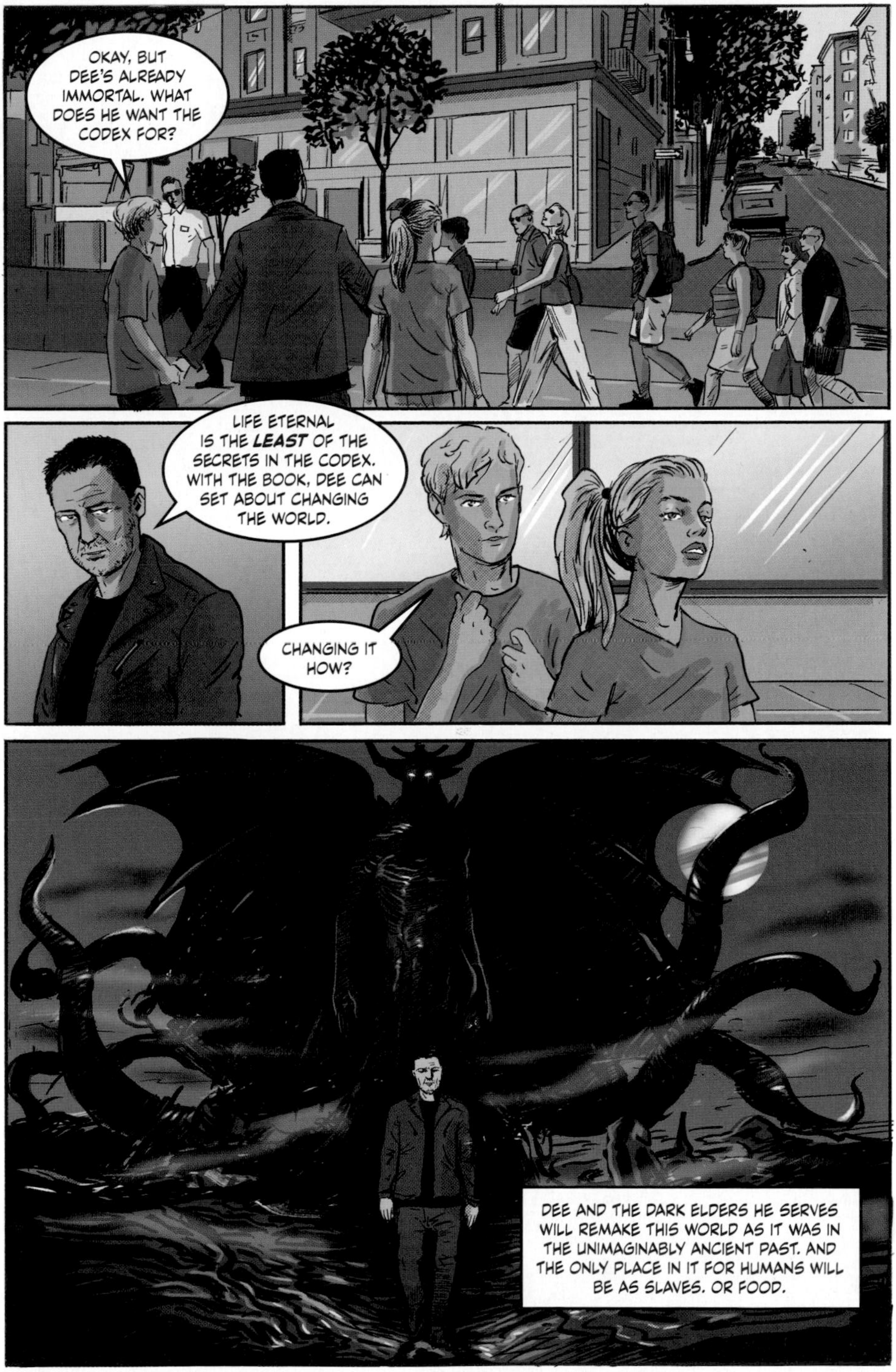
OKAY, BUT DEE'S ALREADY IMMORTAL. WHAT DOES HE WANT THE CODEX FOR?
LIFE ETERNAL IS THE **LEAST** OF THE SECRETS IN THE CODEX. WITH THE BOOK, DEE CAN SET ABOUT CHANGING THE WORLD.
CHANGING IT HOW?
DEE AND THE DARK ELDERS HE SERVES WILL REMAKE THIS WORLD AS IT WAS IN THE UNIMAGINABLY ANCIENT PAST. AND THE ONLY PLACE IN IT FOR HUMANS WILL BE AS SLAVES. OR FOOD.

CHAPTER 6

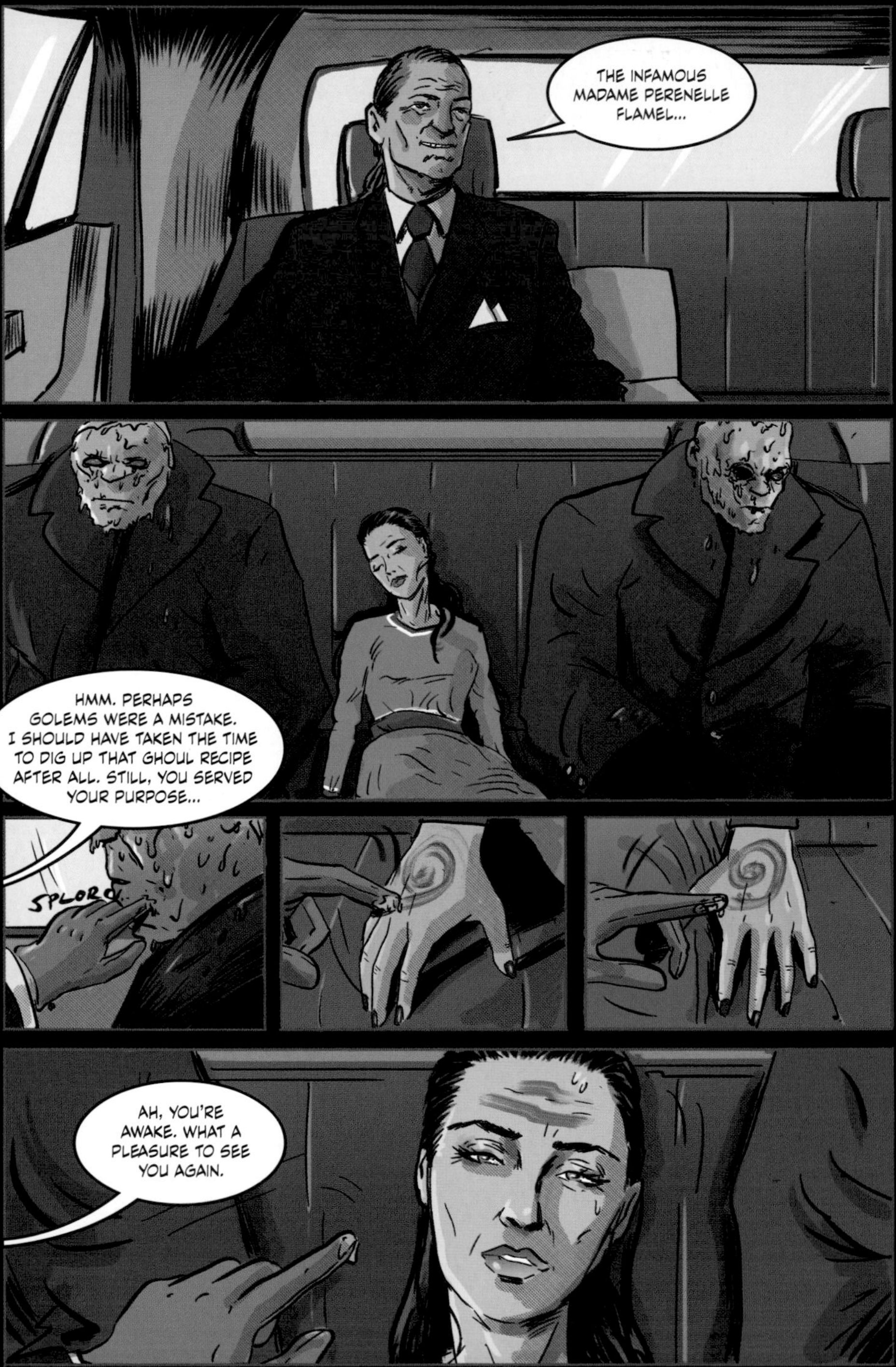
THE INFAMOUS MADAME PERENELLE FLAMEL...
HMM. PERHAPS GOLEMS WERE A MISTAKE. I SHOULD HAVE TAKEN THE TIME TO DIG UP THAT GHOUL RECIPE AFTER ALL. STILL, YOU SERVED YOUR PURPOSE...
SPLORCH
AH, YOU'RE AWAKE. WHAT A PLEASURE TO SEE YOU AGAIN.

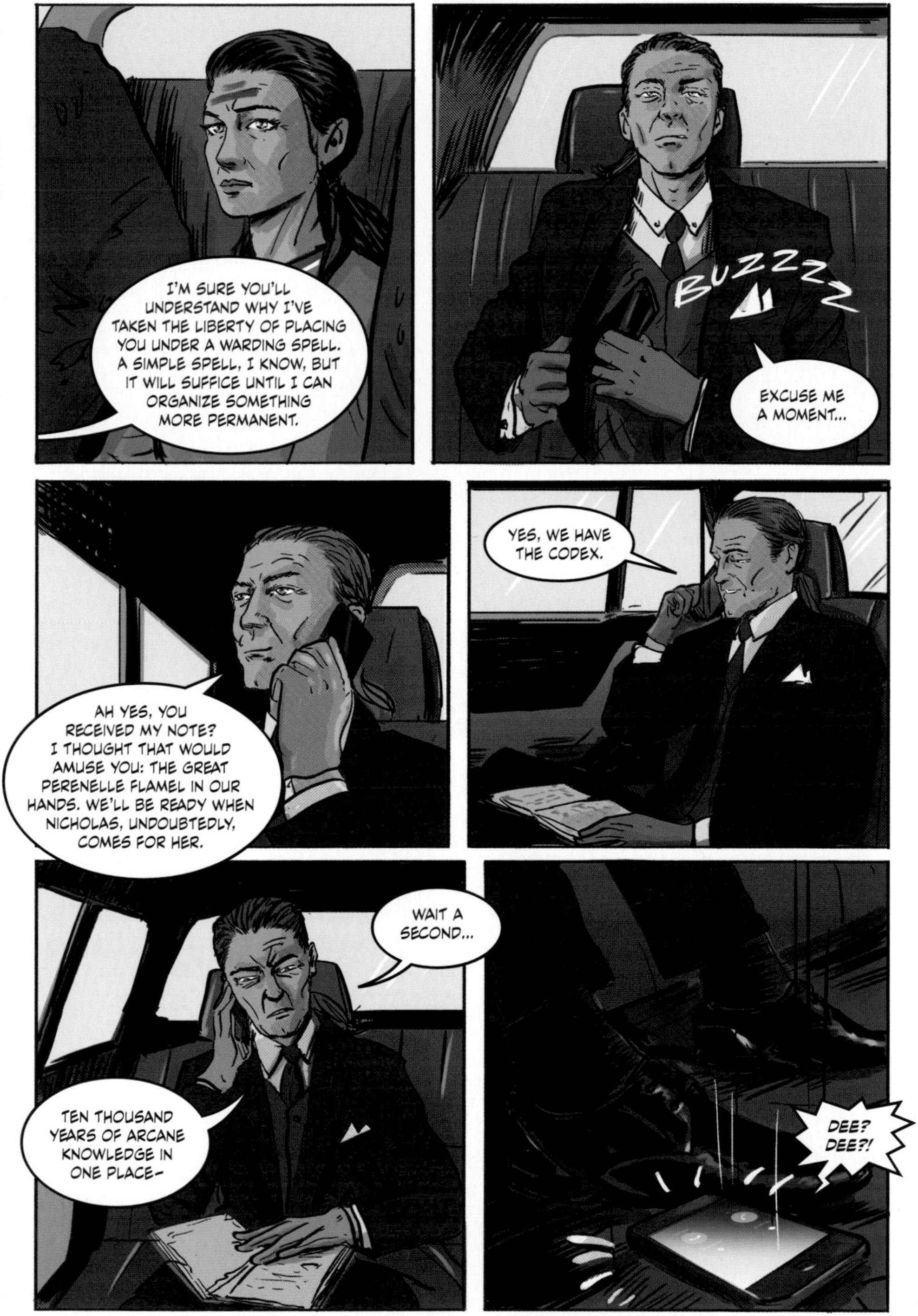
I'M SURE YOU'LL UNDERSTAND WHY I'VE TAKEN THE LIBERTY OF PLACING YOU UNDER A WARDING SPELL. A SIMPLE SPELL, I KNOW, BUT IT WILL SUFFICE UNTIL I CAN ORGANIZE SOMETHING MORE PERMANENT.
BUZZZZ
EXCUSE ME A MOMENT...
AH YES, YOU RECEIVED MY NOTE? I THOUGHT THAT WOULD AMUSE YOU: THE GREAT PERENELLE FLAMEL IN OUR HANDS. WE'LL BE READY WHEN NICHOLAS, UNDOUBTEDLY, COMES FOR HER.
YES, WE HAVE THE CODEX.
WAIT A SECOND...
TEN THOUSAND YEARS OF ARCANE KNOWLEDGE IN ONE PLACE-
DEE? DEE?!

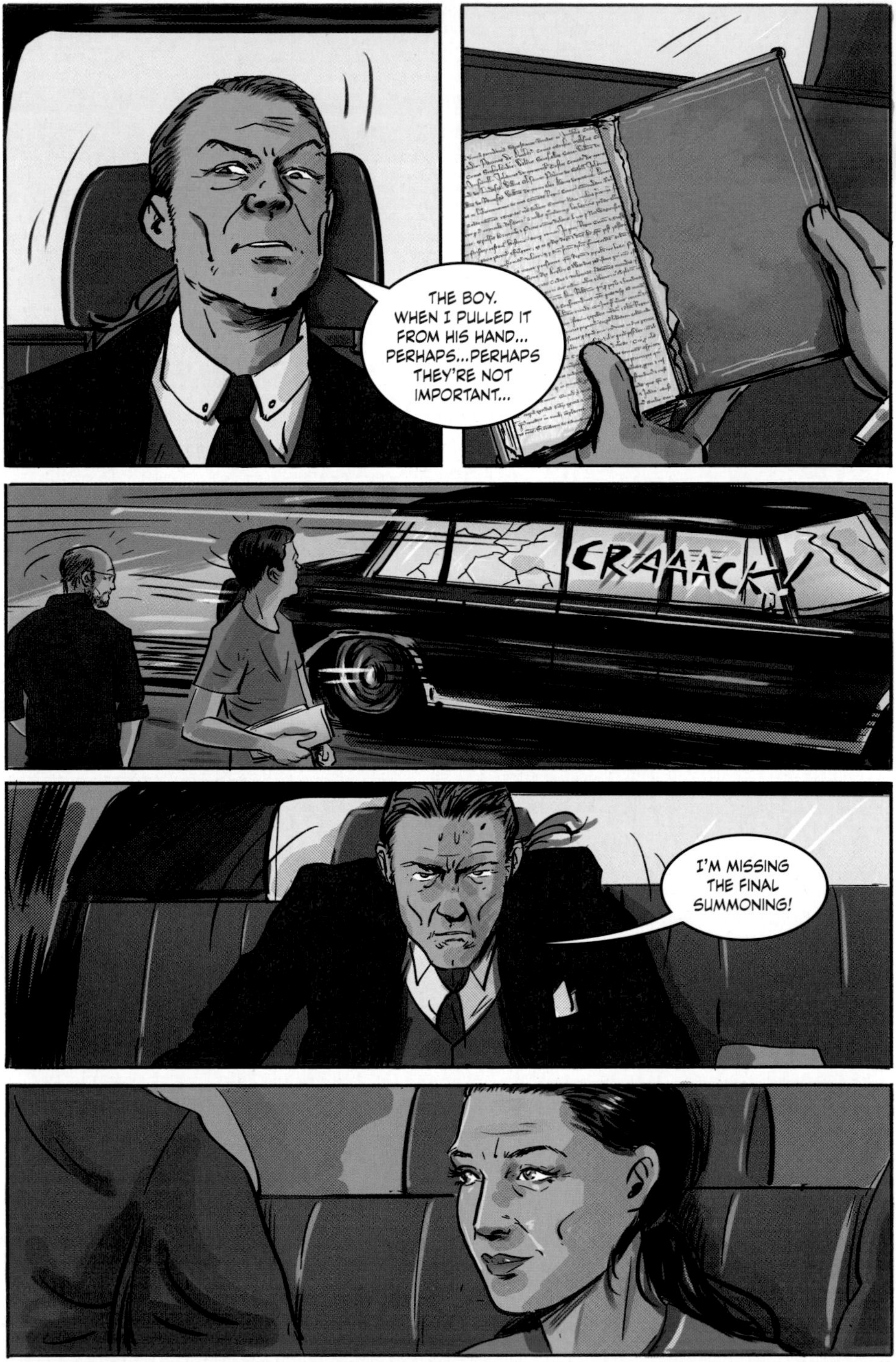

THE BOY. WHEN I PULLED IT FROM HIS HAND... PERHAPS...PERHAPS THEY'RE NOT IMPORTANT...
CRAAACK!
I'M MISSING THE FINAL SUMMONING!

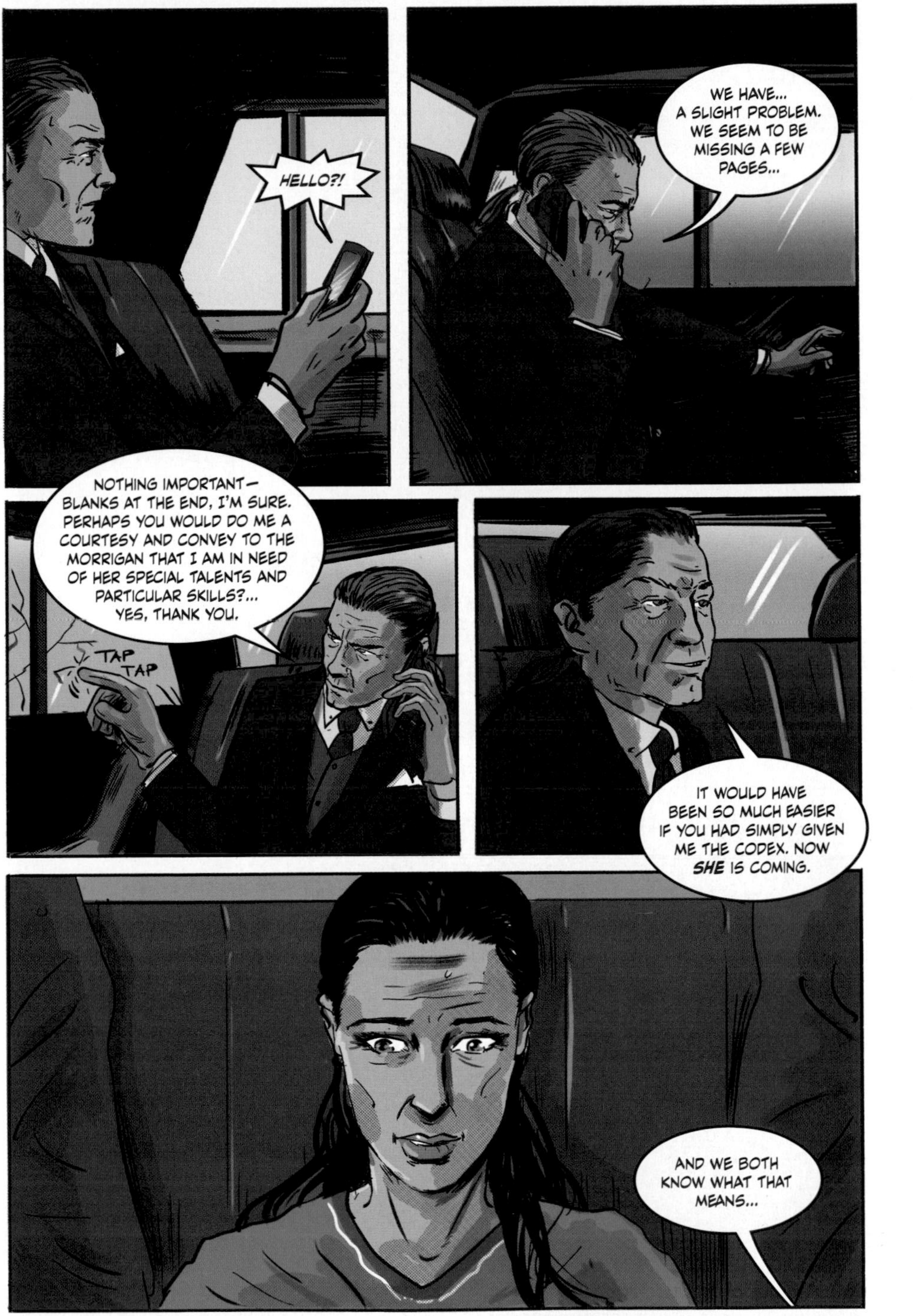
HELLO?!
WE HAVE... A SLIGHT PROBLEM. WE SEEM TO BE MISSING A FEW PAGES...
NOTHING IMPORTANT—BLANKS AT THE END, I'M SURE. PERHAPS YOU WOULD DO ME A COURTESY AND CONVEY TO THE MORRIGAN THAT I AM IN NEED OF HER SPECIAL TALENTS AND PARTICULAR SKILLS?... YES, THANK YOU.
TAP TAP
IT WOULD HAVE BEEN SO MUCH EASIER IF YOU HAD SIMPLY GIVEN ME THE CODEX. NOW ***SHE*** IS COMING.
AND WE BOTH KNOW WHAT THAT MEANS...

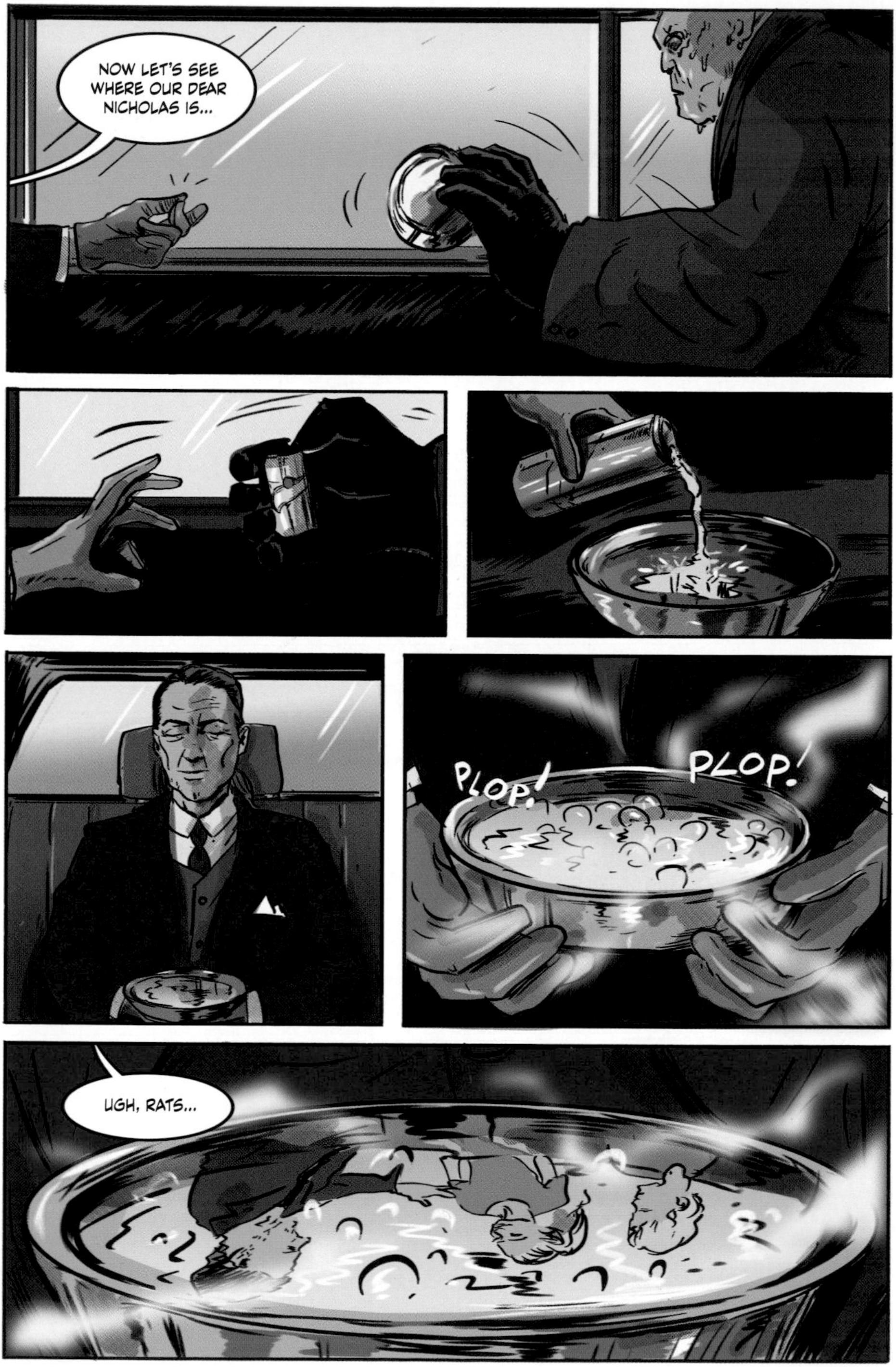
NOW LET'S SEE WHERE OUR DEAR NICHOLAS IS...
PLOP!
PLOP!
UGH, RATS...

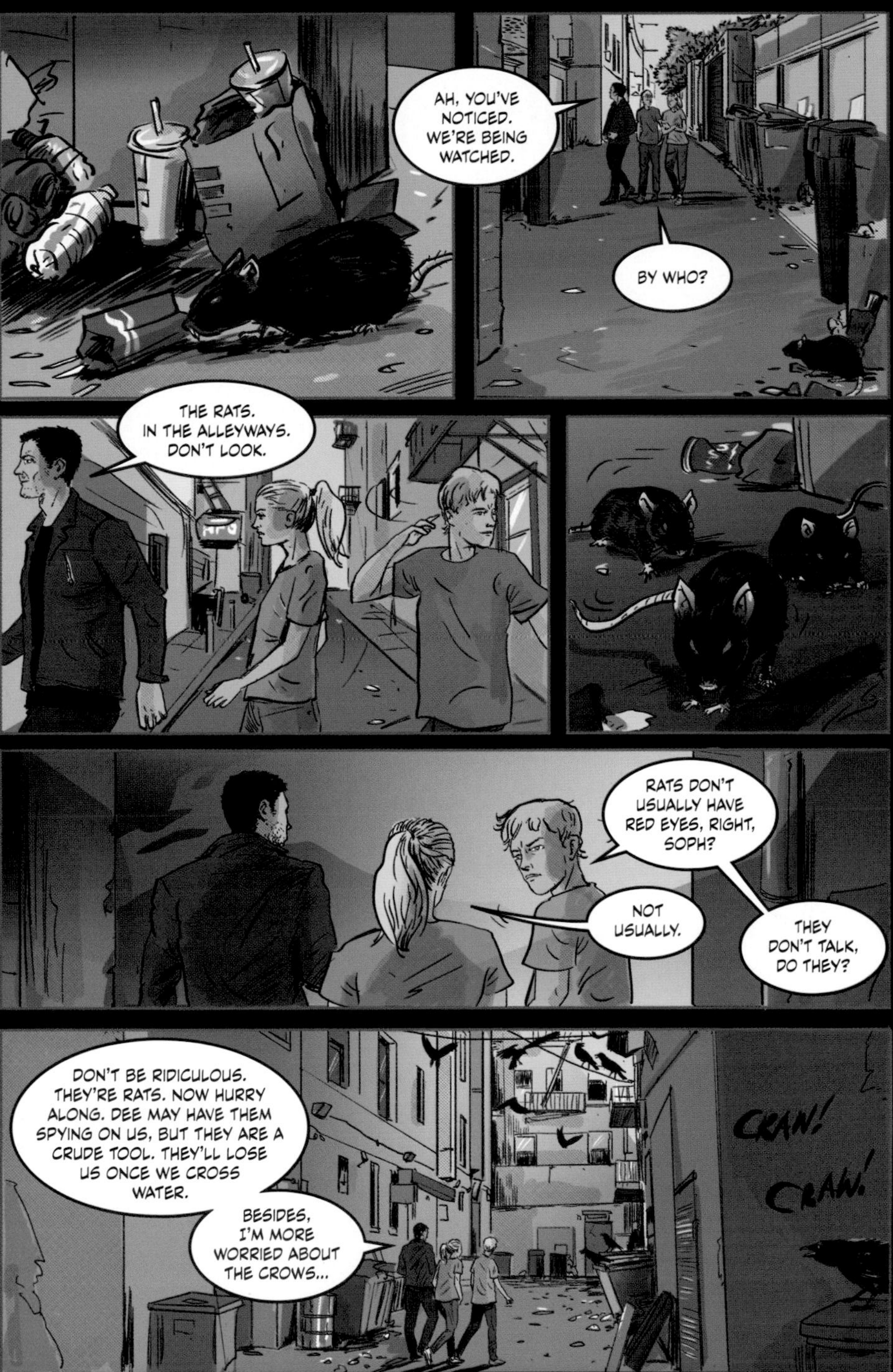
AH, YOU'VE NOTICED. WE'RE BEING WATCHED.
BY WHO?
THE RATS. IN THE ALLEYWAYS. DON'T LOOK.
RATS DON'T USUALLY HAVE RED EYES, RIGHT, SOPH?
NOT USUALLY.
THEY DON'T TALK, DO THEY?
DON'T BE RIDICULOUS. THEY'RE RATS. NOW HURRY ALONG. DEE MAY HAVE THEM SPYING ON US, BUT THEY ARE A CRUDE TOOL. THEY'LL LOSE US ONCE WE CROSS WATER.
BESIDES, I'M MORE WORRIED ABOUT THE CROWS...
CRAW!
CRAW!

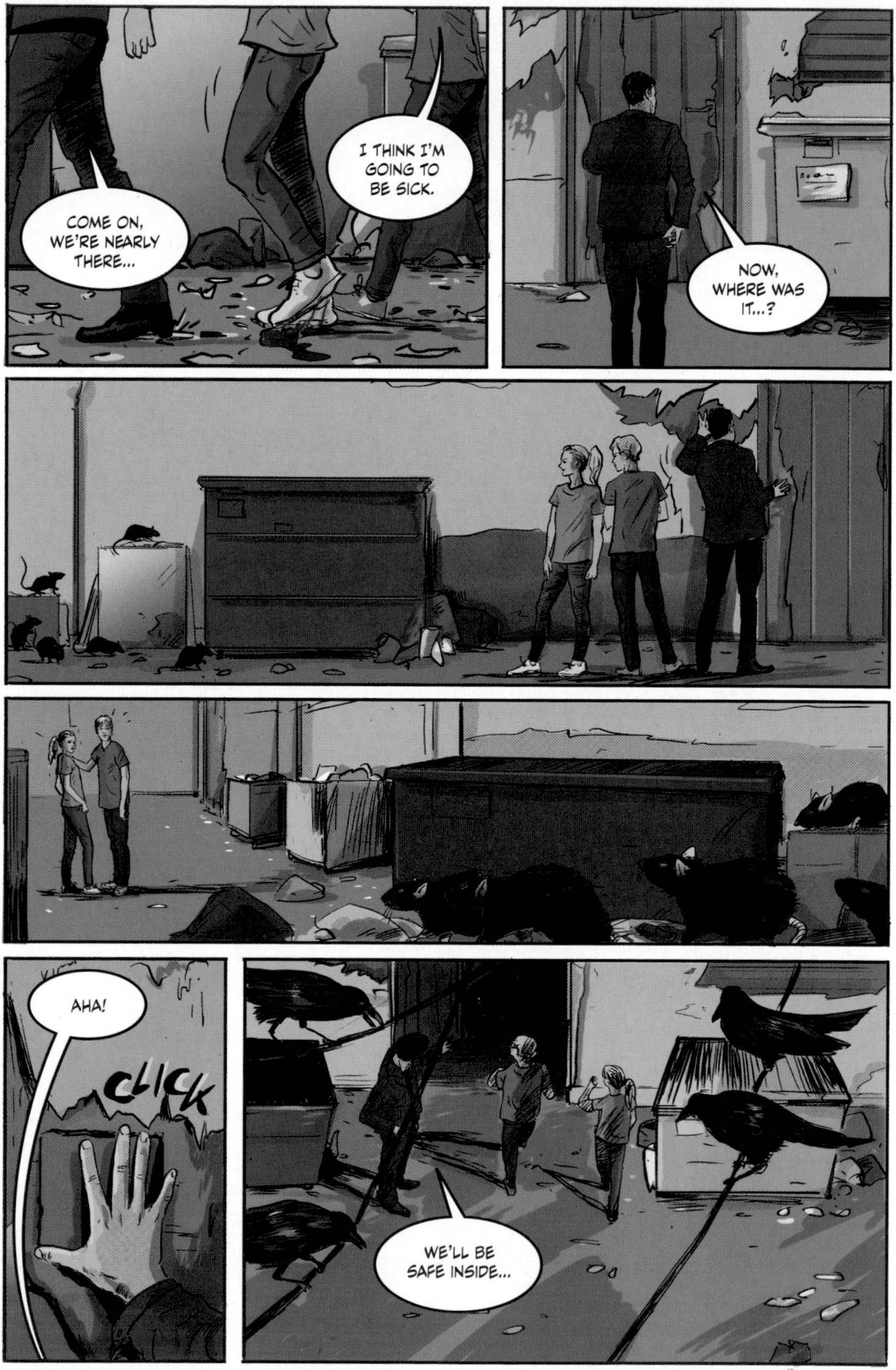
I THINK I'M GOING TO BE SICK.
COME ON, WE'RE NEARLY THERE...
NOW, WHERE WAS IT...?
AHA!
CLICK
WE'LL BE SAFE INSIDE...

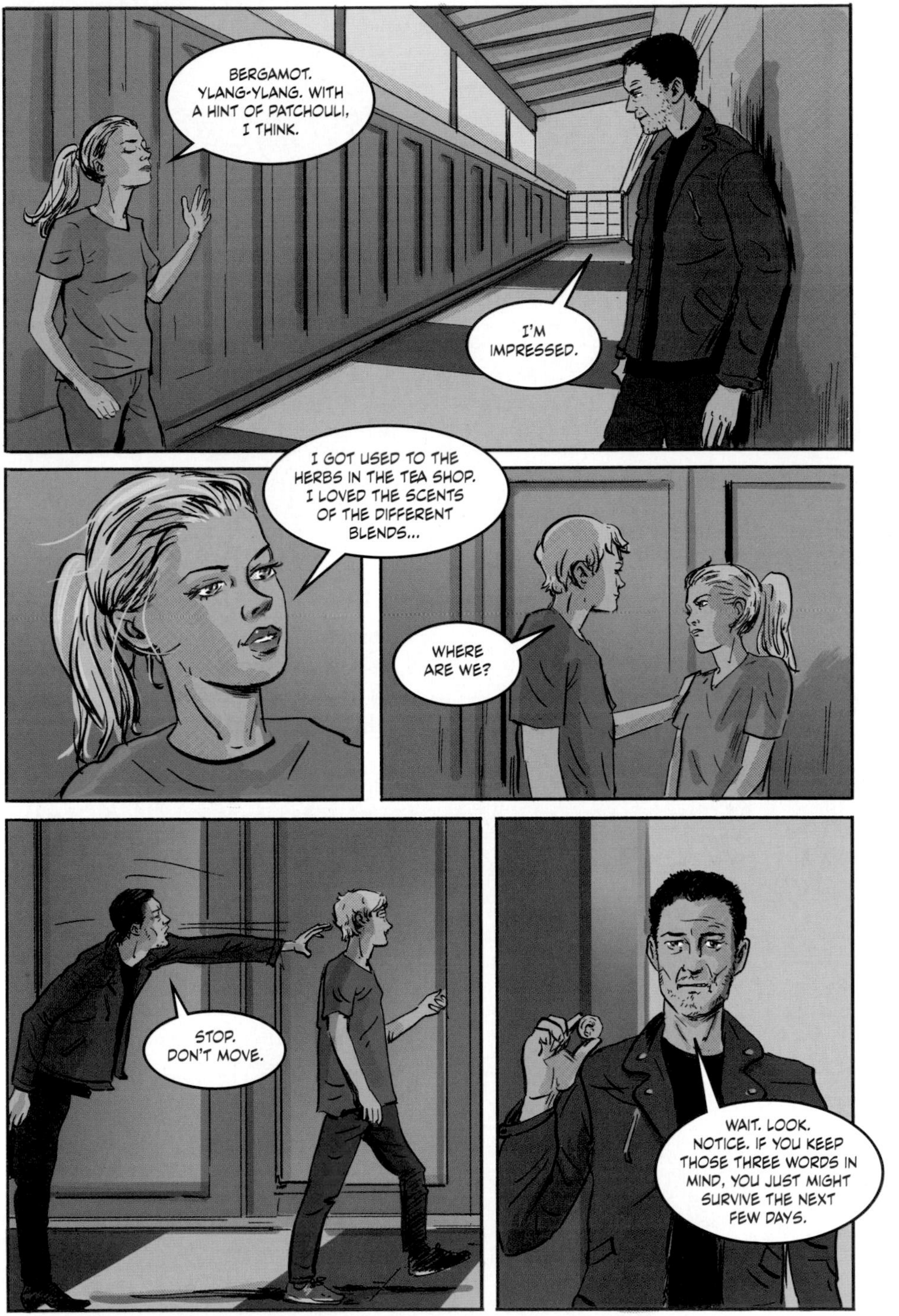
BERGAMOT. YLANG-YLANG. WITH A HINT OF PATCHOULI, I THINK.
I'M IMPRESSED.
I GOT USED TO THE HERBS IN THE TEA SHOP. I LOVED THE SCENTS OF THE DIFFERENT BLENDS...
WHERE ARE WE?
STOP. DON'T MOVE.
WAIT. LOOK. NOTICE. IF YOU KEEP THOSE THREE WORDS IN MIND, YOU JUST MIGHT SURVIVE THE NEXT FEW DAYS.

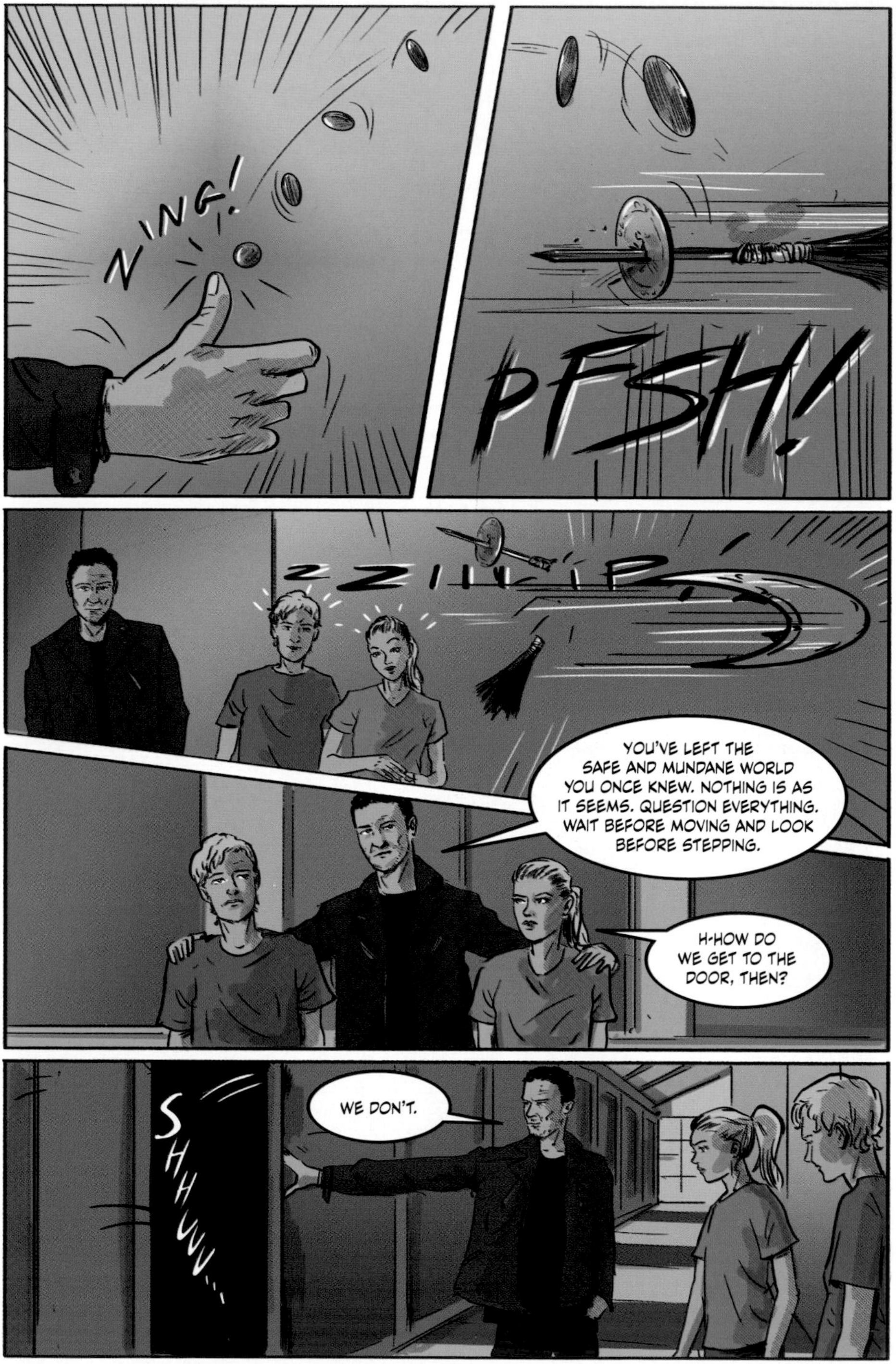
NING!
PFSH!
ZZZIIIIIP
YOU'VE LEFT THE SAFE AND MUNDANE WORLD YOU ONCE KNEW. NOTHING IS AS IT SEEMS. QUESTION EVERYTHING. WAIT BEFORE MOVING AND LOOK BEFORE STEPPING.
H-HOW DO WE GET TO THE DOOR, THEN?
WE DON'T.
SHHUUU...

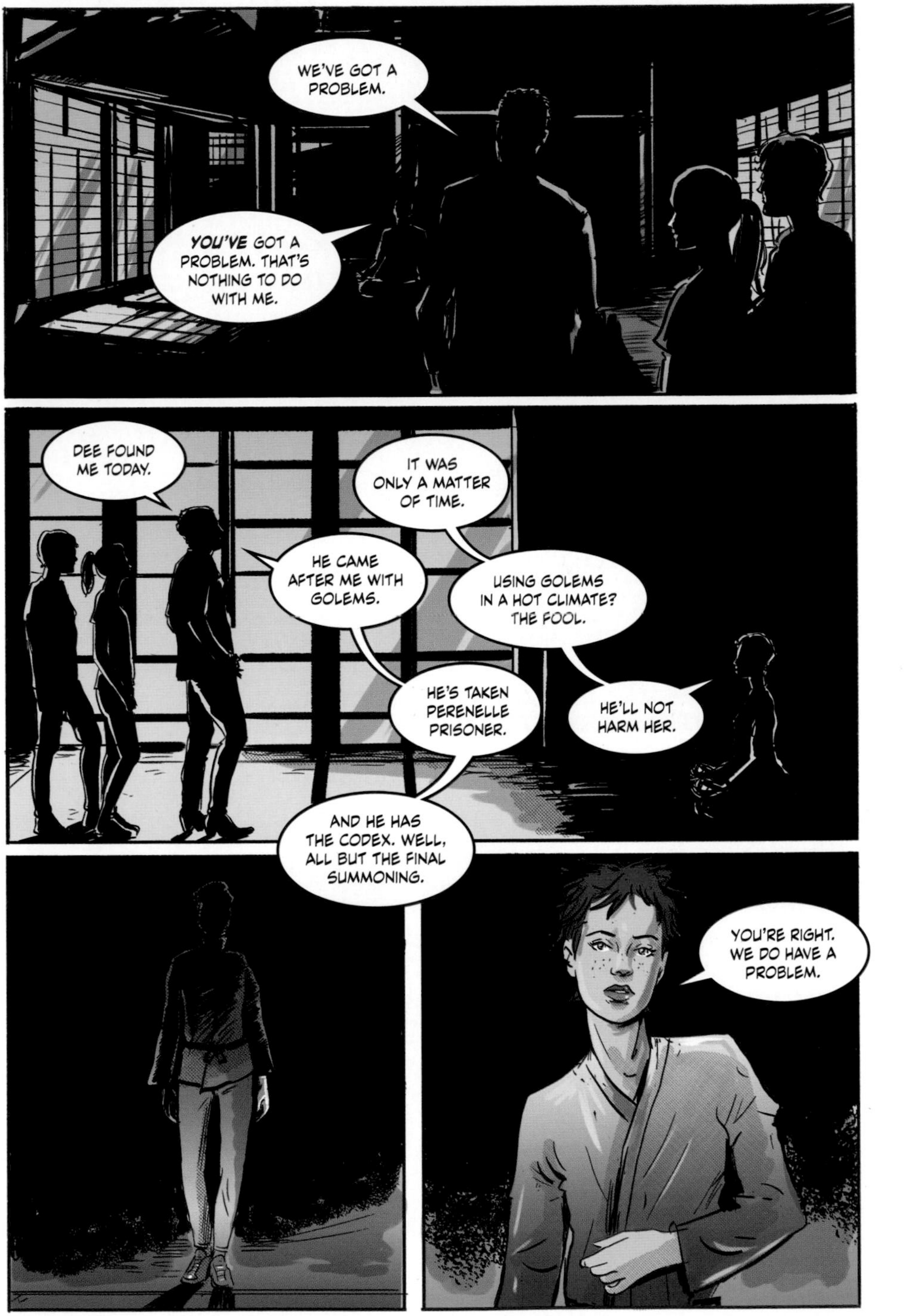
WE'VE GOT A PROBLEM.
YOU'VE GOT A PROBLEM. THAT'S NOTHING TO DO WITH ME.
DEE FOUND ME TODAY.
IT WAS ONLY A MATTER OF TIME.
HE CAME AFTER ME WITH GOLEMS.
USING GOLEMS IN A HOT CLIMATE? THE FOOL.
HE'S TAKEN PERENELLE PRISONER.
HE'LL NOT HARM HER.
AND HE HAS THE CODEX. WELL, ALL BUT THE FINAL SUMMONING.
YOU'RE RIGHT. WE DO HAVE A PROBLEM.

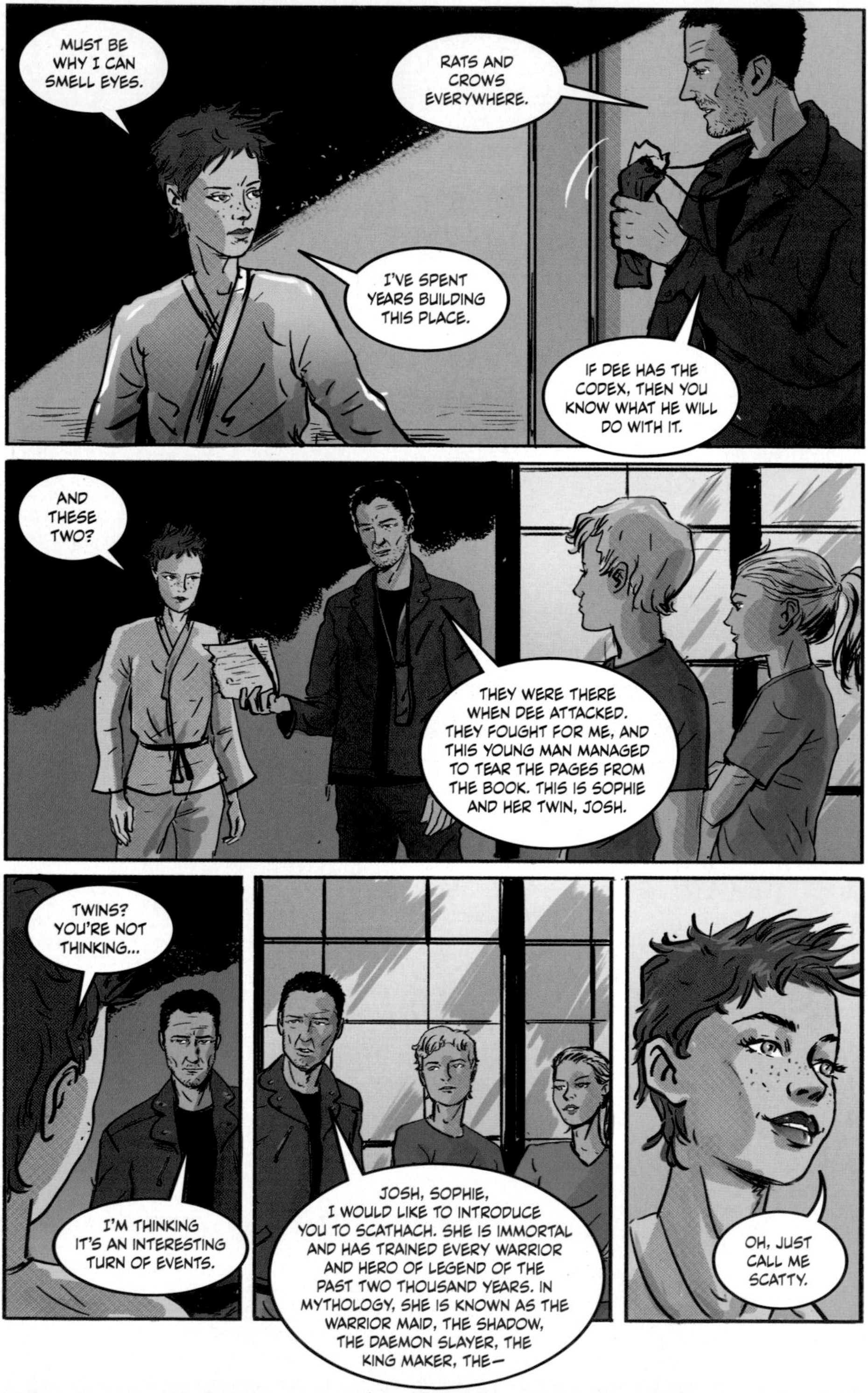
MUST BE WHY I CAN SMELL EYES.
RATS AND CROWS EVERYWHERE.
I'VE SPENT YEARS BUILDING THIS PLACE.
IF DEE HAS THE CODEX, THEN YOU KNOW WHAT HE WILL DO WITH IT.
AND THESE TWO?
THEY WERE THERE WHEN DEE ATTACKED. THEY FOUGHT FOR ME, AND THIS YOUNG MAN MANAGED TO TEAR THE PAGES FROM THE BOOK. THIS IS SOPHIE AND HER TWIN, JOSH.
TWINS? YOU'RE NOT THINKING...
I'M THINKING IT'S AN INTERESTING TURN OF EVENTS.
JOSH, SOPHIE, I WOULD LIKE TO INTRODUCE YOU TO SCATHACH. SHE IS IMMORTAL AND HAS TRAINED EVERY WARRIOR AND HERO OF LEGEND OF THE PAST TWO THOUSAND YEARS. IN MYTHOLOGY, SHE IS KNOWN AS THE WARRIOR MAID, THE SHADOW, THE DAEMON SLAYER, THE KING MAKER, THE—
OH, JUST CALL ME SCATTY.

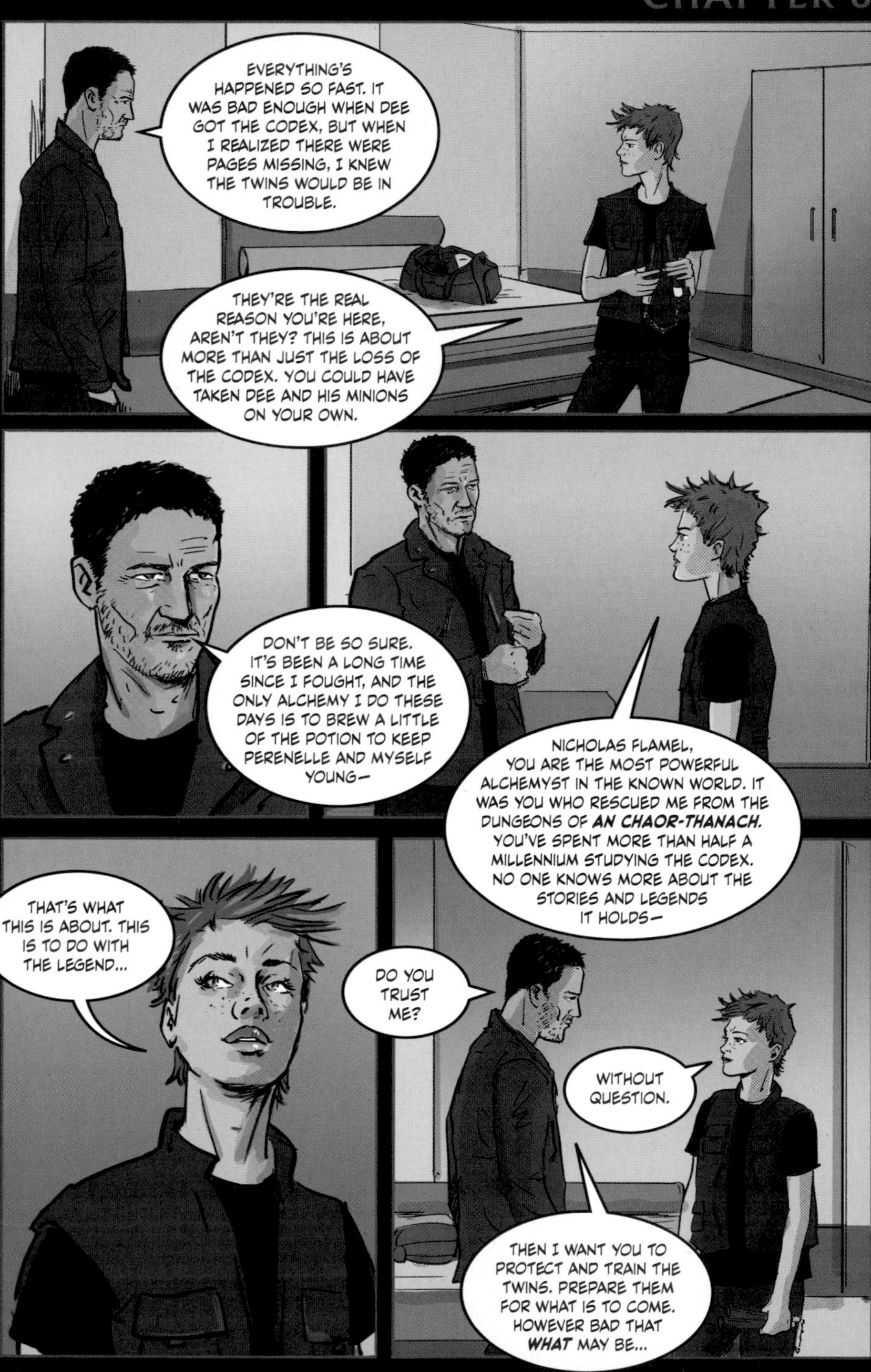
EVERYTHING'S HAPPENED SO FAST. IT WAS BAD ENOUGH WHEN DEE GOT THE CODEX, BUT WHEN I REALIZED THERE WERE PAGES MISSING, I KNEW THE TWINS WOULD BE IN TROUBLE.
THEY'RE THE REAL REASON YOU'RE HERE, AREN'T THEY? THIS IS ABOUT MORE THAN JUST THE LOSS OF THE CODEX. YOU COULD HAVE TAKEN DEE AND HIS MINIONS ON YOUR OWN.
DON'T BE SO SURE. IT'S BEEN A LONG TIME SINCE I FOUGHT, AND THE ONLY ALCHEMY I DO THESE DAYS IS TO BREW A LITTLE OF THE POTION TO KEEP PERENELLE AND MYSELF YOUNG—
NICHOLAS FLAMEL, YOU ARE THE MOST POWERFUL ALCHEMYST IN THE KNOWN WORLD. IT WAS YOU WHO RESCUED ME FROM THE DUNGEONS OF ***AN CHAOR-THANACH.*** YOU'VE SPENT MORE THAN HALF A MILLENNIUM STUDYING THE CODEX. NO ONE KNOWS MORE ABOUT THE STORIES AND LEGENDS IT HOLDS—
THAT'S WHAT THIS IS ABOUT. THIS IS TO DO WITH THE LEGEND...
DO YOU TRUST ME?
WITHOUT QUESTION.
THEN I WANT YOU TO PROTECT AND TRAIN THE TWINS. PREPARE THEM FOR WHAT IS TO COME. HOWEVER BAD THAT ***WHAT*** MAY BE...

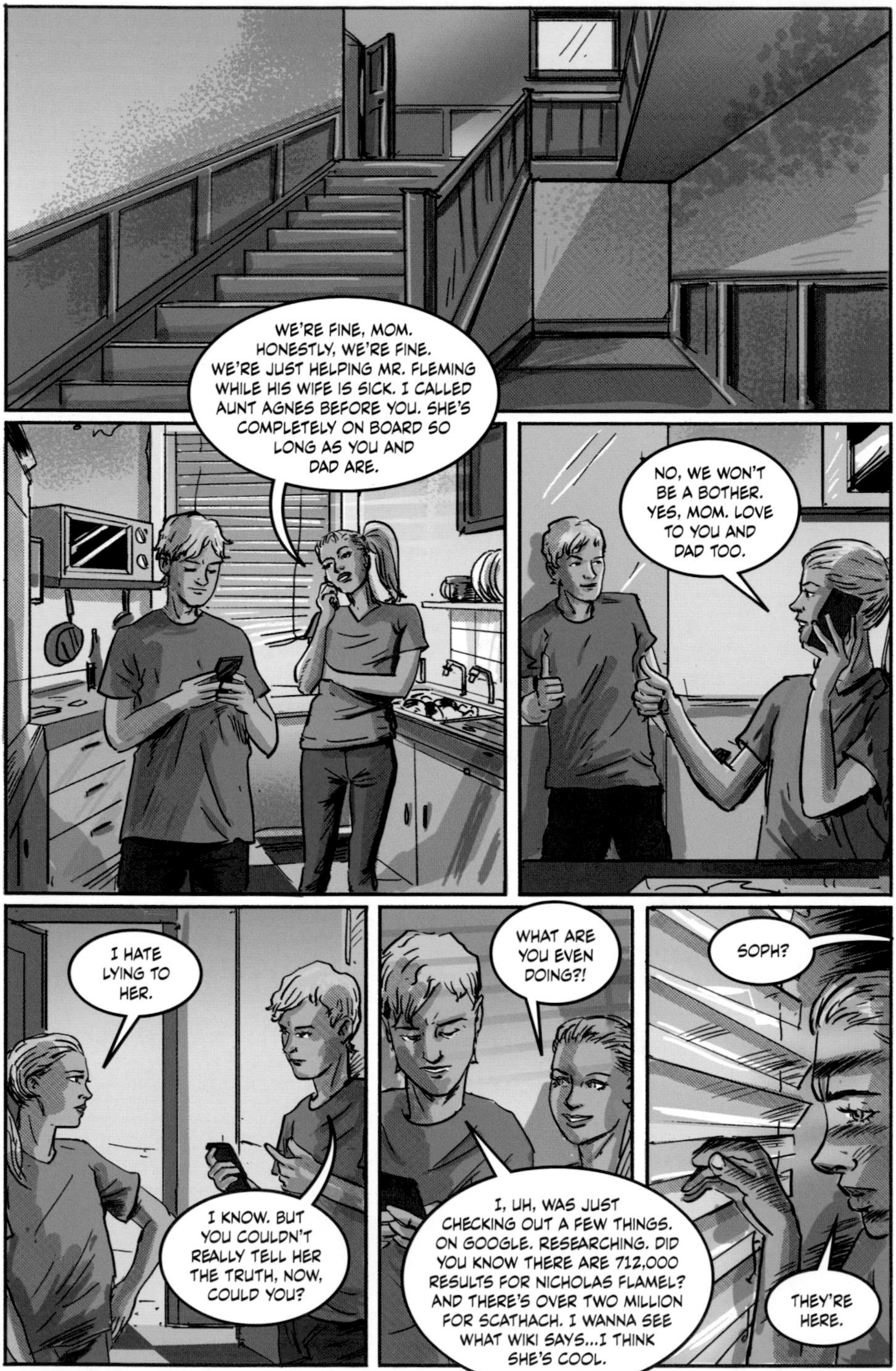
WE'RE FINE, MOM. HONESTLY, WE'RE FINE. WE'RE JUST HELPING MR. FLEMING WHILE HIS WIFE IS SICK. I CALLED AUNT AGNES BEFORE YOU. SHE'S COMPLETELY ON BOARD SO LONG AS YOU AND DAD ARE.
NO, WE WON'T BE A BOTHER. YES, MOM. LOVE TO YOU AND DAD TOO.
I HATE LYING TO HER.
I KNOW. BUT YOU COULDN'T REALLY TELL HER THE TRUTH, NOW, COULD YOU?
WHAT ARE YOU EVEN DOING?!
I, UH, WAS JUST CHECKING OUT A FEW THINGS. ON GOOGLE. RESEARCHING. DID YOU KNOW THERE ARE 712,000 RESULTS FOR NICHOLAS FLAMEL? AND THERE'S OVER TWO MILLION FOR SCATHACH. I WANNA SEE WHAT WIKI SAYS...I THINK SHE'S COOL.
SOPH?
THEY'RE HERE.

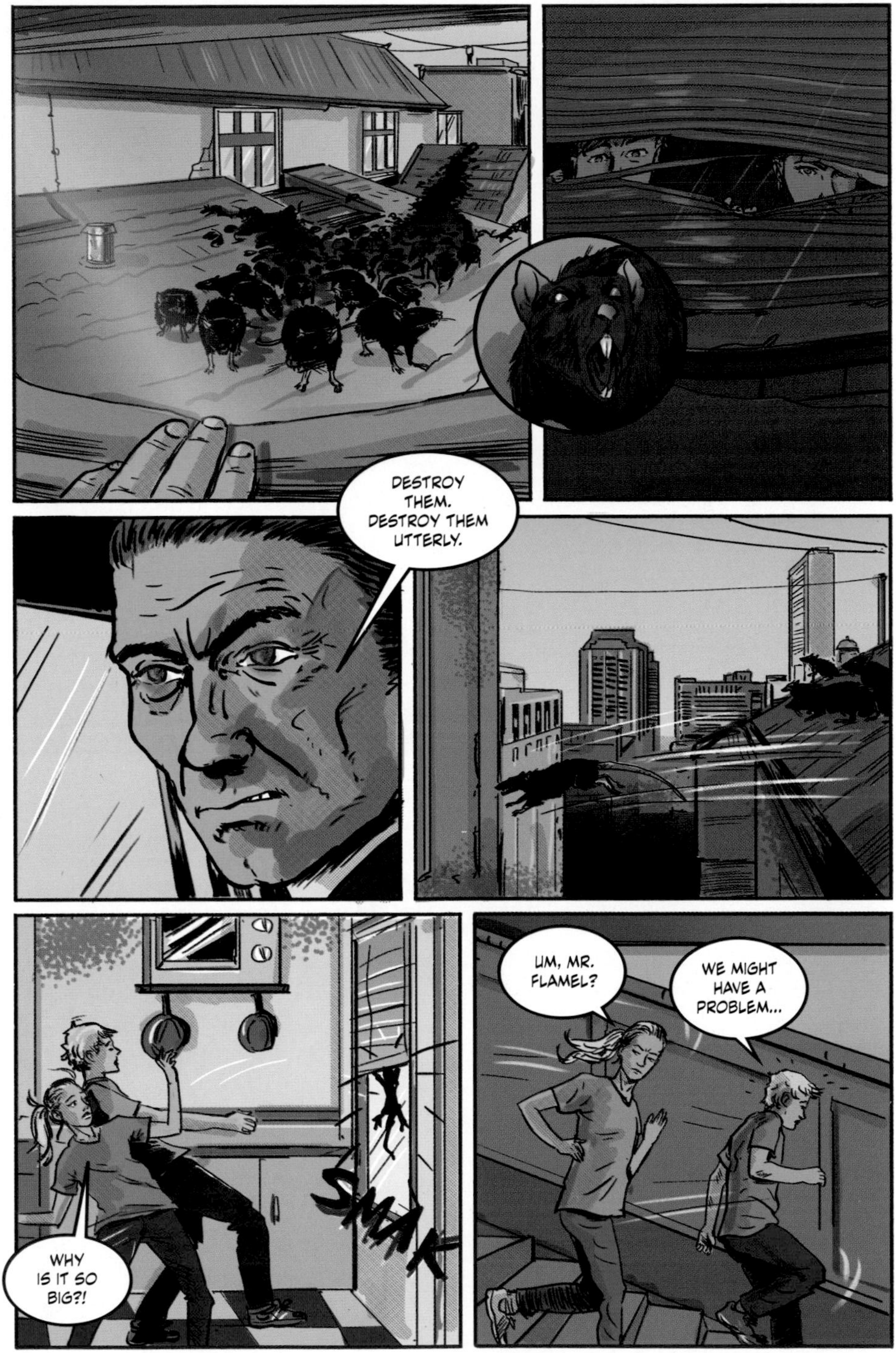
DESTROY THEM. DESTROY THEM UTTERLY.
SMAK
WHY IS IT SO BIG?!
UM, MR. FLAMEL?
WE MIGHT HAVE A PROBLEM...

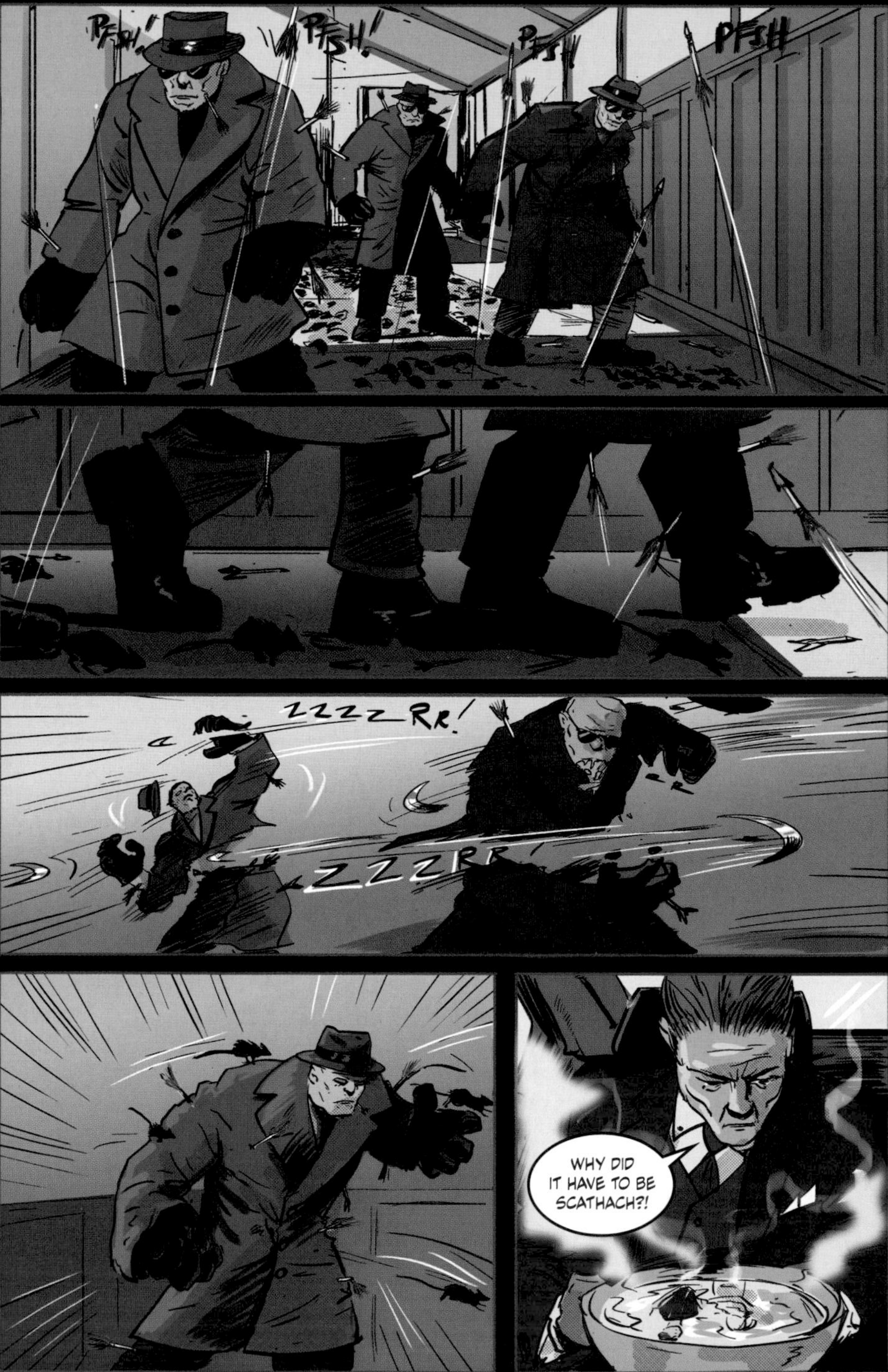
PFSH!
PFSH!
PFSH
PFSH
ZZZZRR!
ZZZRR
WHY DID IT HAVE TO BE SCATHACH?!

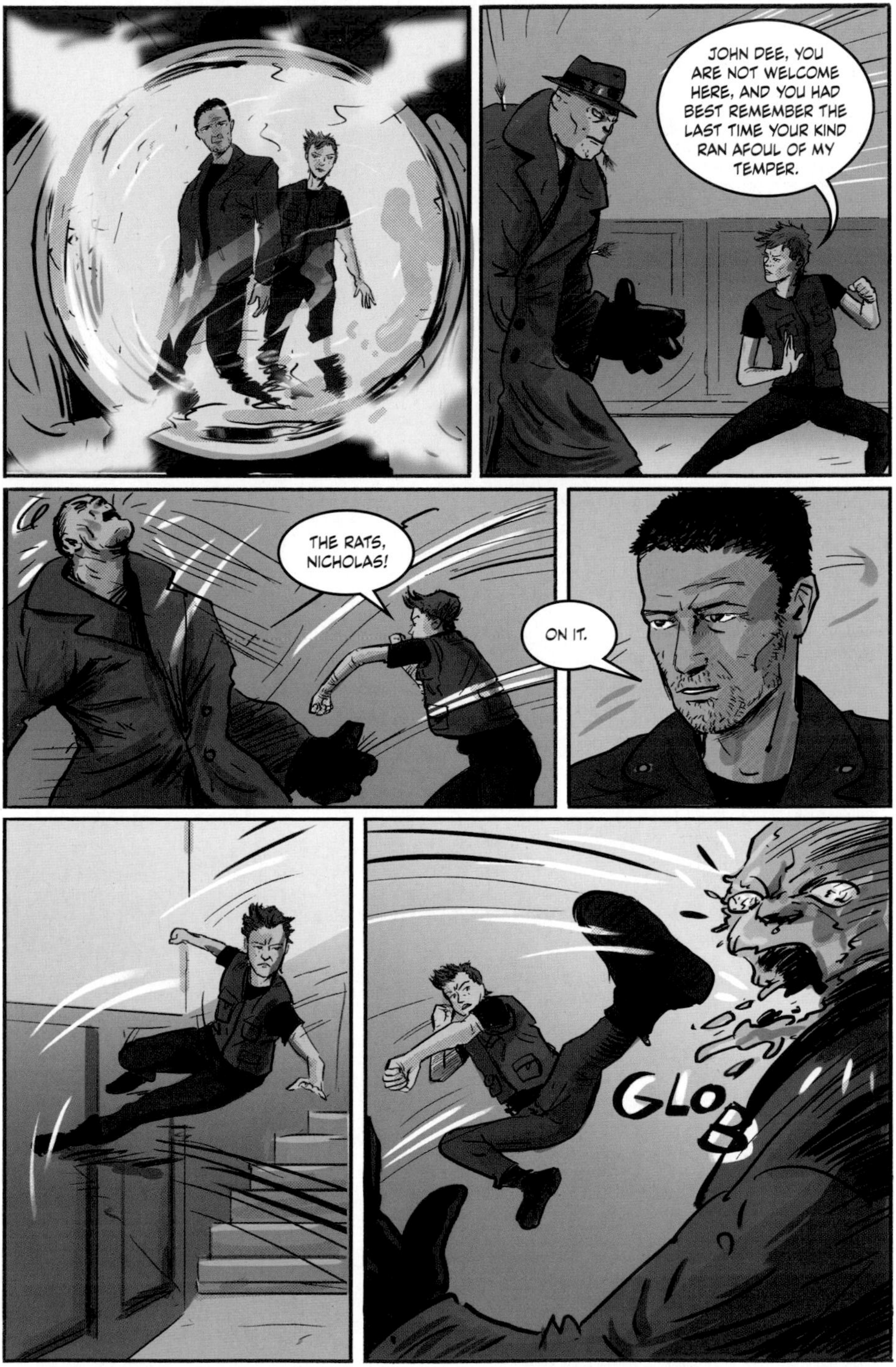
JOHN DEE, YOU ARE NOT WELCOME HERE, AND YOU HAD BEST REMEMBER THE LAST TIME YOUR KIND RAN AFOUL OF MY TEMPER.
THE RATS, NICHOLAS!
ON IT.
GLOB

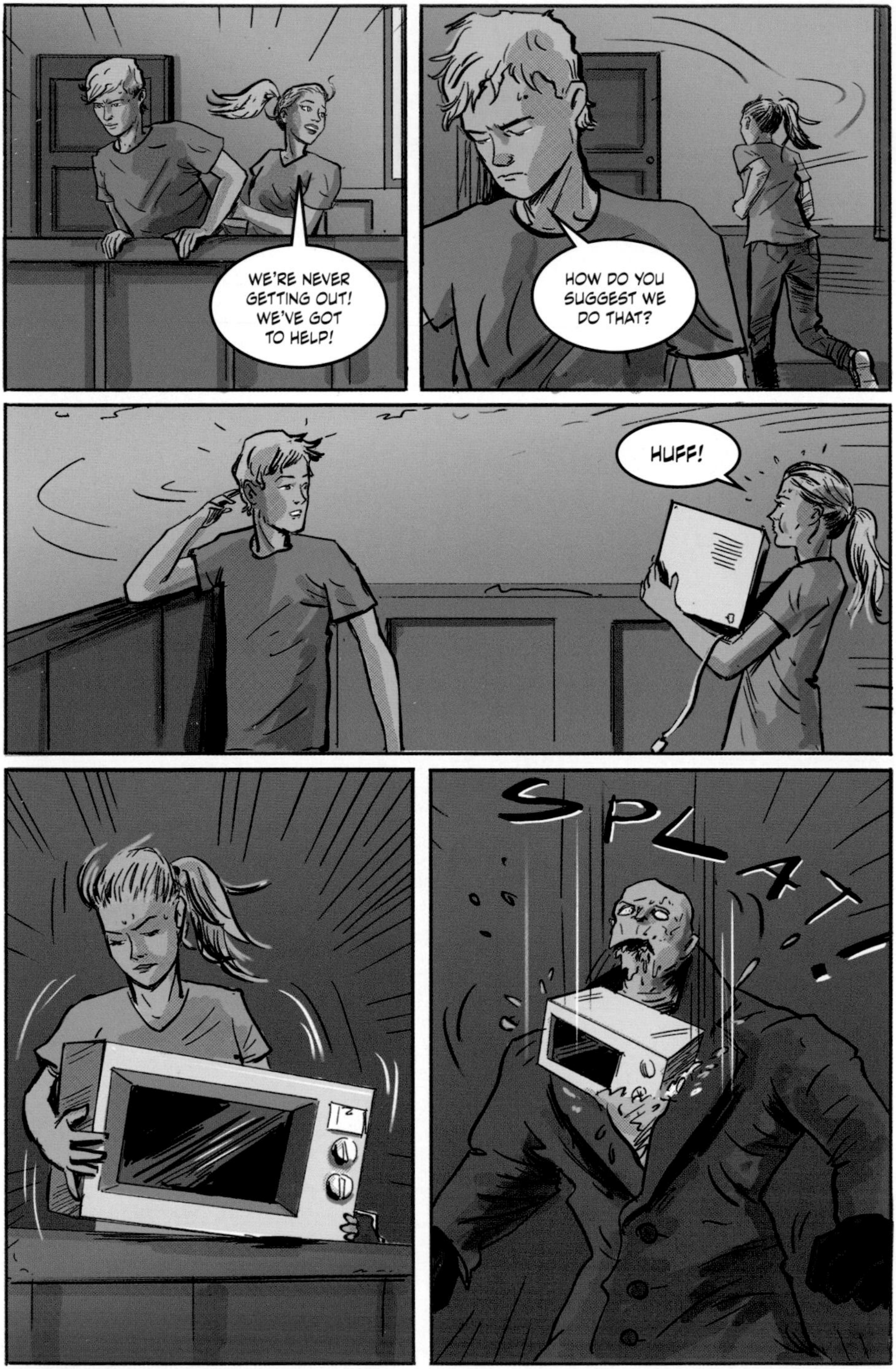
WE'RE NEVER GETTING OUT! WE'VE GOT TO HELP!
HOW DO YOU SUGGEST WE DO THAT?
HUFF!
SPLAT!

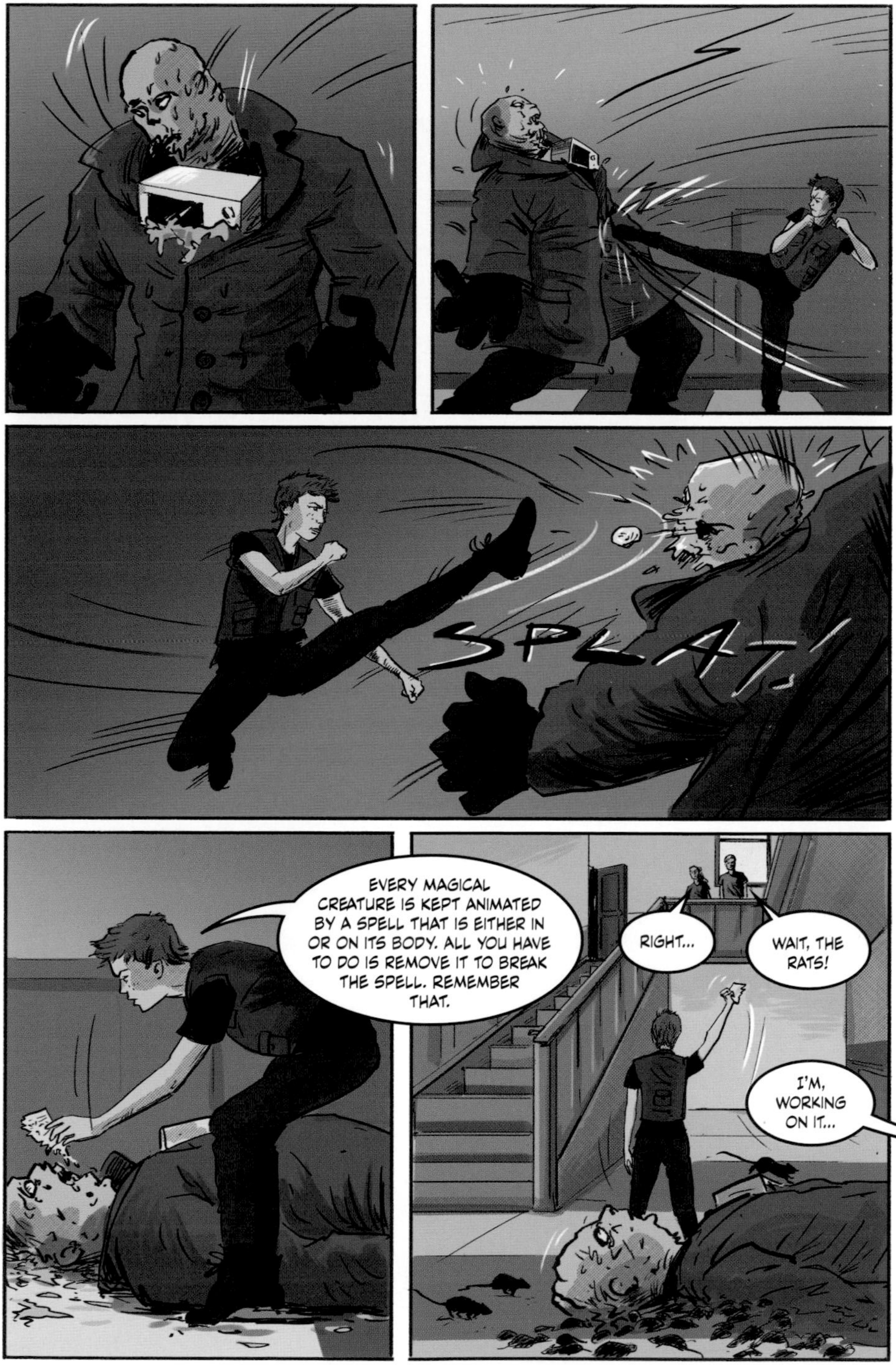
SPLAT!
EVERY MAGICAL CREATURE IS KEPT ANIMATED BY A SPELL THAT IS EITHER IN OR ON ITS BODY. ALL YOU HAVE TO DO IS REMOVE IT TO BREAK THE SPELL. REMEMBER THAT.
RIGHT...
WAIT, THE RATS!
I'M, WORKING ON IT...

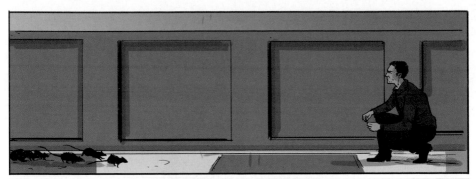

WHOOOOOSH!!

DR. JOHN DEE, YOU HAVE MADE THE BIGGEST MISTAKE OF YOUR LONG LIFE. I WILL BE COMING FOR YOU.

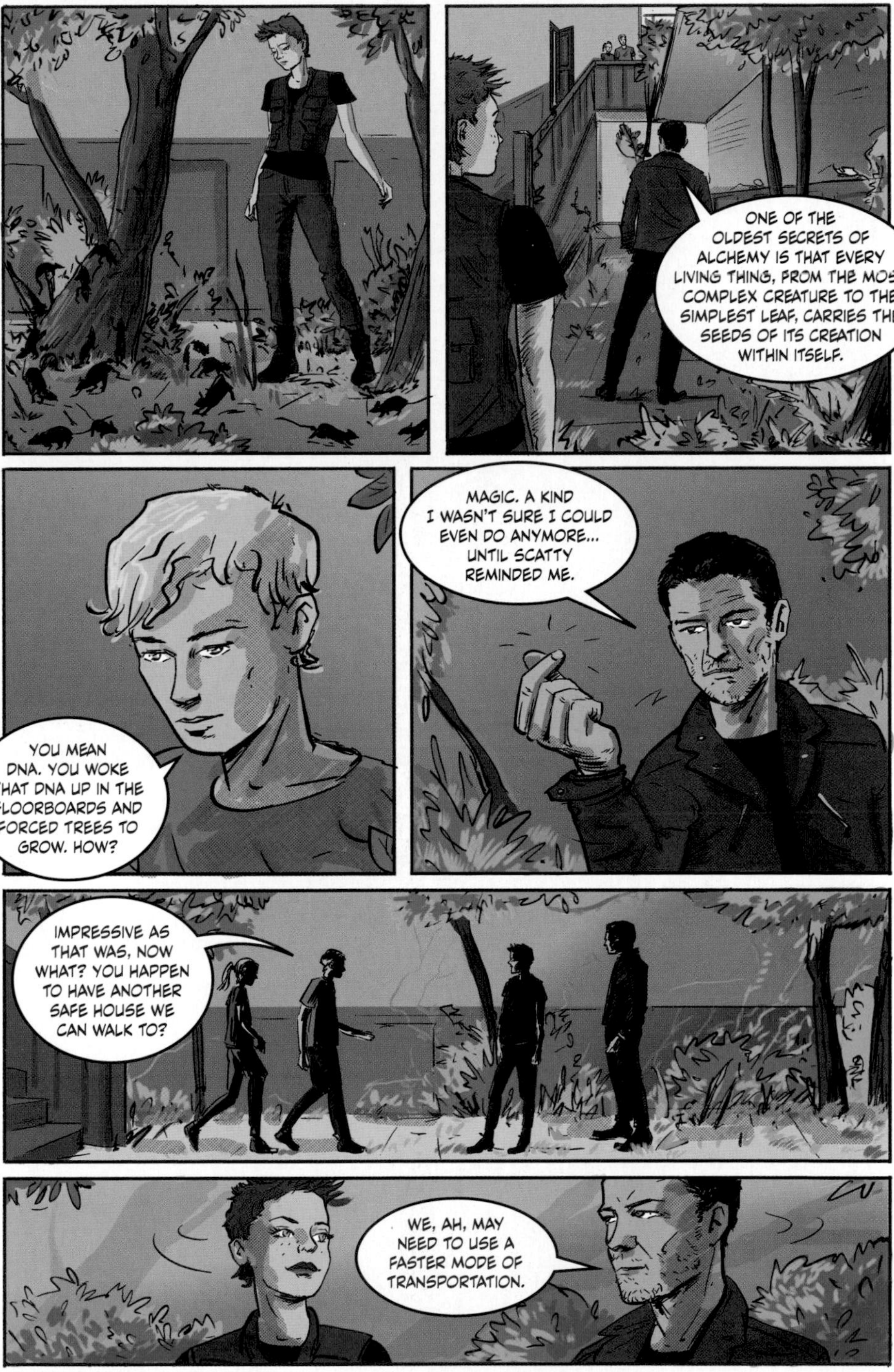
ONE OF THE OLDEST SECRETS OF ALCHEMY IS THAT EVERY LIVING THING, FROM THE MOST COMPLEX CREATURE TO THE SIMPLEST LEAF, CARRIES THE SEEDS OF ITS CREATION WITHIN ITSELF.
YOU MEAN DNA. YOU WOKE THAT DNA UP IN THE FLOORBOARDS AND FORCED TREES TO GROW. HOW?
MAGIC. A KIND I WASN'T SURE I COULD EVEN DO ANYMORE... UNTIL SCATTY REMINDED ME.
IMPRESSIVE AS THAT WAS, NOW WHAT? YOU HAPPEN TO HAVE ANOTHER SAFE HOUSE WE CAN WALK TO?
WE, AH, MAY NEED TO USE A FASTER MODE OF TRANSPORTATION.

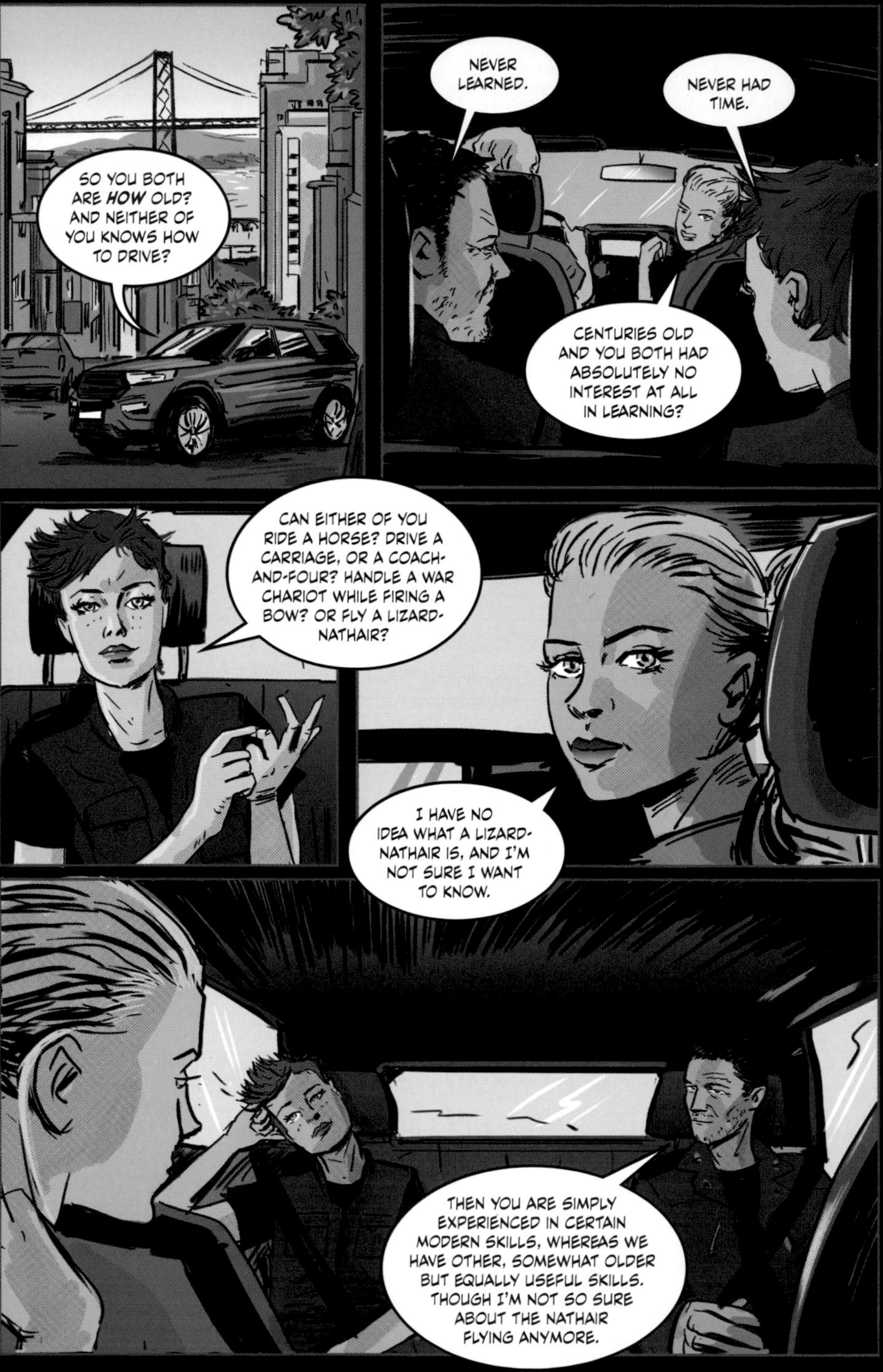
SO YOU BOTH ARE *HOW* OLD? AND NEITHER OF YOU KNOWS HOW TO DRIVE?
NEVER LEARNED.
NEVER HAD TIME.
CENTURIES OLD AND YOU BOTH HAD ABSOLUTELY NO INTEREST AT ALL IN LEARNING?
CAN EITHER OF YOU RIDE A HORSE? DRIVE A CARRIAGE, OR A COACH-AND-FOUR? HANDLE A WAR CHARIOT WHILE FIRING A BOW? OR FLY A LIZARD-NATHAIR?
I HAVE NO IDEA WHAT A LIZARD-NATHAIR IS, AND I'M NOT SURE I WANT TO KNOW.
THEN YOU ARE SIMPLY EXPERIENCED IN CERTAIN MODERN SKILLS, WHEREAS WE HAVE OTHER, SOMEWHAT OLDER BUT EQUALLY USEFUL SKILLS. THOUGH I'M NOT SO SURE ABOUT THE NATHAIR FLYING ANYMORE.

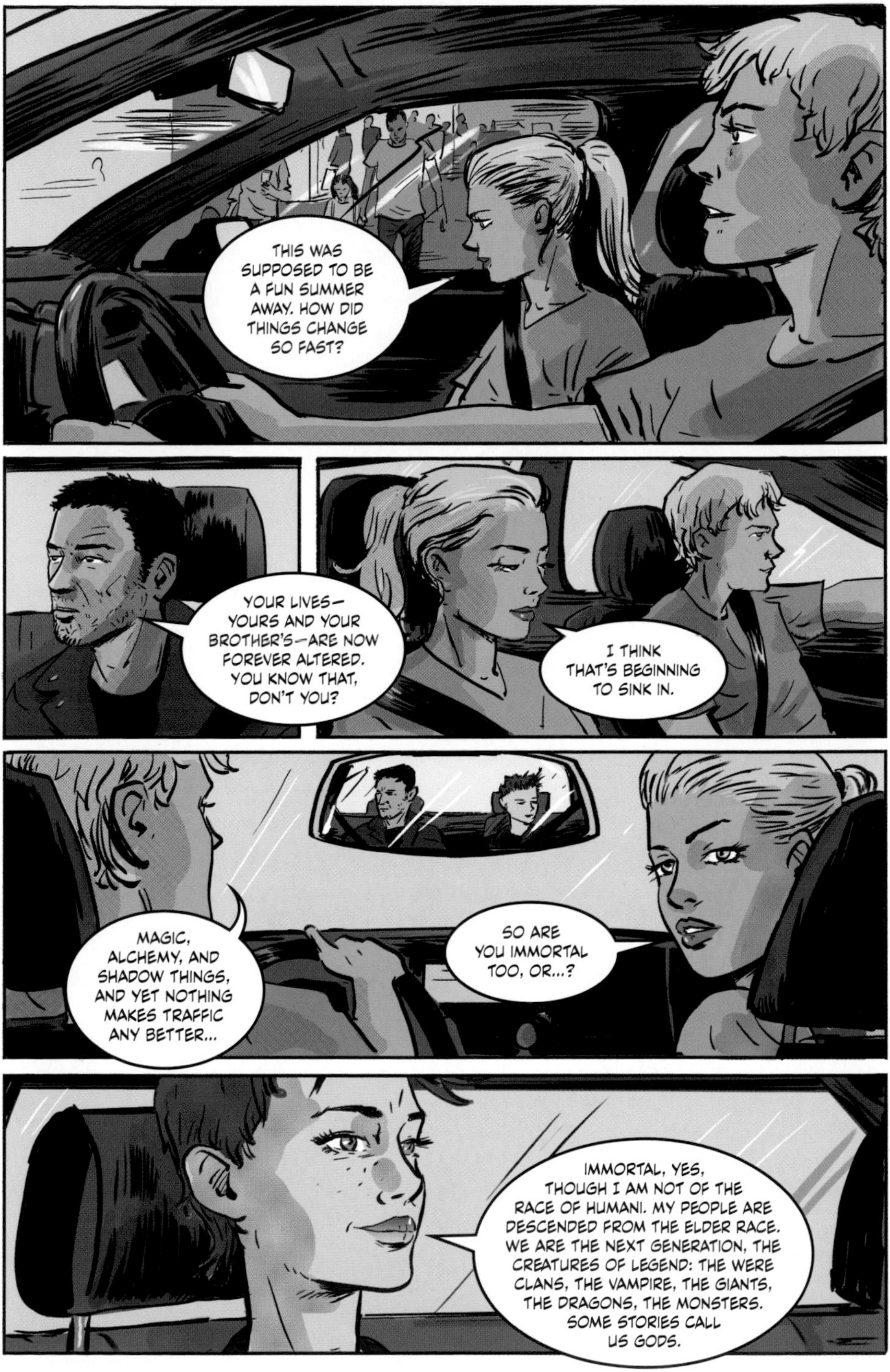
THIS WAS SUPPOSED TO BE A FUN SUMMER AWAY. HOW DID THINGS CHANGE SO FAST?
YOUR LIVES—YOURS AND YOUR BROTHER'S—ARE NOW FOREVER ALTERED. YOU KNOW THAT, DON'T YOU?
I THINK THAT'S BEGINNING TO SINK IN.
MAGIC, ALCHEMY, AND SHADOW THINGS, AND YET NOTHING MAKES TRAFFIC ANY BETTER...
SO ARE YOU IMMORTAL TOO, OR...?
IMMORTAL, YES, THOUGH I AM NOT OF THE RACE OF HUMANI. MY PEOPLE ARE DESCENDED FROM THE ELDER RACE. WE ARE THE NEXT GENERATION, THE CREATURES OF LEGEND: THE WERE CLANS, THE VAMPIRE, THE GIANTS, THE DRAGONS, THE MONSTERS. SOME STORIES CALL US GODS.

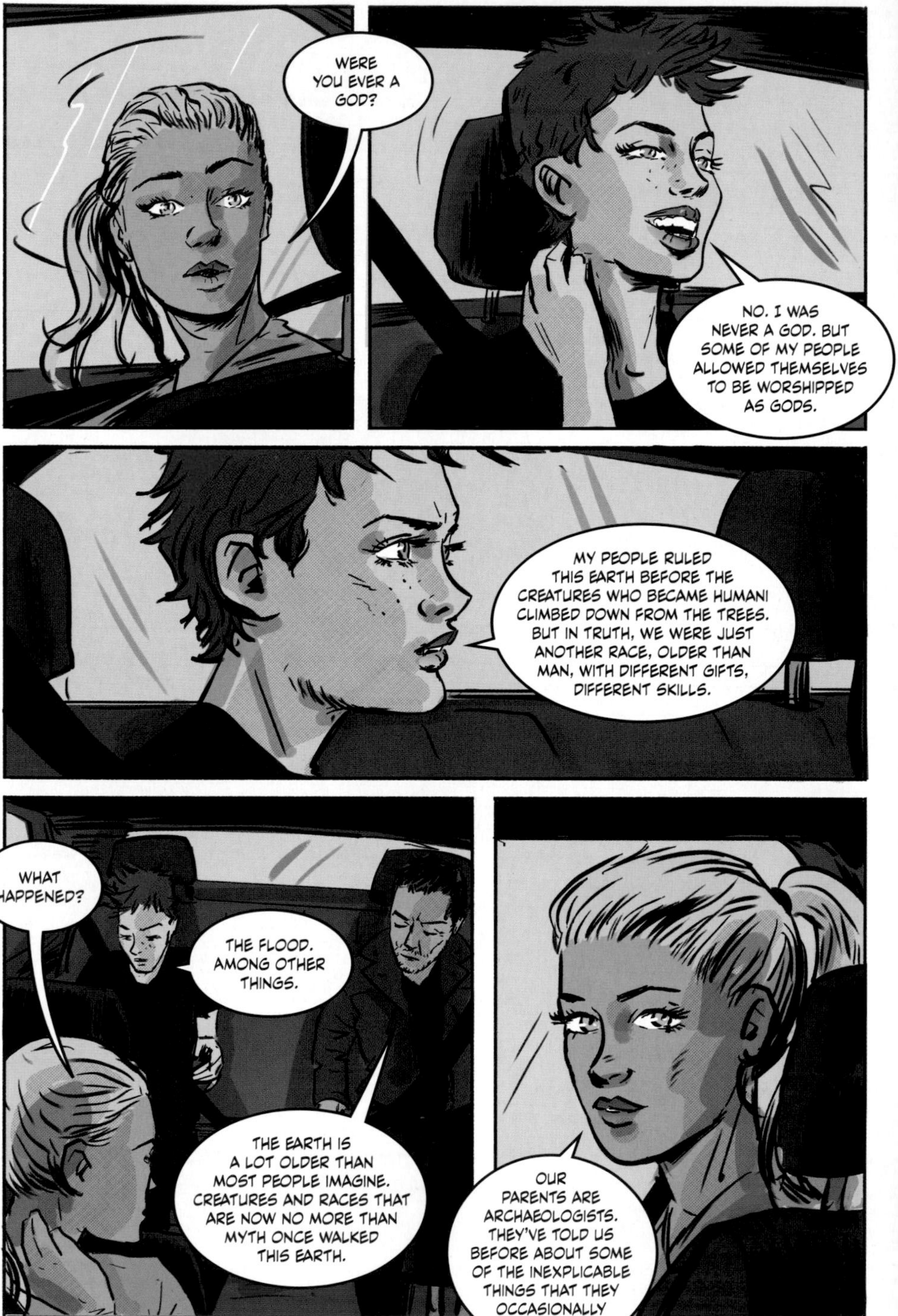
WERE YOU EVER A GOD?
NO. I WAS NEVER A GOD. BUT SOME OF MY PEOPLE ALLOWED THEMSELVES TO BE WORSHIPPED AS GODS.
MY PEOPLE RULED THIS EARTH BEFORE THE CREATURES WHO BECAME HUMANI CLIMBED DOWN FROM THE TREES. BUT IN TRUTH, WE WERE JUST ANOTHER RACE, OLDER THAN MAN, WITH DIFFERENT GIFTS, DIFFERENT SKILLS.
WHAT HAPPENED?
THE FLOOD. AMONG OTHER THINGS.
THE EARTH IS A LOT OLDER THAN MOST PEOPLE IMAGINE. CREATURES AND RACES THAT ARE NOW NO MORE THAN MYTH ONCE WALKED THIS EARTH.
OUR PARENTS ARE ARCHAEOLOGISTS. THEY'VE TOLD US BEFORE ABOUT SOME OF THE INEXPLICABLE THINGS THAT THEY OCCASIONALLY FIND.

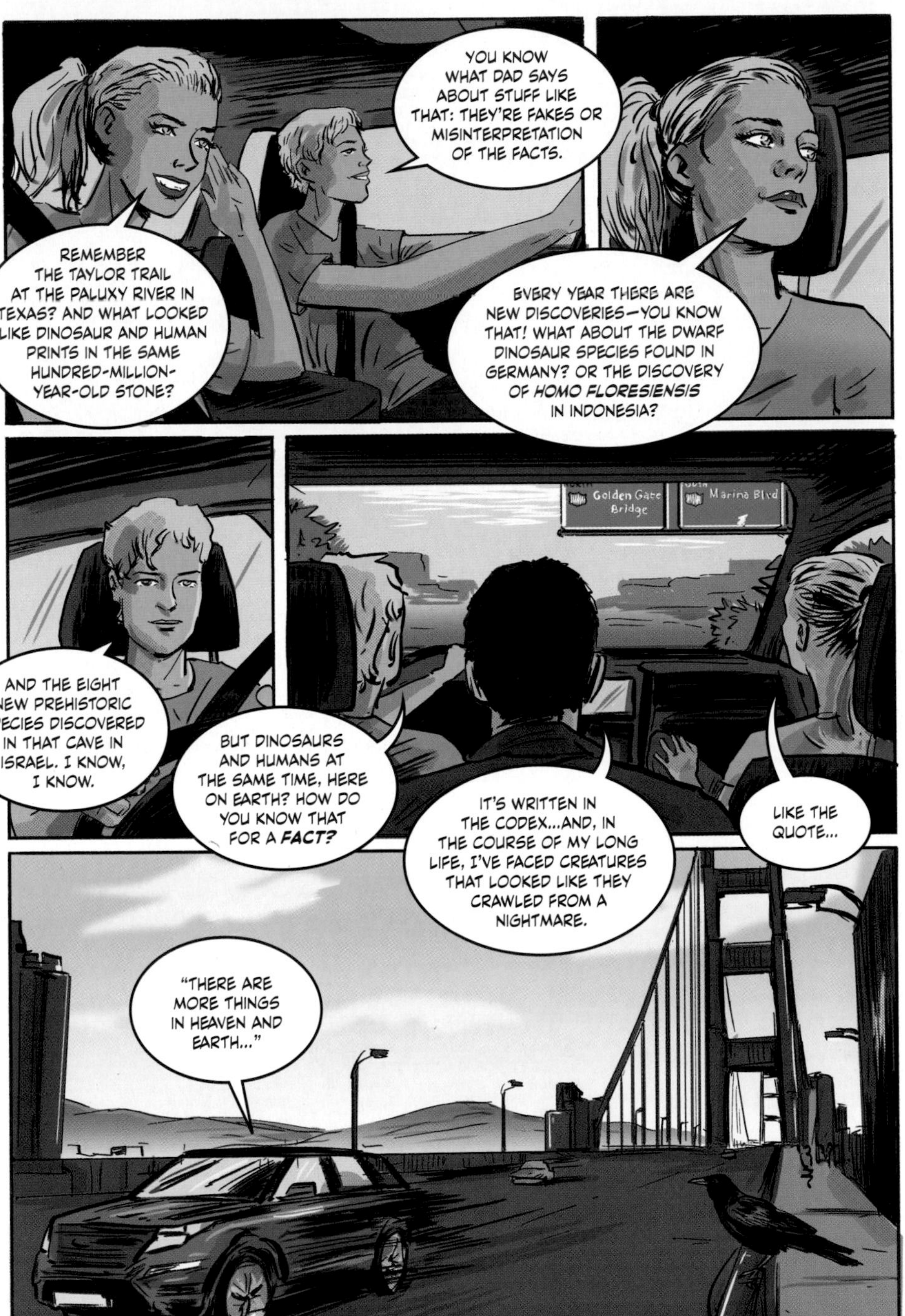

REMEMBER THE TAYLOR TRAIL AT THE PALUXY RIVER IN TEXAS? AND WHAT LOOKED LIKE DINOSAUR AND HUMAN PRINTS IN THE SAME HUNDRED-MILLION-YEAR-OLD STONE?
YOU KNOW WHAT DAD SAYS ABOUT STUFF LIKE THAT: THEY'RE FAKES OR MISINTERPRETATION OF THE FACTS.
EVERY YEAR THERE ARE NEW DISCOVERIES—YOU KNOW THAT! WHAT ABOUT THE DWARF DINOSAUR SPECIES FOUND IN GERMANY? OR THE DISCOVERY OF *HOMO FLORESIENSIS* IN INDONESIA?
AND THE EIGHT NEW PREHISTORIC SPECIES DISCOVERED IN THAT CAVE IN ISRAEL. I KNOW, I KNOW.
Golden Gate Bridge
Marina Blvd
BUT DINOSAURS AND HUMANS AT THE SAME TIME, HERE ON EARTH? HOW DO YOU KNOW THAT FOR A ***FACT?***
IT'S WRITTEN IN THE CODEX...AND, IN THE COURSE OF MY LONG LIFE, I'VE FACED CREATURES THAT LOOKED LIKE THEY CRAWLED FROM A NIGHTMARE.
LIKE THE QUOTE...
"THERE ARE MORE THINGS IN HEAVEN AND EARTH..."

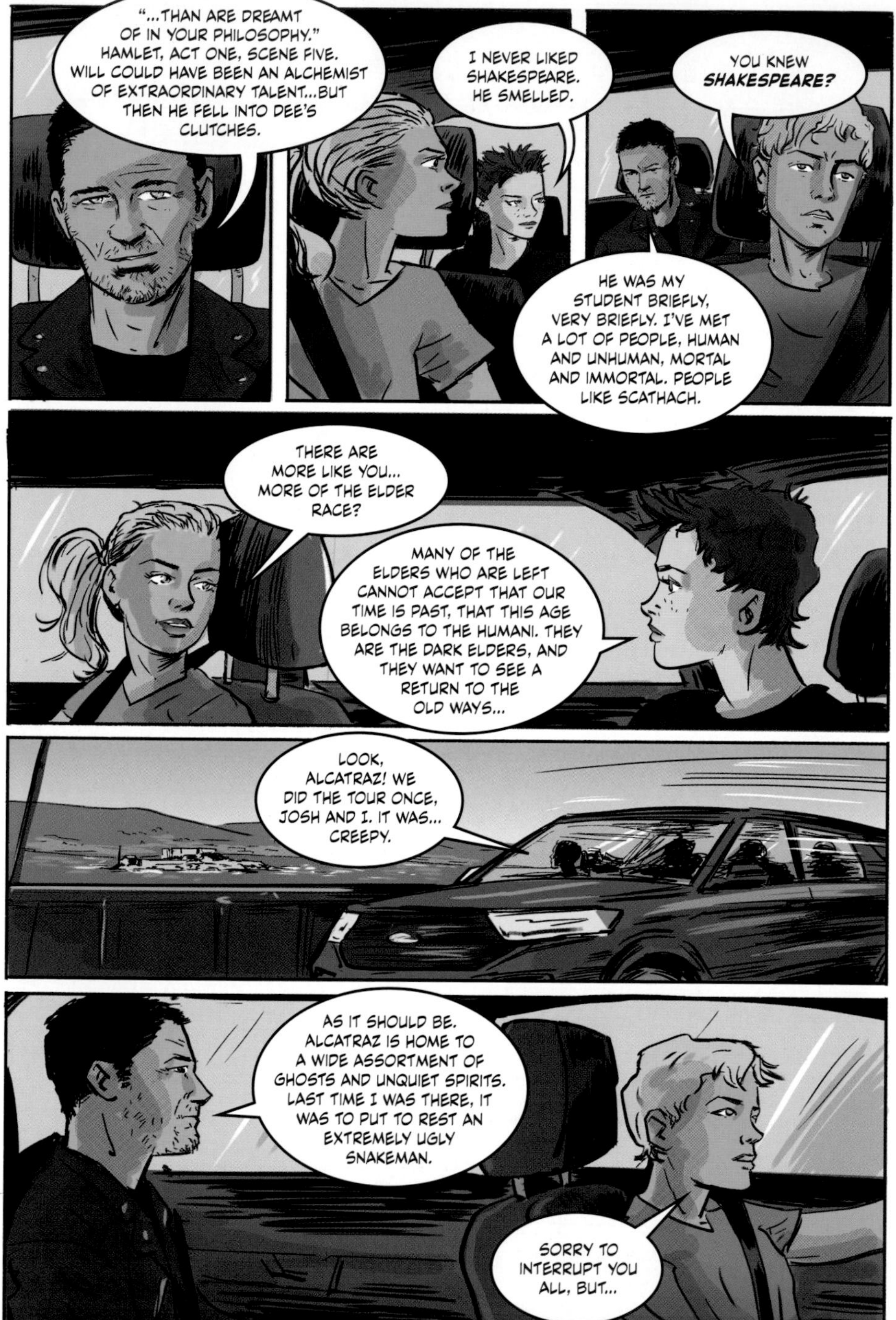
"...THAN ARE DREAMT OF IN YOUR PHILOSOPHY." HAMLET, ACT ONE, SCENE FIVE. WILL COULD HAVE BEEN AN ALCHEMIST OF EXTRAORDINARY TALENT...BUT THEN HE FELL INTO DEE'S CLUTCHES.
I NEVER LIKED SHAKESPEARE. HE SMELLED.
YOU KNEW ***SHAKESPEARE?***
HE WAS MY STUDENT BRIEFLY, VERY BRIEFLY. I'VE MET A LOT OF PEOPLE, HUMAN AND UNHUMAN, MORTAL AND IMMORTAL. PEOPLE LIKE SCATHACH.
THERE ARE MORE LIKE YOU... MORE OF THE ELDER RACE?
MANY OF THE ELDERS WHO ARE LEFT CANNOT ACCEPT THAT OUR TIME IS PAST, THAT THIS AGE BELONGS TO THE HUMANI. THEY ARE THE DARK ELDERS, AND THEY WANT TO SEE A RETURN TO THE OLD WAYS...
LOOK, ALCATRAZ! WE DID THE TOUR ONCE, JOSH AND I. IT WAS... CREEPY.
AS IT SHOULD BE. ALCATRAZ IS HOME TO A WIDE ASSORTMENT OF GHOSTS AND UNQUIET SPIRITS. LAST TIME I WAS THERE, IT WAS TO PUT TO REST AN EXTREMELY UGLY SNAKEMAN.
SORRY TO INTERRUPT YOU ALL, BUT...

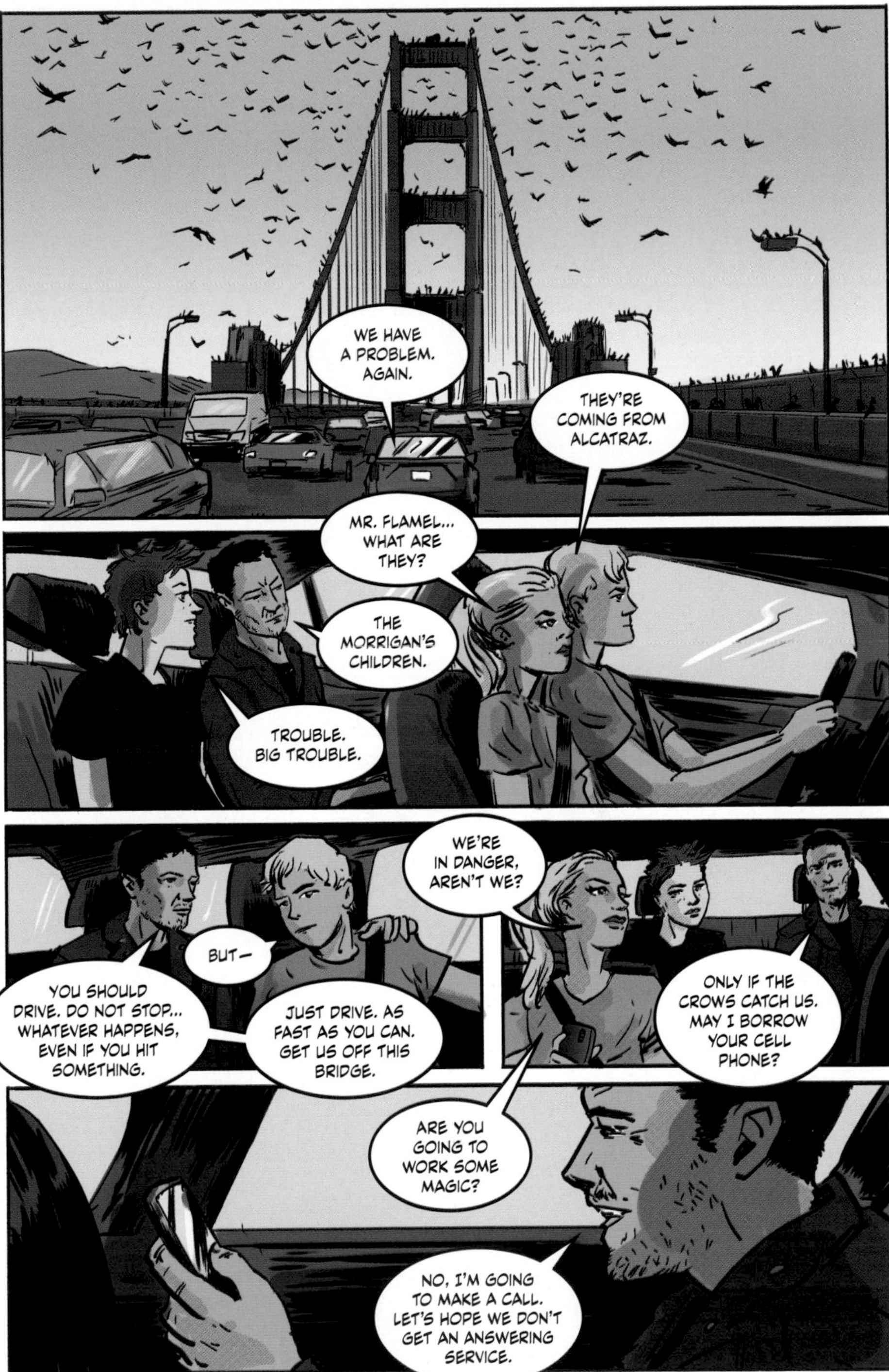
WE HAVE A PROBLEM. AGAIN.
THEY'RE COMING FROM ALCATRAZ.
MR. FLAMEL... WHAT ARE THEY?
THE MORRIGAN'S CHILDREN.
TROUBLE. BIG TROUBLE.
WE'RE IN DANGER, AREN'T WE?
BUT—
YOU SHOULD DRIVE. DO NOT STOP... WHATEVER HAPPENS, EVEN IF YOU HIT SOMETHING.
JUST DRIVE. AS FAST AS YOU CAN. GET US OFF THIS BRIDGE.
ONLY IF THE CROWS CATCH US. MAY I BORROW YOUR CELL PHONE?
ARE YOU GOING TO WORK SOME MAGIC?
NO, I'M GOING TO MAKE A CALL. LET'S HOPE WE DON'T GET AN ANSWERING SERVICE.

CHAPTER 11

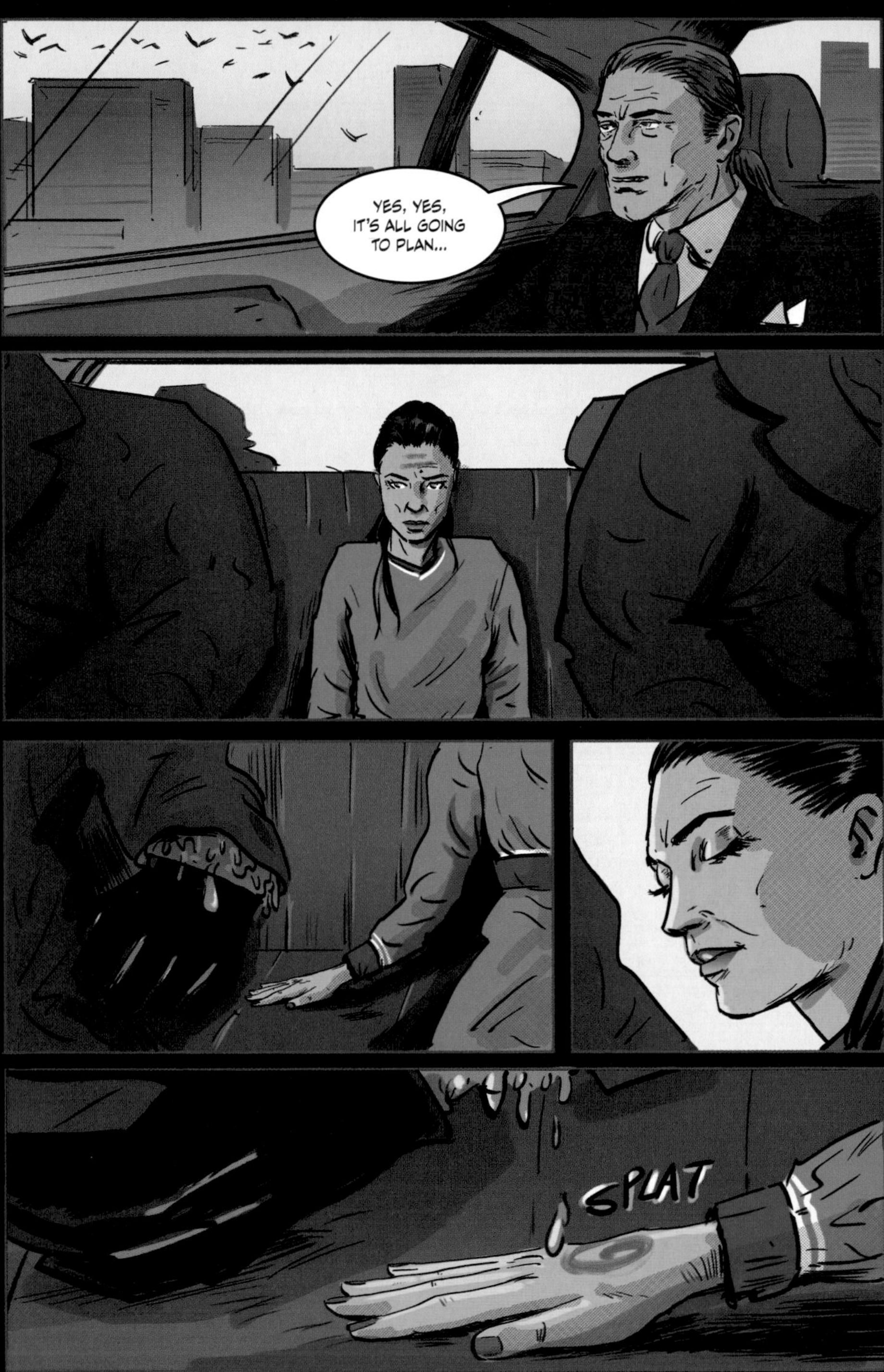
YES, YES, IT'S ALL GOING TO PLAN...
SPLAT

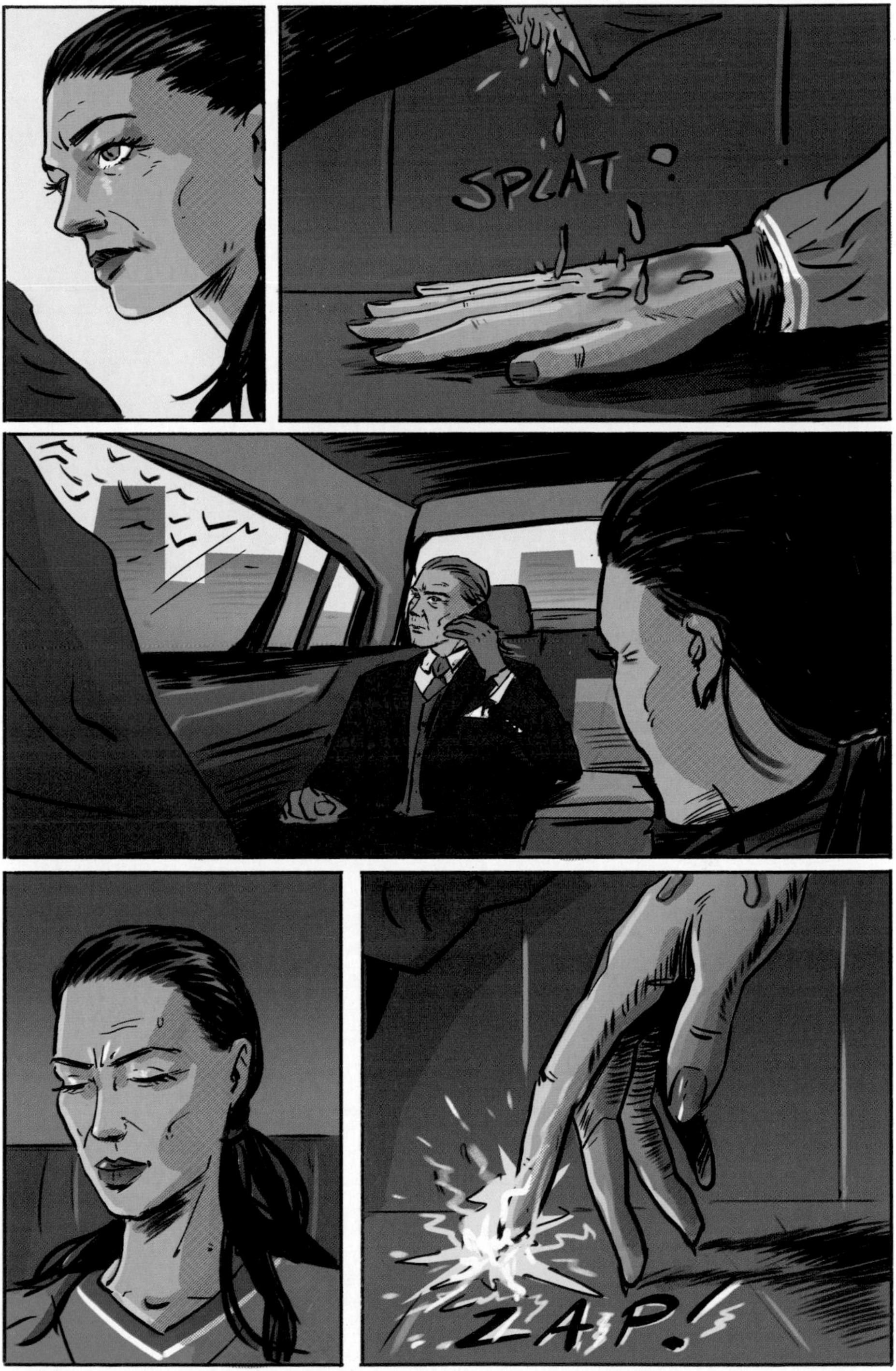
SPLAT!
ZAP!

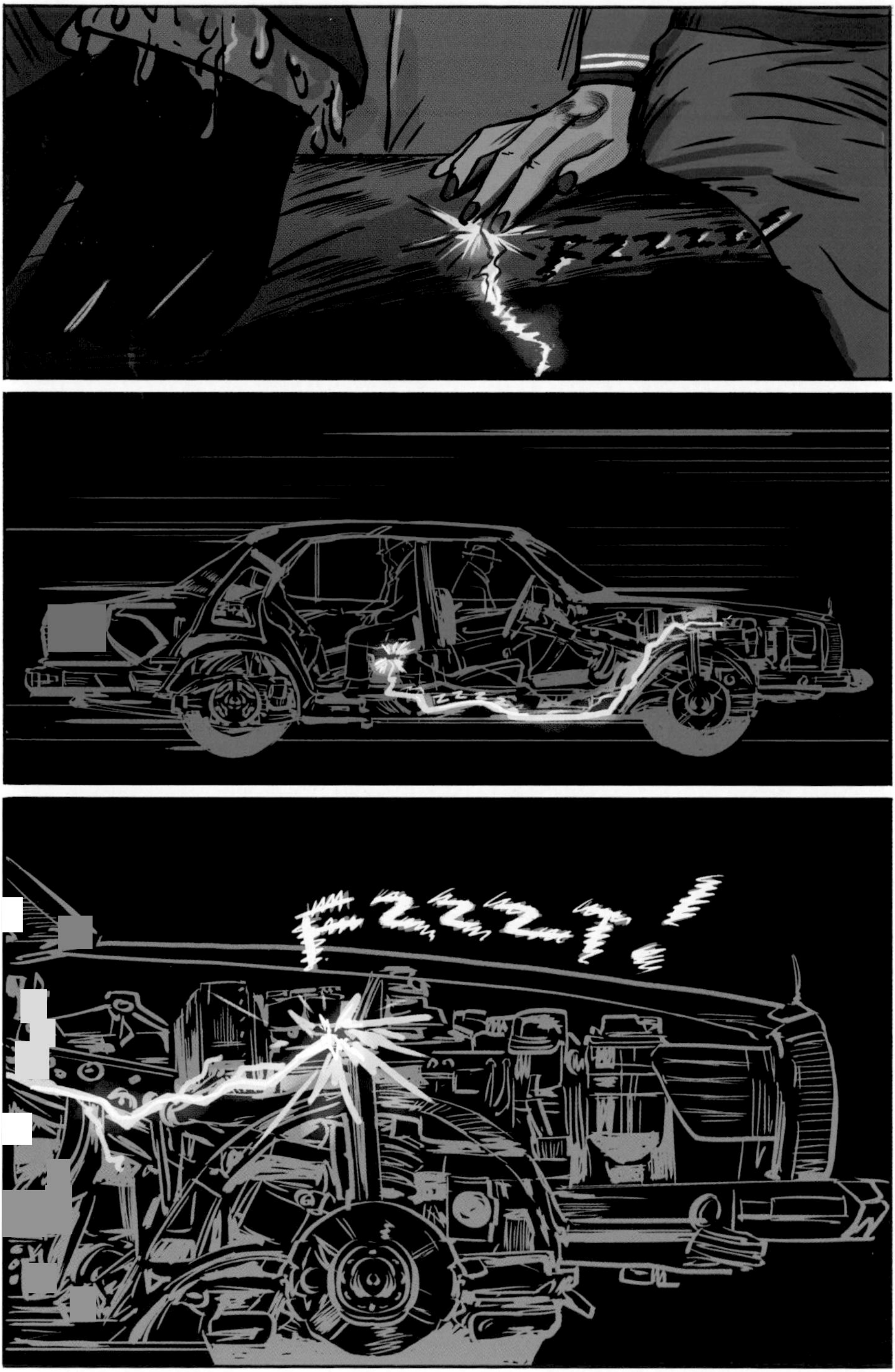
FZZZZT
FZZZT!

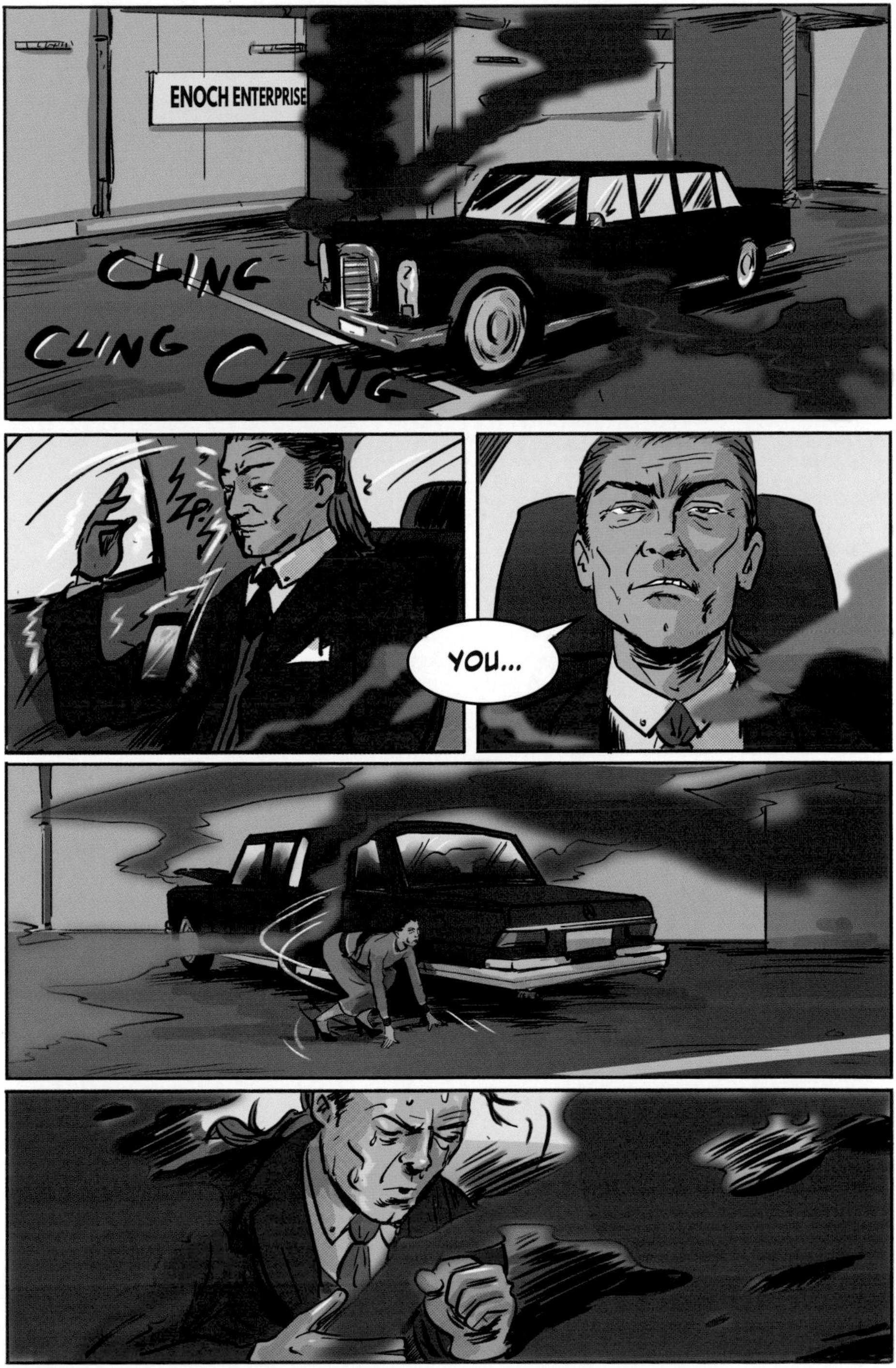
ENOCH ENTERPRISE
CLING
CLING CLING
ZZP
YOU...

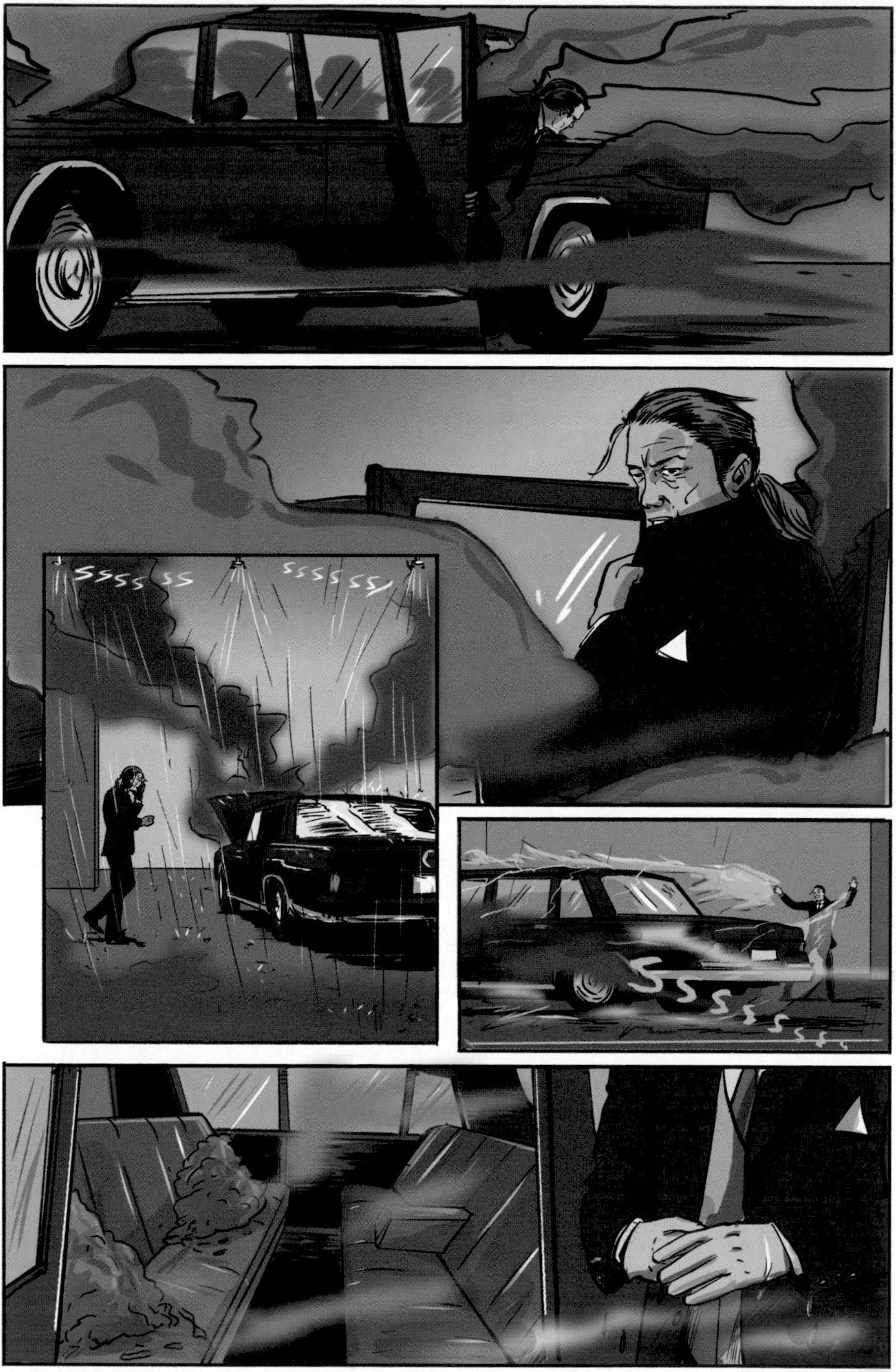
SSSSS SS
SSSSSS
SSSSSSS

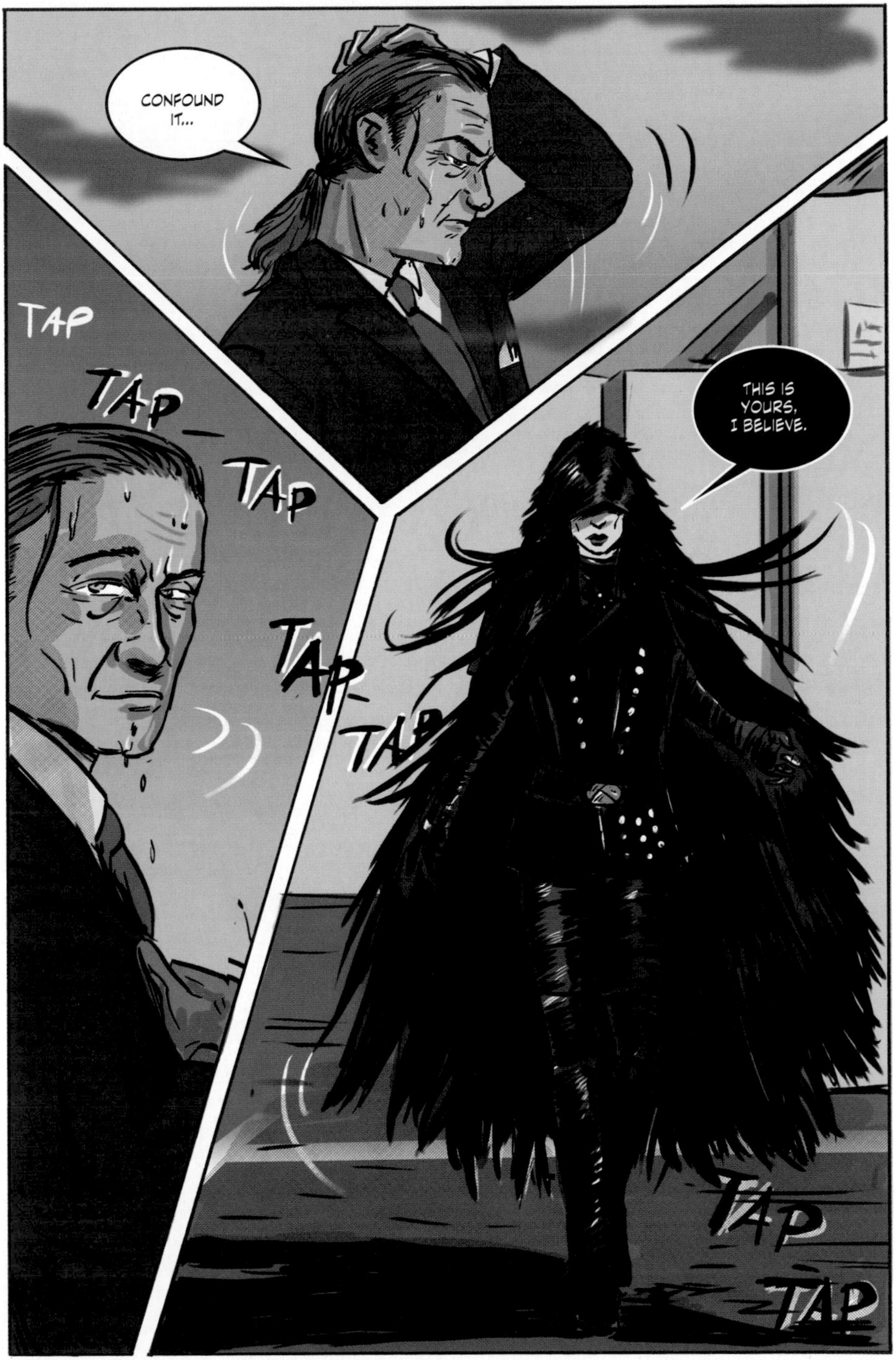
CONFOUND IT...
TAP
TAP
TAP
TAP
TAP
THIS IS YOURS, I BELIEVE.
TAP
TAP

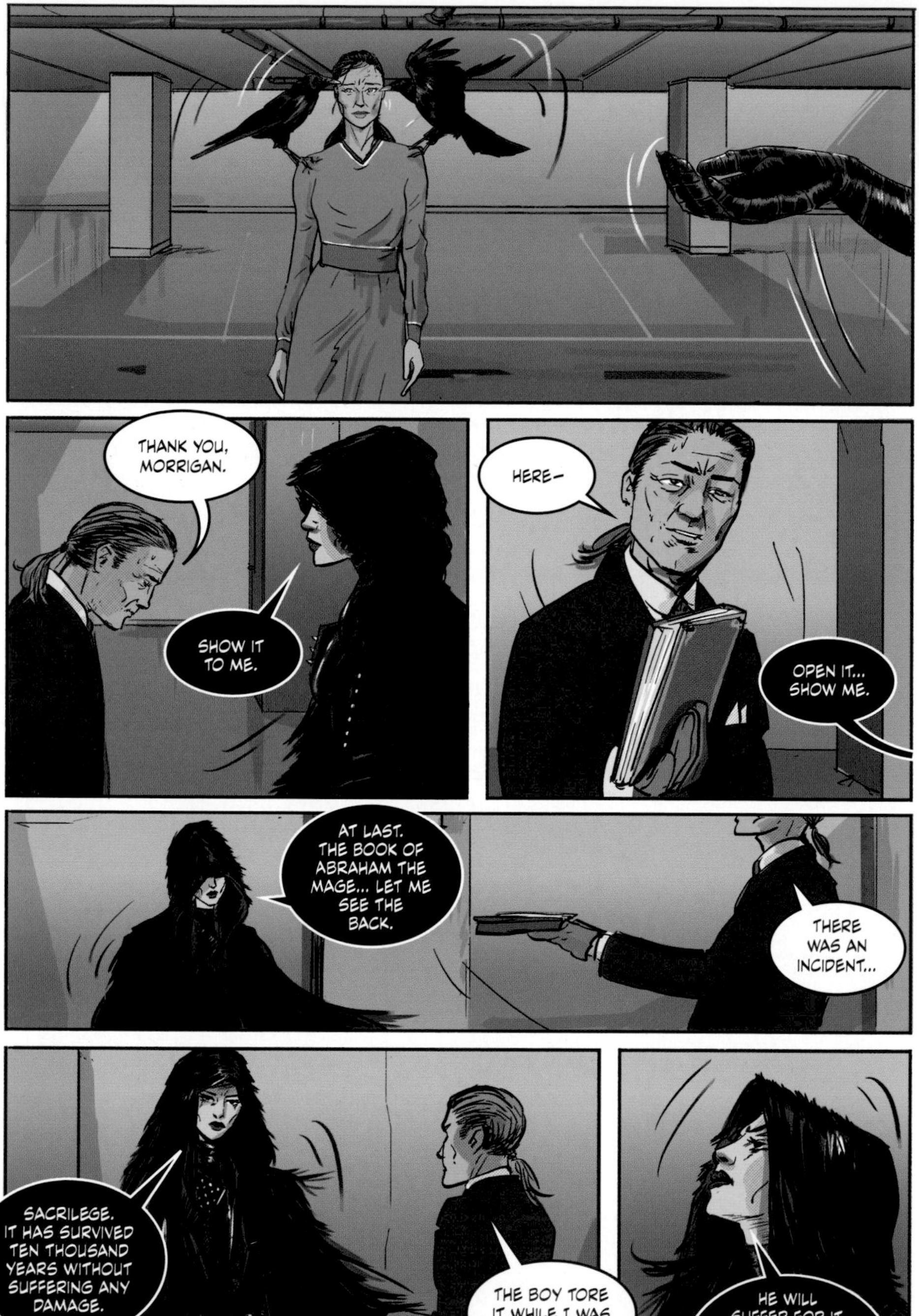
THANK YOU, MORRIGAN.
SHOW IT TO ME.
HERE–
OPEN IT... SHOW ME.
AT LAST. THE BOOK OF ABRAHAM THE MAGE... LET ME SEE THE BACK.
THERE WAS AN INCIDENT...
SACRILEGE. IT HAS SURVIVED TEN THOUSAND YEARS WITHOUT SUFFERING ANY DAMAGE.
THE BOY TORE IT WHILE I WAS RETRIEVING IT.
HE WILL SUFFER FOR IT. MY CHILDREN ARE ALMOST UPON THEM. SOON THEY WILL ALL FEEL MY WRATH.

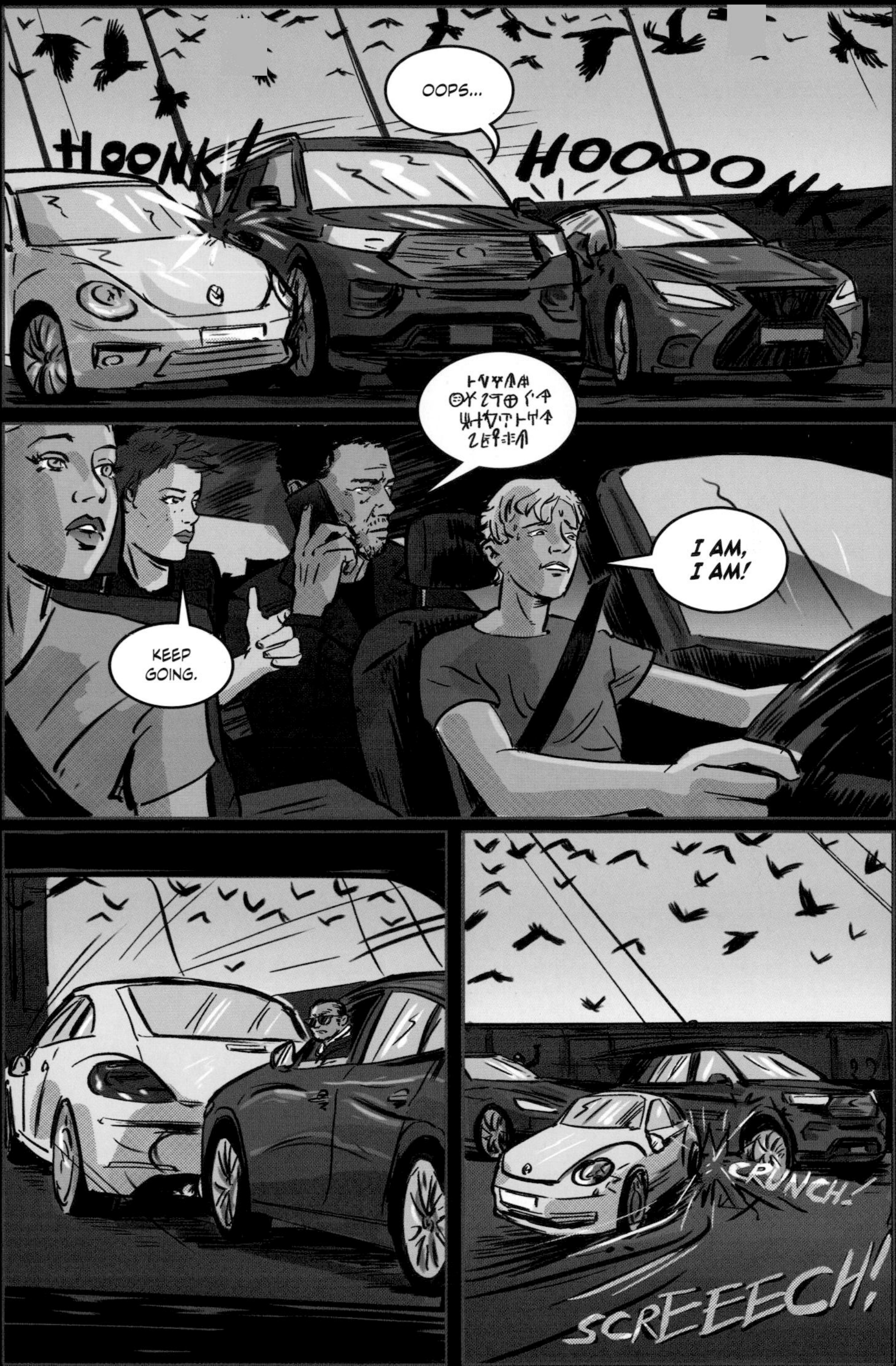
HOONK!
OOPS...
HOOOOONK!
KEEP GOING.
I AM, I AM!
CRUNCH!
SCREEECH!

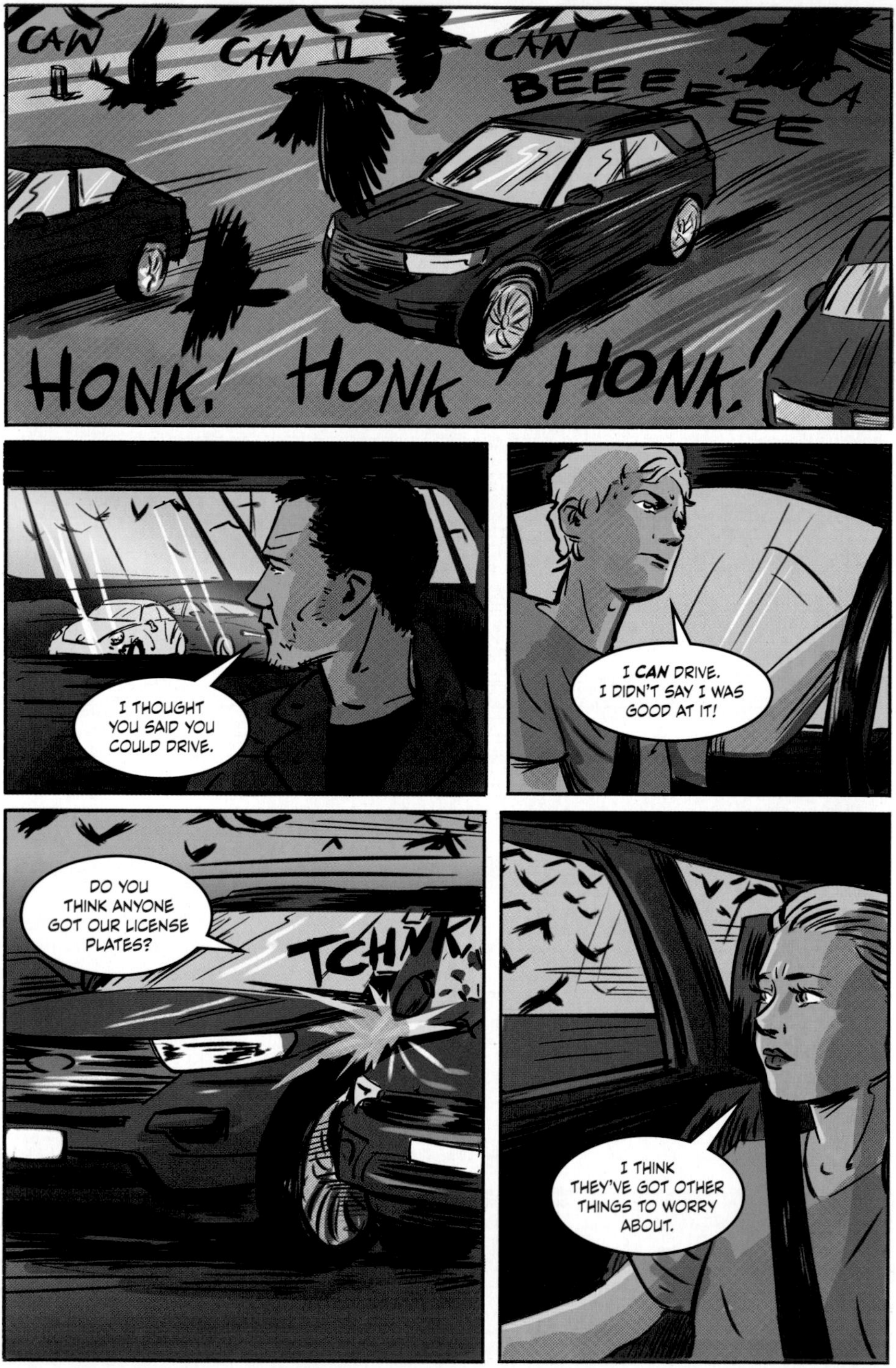
CAW
CAW
CAW
BEEEEEEE
HONK! HONK! HONK!
I THOUGHT YOU SAID YOU COULD DRIVE.
I CAN DRIVE. I DIDN'T SAY I WAS GOOD AT IT!
DO YOU THINK ANYONE GOT OUR LICENSE PLATES?
TCHNK
I THINK THEY'VE GOT OTHER THINGS TO WORRY ABOUT.

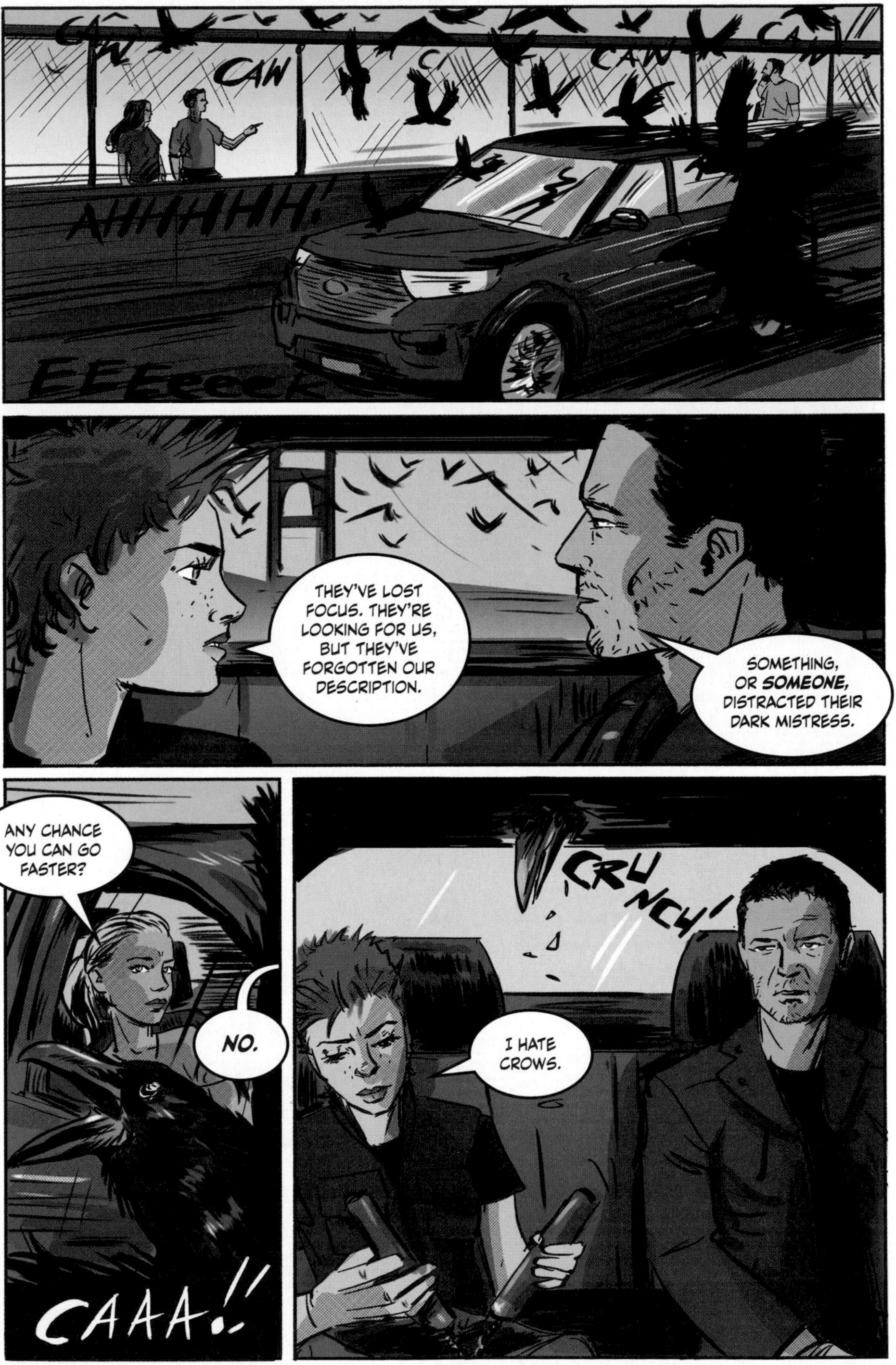
CAW
CAW
CAW
CAW
CAW
AHHHHHH!
EEEEreeck
THEY'VE LOST FOCUS. THEY'RE LOOKING FOR US, BUT THEY'VE FORGOTTEN OUR DESCRIPTION.
SOMETHING, OR **SOMEONE,** DISTRACTED THEIR DARK MISTRESS.
ANY CHANCE YOU CAN GO FASTER?
NO.
CAAA!!
CRUNCH!
I HATE CROWS.

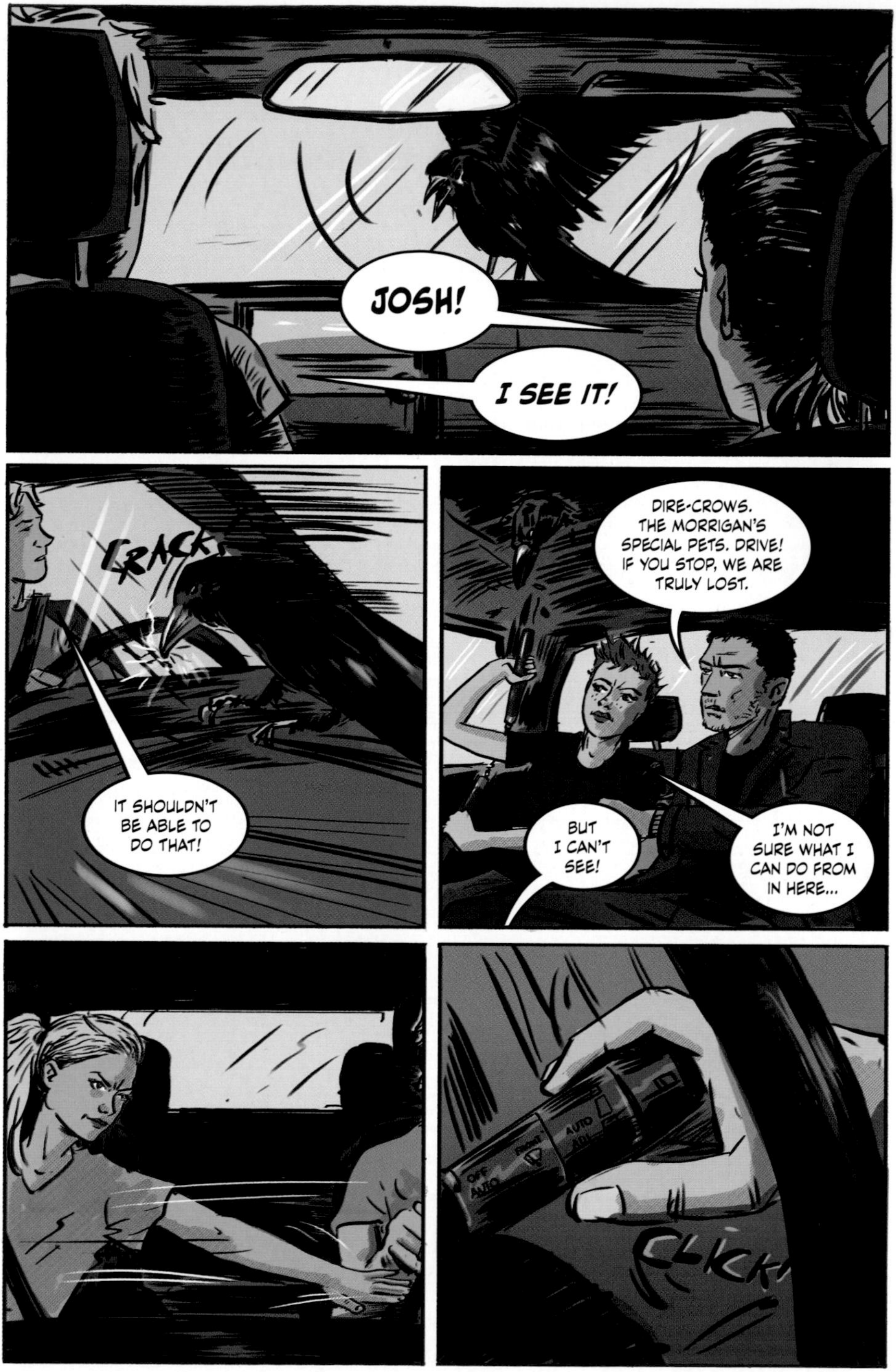
JOSH!
I SEE IT!
CRACK!
IT SHOULDN'T BE ABLE TO DO THAT!
DIRE-CROWS. THE MORRIGAN'S SPECIAL PETS. DRIVE! IF YOU STOP, WE ARE TRULY LOST.
BUT I CAN'T SEE!
I'M NOT SURE WHAT I CAN DO FROM IN HERE...
OFF AUTO
AUTO

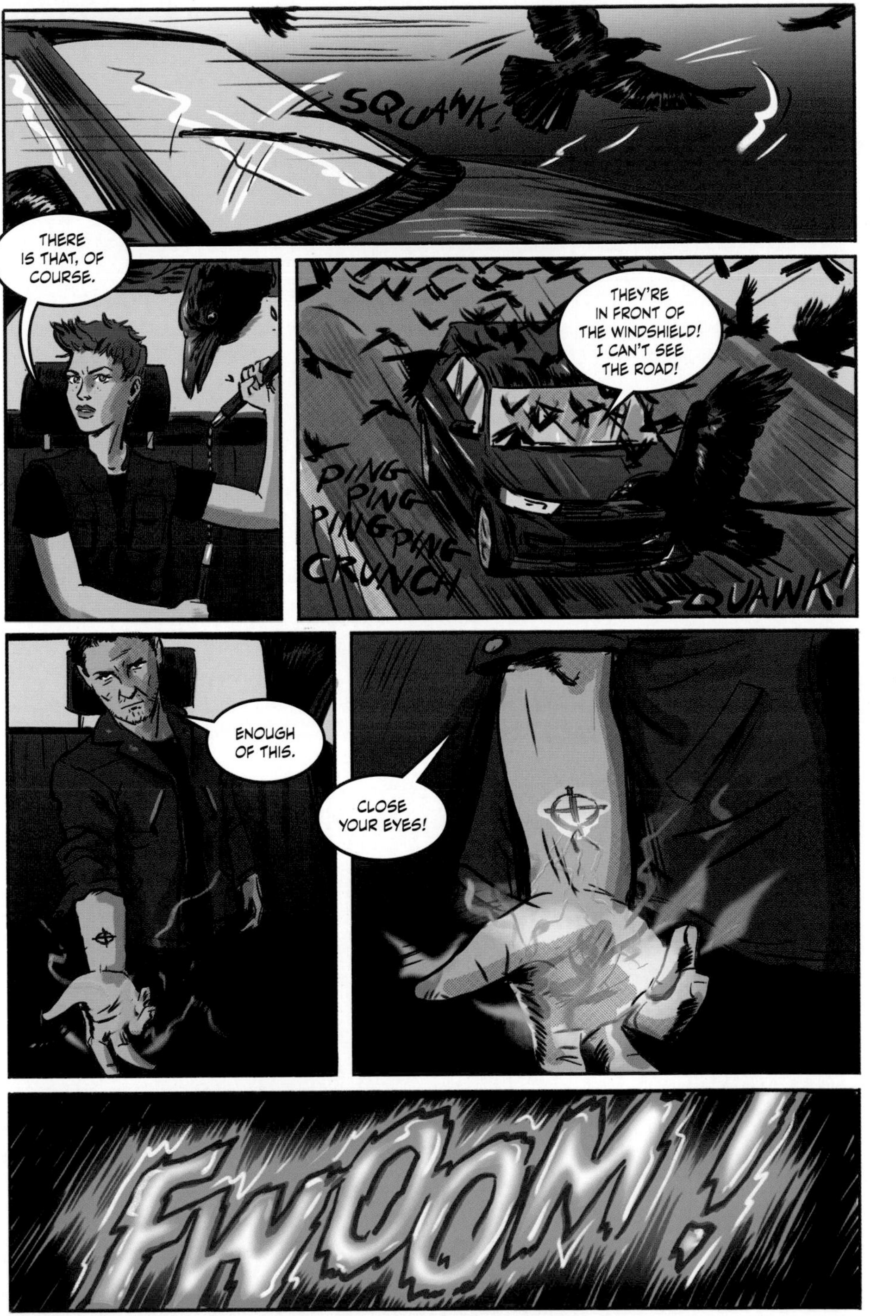
SQUAWK!
THERE IS THAT, OF COURSE.
THEY'RE IN FRONT OF THE WINDSHIELD! I CAN'T SEE THE ROAD!
PING PING PING PING
CRUNCH
SQUAWK!
ENOUGH OF THIS.
CLOSE YOUR EYES!
FWOOM!

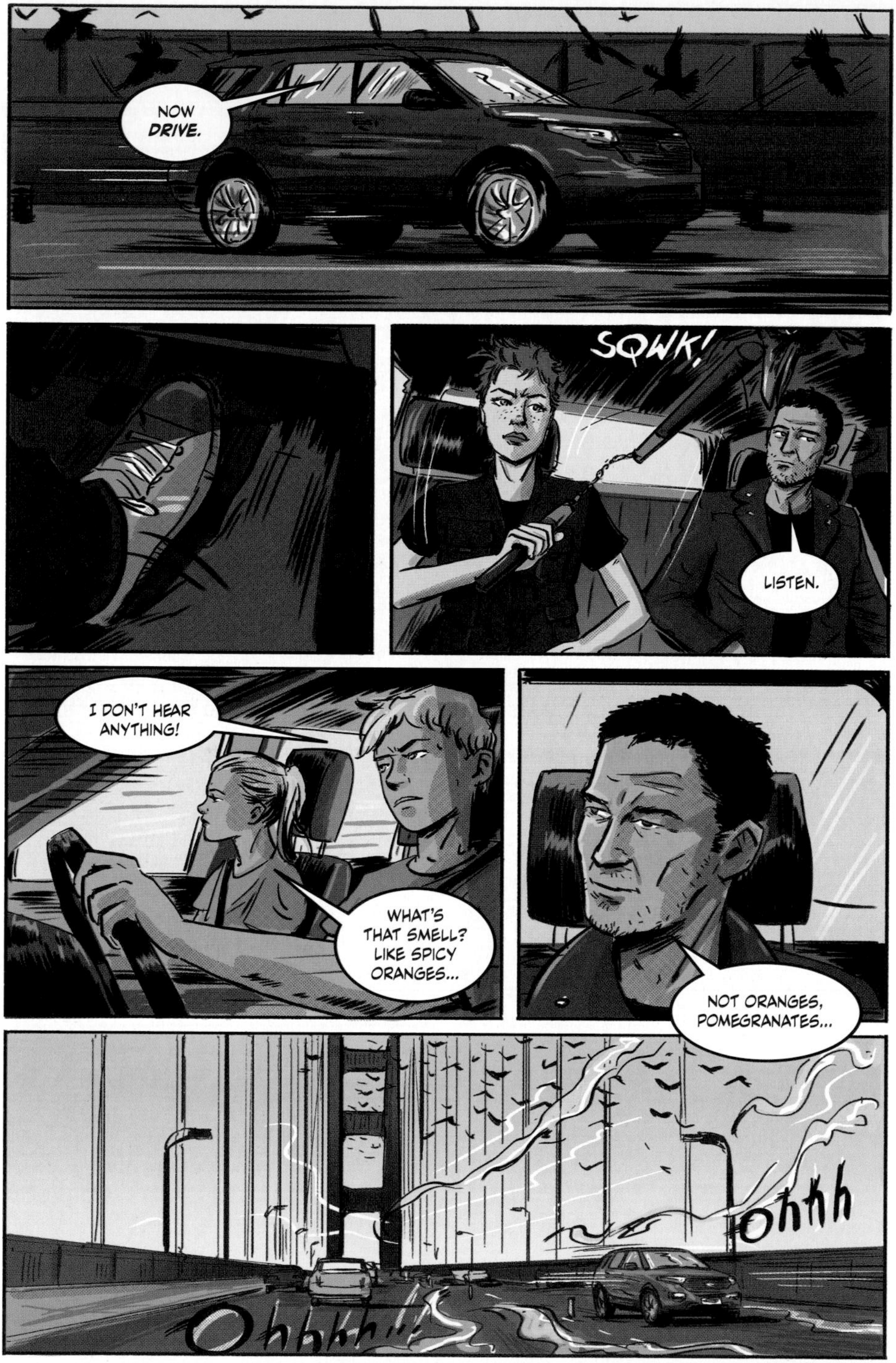
NOW DRIVE.
SQWK!
LISTEN.
I DON'T HEAR ANYTHING!
WHAT'S THAT SMELL? LIKE SPICY ORANGES...
NOT ORANGES, POMEGRANATES...
Ohhh
Ohhhh!!

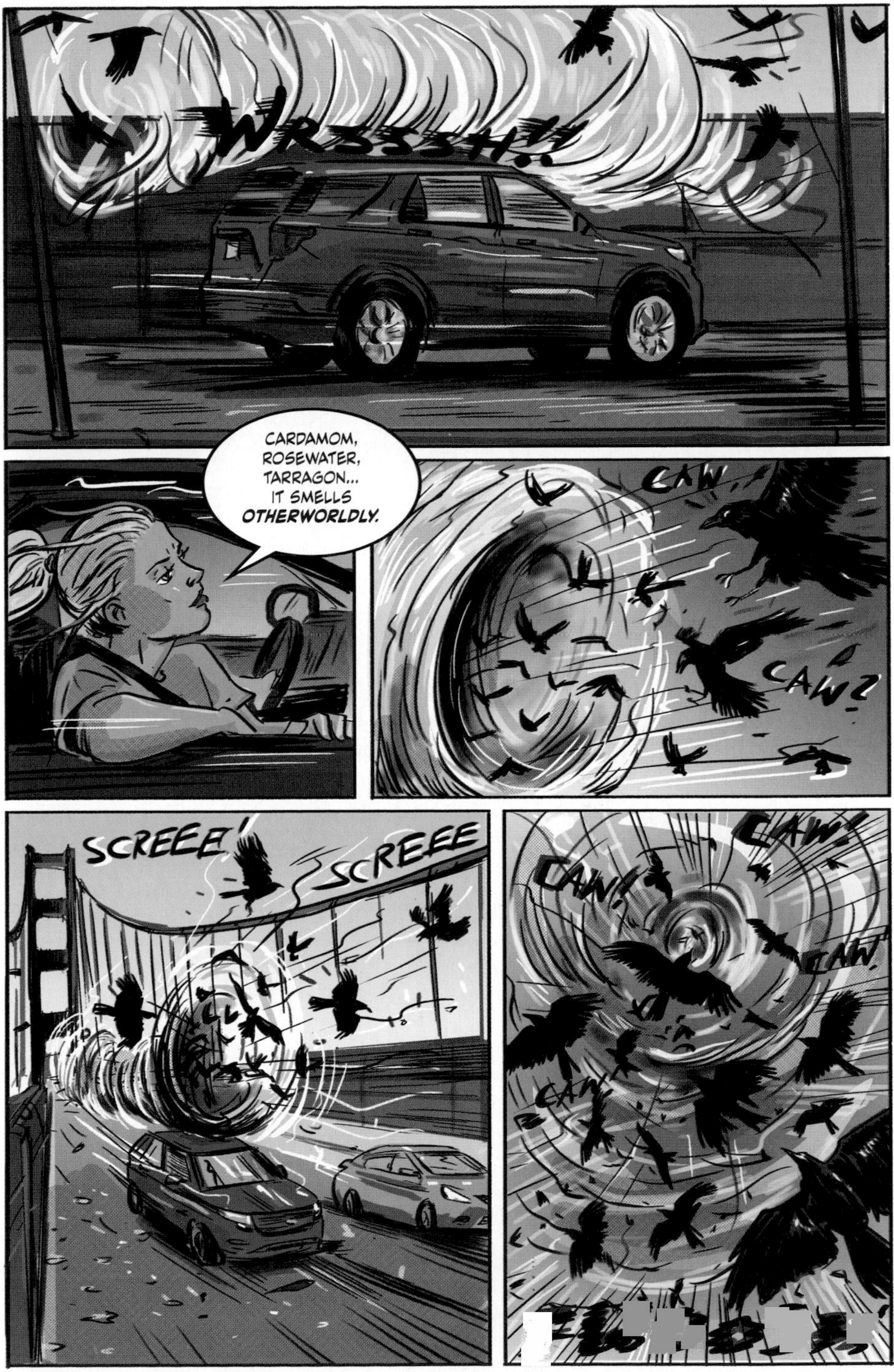
WRSSSH!!
CARDAMOM, ROSEWATER, TARRAGON... IT SMELLS **OTHERWORLDLY.**
CAW
CAW
SCREEE!
SCREEE
CAW!
CAW!
CAW!
CAW

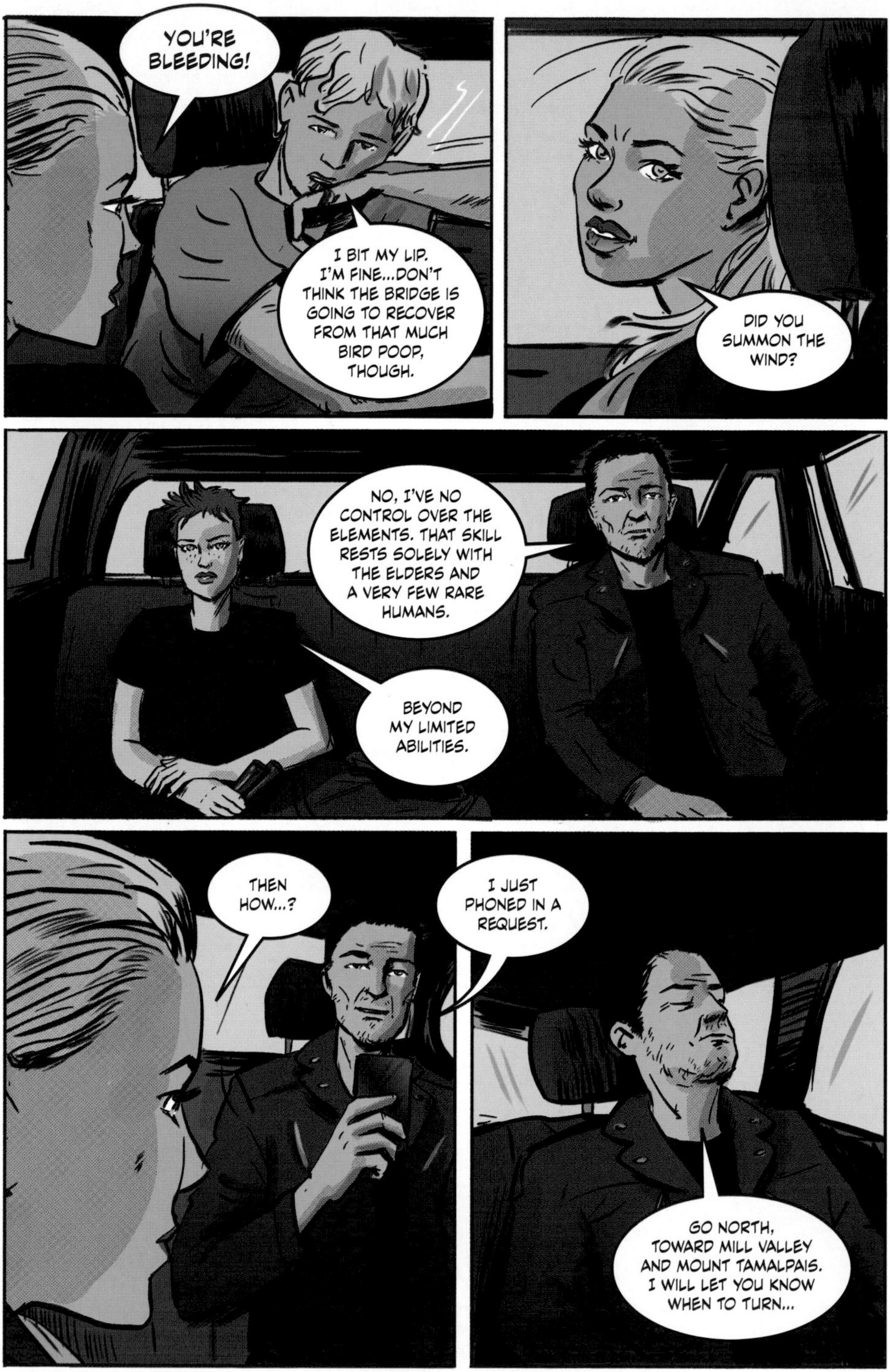
YOU'RE BLEEDING!
I BIT MY LIP. I'M FINE...DON'T THINK THE BRIDGE IS GOING TO RECOVER FROM THAT MUCH BIRD POOP, THOUGH.
DID YOU SUMMON THE WIND?
NO, I'VE NO CONTROL OVER THE ELEMENTS. THAT SKILL RESTS SOLELY WITH THE ELDERS AND A VERY FEW RARE HUMANS.
BEYOND MY LIMITED ABILITIES.
THEN HOW...?
I JUST PHONED IN A REQUEST.
GO NORTH, TOWARD MILL VALLEY AND MOUNT TAMALPAIS. I WILL LET YOU KNOW WHEN TO TURN...

CHAPTER 13

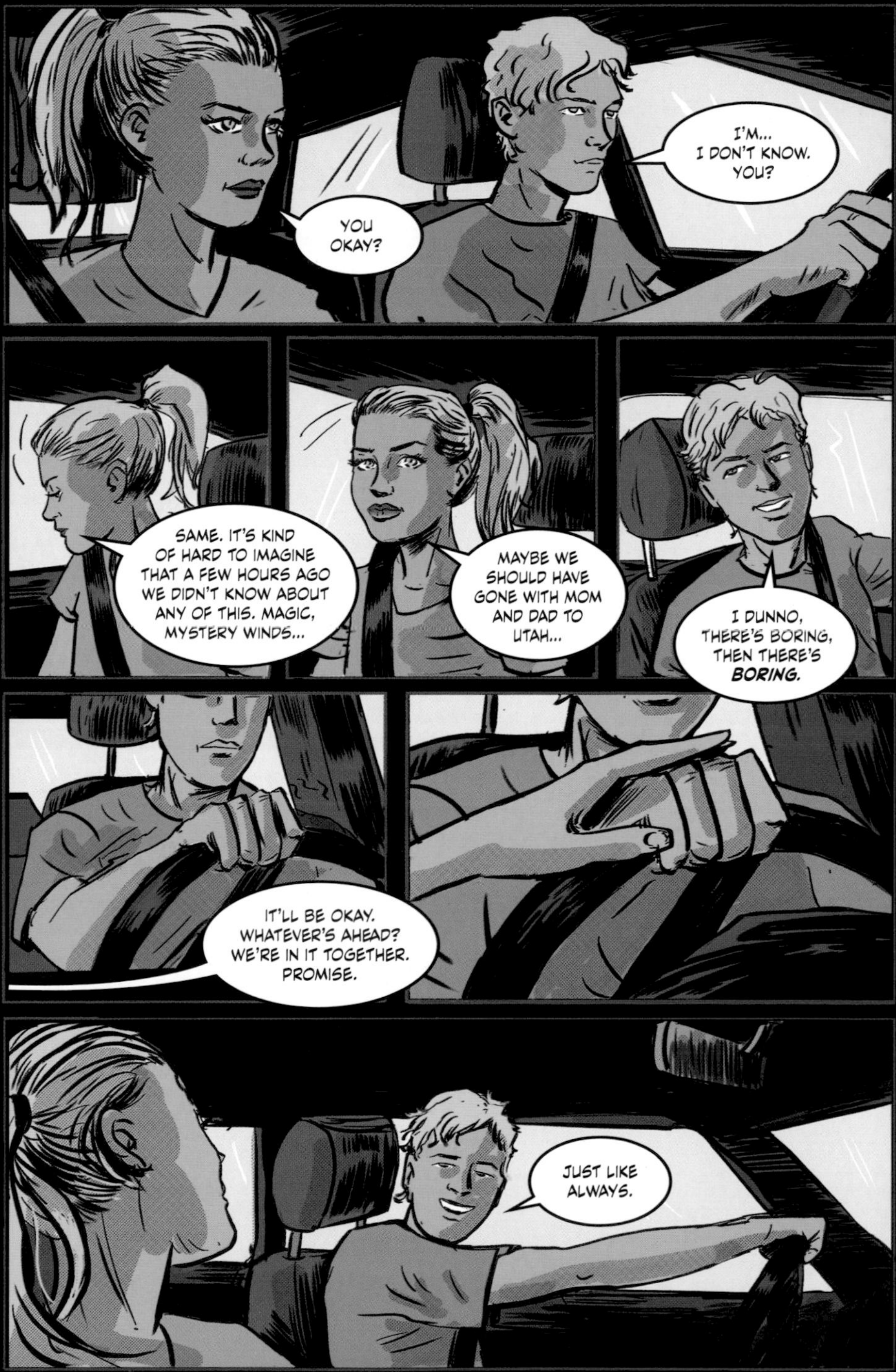
YOU OKAY?
I'M... I DON'T KNOW. YOU?
SAME. IT'S KIND OF HARD TO IMAGINE THAT A FEW HOURS AGO WE DIDN'T KNOW ABOUT ANY OF THIS. MAGIC, MYSTERY WINDS...
MAYBE WE SHOULD HAVE GONE WITH MOM AND DAD TO UTAH...
I DUNNO, THERE'S BORING, THEN THERE'S ***BORING.***
IT'LL BE OKAY. WHATEVER'S AHEAD? WE'RE IN IT TOGETHER. PROMISE.
JUST LIKE ALWAYS.

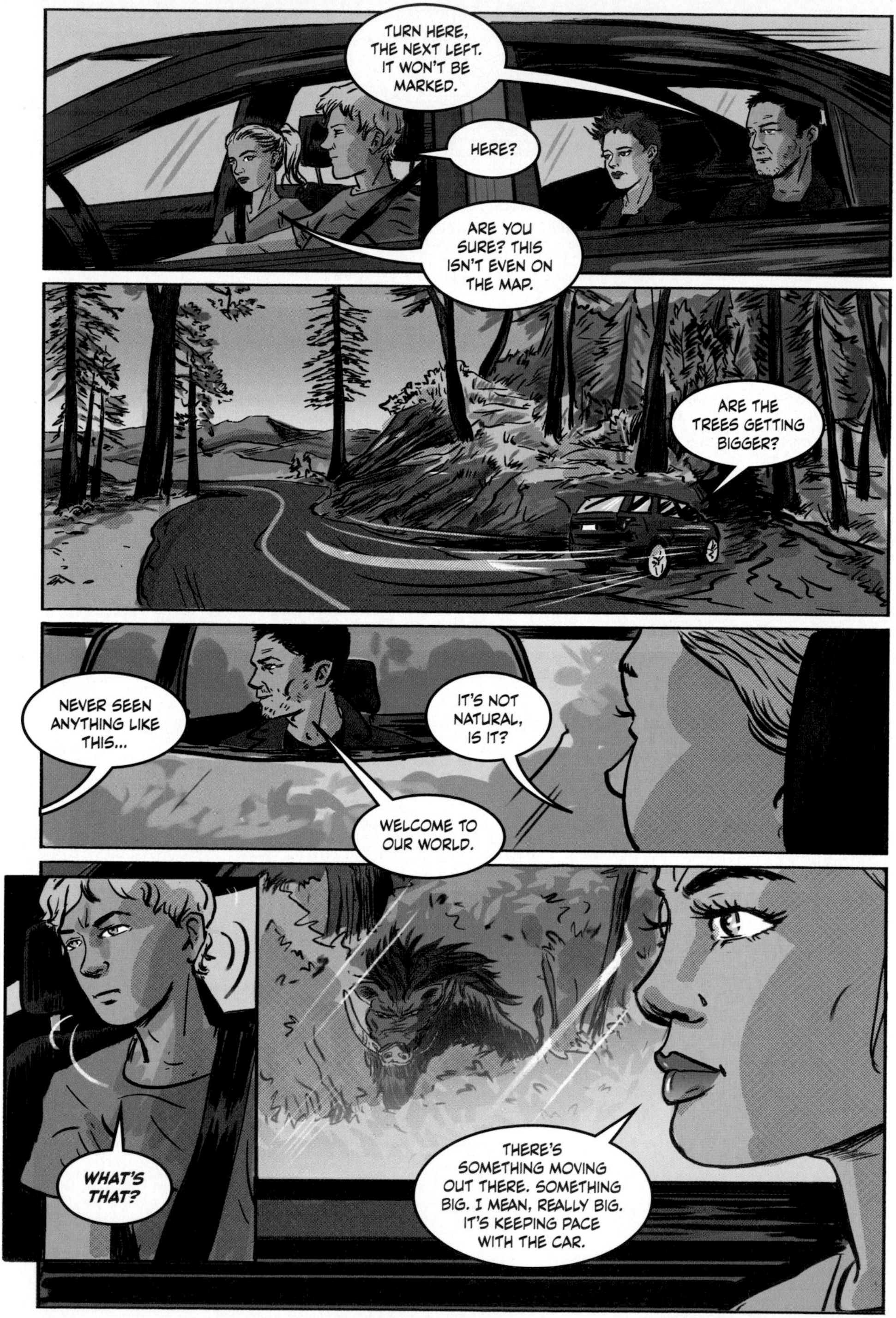
TURN HERE, THE NEXT LEFT. IT WON'T BE MARKED.
HERE?
ARE YOU SURE? THIS ISN'T EVEN ON THE MAP.
ARE THE TREES GETTING BIGGER?
NEVER SEEN ANYTHING LIKE THIS...
IT'S NOT NATURAL, IS IT?
WELCOME TO OUR WORLD.
WHAT'S THAT?
THERE'S SOMETHING MOVING OUT THERE. SOMETHING BIG. I MEAN, REALLY BIG. IT'S KEEPING PACE WITH THE CAR.

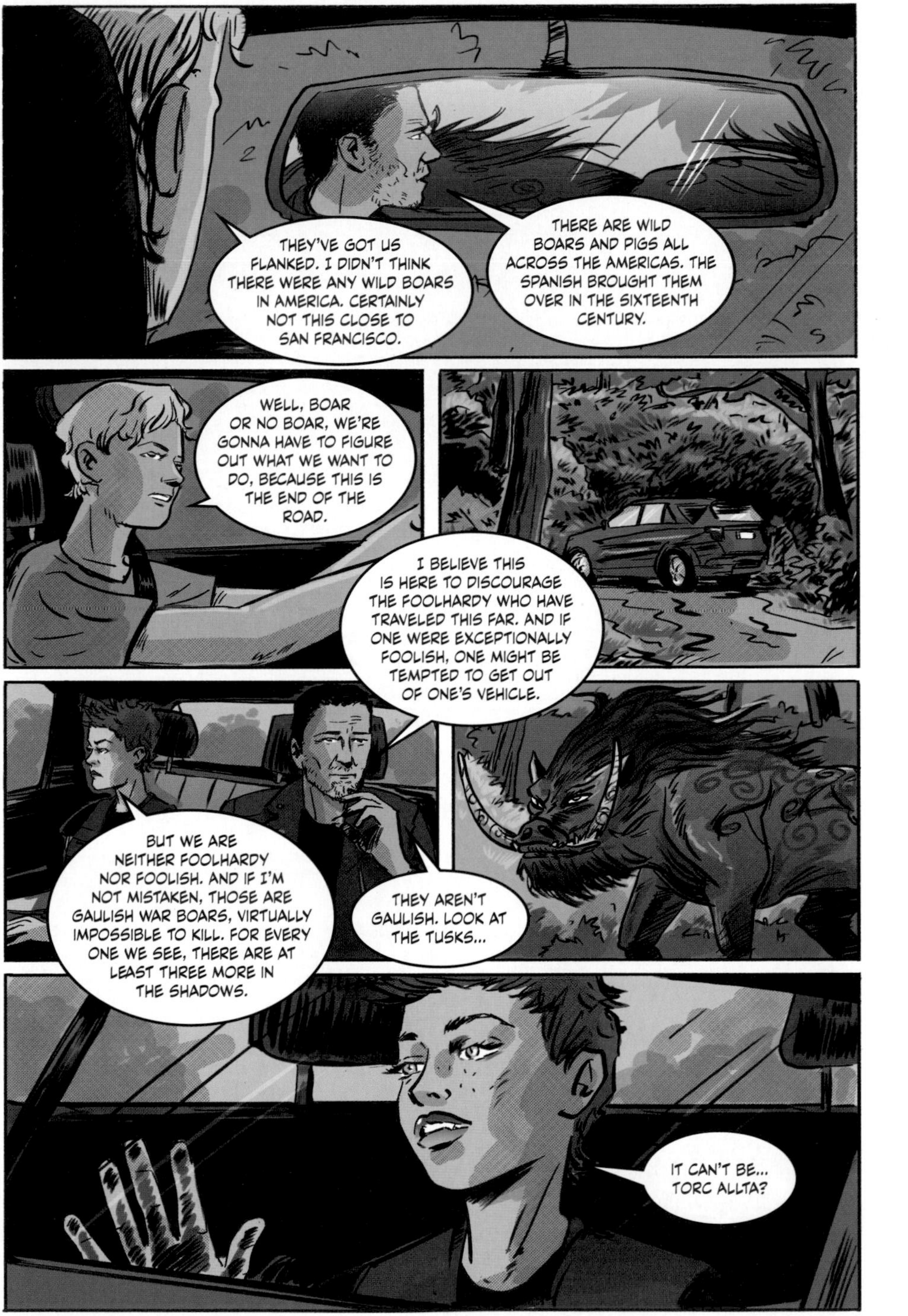
THEY'VE GOT US FLANKED. I DIDN'T THINK THERE WERE ANY WILD BOARS IN AMERICA. CERTAINLY NOT THIS CLOSE TO SAN FRANCISCO.
THERE ARE WILD BOARS AND PIGS ALL ACROSS THE AMERICAS. THE SPANISH BROUGHT THEM OVER IN THE SIXTEENTH CENTURY.
WELL, BOAR OR NO BOAR, WE'RE GONNA HAVE TO FIGURE OUT WHAT WE WANT TO DO, BECAUSE THIS IS THE END OF THE ROAD.
I BELIEVE THIS IS HERE TO DISCOURAGE THE FOOLHARDY WHO HAVE TRAVELED THIS FAR. AND IF ONE WERE EXCEPTIONALLY FOOLISH, ONE MIGHT BE TEMPTED TO GET OUT OF ONE'S VEHICLE.
BUT WE ARE NEITHER FOOLHARDY NOR FOOLISH. AND IF I'M NOT MISTAKEN, THOSE ARE GAULISH WAR BOARS, VIRTUALLY IMPOSSIBLE TO KILL. FOR EVERY ONE WE SEE, THERE ARE AT LEAST THREE MORE IN THE SHADOWS.
THEY AREN'T GAULISH. LOOK AT THE TUSKS...
IT CAN'T BE... TORC ALLTA?

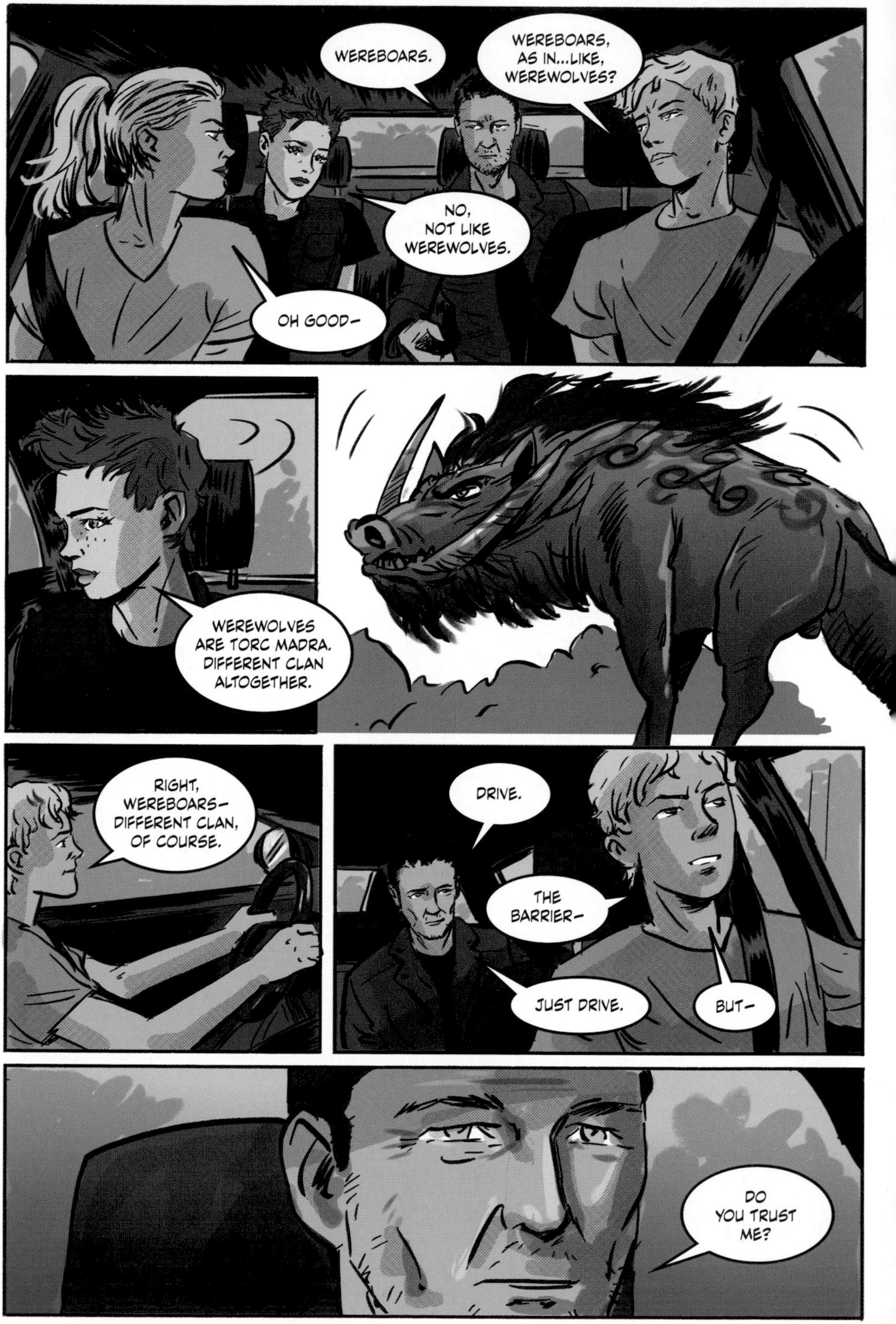
WEREBOARS.
WEREBOARS, AS IN...LIKE, WEREWOLVES?
NO, NOT LIKE WEREWOLVES.
OH GOOD—
WEREWOLVES ARE TORC MADRA. DIFFERENT CLAN ALTOGETHER.
RIGHT, WEREBOARS— DIFFERENT CLAN, OF COURSE.
DRIVE.
THE BARRIER—
JUST DRIVE.
BUT—
DO YOU TRUST ME?

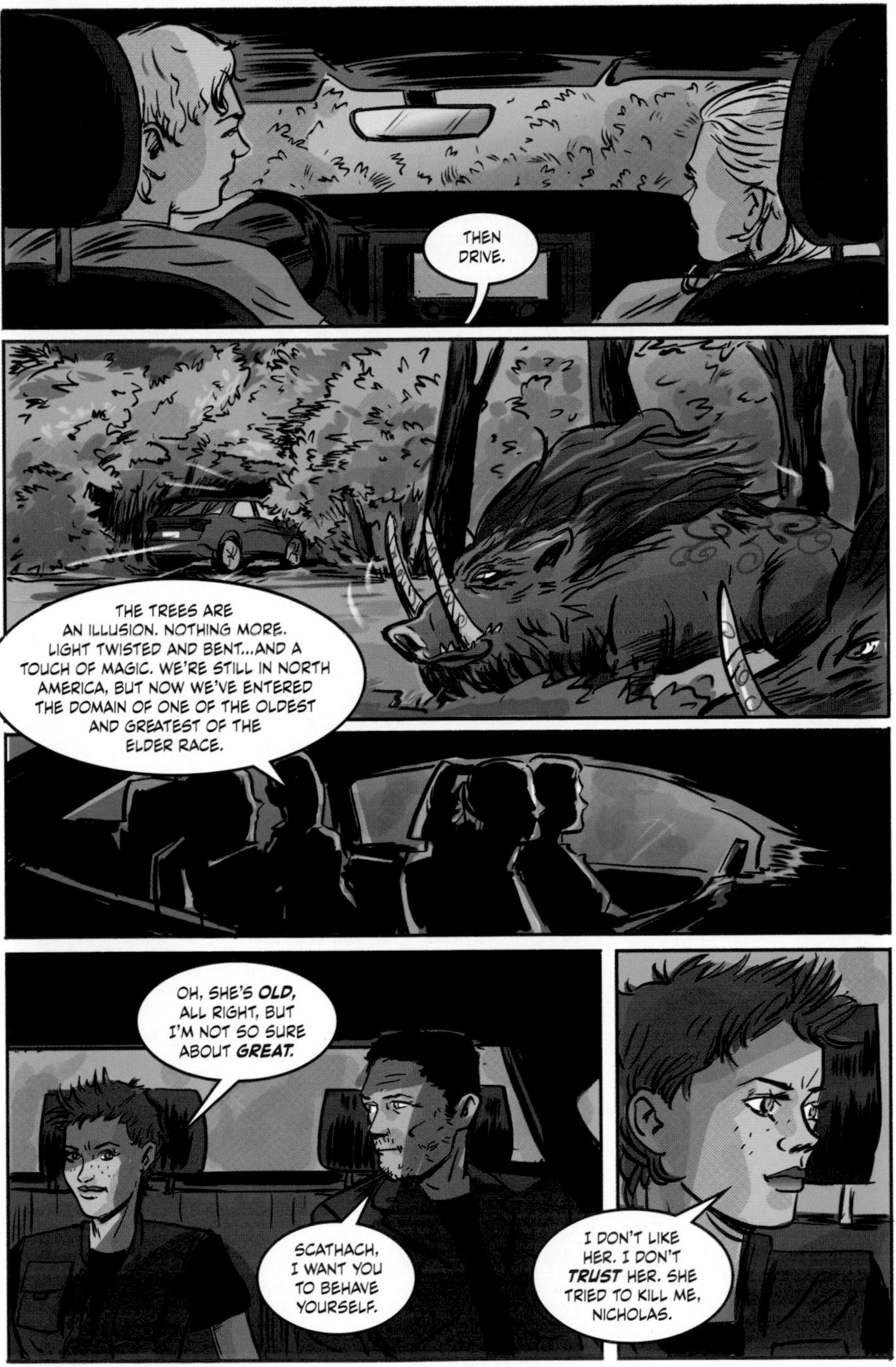
THEN DRIVE.
THE TREES ARE AN ILLUSION. NOTHING MORE. LIGHT TWISTED AND BENT...AND A TOUCH OF MAGIC. WE'RE STILL IN NORTH AMERICA, BUT NOW WE'VE ENTERED THE DOMAIN OF ONE OF THE OLDEST AND GREATEST OF THE ELDER RACE.
OH, SHE'S *OLD*, ALL RIGHT, BUT I'M NOT SO SURE ABOUT *GREAT.*
SCATHACH, I WANT YOU TO BEHAVE YOURSELF.
I DON'T LIKE HER. I DON'T *TRUST* HER. SHE TRIED TO KILL ME, NICHOLAS.

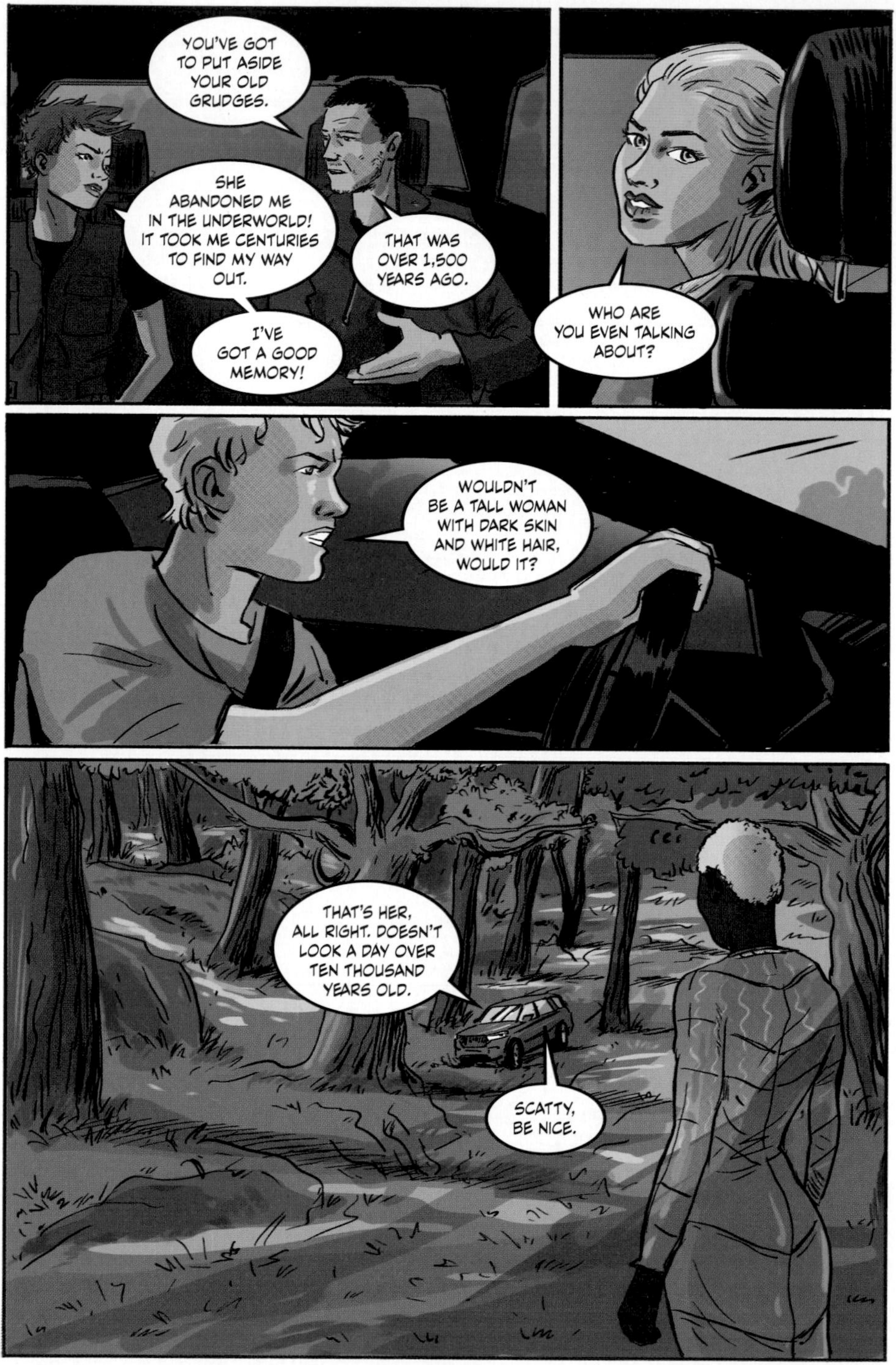
YOU'VE GOT TO PUT ASIDE YOUR OLD GRUDGES.
SHE ABANDONED ME IN THE UNDERWORLD! IT TOOK ME CENTURIES TO FIND MY WAY OUT.
THAT WAS OVER 1,500 YEARS AGO.
I'VE GOT A GOOD MEMORY!
WHO ARE YOU EVEN TALKING ABOUT?
WOULDN'T BE A TALL WOMAN WITH DARK SKIN AND WHITE HAIR, WOULD IT?
THAT'S HER, ALL RIGHT. DOESN'T LOOK A DAY OVER TEN THOUSAND YEARS OLD.
SCATTY, BE NICE.

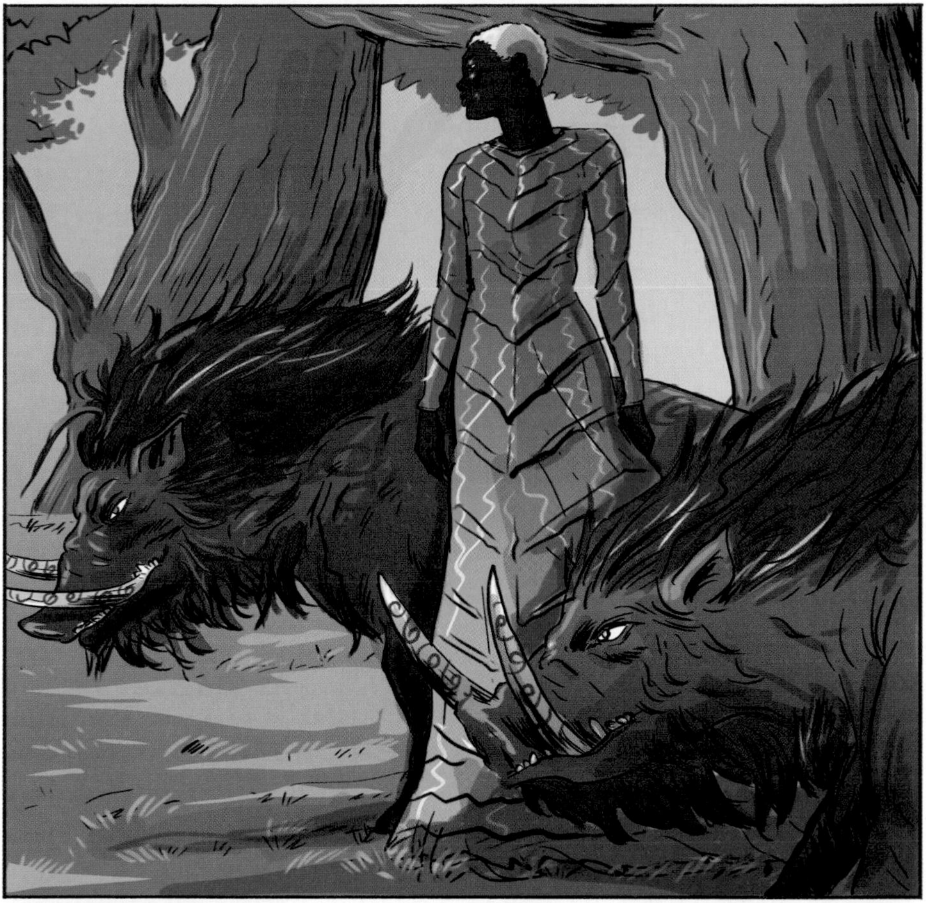

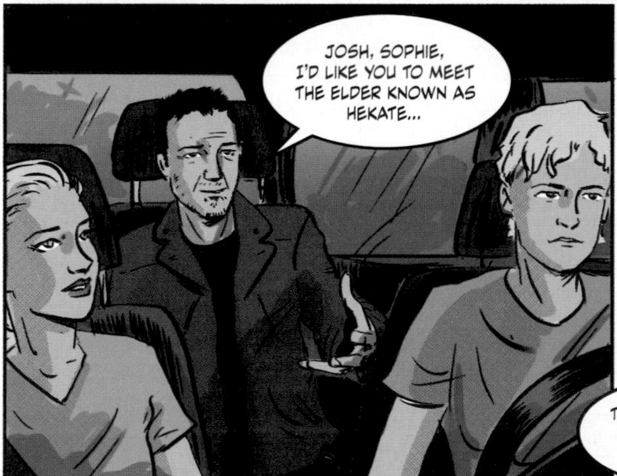
JOSH, SOPHIE, I'D LIKE YOU TO MEET THE ELDER KNOWN AS HEKATE...

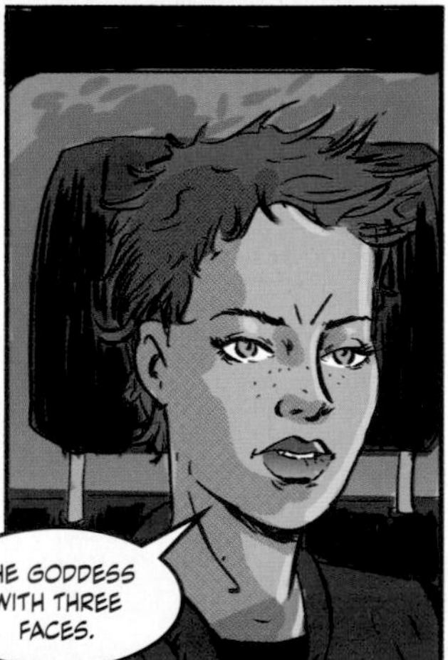
THE GODDESS WITH THREE FACES.

CHAPTER 14

STAY HERE...

I DID NOT THINK THERE WERE ANY OF THE TORC ALLTA CLAN LEFT IN THE AMERICAS.

WHEN WE ARE GONE, WHEN THE ELDER RACE IS NO MORE, WHEN EVEN THE HUMANI HAVE GONE FROM THIS EARTH, THEN THE ALLTA CLANS WILL RECLAIM IT FOR THEMSELVES. THOUGH I DOUBT YOU HAVE COME ALL THIS WAY TO TALK TO ME ABOUT MY CHILDREN.

FIRST, I MUST THANK YOU FOR THE GHOST WIND YOU SENT US.

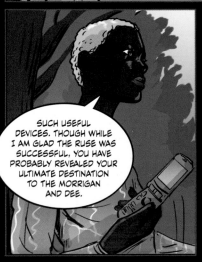

SUCH USEFUL DEVICES. THOUGH WHILE I AM GLAD THE RUSE WAS SUCCESSFUL, YOU HAVE PROBABLY REVEALED YOUR ULTIMATE DESTINATION TO THE MORRIGAN AND DEE.

I KNOW THAT. AND I APOLOGIZE FOR DRAWING THEM DOWN ON YOU.

DEE FEARS ME. HE WILL BLUSTER AND POSTURE; HE WILL THREATEN ME, BUT HE WILL NOT MOVE AGAINST ME. NOT ALONE. NOT EVEN WITH THE MORRIGAN'S ASSISTANCE. HE WOULD NEED ANOTHER.

BUT HE IS ARROGANT. AND NOW HE HAS THE CODEX.

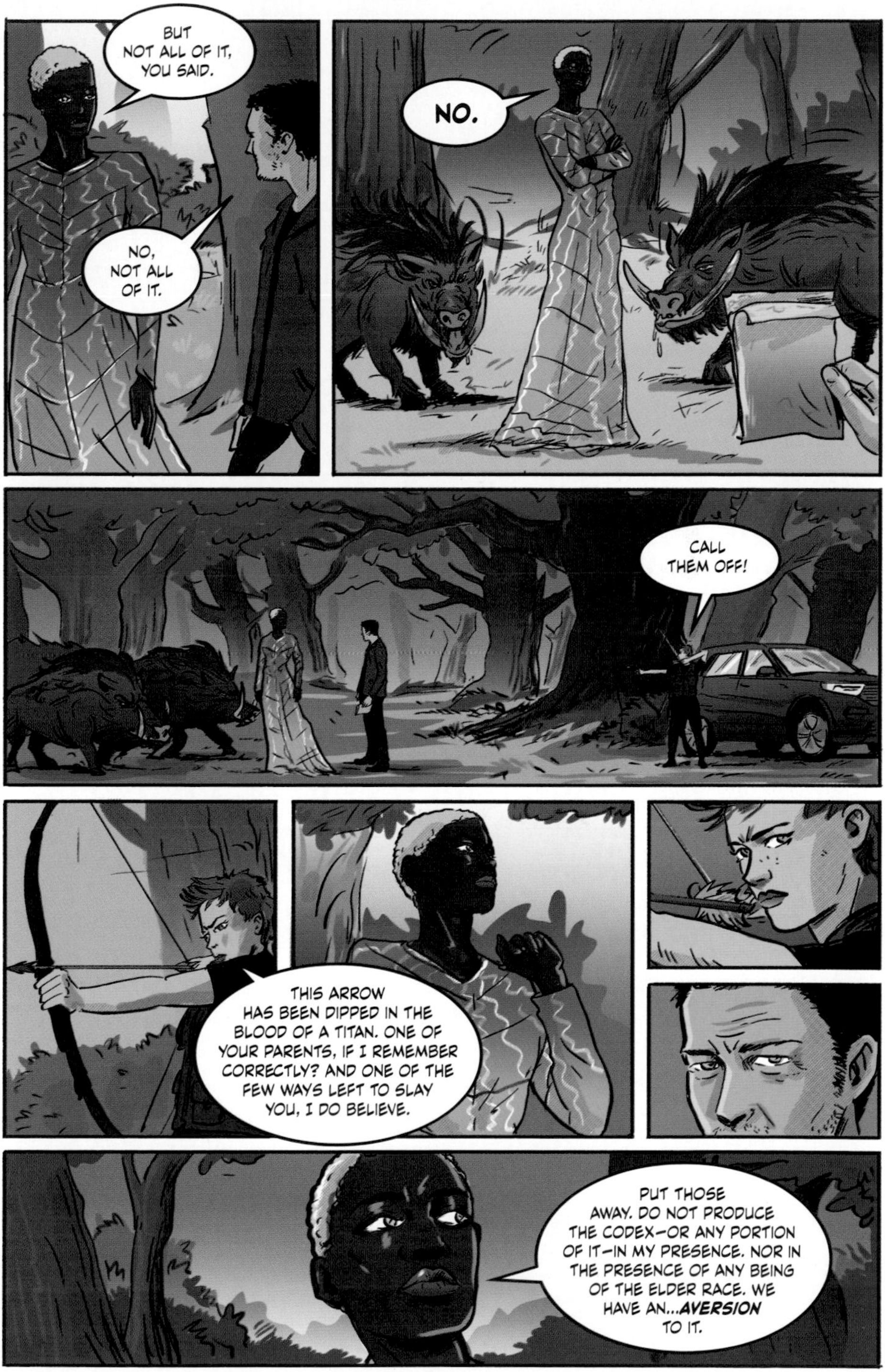
BUT NOT ALL OF IT, YOU SAID.
NO, NOT ALL OF IT.
NO.
CALL THEM OFF!
THIS ARROW HAS BEEN DIPPED IN THE BLOOD OF A TITAN. ONE OF YOUR PARENTS, IF I REMEMBER CORRECTLY? AND ONE OF THE FEW WAYS LEFT TO SLAY YOU, I DO BELIEVE.
PUT THOSE AWAY. DO NOT PRODUCE THE CODEX—OR ANY PORTION OF IT—IN MY PRESENCE. NOR IN THE PRESENCE OF ANY BEING OF THE ELDER RACE. WE HAVE AN...*AVERSION* TO IT.

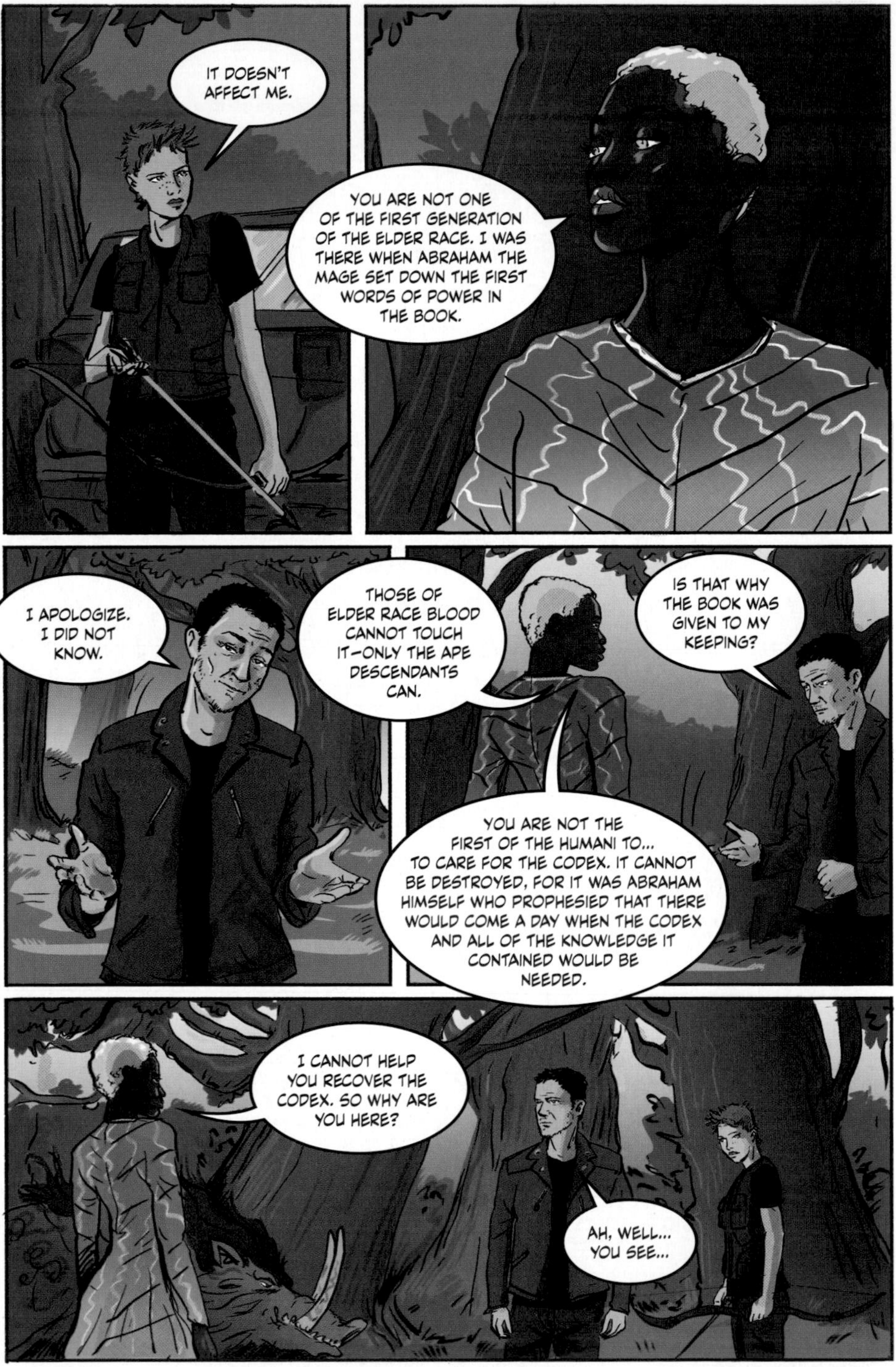
IT DOESN'T AFFECT ME.
YOU ARE NOT ONE OF THE FIRST GENERATION OF THE ELDER RACE. I WAS THERE WHEN ABRAHAM THE MAGE SET DOWN THE FIRST WORDS OF POWER IN THE BOOK.
I APOLOGIZE. I DID NOT KNOW.
THOSE OF ELDER RACE BLOOD CANNOT TOUCH IT—ONLY THE APE DESCENDANTS CAN.
IS THAT WHY THE BOOK WAS GIVEN TO MY KEEPING?
YOU ARE NOT THE FIRST OF THE HUMANI TO... TO CARE FOR THE CODEX. IT CANNOT BE DESTROYED, FOR IT WAS ABRAHAM HIMSELF WHO PROPHESIED THAT THERE WOULD COME A DAY WHEN THE CODEX AND ALL OF THE KNOWLEDGE IT CONTAINED WOULD BE NEEDED.
I CANNOT HELP YOU RECOVER THE CODEX. SO WHY ARE YOU HERE?
AH, WELL... YOU SEE...

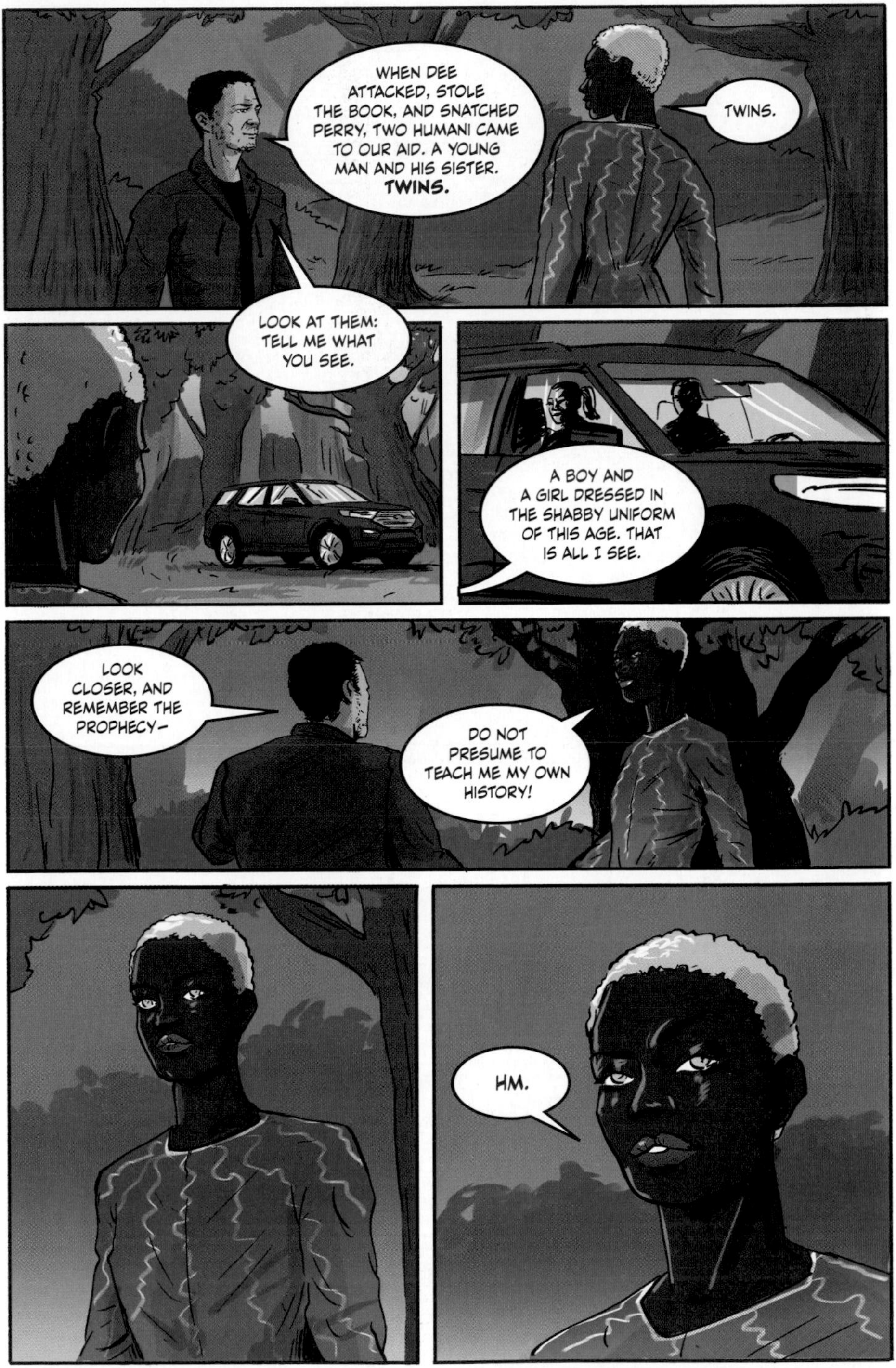
WHEN DEE ATTACKED, STOLE THE BOOK, AND SNATCHED PERRY, TWO HUMANI CAME TO OUR AID. A YOUNG MAN AND HIS SISTER. **TWINS.**
TWINS.
LOOK AT THEM: TELL ME WHAT YOU SEE.
A BOY AND A GIRL DRESSED IN THE SHABBY UNIFORM OF THIS AGE. THAT IS ALL I SEE.
LOOK CLOSER, AND REMEMBER THE PROPHECY–
DO NOT PRESUME TO TEACH ME MY OWN HISTORY!
HM.

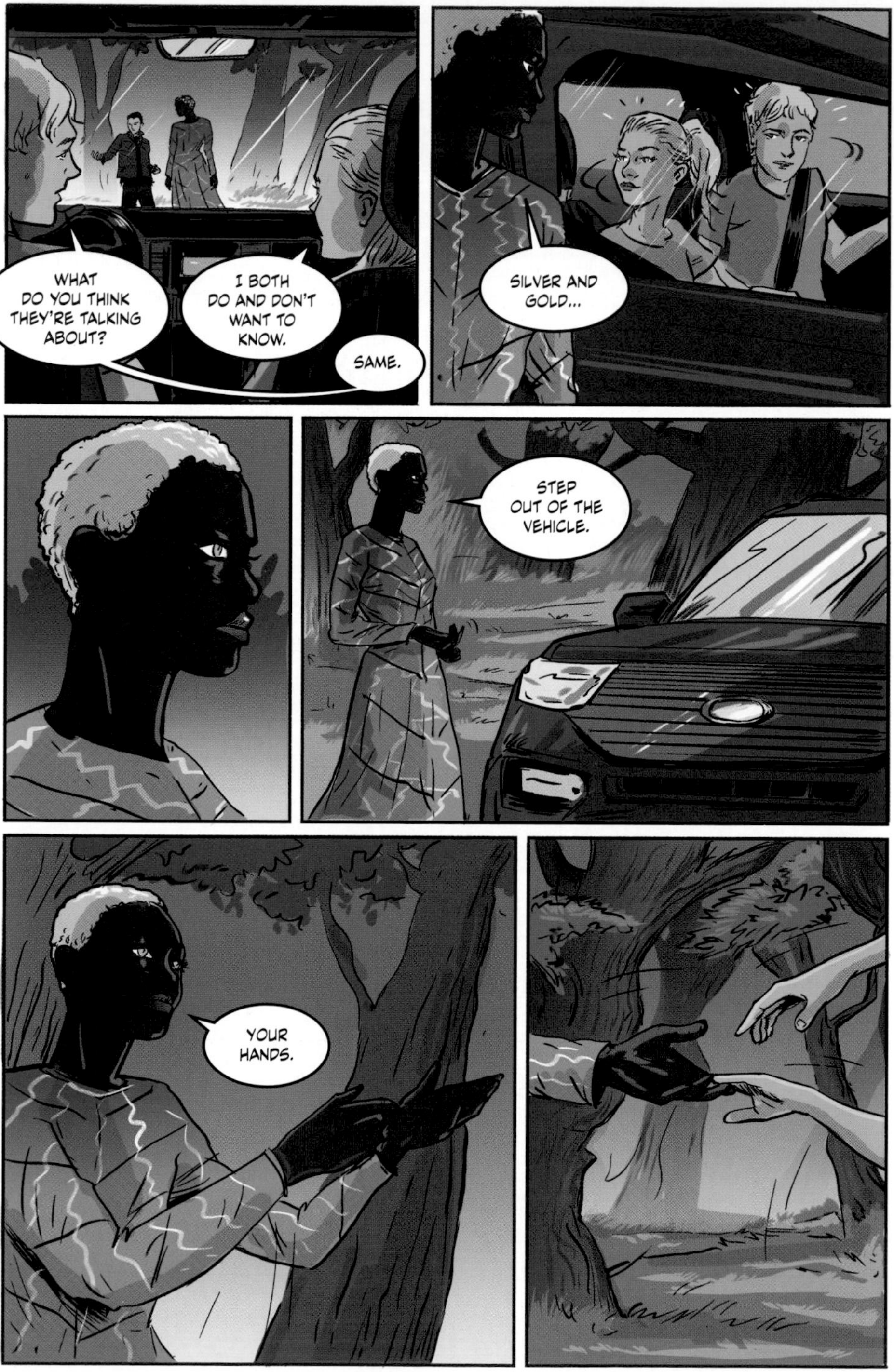
WHAT DO YOU THINK THEY'RE TALKING ABOUT?
I BOTH DO AND DON'T WANT TO KNOW.
SAME.
SILVER AND GOLD...
STEP OUT OF THE VEHICLE.
YOUR HANDS.

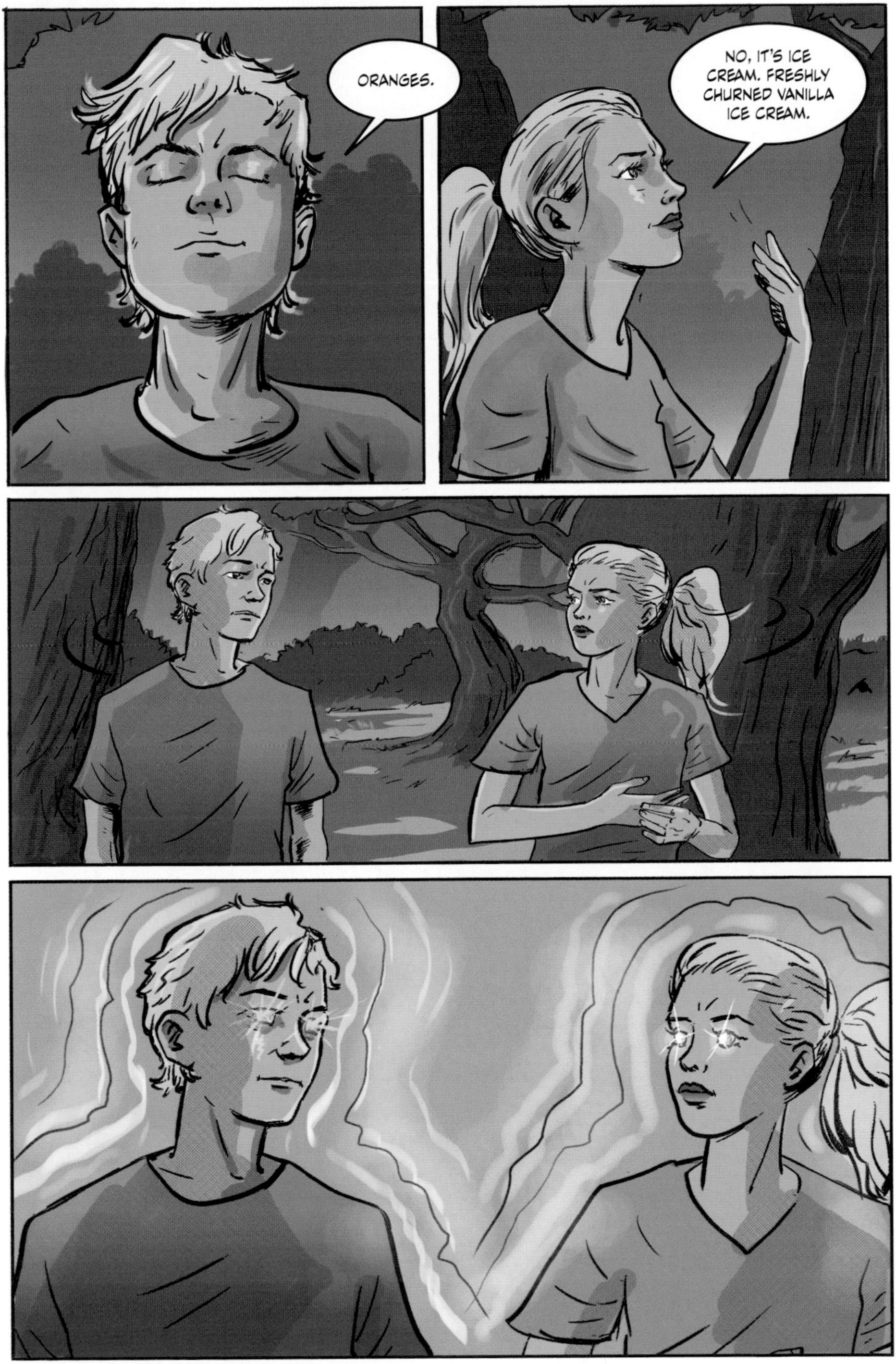
ORANGES.
NO, IT'S ICE CREAM. FRESHLY CHURNED VANILLA ICE CREAM.

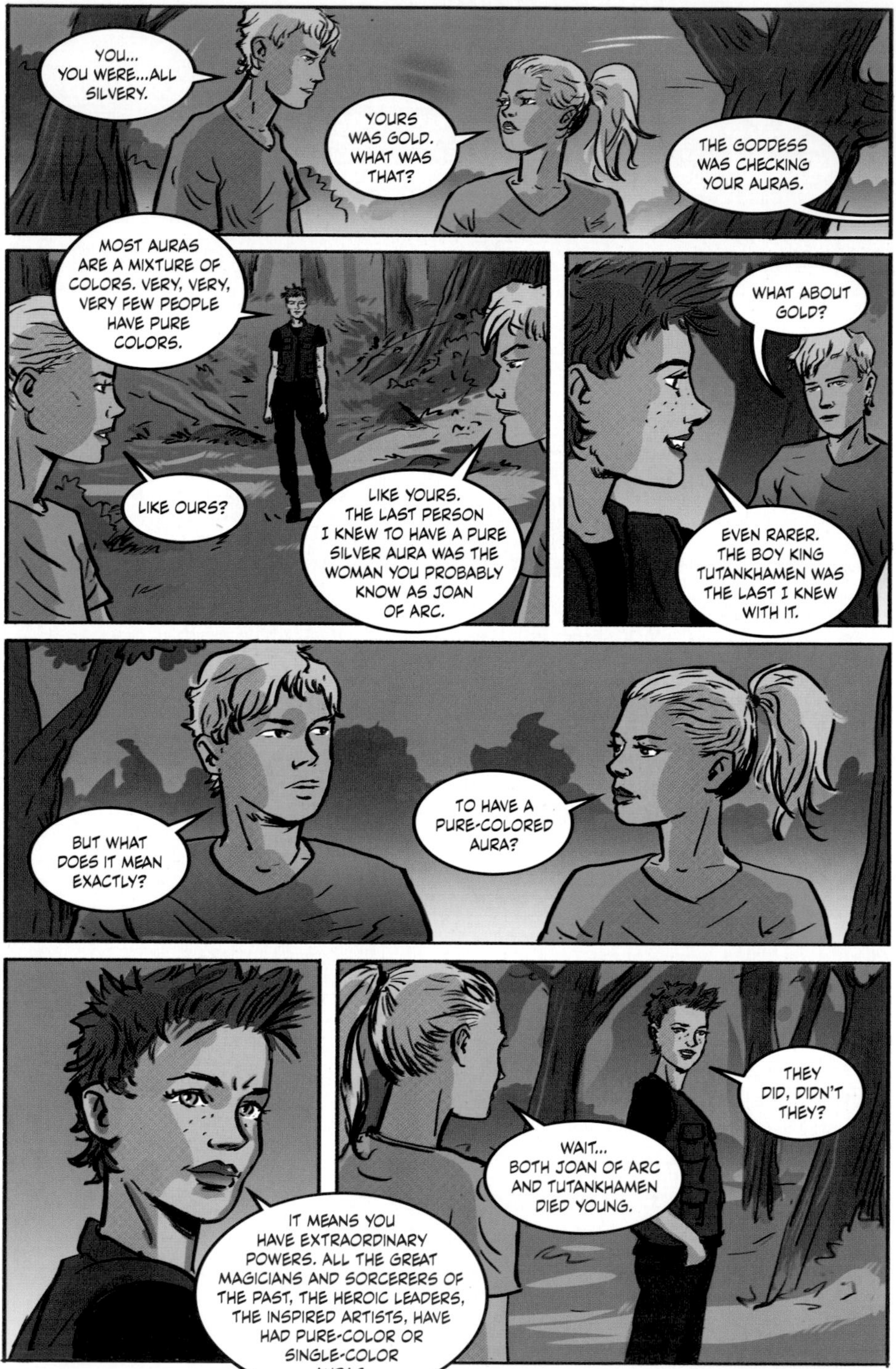
YOU... YOU WERE...ALL SILVERY.
YOURS WAS GOLD. WHAT WAS THAT?
THE GODDESS WAS CHECKING YOUR AURAS.
MOST AURAS ARE A MIXTURE OF COLORS. VERY, VERY, VERY FEW PEOPLE HAVE PURE COLORS.
LIKE OURS?
LIKE YOURS. THE LAST PERSON I KNEW TO HAVE A PURE SILVER AURA WAS THE WOMAN YOU PROBABLY KNOW AS JOAN OF ARC.
WHAT ABOUT GOLD?
EVEN RARER. THE BOY KING TUTANKHAMEN WAS THE LAST I KNEW WITH IT.
BUT WHAT DOES IT MEAN EXACTLY?
TO HAVE A PURE-COLORED AURA?
IT MEANS YOU HAVE EXTRAORDINARY POWERS. ALL THE GREAT MAGICIANS AND SORCERERS OF THE PAST, THE HEROIC LEADERS, THE INSPIRED ARTISTS, HAVE HAD PURE-COLOR OR SINGLE-COLOR AURAS.
WAIT... BOTH JOAN OF ARC AND TUTANKHAMEN DIED YOUNG.
THEY DID, DIDN'T THEY?

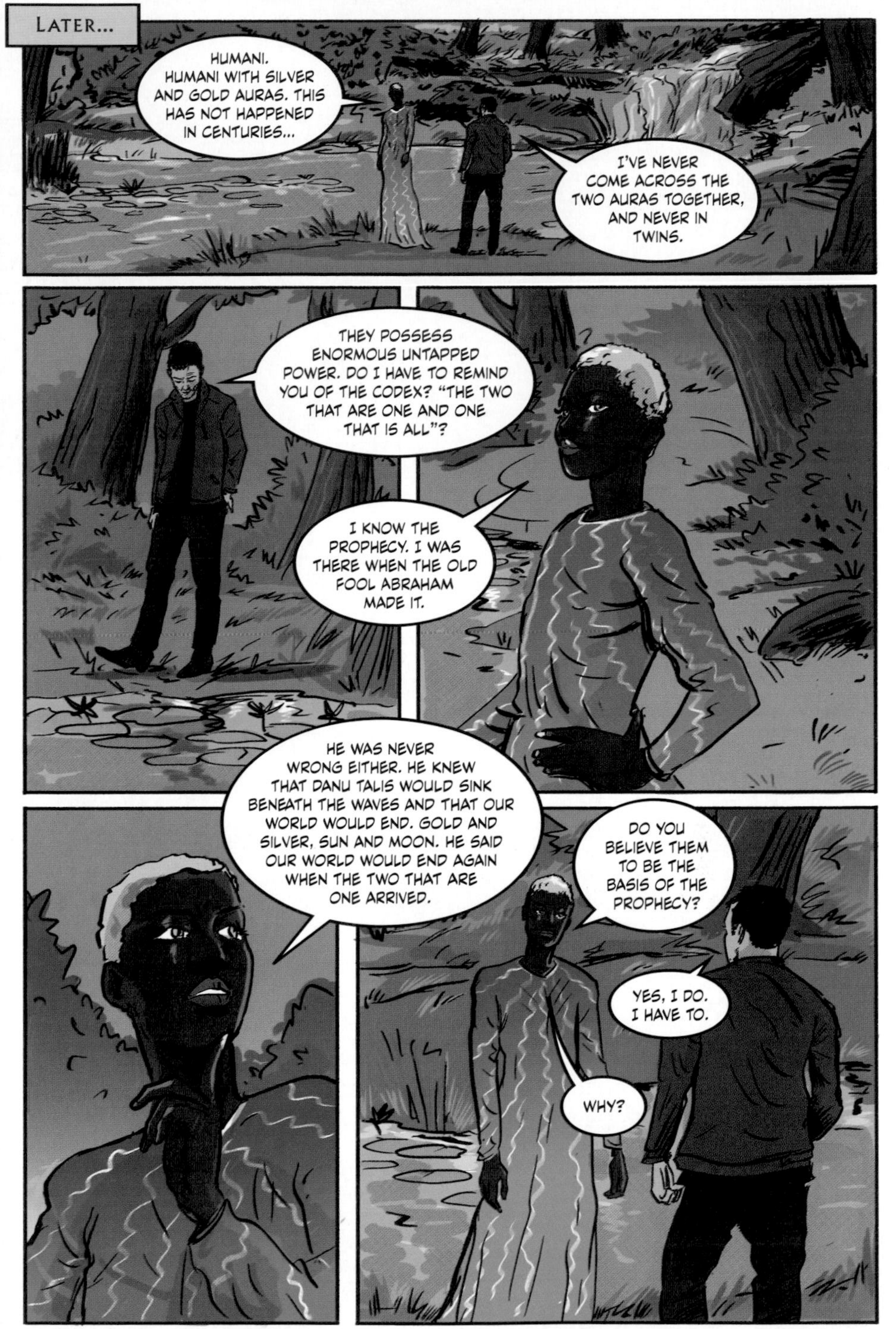
LATER...
HUMANI. HUMANI WITH SILVER AND GOLD AURAS. THIS HAS NOT HAPPENED IN CENTURIES...
I'VE NEVER COME ACROSS THE TWO AURAS TOGETHER, AND NEVER IN TWINS.
THEY POSSESS ENORMOUS UNTAPPED POWER. DO I HAVE TO REMIND YOU OF THE CODEX? "THE TWO THAT ARE ONE AND ONE THAT IS ALL"?
I KNOW THE PROPHECY. I WAS THERE WHEN THE OLD FOOL ABRAHAM MADE IT.
HE WAS NEVER WRONG EITHER. HE KNEW THAT DANU TALIS WOULD SINK BENEATH THE WAVES AND THAT OUR WORLD WOULD END. GOLD AND SILVER, SUN AND MOON. HE SAID OUR WORLD WOULD END AGAIN WHEN THE TWO THAT ARE ONE ARRIVED.
DO YOU BELIEVE THEM TO BE THE BASIS OF THE PROPHECY?
YES, I DO. I HAVE TO.
WHY?

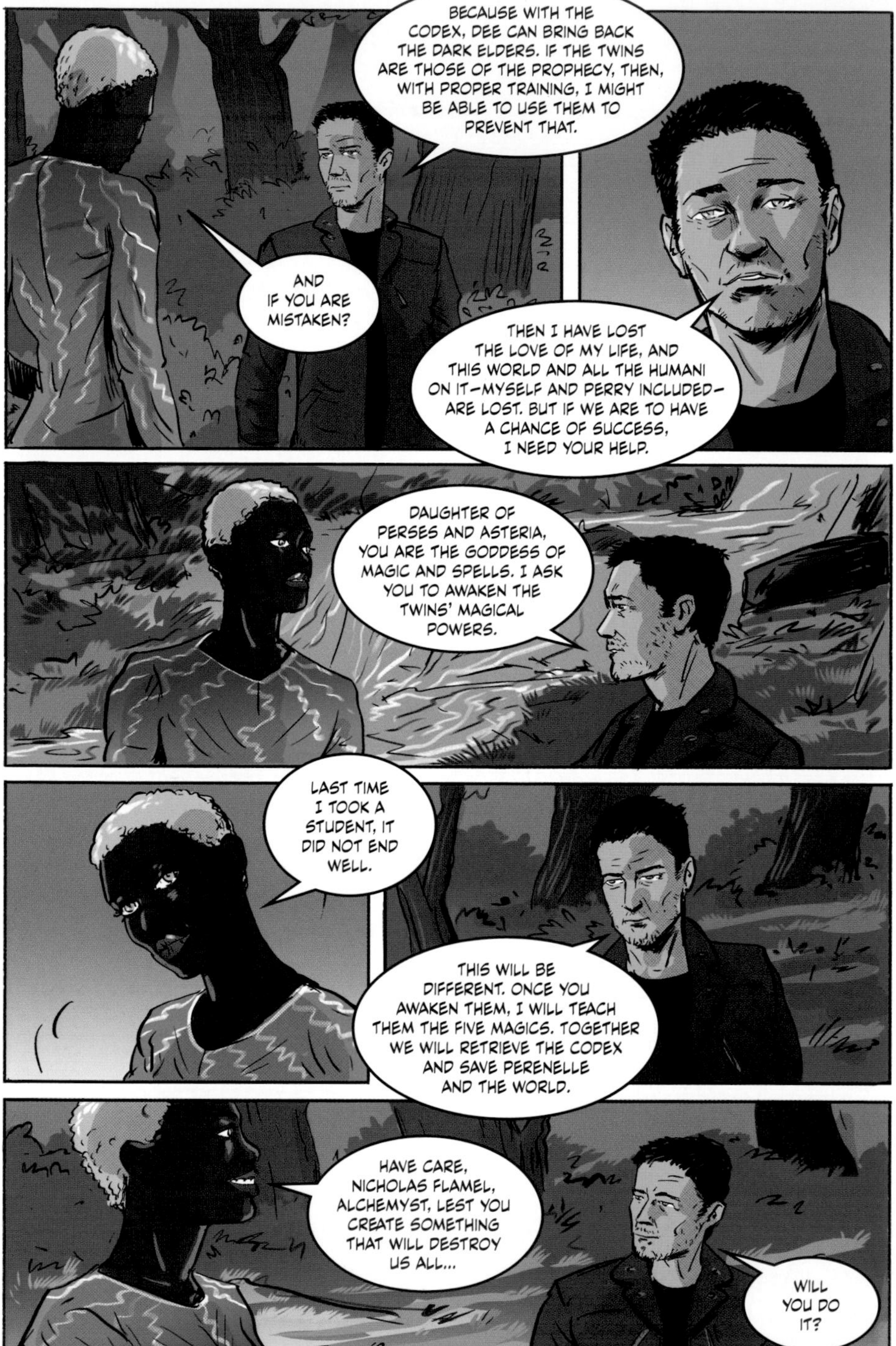
BECAUSE WITH THE CODEX, DEE CAN BRING BACK THE DARK ELDERS. IF THE TWINS ARE THOSE OF THE PROPHECY, THEN, WITH PROPER TRAINING, I MIGHT BE ABLE TO USE THEM TO PREVENT THAT.
AND IF YOU ARE MISTAKEN?
THEN I HAVE LOST THE LOVE OF MY LIFE, AND THIS WORLD AND ALL THE HUMANI ON IT—MYSELF AND PERRY INCLUDED—ARE LOST. BUT IF WE ARE TO HAVE A CHANCE OF SUCCESS, I NEED YOUR HELP.
DAUGHTER OF PERSES AND ASTERIA, YOU ARE THE GODDESS OF MAGIC AND SPELLS. I ASK YOU TO AWAKEN THE TWINS' MAGICAL POWERS.
LAST TIME I TOOK A STUDENT, IT DID NOT END WELL.
THIS WILL BE DIFFERENT. ONCE YOU AWAKEN THEM, I WILL TEACH THEM THE FIVE MAGICS. TOGETHER WE WILL RETRIEVE THE CODEX AND SAVE PERENELLE AND THE WORLD.
HAVE CARE, NICHOLAS FLAMEL, ALCHEMYST, LEST YOU CREATE SOMETHING THAT WILL DESTROY US ALL...
WILL YOU DO IT?

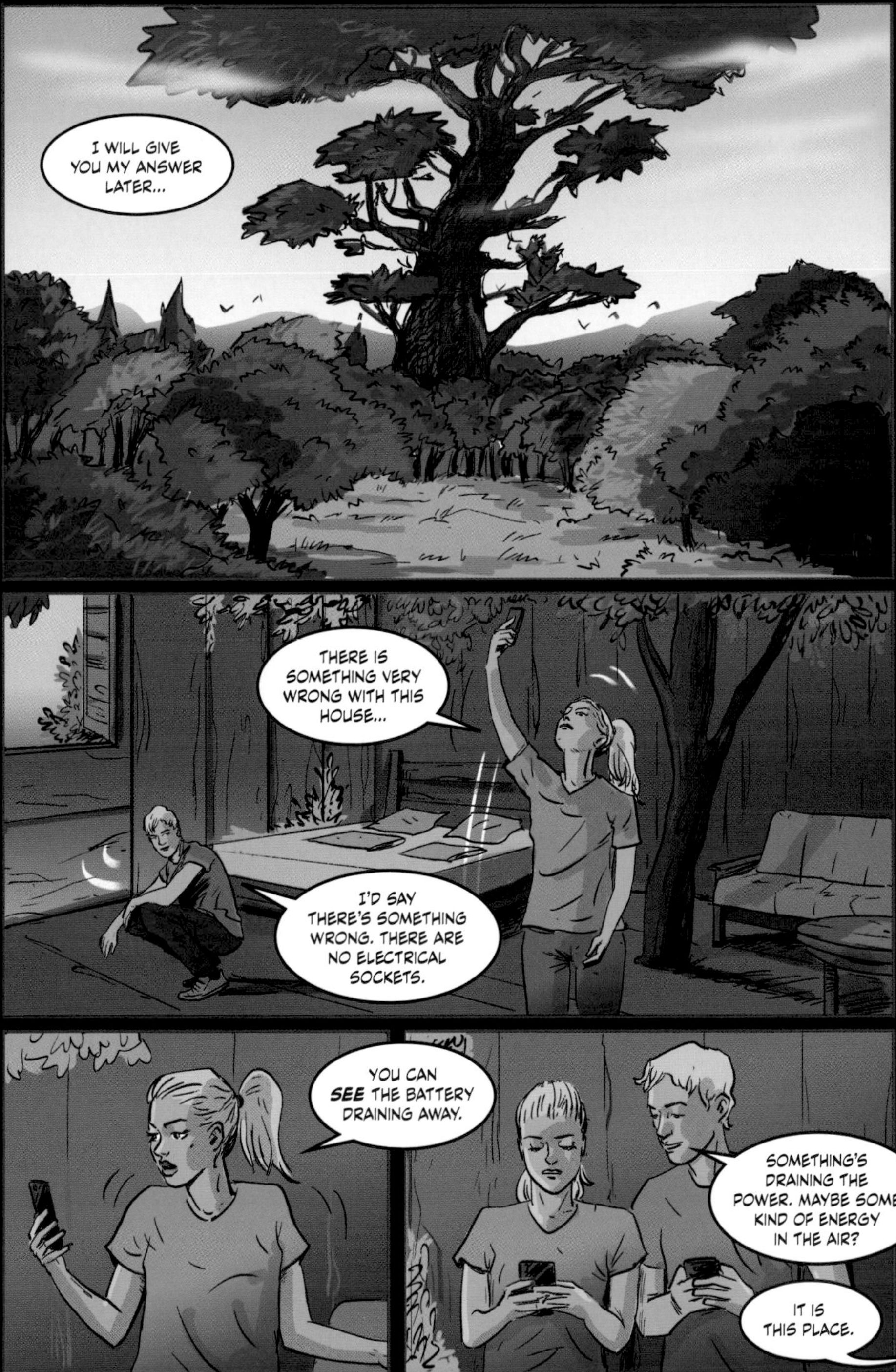
I WILL GIVE YOU MY ANSWER LATER...
THERE IS SOMETHING VERY WRONG WITH THIS HOUSE...
I'D SAY THERE'S SOMETHING WRONG. THERE ARE NO ELECTRICAL SOCKETS.
YOU CAN SEE THE BATTERY DRAINING AWAY.
SOMETHING'S DRAINING THE POWER. MAYBE SOME KIND OF ENERGY IN THE AIR?
IT IS THIS PLACE.

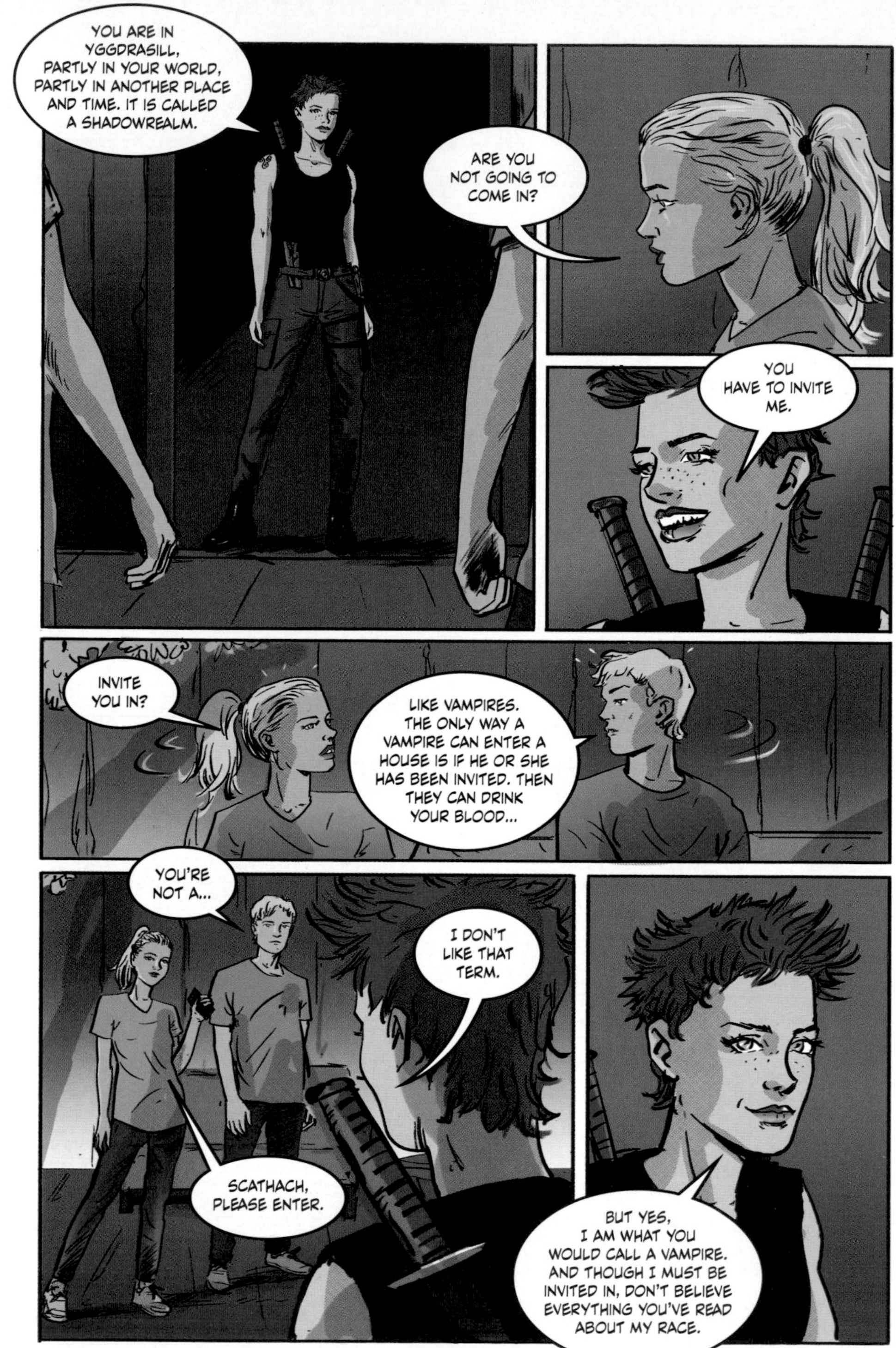
YOU ARE IN YGGDRASILL, PARTLY IN YOUR WORLD, PARTLY IN ANOTHER PLACE AND TIME. IT IS CALLED A SHADOWREALM.
ARE YOU NOT GOING TO COME IN?
YOU HAVE TO INVITE ME.
INVITE YOU IN?
LIKE VAMPIRES. THE ONLY WAY A VAMPIRE CAN ENTER A HOUSE IS IF HE OR SHE HAS BEEN INVITED. THEN THEY CAN DRINK YOUR BLOOD...
YOU'RE NOT A...
I DON'T LIKE THAT TERM.
SCATHACH, PLEASE ENTER.
BUT YES, I AM WHAT YOU WOULD CALL A VAMPIRE. AND THOUGH I MUST BE INVITED IN, DON'T BELIEVE EVERYTHING YOU'VE READ ABOUT MY RACE.

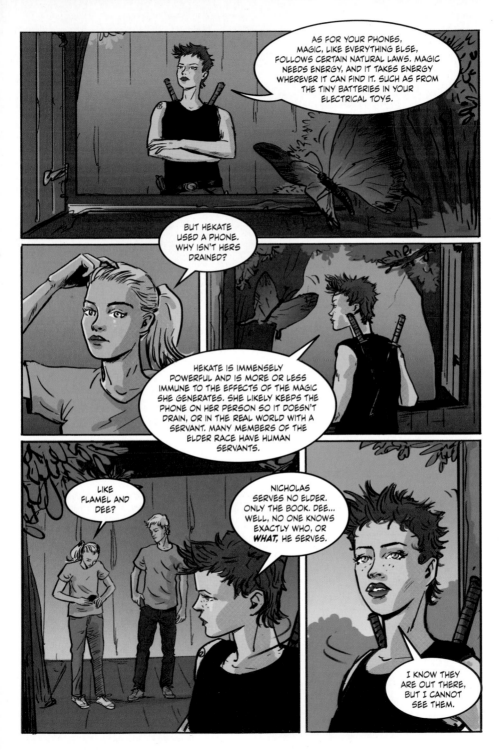

AS FOR YOUR PHONES, MAGIC, LIKE EVERYTHING ELSE, FOLLOWS CERTAIN NATURAL LAWS. MAGIC NEEDS ENERGY, AND IT TAKES ENERGY WHEREVER IT CAN FIND IT. SUCH AS FROM THE TINY BATTERIES IN YOUR ELECTRICAL TOYS.

BUT HEKATE USED A PHONE. WHY ISN'T HERS DRAINED?

HEKATE IS IMMENSELY POWERFUL AND IS MORE OR LESS IMMUNE TO THE EFFECTS OF THE MAGIC SHE GENERATES. SHE LIKELY KEEPS THE PHONE ON HER PERSON SO IT DOESN'T DRAIN, OR IN THE REAL WORLD WITH A SERVANT. MANY MEMBERS OF THE ELDER RACE HAVE HUMAN SERVANTS.

LIKE FLAMEL AND DEE?

NICHOLAS SERVES NO ELDER. ONLY THE BOOK. DEE... WELL, NO ONE KNOWS EXACTLY WHO, OR **WHAT**, HE SERVES.

I KNOW THEY ARE OUT THERE, BUT I CANNOT SEE THEM.

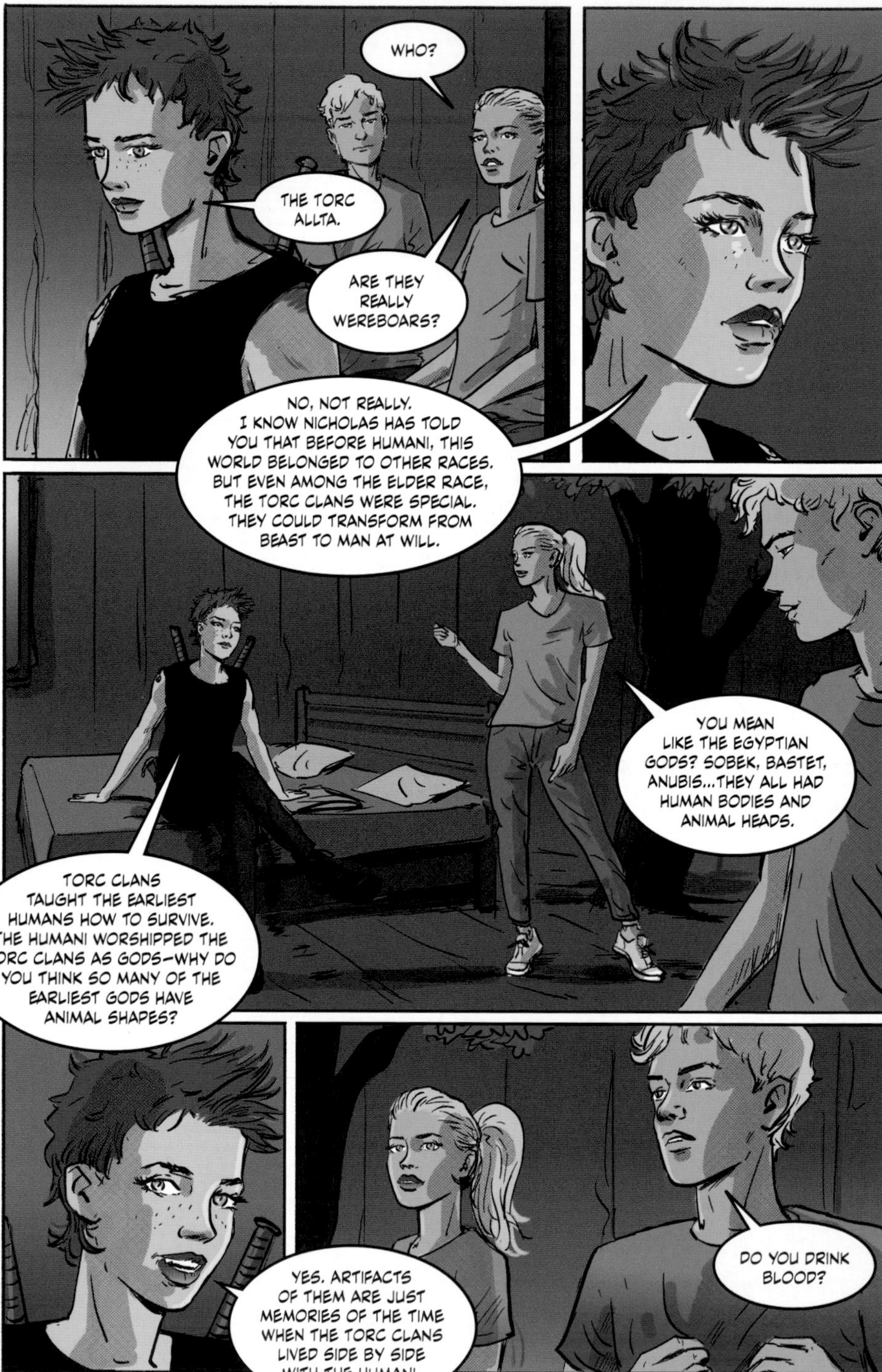
WHO?
THE TORC ALLTA.
ARE THEY REALLY WEREBOARS?
NO, NOT REALLY. I KNOW NICHOLAS HAS TOLD YOU THAT BEFORE HUMANI, THIS WORLD BELONGED TO OTHER RACES. BUT EVEN AMONG THE ELDER RACE, THE TORC CLANS WERE SPECIAL. THEY COULD TRANSFORM FROM BEAST TO MAN AT WILL.
YOU MEAN LIKE THE EGYPTIAN GODS? SOBEK, BASTET, ANUBIS...THEY ALL HAD HUMAN BODIES AND ANIMAL HEADS.
TORC CLANS TAUGHT THE EARLIEST HUMANS HOW TO SURVIVE. THE HUMANI WORSHIPPED THE TORC CLANS AS GODS—WHY DO YOU THINK SO MANY OF THE EARLIEST GODS HAVE ANIMAL SHAPES?
YES. ARTIFACTS OF THEM ARE JUST MEMORIES OF THE TIME WHEN THE TORC CLANS LIVED SIDE BY SIDE WITH THE HUMANI.
DO YOU DRINK BLOOD?

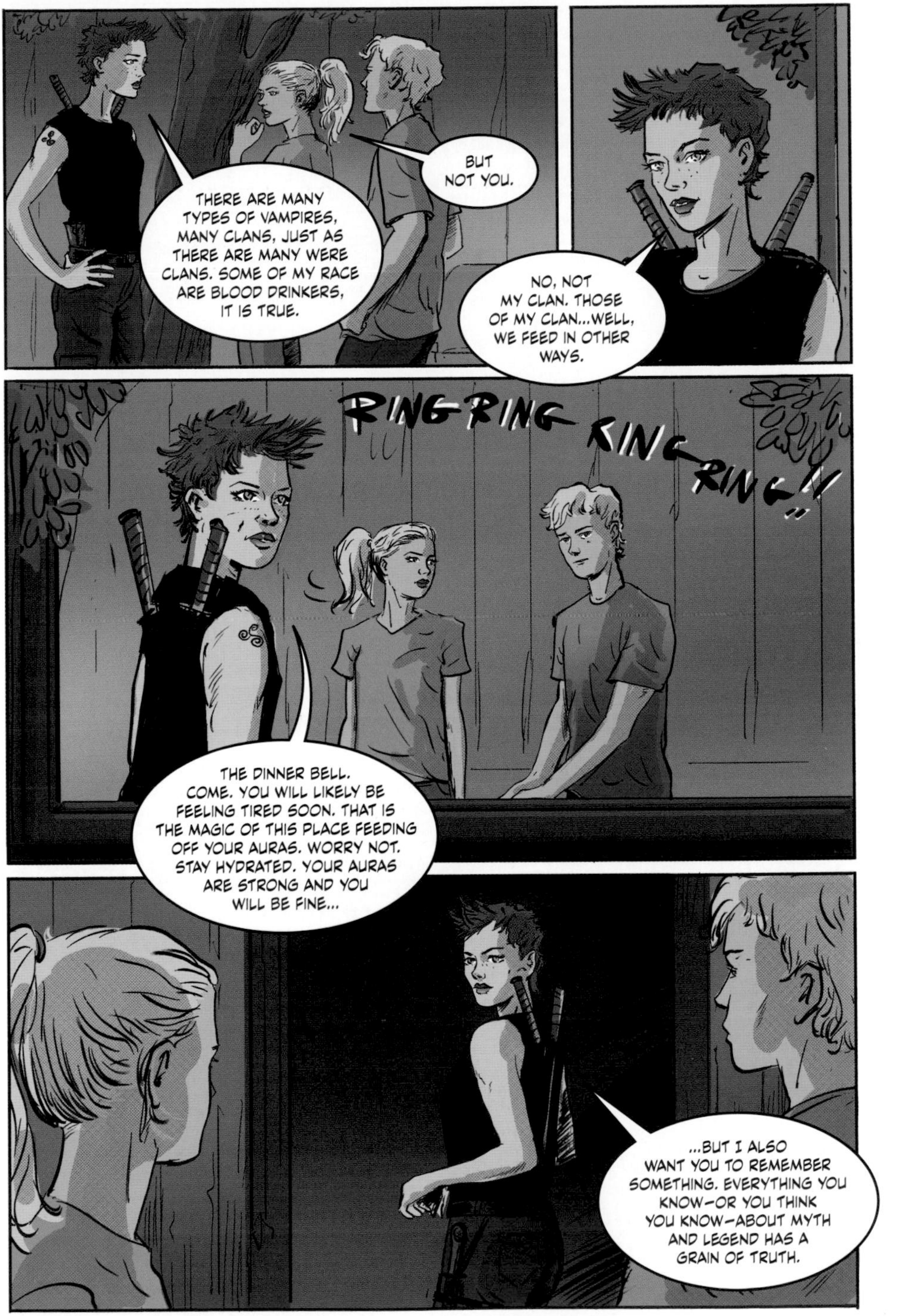
THERE ARE MANY TYPES OF VAMPIRES, MANY CLANS, JUST AS THERE ARE MANY WERE CLANS. SOME OF MY RACE ARE BLOOD DRINKERS, IT IS TRUE.
BUT NOT YOU.
NO, NOT MY CLAN. THOSE OF MY CLAN...WELL, WE FEED IN OTHER WAYS.
RINGRING RINGRING!!
THE DINNER BELL. COME. YOU WILL LIKELY BE FEELING TIRED SOON. THAT IS THE MAGIC OF THIS PLACE FEEDING OFF YOUR AURAS. WORRY NOT. STAY HYDRATED. YOUR AURAS ARE STRONG AND YOU WILL BE FINE...
...BUT I ALSO WANT YOU TO REMEMBER SOMETHING. EVERYTHING YOU KNOW—OR YOU THINK YOU KNOW—ABOUT MYTH AND LEGEND HAS A GRAIN OF TRUTH.

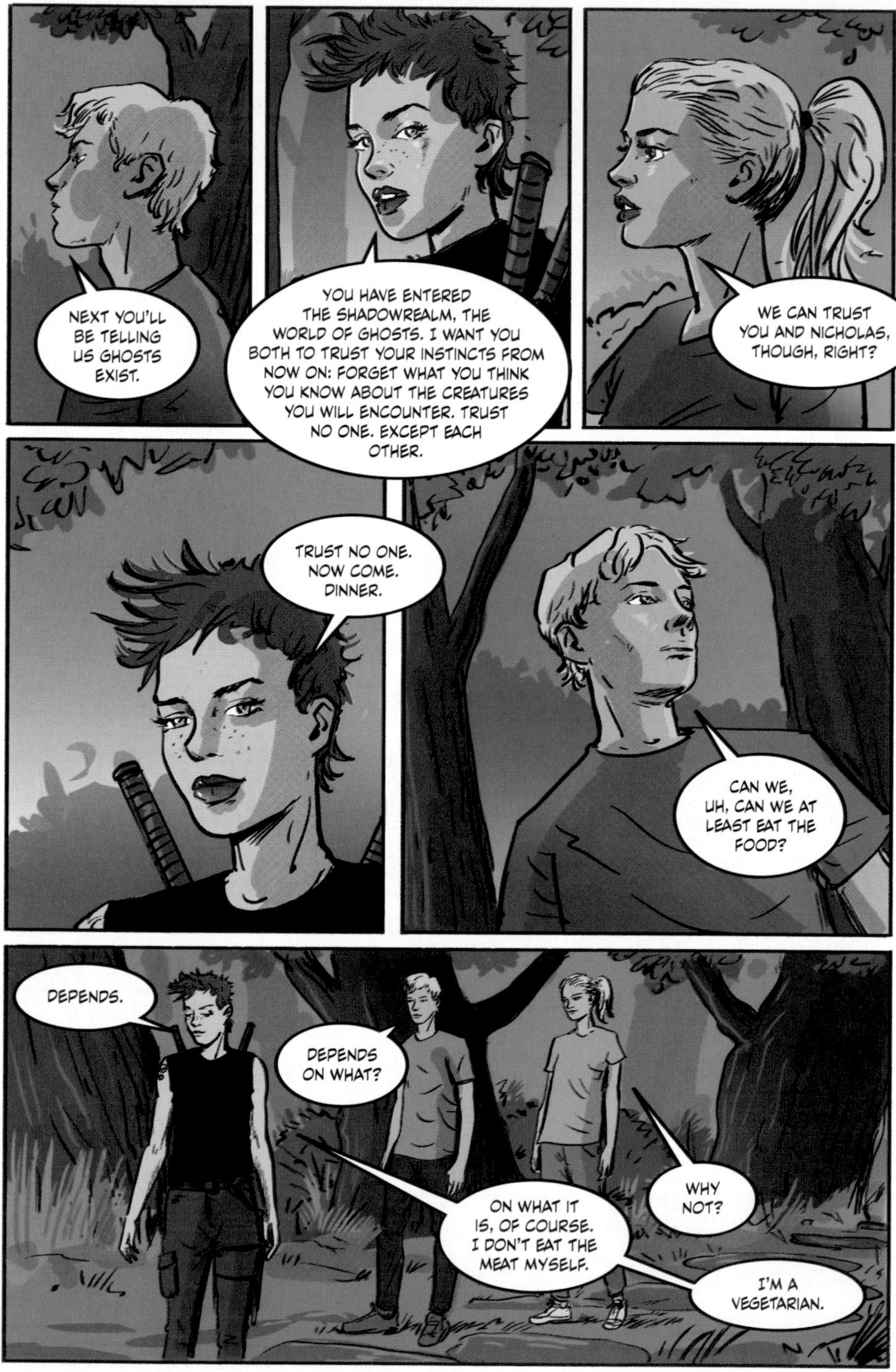
NEXT YOU'LL BE TELLING US GHOSTS EXIST.
YOU HAVE ENTERED THE SHADOWREALM, THE WORLD OF GHOSTS. I WANT YOU BOTH TO TRUST YOUR INSTINCTS FROM NOW ON: FORGET WHAT YOU THINK YOU KNOW ABOUT THE CREATURES YOU WILL ENCOUNTER. TRUST NO ONE. EXCEPT EACH OTHER.
WE CAN TRUST YOU AND NICHOLAS, THOUGH, RIGHT?
TRUST NO ONE. NOW COME. DINNER.
CAN WE, UH, CAN WE AT LEAST EAT THE FOOD?
DEPENDS.
DEPENDS ON WHAT?
ON WHAT IT IS, OF COURSE. I DON'T EAT THE MEAT MYSELF.
WHY NOT?
I'M A VEGETARIAN.

CHAPTER 16

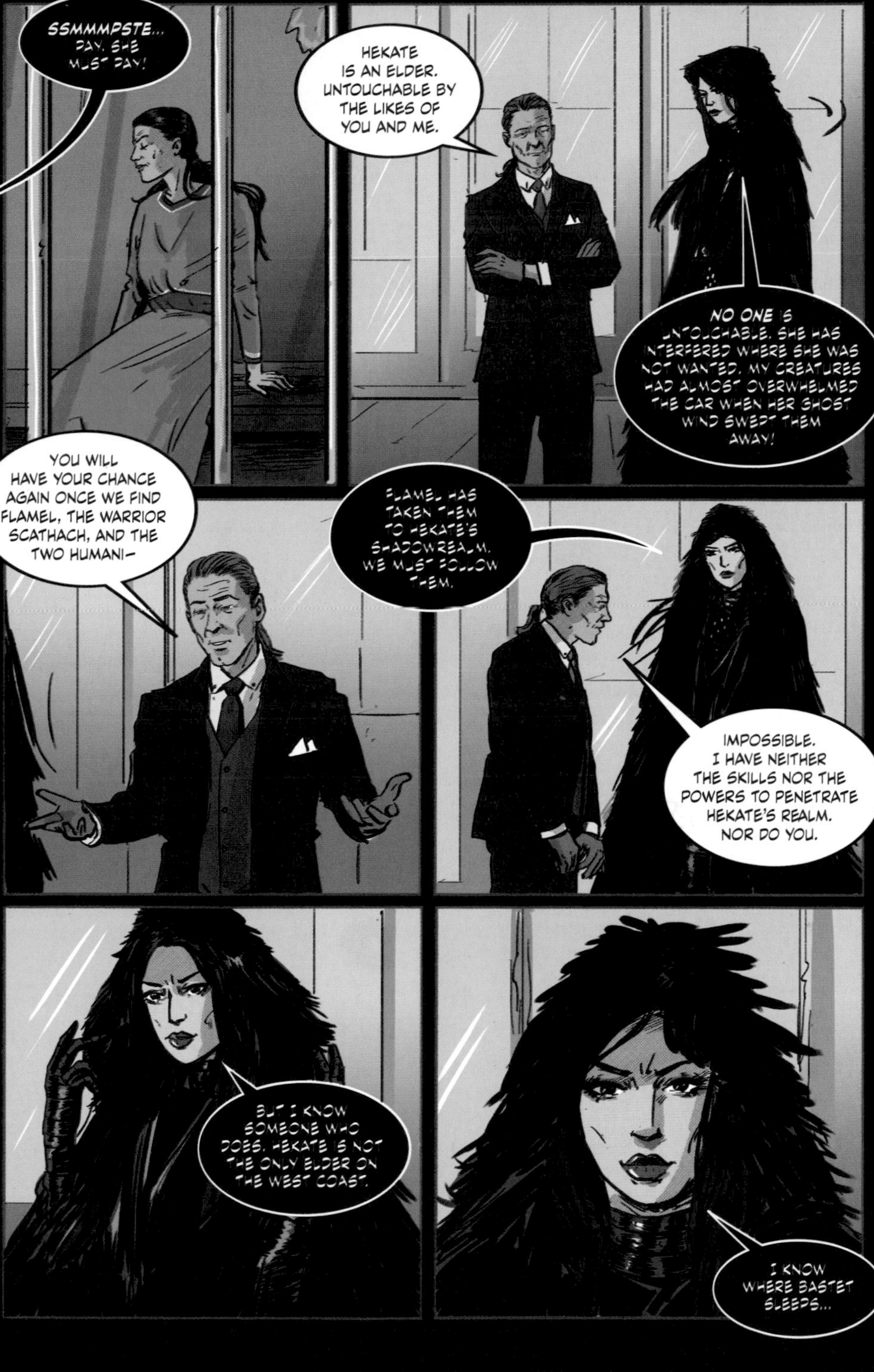
SSMMMPSTE... PAY. SHE MUST PAY!
HEKATE IS AN ELDER. UNTOUCHABLE BY THE LIKES OF YOU AND ME.
NO ONE IS UNTOUCHABLE. SHE HAS INTERFERED WHERE SHE WAS NOT WANTED. MY CREATURES HAD ALMOST OVERWHELMED THE CAR WHEN HER GHOST WIND SWEPT THEM AWAY!
YOU WILL HAVE YOUR CHANCE AGAIN ONCE WE FIND FLAMEL, THE WARRIOR SCATHACH, AND THE TWO HUMANI—
FLAMEL HAS TAKEN THEM TO HEKATE'S SHADOWREALM. WE MUST FOLLOW THEM.
IMPOSSIBLE. I HAVE NEITHER THE SKILLS NOR THE POWERS TO PENETRATE HEKATE'S REALM. NOR DO YOU.
BUT I KNOW SOMEONE WHO DOES. HEKATE IS NOT THE ONLY ELDER ON THE WEST COAST.
I KNOW WHERE BASTET SLEEPS...

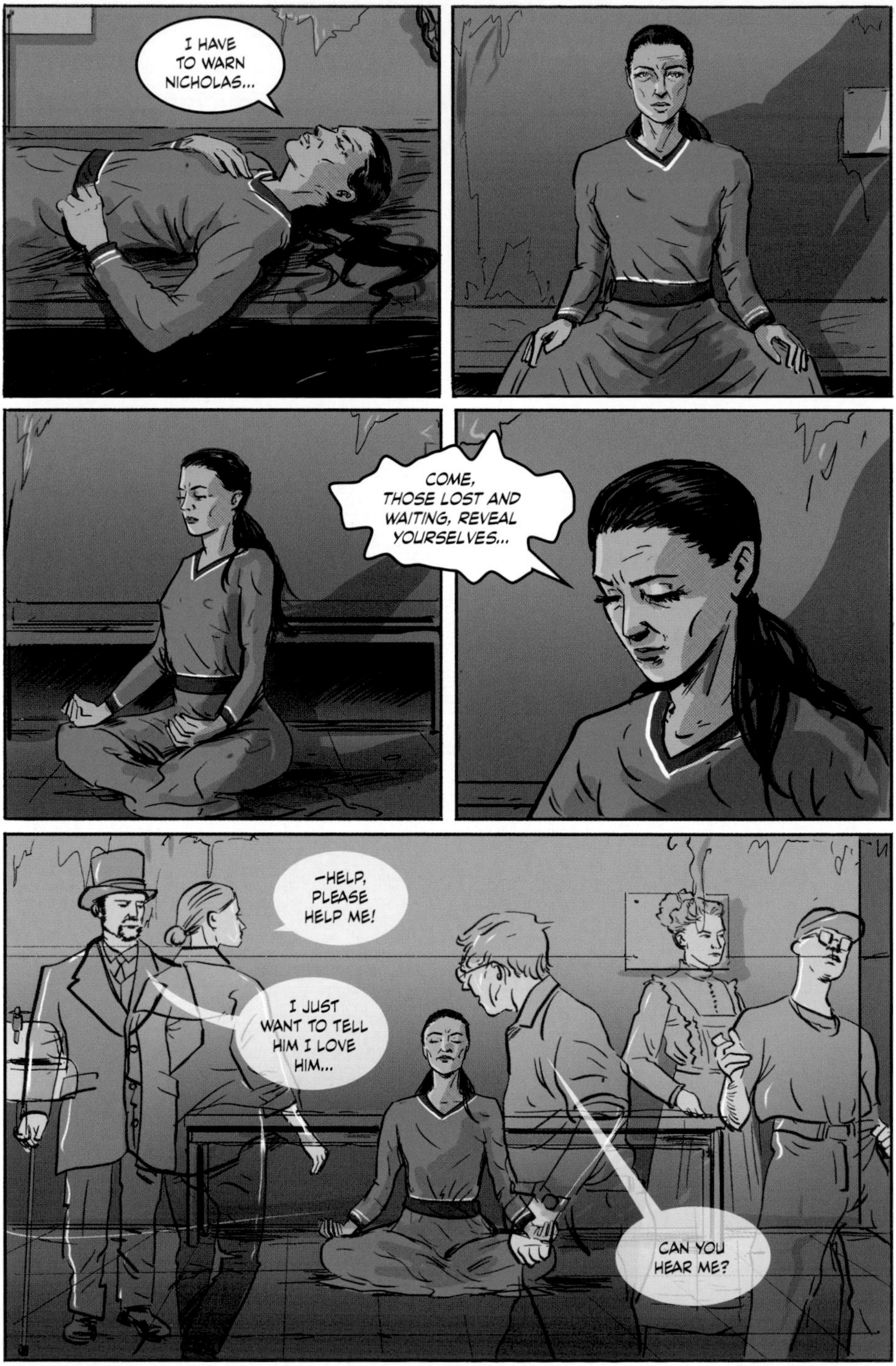
I HAVE TO WARN NICHOLAS...
COME, THOSE LOST AND WAITING, REVEAL YOURSELVES...
-HELP, PLEASE HELP ME!
I JUST WANT TO TELL HIM I LOVE HIM...
CAN YOU HEAR ME?

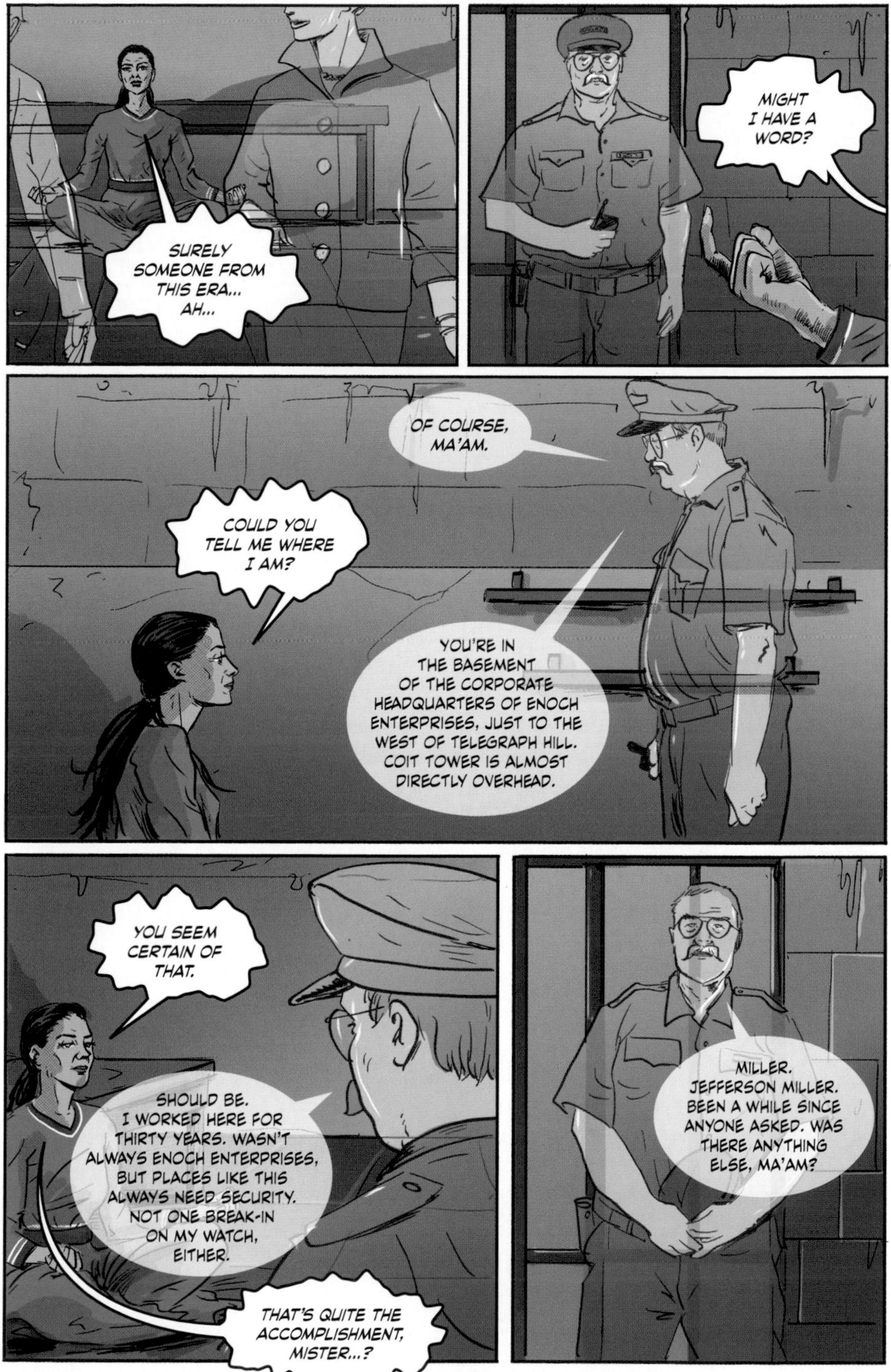
SURELY SOMEONE FROM THIS ERA... AH...
MIGHT I HAVE A WORD?
OF COURSE, MA'AM.
COULD YOU TELL ME WHERE I AM?
YOU'RE IN THE BASEMENT OF THE CORPORATE HEADQUARTERS OF ENOCH ENTERPRISES, JUST TO THE WEST OF TELEGRAPH HILL. COIT TOWER IS ALMOST DIRECTLY OVERHEAD.
YOU SEEM CERTAIN OF THAT.
SHOULD BE. I WORKED HERE FOR THIRTY YEARS. WASN'T ALWAYS ENOCH ENTERPRISES, BUT PLACES LIKE THIS ALWAYS NEED SECURITY. NOT ONE BREAK-IN ON MY WATCH, EITHER.
THAT'S QUITE THE ACCOMPLISHMENT, MISTER...?
MILLER. JEFFERSON MILLER. BEEN A WHILE SINCE ANYONE ASKED. WAS THERE ANYTHING ELSE, MA'AM?

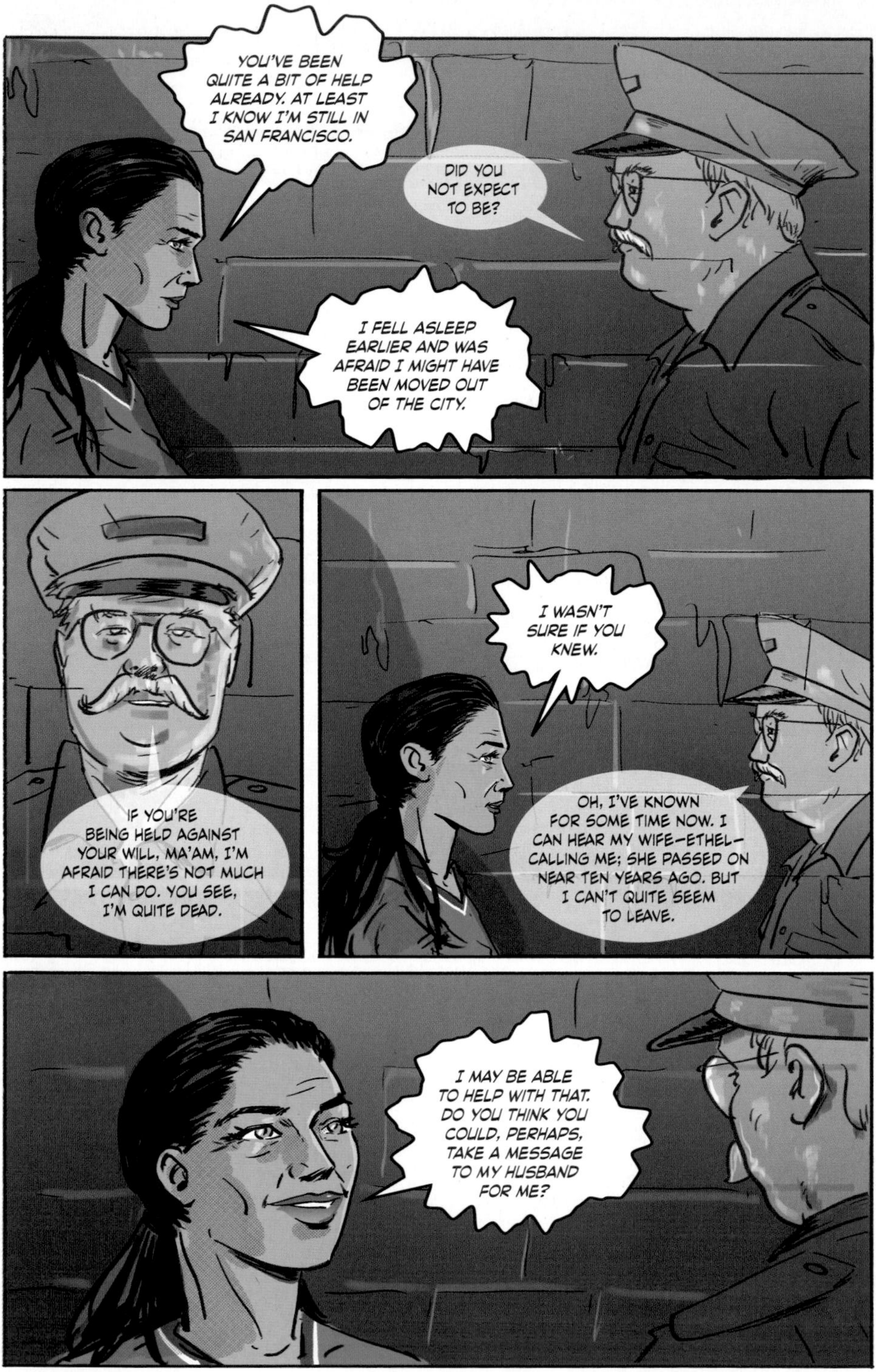
YOU'VE BEEN QUITE A BIT OF HELP ALREADY. AT LEAST I KNOW I'M STILL IN SAN FRANCISCO.
DID YOU NOT EXPECT TO BE?
I FELL ASLEEP EARLIER AND WAS AFRAID I MIGHT HAVE BEEN MOVED OUT OF THE CITY.
IF YOU'RE BEING HELD AGAINST YOUR WILL, MA'AM, I'M AFRAID THERE'S NOT MUCH I CAN DO. YOU SEE, I'M QUITE DEAD.
I WASN'T SURE IF YOU KNEW.
OH, I'VE KNOWN FOR SOME TIME NOW. I CAN HEAR MY WIFE—ETHEL—CALLING ME; SHE PASSED ON NEAR TEN YEARS AGO. BUT I CAN'T QUITE SEEM TO LEAVE.
I MAY BE ABLE TO HELP WITH THAT. DO YOU THINK YOU COULD, PERHAPS, TAKE A MESSAGE TO MY HUSBAND FOR ME?

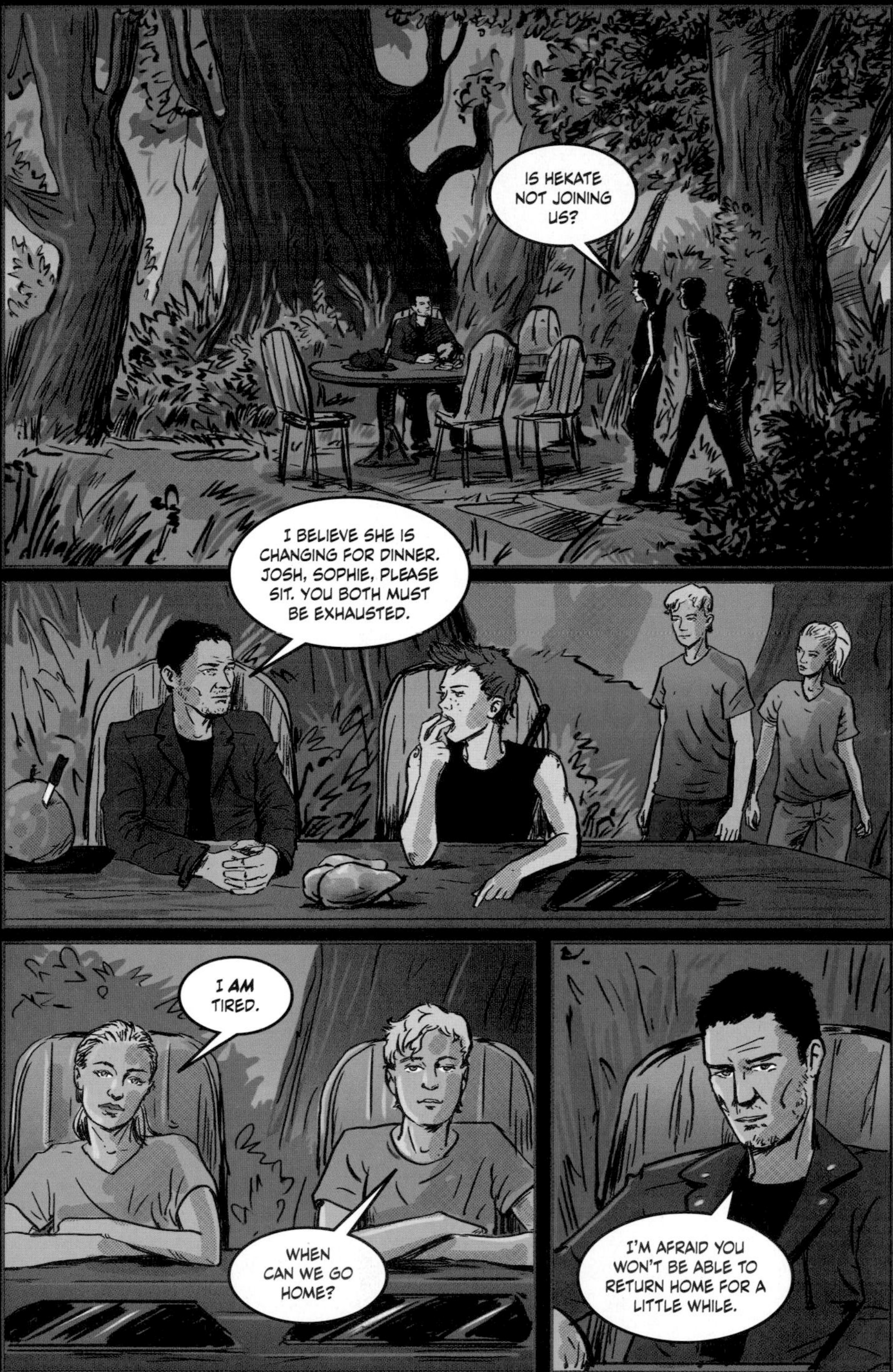
IS HEKATE NOT JOINING US?
I BELIEVE SHE IS CHANGING FOR DINNER. JOSH, SOPHIE, PLEASE SIT. YOU BOTH MUST BE EXHAUSTED.
I *AM* TIRED.
WHEN CAN WE GO HOME?
I'M AFRAID YOU WON'T BE ABLE TO RETURN HOME FOR A LITTLE WHILE.

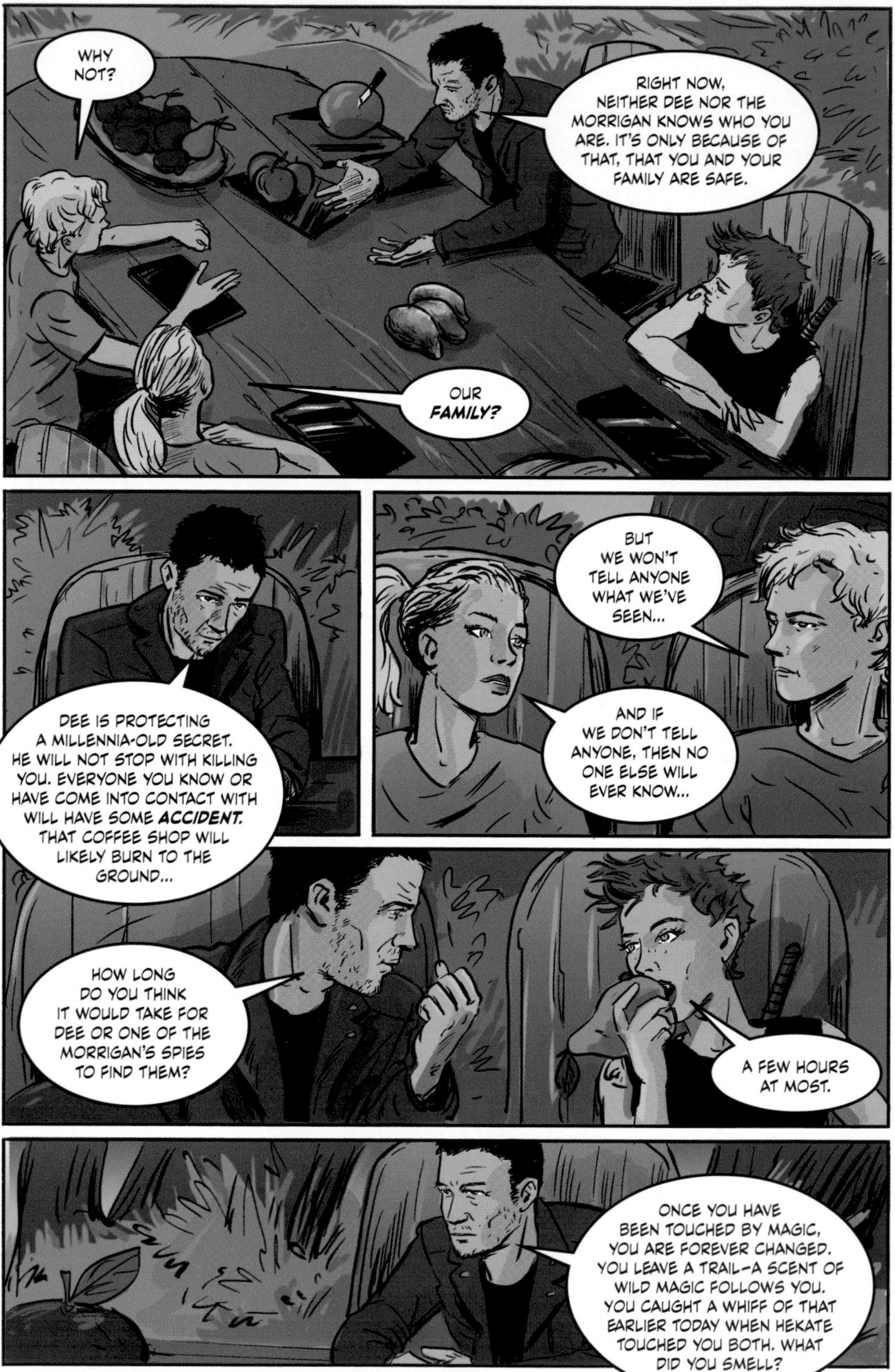
WHY NOT?
RIGHT NOW, NEITHER DEE NOR THE MORRIGAN KNOWS WHO YOU ARE. IT'S ONLY BECAUSE OF THAT, THAT YOU AND YOUR FAMILY ARE SAFE.
OUR FAMILY?
DEE IS PROTECTING A MILLENNIA-OLD SECRET. HE WILL NOT STOP WITH KILLING YOU. EVERYONE YOU KNOW OR HAVE COME INTO CONTACT WITH WILL HAVE SOME ACCIDENT. THAT COFFEE SHOP WILL LIKELY BURN TO THE GROUND...
BUT WE WON'T TELL ANYONE WHAT WE'VE SEEN...
AND IF WE DON'T TELL ANYONE, THEN NO ONE ELSE WILL EVER KNOW...
HOW LONG DO YOU THINK IT WOULD TAKE FOR DEE OR ONE OF THE MORRIGAN'S SPIES TO FIND THEM?
A FEW HOURS AT MOST.
ONCE YOU HAVE BEEN TOUCHED BY MAGIC, YOU ARE FOREVER CHANGED. YOU LEAVE A TRAIL–A SCENT OF WILD MAGIC FOLLOWS YOU. YOU CAUGHT A WHIFF OF THAT EARLIER TODAY WHEN HEKATE TOUCHED YOU BOTH. WHAT DID YOU SMELL?

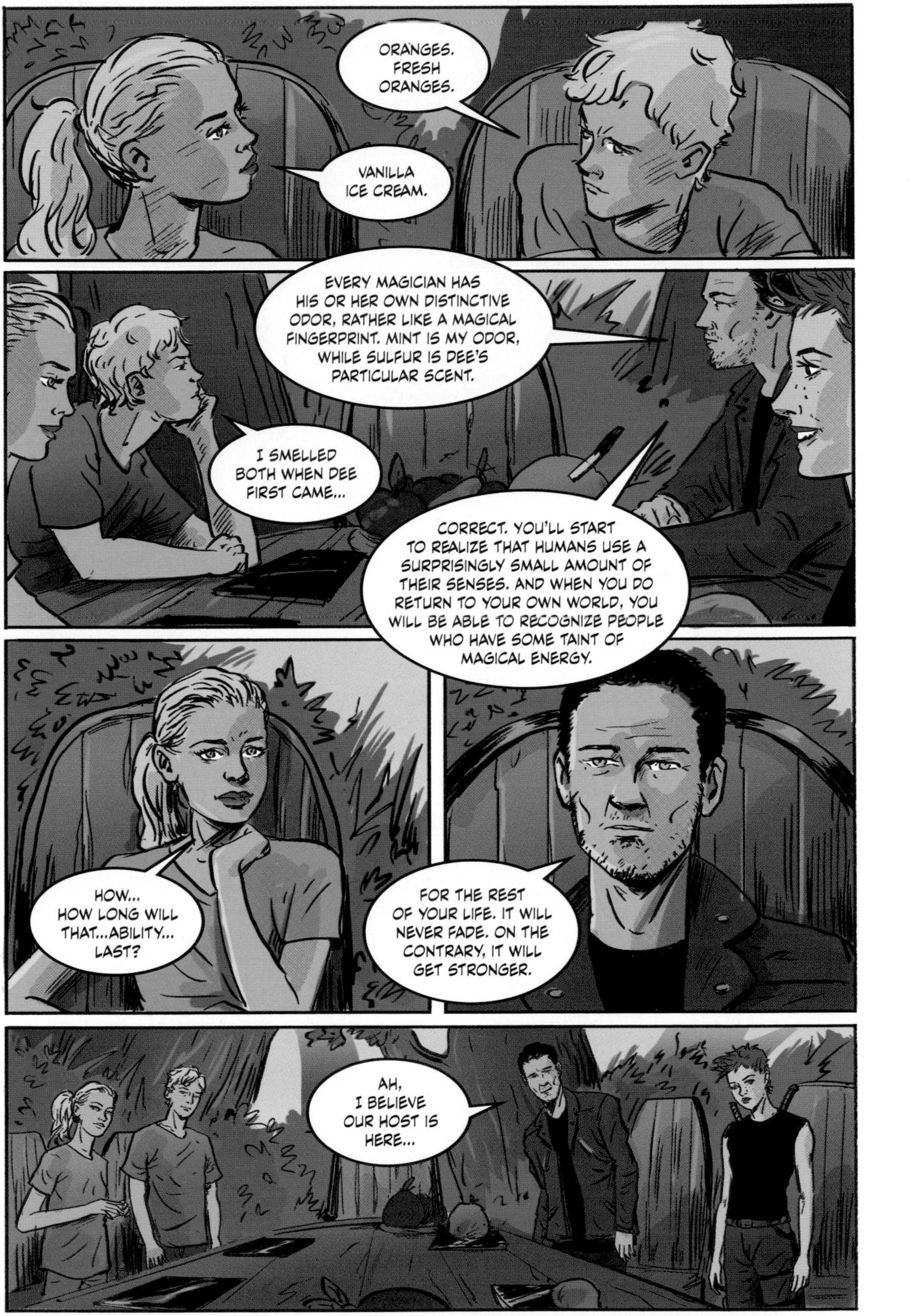
ORANGES. FRESH ORANGES.
VANILLA ICE CREAM.
EVERY MAGICIAN HAS HIS OR HER OWN DISTINCTIVE ODOR, RATHER LIKE A MAGICAL FINGERPRINT. MINT IS MY ODOR, WHILE SULFUR IS DEE'S PARTICULAR SCENT.
I SMELLED BOTH WHEN DEE FIRST CAME...
CORRECT. YOU'LL START TO REALIZE THAT HUMANS USE A SURPRISINGLY SMALL AMOUNT OF THEIR SENSES. AND WHEN YOU DO RETURN TO YOUR OWN WORLD, YOU WILL BE ABLE TO RECOGNIZE PEOPLE WHO HAVE SOME TAINT OF MAGICAL ENERGY.
HOW... HOW LONG WILL THAT...ABILITY... LAST?
FOR THE REST OF YOUR LIFE. IT WILL NEVER FADE. ON THE CONTRARY, IT WILL GET STRONGER.
AH, I BELIEVE OUR HOST IS HERE...

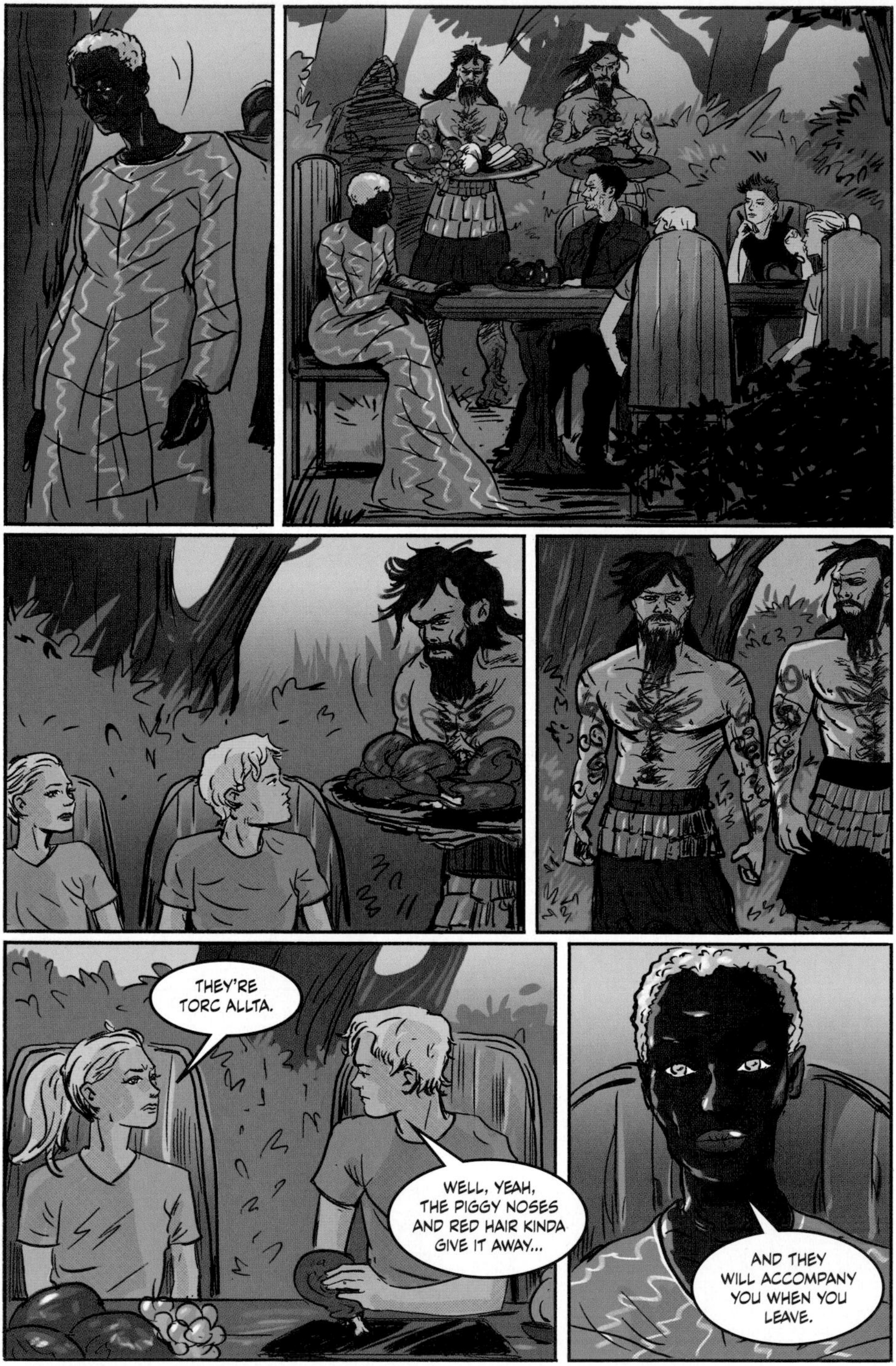
THEY'RE TORC ALLTA.
WELL, YEAH, THE PIGGY NOSES AND RED HAIR KINDA GIVE IT AWAY...
AND THEY WILL ACCOMPANY YOU WHEN YOU LEAVE.

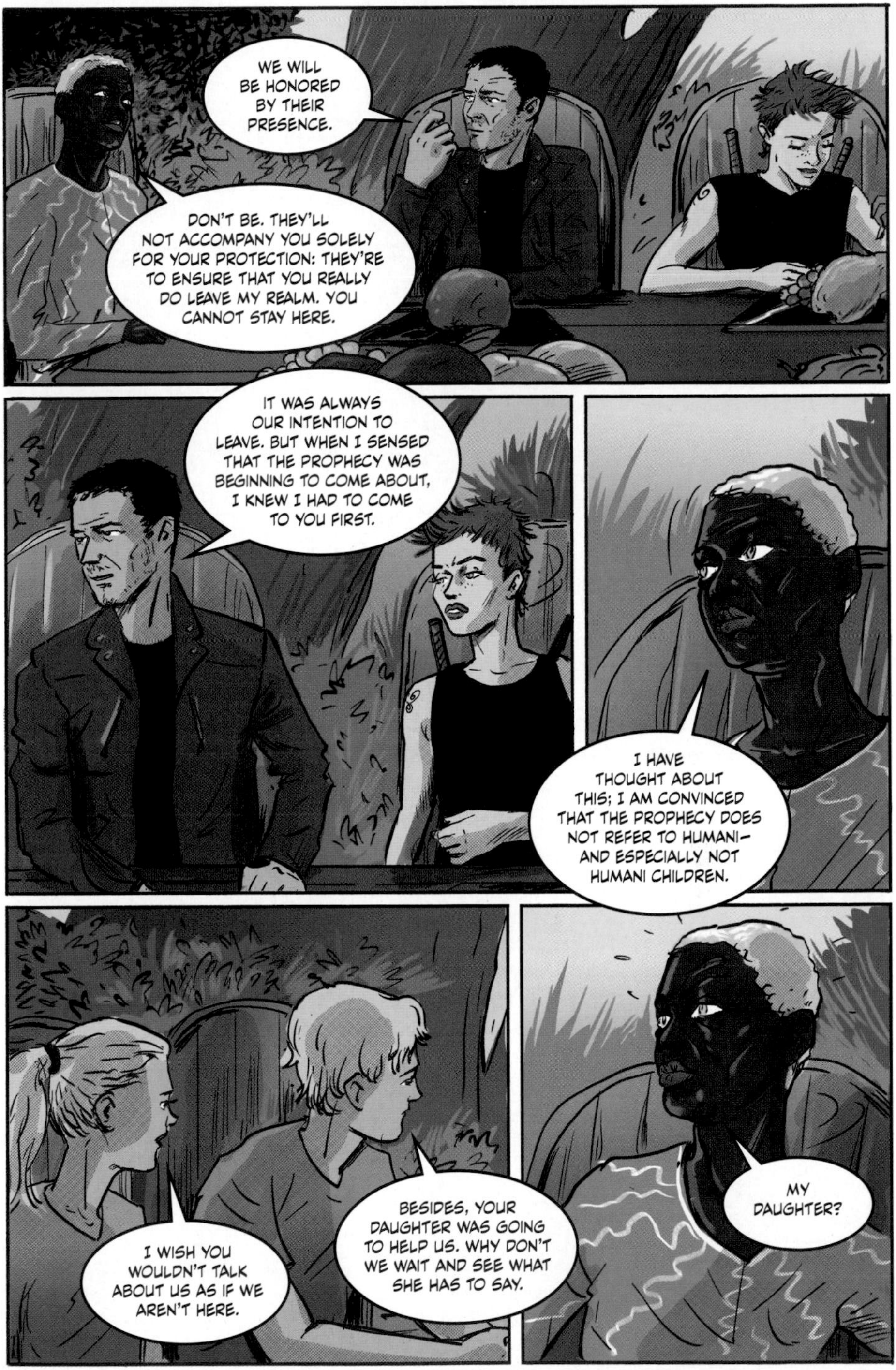
WE WILL BE HONORED BY THEIR PRESENCE.
DON'T BE. THEY'LL NOT ACCOMPANY YOU SOLELY FOR YOUR PROTECTION: THEY'RE TO ENSURE THAT YOU REALLY DO LEAVE MY REALM. YOU CANNOT STAY HERE.
IT WAS ALWAYS OUR INTENTION TO LEAVE. BUT WHEN I SENSED THAT THE PROPHECY WAS BEGINNING TO COME ABOUT, I KNEW I HAD TO COME TO YOU FIRST.
I HAVE THOUGHT ABOUT THIS; I AM CONVINCED THAT THE PROPHECY DOES NOT REFER TO HUMANI— AND ESPECIALLY NOT HUMANI CHILDREN.
I WISH YOU WOULDN'T TALK ABOUT US AS IF WE AREN'T HERE.
BESIDES, YOUR DAUGHTER WAS GOING TO HELP US. WHY DON'T WE WAIT AND SEE WHAT SHE HAS TO SAY.
MY DAUGHTER?

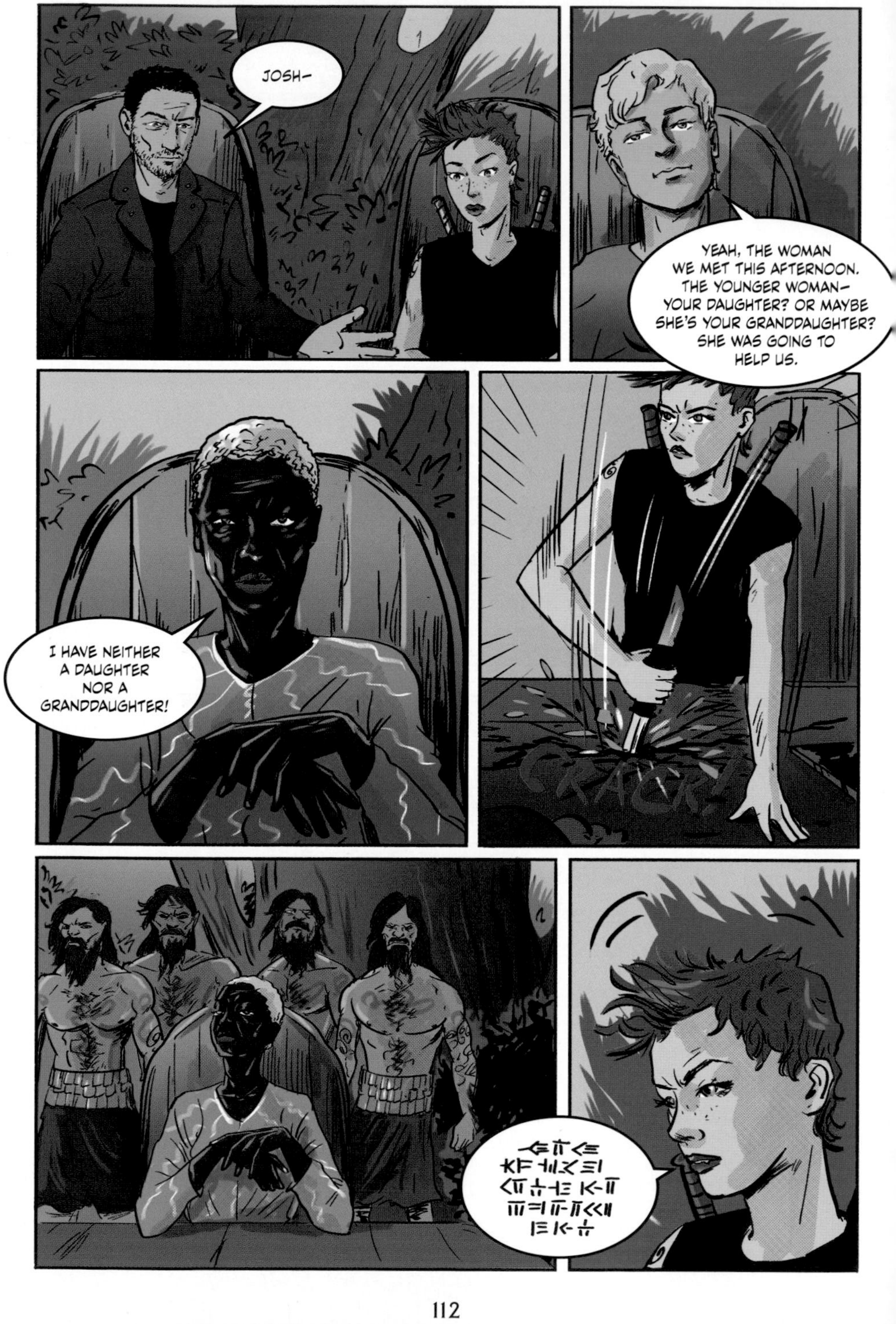
JOSH–
YEAH, THE WOMAN WE MET THIS AFTERNOON. THE YOUNGER WOMAN– YOUR DAUGHTER? OR MAYBE SHE'S YOUR GRANDDAUGHTER? SHE WAS GOING TO HELP US.
I HAVE NEITHER A DAUGHTER NOR A GRANDDAUGHTER!
CRACK!

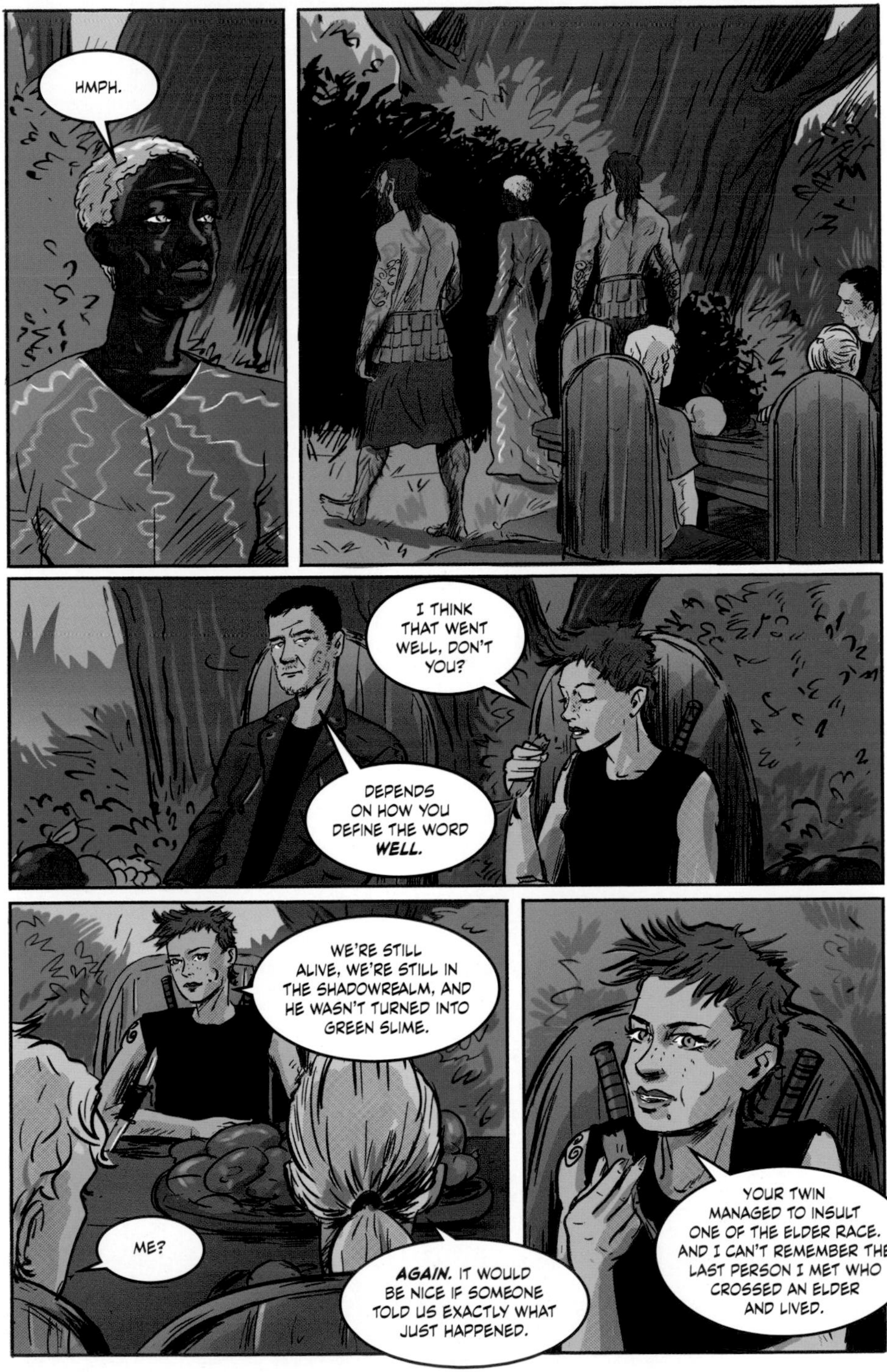
HMPH.
I THINK THAT WENT WELL, DON'T YOU?
DEPENDS ON HOW YOU DEFINE THE WORD **WELL.**
WE'RE STILL ALIVE, WE'RE STILL IN THE SHADOWREALM, AND HE WASN'T TURNED INTO GREEN SLIME.
ME?
AGAIN. IT WOULD BE NICE IF SOMEONE TOLD US EXACTLY WHAT JUST HAPPENED.
YOUR TWIN MANAGED TO INSULT ONE OF THE ELDER RACE. AND I CAN'T REMEMBER THE LAST PERSON I MET WHO CROSSED AN ELDER AND LIVED.

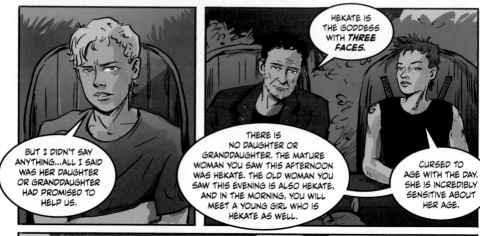

HEKATE IS THE GODDESS WITH *THREE* FACES.

BUT I DIDN'T SAY ANYTHING...ALL I SAID WAS HER DAUGHTER OR GRANDDAUGHTER HAD PROMISED TO HELP US.

THERE IS NO DAUGHTER OR GRANDDAUGHTER. THE MATURE WOMAN YOU SAW THIS AFTERNOON WAS HEKATE. THE OLD WOMAN YOU SAW THIS EVENING IS ALSO HEKATE, AND IN THE MORNING, YOU WILL MEET A YOUNG GIRL WHO IS HEKATE AS WELL.

CURSED TO AGE WITH THE DAY. SHE IS INCREDIBLY SENSITIVE ABOUT HER AGE.

I DIDN'T KNOW.

NO REASON WHY YOU SHOULD HAVE. BUT YOUR IGNORANCE COULD HAVE GOTTEN YOU KILLED... OR WORSE.

BUT WHAT DID YOU DO TO THE TABLE?

IRON.

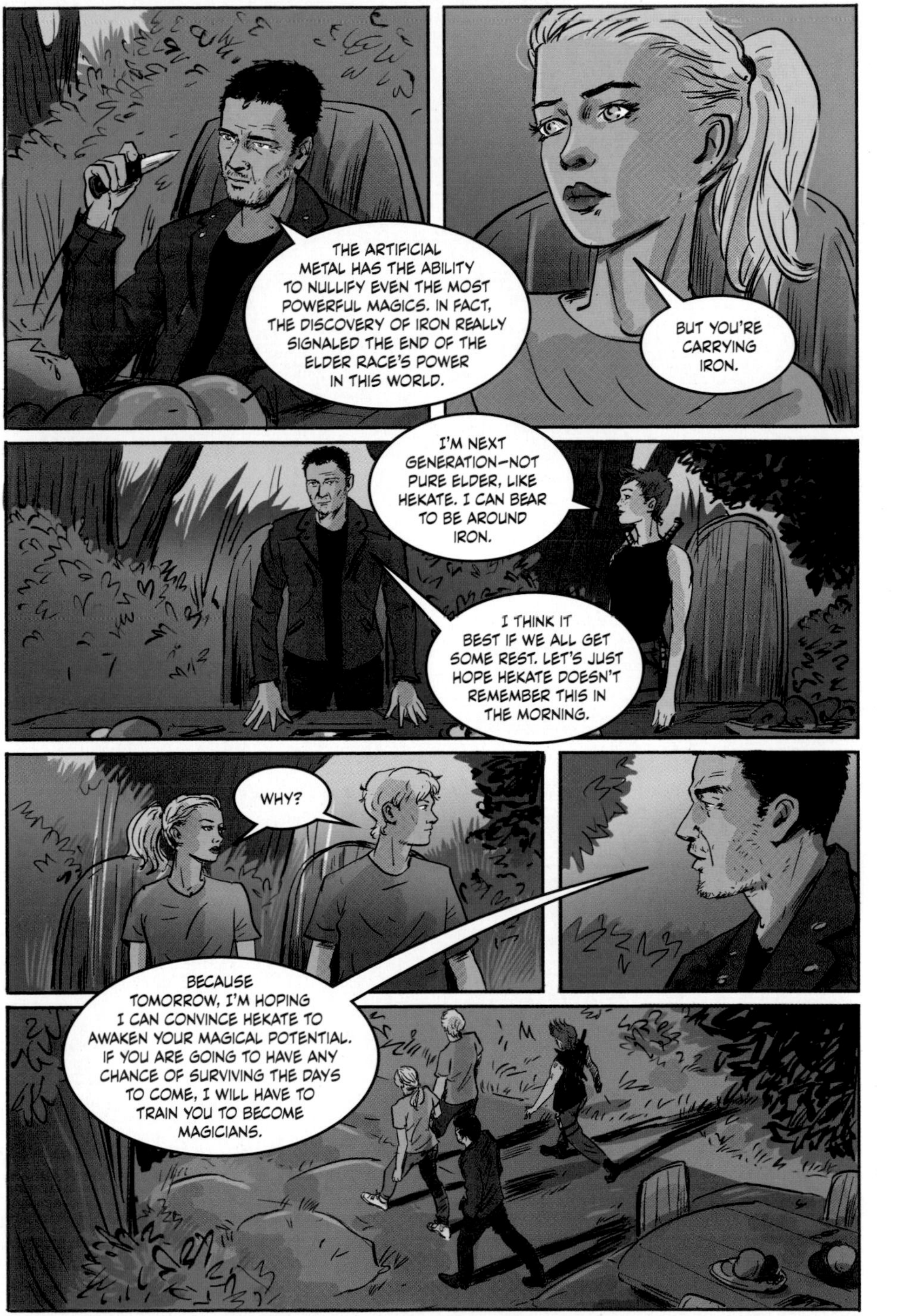
THE ARTIFICIAL METAL HAS THE ABILITY TO NULLIFY EVEN THE MOST POWERFUL MAGICS. IN FACT, THE DISCOVERY OF IRON REALLY SIGNALED THE END OF THE ELDER RACE'S POWER IN THIS WORLD.
BUT YOU'RE CARRYING IRON.
I'M NEXT GENERATION—NOT PURE ELDER, LIKE HEKATE. I CAN BEAR TO BE AROUND IRON.
I THINK IT BEST IF WE ALL GET SOME REST. LET'S JUST HOPE HEKATE DOESN'T REMEMBER THIS IN THE MORNING.
WHY?
BECAUSE TOMORROW, I'M HOPING I CAN CONVINCE HEKATE TO AWAKEN YOUR MAGICAL POTENTIAL. IF YOU ARE GOING TO HAVE ANY CHANCE OF SURVIVING THE DAYS TO COME, I WILL HAVE TO TRAIN YOU TO BECOME MAGICIANS.

CHAPTER 18

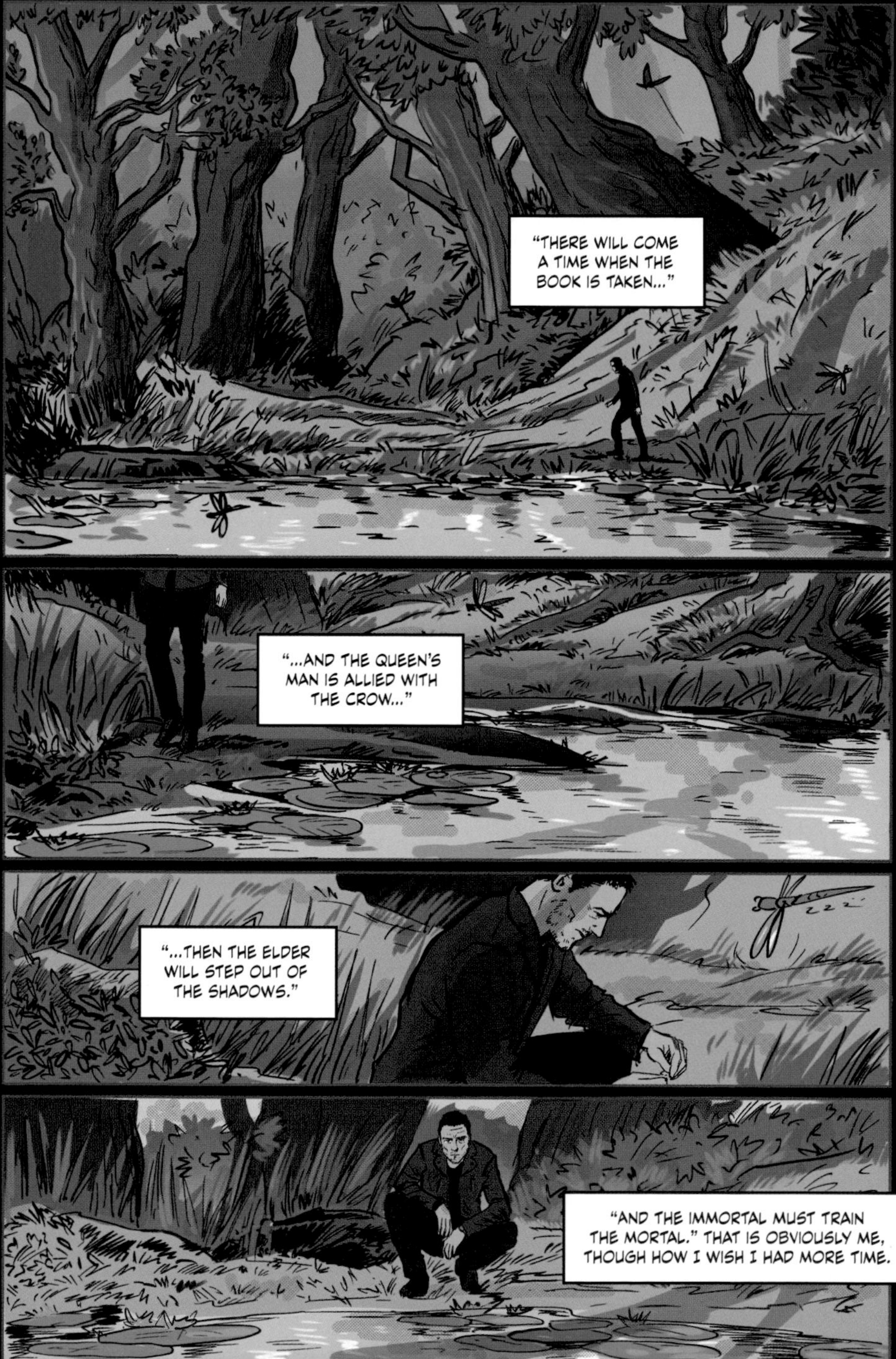

"THERE WILL COME A TIME WHEN THE BOOK IS TAKEN..."
"...AND THE QUEEN'S MAN IS ALLIED WITH THE CROW..."
"...THEN THE ELDER WILL STEP OUT OF THE SHADOWS."
"AND THE IMMORTAL MUST TRAIN THE MORTAL." THAT IS OBVIOUSLY ME, THOUGH HOW I WISH I HAD MORE TIME.

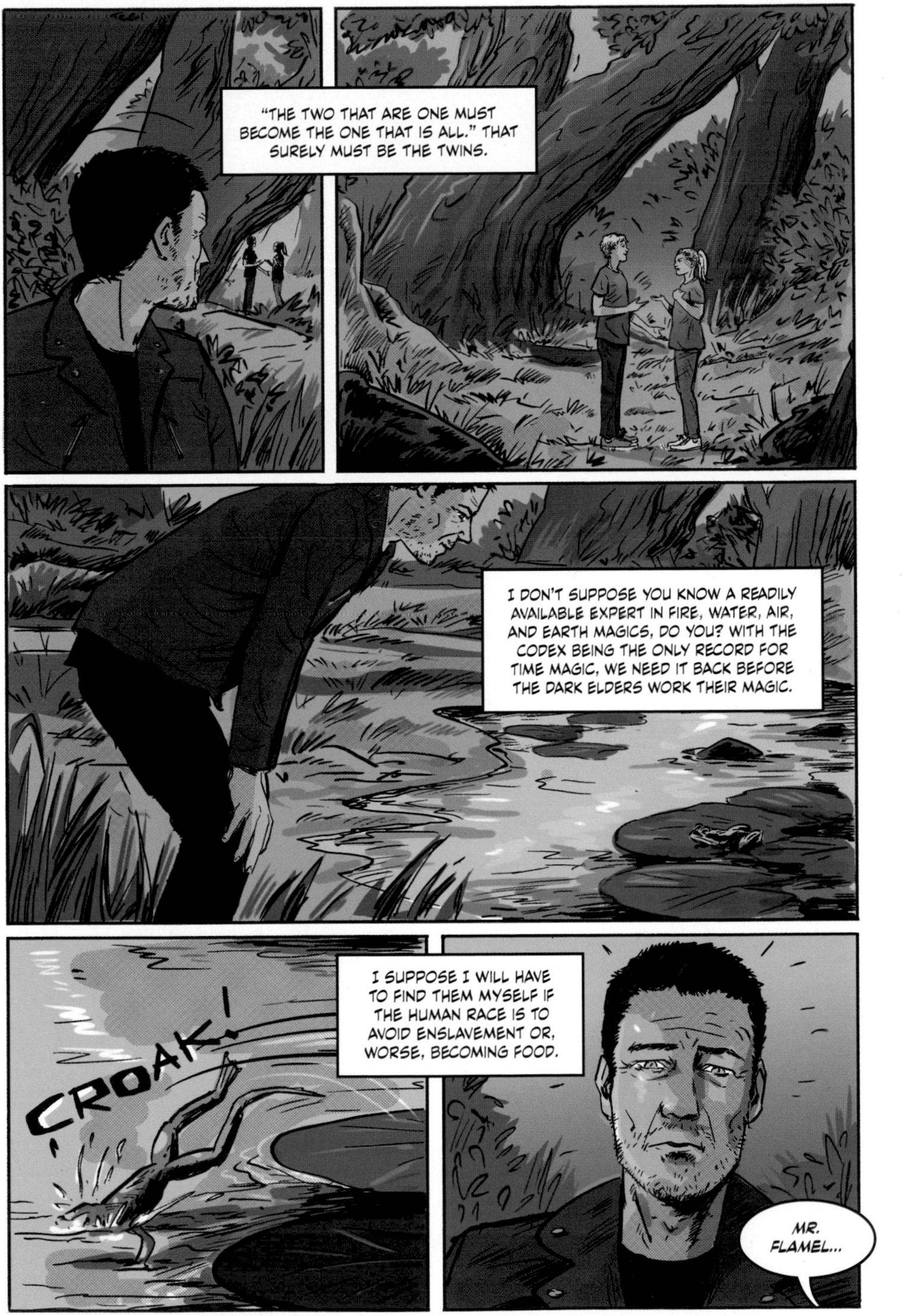
"THE TWO THAT ARE ONE MUST BECOME THE ONE THAT IS ALL." THAT SURELY MUST BE THE TWINS.
I DON'T SUPPOSE YOU KNOW A READILY AVAILABLE EXPERT IN FIRE, WATER, AIR, AND EARTH MAGICS, DO YOU? WITH THE CODEX BEING THE ONLY RECORD FOR TIME MAGIC, WE NEED IT BACK BEFORE THE DARK ELDERS WORK THEIR MAGIC.
CROAK!
I SUPPOSE I WILL HAVE TO FIND THEM MYSELF IF THE HUMAN RACE IS TO AVOID ENSLAVEMENT OR, WORSE, BECOMING FOOD.
MR. FLAMEL...

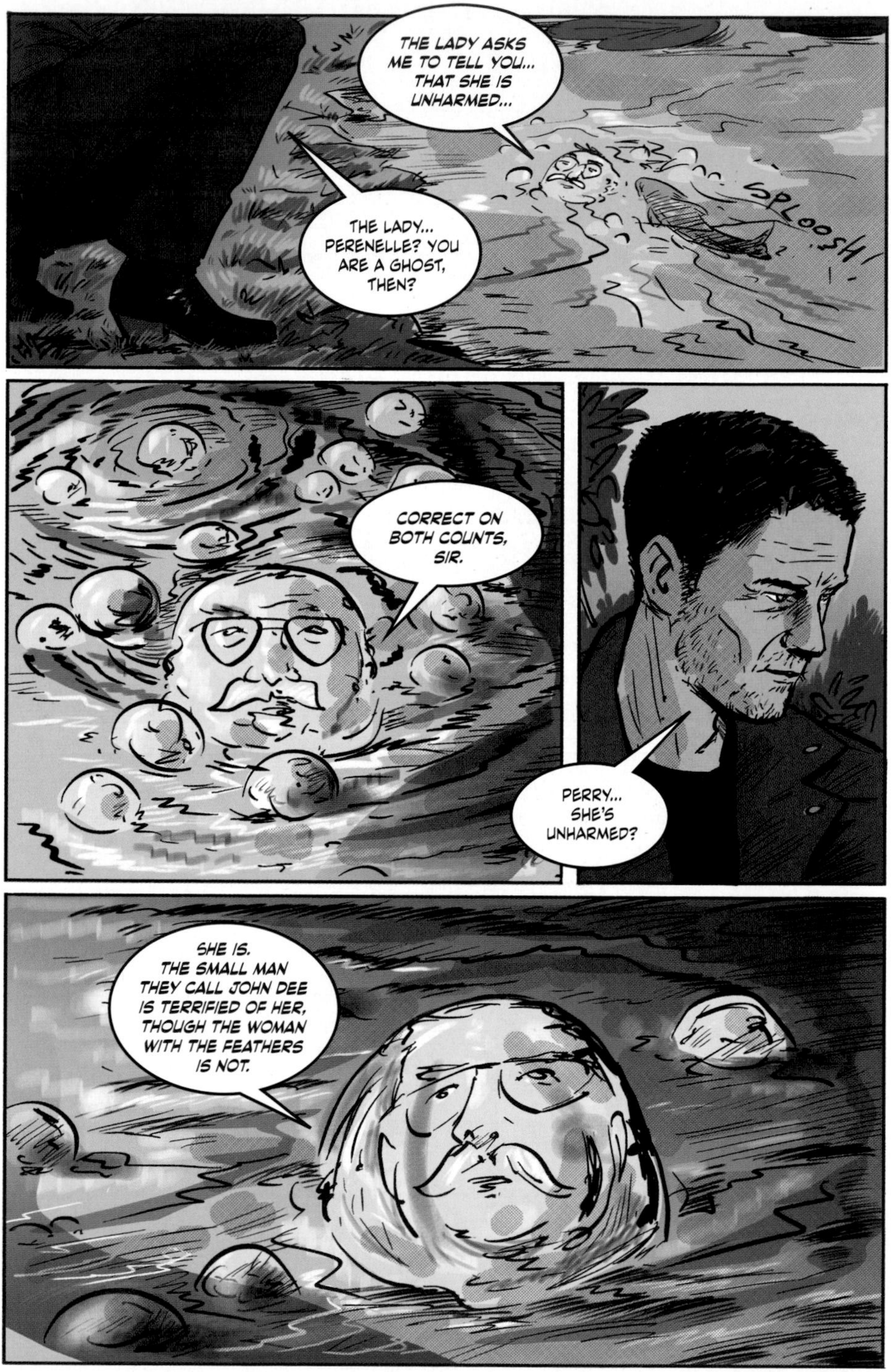
THE LADY ASKS ME TO TELL YOU... THAT SHE IS UNHARMED...
THE LADY... PERENELLE? YOU ARE A GHOST, THEN?
SPLOOSH!
CORRECT ON BOTH COUNTS, SIR.
PERRY... SHE'S UNHARMED?
SHE IS. THE SMALL MAN THEY CALL JOHN DEE IS TERRIFIED OF HER, THOUGH THE WOMAN WITH THE FEATHERS IS NOT.

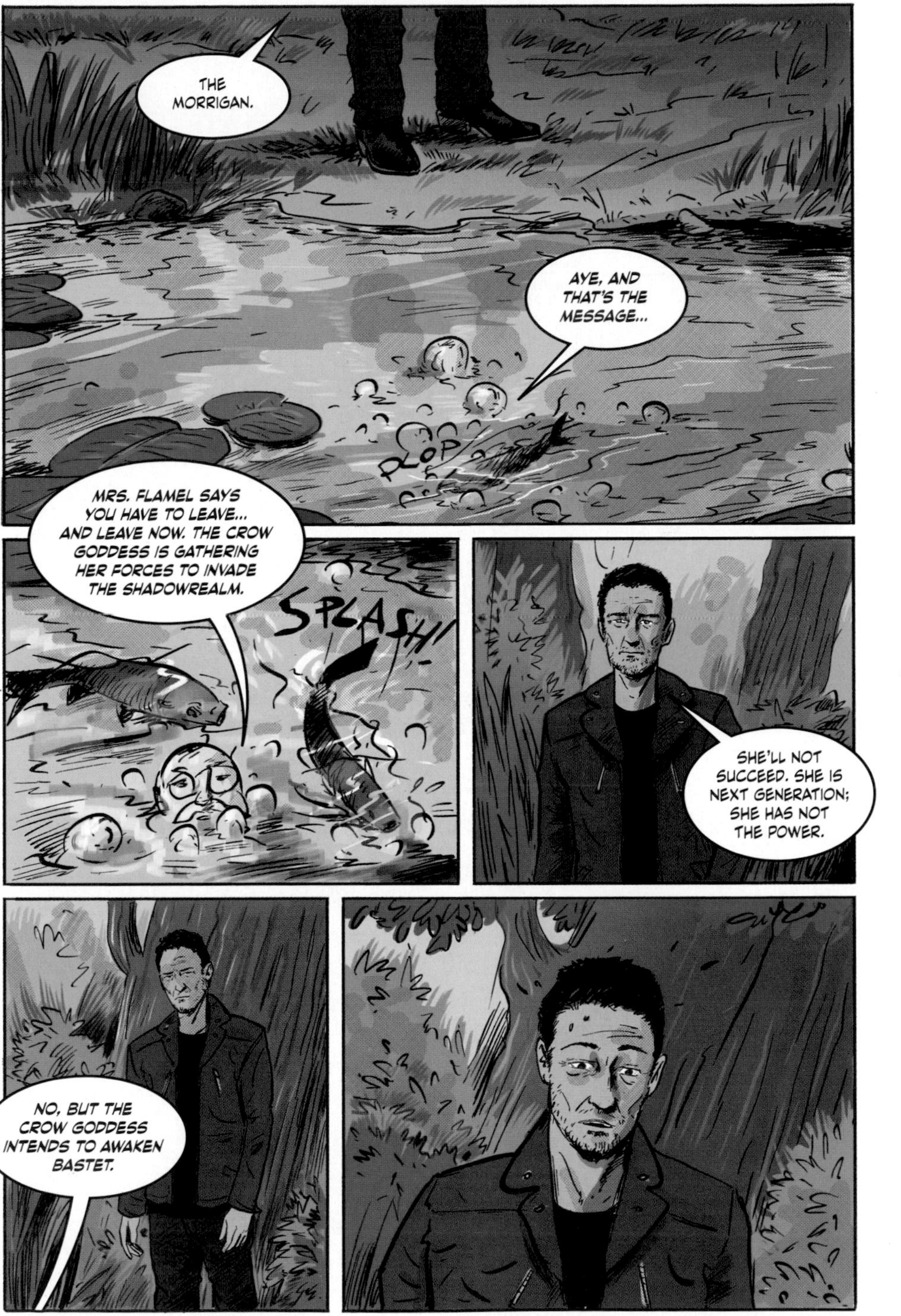
THE MORRIGAN.
AYE, AND THAT'S THE MESSAGE...
PLOP
MRS. FLAMEL SAYS YOU HAVE TO LEAVE... AND LEAVE NOW. THE CROW GODDESS IS GATHERING HER FORCES TO INVADE THE SHADOWREALM.
SPLASH!
SHE'LL NOT SUCCEED. SHE IS NEXT GENERATION; SHE HAS NOT THE POWER.
NO, BUT THE CROW GODDESS INTENDS TO AWAKEN BASTET.

CHAPTER 19

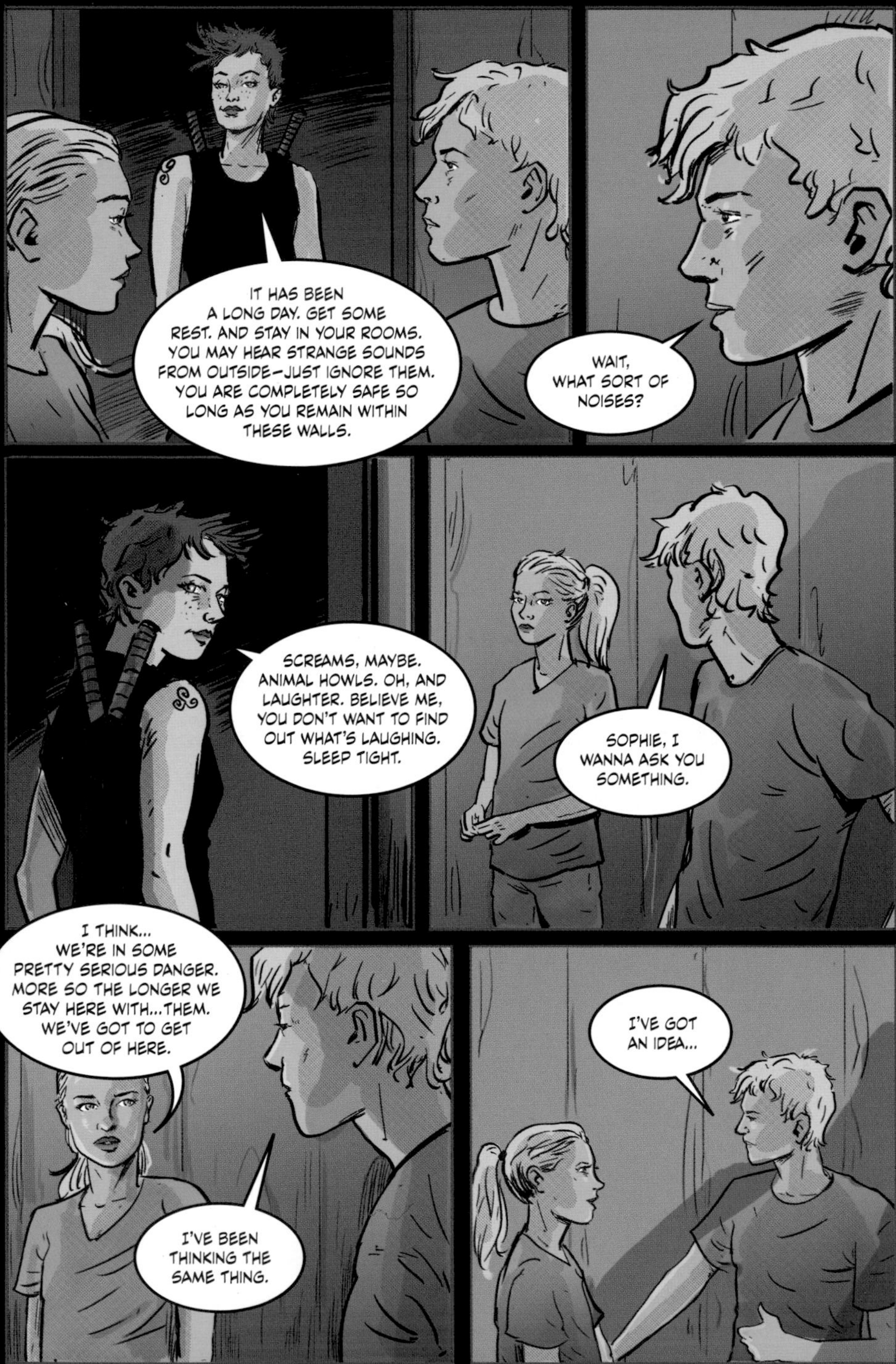

IT HAS BEEN A LONG DAY. GET SOME REST. AND STAY IN YOUR ROOMS. YOU MAY HEAR STRANGE SOUNDS FROM OUTSIDE—JUST IGNORE THEM. YOU ARE COMPLETELY SAFE SO LONG AS YOU REMAIN WITHIN THESE WALLS.
WAIT, WHAT SORT OF NOISES?
SCREAMS, MAYBE. ANIMAL HOWLS. OH, AND LAUGHTER. BELIEVE ME, YOU DON'T WANT TO FIND OUT WHAT'S LAUGHING. SLEEP TIGHT.
SOPHIE, I WANNA ASK YOU SOMETHING.
I THINK... WE'RE IN SOME PRETTY SERIOUS DANGER. MORE SO THE LONGER WE STAY HERE WITH...THEM. WE'VE GOT TO GET OUT OF HERE.
I'VE BEEN THINKING THE SAME THING.
I'VE GOT AN IDEA...

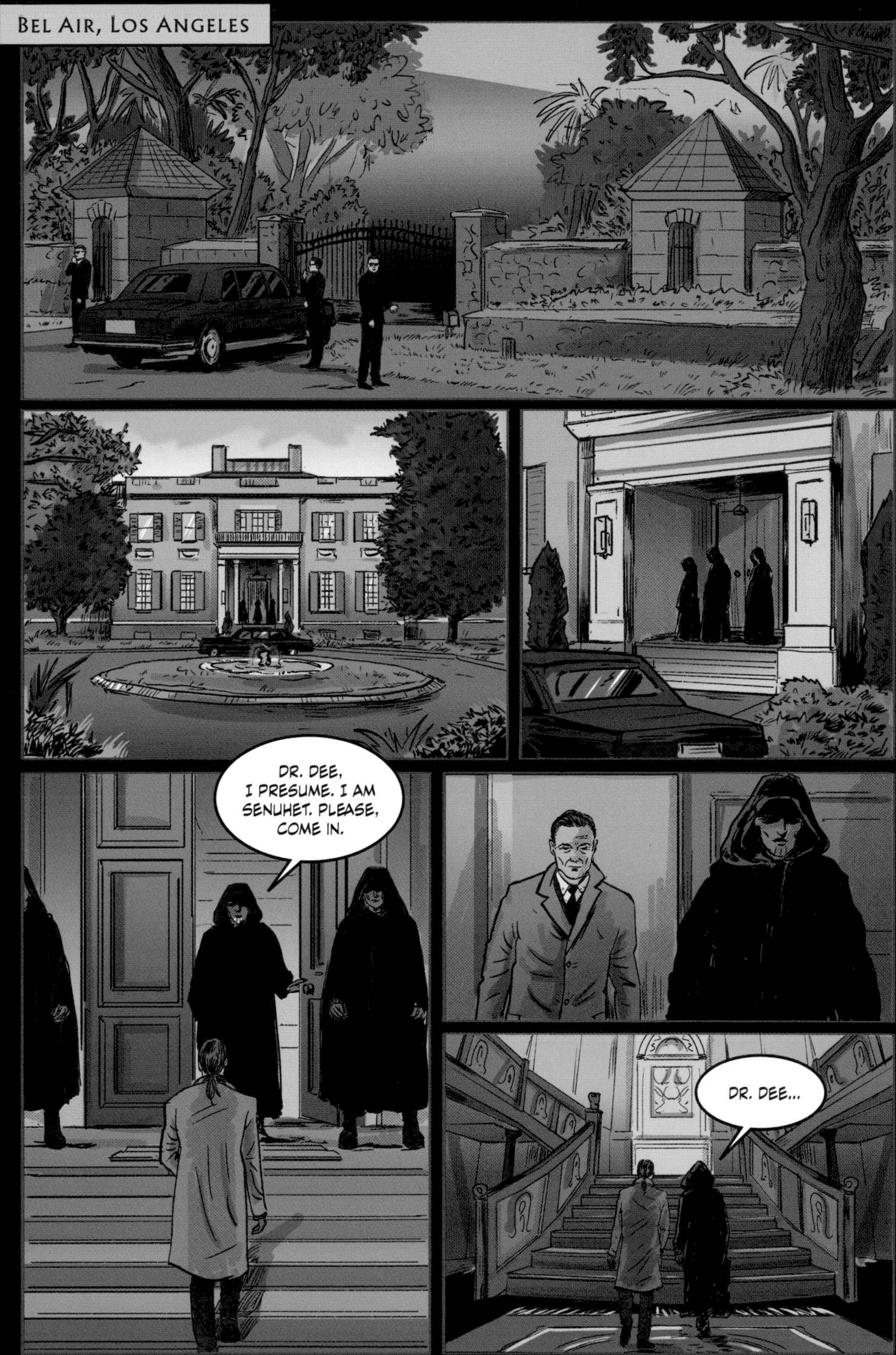
BEL AIR, LOS ANGELES
DR. DEE, I PRESUME. I AM SENUHET. PLEASE, COME IN.
DR. DEE...

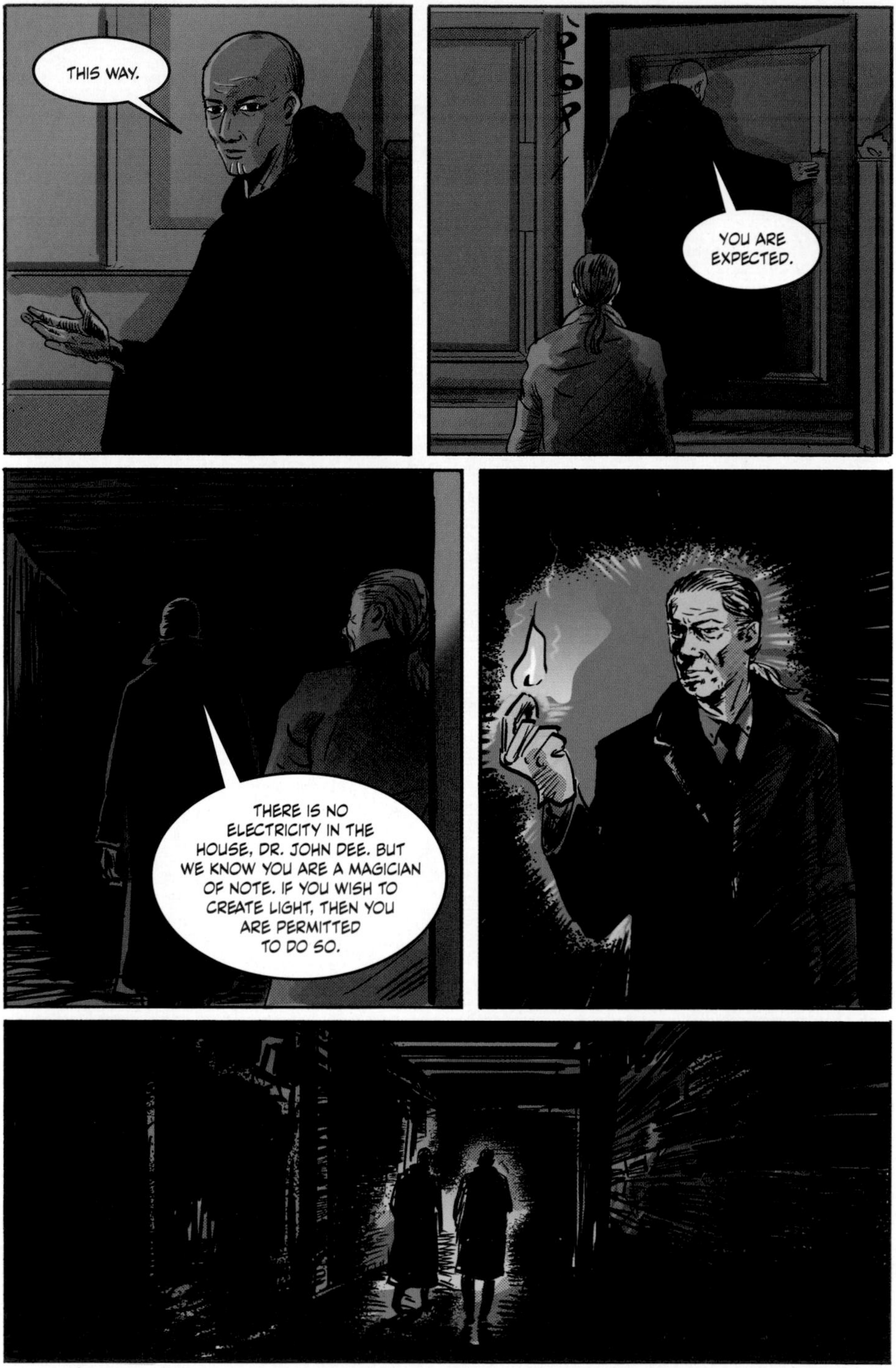
THIS WAY.
YOU ARE EXPECTED.
THERE IS NO ELECTRICITY IN THE HOUSE, DR. JOHN DEE. BUT WE KNOW YOU ARE A MAGICIAN OF NOTE. IF YOU WISH TO CREATE LIGHT, THEN YOU ARE PERMITTED TO DO SO.

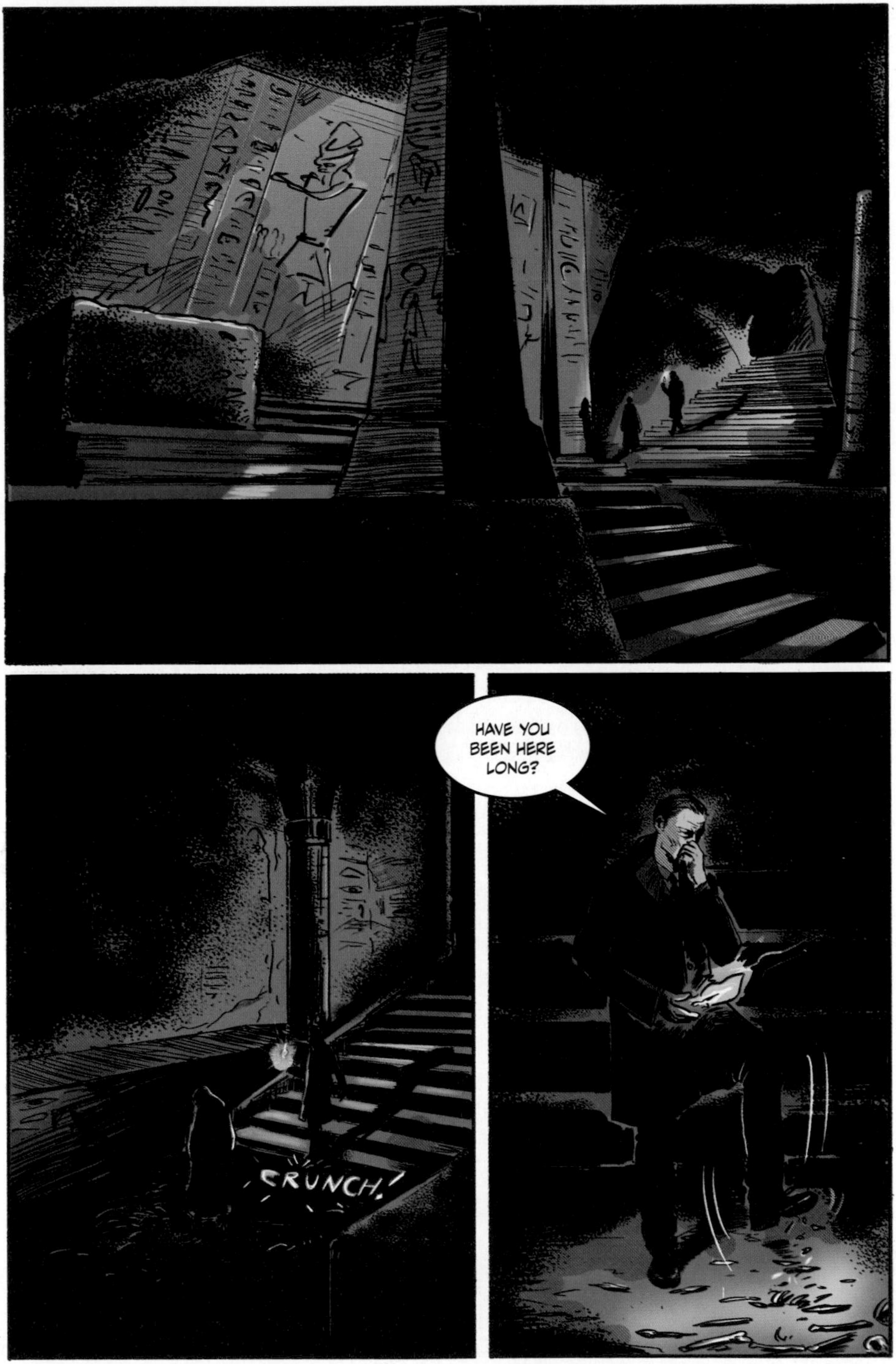
CRUNCH!
HAVE YOU BEEN HERE LONG?

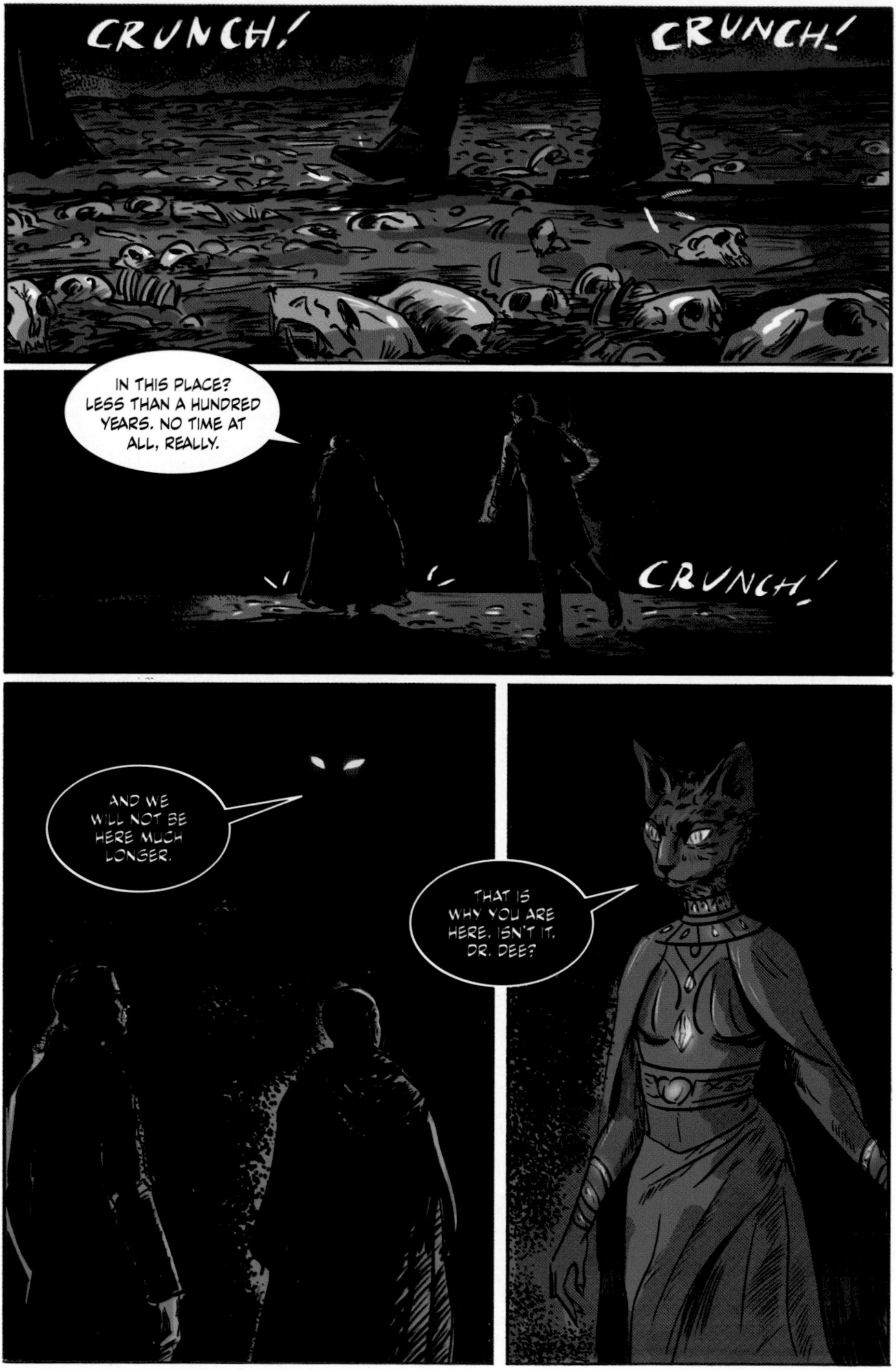
CRUNCH!
CRUNCH!
IN THIS PLACE? LESS THAN A HUNDRED YEARS. NO TIME AT ALL, REALLY.
CRUNCH!
AND WE WILL NOT BE HERE MUCH LONGER.
THAT IS WHY YOU ARE HERE, ISN'T IT, DR. DEE?

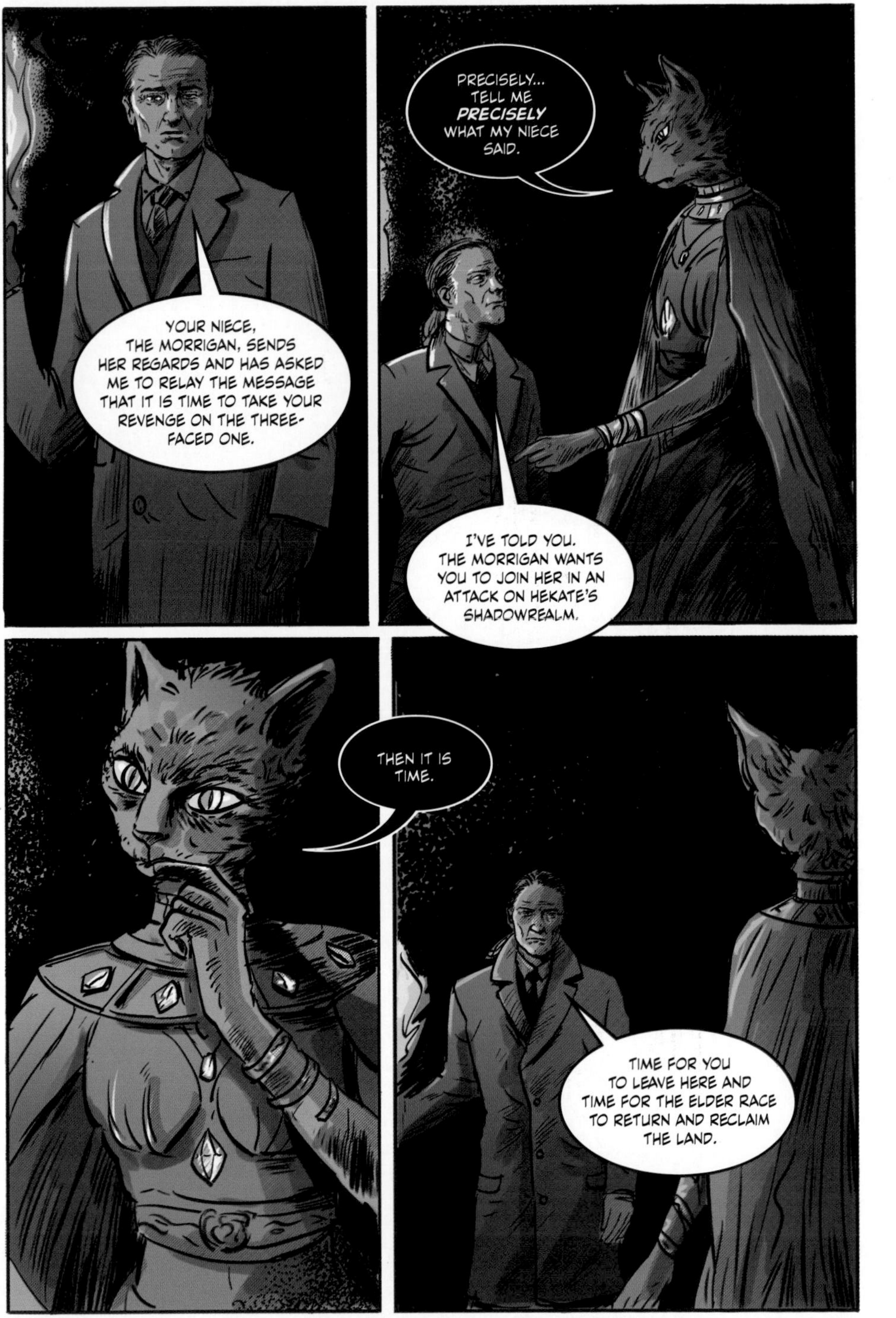
YOUR NIECE, THE MORRIGAN, SENDS HER REGARDS AND HAS ASKED ME TO RELAY THE MESSAGE THAT IT IS TIME TO TAKE YOUR REVENGE ON THE THREE-FACED ONE.
PRECISELY... TELL ME *PRECISELY* WHAT MY NIECE SAID.
I'VE TOLD YOU. THE MORRIGAN WANTS YOU TO JOIN HER IN AN ATTACK ON HEKATE'S SHADOWREALM.
THEN IT IS TIME.
TIME FOR YOU TO LEAVE HERE AND TIME FOR THE ELDER RACE TO RETURN AND RECLAIM THE LAND.

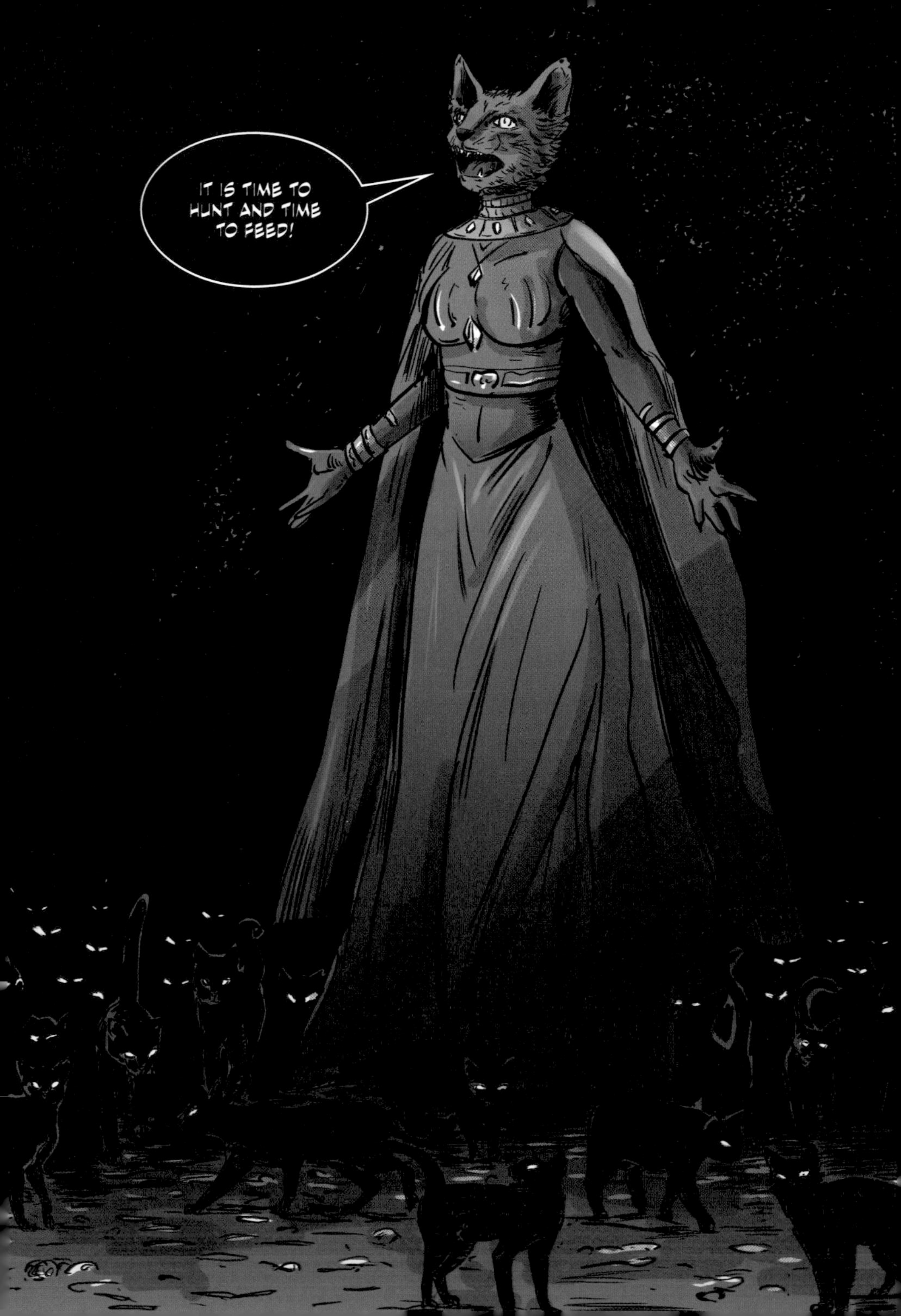
IT IS TIME TO HUNT AND TIME TO FEED!

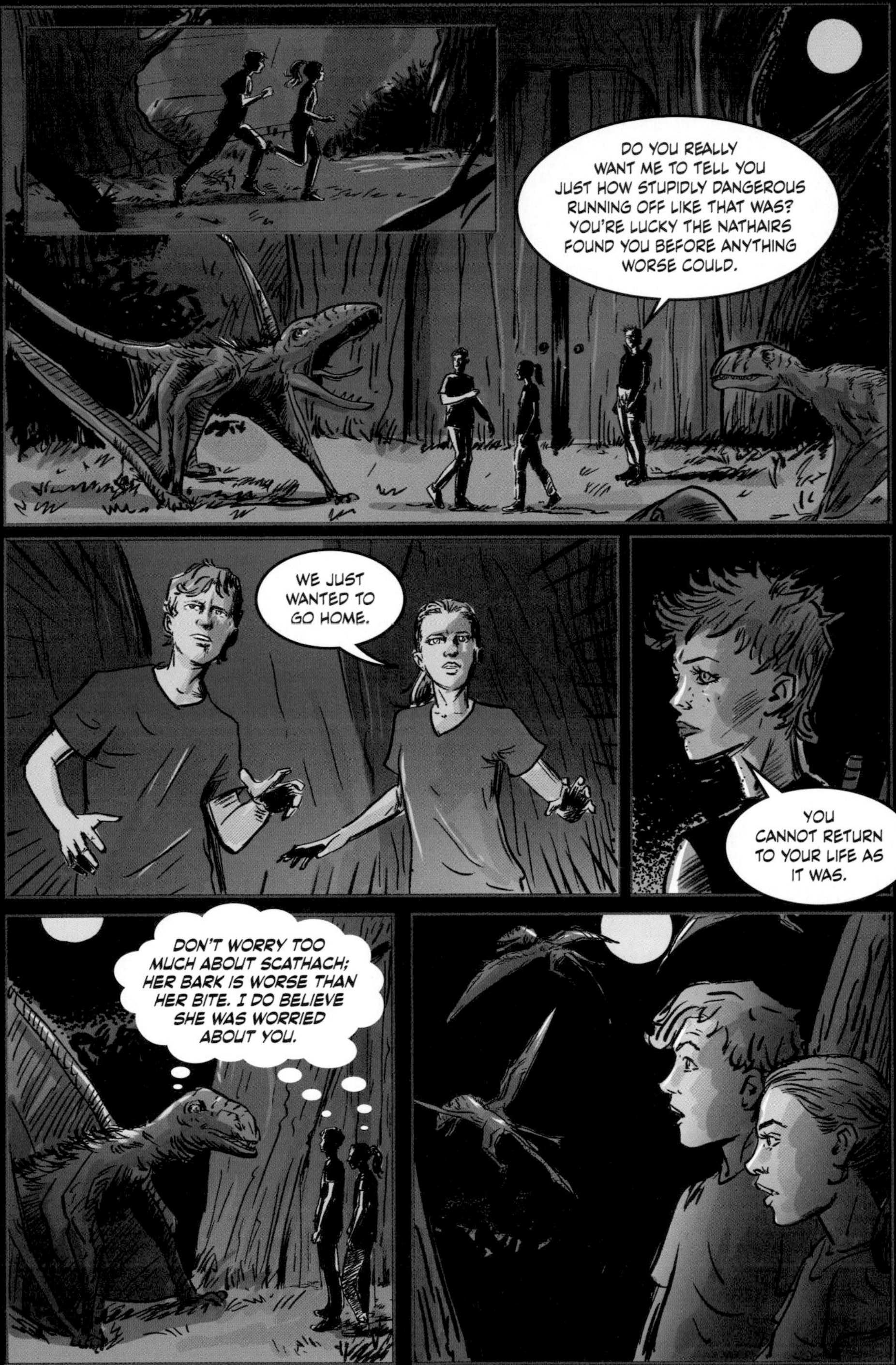
DO YOU REALLY WANT ME TO TELL YOU JUST HOW STUPIDLY DANGEROUS RUNNING OFF LIKE THAT WAS? YOU'RE LUCKY THE NATHAIRS FOUND YOU BEFORE ANYTHING WORSE COULD.
WE JUST WANTED TO GO HOME.
YOU CANNOT RETURN TO YOUR LIFE AS IT WAS.
DON'T WORRY TOO MUCH ABOUT SCATHACH; HER BARK IS WORSE THAN HER BITE. I DO BELIEVE SHE WAS WORRIED ABOUT YOU.

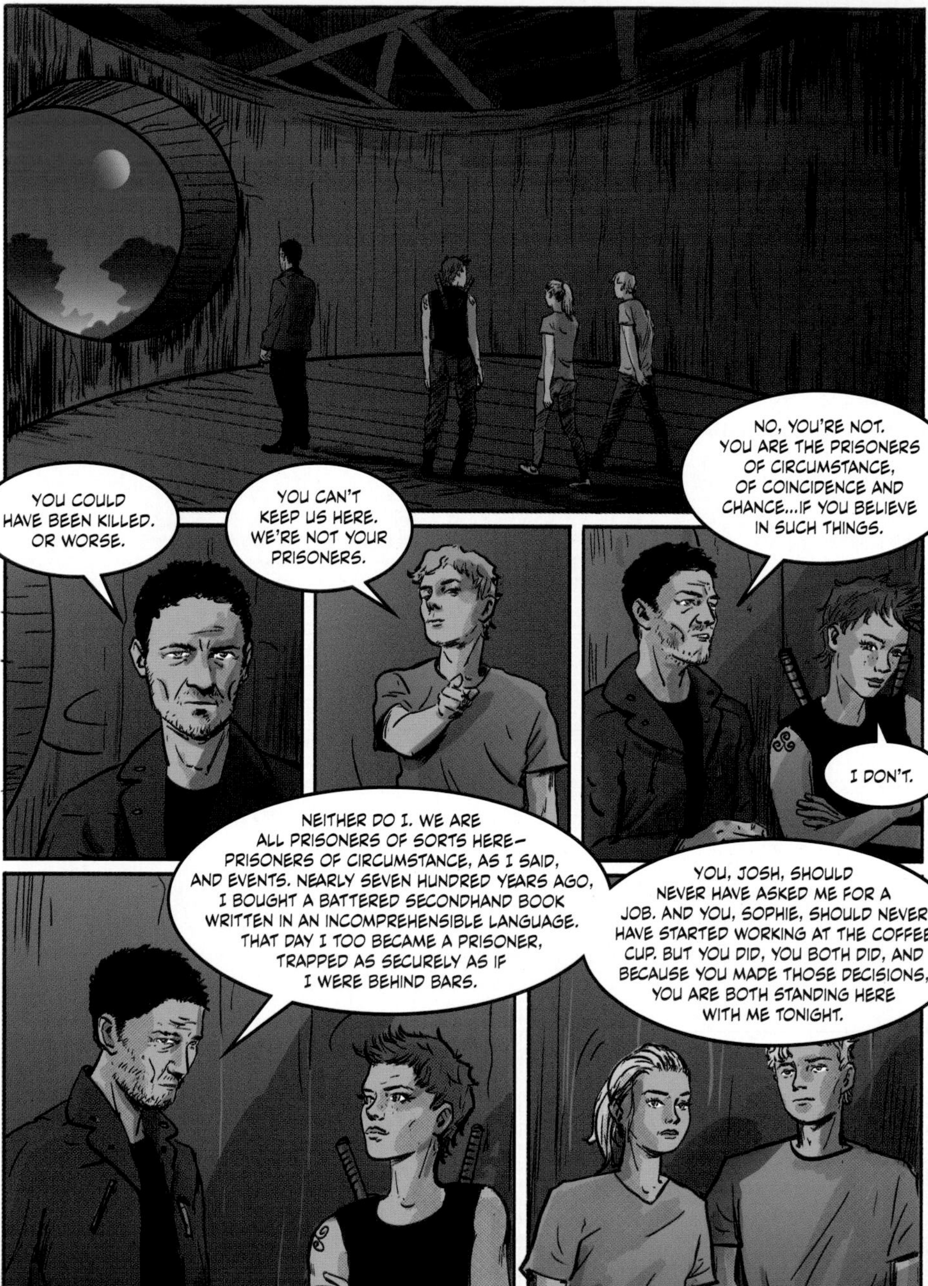
YOU COULD HAVE BEEN KILLED. OR WORSE.
YOU CAN'T KEEP US HERE. WE'RE NOT YOUR PRISONERS.
NO, YOU'RE NOT. YOU ARE THE PRISONERS OF CIRCUMSTANCE, OF COINCIDENCE AND CHANCE...IF YOU BELIEVE IN SUCH THINGS.
I DON'T.
NEITHER DO I. WE ARE ALL PRISONERS OF SORTS HERE—PRISONERS OF CIRCUMSTANCE, AS I SAID, AND EVENTS. NEARLY SEVEN HUNDRED YEARS AGO, I BOUGHT A BATTERED SECONDHAND BOOK WRITTEN IN AN INCOMPREHENSIBLE LANGUAGE. THAT DAY I TOO BECAME A PRISONER, TRAPPED AS SECURELY AS IF I WERE BEHIND BARS.
YOU, JOSH, SHOULD NEVER HAVE ASKED ME FOR A JOB. AND YOU, SOPHIE, SHOULD NEVER HAVE STARTED WORKING AT THE COFFEE CUP. BUT YOU DID, YOU BOTH DID, AND BECAUSE YOU MADE THOSE DECISIONS, YOU ARE BOTH STANDING HERE WITH ME TONIGHT.

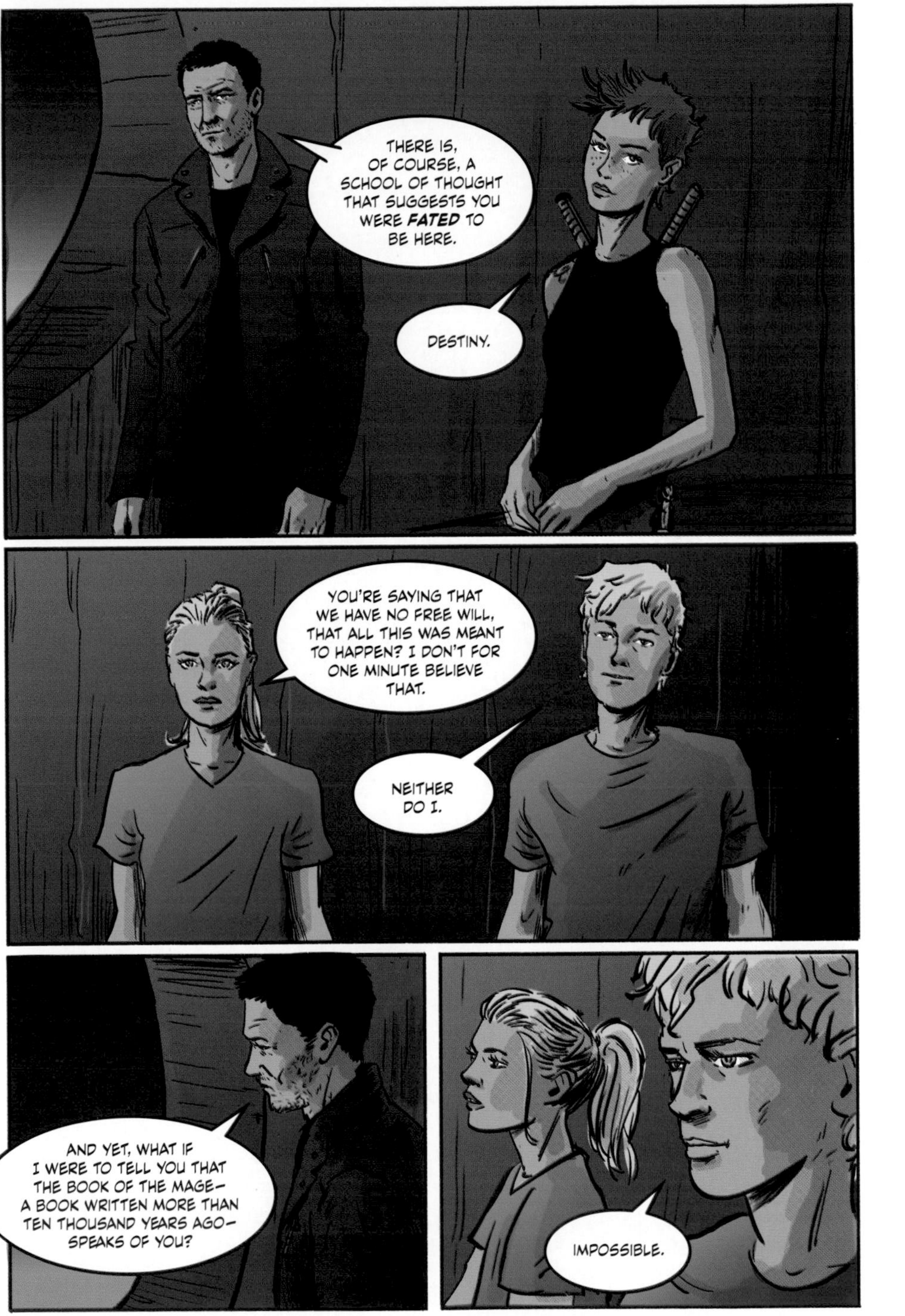
THERE IS, OF COURSE, A SCHOOL OF THOUGHT THAT SUGGESTS YOU WERE **FATED** TO BE HERE.
DESTINY.
YOU'RE SAYING THAT WE HAVE NO FREE WILL, THAT ALL THIS WAS MEANT TO HAPPEN? I DON'T FOR ONE MINUTE BELIEVE THAT.
NEITHER DO I.
AND YET, WHAT IF I WERE TO TELL YOU THAT THE BOOK OF THE MAGE— A BOOK WRITTEN MORE THAN TEN THOUSAND YEARS AGO— SPEAKS OF YOU?
IMPOSSIBLE.

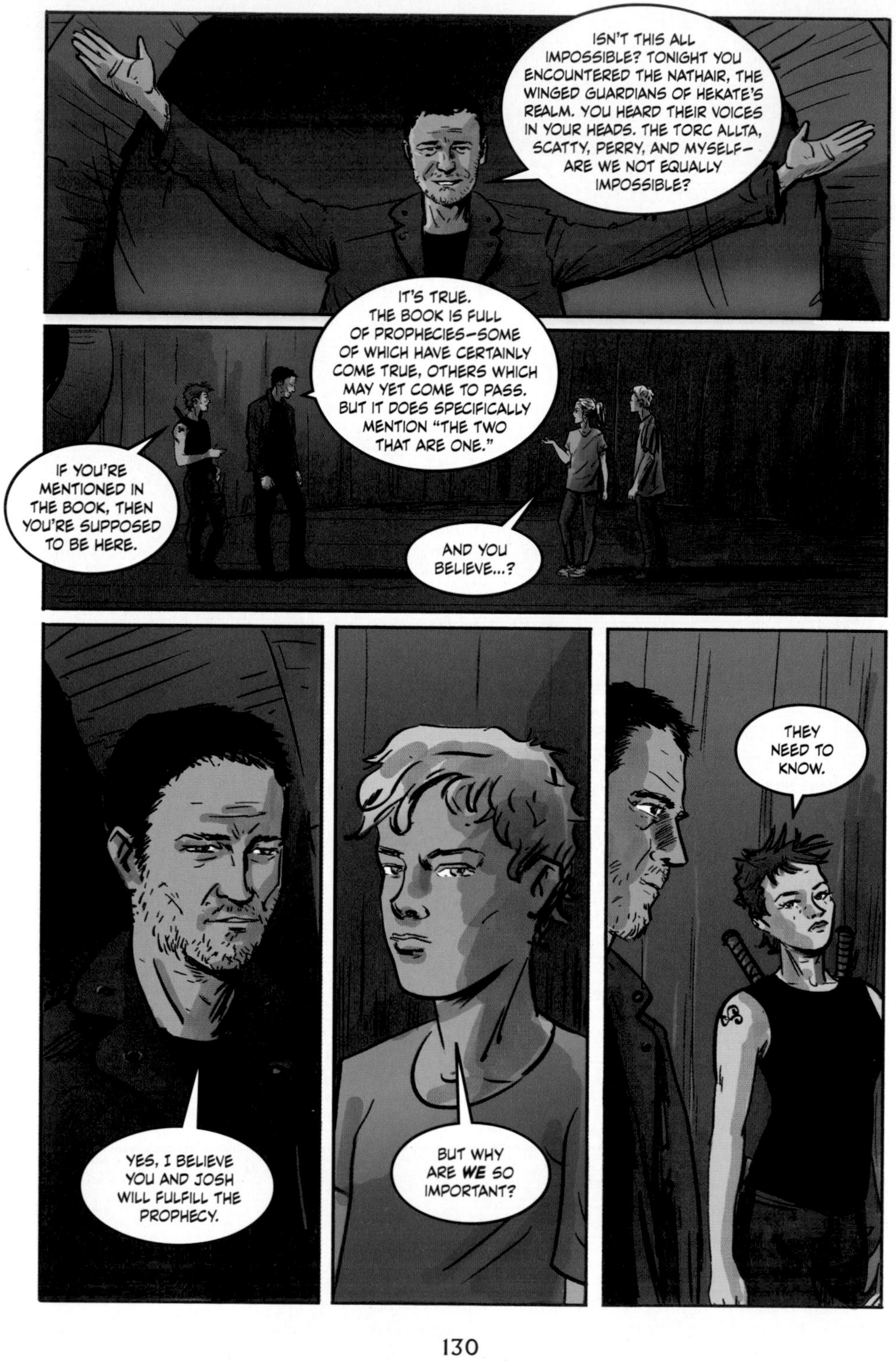

ISN'T THIS ALL IMPOSSIBLE? TONIGHT YOU ENCOUNTERED THE NATHAIR, THE WINGED GUARDIANS OF HEKATE'S REALM. YOU HEARD THEIR VOICES IN YOUR HEADS. THE TORC ALLTA, SCATTY, PERRY, AND MYSELF—ARE WE NOT EQUALLY IMPOSSIBLE?
IT'S TRUE. THE BOOK IS FULL OF PROPHECIES—SOME OF WHICH HAVE CERTAINLY COME TRUE, OTHERS WHICH MAY YET COME TO PASS. BUT IT DOES SPECIFICALLY MENTION "THE TWO THAT ARE ONE."
IF YOU'RE MENTIONED IN THE BOOK, THEN YOU'RE SUPPOSED TO BE HERE.
AND YOU BELIEVE...?
YES, I BELIEVE YOU AND JOSH WILL FULFILL THE PROPHECY.
BUT WHY ARE **WE** SO IMPORTANT?
THEY NEED TO KNOW.

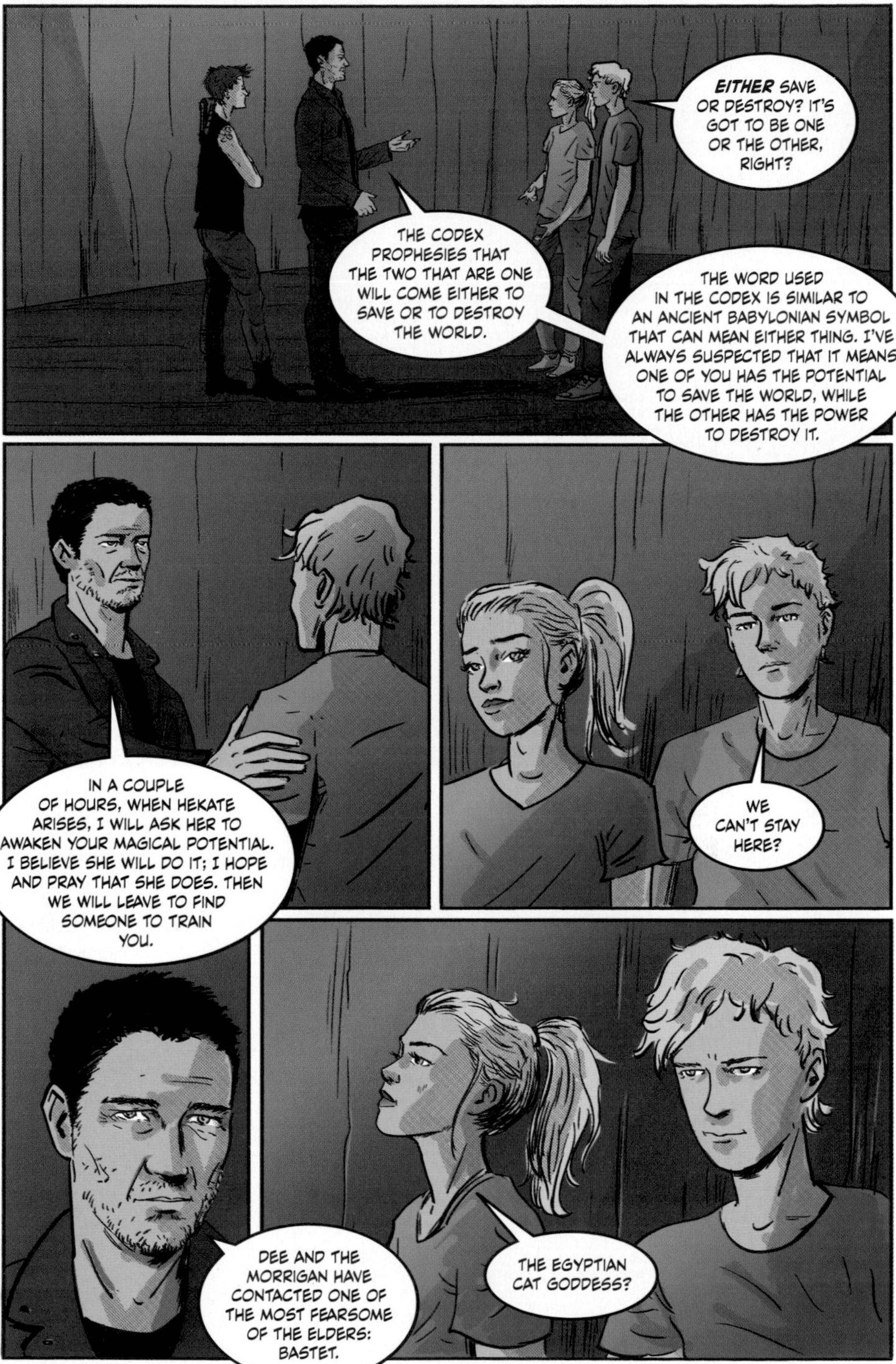
EITHER SAVE OR DESTROY? IT'S GOT TO BE ONE OR THE OTHER, RIGHT?
THE CODEX PROPHESIES THAT THE TWO THAT ARE ONE WILL COME EITHER TO SAVE OR TO DESTROY THE WORLD.
THE WORD USED IN THE CODEX IS SIMILAR TO AN ANCIENT BABYLONIAN SYMBOL THAT CAN MEAN EITHER THING. I'VE ALWAYS SUSPECTED THAT IT MEANS ONE OF YOU HAS THE POTENTIAL TO SAVE THE WORLD, WHILE THE OTHER HAS THE POWER TO DESTROY IT.
IN A COUPLE OF HOURS, WHEN HEKATE ARISES, I WILL ASK HER TO AWAKEN YOUR MAGICAL POTENTIAL. I BELIEVE SHE WILL DO IT; I HOPE AND PRAY THAT SHE DOES. THEN WE WILL LEAVE TO FIND SOMEONE TO TRAIN YOU.
WE CAN'T STAY HERE?
DEE AND THE MORRIGAN HAVE CONTACTED ONE OF THE MOST FEARSOME OF THE ELDERS: BASTET.
THE EGYPTIAN CAT GODDESS?

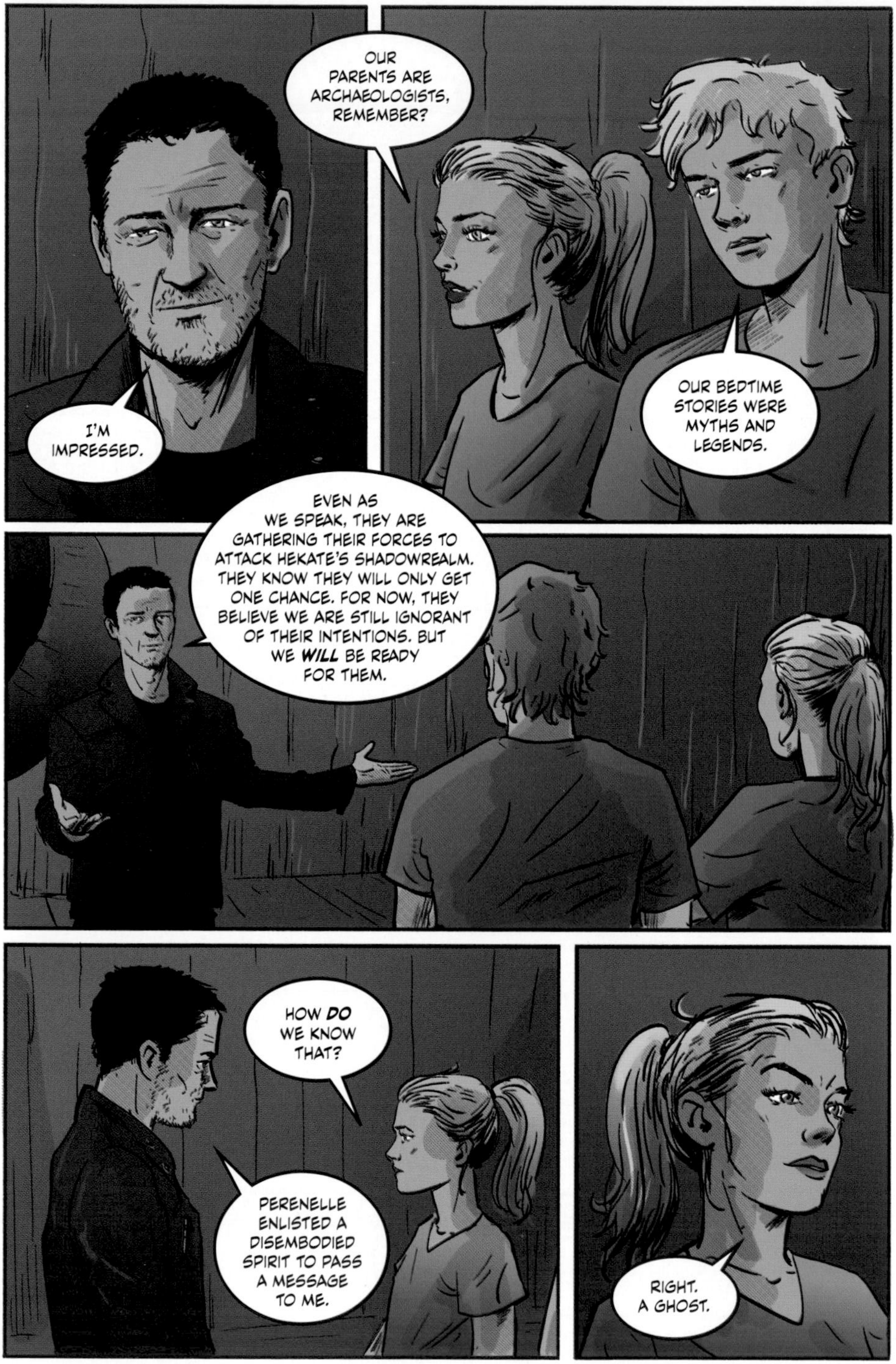
I'M IMPRESSED.
OUR PARENTS ARE ARCHAEOLOGISTS, REMEMBER?
OUR BEDTIME STORIES WERE MYTHS AND LEGENDS.
EVEN AS WE SPEAK, THEY ARE GATHERING THEIR FORCES TO ATTACK HEKATE'S SHADOWREALM. THEY KNOW THEY WILL ONLY GET ONE CHANCE. FOR NOW, THEY BELIEVE WE ARE STILL IGNORANT OF THEIR INTENTIONS. BUT WE WILL BE READY FOR THEM.
HOW DO WE KNOW THAT?
PERENELLE ENLISTED A DISEMBODIED SPIRIT TO PASS A MESSAGE TO ME.
RIGHT. A GHOST.

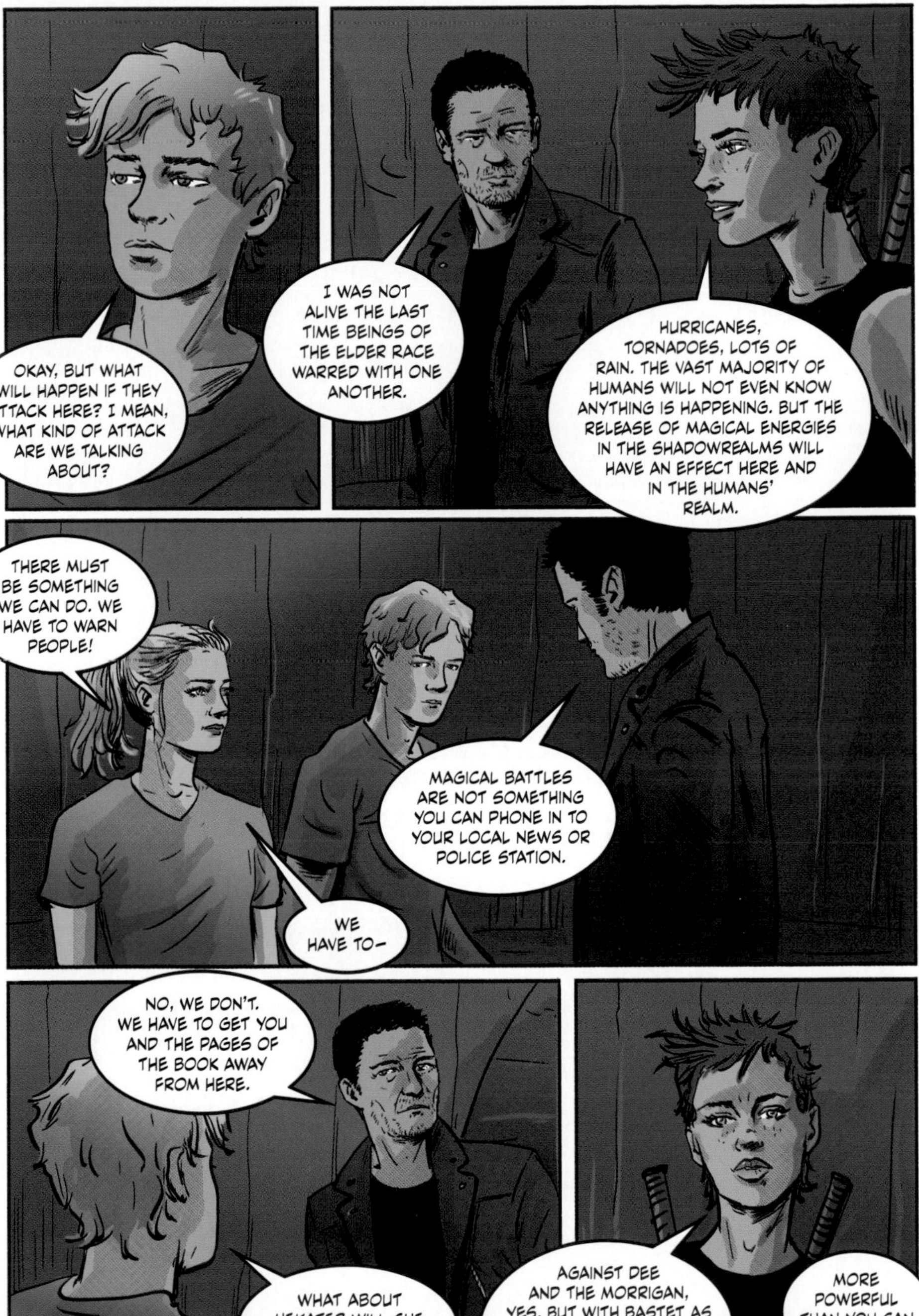
OKAY, BUT WHAT WILL HAPPEN IF THEY ATTACK HERE? I MEAN, WHAT KIND OF ATTACK ARE WE TALKING ABOUT?
I WAS NOT ALIVE THE LAST TIME BEINGS OF THE ELDER RACE WARRED WITH ONE ANOTHER.
HURRICANES, TORNADOES, LOTS OF RAIN. THE VAST MAJORITY OF HUMANS WILL NOT EVEN KNOW ANYTHING IS HAPPENING. BUT THE RELEASE OF MAGICAL ENERGIES IN THE SHADOWREALMS WILL HAVE AN EFFECT HERE AND IN THE HUMANS' REALM.
THERE MUST BE SOMETHING WE CAN DO. WE HAVE TO WARN PEOPLE!
MAGICAL BATTLES ARE NOT SOMETHING YOU CAN PHONE IN TO YOUR LOCAL NEWS OR POLICE STATION.
WE HAVE TO—
NO, WE DON'T. WE HAVE TO GET YOU AND THE PAGES OF THE BOOK AWAY FROM HERE.
WHAT ABOUT HEKATE? WILL SHE BE ABLE TO DEFEND HERSELF?
AGAINST DEE AND THE MORRIGAN, YES. BUT WITH BASTET AS THEIR ALLY, I SIMPLY CAN'T SAY. EVEN I DON'T KNOW HOW POWERFUL THE GODDESS IS.
MORE POWERFUL THAN YOU CAN IMAGINE.

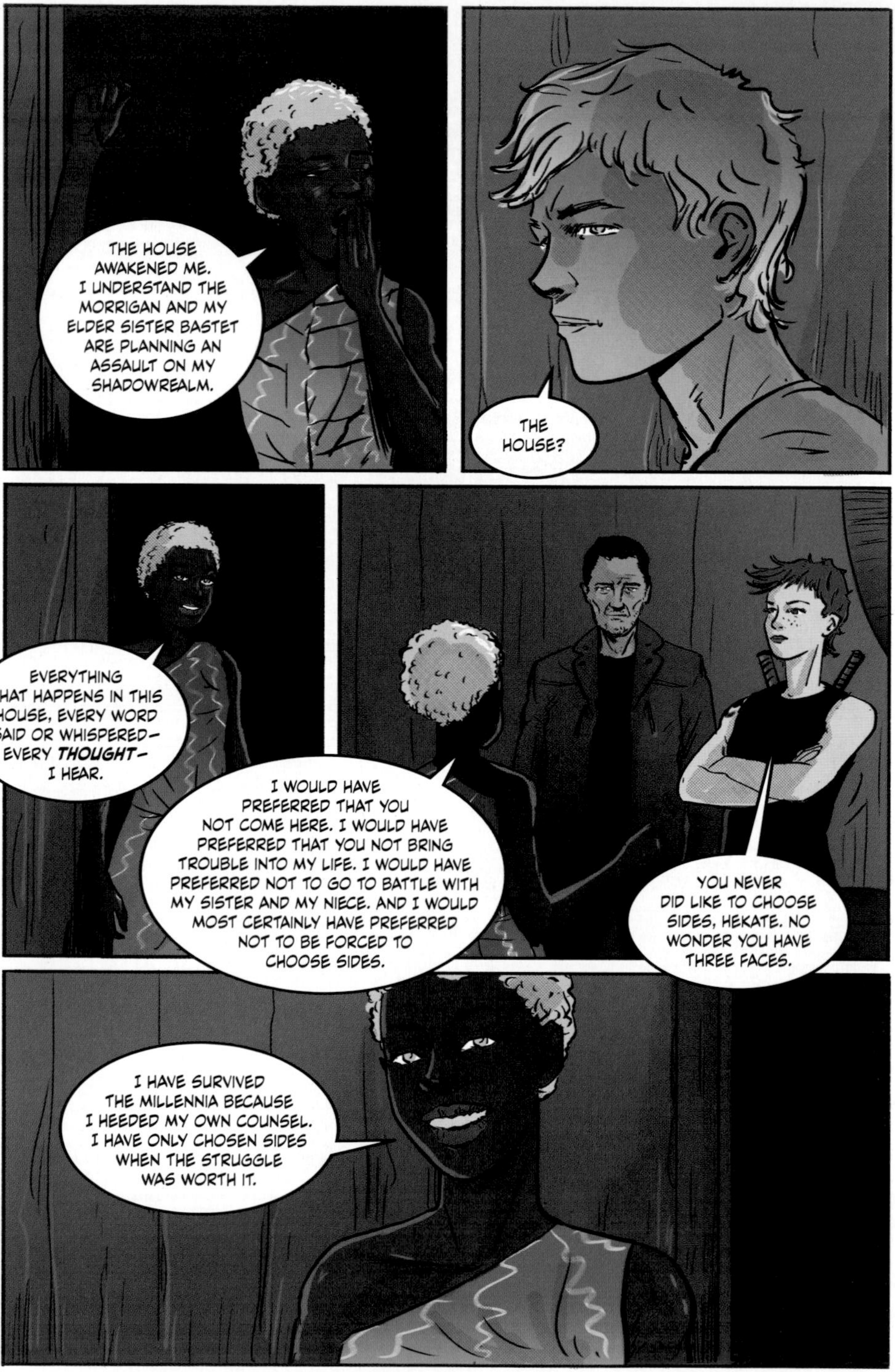
THE HOUSE AWAKENED ME. I UNDERSTAND THE MORRIGAN AND MY ELDER SISTER BASTET ARE PLANNING AN ASSAULT ON MY SHADOWREALM.
THE HOUSE?
EVERYTHING THAT HAPPENS IN THIS HOUSE, EVERY WORD SAID OR WHISPERED— EVERY *THOUGHT*— I HEAR.
I WOULD HAVE PREFERRED THAT YOU NOT COME HERE. I WOULD HAVE PREFERRED THAT YOU NOT BRING TROUBLE INTO MY LIFE. I WOULD HAVE PREFERRED NOT TO GO TO BATTLE WITH MY SISTER AND MY NIECE. AND I WOULD MOST CERTAINLY HAVE PREFERRED NOT TO BE FORCED TO CHOOSE SIDES.
YOU NEVER DID LIKE TO CHOOSE SIDES, HEKATE. NO WONDER YOU HAVE THREE FACES.
I HAVE SURVIVED THE MILLENNIA BECAUSE I HEEDED MY OWN COUNSEL. I HAVE ONLY CHOSEN SIDES WHEN THE STRUGGLE WAS WORTH IT.

AND NOW I THINK IT IS TIME TO CHOOSE AGAIN.

I SEE.

YOU MAY BE RIGHT. THESE MAY INDEED BE THE ONES SPOKEN OF IN THE CURSED CODEX. THEY POSSESS INCREDIBLE UNTAPPED POTENTIAL.

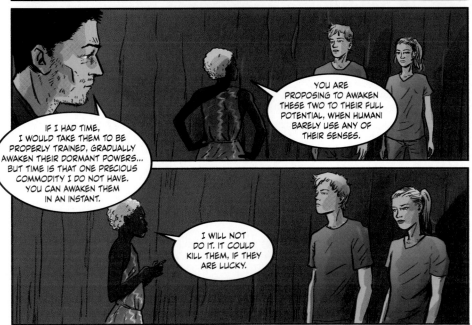

YOU ARE PROPOSING TO AWAKEN THESE TWO TO THEIR FULL POTENTIAL, WHEN HUMANI BARELY USE ANY OF THEIR SENSES.

IF I HAD TIME, I WOULD TAKE THEM TO BE PROPERLY TRAINED, GRADUALLY AWAKEN THEIR DORMANT POWERS... BUT TIME IS THAT ONE PRECIOUS COMMODITY I DO NOT HAVE. YOU CAN AWAKEN THEM IN AN INSTANT.

I WILL NOT DO IT. IT COULD KILL THEM, IF THEY ARE LUCKY.

CHAPTER 22

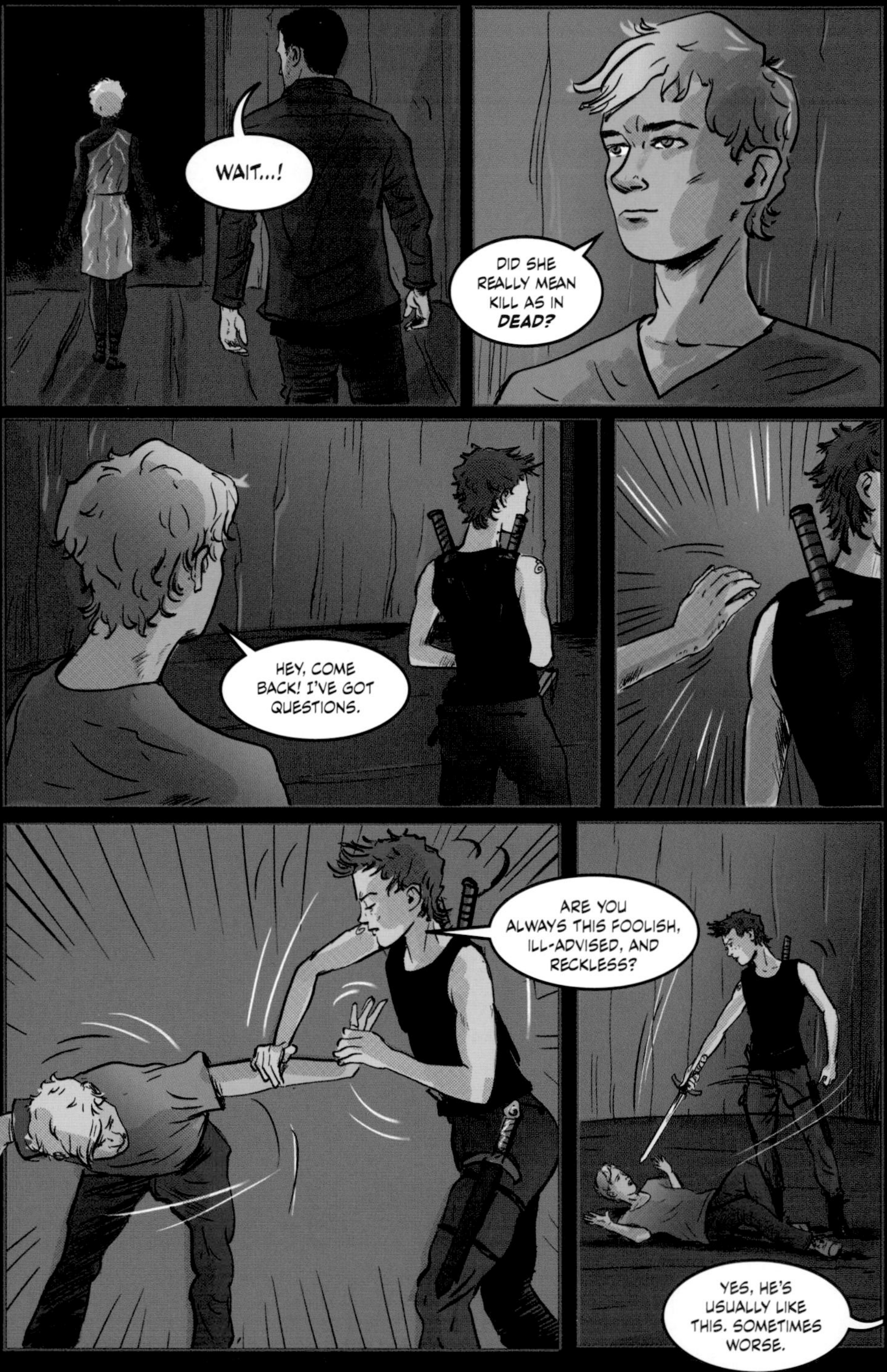
WAIT...!
DID SHE REALLY MEAN KILL AS IN *DEAD?*
HEY, COME BACK! I'VE GOT QUESTIONS.
ARE YOU ALWAYS THIS FOOLISH, ILL-ADVISED, AND RECKLESS?
YES, HE'S USUALLY LIKE THIS. SOMETIMES WORSE.

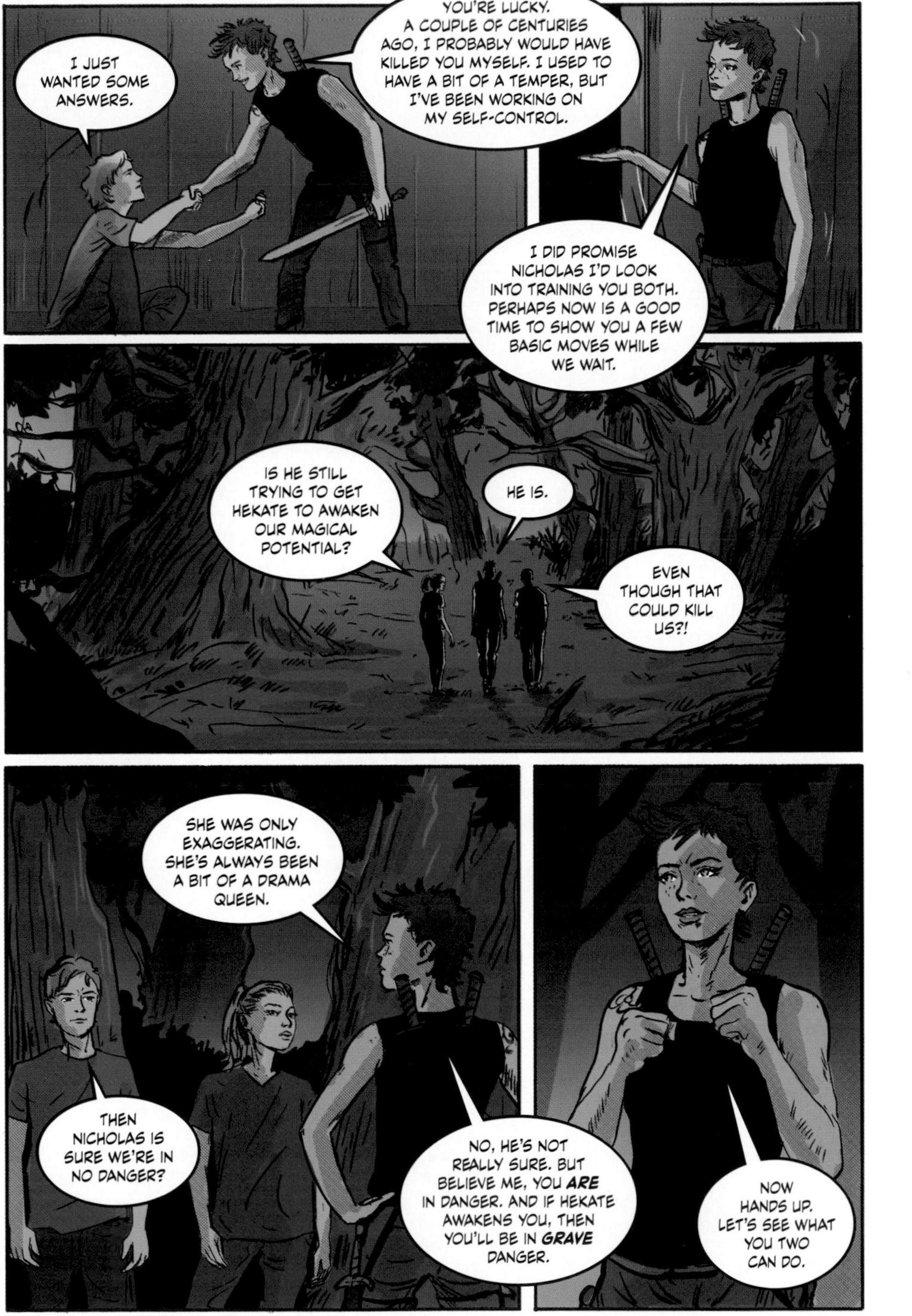
I JUST WANTED SOME ANSWERS.
YOU'RE LUCKY. A COUPLE OF CENTURIES AGO, I PROBABLY WOULD HAVE KILLED YOU MYSELF. I USED TO HAVE A BIT OF A TEMPER, BUT I'VE BEEN WORKING ON MY SELF-CONTROL.
I DID PROMISE NICHOLAS I'D LOOK INTO TRAINING YOU BOTH. PERHAPS NOW IS A GOOD TIME TO SHOW YOU A FEW BASIC MOVES WHILE WE WAIT.
IS HE STILL TRYING TO GET HEKATE TO AWAKEN OUR MAGICAL POTENTIAL?
HE IS.
EVEN THOUGH THAT COULD KILL US?!
SHE WAS ONLY EXAGGERATING. SHE'S ALWAYS BEEN A BIT OF A DRAMA QUEEN.
THEN NICHOLAS IS SURE WE'RE IN NO DANGER?
NO, HE'S NOT REALLY SURE. BUT BELIEVE ME, YOU ***ARE*** IN DANGER. AND IF HEKATE AWAKENS YOU, THEN YOU'LL BE IN ***GRAVE*** DANGER.
NOW HANDS UP. LET'S SEE WHAT YOU TWO CAN DO.

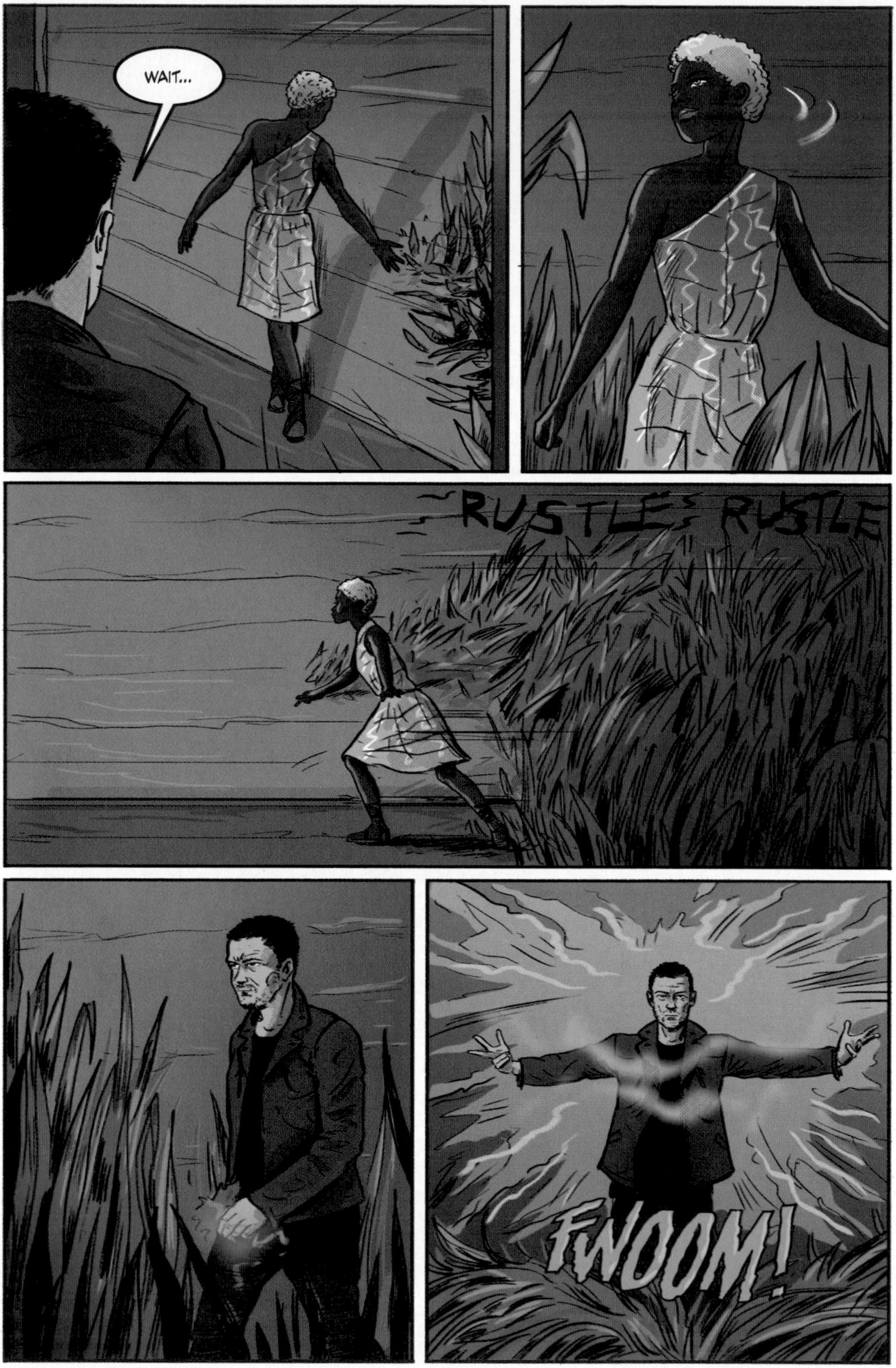
WAIT...
RUSTLE RUSTLE
FWOOM!

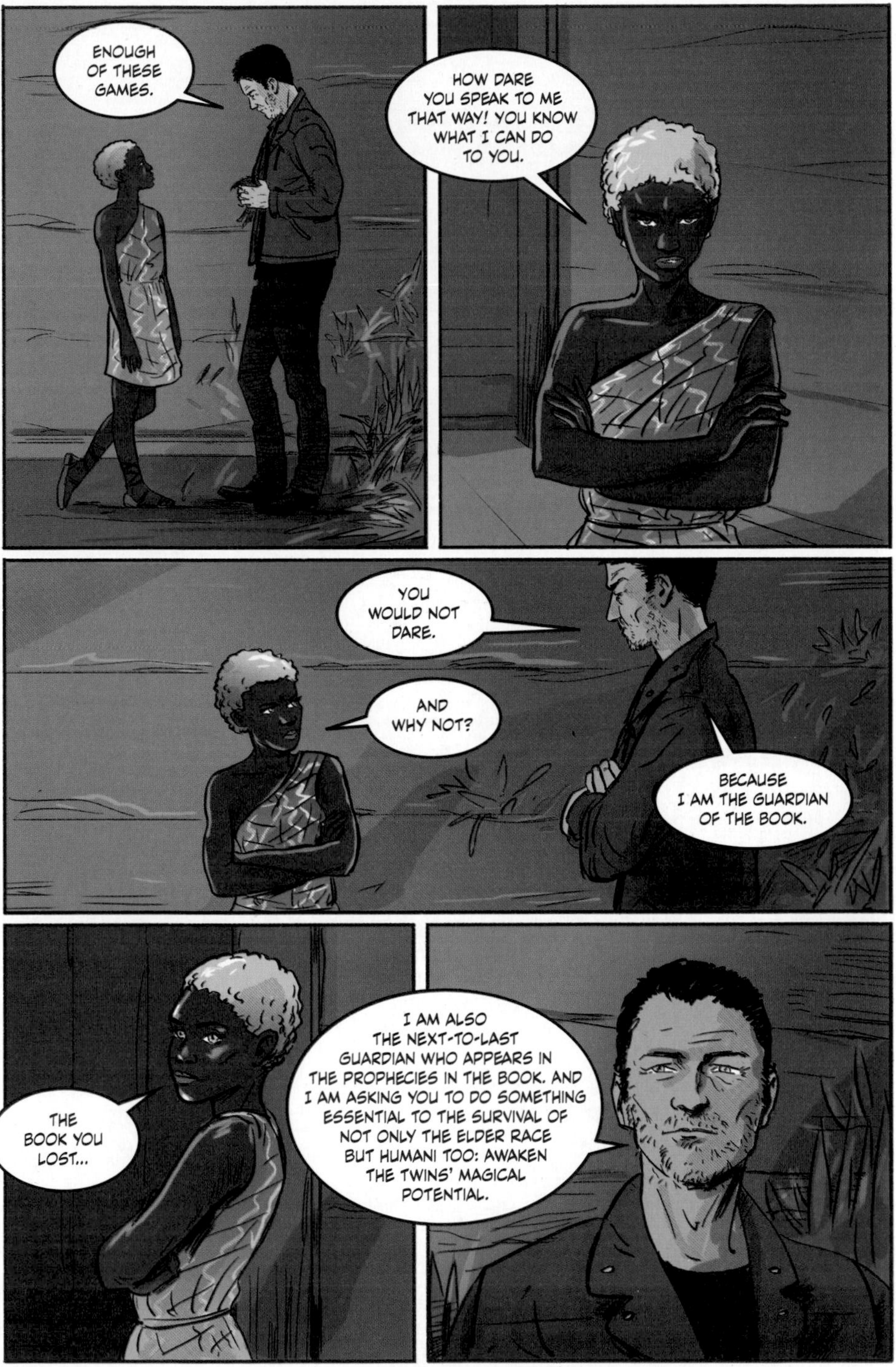
ENOUGH OF THESE GAMES.
HOW DARE YOU SPEAK TO ME THAT WAY! YOU KNOW WHAT I CAN DO TO YOU.
YOU WOULD NOT DARE.
AND WHY NOT?
BECAUSE I AM THE GUARDIAN OF THE BOOK.
THE BOOK YOU LOST...
I AM ALSO THE NEXT-TO-LAST GUARDIAN WHO APPEARS IN THE PROPHECIES IN THE BOOK. AND I AM ASKING YOU TO DO SOMETHING ESSENTIAL TO THE SURVIVAL OF NOT ONLY THE ELDER RACE BUT HUMANI TOO: AWAKEN THE TWINS' MAGICAL POTENTIAL.

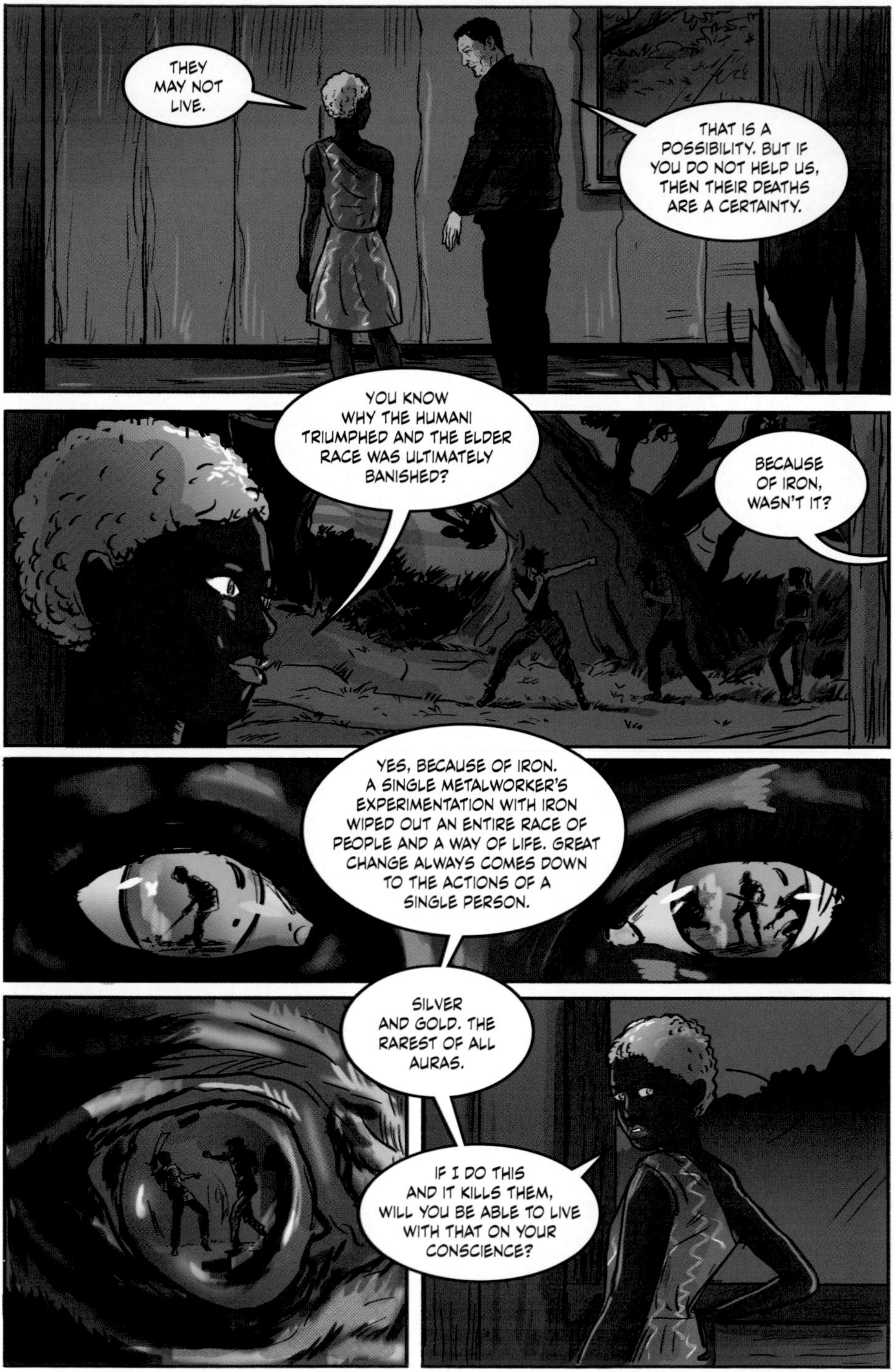
THEY MAY NOT LIVE.
THAT IS A POSSIBILITY. BUT IF YOU DO NOT HELP US, THEN THEIR DEATHS ARE A CERTAINTY.
YOU KNOW WHY THE HUMANI TRIUMPHED AND THE ELDER RACE WAS ULTIMATELY BANISHED?
BECAUSE OF IRON, WASN'T IT?
YES, BECAUSE OF IRON. A SINGLE METALWORKER'S EXPERIMENTATION WITH IRON WIPED OUT AN ENTIRE RACE OF PEOPLE AND A WAY OF LIFE. GREAT CHANGE ALWAYS COMES DOWN TO THE ACTIONS OF A SINGLE PERSON.
SILVER AND GOLD. THE RAREST OF ALL AURAS.
IF I DO THIS AND IT KILLS THEM, WILL YOU BE ABLE TO LIVE WITH THAT ON YOUR CONSCIENCE?

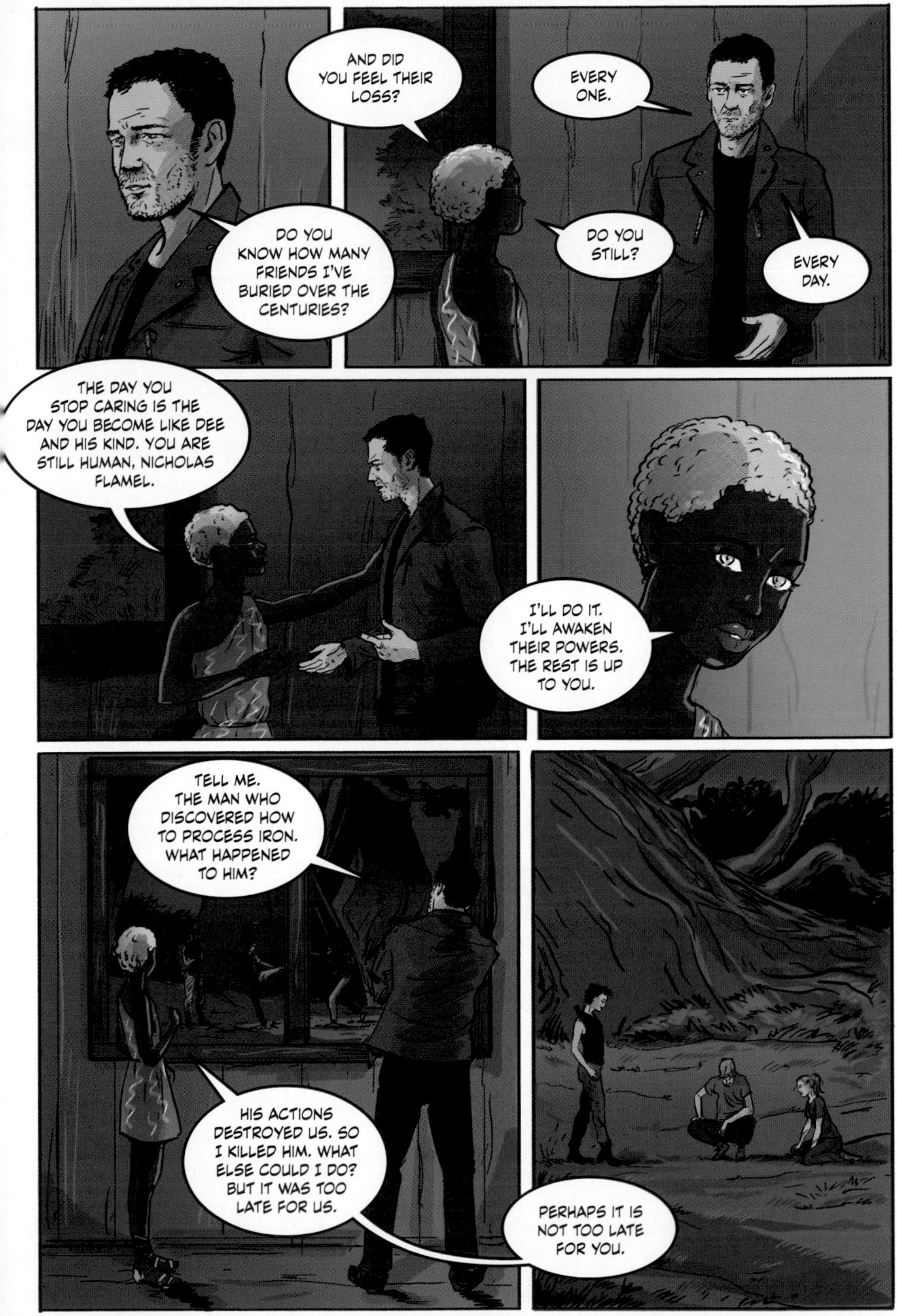
DO YOU KNOW HOW MANY FRIENDS I'VE BURIED OVER THE CENTURIES?
AND DID YOU FEEL THEIR LOSS?
EVERY ONE.
DO YOU STILL?
EVERY DAY.
THE DAY YOU STOP CARING IS THE DAY YOU BECOME LIKE DEE AND HIS KIND. YOU ARE STILL HUMAN, NICHOLAS FLAMEL.
I'LL DO IT. I'LL AWAKEN THEIR POWERS. THE REST IS UP TO YOU.
TELL ME. THE MAN WHO DISCOVERED HOW TO PROCESS IRON. WHAT HAPPENED TO HIM?
HIS ACTIONS DESTROYED US. SO I KILLED HIM. WHAT ELSE COULD I DO? BUT IT WAS TOO LATE FOR US.
PERHAPS IT IS NOT TOO LATE FOR YOU.

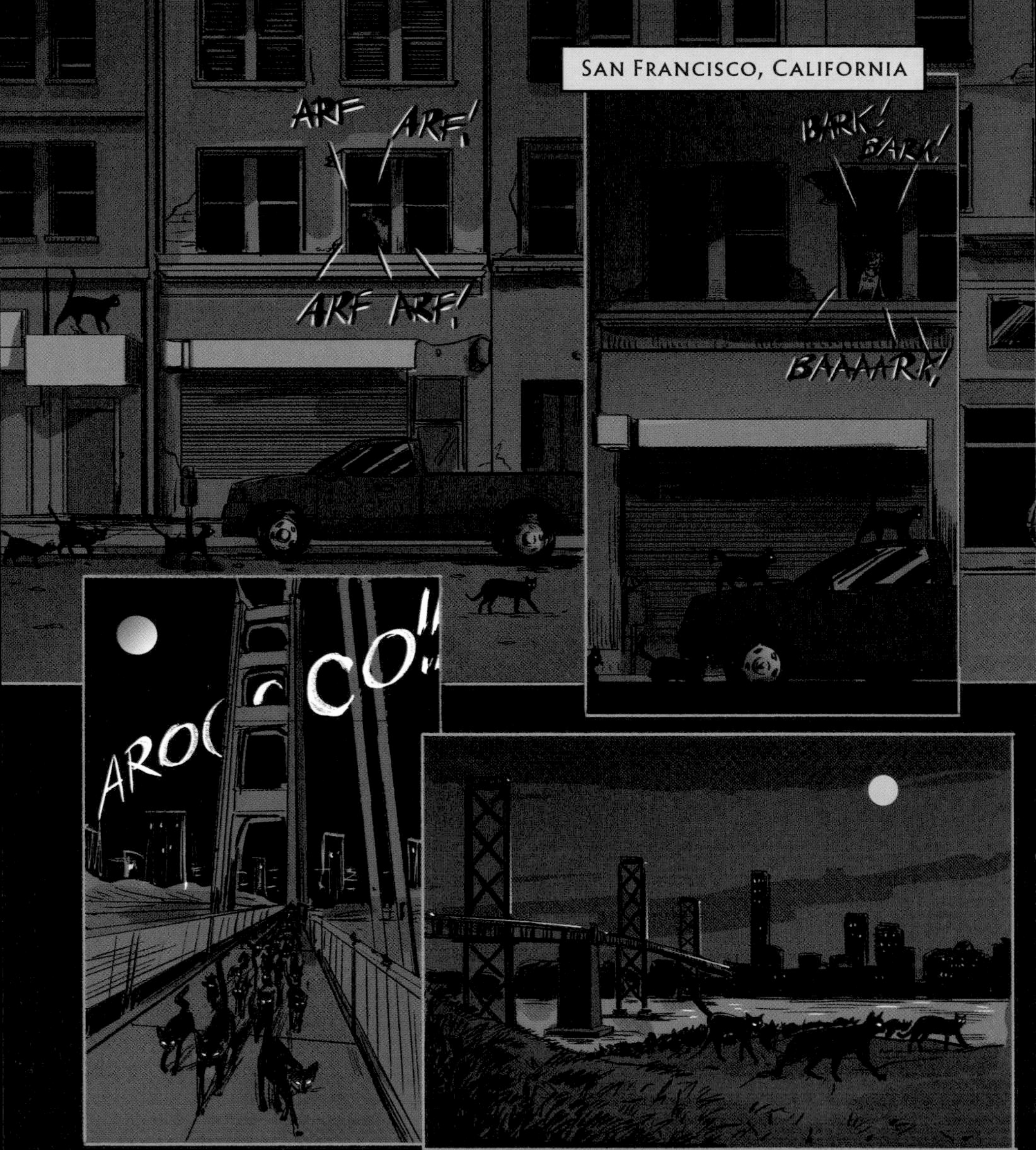
SAN FRANCISCO, CALIFORNIA
ARF
ARF!
ARF ARF!
BARK! BARK!
BAAAARK!
AROOOOO!!

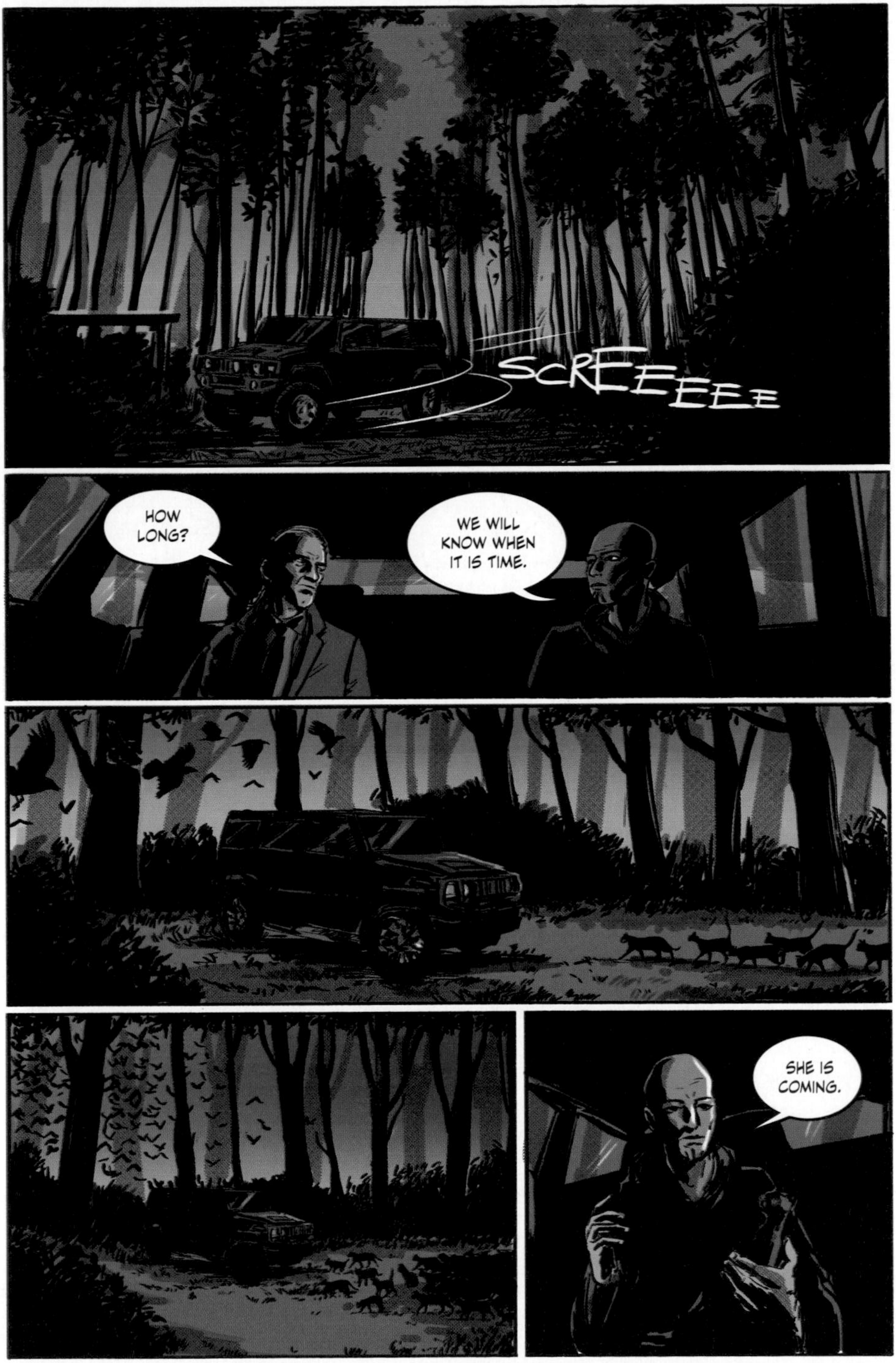
SCREEEEEE
HOW LONG?
WE WILL KNOW WHEN IT IS TIME.
SHE IS COMING.

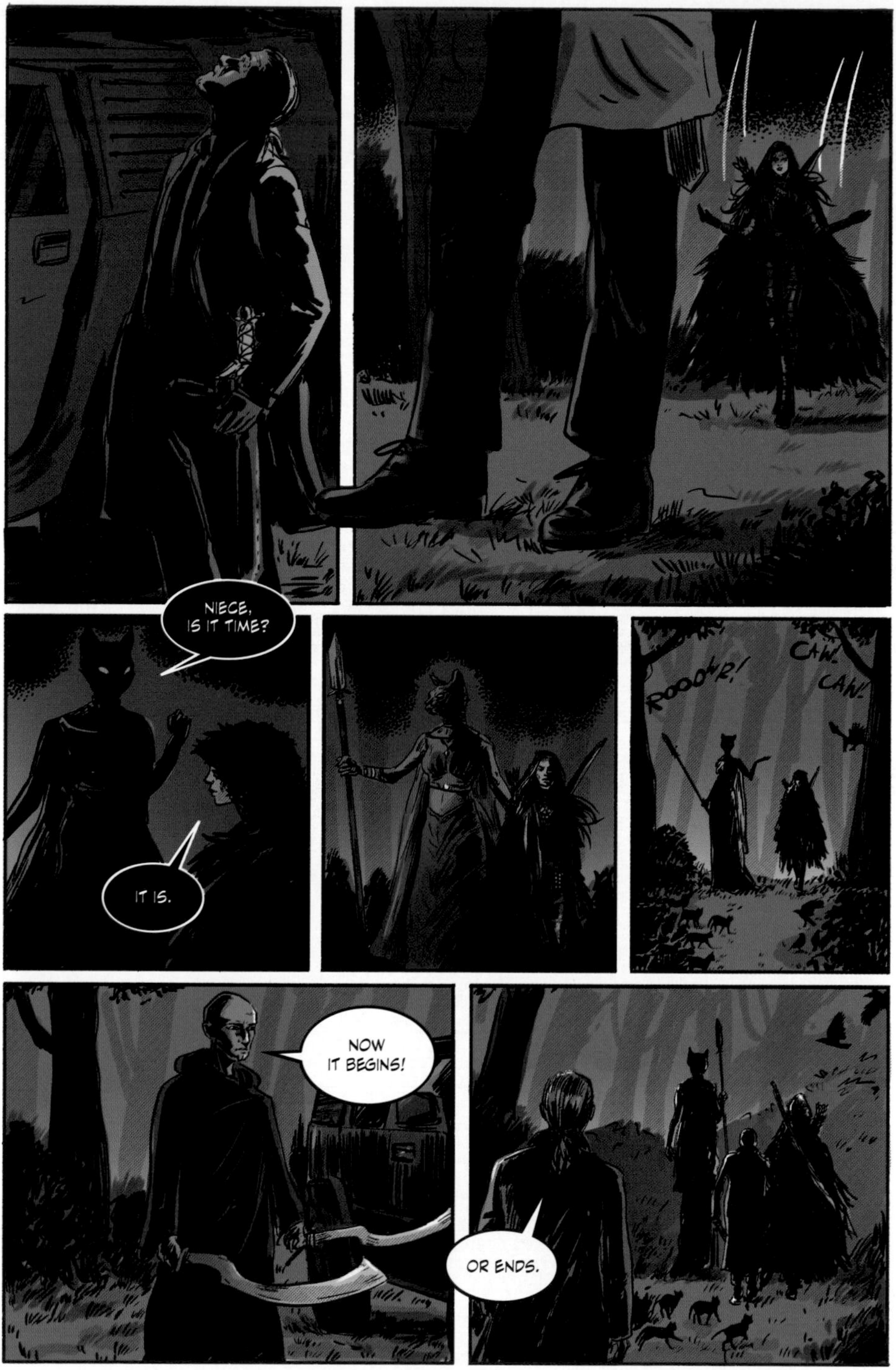
NIECE, IS IT TIME?
IT IS.
ROOOWR!
CAW!
CAW!
NOW IT BEGINS!
OR ENDS.

CHAPTER 24

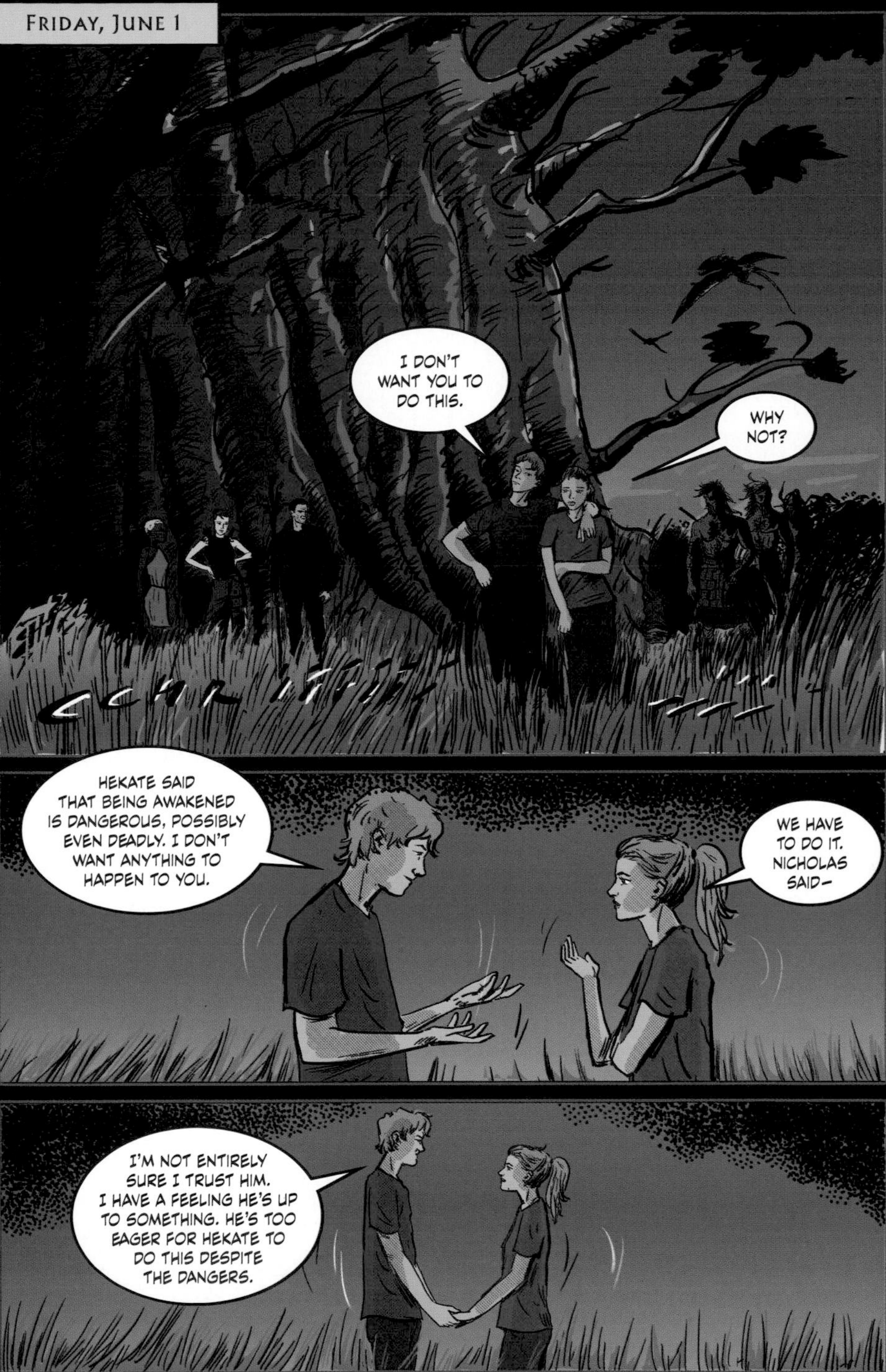
FRIDAY, JUNE 1
I DON'T WANT YOU TO DO THIS.
WHY NOT?
HEKATE SAID THAT BEING AWAKENED IS DANGEROUS, POSSIBLY EVEN DEADLY. I DON'T WANT ANYTHING TO HAPPEN TO YOU.
WE HAVE TO DO IT. NICHOLAS SAID–
I'M NOT ENTIRELY SURE I TRUST HIM. I HAVE A FEELING HE'S UP TO SOMETHING. HE'S TOO EAGER FOR HEKATE TO DO THIS DESPITE THE DANGERS.

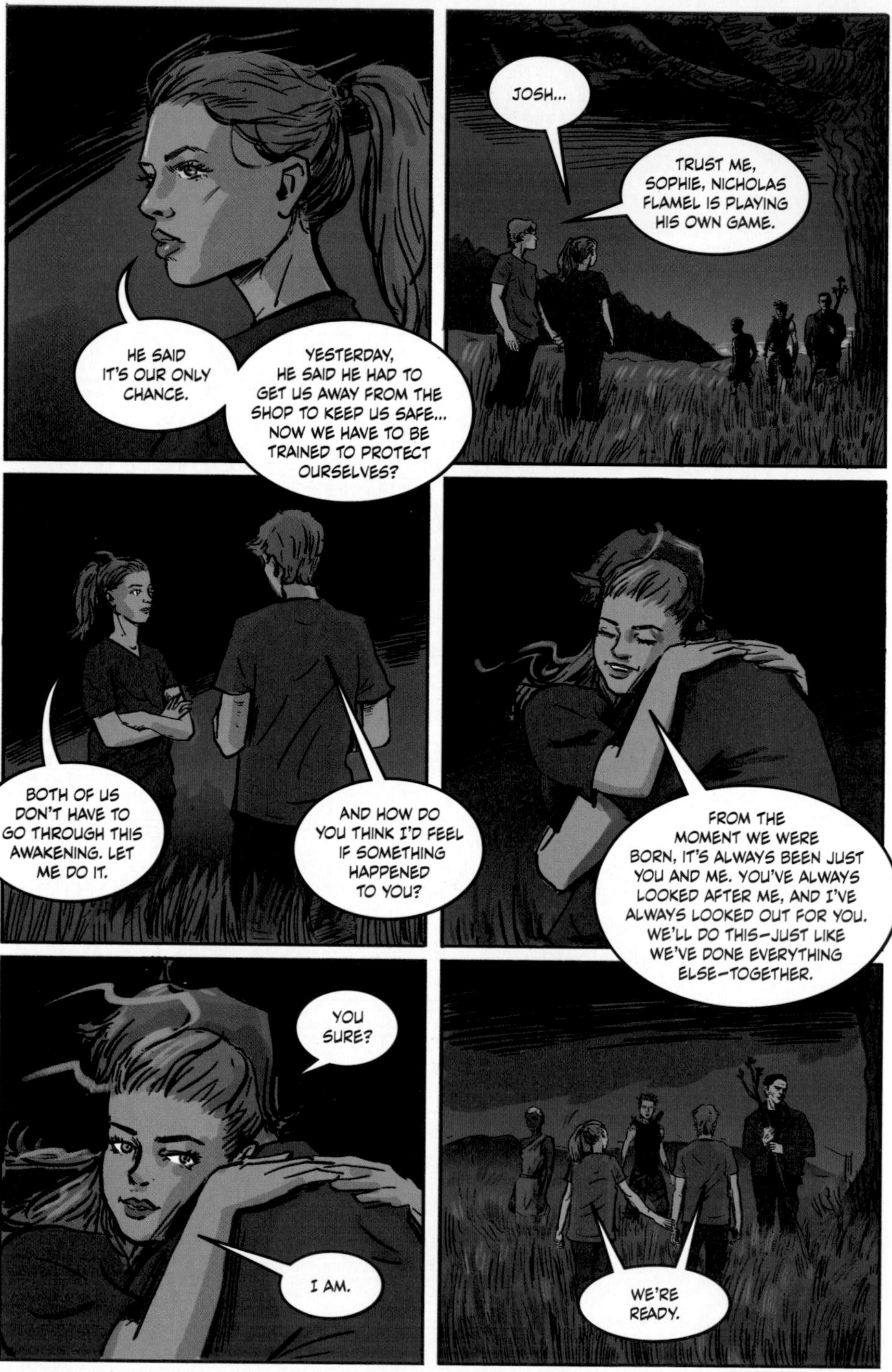
HE SAID IT'S OUR ONLY CHANCE.
YESTERDAY, HE SAID HE HAD TO GET US AWAY FROM THE SHOP TO KEEP US SAFE... NOW WE HAVE TO BE TRAINED TO PROTECT OURSELVES?
JOSH...
TRUST ME, SOPHIE, NICHOLAS FLAMEL IS PLAYING HIS OWN GAME.
BOTH OF US DON'T HAVE TO GO THROUGH THIS AWAKENING. LET ME DO IT.
AND HOW DO YOU THINK I'D FEEL IF SOMETHING HAPPENED TO YOU?
FROM THE MOMENT WE WERE BORN, IT'S ALWAYS BEEN JUST YOU AND ME. YOU'VE ALWAYS LOOKED AFTER ME, AND I'VE ALWAYS LOOKED OUT FOR YOU. WE'LL DO THIS—JUST LIKE WE'VE DONE EVERYTHING ELSE—TOGETHER.
YOU SURE?
I AM.
WE'RE READY.

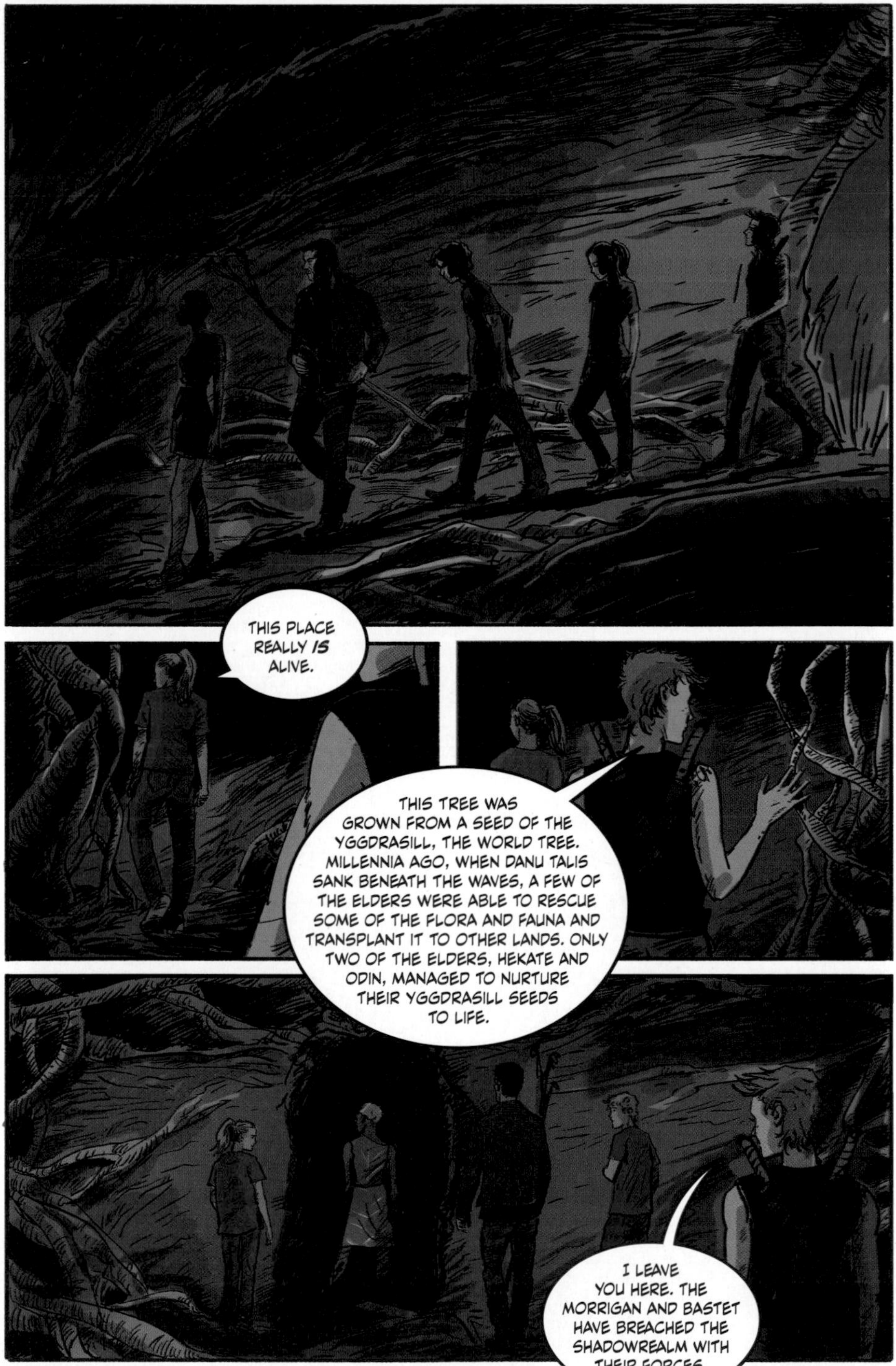
THIS PLACE REALLY *IS* ALIVE.
THIS TREE WAS GROWN FROM A SEED OF THE YGGDRASILL, THE WORLD TREE. MILLENNIA AGO, WHEN DANU TALIS SANK BENEATH THE WAVES, A FEW OF THE ELDERS WERE ABLE TO RESCUE SOME OF THE FLORA AND FAUNA AND TRANSPLANT IT TO OTHER LANDS. ONLY TWO OF THE ELDERS, HEKATE AND ODIN, MANAGED TO NURTURE THEIR YGGDRASILL SEEDS TO LIFE.
I LEAVE YOU HERE. THE MORRIGAN AND BASTET HAVE BREACHED THE SHADOWREALM WITH THEIR FORCES.

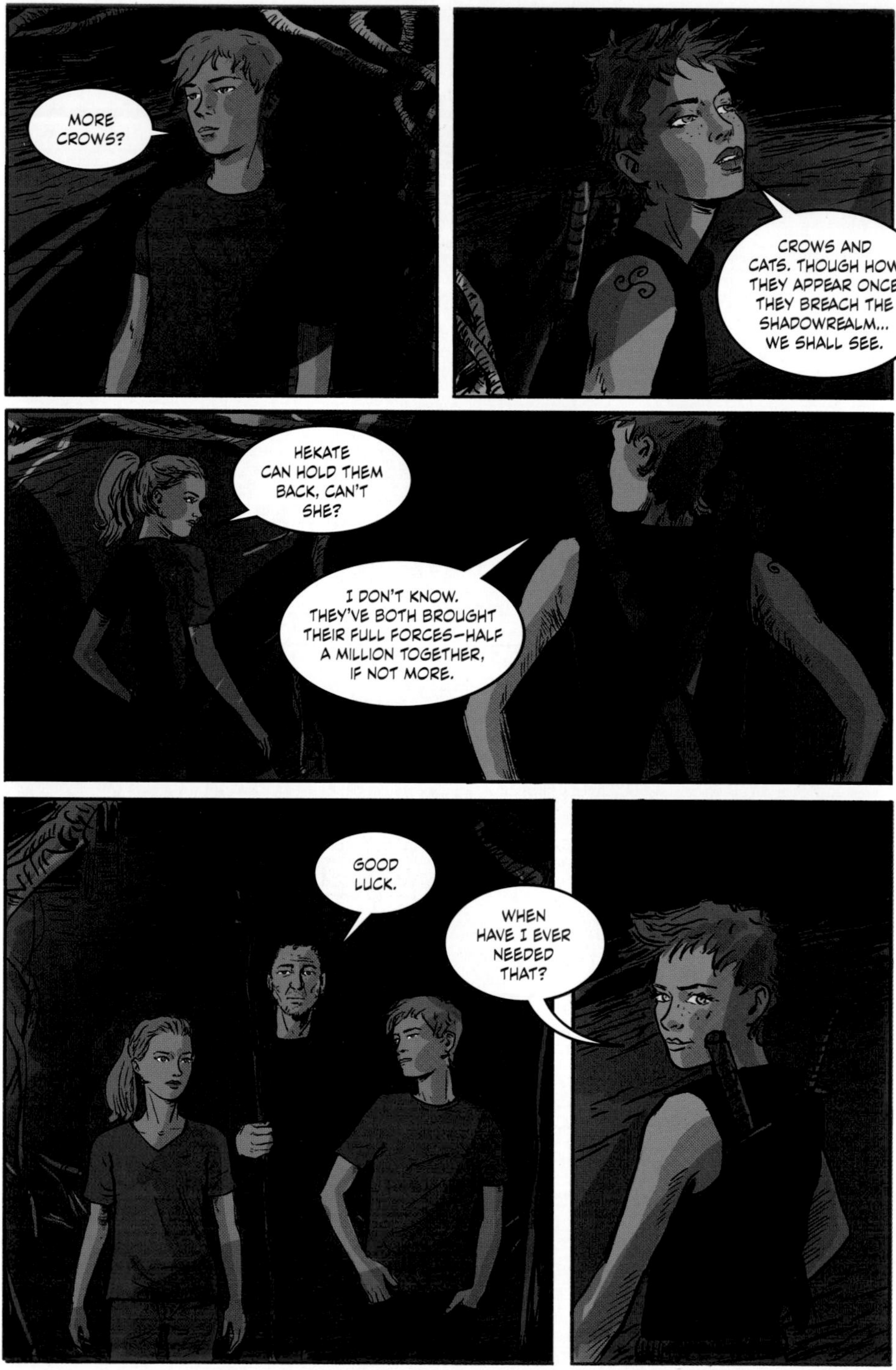
MORE CROWS?
CROWS AND CATS. THOUGH HOW THEY APPEAR ONCE THEY BREACH THE SHADOWREALM... WE SHALL SEE.
HEKATE CAN HOLD THEM BACK, CAN'T SHE?
I DON'T KNOW. THEY'VE BOTH BROUGHT THEIR FULL FORCES—HALF A MILLION TOGETHER, IF NOT MORE.
GOOD LUCK.
WHEN HAVE I EVER NEEDED THAT?

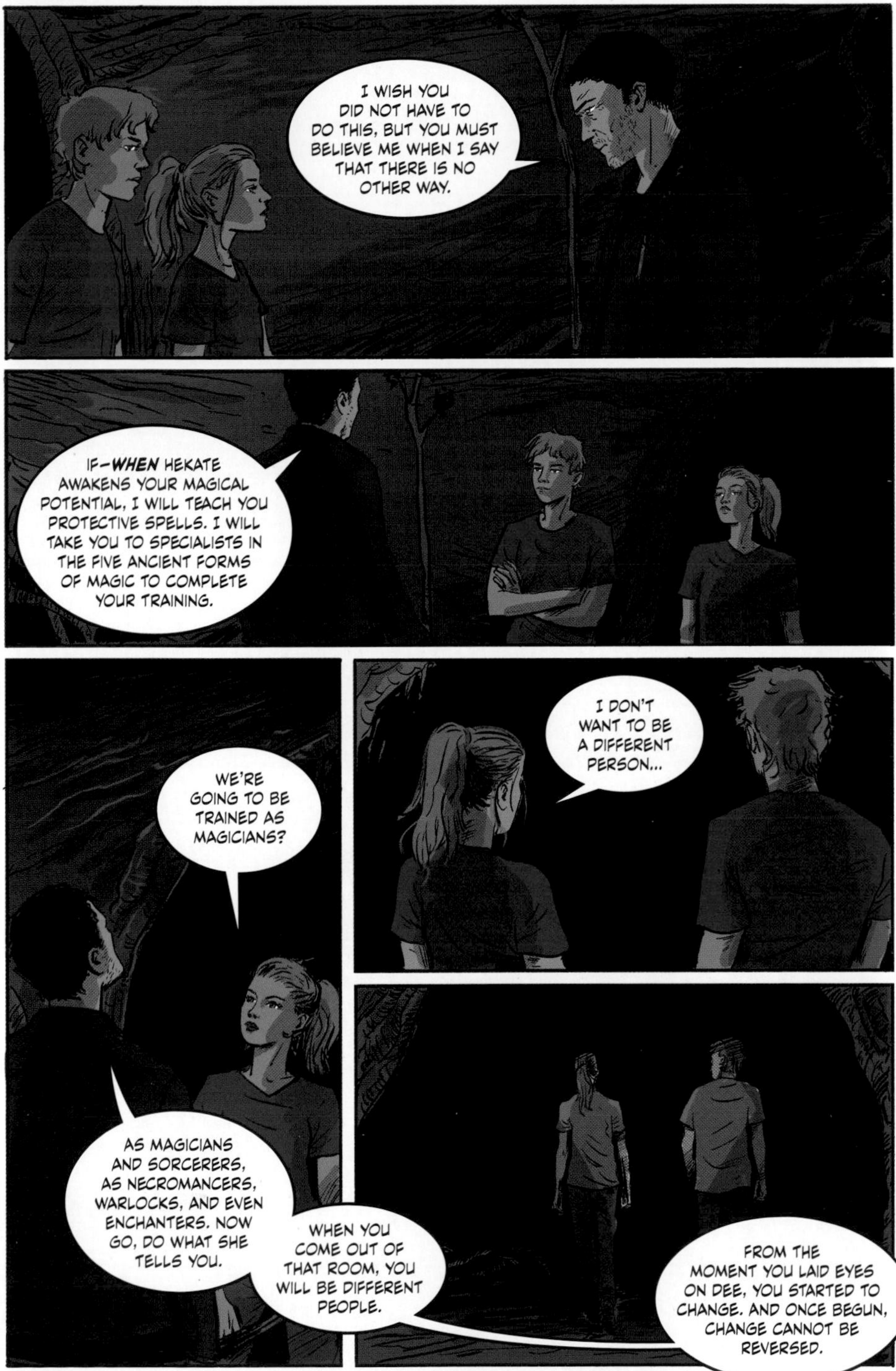
I WISH YOU DID NOT HAVE TO DO THIS, BUT YOU MUST BELIEVE ME WHEN I SAY THAT THERE IS NO OTHER WAY.
IF—*WHEN* HEKATE AWAKENS YOUR MAGICAL POTENTIAL, I WILL TEACH YOU PROTECTIVE SPELLS. I WILL TAKE YOU TO SPECIALISTS IN THE FIVE ANCIENT FORMS OF MAGIC TO COMPLETE YOUR TRAINING.
WE'RE GOING TO BE TRAINED AS MAGICIANS?
AS MAGICIANS AND SORCERERS, AS NECROMANCERS, WARLOCKS, AND EVEN ENCHANTERS. NOW GO, DO WHAT SHE TELLS YOU.
I DON'T WANT TO BE A DIFFERENT PERSON...
WHEN YOU COME OUT OF THAT ROOM, YOU WILL BE DIFFERENT PEOPLE.
FROM THE MOMENT YOU LAID EYES ON DEE, YOU STARTED TO CHANGE. AND ONCE BEGUN, CHANGE CANNOT BE REVERSED.

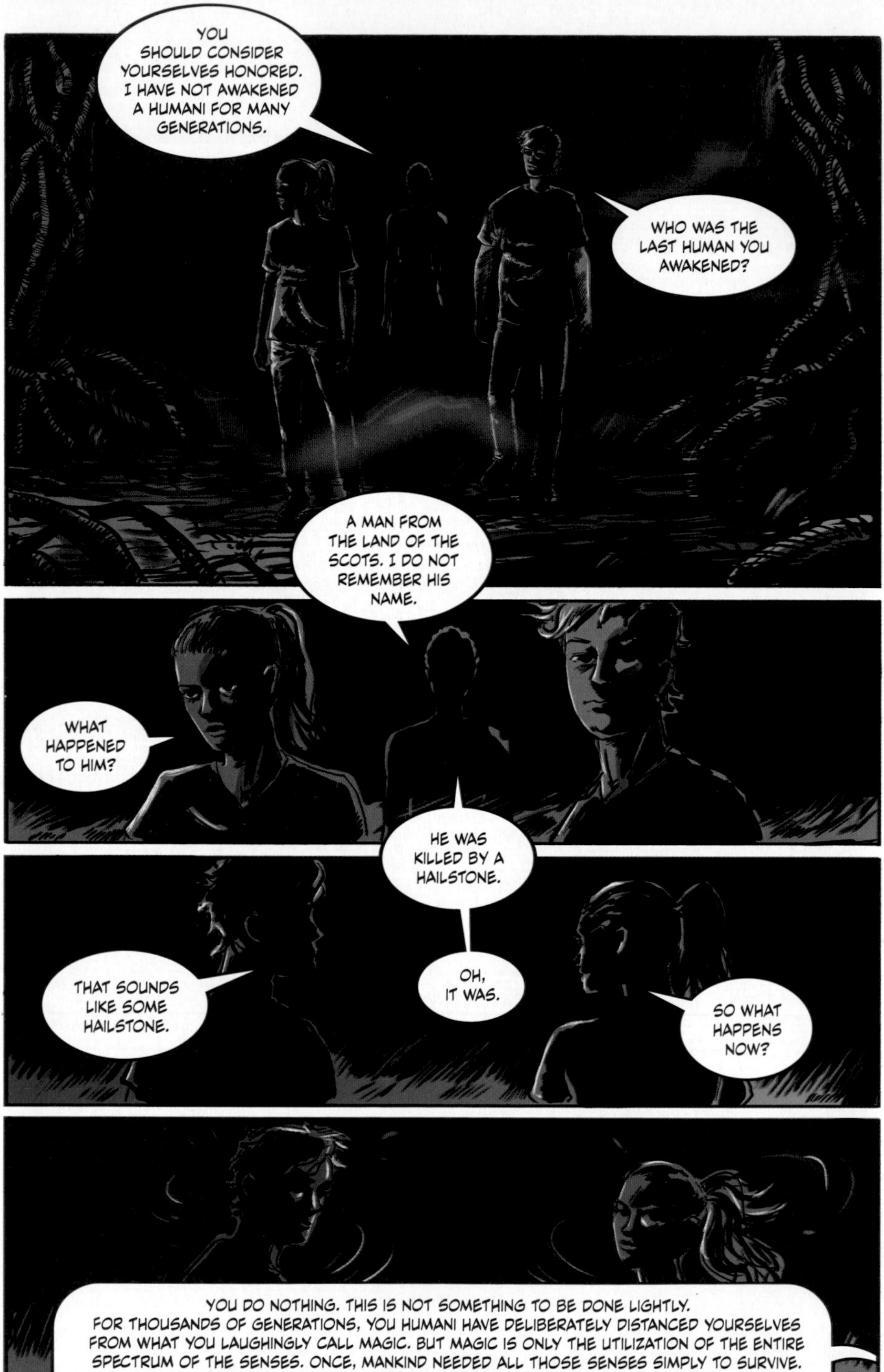
YOU SHOULD CONSIDER YOURSELVES HONORED. I HAVE NOT AWAKENED A HUMANI FOR MANY GENERATIONS.
WHO WAS THE LAST HUMAN YOU AWAKENED?
A MAN FROM THE LAND OF THE SCOTS. I DO NOT REMEMBER HIS NAME.
WHAT HAPPENED TO HIM?
HE WAS KILLED BY A HAILSTONE.
THAT SOUNDS LIKE SOME HAILSTONE.
OH, IT WAS.
SO WHAT HAPPENS NOW?
YOU DO NOTHING. THIS IS NOT SOMETHING TO BE DONE LIGHTLY. FOR THOUSANDS OF GENERATIONS, YOU HUMANI HAVE DELIBERATELY DISTANCED YOURSELVES FROM WHAT YOU LAUGHINGLY CALL MAGIC. BUT MAGIC IS ONLY THE UTILIZATION OF THE ENTIRE SPECTRUM OF THE SENSES. ONCE, MANKIND NEEDED ALL THOSE SENSES SIMPLY TO SURVIVE. THEN DANU TALIS SANK BENEATH THE WAVES, THE AGE OF THE LIZARDS PASSED, THE TIME OF ICE CAME, AND THE HUMANI BECAME ***SOPHISTICATED.*** THEY GREW INDOLENT AND ARROGANT. THEY FOUND THEY DID NOT NEED ALL THEIR SENSES, AND GRADUALLY, THEY LOST THEM.

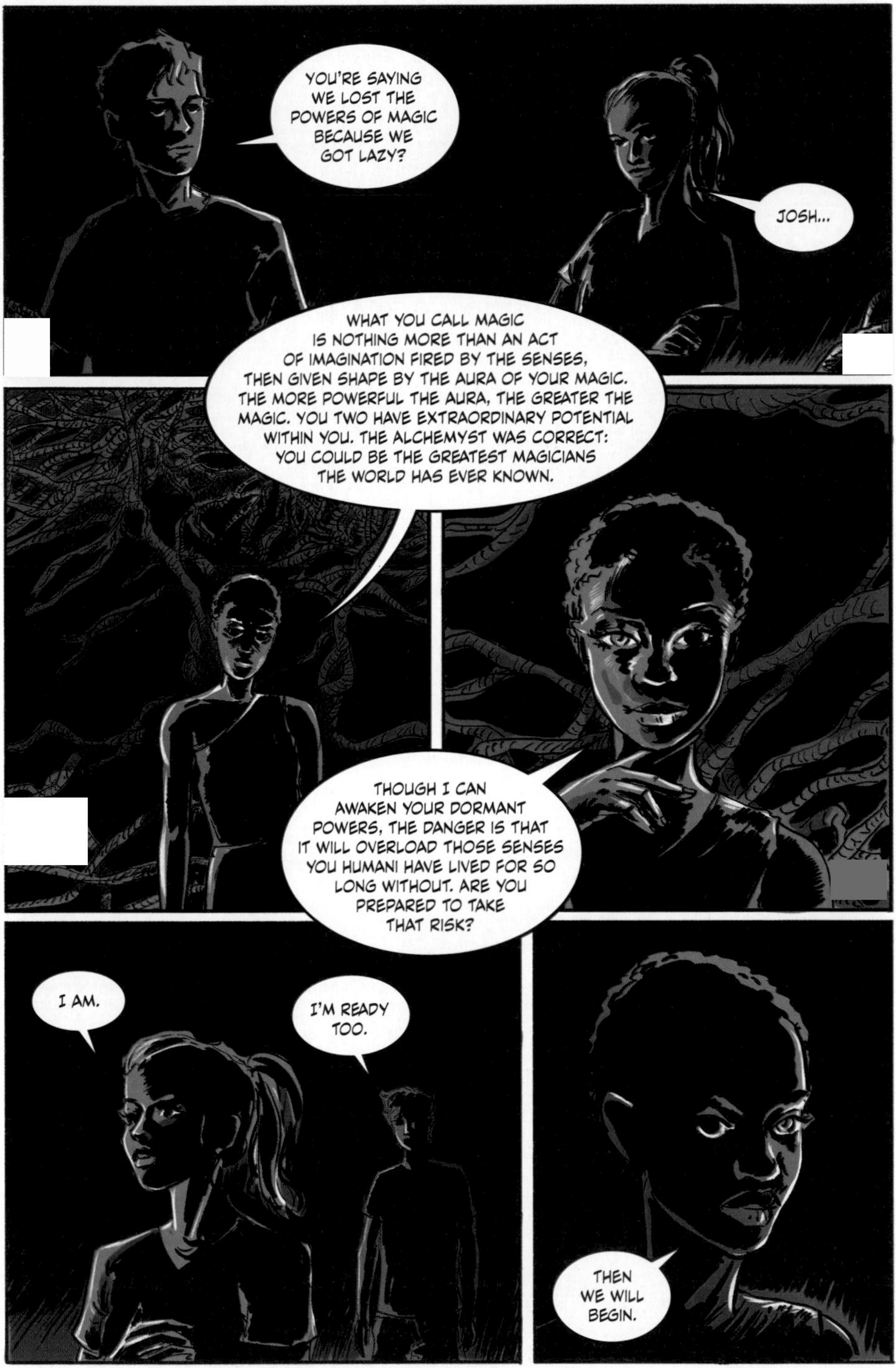
YOU'RE SAYING WE LOST THE POWERS OF MAGIC BECAUSE WE GOT LAZY?
JOSH...
WHAT YOU CALL MAGIC IS NOTHING MORE THAN AN ACT OF IMAGINATION FIRED BY THE SENSES, THEN GIVEN SHAPE BY THE AURA OF YOUR MAGIC. THE MORE POWERFUL THE AURA, THE GREATER THE MAGIC. YOU TWO HAVE EXTRAORDINARY POTENTIAL WITHIN YOU. THE ALCHEMYST WAS CORRECT: YOU COULD BE THE GREATEST MAGICIANS THE WORLD HAS EVER KNOWN.
THOUGH I CAN AWAKEN YOUR DORMANT POWERS, THE DANGER IS THAT IT WILL OVERLOAD THOSE SENSES YOU HUMANI HAVE LIVED FOR SO LONG WITHOUT. ARE YOU PREPARED TO TAKE THAT RISK?
I AM.
I'M READY TOO.
THEN WE WILL BEGIN.

CHAPTER 25

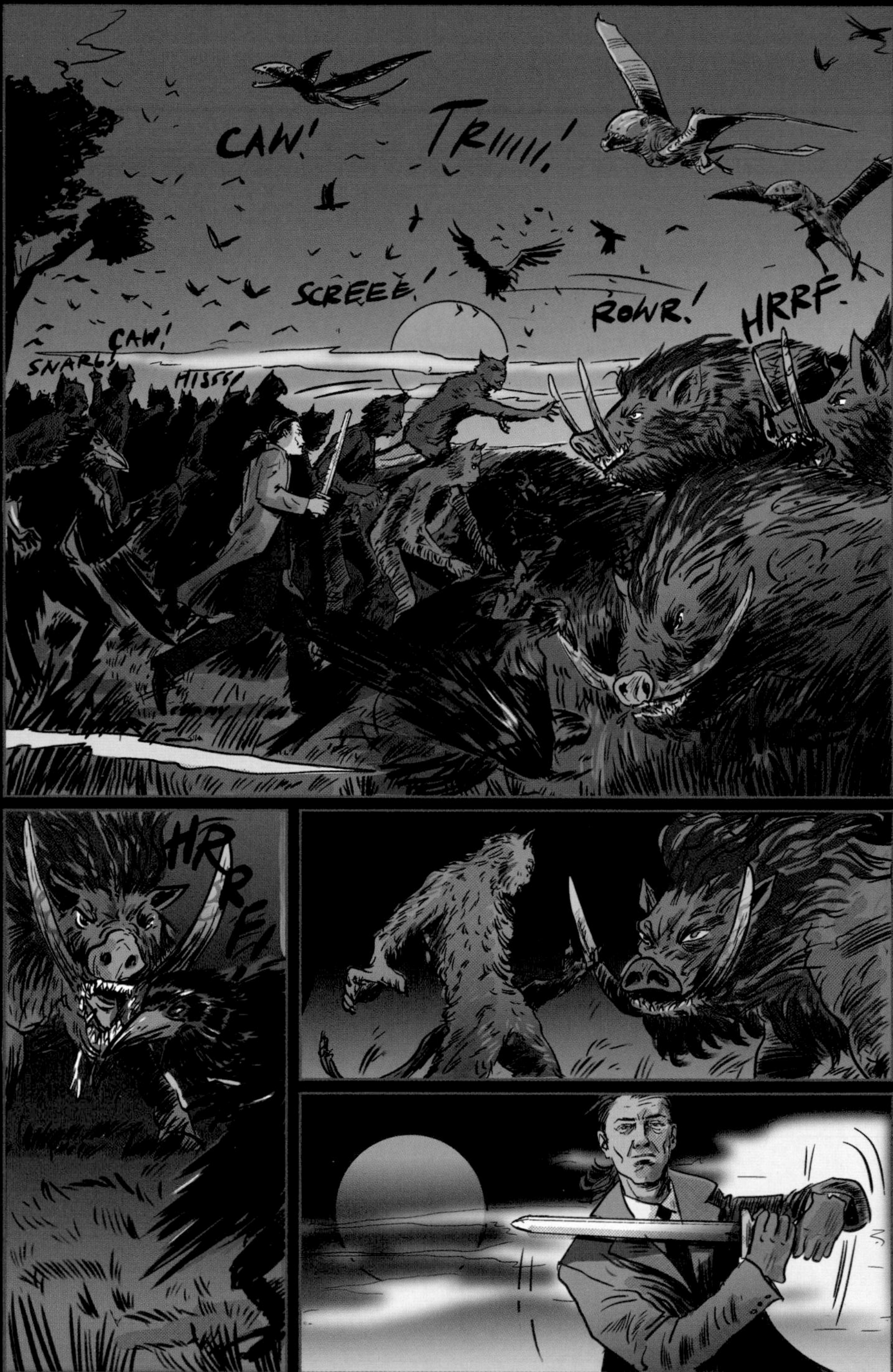
CAW!
TRIIIII!
SCREEE
ROWR!
HRRF.
CAW!
SNARL!
HISSS
HRRF!

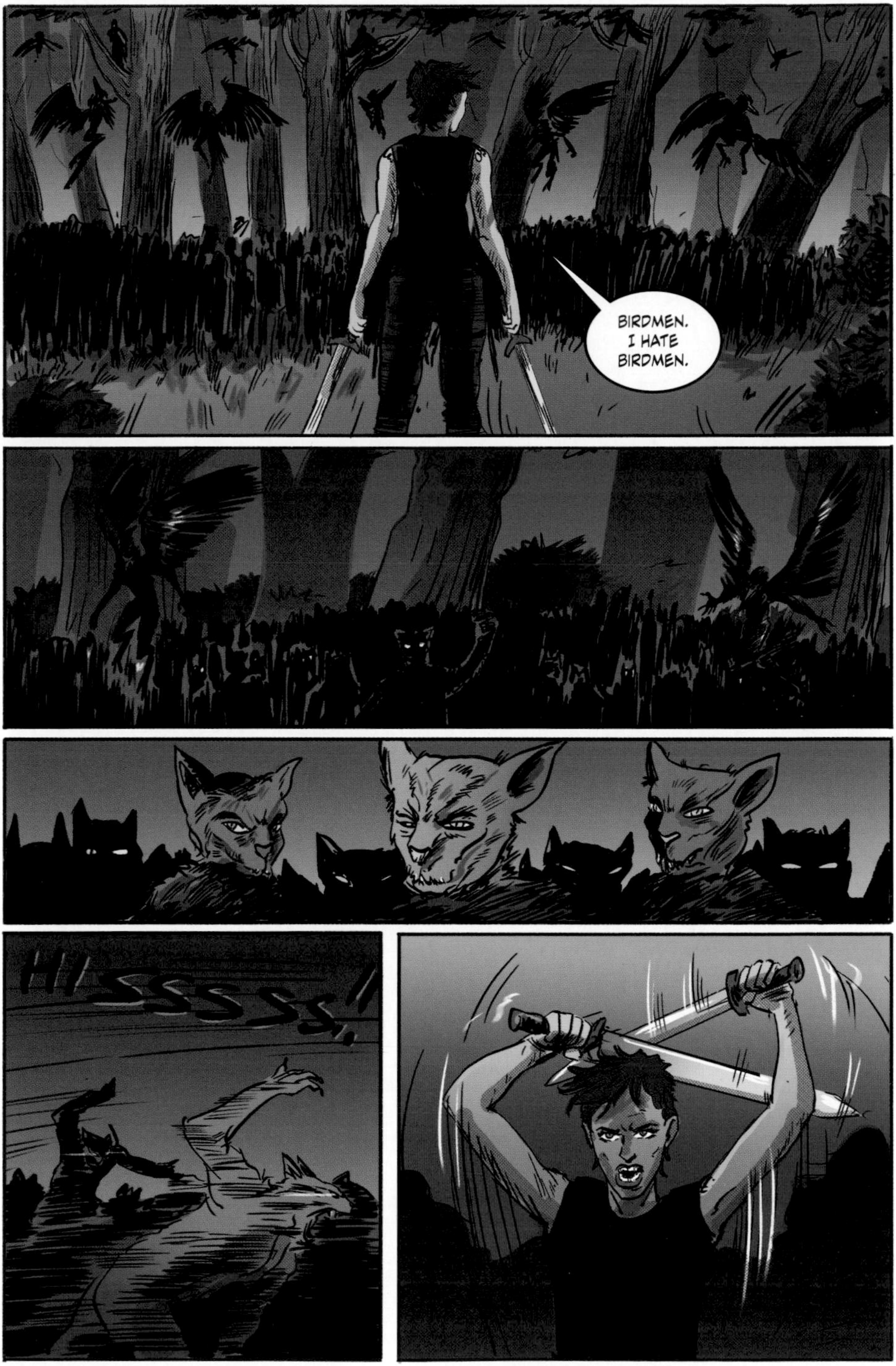
BIRDMEN. I HATE BIRDMEN.
HISSSSSS!!

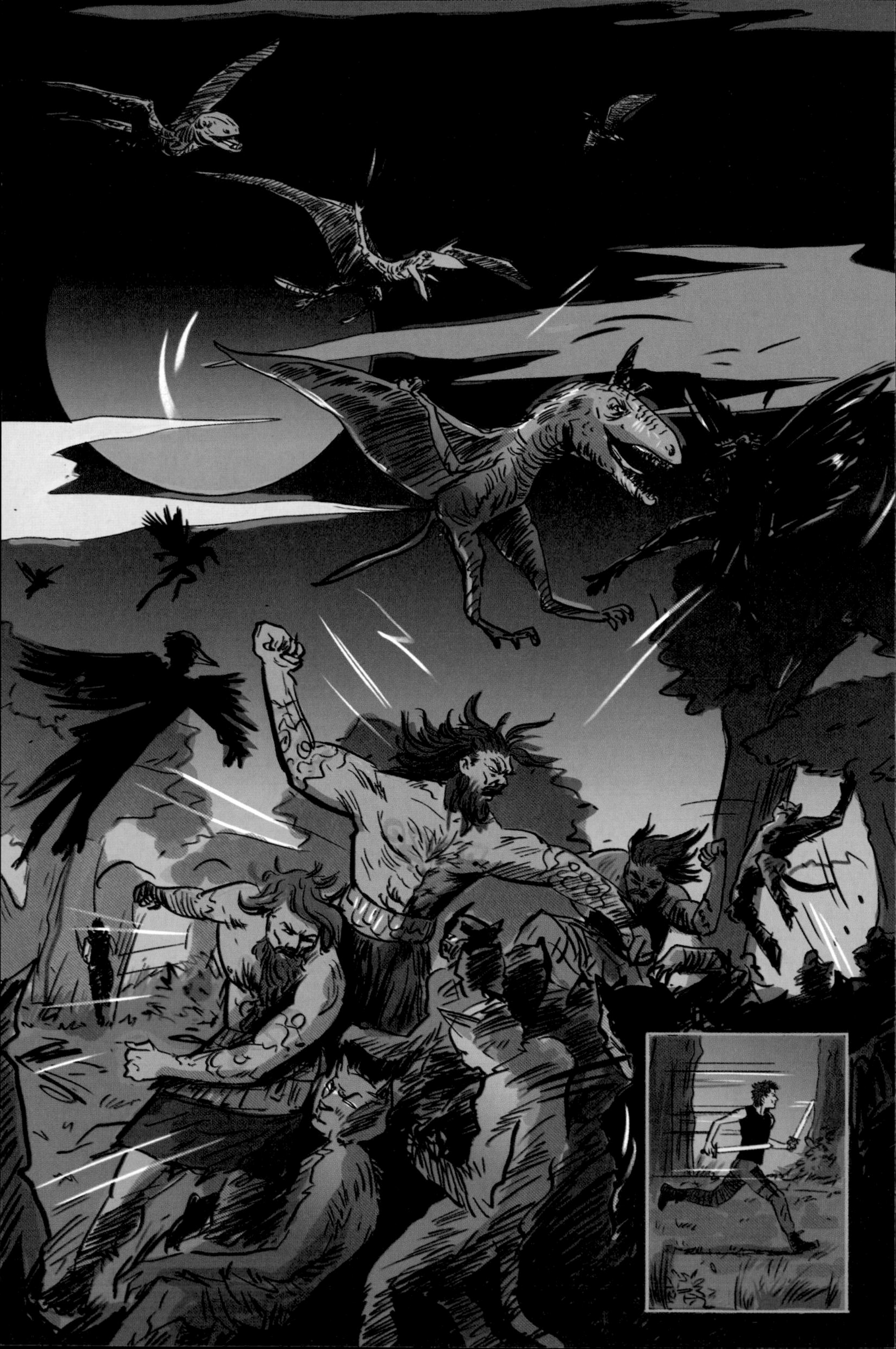

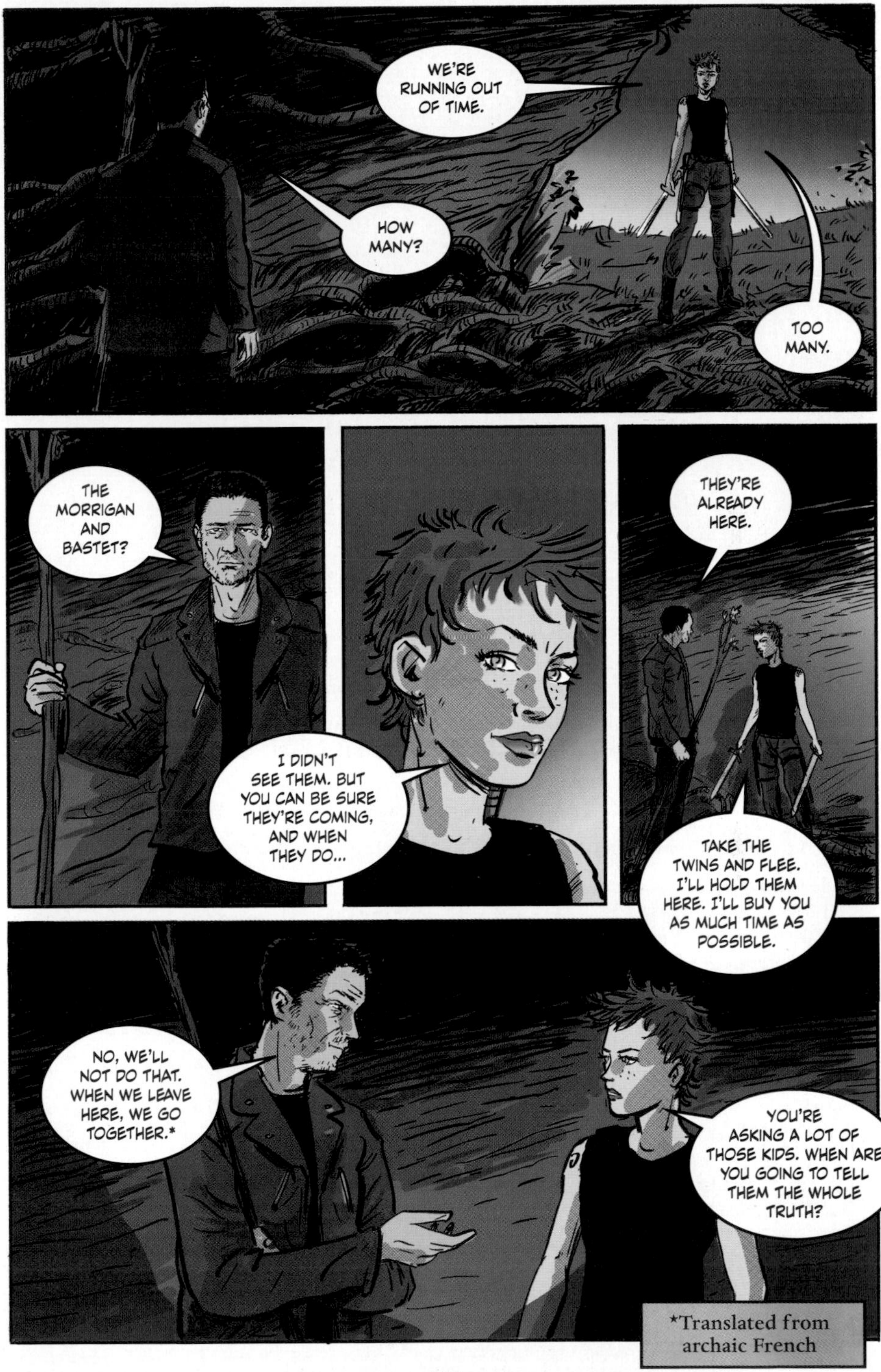
WE'RE RUNNING OUT OF TIME.
HOW MANY?
TOO MANY.
THE MORRIGAN AND BASTET?
I DIDN'T SEE THEM. BUT YOU CAN BE SURE THEY'RE COMING, AND WHEN THEY DO...
THEY'RE ALREADY HERE.
TAKE THE TWINS AND FLEE. I'LL HOLD THEM HERE. I'LL BUY YOU AS MUCH TIME AS POSSIBLE.
NO, WE'LL NOT DO THAT. WHEN WE LEAVE HERE, WE GO TOGETHER.*
YOU'RE ASKING A LOT OF THOSE KIDS. WHEN ARE YOU GOING TO TELL THEM THE WHOLE TRUTH?

*Translated from archaic French

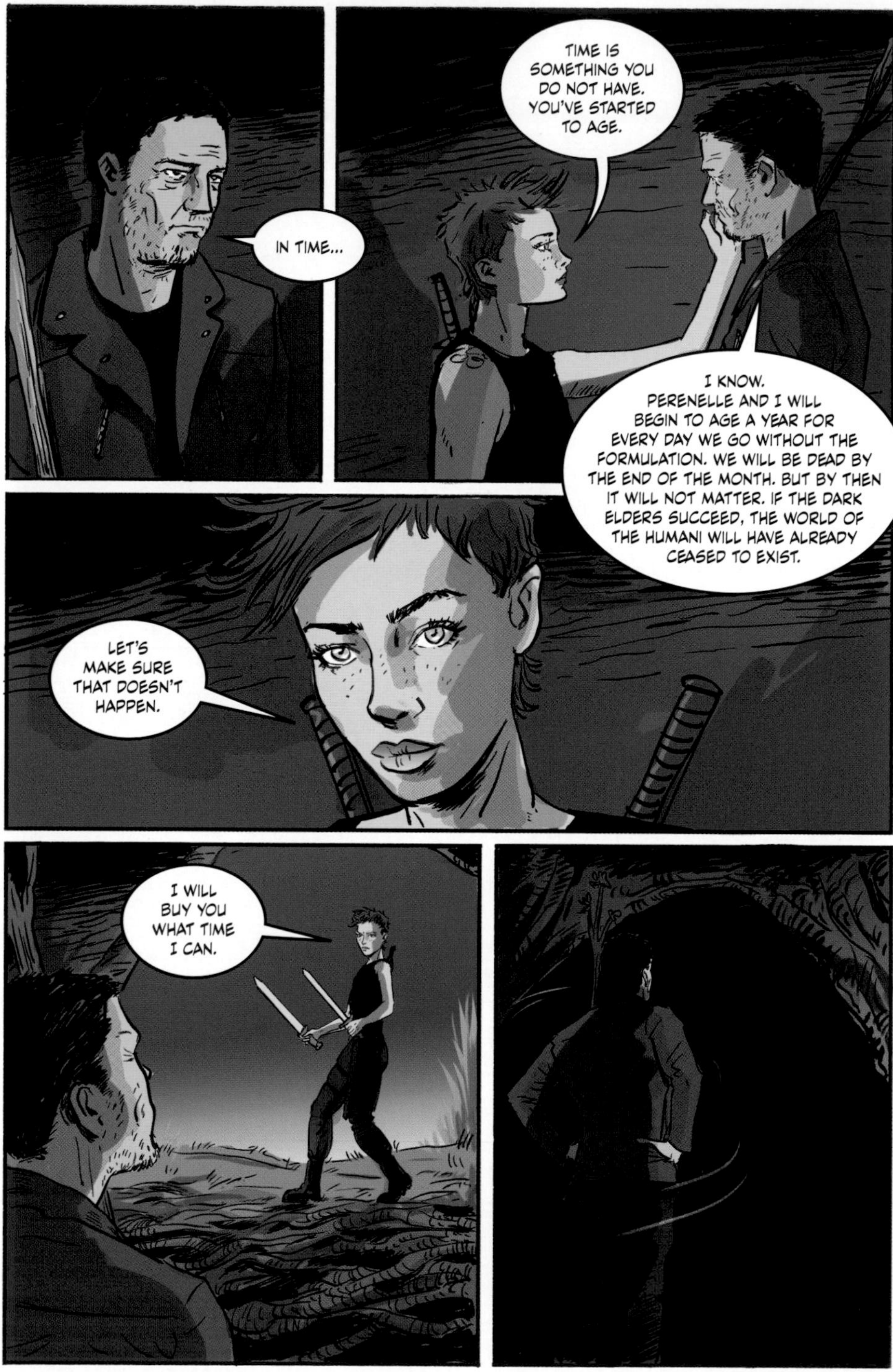
IN TIME...
TIME IS SOMETHING YOU DO NOT HAVE. YOU'VE STARTED TO AGE.
I KNOW. PERENELLE AND I WILL BEGIN TO AGE A YEAR FOR EVERY DAY WE GO WITHOUT THE FORMULATION. WE WILL BE DEAD BY THE END OF THE MONTH. BUT BY THEN IT WILL NOT MATTER. IF THE DARK ELDERS SUCCEED, THE WORLD OF THE HUMANI WILL HAVE ALREADY CEASED TO EXIST.
LET'S MAKE SURE THAT DOESN'T HAPPEN.
I WILL BUY YOU WHAT TIME I CAN.

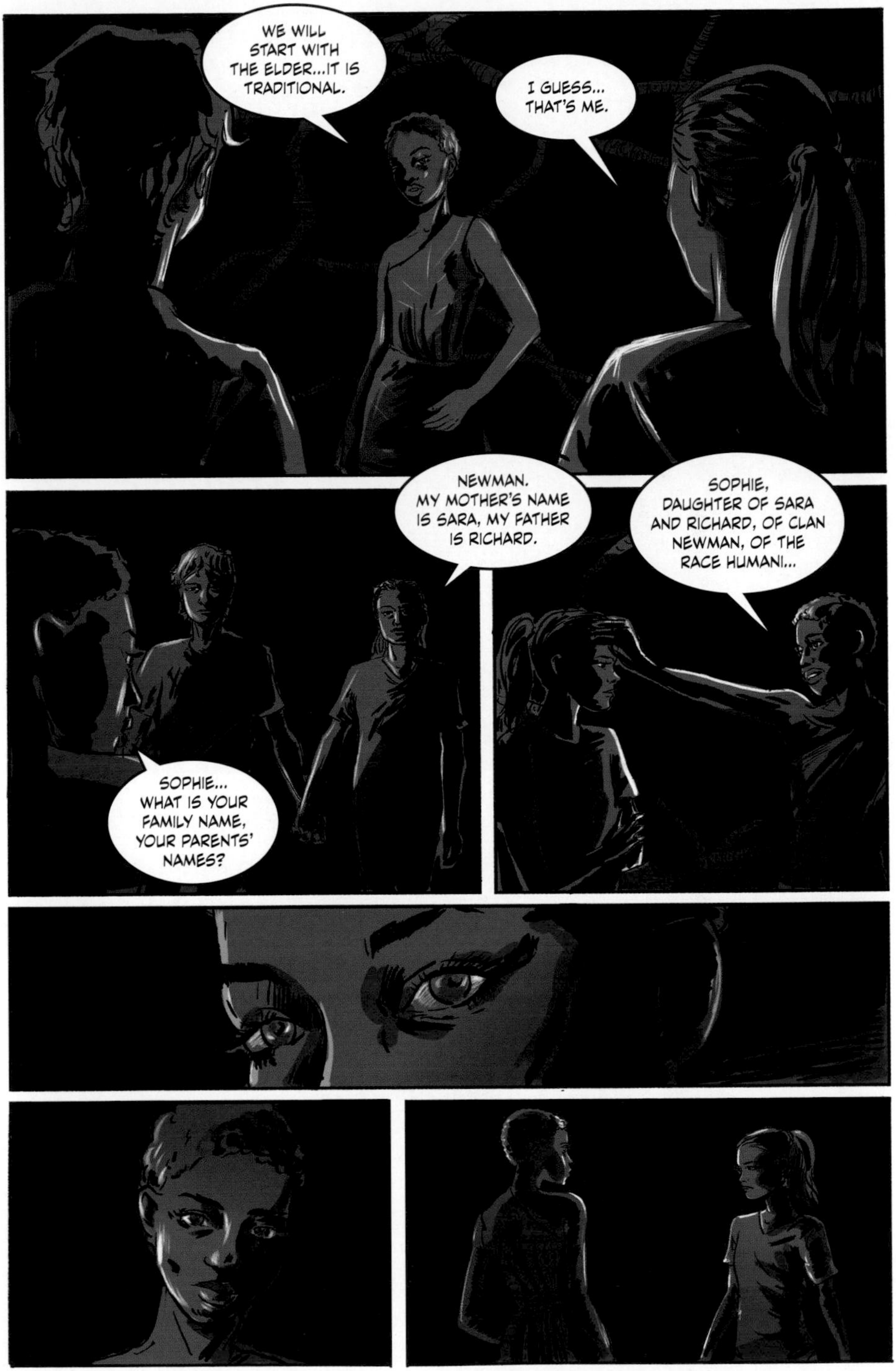
WE WILL START WITH THE ELDER...IT IS TRADITIONAL.
I GUESS... THAT'S ME.
SOPHIE... WHAT IS YOUR FAMILY NAME, YOUR PARENTS' NAMES?
NEWMAN. MY MOTHER'S NAME IS SARA, MY FATHER IS RICHARD.
SOPHIE, DAUGHTER OF SARA AND RICHARD, OF CLAN NEWMAN, OF THE RACE HUMANI...

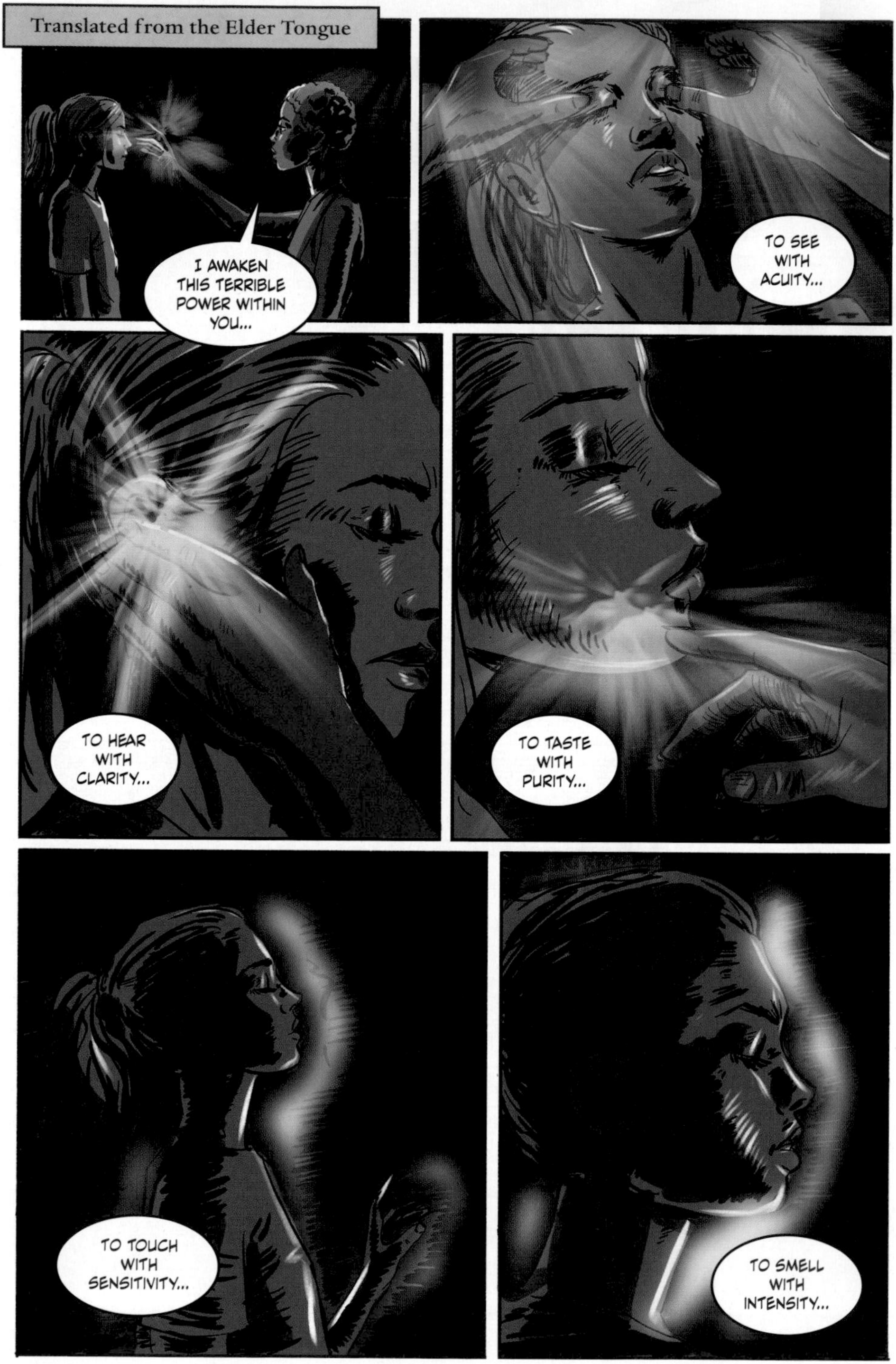
Translated from the Elder Tongue
I AWAKEN THIS TERRIBLE POWER WITHIN YOU...
TO SEE WITH ACUITY...
TO HEAR WITH CLARITY...
TO TASTE WITH PURITY...
TO TOUCH WITH SENSITIVITY...
TO SMELL WITH INTENSITY...

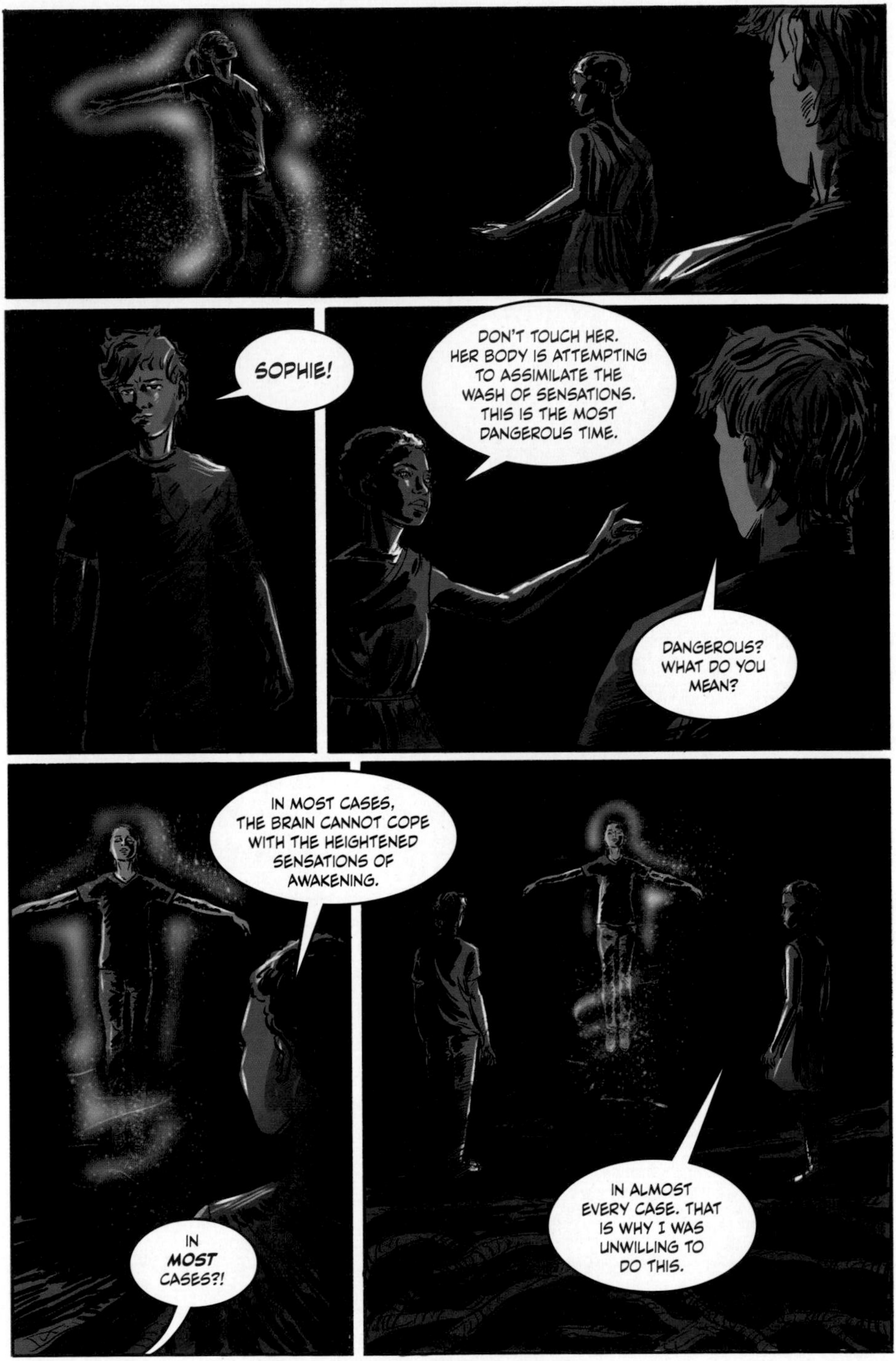
SOPHIE!
DON'T TOUCH HER. HER BODY IS ATTEMPTING TO ASSIMILATE THE WASH OF SENSATIONS. THIS IS THE MOST DANGEROUS TIME.
DANGEROUS? WHAT DO YOU MEAN?
IN MOST CASES, THE BRAIN CANNOT COPE WITH THE HEIGHTENED SENSATIONS OF AWAKENING.
IN MOST CASES?!
IN ALMOST EVERY CASE. THAT IS WHY I WAS UNWILLING TO DO THIS.

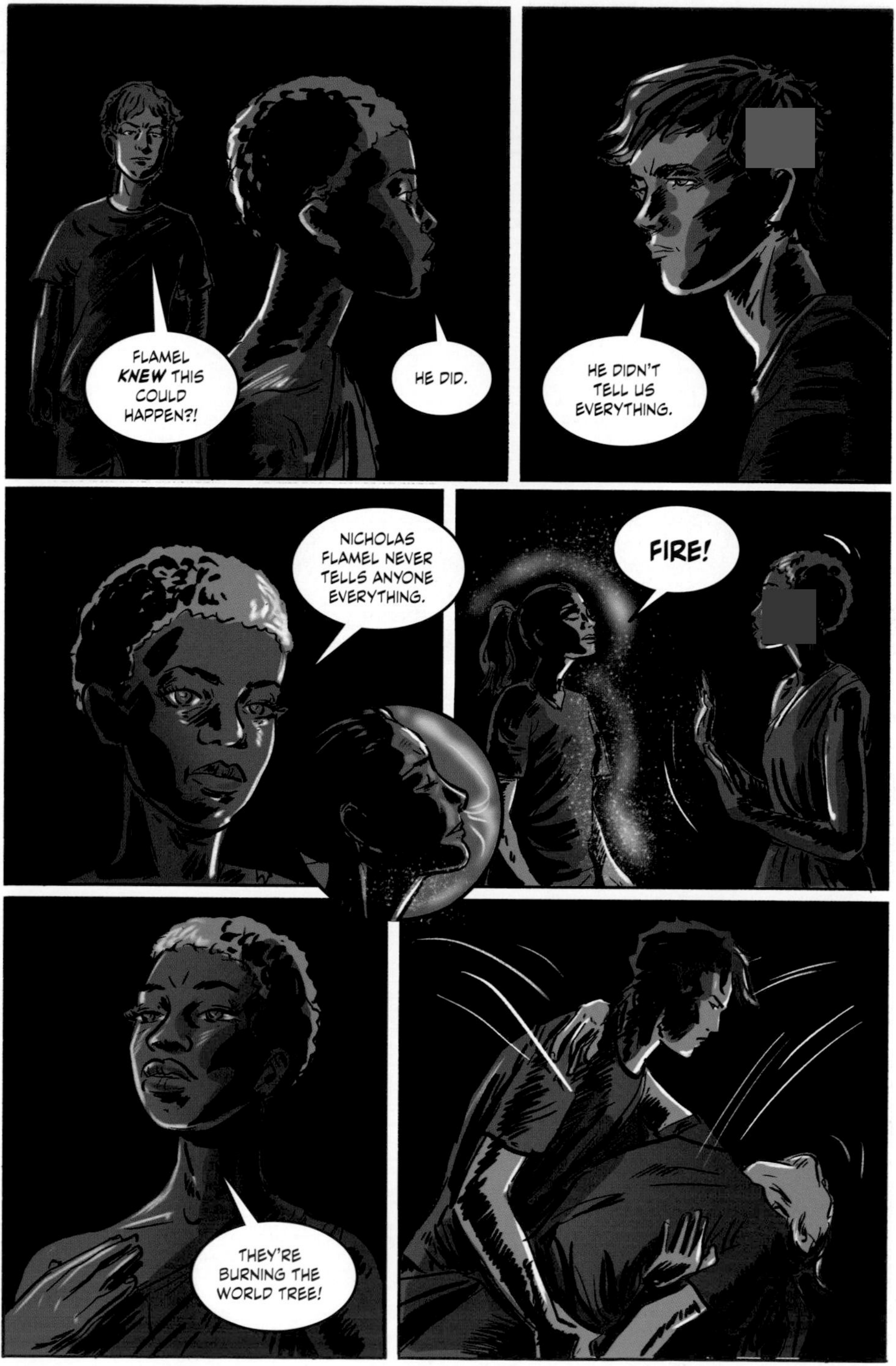
FLAMEL **KNEW** THIS COULD HAPPEN?!
HE DID.
HE DIDN'T TELL US EVERYTHING.
NICHOLAS FLAMEL NEVER TELLS ANYONE EVERYTHING.
FIRE!
THEY'RE BURNING THE WORLD TREE!

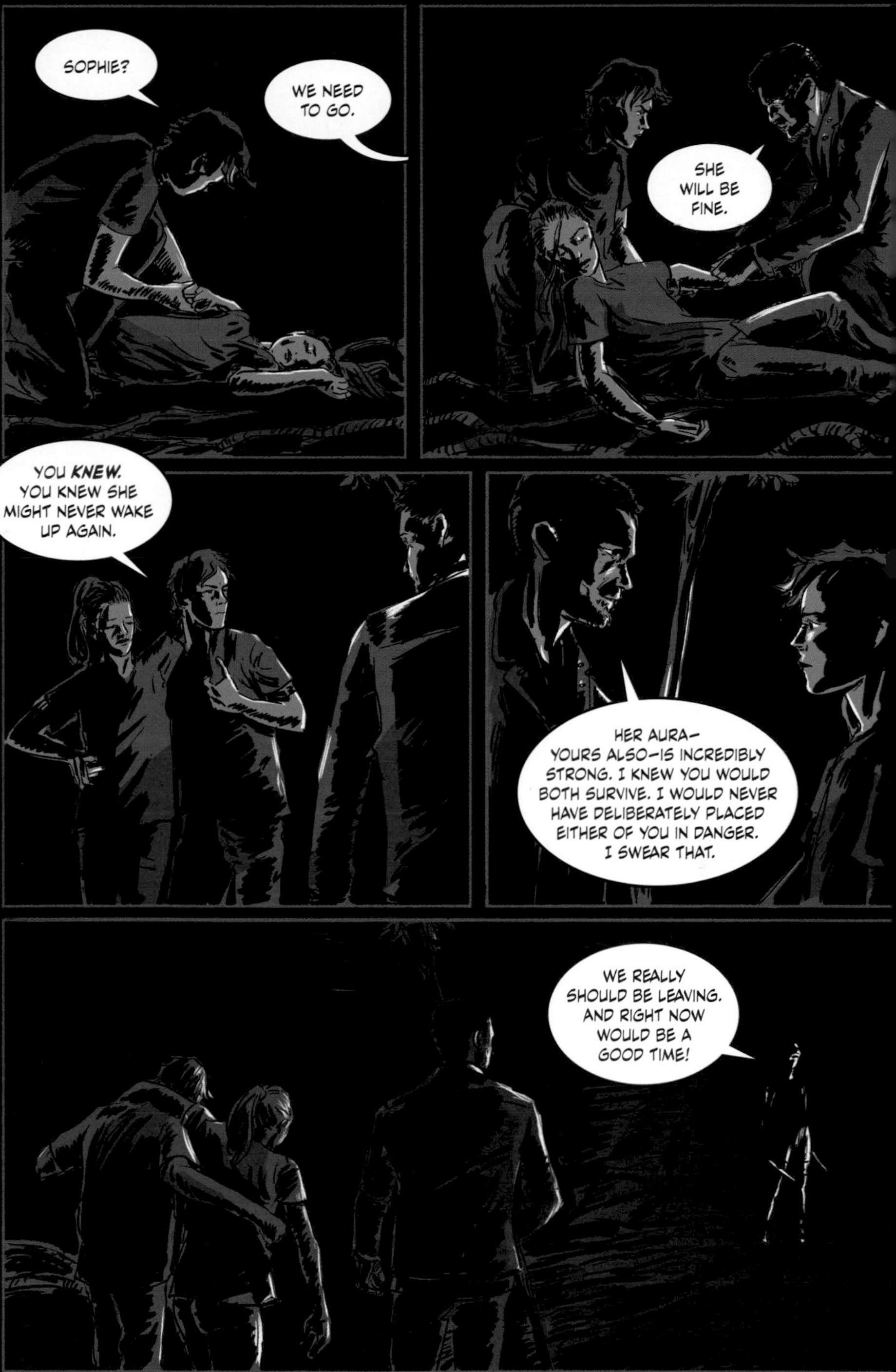
SOPHIE?
WE NEED TO GO.
SHE WILL BE FINE.
YOU **KNEW.** YOU KNEW SHE MIGHT NEVER WAKE UP AGAIN.
HER AURA— YOURS ALSO—IS INCREDIBLY STRONG. I KNEW YOU WOULD BOTH SURVIVE. I WOULD NEVER HAVE DELIBERATELY PLACED EITHER OF YOU IN DANGER. I SWEAR THAT.
WE REALLY SHOULD BE LEAVING. AND RIGHT NOW WOULD BE A GOOD TIME!

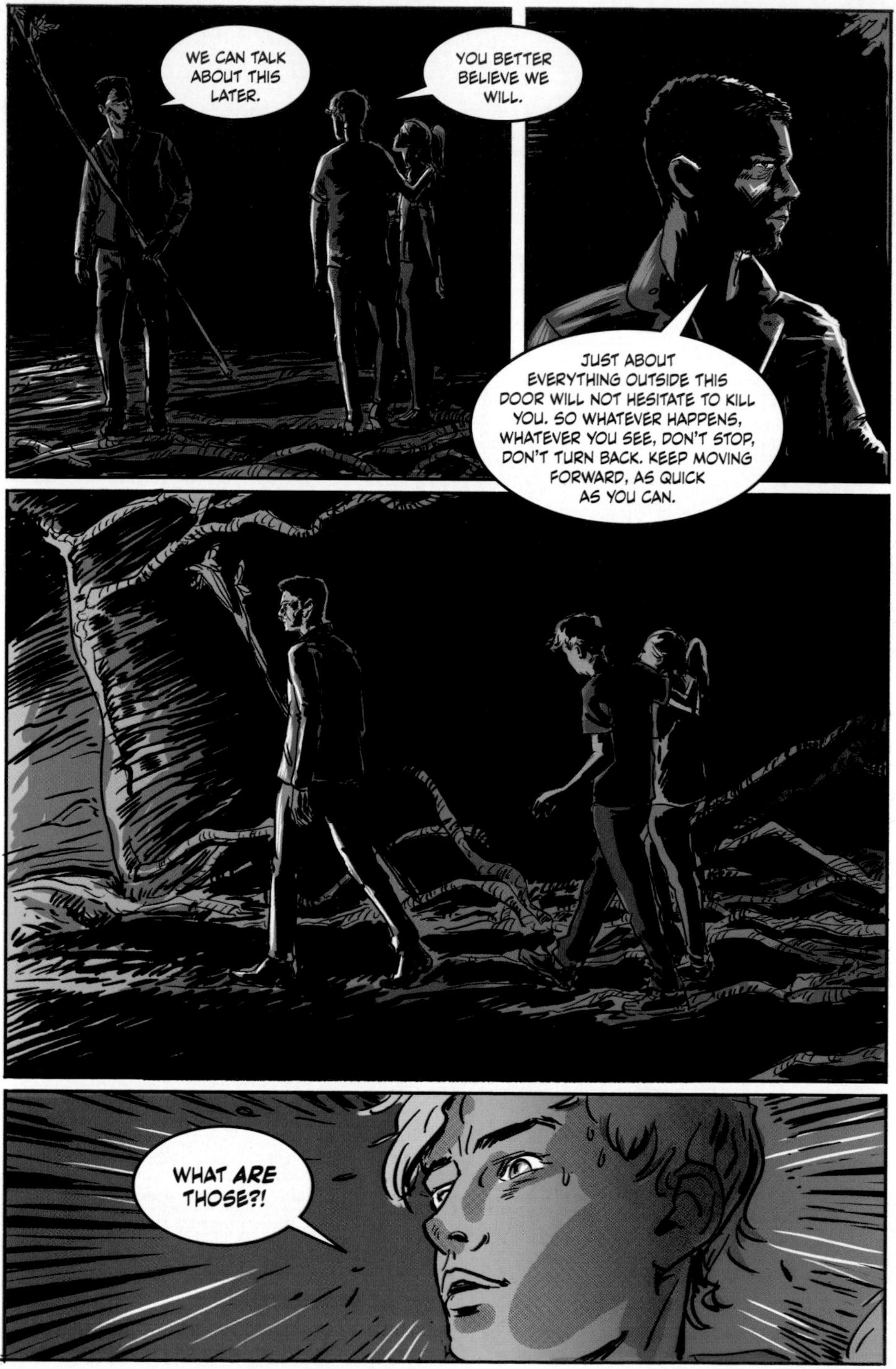
WE CAN TALK ABOUT THIS LATER.
YOU BETTER BELIEVE WE WILL.
JUST ABOUT EVERYTHING OUTSIDE THIS DOOR WILL NOT HESITATE TO KILL YOU. SO WHATEVER HAPPENS, WHATEVER YOU SEE, DON'T STOP, DON'T TURN BACK. KEEP MOVING FORWARD, AS QUICK AS YOU CAN.
WHAT ARE THOSE?!

SCATTY-
DOWN!

SCREEE!

YoOOOWL!

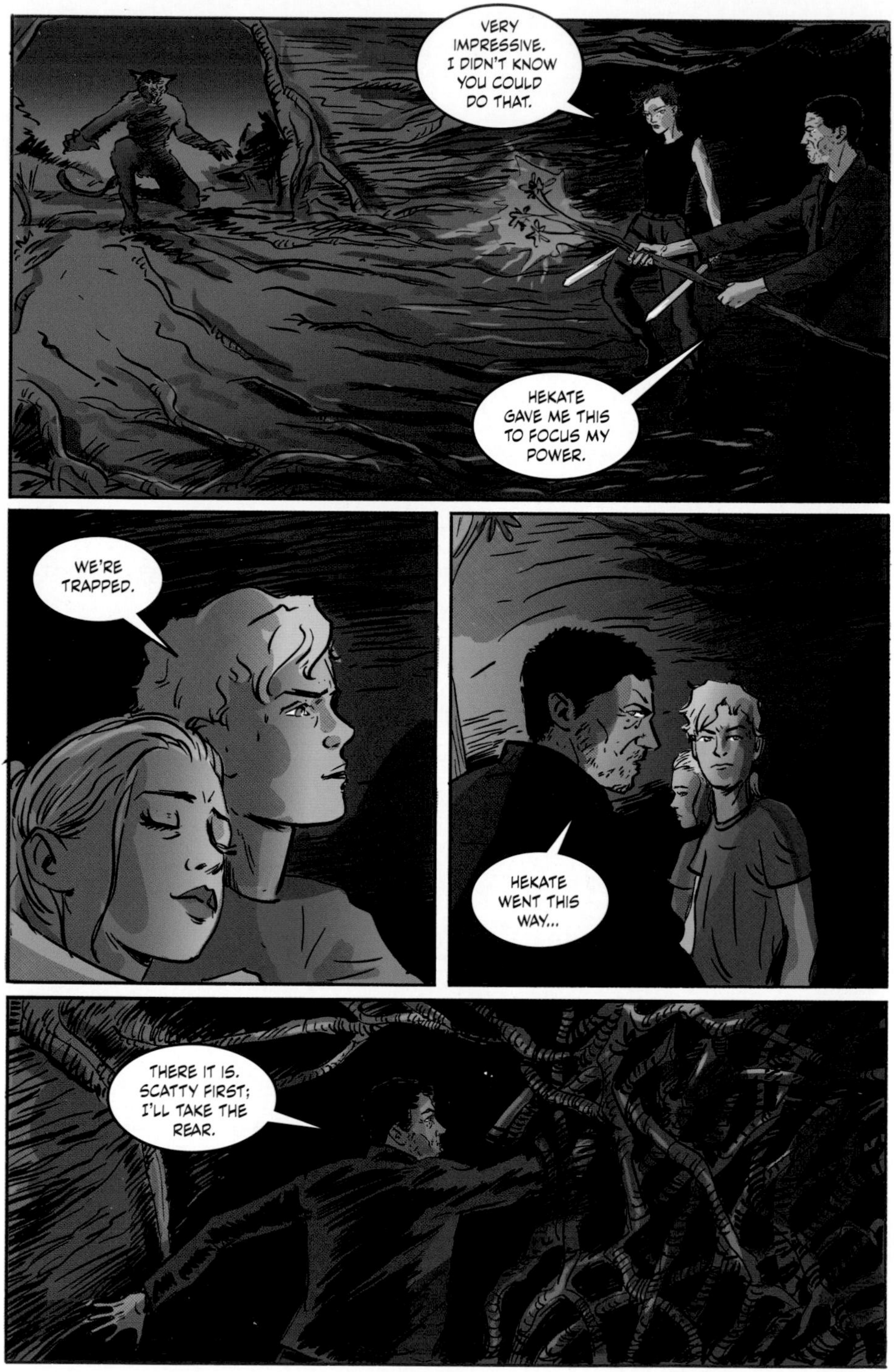
VERY IMPRESSIVE. I DIDN'T KNOW YOU COULD DO THAT.
HEKATE GAVE ME THIS TO FOCUS MY POWER.
WE'RE TRAPPED.
HEKATE WENT THIS WAY...
THERE IT IS. SCATTY FIRST; I'LL TAKE THE REAR.

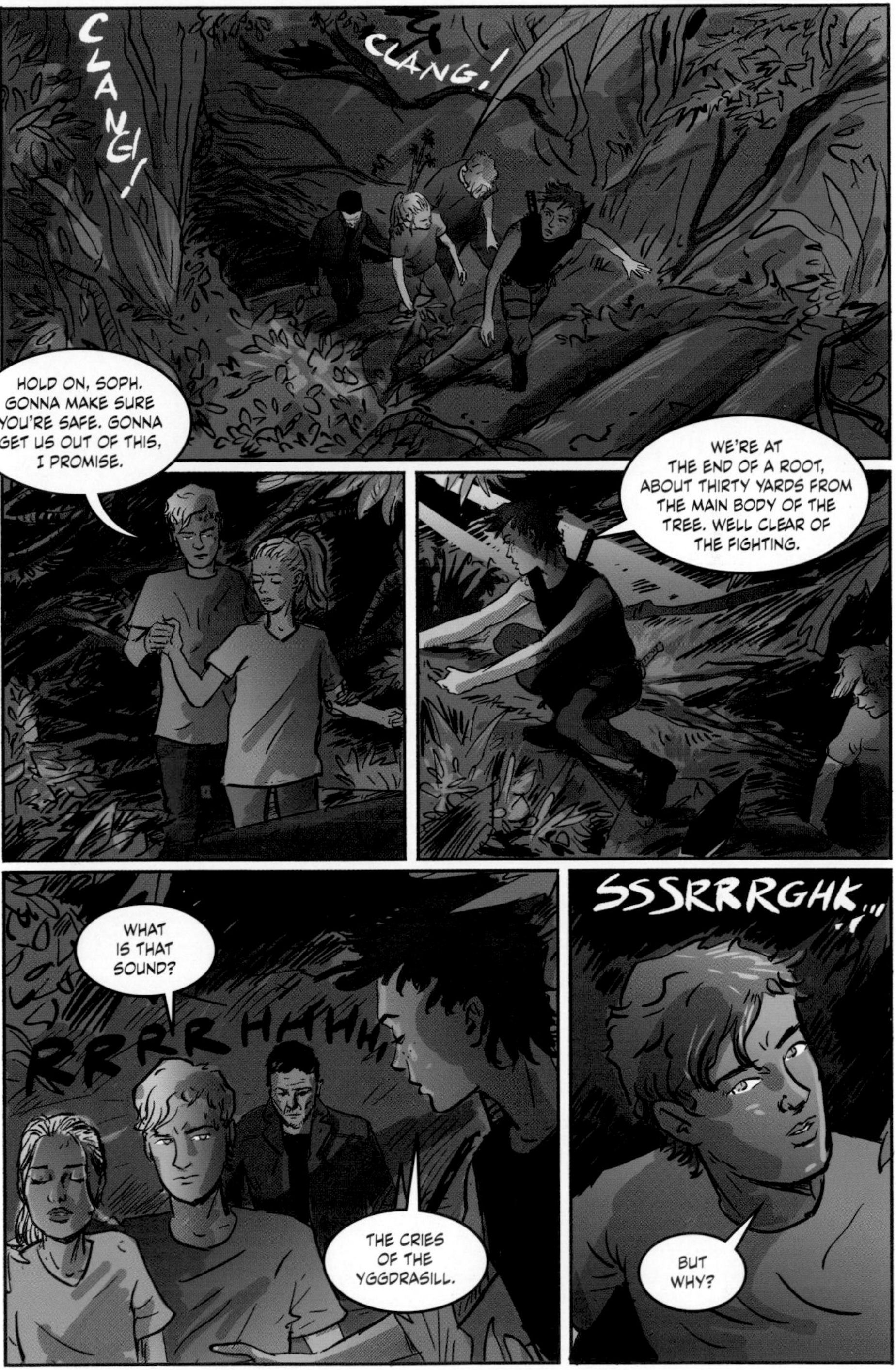
CLANG!
CLANG!
HOLD ON, SOPH. GONNA MAKE SURE YOU'RE SAFE. GONNA GET US OUT OF THIS, I PROMISE.
WE'RE AT THE END OF A ROOT, ABOUT THIRTY YARDS FROM THE MAIN BODY OF THE TREE. WELL CLEAR OF THE FIGHTING.
WHAT IS THAT SOUND?
RRRRHHHH
THE CRIES OF THE YGGDRASILL.
SSSRRRGHK...
BUT WHY?

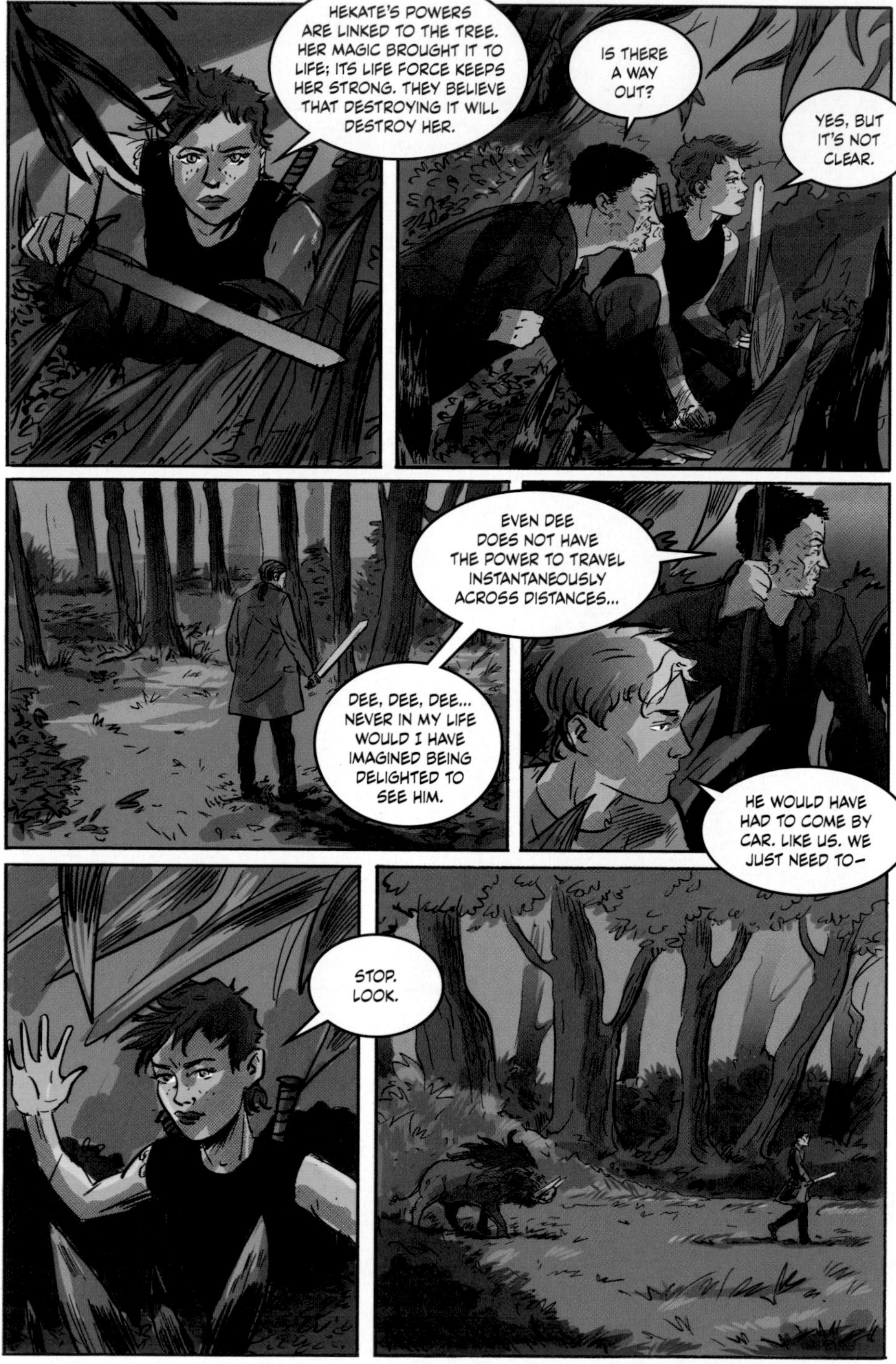
HEKATE'S POWERS ARE LINKED TO THE TREE. HER MAGIC BROUGHT IT TO LIFE; ITS LIFE FORCE KEEPS HER STRONG. THEY BELIEVE THAT DESTROYING IT WILL DESTROY HER.
IS THERE A WAY OUT?
YES, BUT IT'S NOT CLEAR.
EVEN DEE DOES NOT HAVE THE POWER TO TRAVEL INSTANTANEOUSLY ACROSS DISTANCES...
DEE, DEE, DEE... NEVER IN MY LIFE WOULD I HAVE IMAGINED BEING DELIGHTED TO SEE HIM.
HE WOULD HAVE HAD TO COME BY CAR. LIKE US. WE JUST NEED TO—
STOP. LOOK.

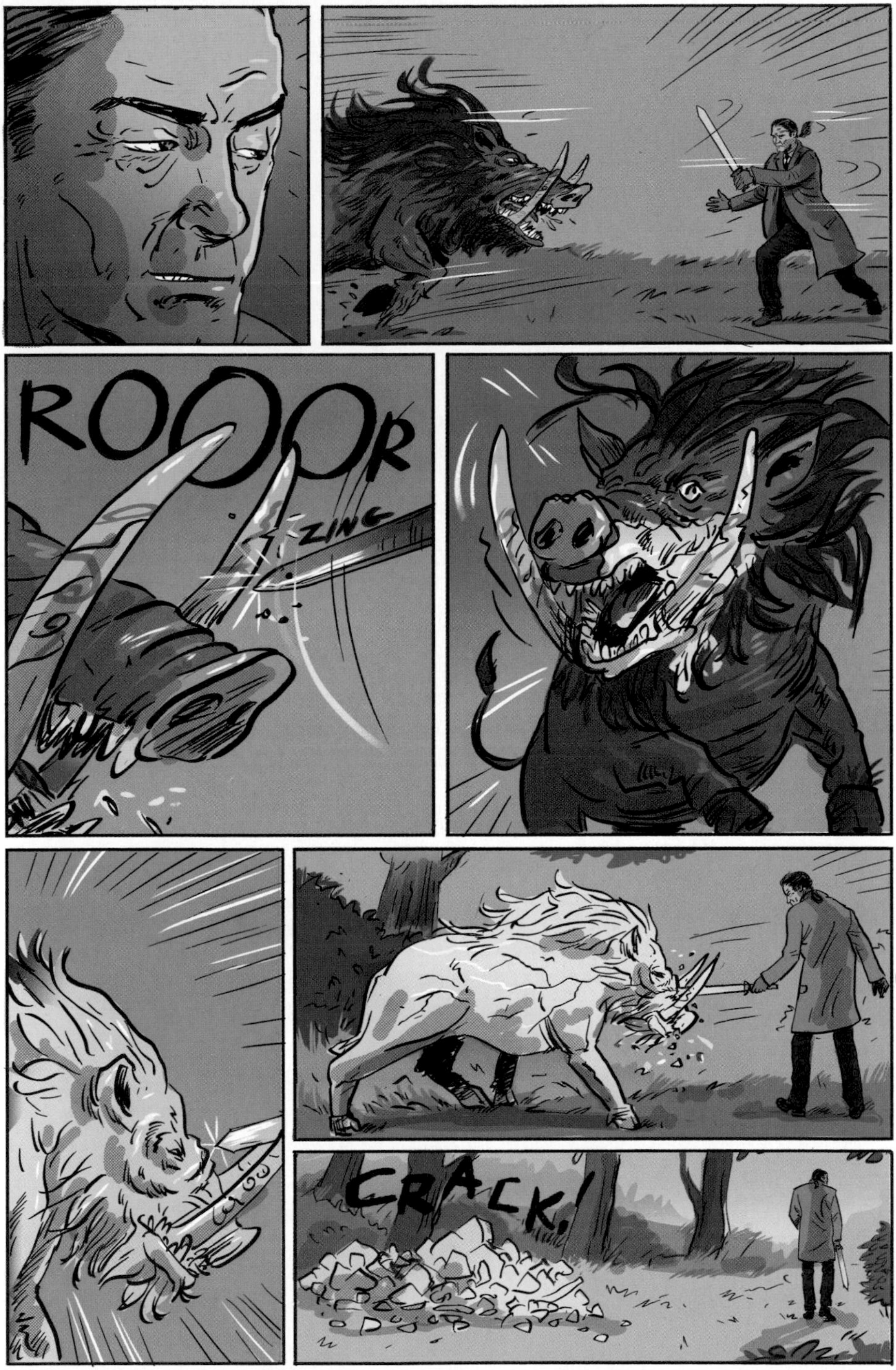
ROOOR
ZING
CRACK!

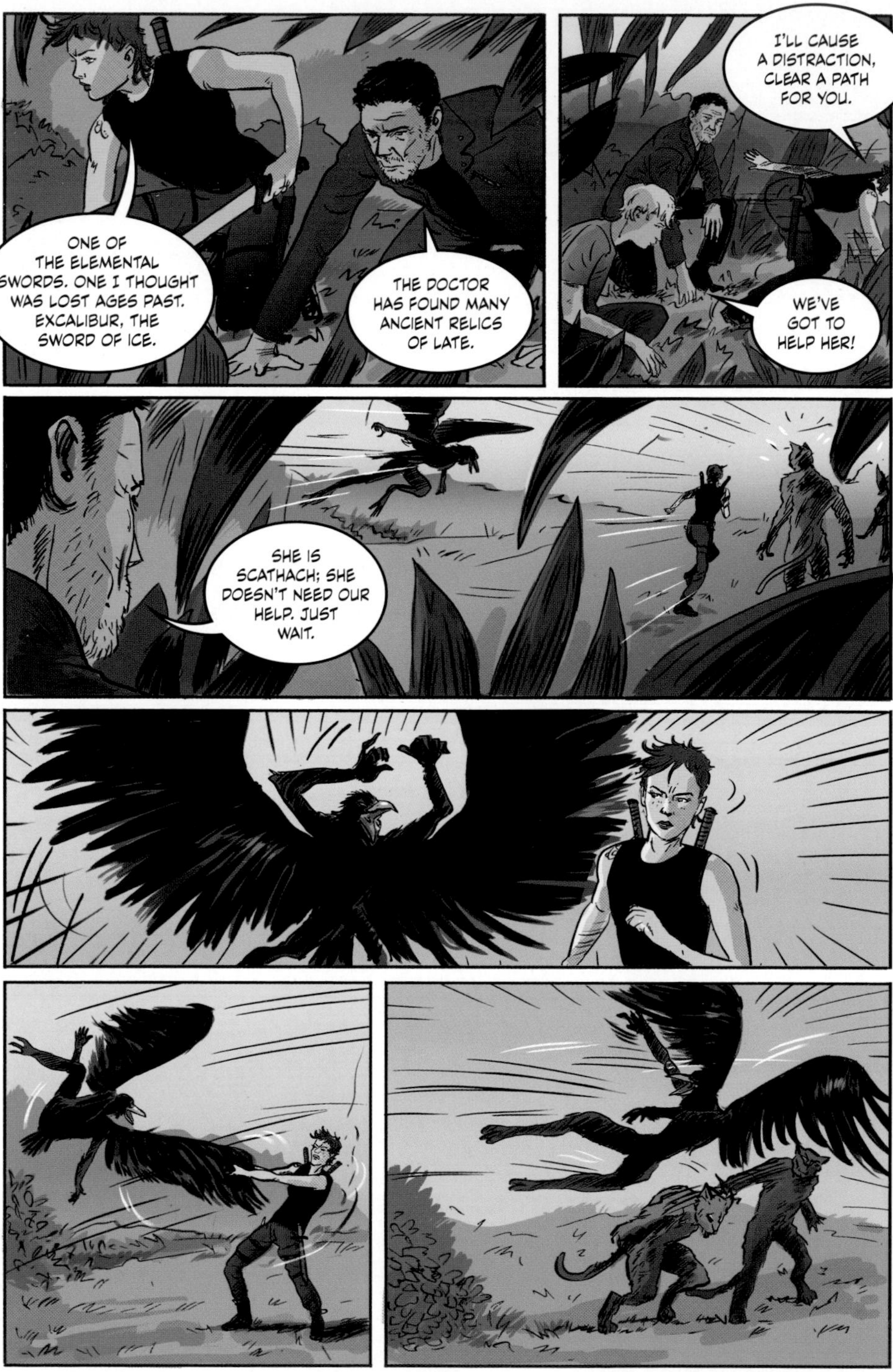
ONE OF THE ELEMENTAL SWORDS. ONE I THOUGHT WAS LOST AGES PAST. EXCALIBUR, THE SWORD OF ICE.
THE DOCTOR HAS FOUND MANY ANCIENT RELICS OF LATE.
I'LL CAUSE A DISTRACTION, CLEAR A PATH FOR YOU.
WE'VE GOT TO HELP HER!
SHE IS SCATHACH; SHE DOESN'T NEED OUR HELP. JUST WAIT.

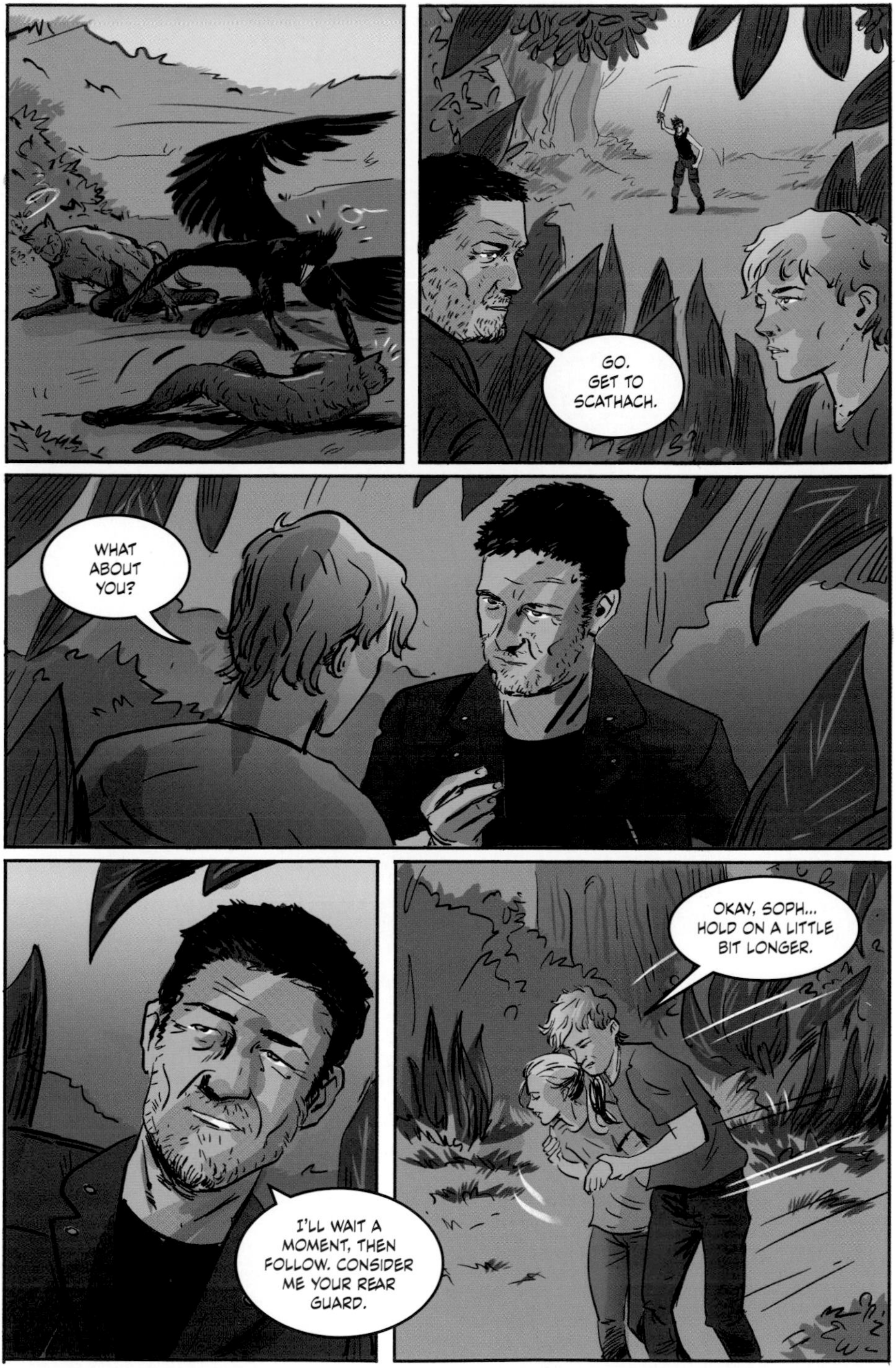
GO. GET TO SCATHACH.
WHAT ABOUT YOU?
I'LL WAIT A MOMENT, THEN FOLLOW. CONSIDER ME YOUR REAR GUARD.
OKAY, SOPH... HOLD ON A LITTLE BIT LONGER.

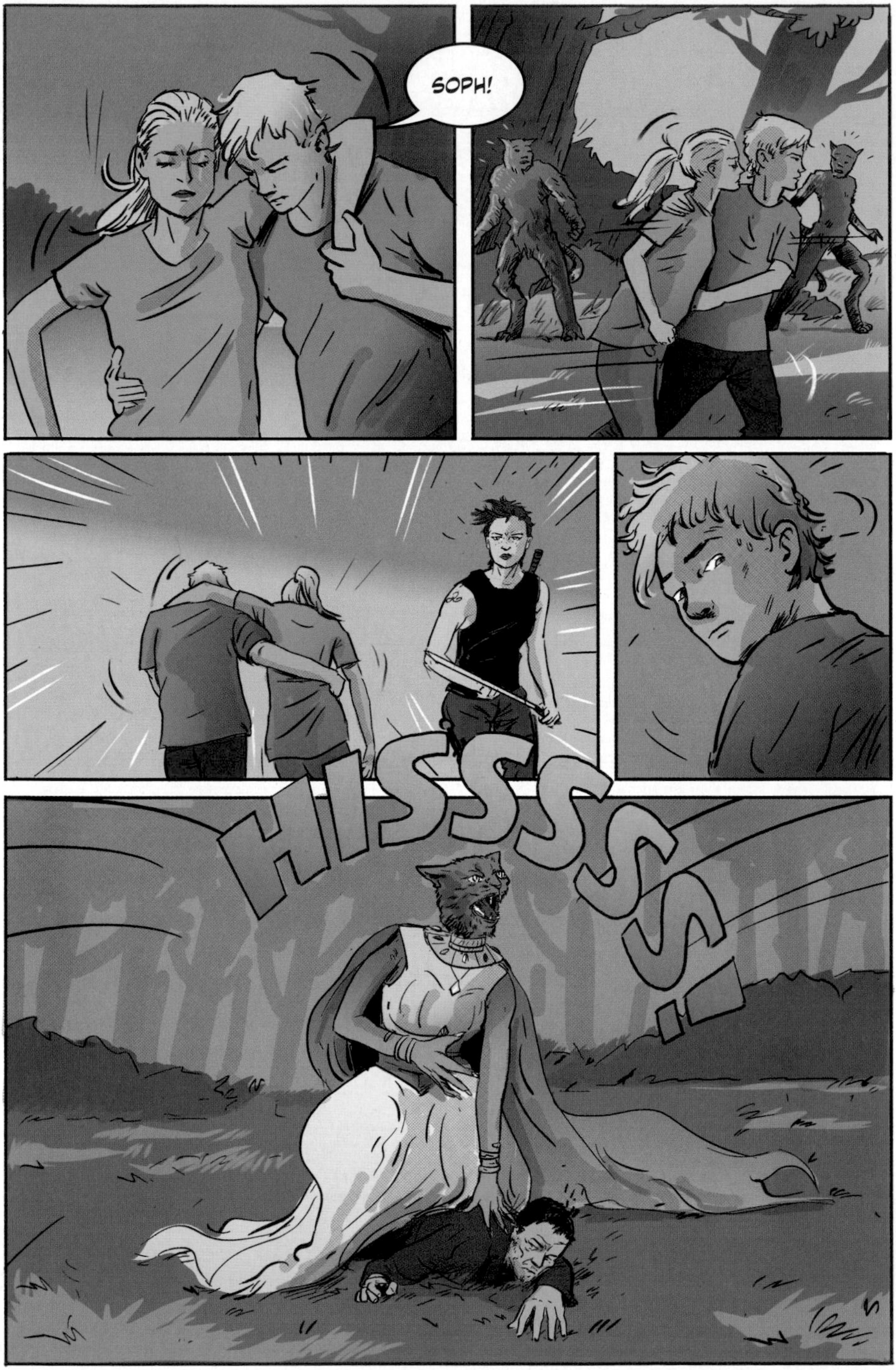
SOPH!
HISSSSS!!

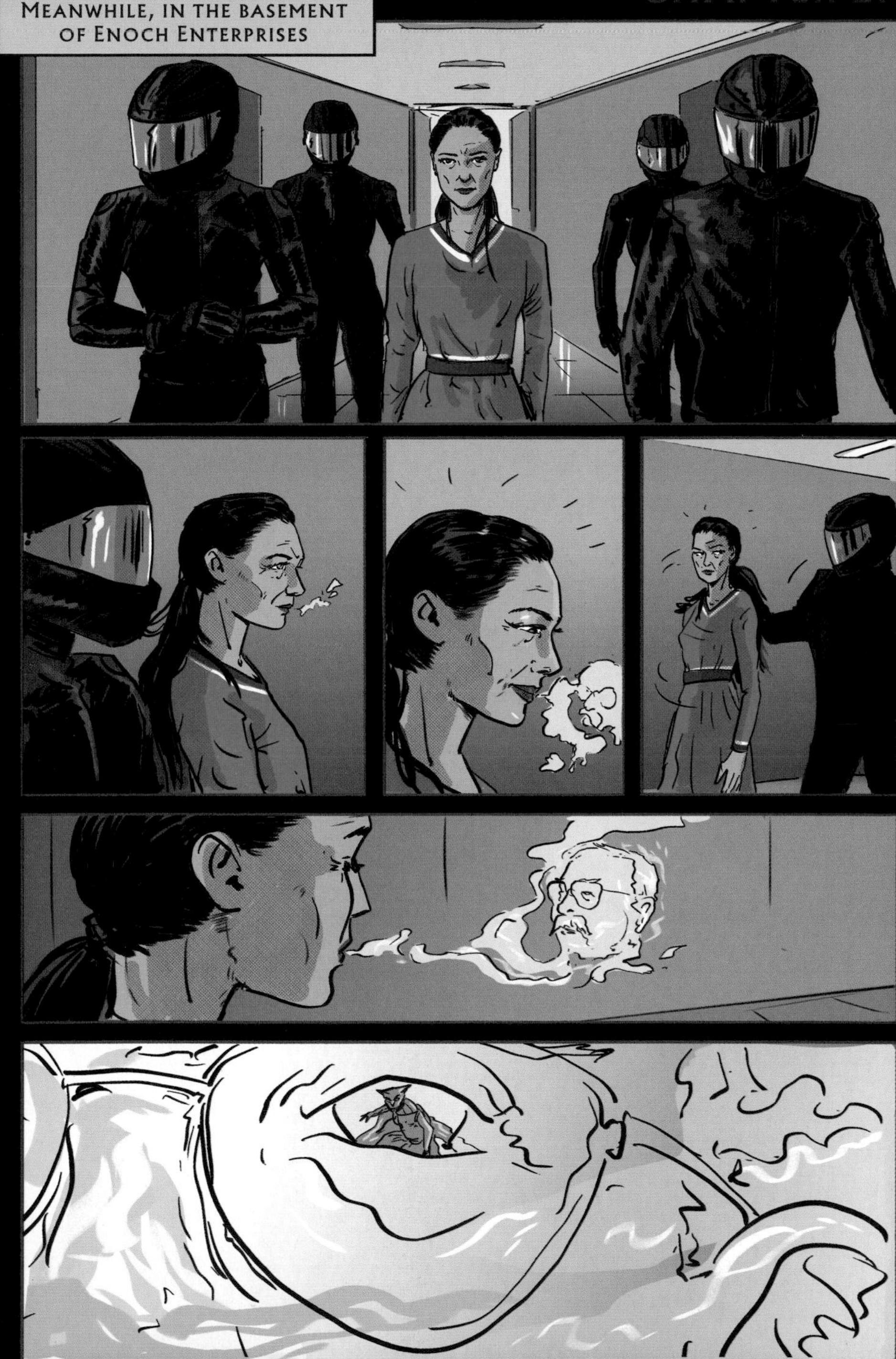
MEANWHILE, IN THE BASEMENT
OF ENOCH ENTERPRISES

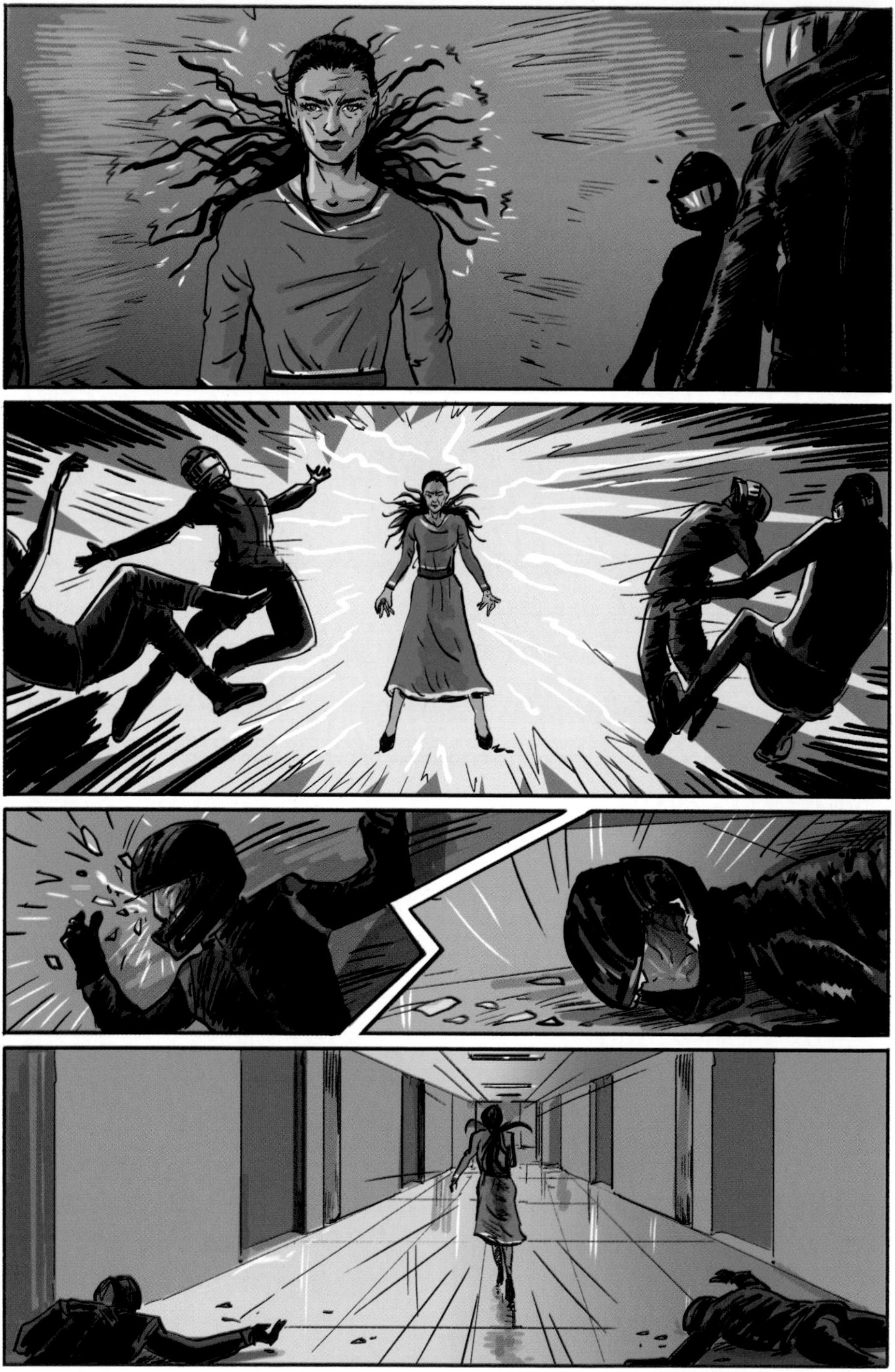

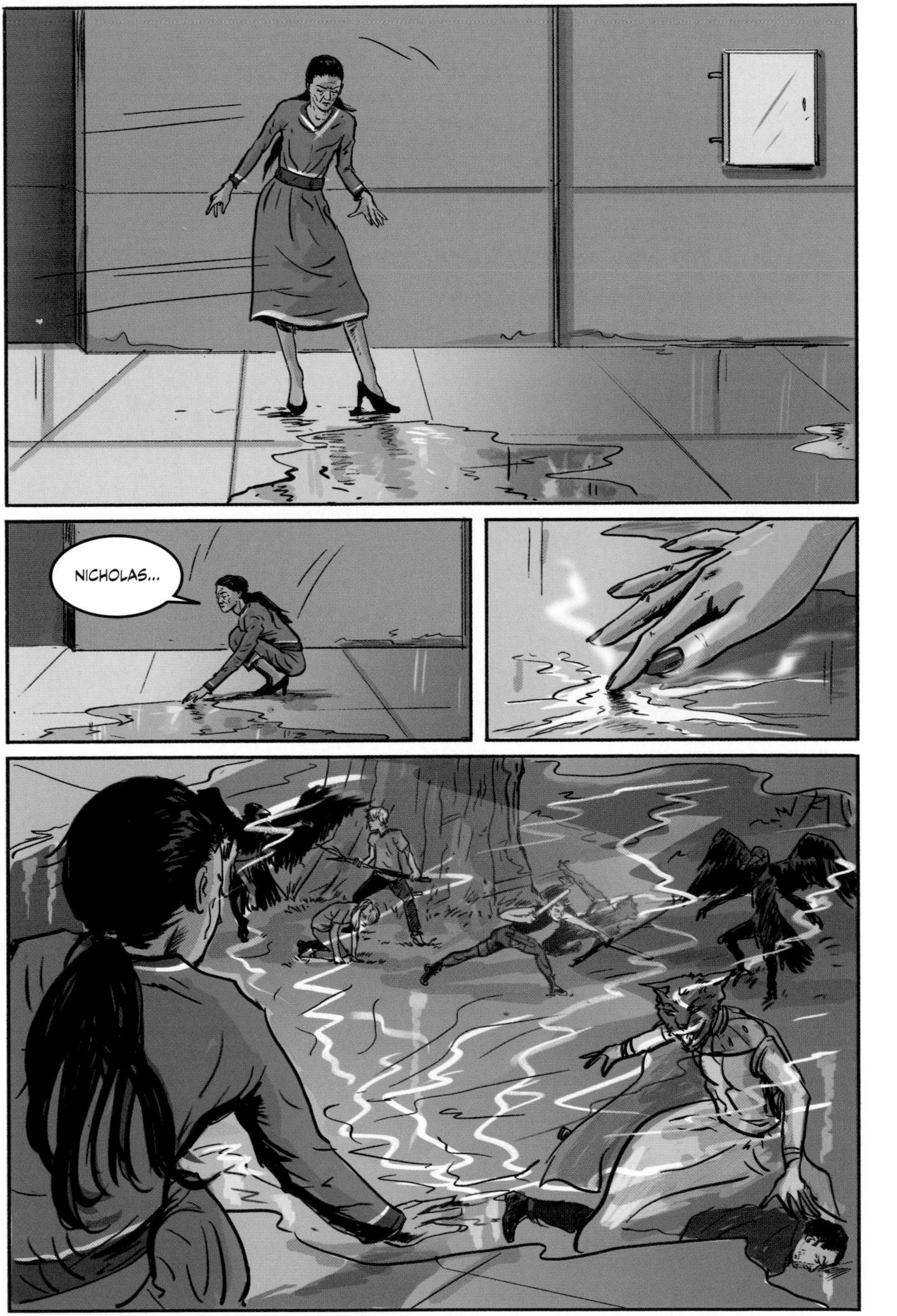
NICHOLAS...

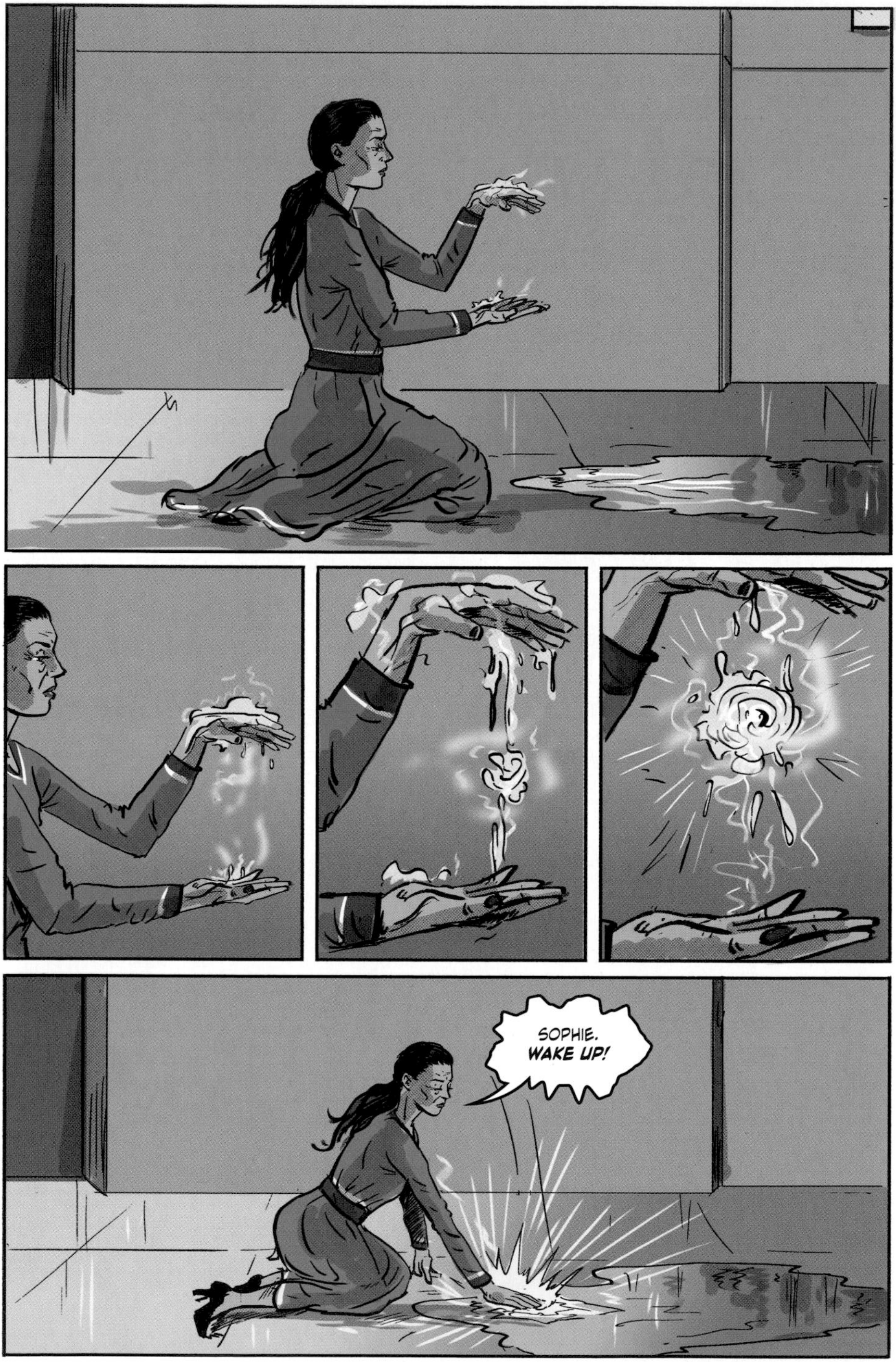
SOPHIE.
WAKE UP!

CHAPTER 28

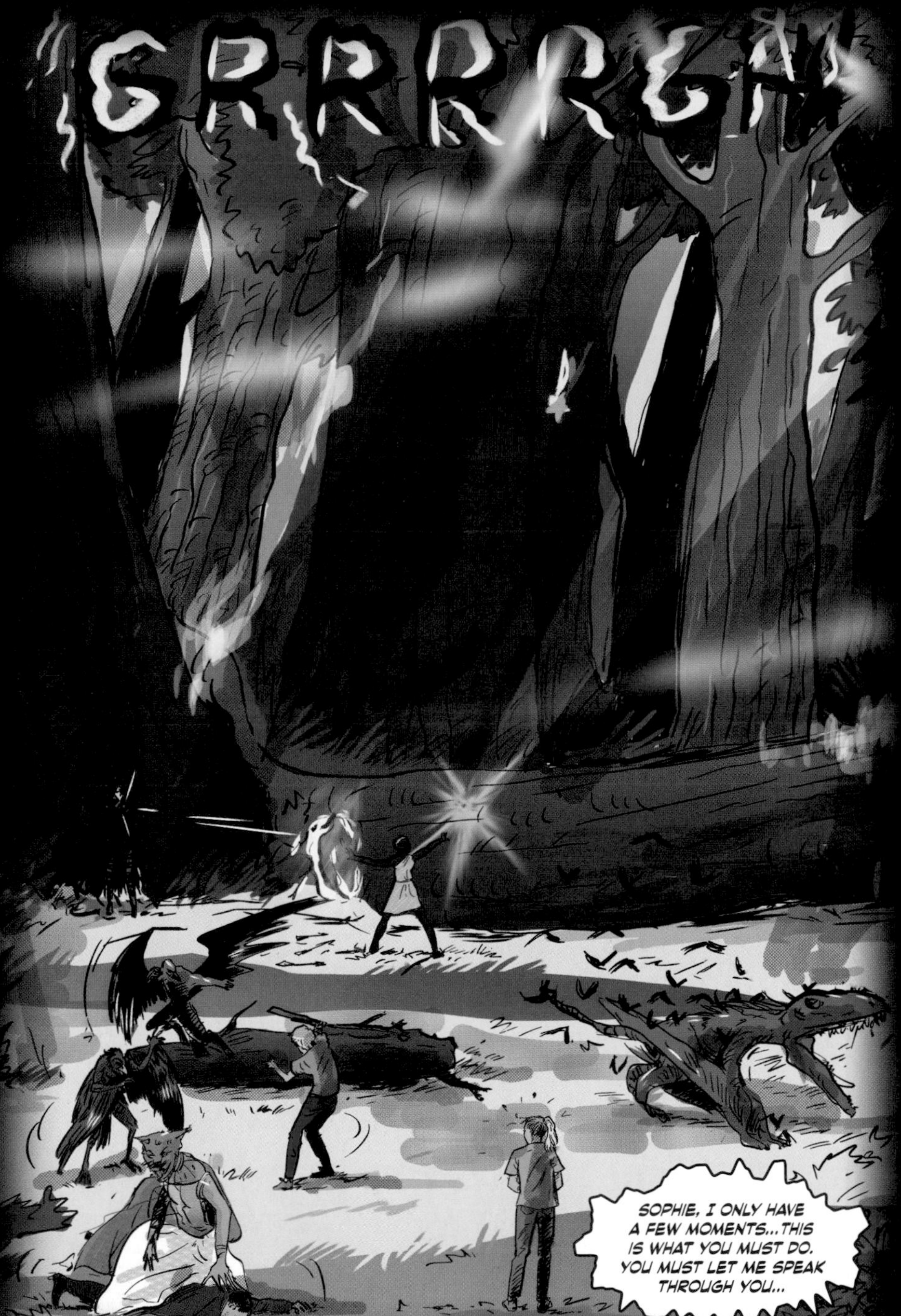
GRRRRGH
SOPHIE, I ONLY HAVE A FEW MOMENTS...THIS IS WHAT YOU MUST DO. YOU MUST LET ME SPEAK THROUGH YOU...

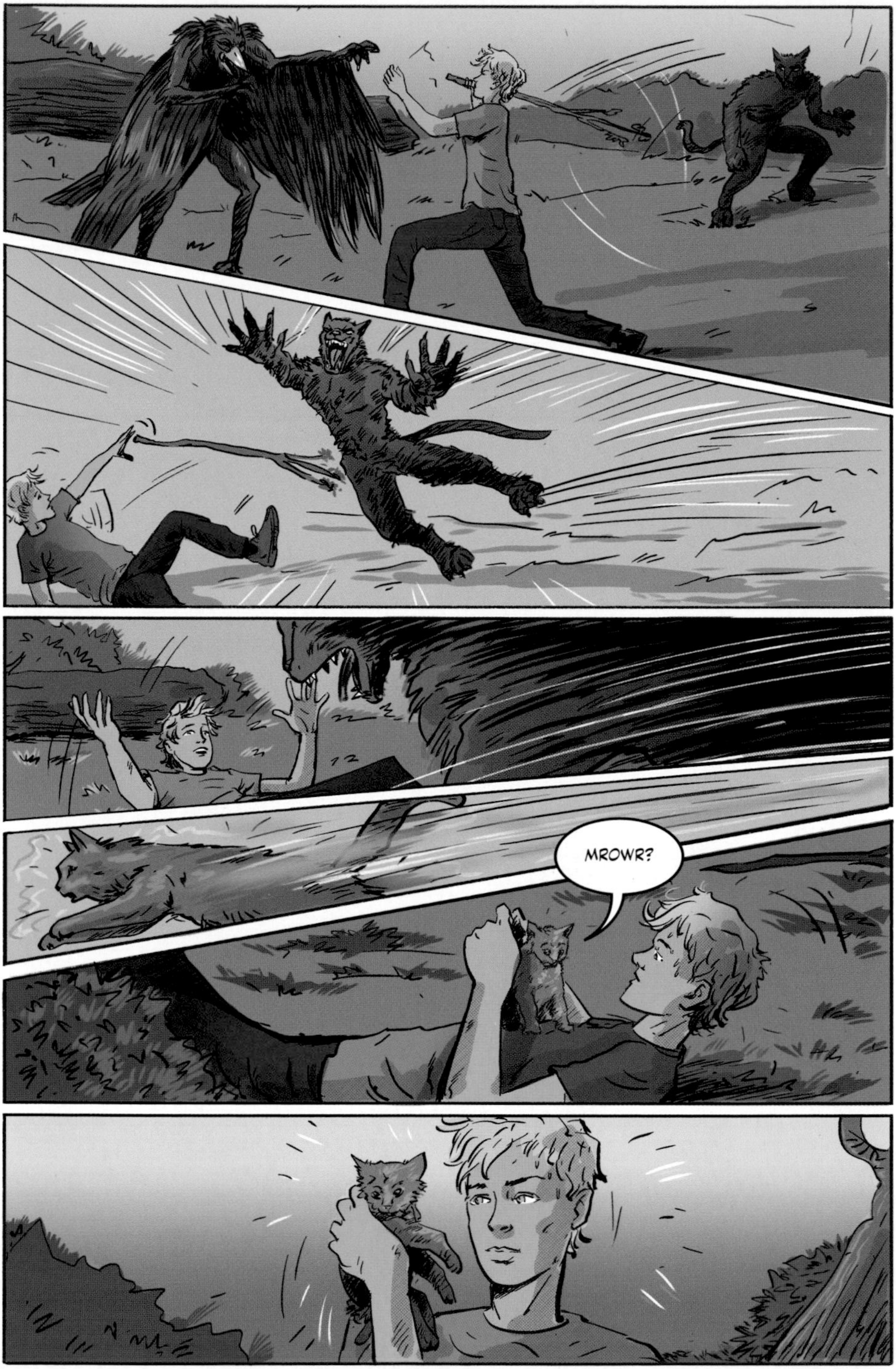
MROWR?

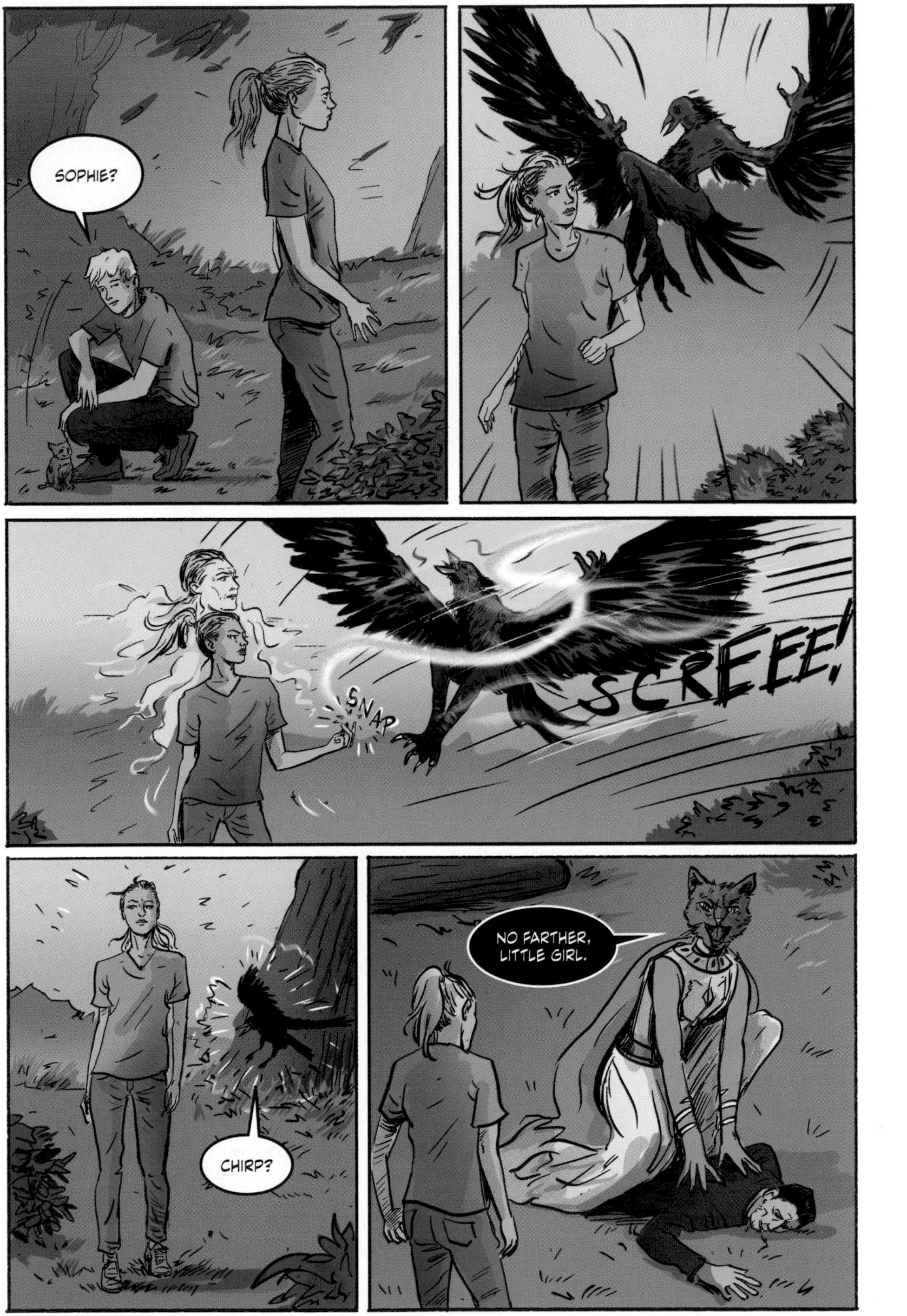
SOPHIE?
SNAP
SCREEE!
CHIRP?
NO FARTHER, LITTLE GIRL.

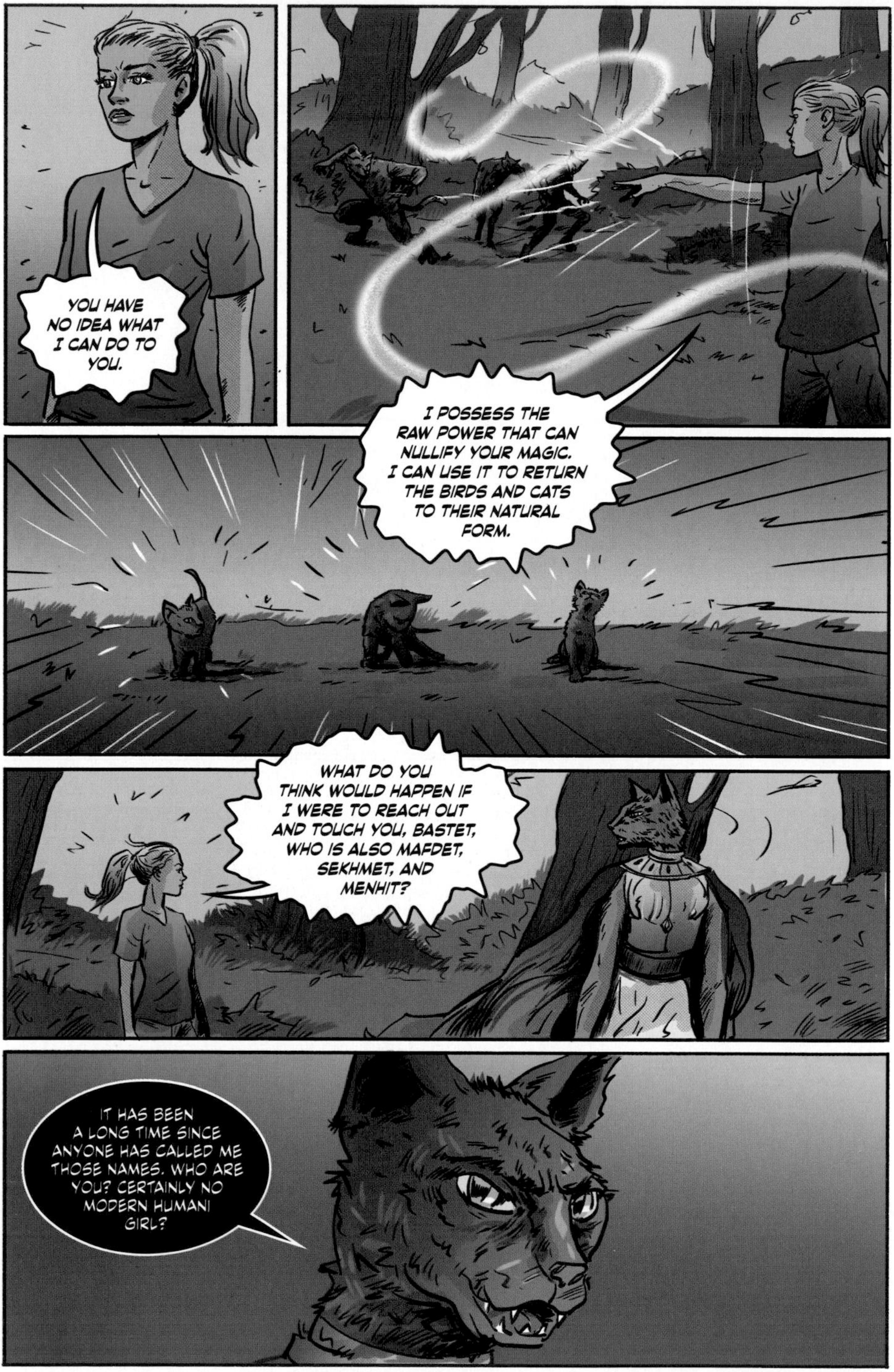
YOU HAVE NO IDEA WHAT I CAN DO TO YOU.
I POSSESS THE RAW POWER THAT CAN NULLIFY YOUR MAGIC. I CAN USE IT TO RETURN THE BIRDS AND CATS TO THEIR NATURAL FORM.
WHAT DO YOU THINK WOULD HAPPEN IF I WERE TO REACH OUT AND TOUCH YOU, BASTET, WHO IS ALSO MAFDET, SEKHMET, AND MENHIT?
IT HAS BEEN A LONG TIME SINCE ANYONE HAS CALLED ME THOSE NAMES. WHO ARE YOU? CERTAINLY NO MODERN HUMANI GIRL?

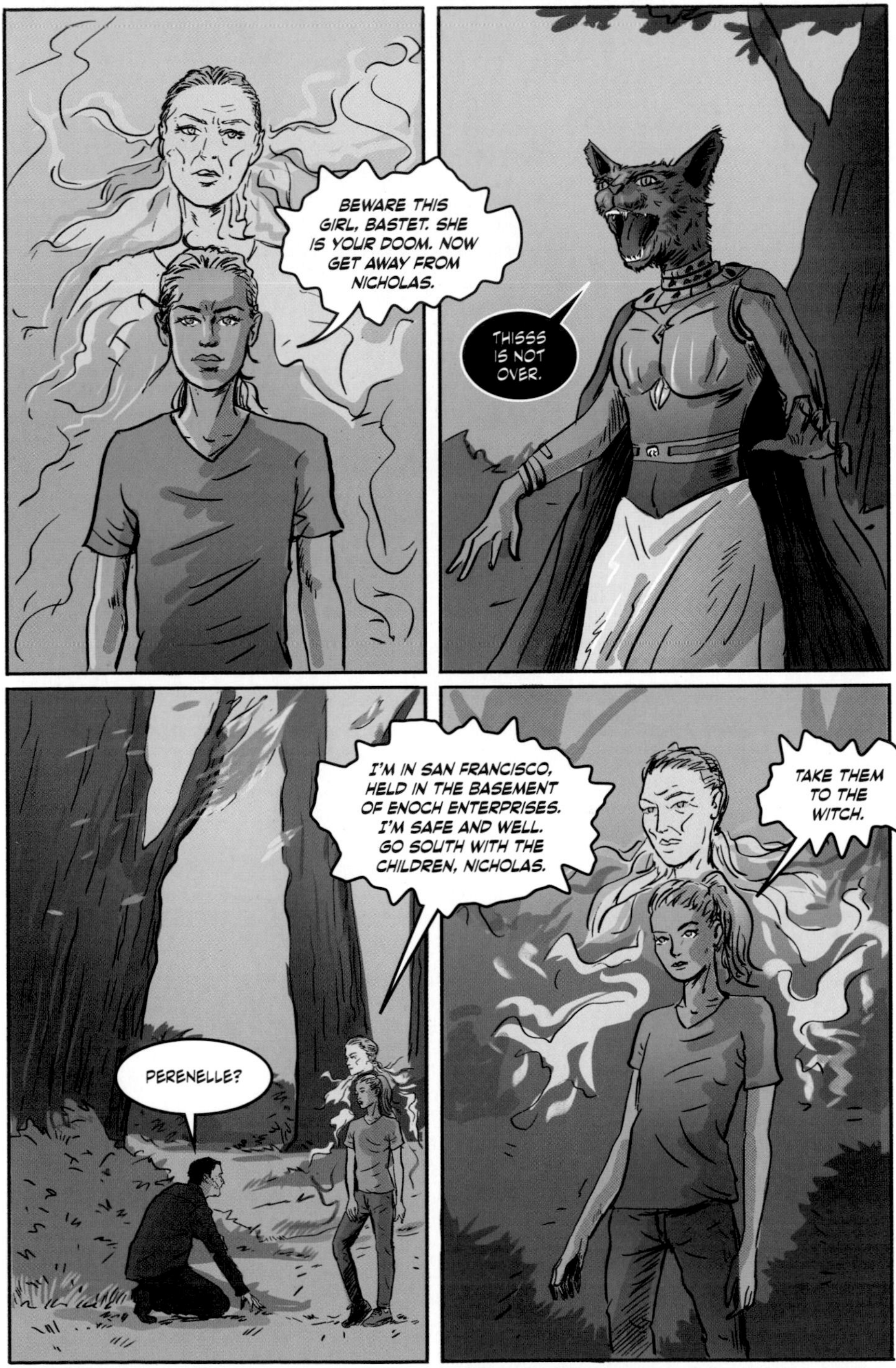
BEWARE THIS GIRL, BASTET. SHE IS YOUR DOOM. NOW GET AWAY FROM NICHOLAS.
THISSS IS NOT OVER.
I'M IN SAN FRANCISCO, HELD IN THE BASEMENT OF ENOCH ENTERPRISES. I'M SAFE AND WELL. GO SOUTH WITH THE CHILDREN, NICHOLAS.
PERENELLE?
TAKE THEM TO THE WITCH.

CHAPTER 29

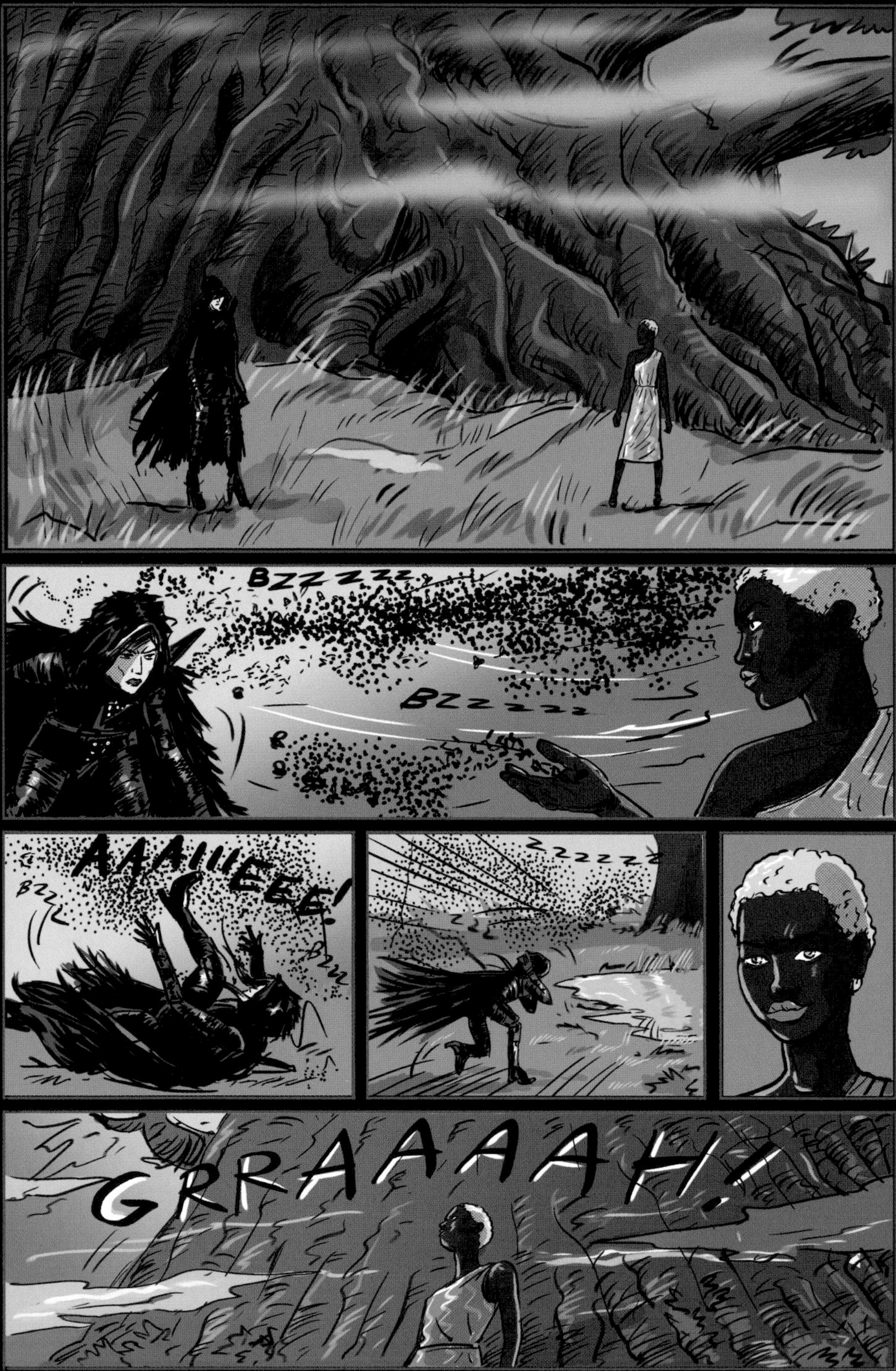
BZZZZZZ
BZZZZZZ
AAAIIIEEEE!
BZZ
BZZ
ZZZZZZ
GRRAAAAAH!!

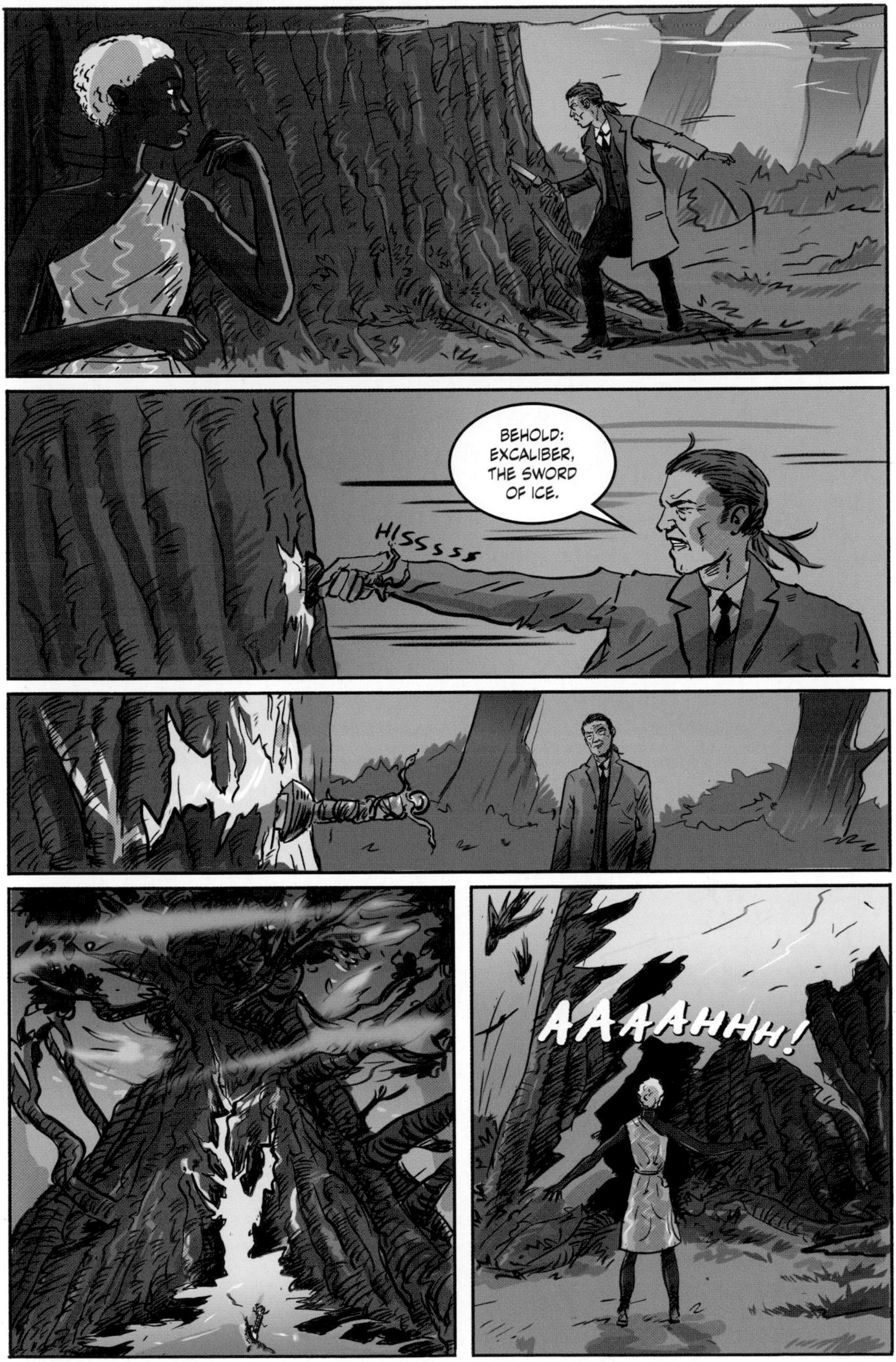

BEHOLD: EXCALIBER, THE SWORD OF ICE.
HISSSSSS
AAAAHHH!

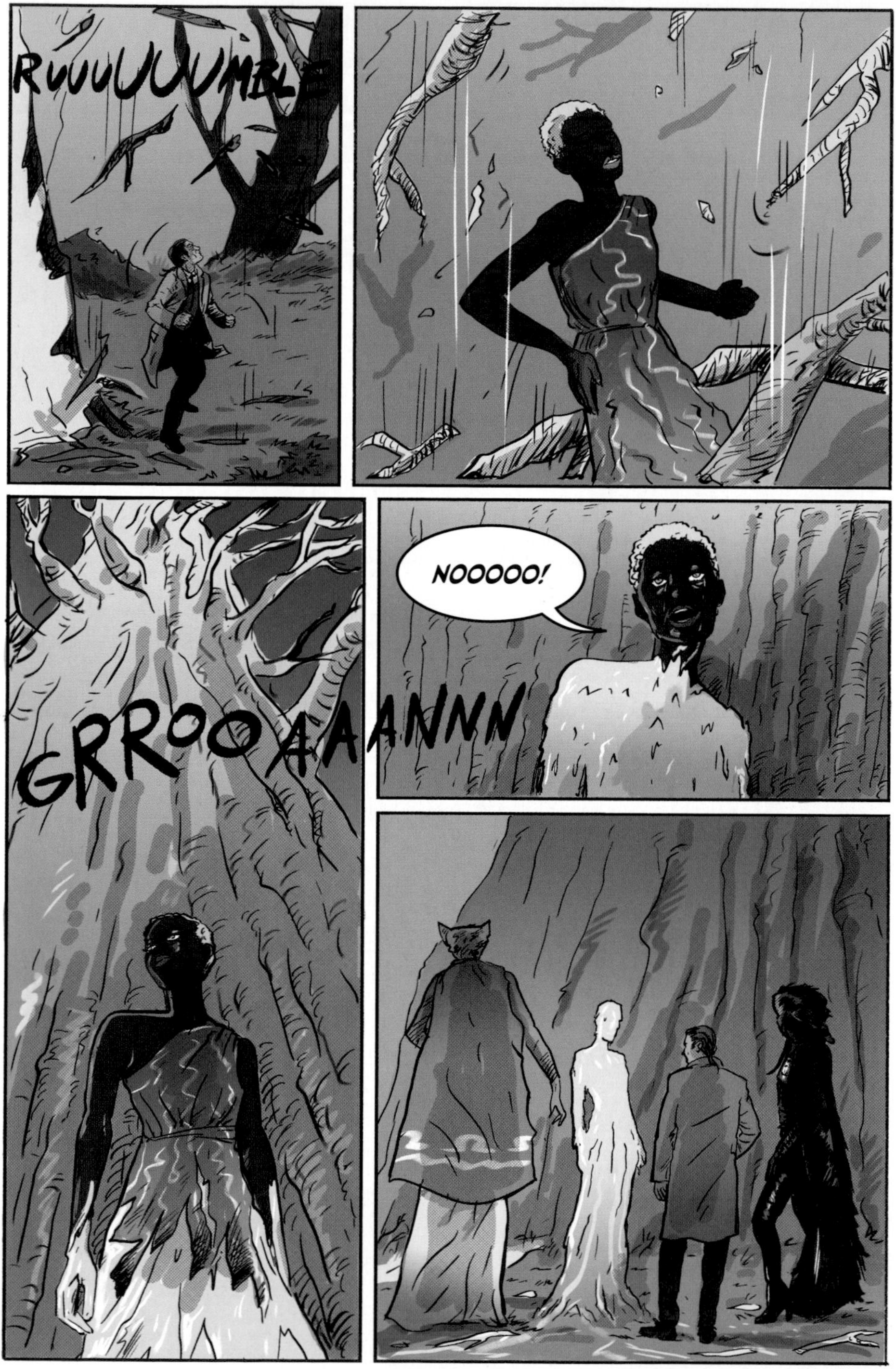
RUUUUUUMBLE
GRROOAAANNN
NOOOOO!

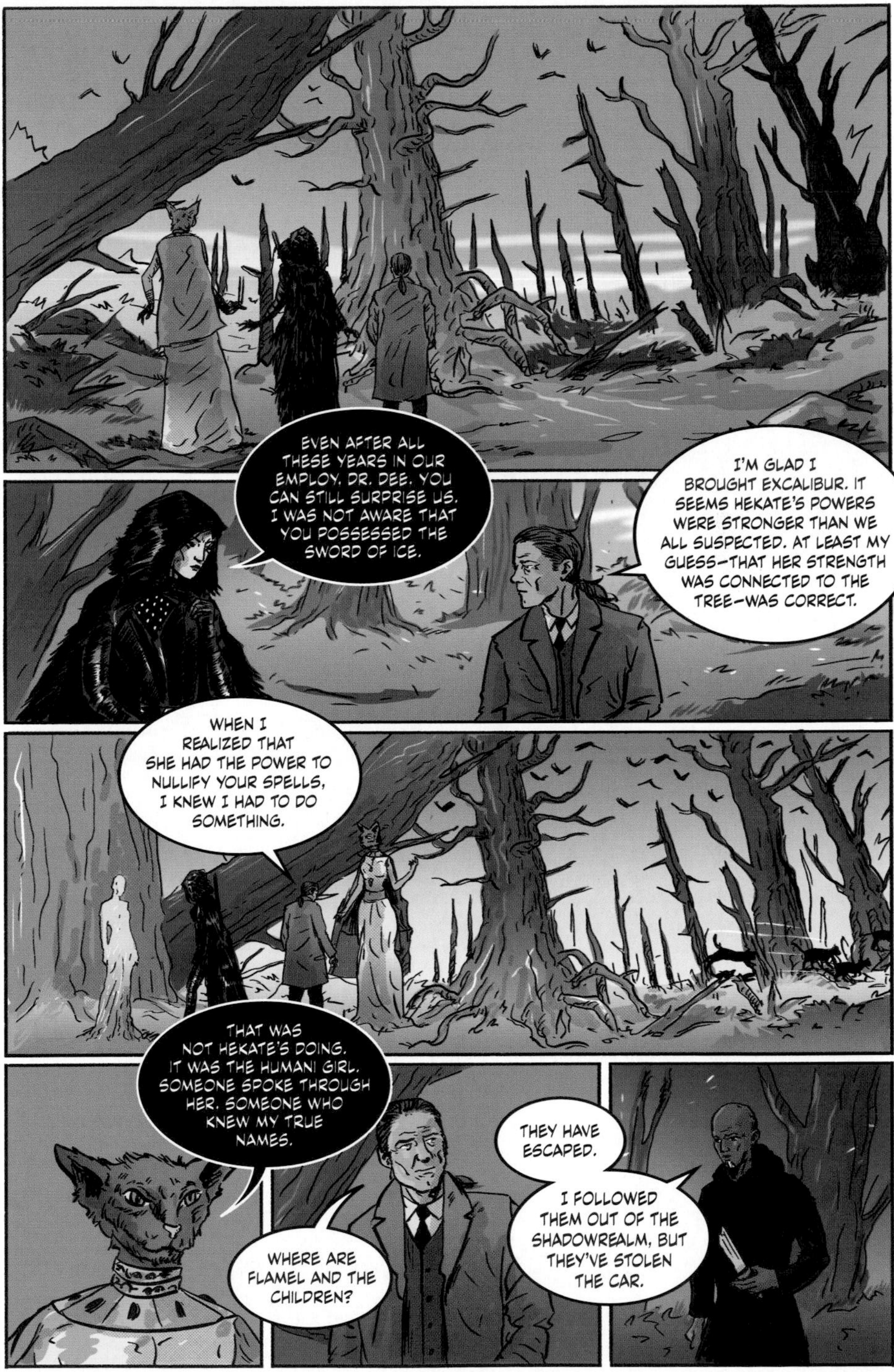

EVEN AFTER ALL THESE YEARS IN OUR EMPLOY, DR. DEE, YOU CAN STILL SURPRISE US. I WAS NOT AWARE THAT YOU POSSESSED THE SWORD OF ICE.
I'M GLAD I BROUGHT EXCALIBUR. IT SEEMS HEKATE'S POWERS WERE STRONGER THAN WE ALL SUSPECTED. AT LEAST MY GUESS—THAT HER STRENGTH WAS CONNECTED TO THE TREE—WAS CORRECT.
WHEN I REALIZED THAT SHE HAD THE POWER TO NULLIFY YOUR SPELLS, I KNEW I HAD TO DO SOMETHING.
THAT WAS NOT HEKATE'S DOING. IT WAS THE HUMANI GIRL. SOMEONE SPOKE THROUGH HER. SOMEONE WHO KNEW MY TRUE NAMES.
WHERE ARE FLAMEL AND THE CHILDREN?
THEY HAVE ESCAPED.
I FOLLOWED THEM OUT OF THE SHADOWREALM, BUT THEY'VE STOLEN THE CAR.

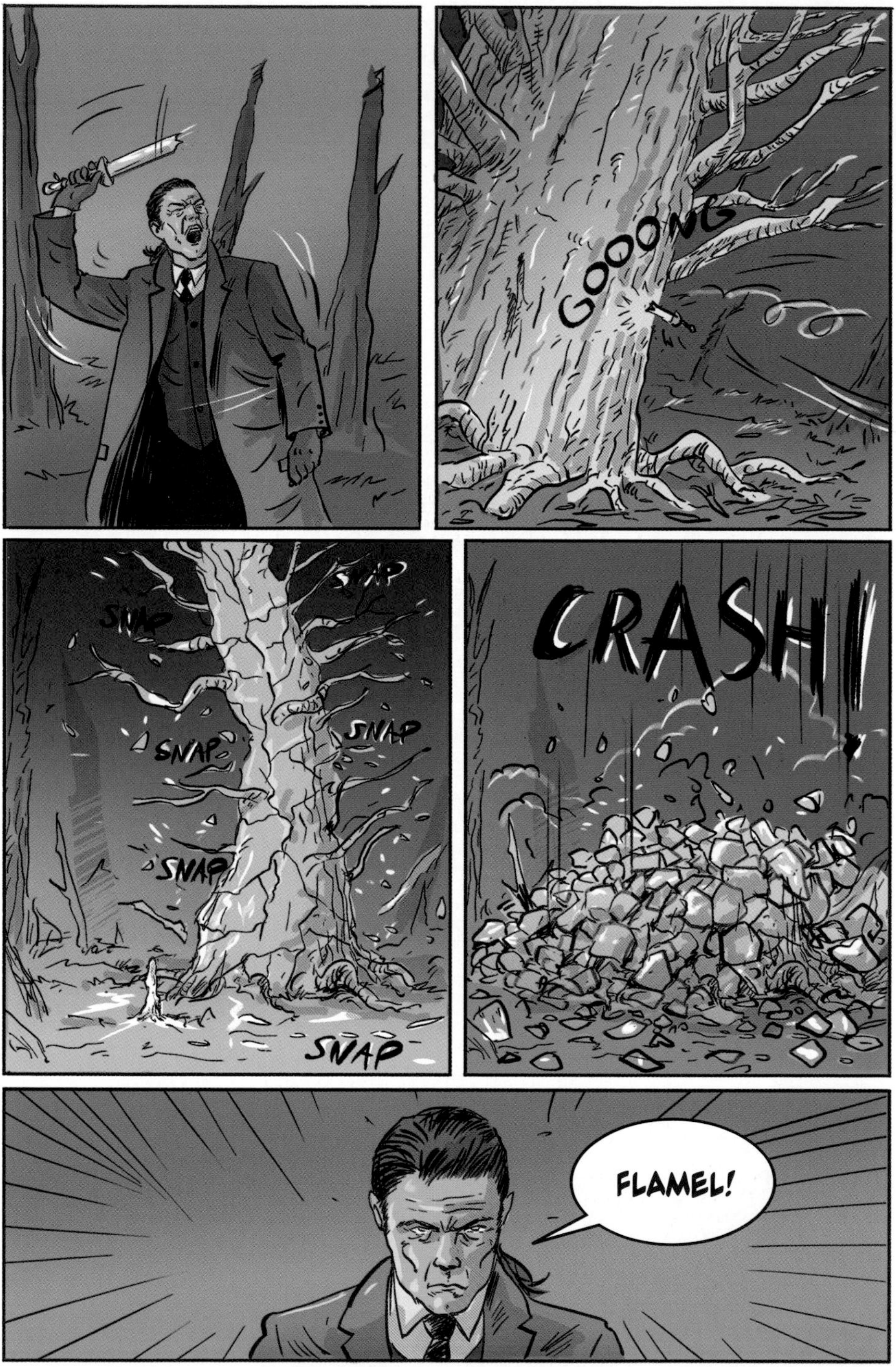
GOOONG
SNAP
SNAP
SNAP
SNAP
SNAP
SNAP
CRASH!
FLAMEL!

CHAPTER 30

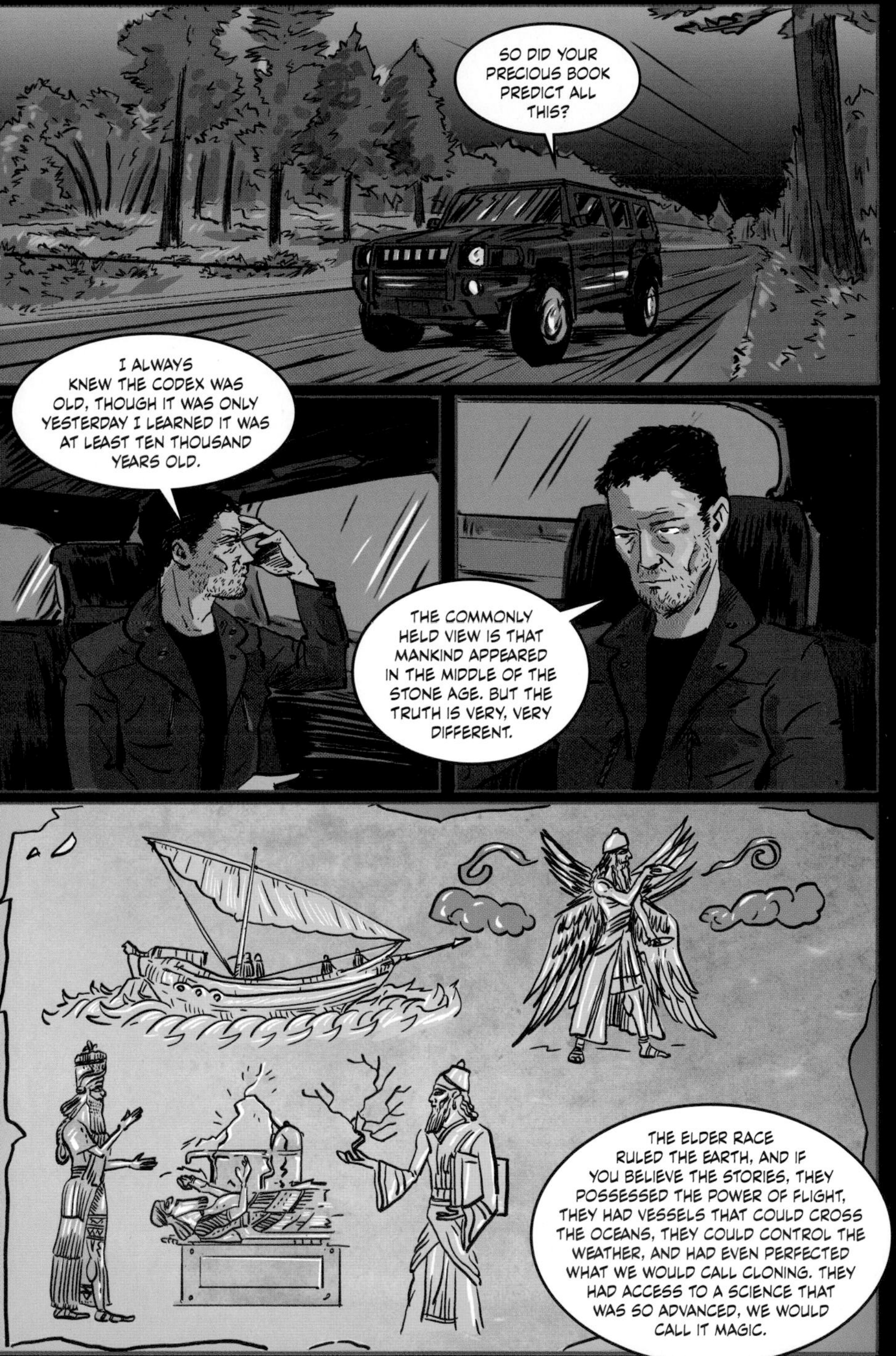
SO DID YOUR PRECIOUS BOOK PREDICT ALL THIS?
I ALWAYS KNEW THE CODEX WAS OLD, THOUGH IT WAS ONLY YESTERDAY I LEARNED IT WAS AT LEAST TEN THOUSAND YEARS OLD.
THE COMMONLY HELD VIEW IS THAT MANKIND APPEARED IN THE MIDDLE OF THE STONE AGE. BUT THE TRUTH IS VERY, VERY DIFFERENT.
THE ELDER RACE RULED THE EARTH, AND IF YOU BELIEVE THE STORIES, THEY POSSESSED THE POWER OF FLIGHT, THEY HAD VESSELS THAT COULD CROSS THE OCEANS, THEY COULD CONTROL THE WEATHER, AND HAD EVEN PERFECTED WHAT WE WOULD CALL CLONING. THEY HAD ACCESS TO A SCIENCE THAT WAS SO ADVANCED, WE WOULD CALL IT MAGIC.

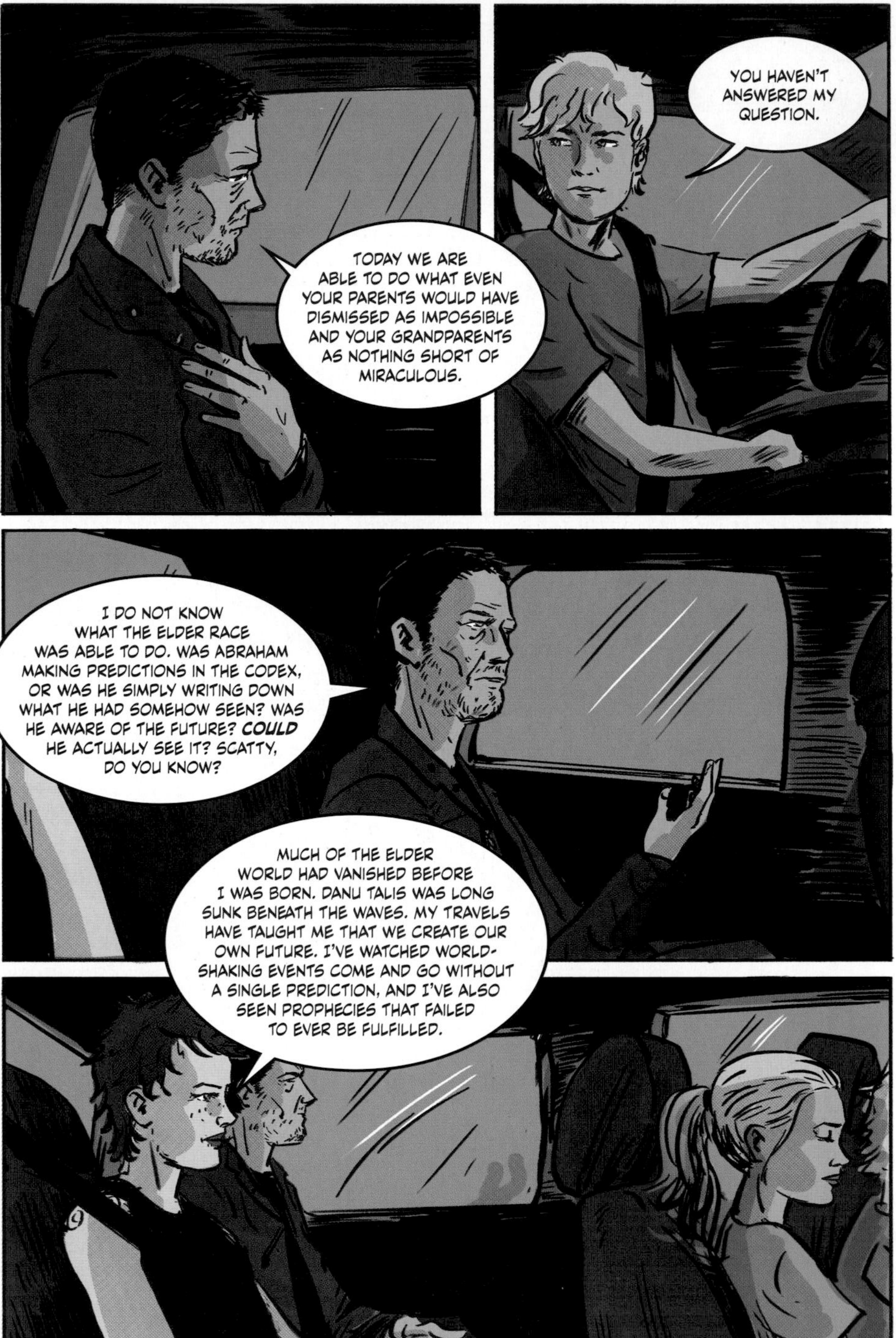
YOU HAVEN'T ANSWERED MY QUESTION.
TODAY WE ARE ABLE TO DO WHAT EVEN YOUR PARENTS WOULD HAVE DISMISSED AS IMPOSSIBLE AND YOUR GRANDPARENTS AS NOTHING SHORT OF MIRACULOUS.
I DO NOT KNOW WHAT THE ELDER RACE WAS ABLE TO DO. WAS ABRAHAM MAKING PREDICTIONS IN THE CODEX, OR WAS HE SIMPLY WRITING DOWN WHAT HE HAD SOMEHOW SEEN? WAS HE AWARE OF THE FUTURE? ***COULD*** HE ACTUALLY SEE IT? SCATTY, DO YOU KNOW?
MUCH OF THE ELDER WORLD HAD VANISHED BEFORE I WAS BORN. DANU TALIS WAS LONG SUNK BENEATH THE WAVES. MY TRAVELS HAVE TAUGHT ME THAT WE CREATE OUR OWN FUTURE. I'VE WATCHED WORLD-SHAKING EVENTS COME AND GO WITHOUT A SINGLE PREDICTION, AND I'VE ALSO SEEN PROPHECIES THAT FAILED TO EVER BE FULFILLED.

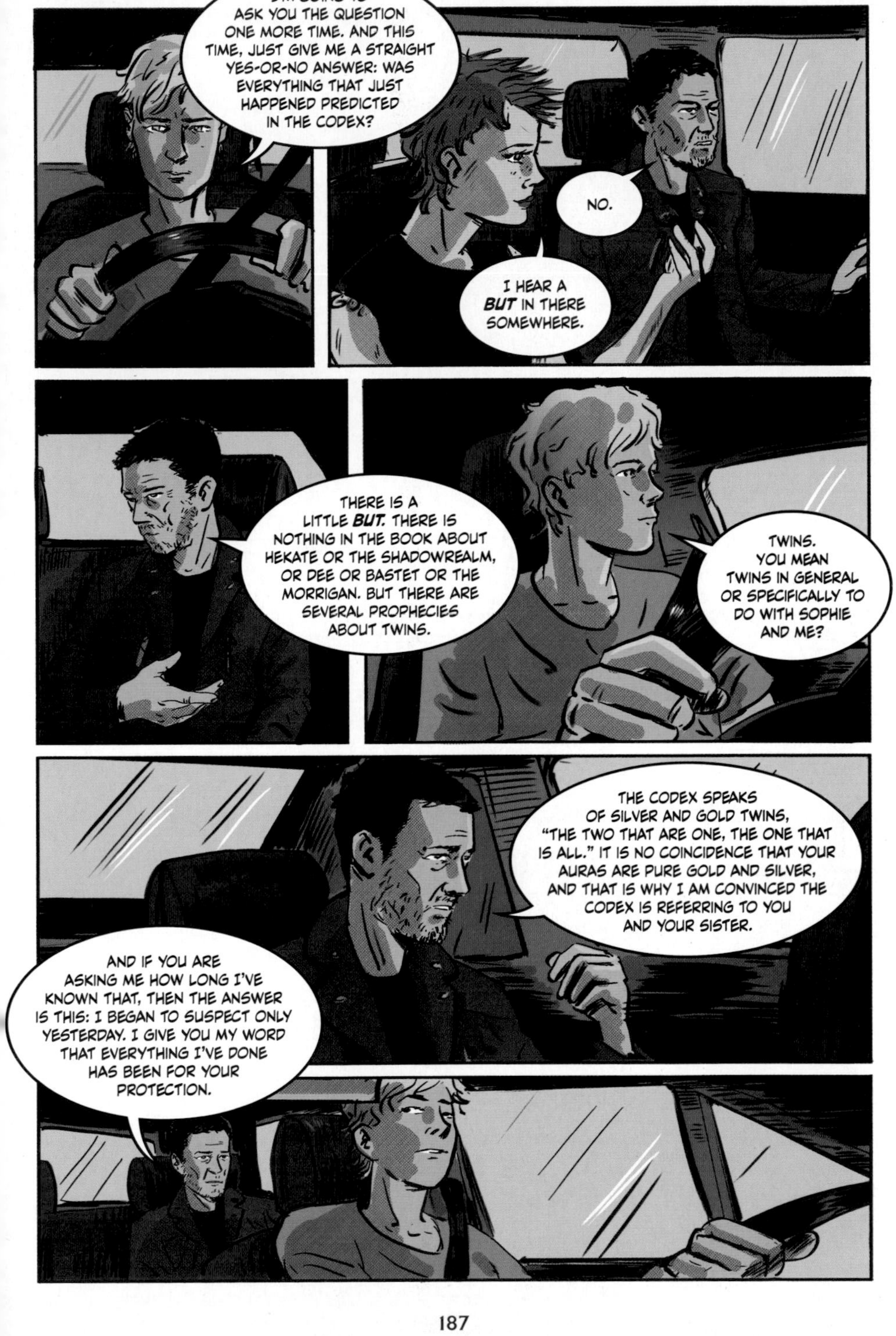
I'M GOING TO ASK YOU THE QUESTION ONE MORE TIME. AND THIS TIME, JUST GIVE ME A STRAIGHT YES-OR-NO ANSWER: WAS EVERYTHING THAT JUST HAPPENED PREDICTED IN THE CODEX?
NO.
I HEAR A *BUT* IN THERE SOMEWHERE.
THERE IS A LITTLE *BUT.* THERE IS NOTHING IN THE BOOK ABOUT HEKATE OR THE SHADOWREALM, OR DEE OR BASTET OR THE MORRIGAN. BUT THERE ARE SEVERAL PROPHECIES ABOUT TWINS.
TWINS. YOU MEAN TWINS IN GENERAL OR SPECIFICALLY TO DO WITH SOPHIE AND ME?
THE CODEX SPEAKS OF SILVER AND GOLD TWINS, "THE TWO THAT ARE ONE, THE ONE THAT IS ALL." IT IS NO COINCIDENCE THAT YOUR AURAS ARE PURE GOLD AND SILVER, AND THAT IS WHY I AM CONVINCED THE CODEX IS REFERRING TO YOU AND YOUR SISTER.
AND IF YOU ARE ASKING ME HOW LONG I'VE KNOWN THAT, THEN THE ANSWER IS THIS: I BEGAN TO SUSPECT ONLY YESTERDAY. I GIVE YOU MY WORD THAT EVERYTHING I'VE DONE HAS BEEN FOR YOUR PROTECTION.

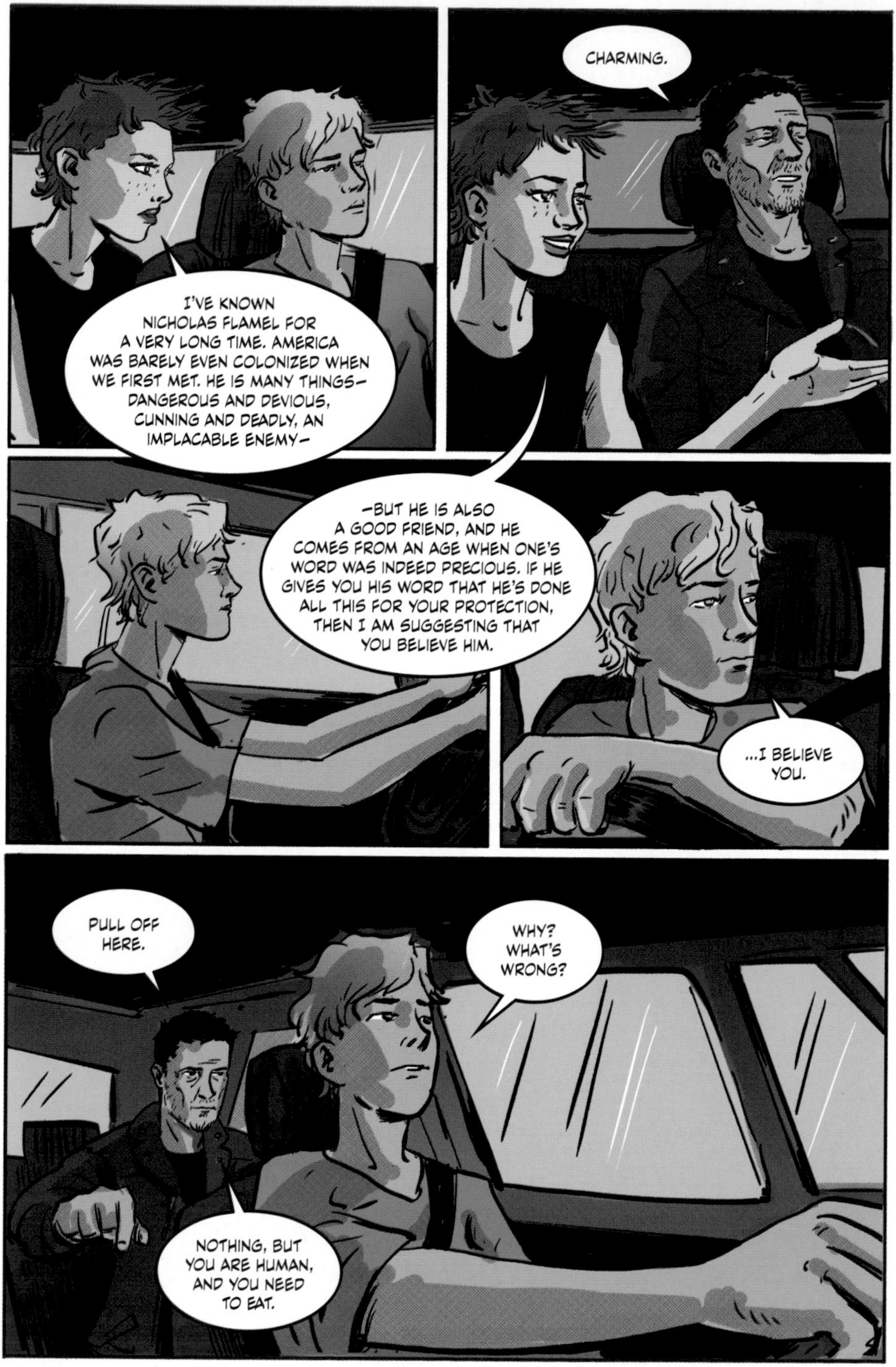
I'VE KNOWN NICHOLAS FLAMEL FOR A VERY LONG TIME. AMERICA WAS BARELY EVEN COLONIZED WHEN WE FIRST MET. HE IS MANY THINGS— DANGEROUS AND DEVIOUS, CUNNING AND DEADLY, AN IMPLACABLE ENEMY—
CHARMING.
—BUT HE IS ALSO A GOOD FRIEND, AND HE COMES FROM AN AGE WHEN ONE'S WORD WAS INDEED PRECIOUS. IF HE GIVES YOU HIS WORD THAT HE'S DONE ALL THIS FOR YOUR PROTECTION, THEN I AM SUGGESTING THAT YOU BELIEVE HIM.
...I BELIEVE YOU.
PULL OFF HERE.
WHY? WHAT'S WRONG?
NOTHING, BUT YOU ARE HUMAN, AND YOU NEED TO EAT.

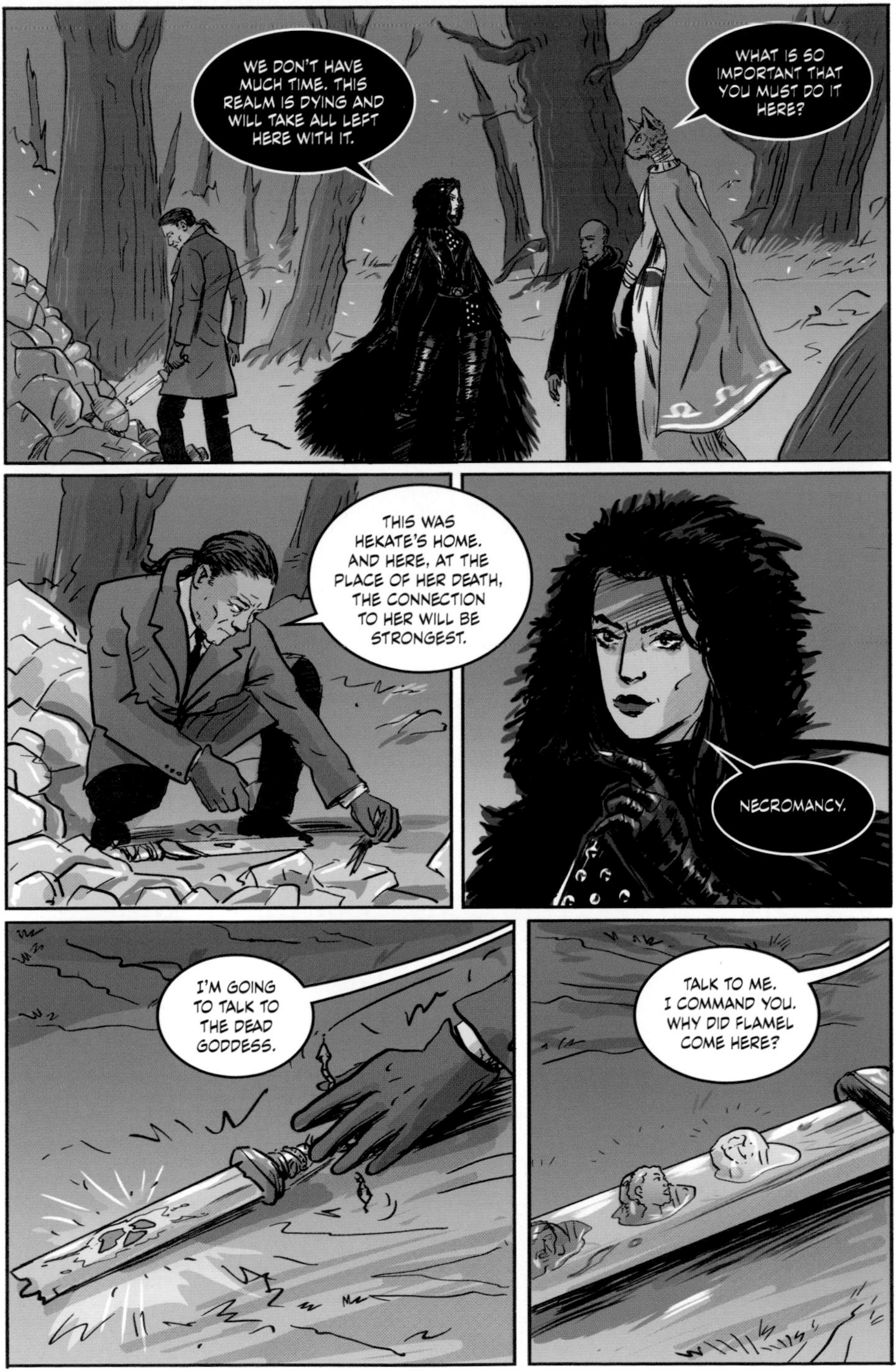
WE DON'T HAVE MUCH TIME. THIS REALM IS DYING AND WILL TAKE ALL LEFT HERE WITH IT.
WHAT IS SO IMPORTANT THAT YOU MUST DO IT HERE?
THIS WAS HEKATE'S HOME. AND HERE, AT THE PLACE OF HER DEATH, THE CONNECTION TO HER WILL BE STRONGEST.
NECROMANCY.
I'M GOING TO TALK TO THE DEAD GODDESS.
TALK TO ME. I COMMAND YOU. WHY DID FLAMEL COME HERE?

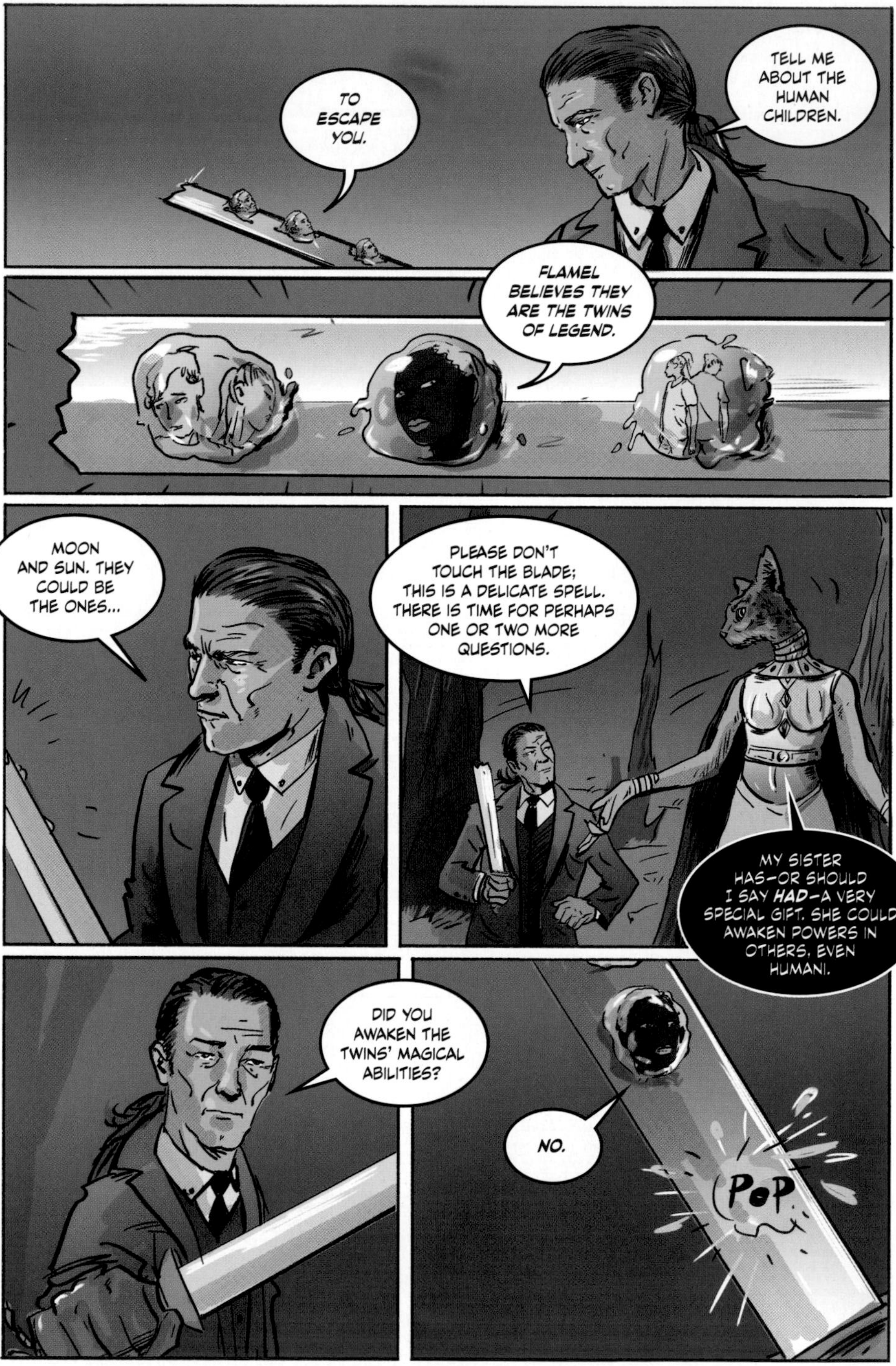
TO ESCAPE YOU.
TELL ME ABOUT THE HUMAN CHILDREN.
FLAMEL BELIEVES THEY ARE THE TWINS OF LEGEND.
MOON AND SUN. THEY COULD BE THE ONES...
PLEASE DON'T TOUCH THE BLADE; THIS IS A DELICATE SPELL. THERE IS TIME FOR PERHAPS ONE OR TWO MORE QUESTIONS.
MY SISTER HAS—OR SHOULD I SAY *HAD*—A VERY SPECIAL GIFT. SHE COULD AWAKEN POWERS IN OTHERS. EVEN HUMANI.
DID YOU AWAKEN THE TWINS' MAGICAL ABILITIES?
NO.
POP

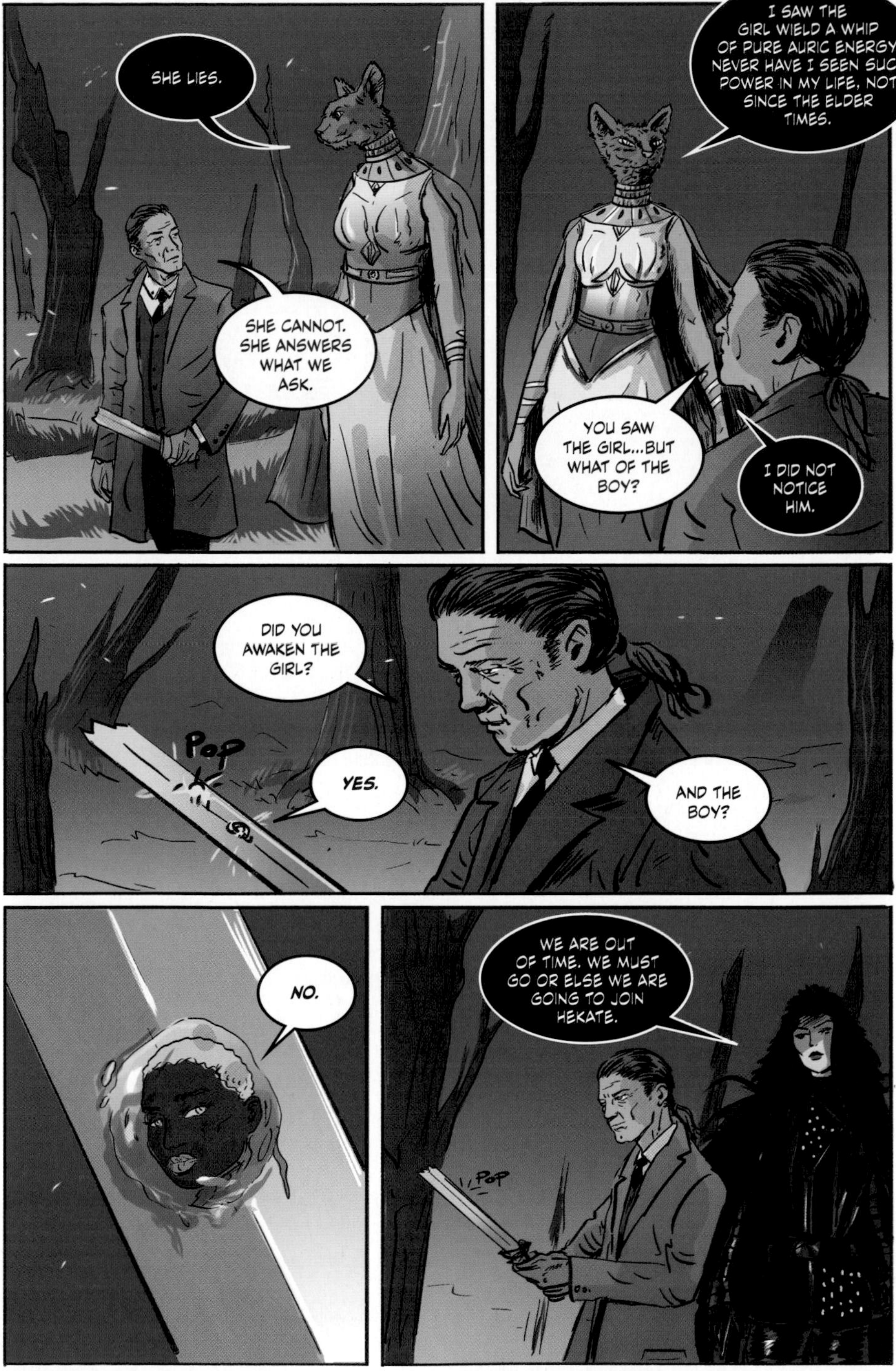
SHE LIES.
SHE CANNOT. SHE ANSWERS WHAT WE ASK.
I SAW THE GIRL WIELD A WHIP OF PURE AURIC ENERGY. NEVER HAVE I SEEN SUCH POWER IN MY LIFE, NOT SINCE THE ELDER TIMES.
YOU SAW THE GIRL...BUT WHAT OF THE BOY?
I DID NOT NOTICE HIM.
DID YOU AWAKEN THE GIRL?
POP
YES.
AND THE BOY?
NO.
WE ARE OUT OF TIME. WE MUST GO OR ELSE WE ARE GOING TO JOIN HEKATE.
POP

CHAPTER 31

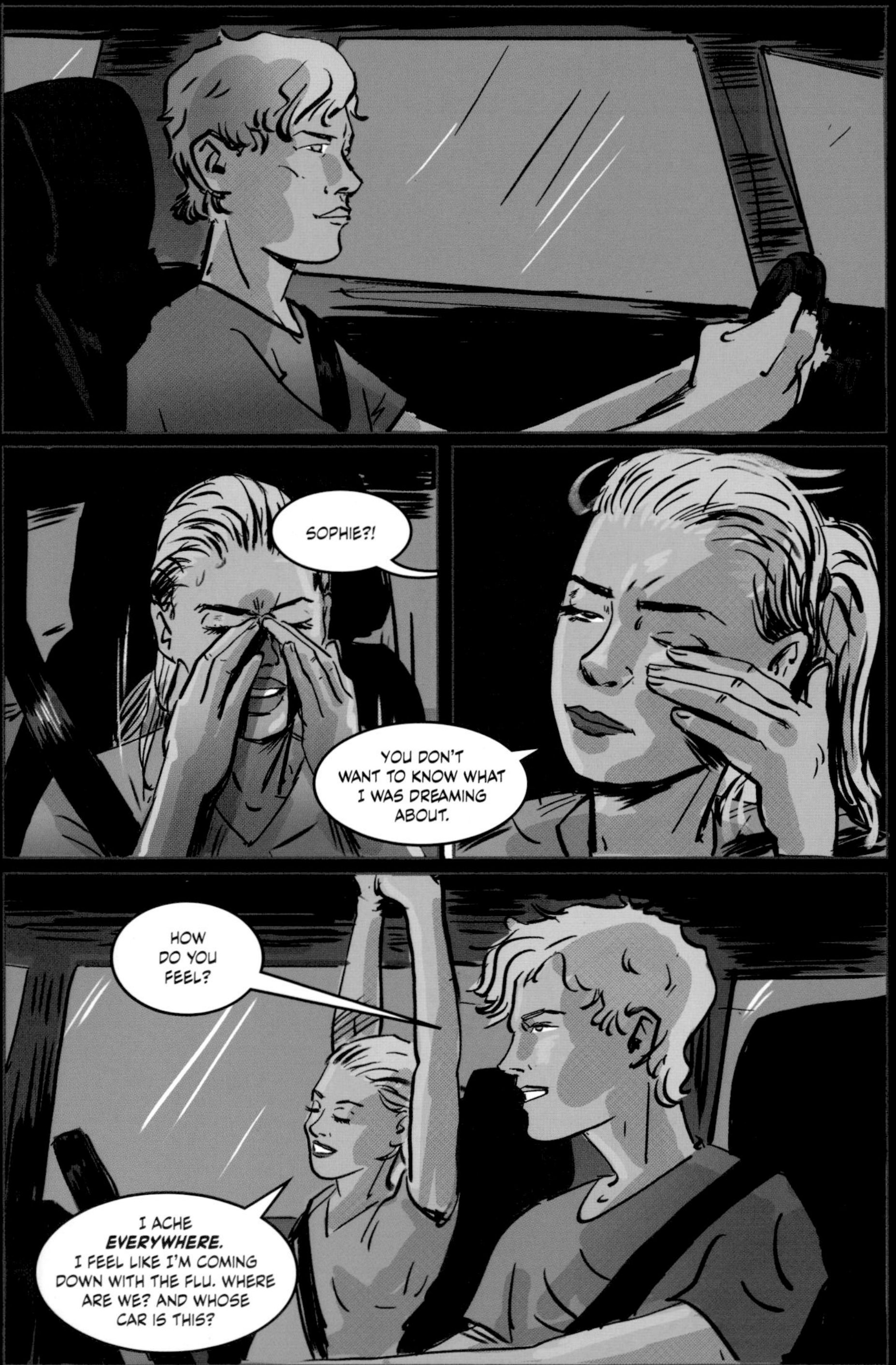
SOPHIE?!
YOU DON'T WANT TO KNOW WHAT I WAS DREAMING ABOUT.
HOW DO YOU FEEL?
I ACHE ***EVERYWHERE.*** I FEEL LIKE I'M COMING DOWN WITH THE FLU. WHERE ARE WE? AND WHOSE CAR IS THIS?

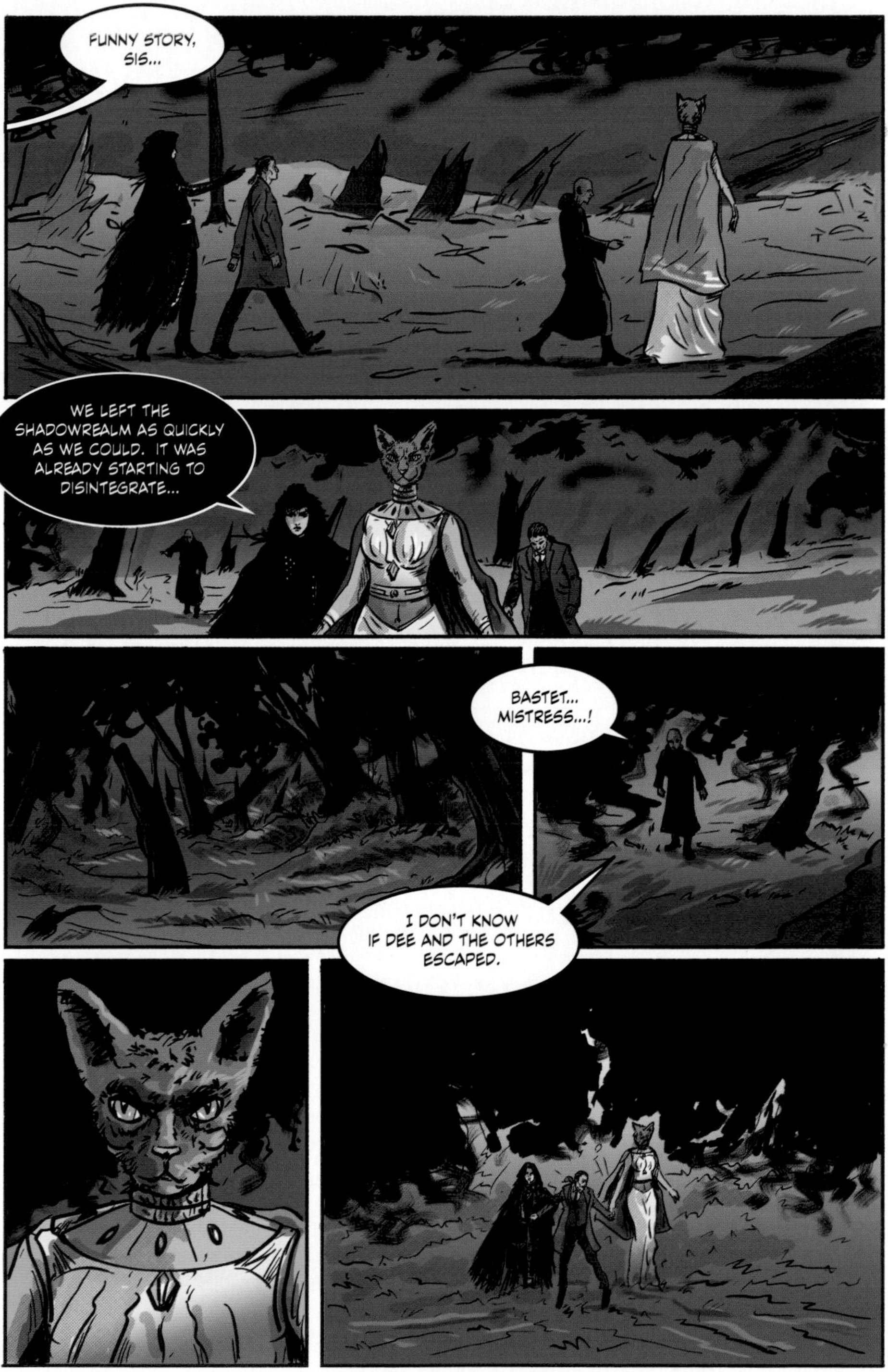
FUNNY STORY, SIS...
WE LEFT THE SHADOWREALM AS QUICKLY AS WE COULD. IT WAS ALREADY STARTING TO DISINTEGRATE...
BASTET... MISTRESS...!
I DON'T KNOW IF DEE AND THE OTHERS ESCAPED.

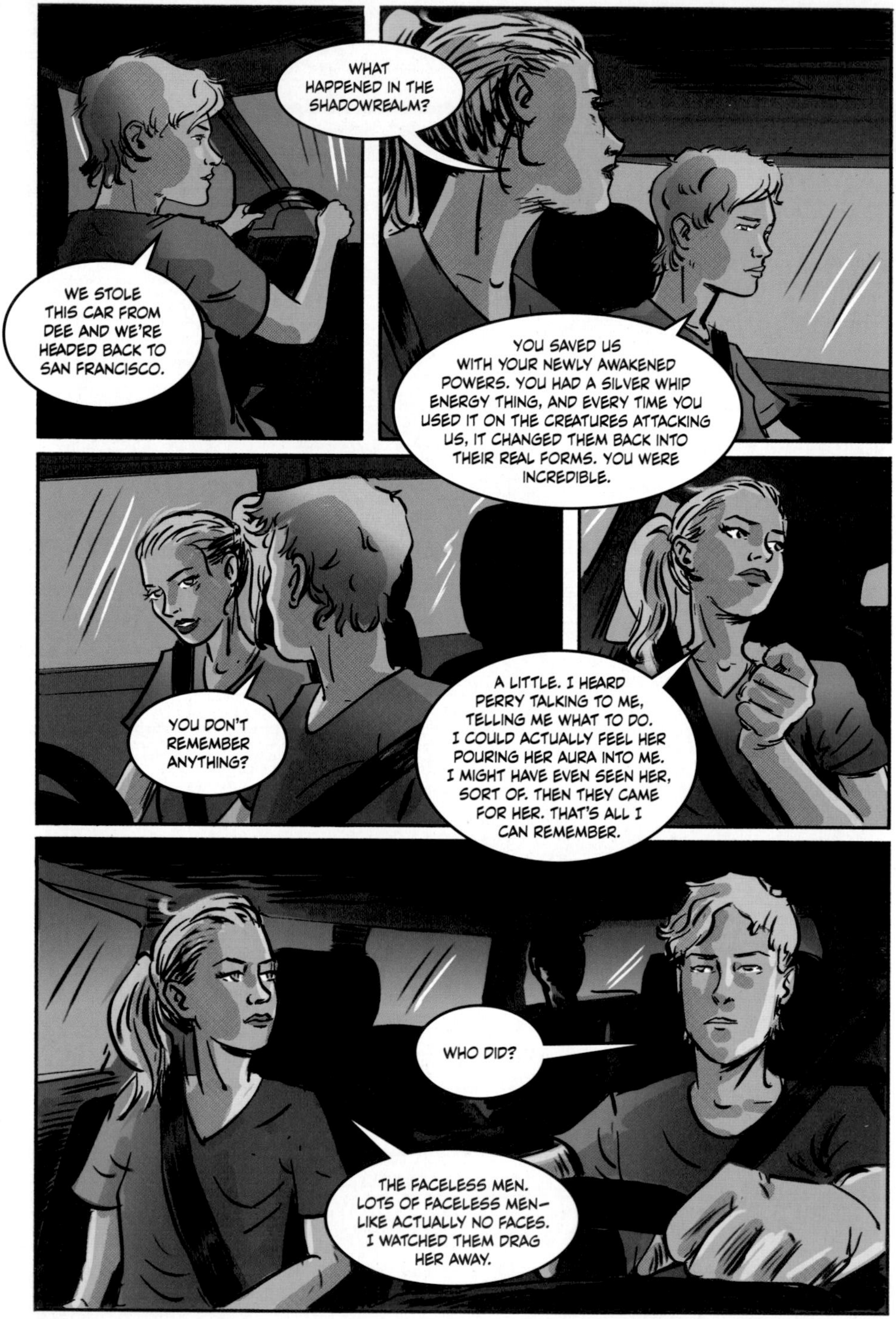

WHAT HAPPENED IN THE SHADOWREALM?
WE STOLE THIS CAR FROM DEE AND WE'RE HEADED BACK TO SAN FRANCISCO.
YOU SAVED US WITH YOUR NEWLY AWAKENED POWERS. YOU HAD A SILVER WHIP ENERGY THING, AND EVERY TIME YOU USED IT ON THE CREATURES ATTACKING US, IT CHANGED THEM BACK INTO THEIR REAL FORMS. YOU WERE INCREDIBLE.
YOU DON'T REMEMBER ANYTHING?
A LITTLE. I HEARD PERRY TALKING TO ME, TELLING ME WHAT TO DO. I COULD ACTUALLY FEEL HER POURING HER AURA INTO ME. I MIGHT HAVE EVEN SEEN HER, SORT OF. THEN THEY CAME FOR HER. THAT'S ALL I CAN REMEMBER.
WHO DID?
THE FACELESS MEN. LOTS OF FACELESS MEN—LIKE ACTUALLY NO FACES. I WATCHED THEM DRAG HER AWAY.

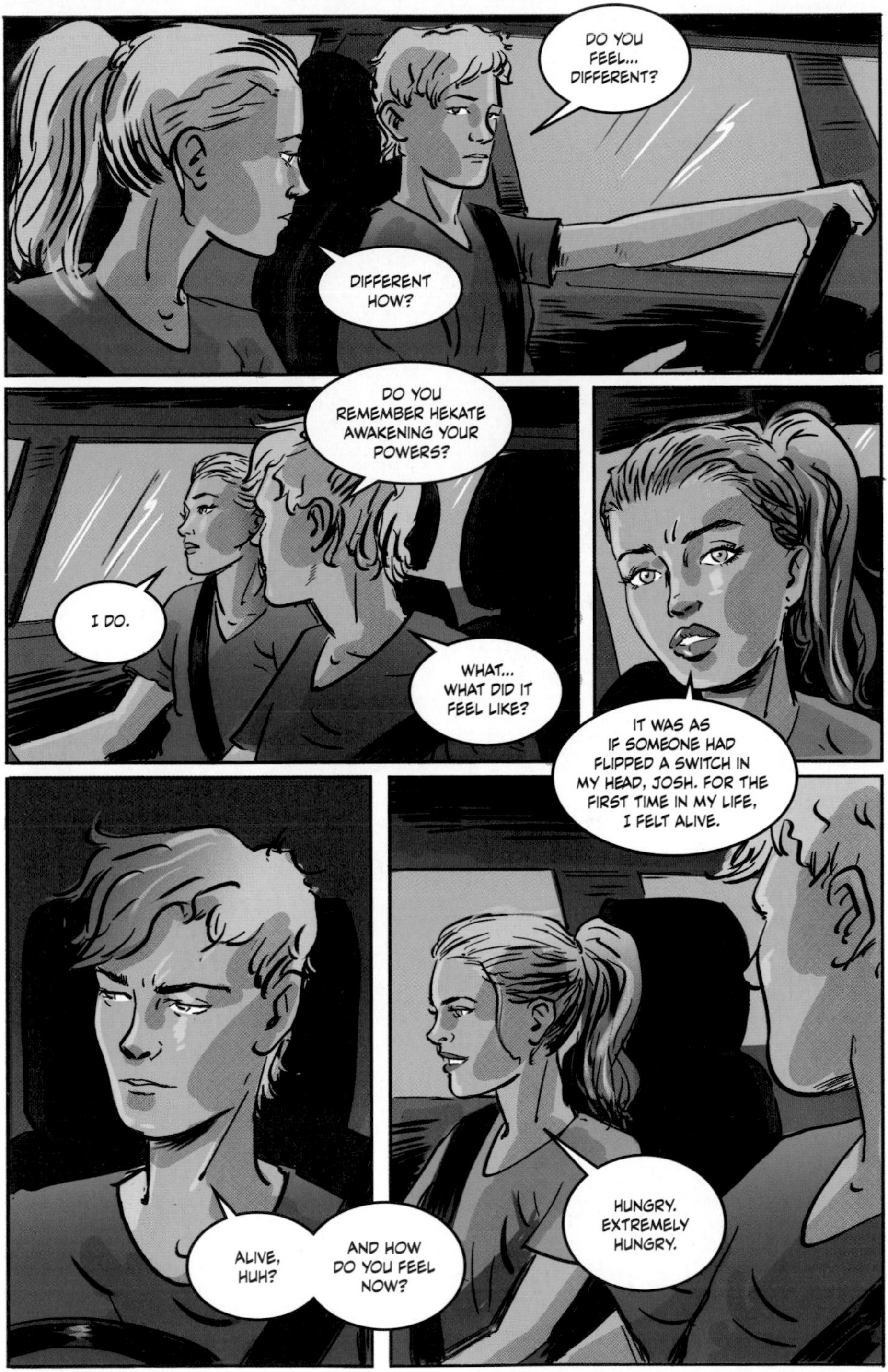
DO YOU FEEL... DIFFERENT?
DIFFERENT HOW?
DO YOU REMEMBER HEKATE AWAKENING YOUR POWERS?
I DO.
WHAT... WHAT DID IT FEEL LIKE?
IT WAS AS IF SOMEONE HAD FLIPPED A SWITCH IN MY HEAD, JOSH. FOR THE FIRST TIME IN MY LIFE, I FELT ALIVE.
ALIVE, HUH?
AND HOW DO YOU FEEL NOW?
HUNGRY. EXTREMELY HUNGRY.

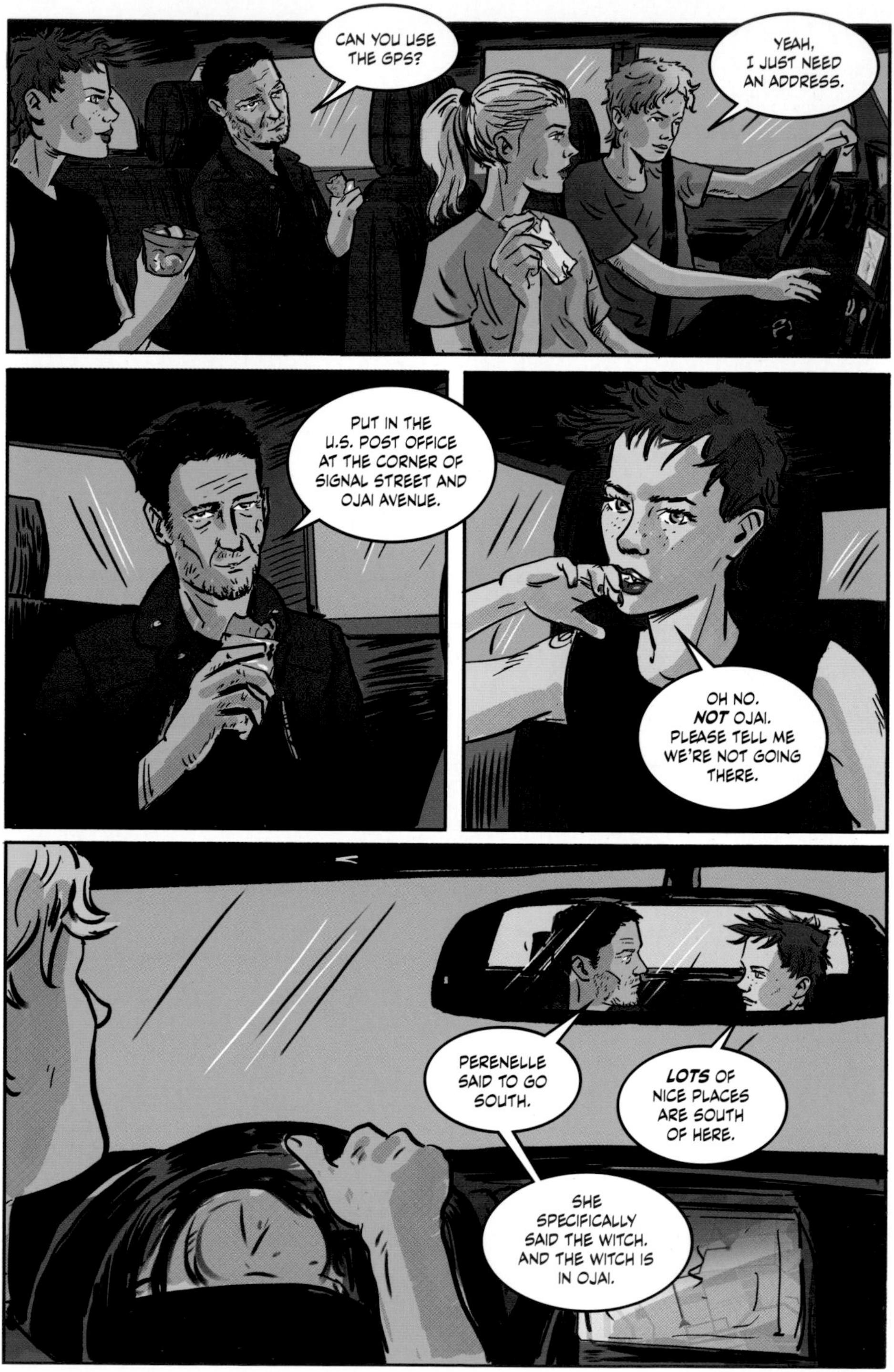
CAN YOU USE THE GPS?
YEAH, I JUST NEED AN ADDRESS.
PUT IN THE U.S. POST OFFICE AT THE CORNER OF SIGNAL STREET AND OJAI AVENUE.
OH NO. **NOT** OJAI. PLEASE TELL ME WE'RE NOT GOING THERE.
PERENELLE SAID TO GO SOUTH.
LOTS OF NICE PLACES ARE SOUTH OF HERE.
SHE SPECIFICALLY SAID THE WITCH. AND THE WITCH IS IN OJAI.

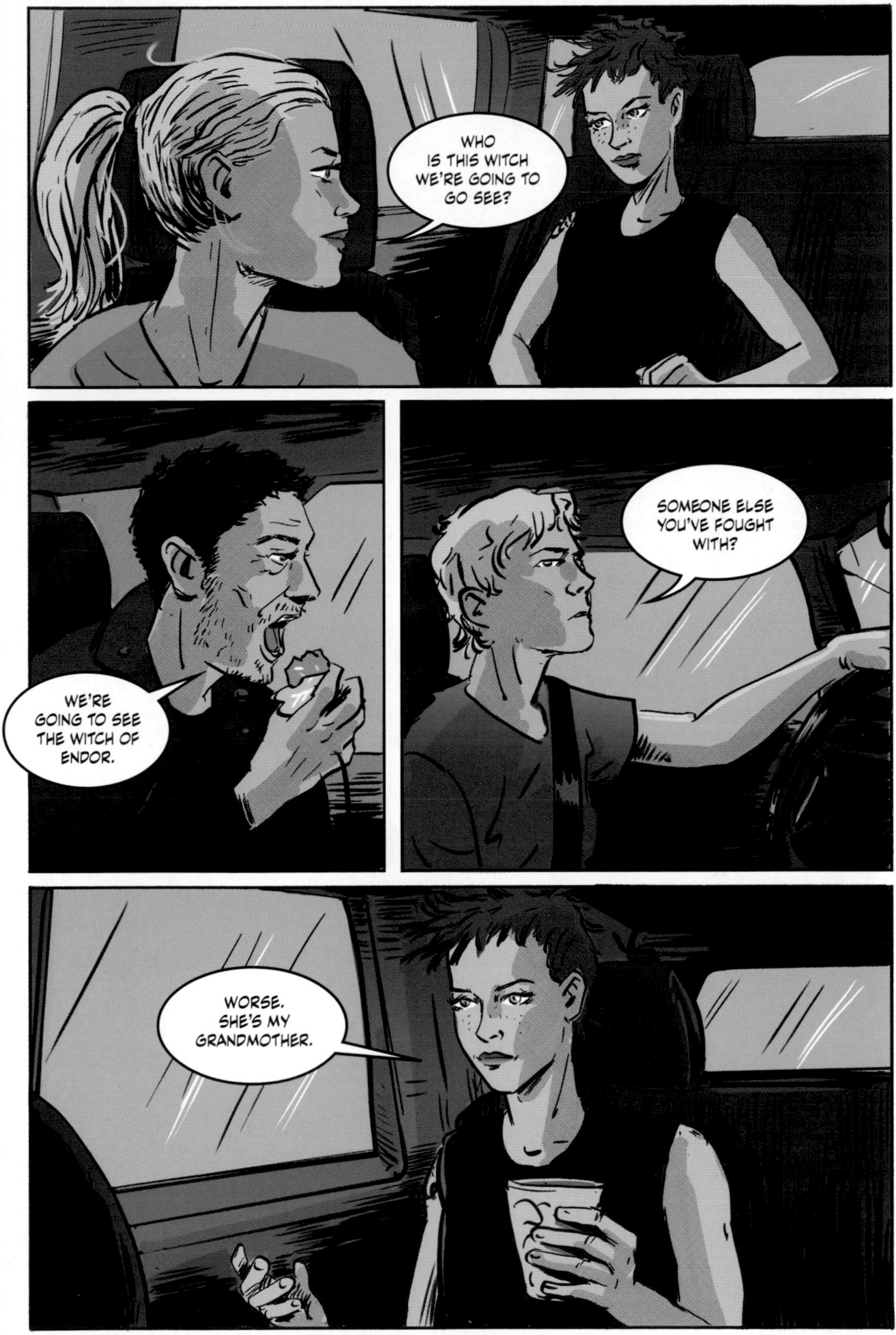
WHO IS THIS WITCH WE'RE GOING TO GO SEE?
WE'RE GOING TO SEE THE WITCH OF ENDOR.
SOMEONE ELSE YOU'VE FOUGHT WITH?
WORSE. SHE'S MY GRANDMOTHER.

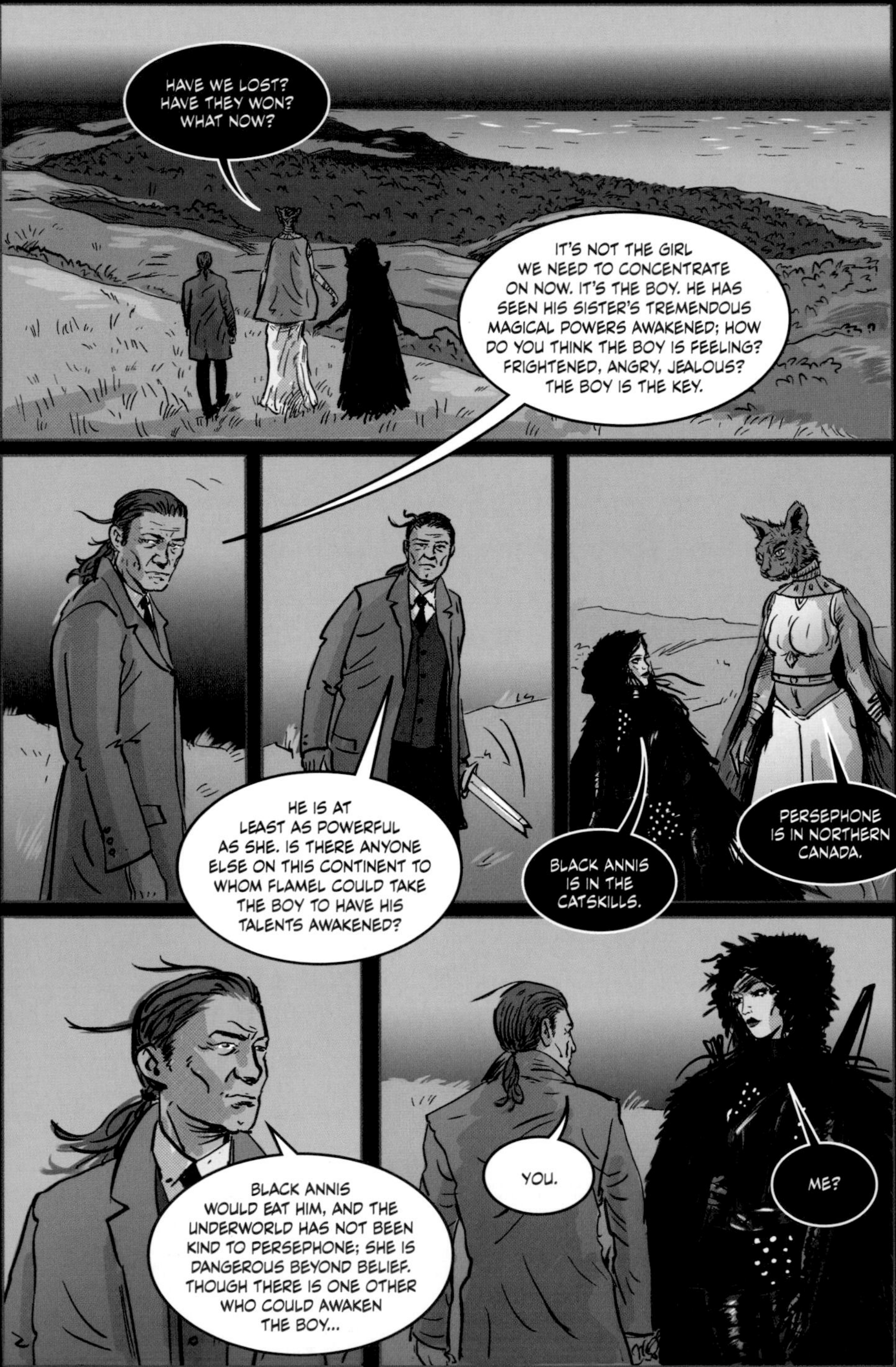
HAVE WE LOST? HAVE THEY WON? WHAT NOW?
IT'S NOT THE GIRL WE NEED TO CONCENTRATE ON NOW. IT'S THE BOY. HE HAS SEEN HIS SISTER'S TREMENDOUS MAGICAL POWERS AWAKENED; HOW DO YOU THINK THE BOY IS FEELING? FRIGHTENED, ANGRY, JEALOUS? THE BOY IS THE KEY.
HE IS AT LEAST AS POWERFUL AS SHE. IS THERE ANYONE ELSE ON THIS CONTINENT TO WHOM FLAMEL COULD TAKE THE BOY TO HAVE HIS TALENTS AWAKENED?
BLACK ANNIS IS IN THE CATSKILLS.
PERSEPHONE IS IN NORTHERN CANADA.
BLACK ANNIS WOULD EAT HIM, AND THE UNDERWORLD HAS NOT BEEN KIND TO PERSEPHONE; SHE IS DANGEROUS BEYOND BELIEF. THOUGH THERE IS ONE OTHER WHO COULD AWAKEN THE BOY...
YOU.
ME?

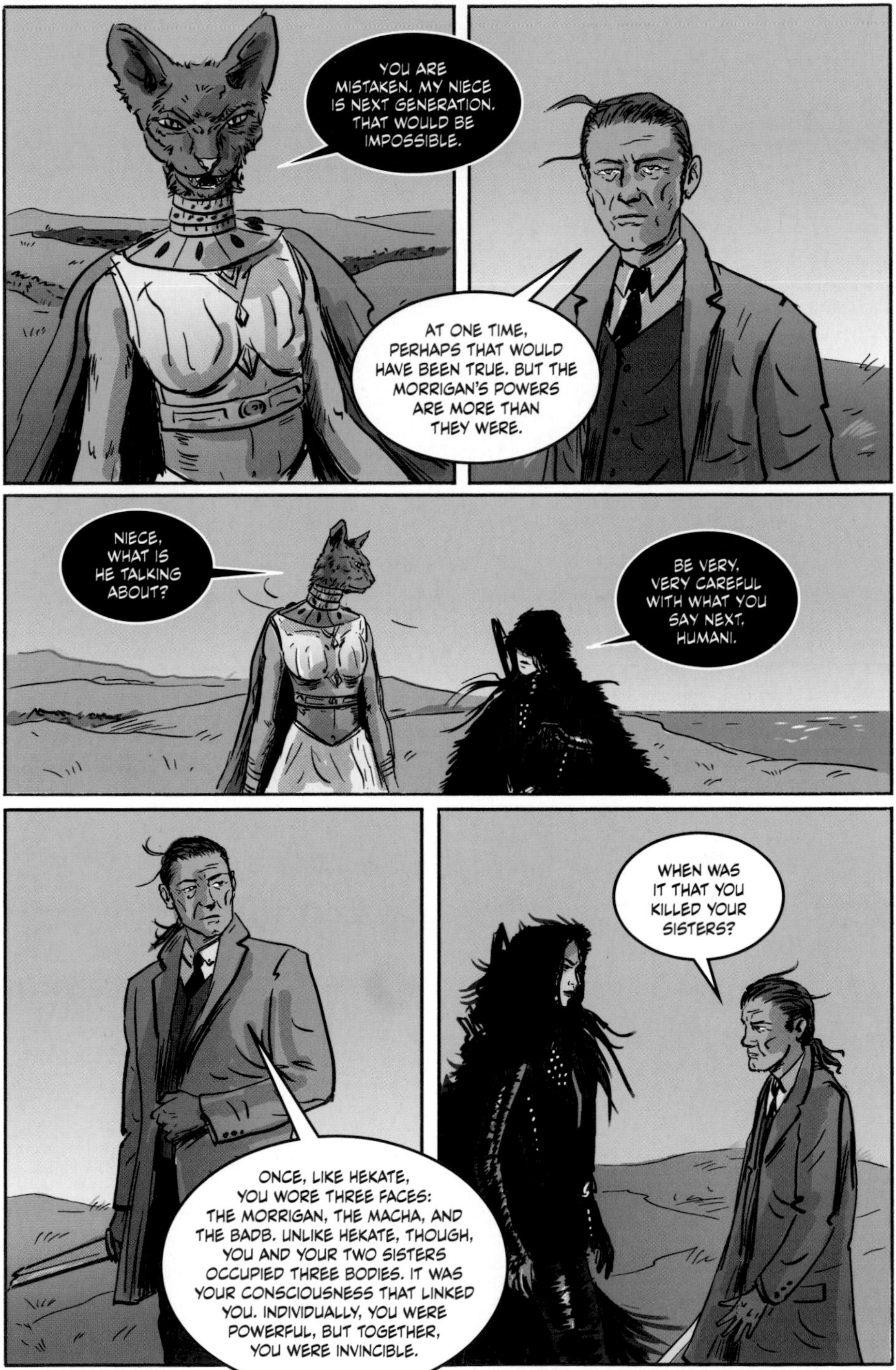
YOU ARE MISTAKEN. MY NIECE IS NEXT GENERATION. THAT WOULD BE IMPOSSIBLE.
AT ONE TIME, PERHAPS THAT WOULD HAVE BEEN TRUE. BUT THE MORRIGAN'S POWERS ARE MORE THAN THEY WERE.
NIECE, WHAT IS HE TALKING ABOUT?
BE VERY, VERY CAREFUL WITH WHAT YOU SAY NEXT, HUMAN.
ONCE, LIKE HEKATE, YOU WORE THREE FACES: THE MORRIGAN, THE MACHA, AND THE BADB. UNLIKE HEKATE, THOUGH, YOU AND YOUR TWO SISTERS OCCUPIED THREE BODIES. IT WAS YOUR CONSCIOUSNESS THAT LINKED YOU. INDIVIDUALLY, YOU WERE POWERFUL, BUT TOGETHER, YOU WERE INVINCIBLE.
WHEN WAS IT THAT YOU KILLED YOUR SISTERS?

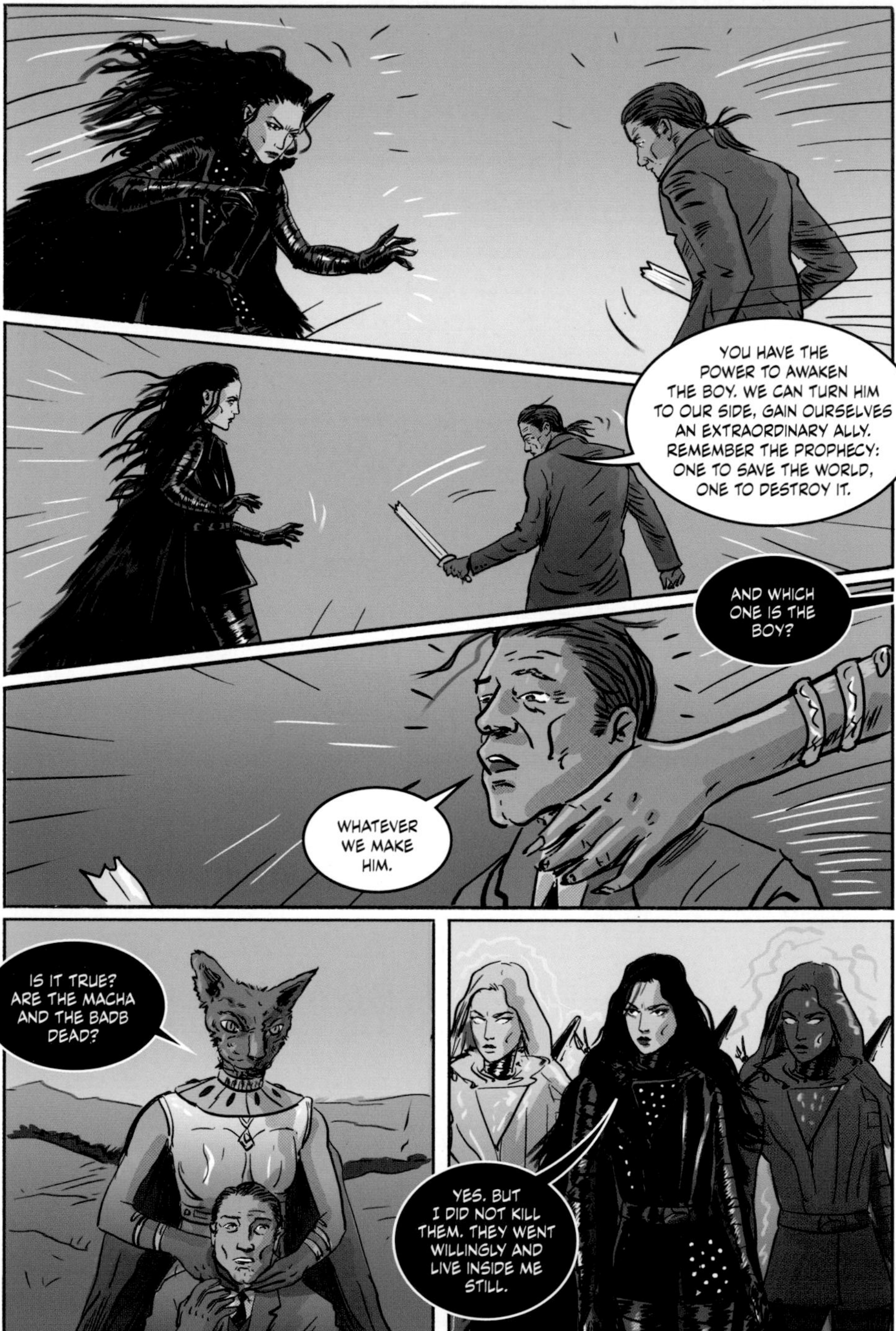
YOU HAVE THE POWER TO AWAKEN THE BOY. WE CAN TURN HIM TO OUR SIDE, GAIN OURSELVES AN EXTRAORDINARY ALLY. REMEMBER THE PROPHECY: ONE TO SAVE THE WORLD, ONE TO DESTROY IT.
AND WHICH ONE IS THE BOY?
WHATEVER WE MAKE HIM.
IS IT TRUE? ARE THE MACHA AND THE BADB DEAD?
YES. BUT I DID NOT KILL THEM. THEY WENT WILLINGLY AND LIVE INSIDE ME STILL.

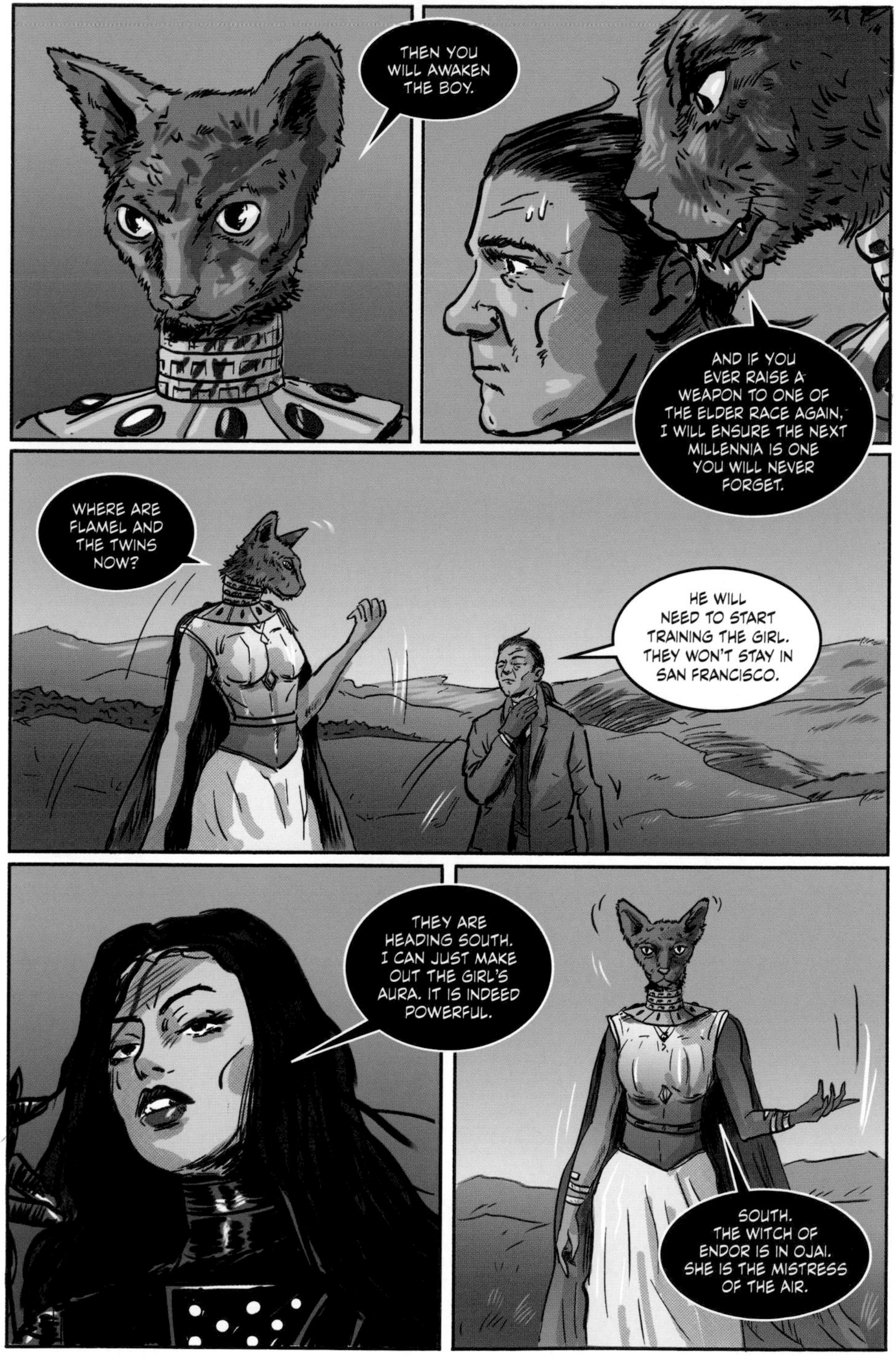
THEN YOU WILL AWAKEN THE BOY.
AND IF YOU EVER RAISE A WEAPON TO ONE OF THE ELDER RACE AGAIN, I WILL ENSURE THE NEXT MILLENNIA IS ONE YOU WILL NEVER FORGET.
WHERE ARE FLAMEL AND THE TWINS NOW?
HE WILL NEED TO START TRAINING THE GIRL. THEY WON'T STAY IN SAN FRANCISCO.
THEY ARE HEADING SOUTH. I CAN JUST MAKE OUT THE GIRL'S AURA. IT IS INDEED POWERFUL.
SOUTH. THE WITCH OF ENDOR IS IN OJAI. SHE IS THE MISTRESS OF THE AIR.

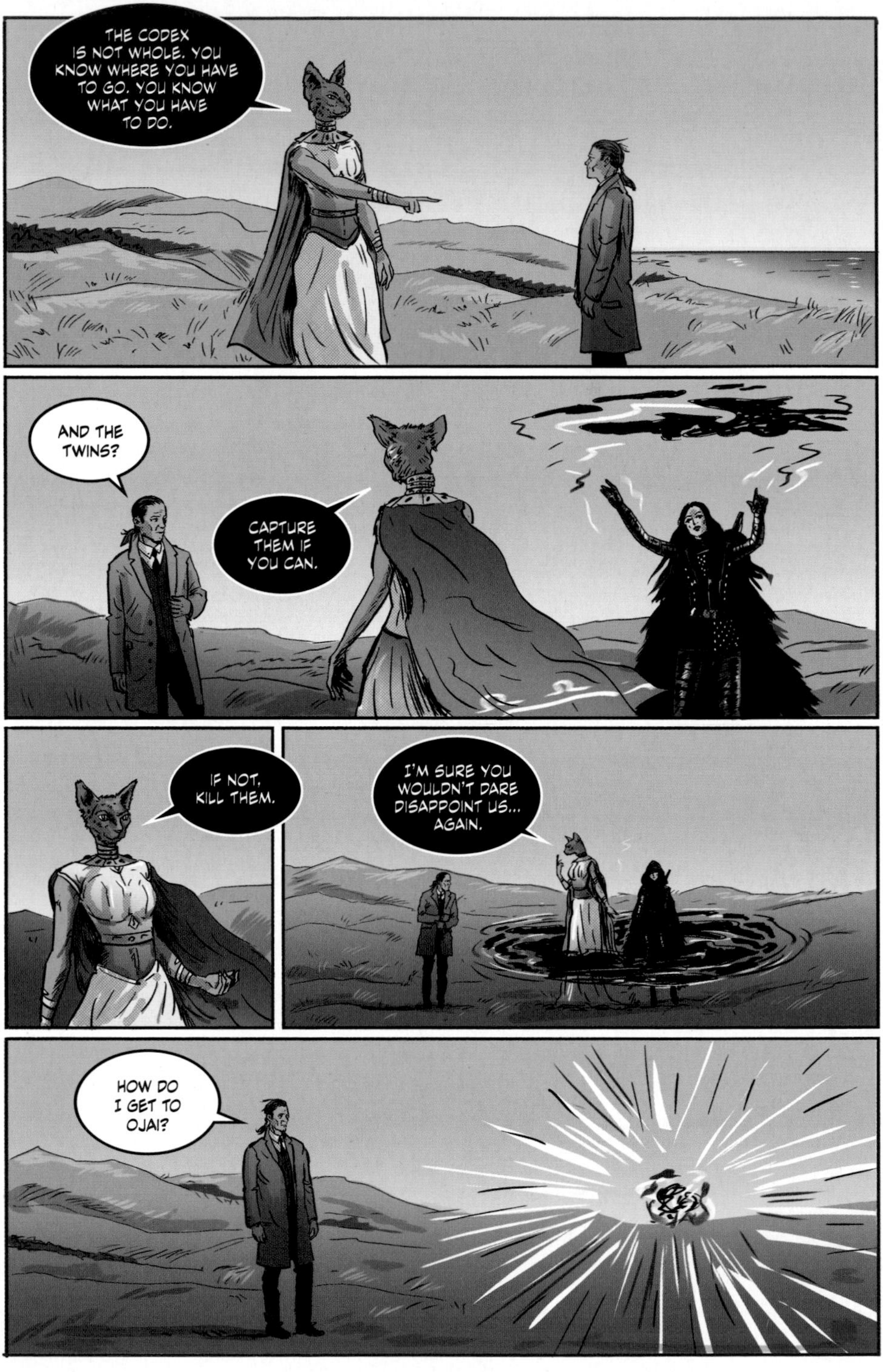
THE CODEX IS NOT WHOLE. YOU KNOW WHERE YOU HAVE TO GO. YOU KNOW WHAT YOU HAVE TO DO.
AND THE TWINS?
CAPTURE THEM IF YOU CAN.
IF NOT, KILL THEM.
I'M SURE YOU WOULDN'T DARE DISAPPOINT US... AGAIN.
HOW DO I GET TO OJAI?

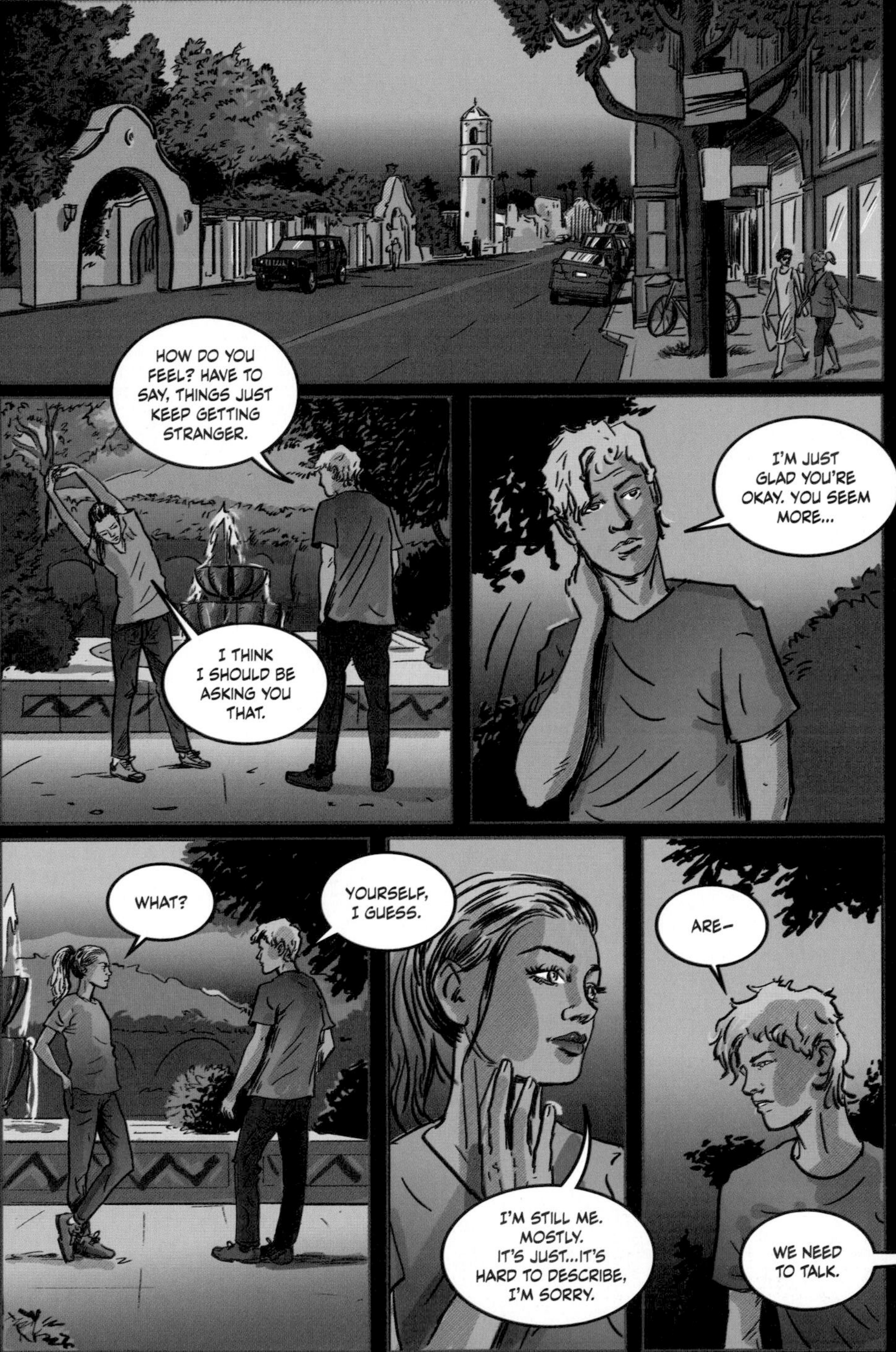
HOW DO YOU FEEL? HAVE TO SAY, THINGS JUST KEEP GETTING STRANGER.
I THINK I SHOULD BE ASKING YOU THAT.
I'M JUST GLAD YOU'RE OKAY. YOU SEEM MORE...
WHAT?
YOURSELF, I GUESS.
I'M STILL ME. MOSTLY. IT'S JUST...IT'S HARD TO DESCRIBE, I'M SORRY.
ARE-
WE NEED TO TALK.

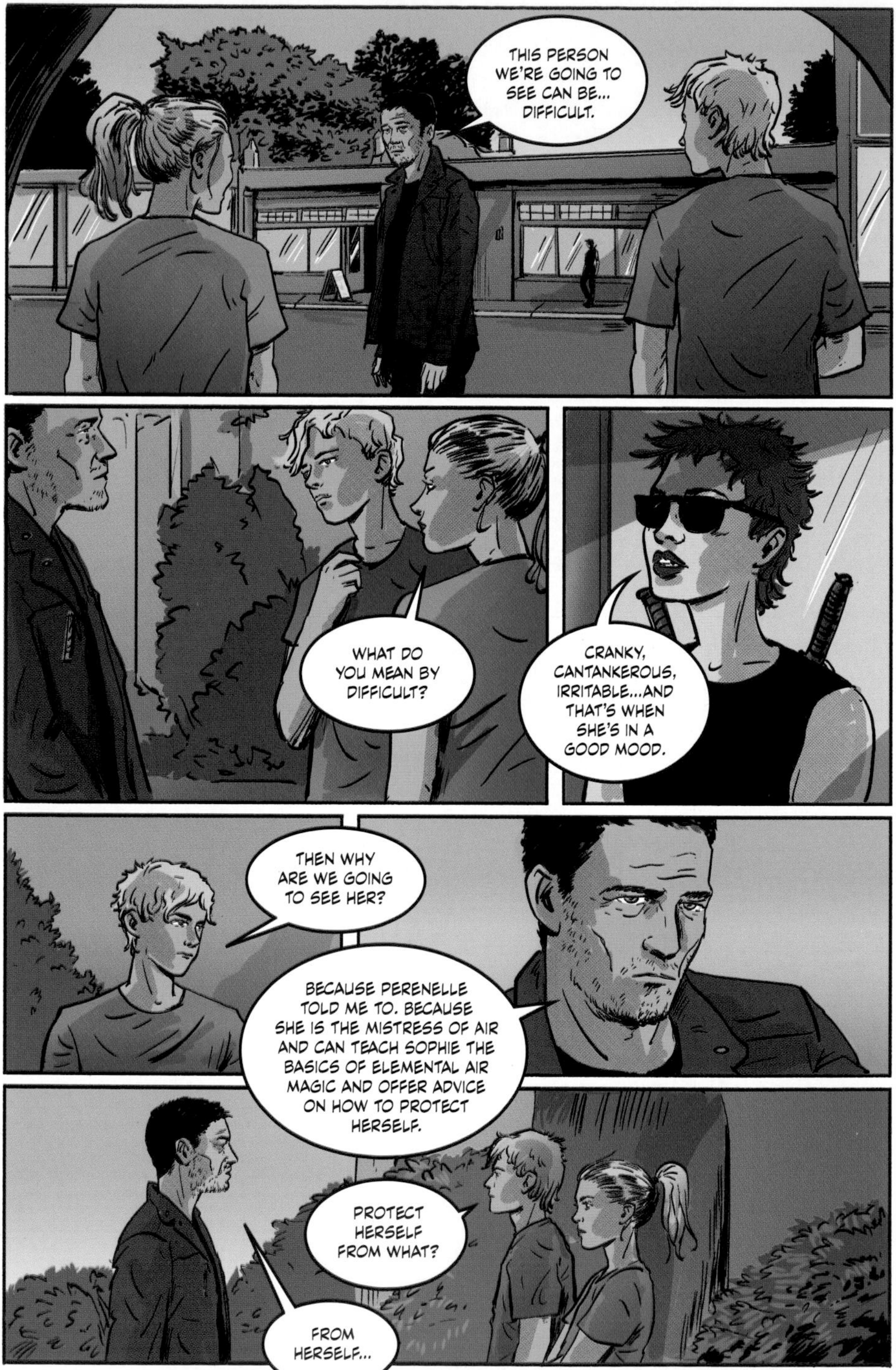
THIS PERSON WE'RE GOING TO SEE CAN BE... DIFFICULT.
WHAT DO YOU MEAN BY DIFFICULT?
CRANKY, CANTANKEROUS, IRRITABLE...AND THAT'S WHEN SHE'S IN A GOOD MOOD.
THEN WHY ARE WE GOING TO SEE HER?
BECAUSE PERENELLE TOLD ME TO. BECAUSE SHE IS THE MISTRESS OF AIR AND CAN TEACH SOPHIE THE BASICS OF ELEMENTAL AIR MAGIC AND OFFER ADVICE ON HOW TO PROTECT HERSELF.
PROTECT HERSELF FROM WHAT?
FROM HERSELF...

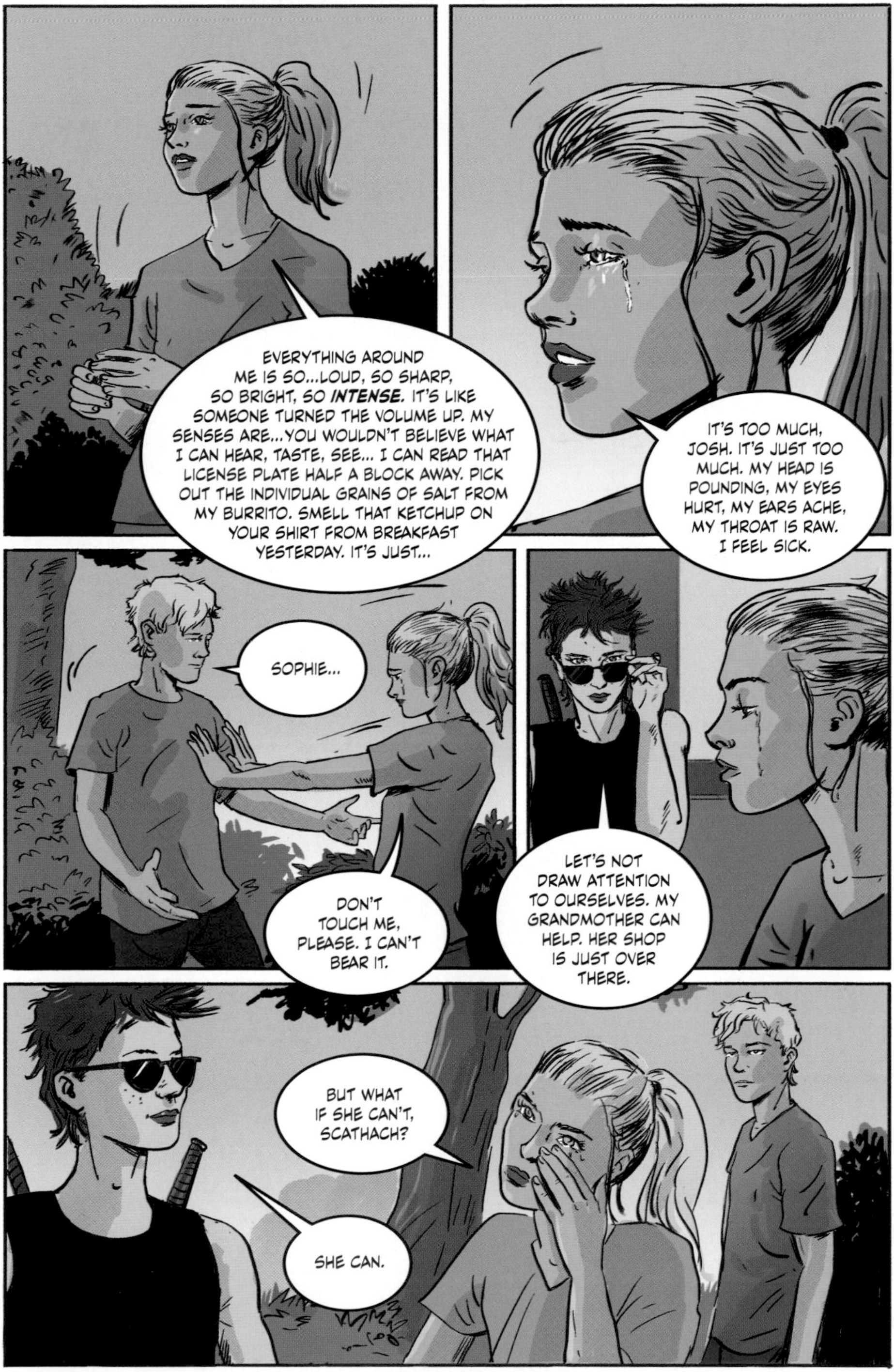
EVERYTHING AROUND ME IS SO...LOUD, SO SHARP, SO BRIGHT, SO *INTENSE.* IT'S LIKE SOMEONE TURNED THE VOLUME UP. MY SENSES ARE...YOU WOULDN'T BELIEVE WHAT I CAN HEAR, TASTE, SEE... I CAN READ THAT LICENSE PLATE HALF A BLOCK AWAY. PICK OUT THE INDIVIDUAL GRAINS OF SALT FROM MY BURRITO. SMELL THAT KETCHUP ON YOUR SHIRT FROM BREAKFAST YESTERDAY. IT'S JUST...
IT'S TOO MUCH, JOSH. IT'S JUST TOO MUCH. MY HEAD IS POUNDING, MY EYES HURT, MY EARS ACHE, MY THROAT IS RAW. I FEEL SICK.
SOPHIE...
DON'T TOUCH ME, PLEASE. I CAN'T BEAR IT.
LET'S NOT DRAW ATTENTION TO OURSELVES. MY GRANDMOTHER CAN HELP. HER SHOP IS JUST OVER THERE.
BUT WHAT IF SHE CAN'T, SCATHACH?
SHE CAN.

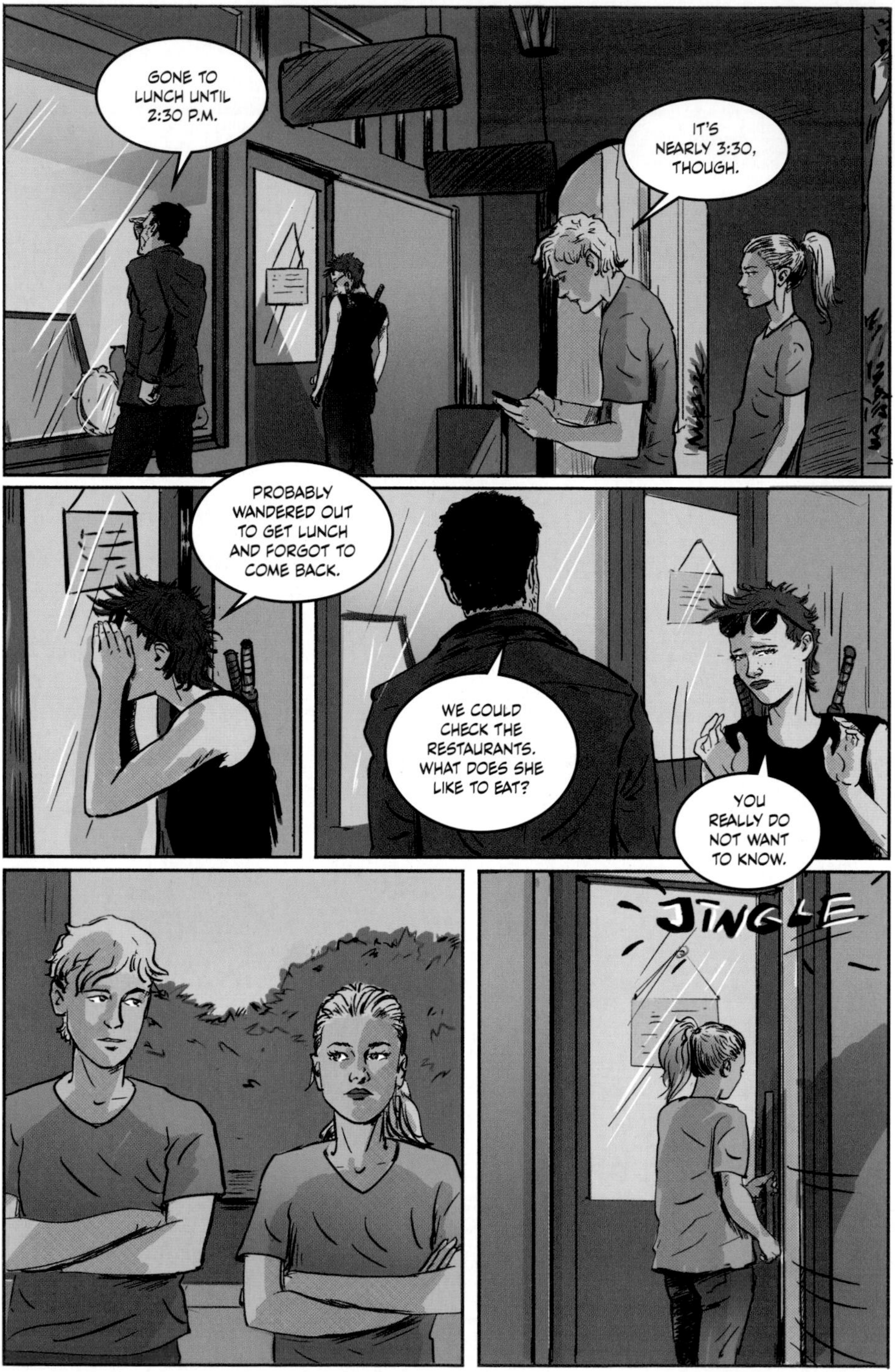
GONE TO LUNCH UNTIL 2:30 P.M.
IT'S NEARLY 3:30, THOUGH.
PROBABLY WANDERED OUT TO GET LUNCH AND FORGOT TO COME BACK.
WE COULD CHECK THE RESTAURANTS. WHAT DOES SHE LIKE TO EAT?
YOU REALLY DO NOT WANT TO KNOW.
JINGLE

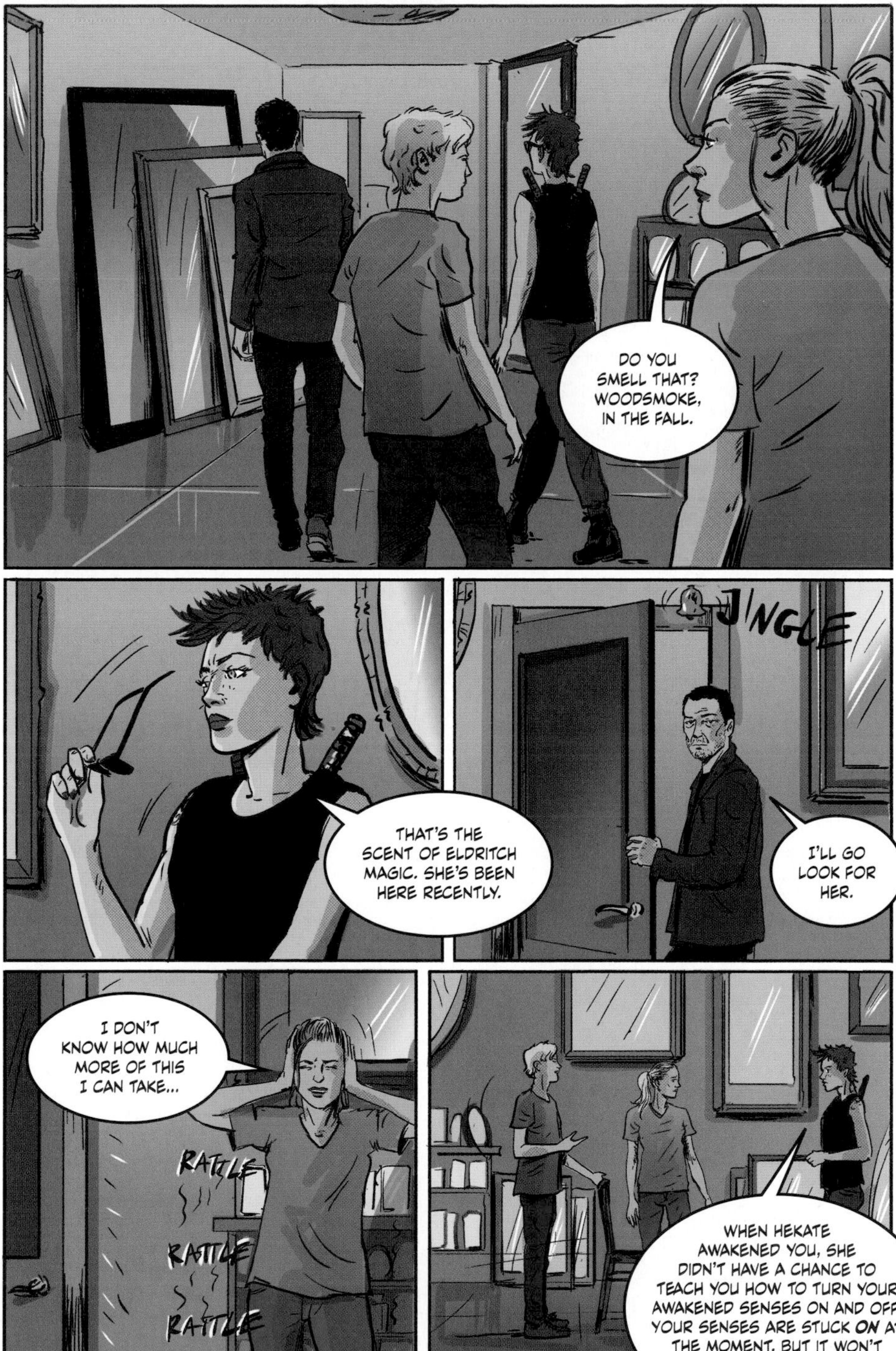
DO YOU SMELL THAT? WOODSMOKE, IN THE FALL.
THAT'S THE SCENT OF ELDRITCH MAGIC. SHE'S BEEN HERE RECENTLY.
JINGLE
I'LL GO LOOK FOR HER.
I DON'T KNOW HOW MUCH MORE OF THIS I CAN TAKE...
RATTLE
RATTLE
RATTLE
WHEN HEKATE AWAKENED YOU, SHE DIDN'T HAVE A CHANCE TO TEACH YOU HOW TO TURN YOUR AWAKENED SENSES ON AND OFF. YOUR SENSES ARE STUCK ON AT THE MOMENT, BUT IT WON'T BE LIKE THAT ALL THE TIME, I PROMISE.

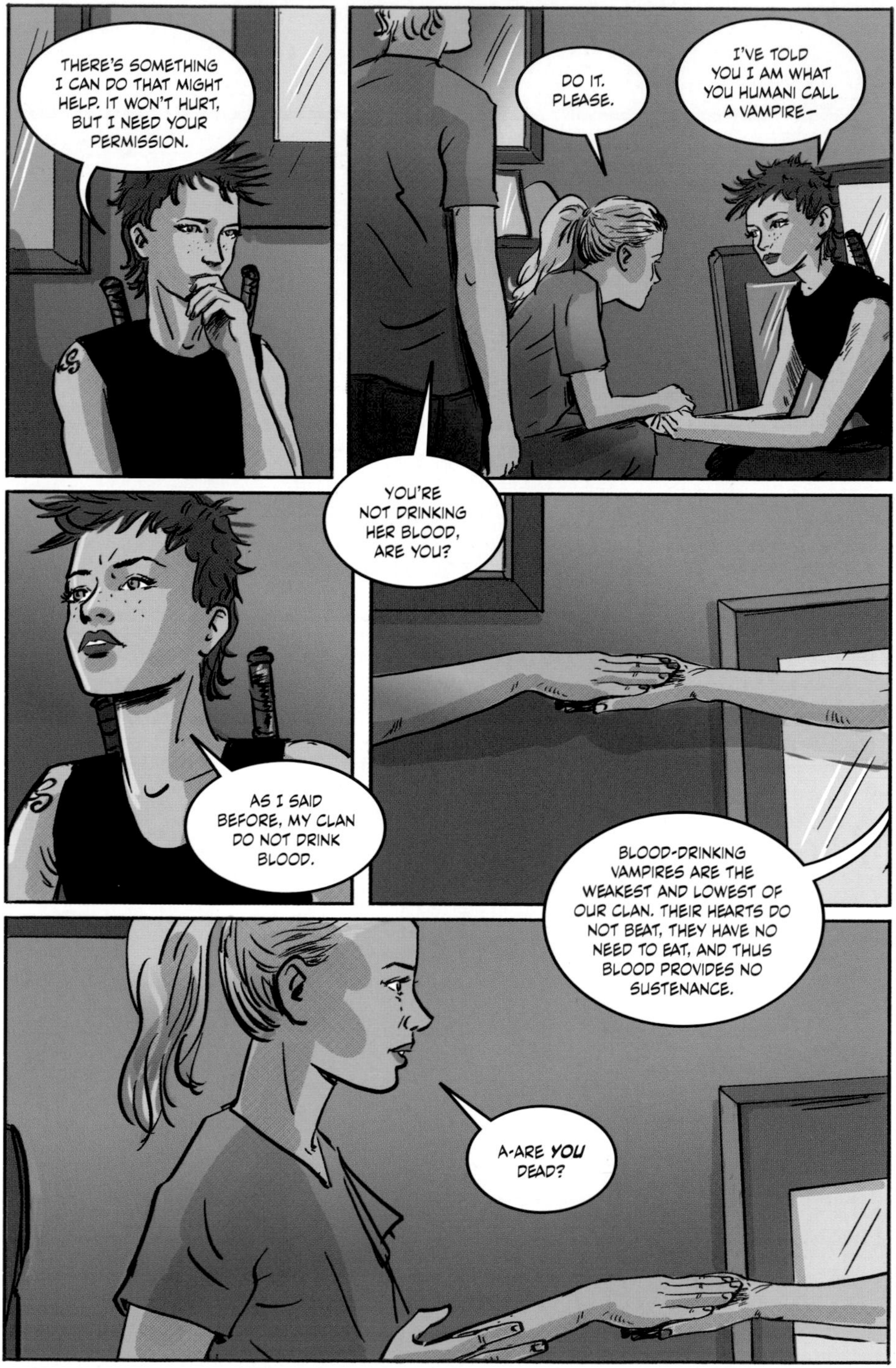
THERE'S SOMETHING I CAN DO THAT MIGHT HELP. IT WON'T HURT, BUT I NEED YOUR PERMISSION.
DO IT. PLEASE.
I'VE TOLD YOU I AM WHAT YOU HUMANI CALL A VAMPIRE—
YOU'RE NOT DRINKING HER BLOOD, ARE YOU?
AS I SAID BEFORE, MY CLAN DO NOT DRINK BLOOD.
BLOOD-DRINKING VAMPIRES ARE THE WEAKEST AND LOWEST OF OUR CLAN. THEIR HEARTS DO NOT BEAT, THEY HAVE NO NEED TO EAT, AND THUS BLOOD PROVIDES NO SUSTENANCE.
A-ARE *YOU* DEAD?

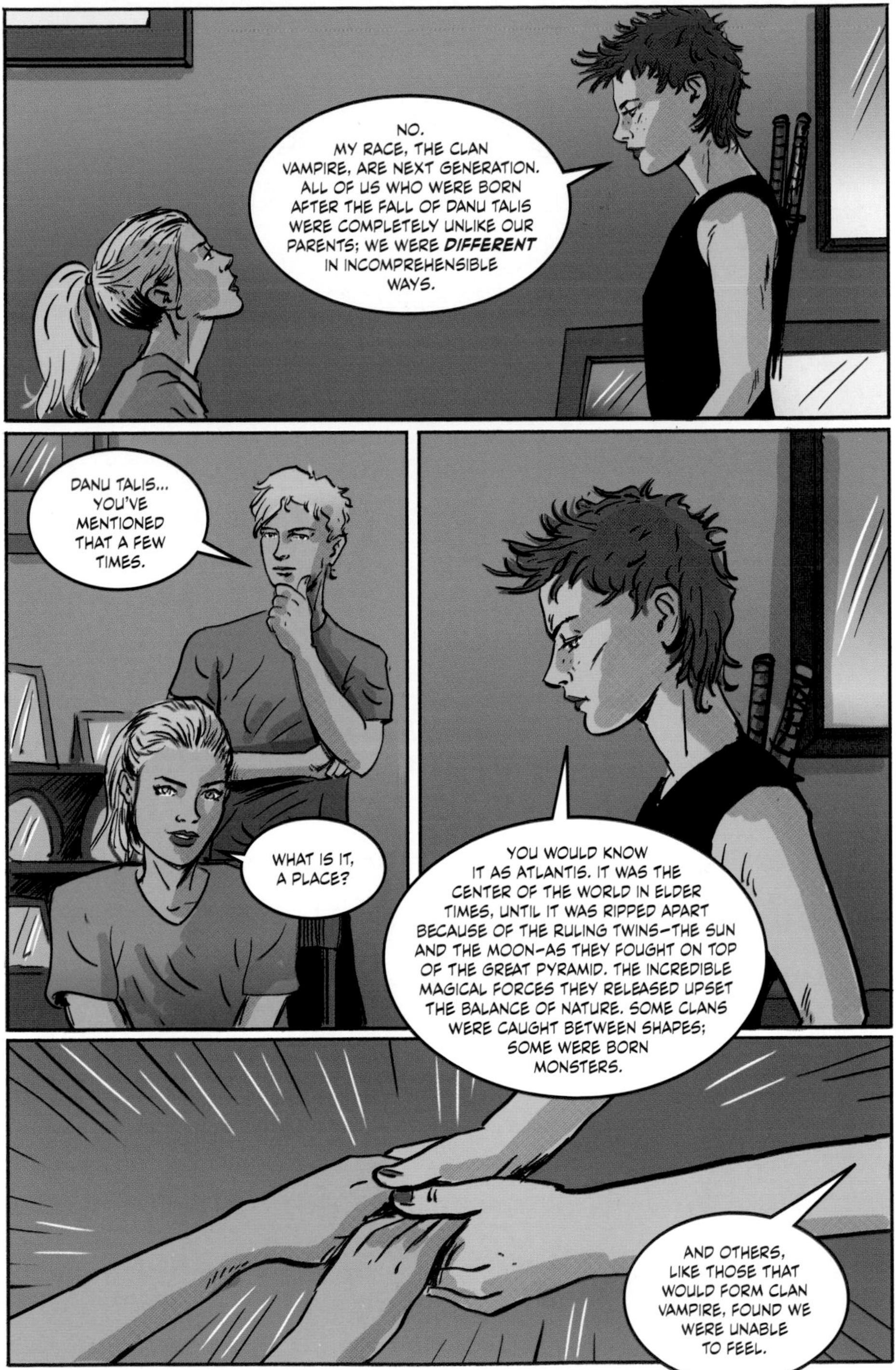
NO. MY RACE, THE CLAN VAMPIRE, ARE NEXT GENERATION. ALL OF US WHO WERE BORN AFTER THE FALL OF DANU TALIS WERE COMPLETELY UNLIKE OUR PARENTS; WE WERE ***DIFFERENT*** IN INCOMPREHENSIBLE WAYS.
DANU TALIS... YOU'VE MENTIONED THAT A FEW TIMES.
WHAT IS IT, A PLACE?
YOU WOULD KNOW IT AS ATLANTIS. IT WAS THE CENTER OF THE WORLD IN ELDER TIMES, UNTIL IT WAS RIPPED APART BECAUSE OF THE RULING TWINS—THE SUN AND THE MOON—AS THEY FOUGHT ON TOP OF THE GREAT PYRAMID. THE INCREDIBLE MAGICAL FORCES THEY RELEASED UPSET THE BALANCE OF NATURE. SOME CLANS WERE CAUGHT BETWEEN SHAPES; SOME WERE BORN MONSTERS.
AND OTHERS, LIKE THOSE THAT WOULD FORM CLAN VAMPIRE, FOUND WE WERE UNABLE TO FEEL.

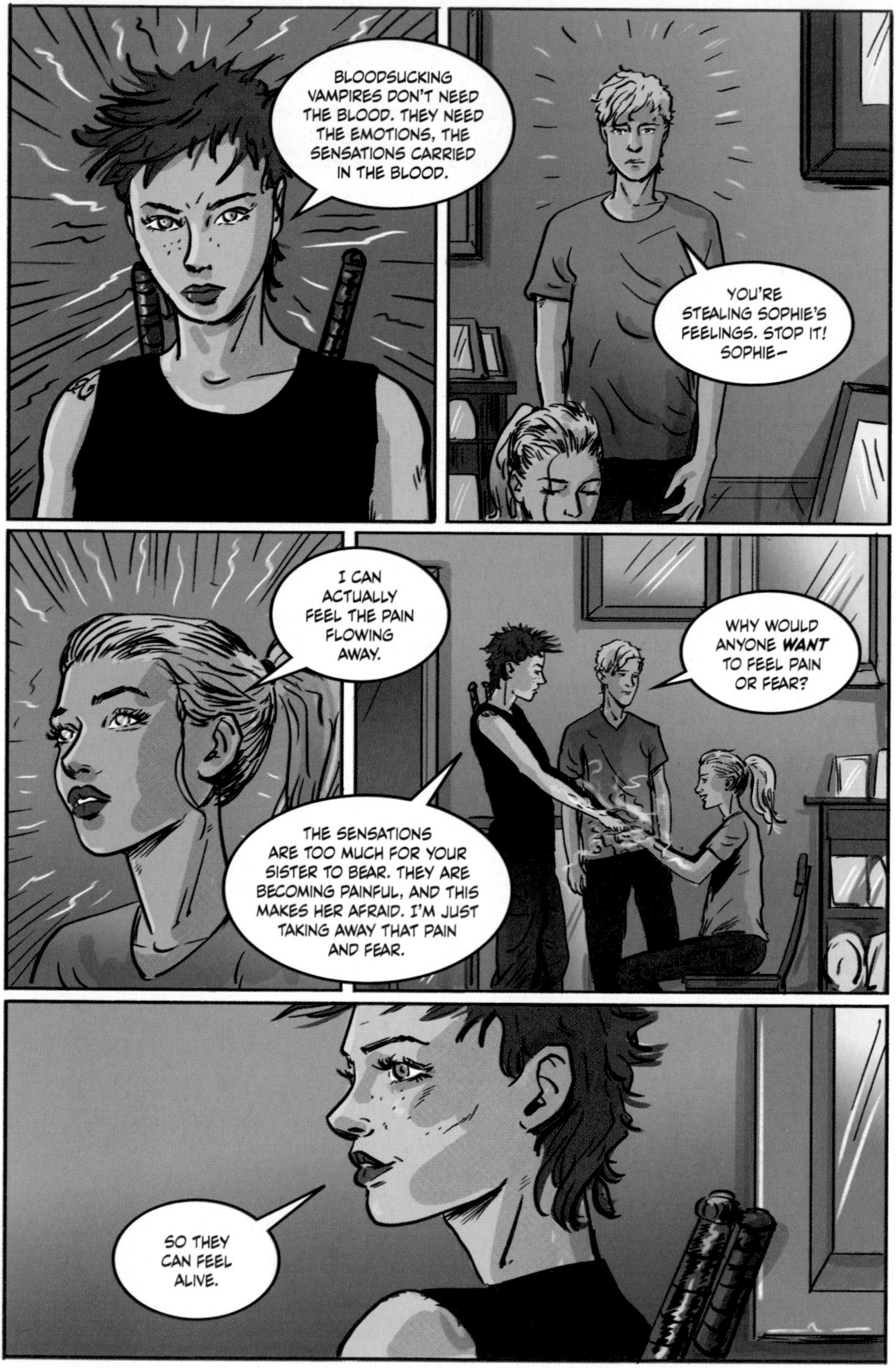
BLOODSUCKING VAMPIRES DON'T NEED THE BLOOD. THEY NEED THE EMOTIONS, THE SENSATIONS CARRIED IN THE BLOOD.
YOU'RE STEALING SOPHIE'S FEELINGS. STOP IT! SOPHIE–
I CAN ACTUALLY FEEL THE PAIN FLOWING AWAY.
WHY WOULD ANYONE **WANT** TO FEEL PAIN OR FEAR?
THE SENSATIONS ARE TOO MUCH FOR YOUR SISTER TO BEAR. THEY ARE BECOMING PAINFUL, AND THIS MAKES HER AFRAID. I'M JUST TAKING AWAY THAT PAIN AND FEAR.
SO THEY CAN FEEL ALIVE.

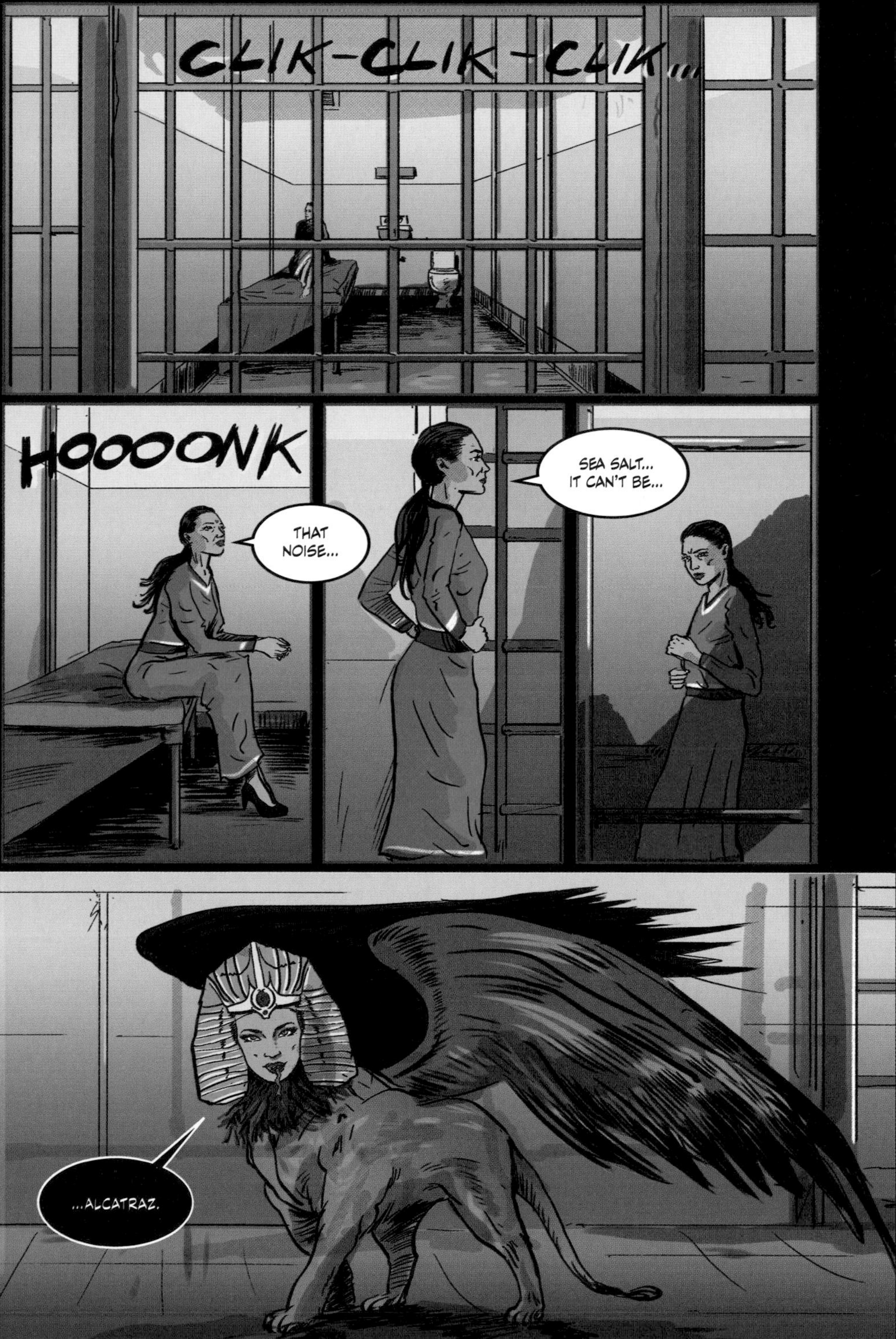
CLIK-CLIK-CLIK...
HOOOONK
THAT NOISE...
SEA SALT... IT CAN'T BE...
...ALCATRAZ.

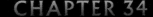

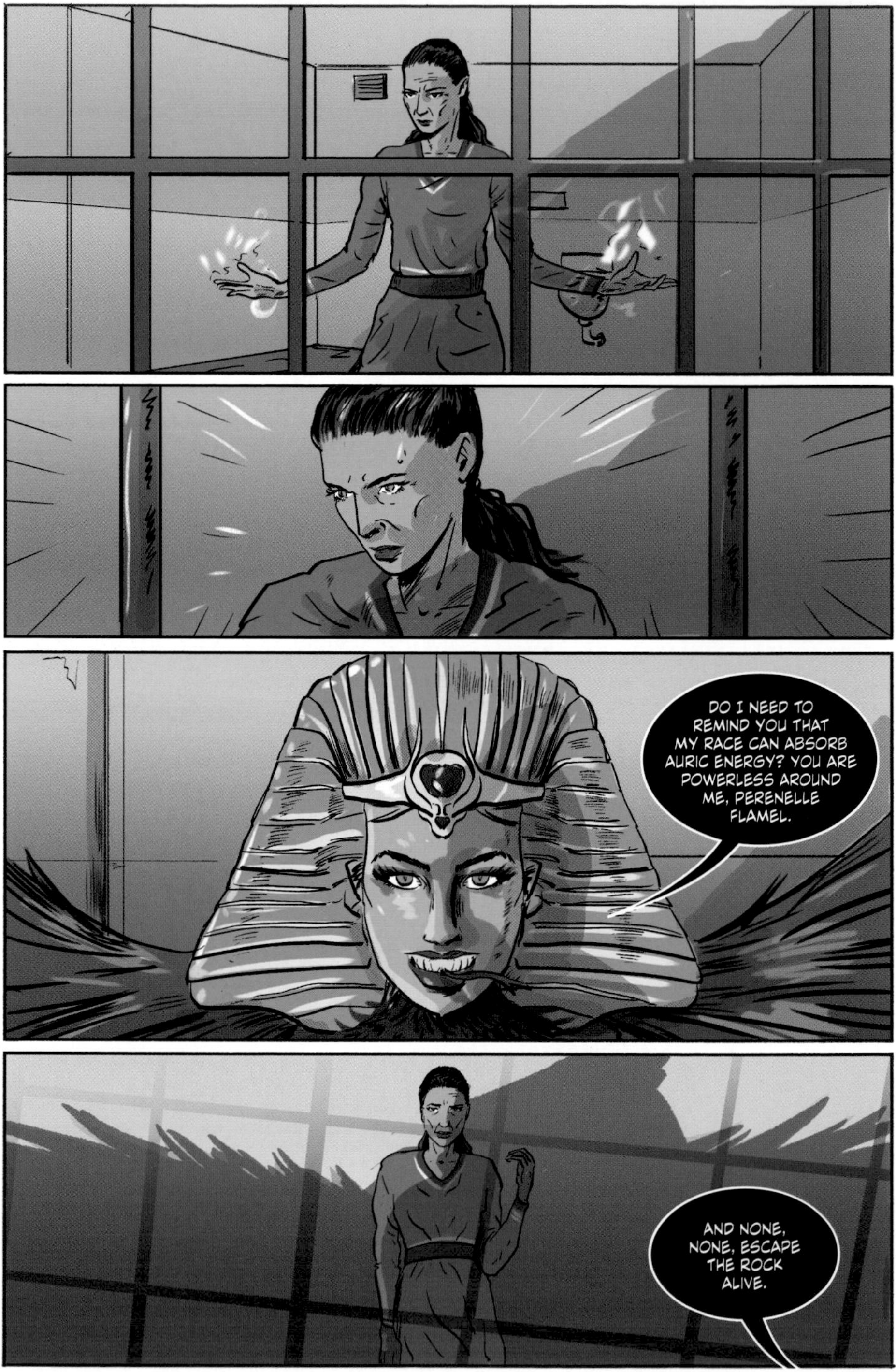
DO I NEED TO REMIND YOU THAT MY RACE CAN ABSORB AURIC ENERGY? YOU ARE POWERLESS AROUND ME, PERENELLE FLAMEL.
AND NONE, NONE, ESCAPE THE ROCK ALIVE.

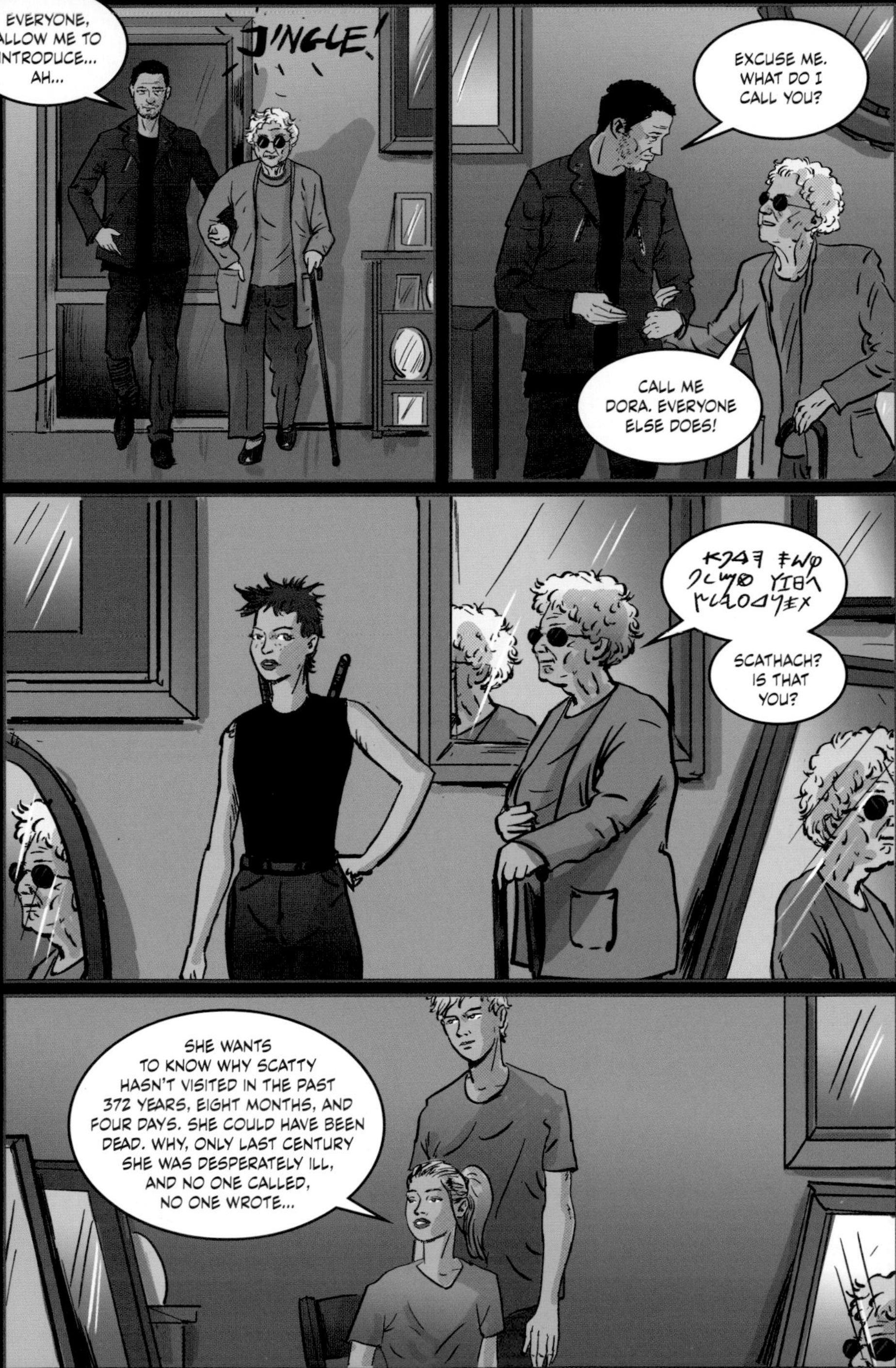
EVERYONE, ALLOW ME TO INTRODUCE... AH...
JINGLE!
EXCUSE ME. WHAT DO I CALL YOU?
CALL ME DORA. EVERYONE ELSE DOES!
SCATHACH? IS THAT YOU?
SHE WANTS TO KNOW WHY SCATTY HASN'T VISITED IN THE PAST 372 YEARS, EIGHT MONTHS, AND FOUR DAYS. SHE COULD HAVE BEEN DEAD. WHY, ONLY LAST CENTURY SHE WAS DESPERATELY ILL, AND NO ONE CALLED, NO ONE WROTE...

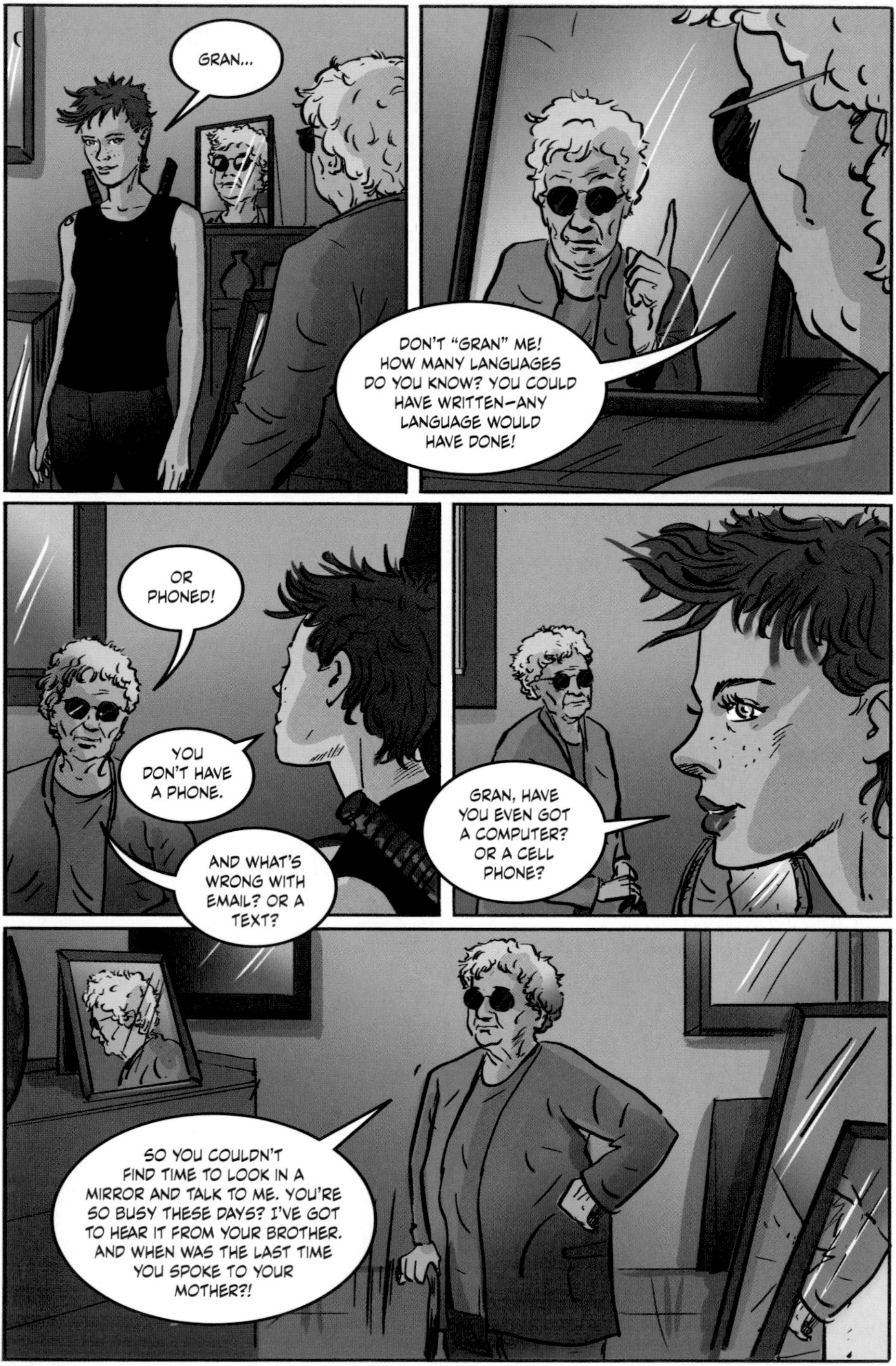
GRAN...
DON'T "GRAN" ME! HOW MANY LANGUAGES DO YOU KNOW? YOU COULD HAVE WRITTEN—ANY LANGUAGE WOULD HAVE DONE!
OR PHONED!
YOU DON'T HAVE A PHONE.
AND WHAT'S WRONG WITH EMAIL? OR A TEXT?
GRAN, HAVE YOU EVEN GOT A COMPUTER? OR A CELL PHONE?
SO YOU COULDN'T FIND TIME TO LOOK IN A MIRROR AND TALK TO ME. YOU'RE SO BUSY THESE DAYS? I'VE GOT TO HEAR IT FROM YOUR BROTHER. AND WHEN WAS THE LAST TIME YOU SPOKE TO YOUR MOTHER?!

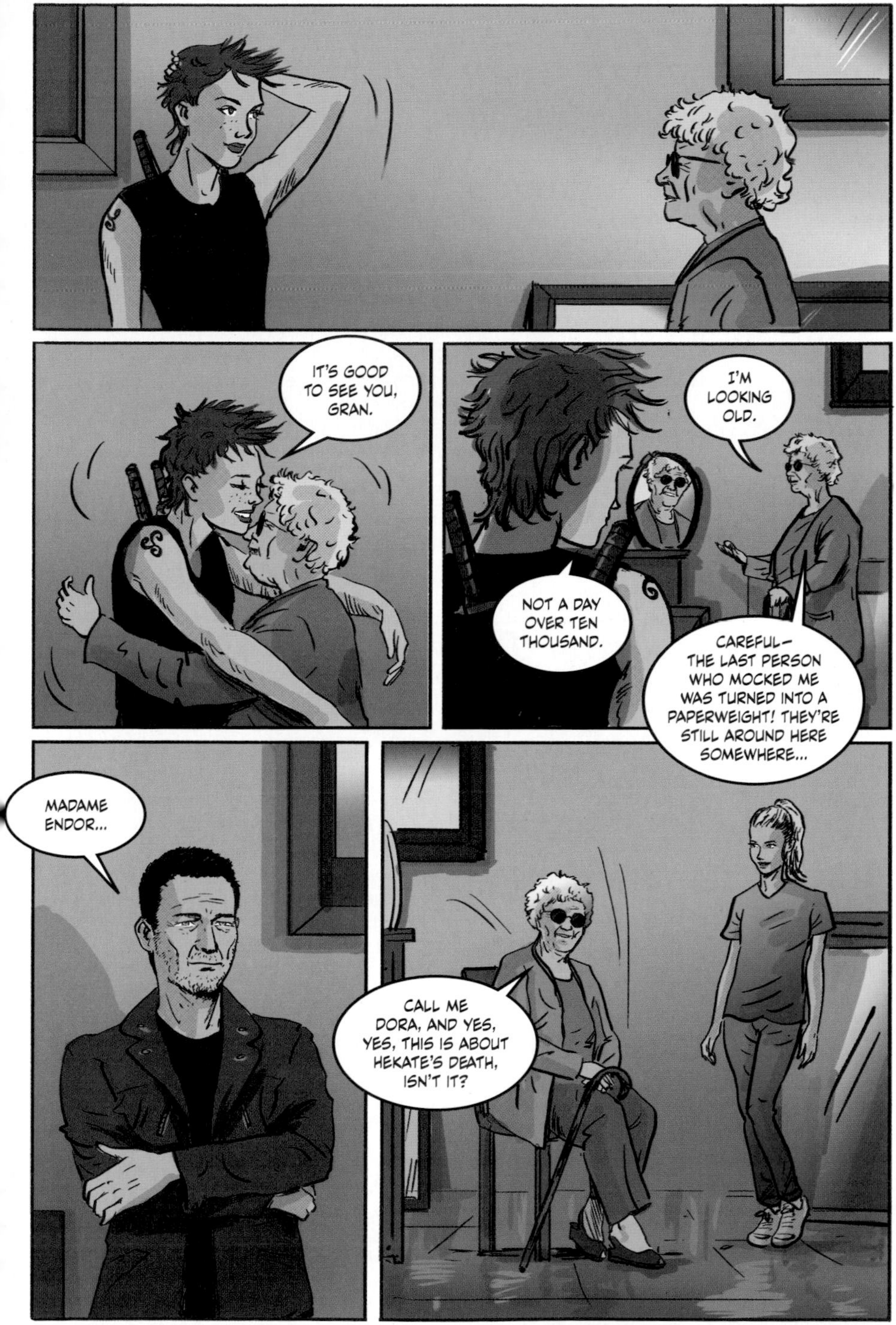
IT'S GOOD TO SEE YOU, GRAN.
I'M LOOKING OLD.
NOT A DAY OVER TEN THOUSAND.
CAREFUL— THE LAST PERSON WHO MOCKED ME WAS TURNED INTO A PAPERWEIGHT! THEY'RE STILL AROUND HERE SOMEWHERE...
MADAME ENDOR...
CALL ME DORA, AND YES, YES, THIS IS ABOUT HEKATE'S DEATH, ISN'T IT?

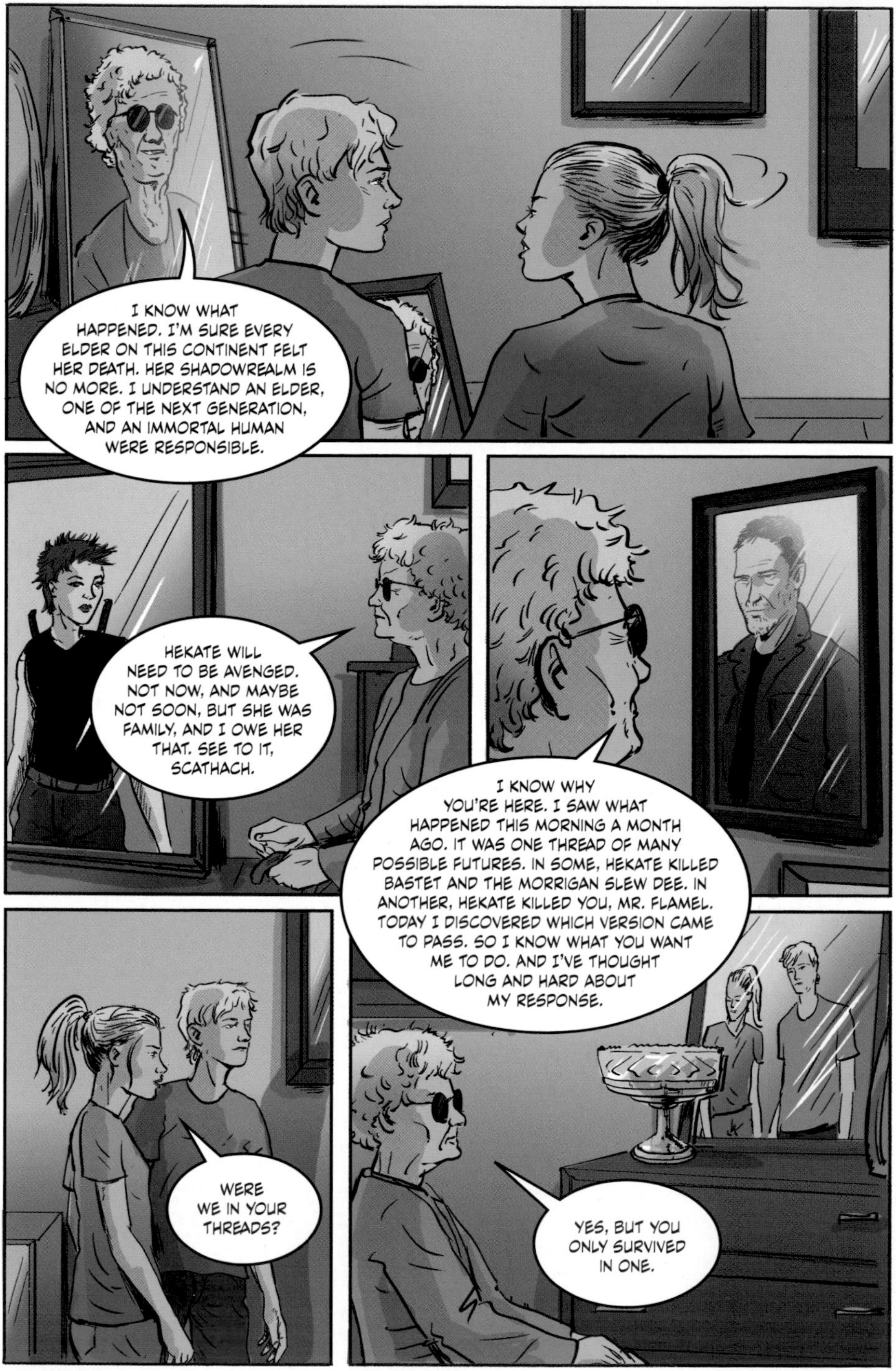
I KNOW WHAT HAPPENED. I'M SURE EVERY ELDER ON THIS CONTINENT FELT HER DEATH. HER SHADOWREALM IS NO MORE. I UNDERSTAND AN ELDER, ONE OF THE NEXT GENERATION, AND AN IMMORTAL HUMAN WERE RESPONSIBLE.
HEKATE WILL NEED TO BE AVENGED. NOT NOW, AND MAYBE NOT SOON, BUT SHE WAS FAMILY, AND I OWE HER THAT. SEE TO IT, SCATHACH.
I KNOW WHY YOU'RE HERE. I SAW WHAT HAPPENED THIS MORNING A MONTH AGO. IT WAS ONE THREAD OF MANY POSSIBLE FUTURES. IN SOME, HEKATE KILLED BASTET AND THE MORRIGAN SLEW DEE. IN ANOTHER, HEKATE KILLED YOU, MR. FLAMEL. TODAY I DISCOVERED WHICH VERSION CAME TO PASS. SO I KNOW WHAT YOU WANT ME TO DO. AND I'VE THOUGHT LONG AND HARD ABOUT MY RESPONSE.
WERE WE IN YOUR THREADS?
YES, BUT YOU ONLY SURVIVED IN ONE.

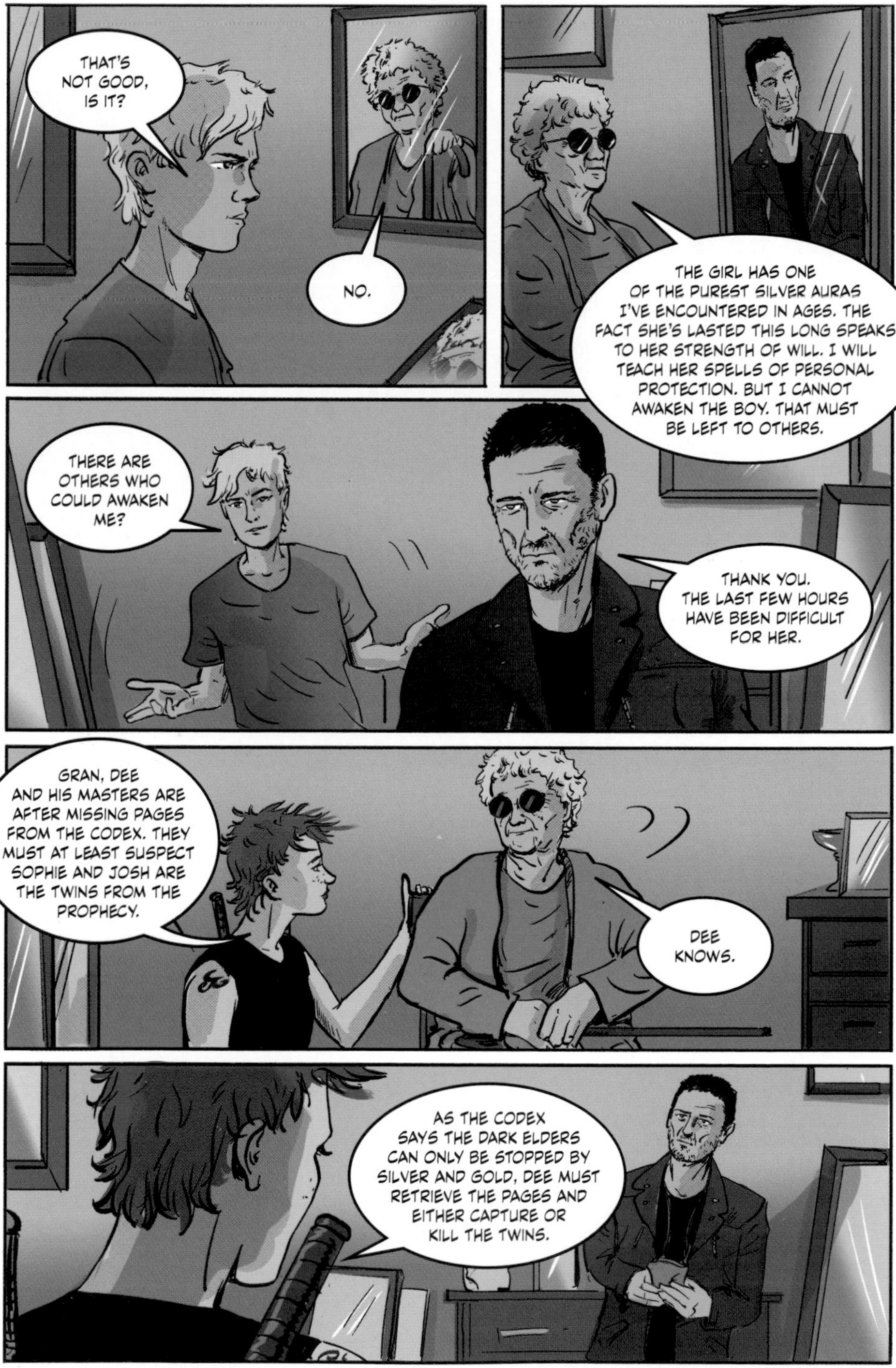
THAT'S NOT GOOD, IS IT?
NO.
THE GIRL HAS ONE OF THE PUREST SILVER AURAS I'VE ENCOUNTERED IN AGES. THE FACT SHE'S LASTED THIS LONG SPEAKS TO HER STRENGTH OF WILL. I WILL TEACH HER SPELLS OF PERSONAL PROTECTION. BUT I CANNOT AWAKEN THE BOY. THAT MUST BE LEFT TO OTHERS.
THERE ARE OTHERS WHO COULD AWAKEN ME?
THANK YOU. THE LAST FEW HOURS HAVE BEEN DIFFICULT FOR HER.
GRAN, DEE AND HIS MASTERS ARE AFTER MISSING PAGES FROM THE CODEX. THEY MUST AT LEAST SUSPECT SOPHIE AND JOSH ARE THE TWINS FROM THE PROPHECY.
DEE KNOWS.
AS THE CODEX SAYS THE DARK ELDERS CAN ONLY BE STOPPED BY SILVER AND GOLD, DEE MUST RETRIEVE THE PAGES AND EITHER CAPTURE OR KILL THE TWINS.

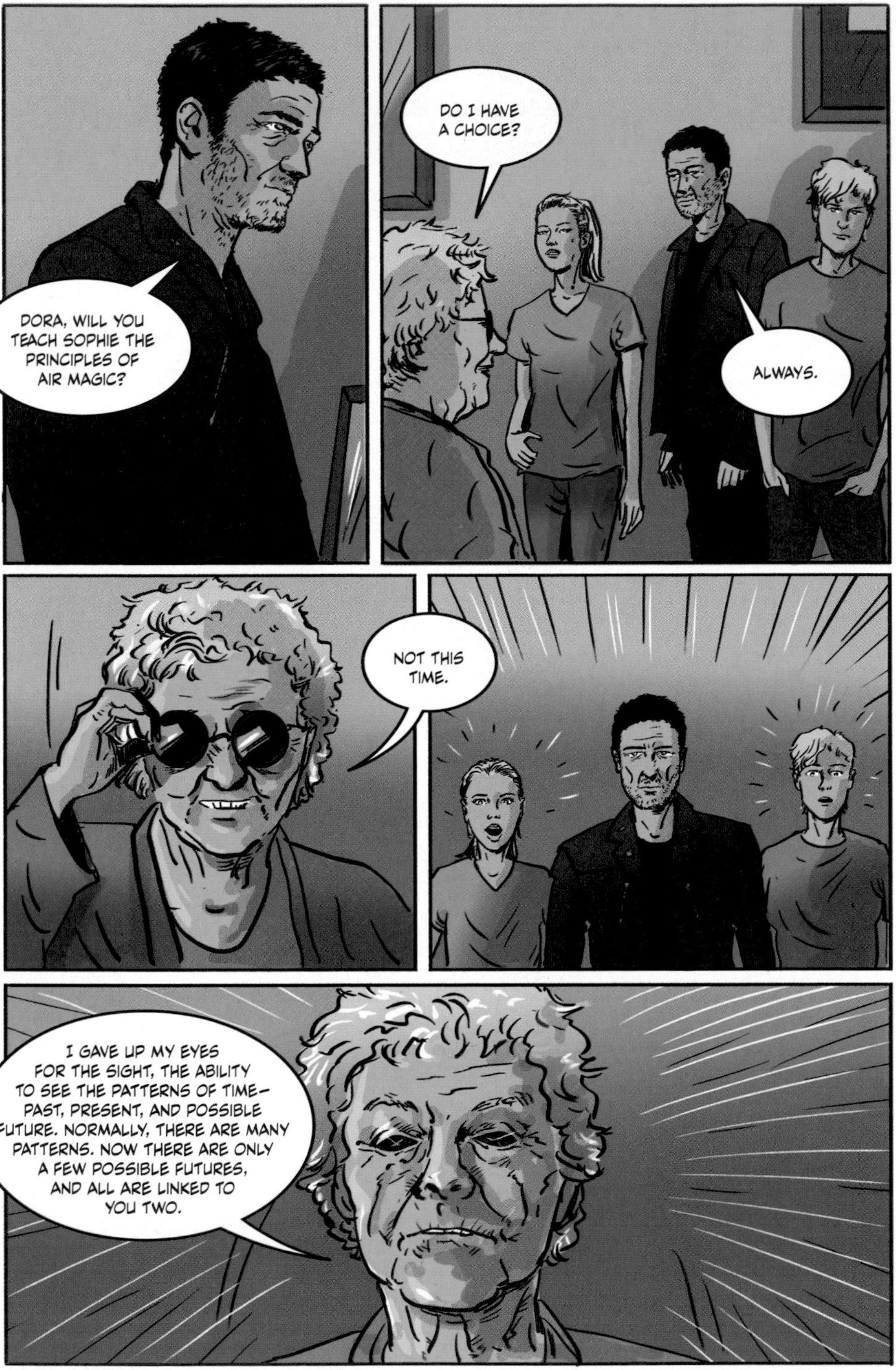
DORA, WILL YOU TEACH SOPHIE THE PRINCIPLES OF AIR MAGIC?
DO I HAVE A CHOICE?
ALWAYS.
NOT THIS TIME.
I GAVE UP MY EYES FOR THE SIGHT, THE ABILITY TO SEE THE PATTERNS OF TIME—PAST, PRESENT, AND POSSIBLE FUTURE. NORMALLY, THERE ARE MANY PATTERNS. NOW THERE ARE ONLY A FEW POSSIBLE FUTURES, AND ALL ARE LINKED TO YOU TWO.

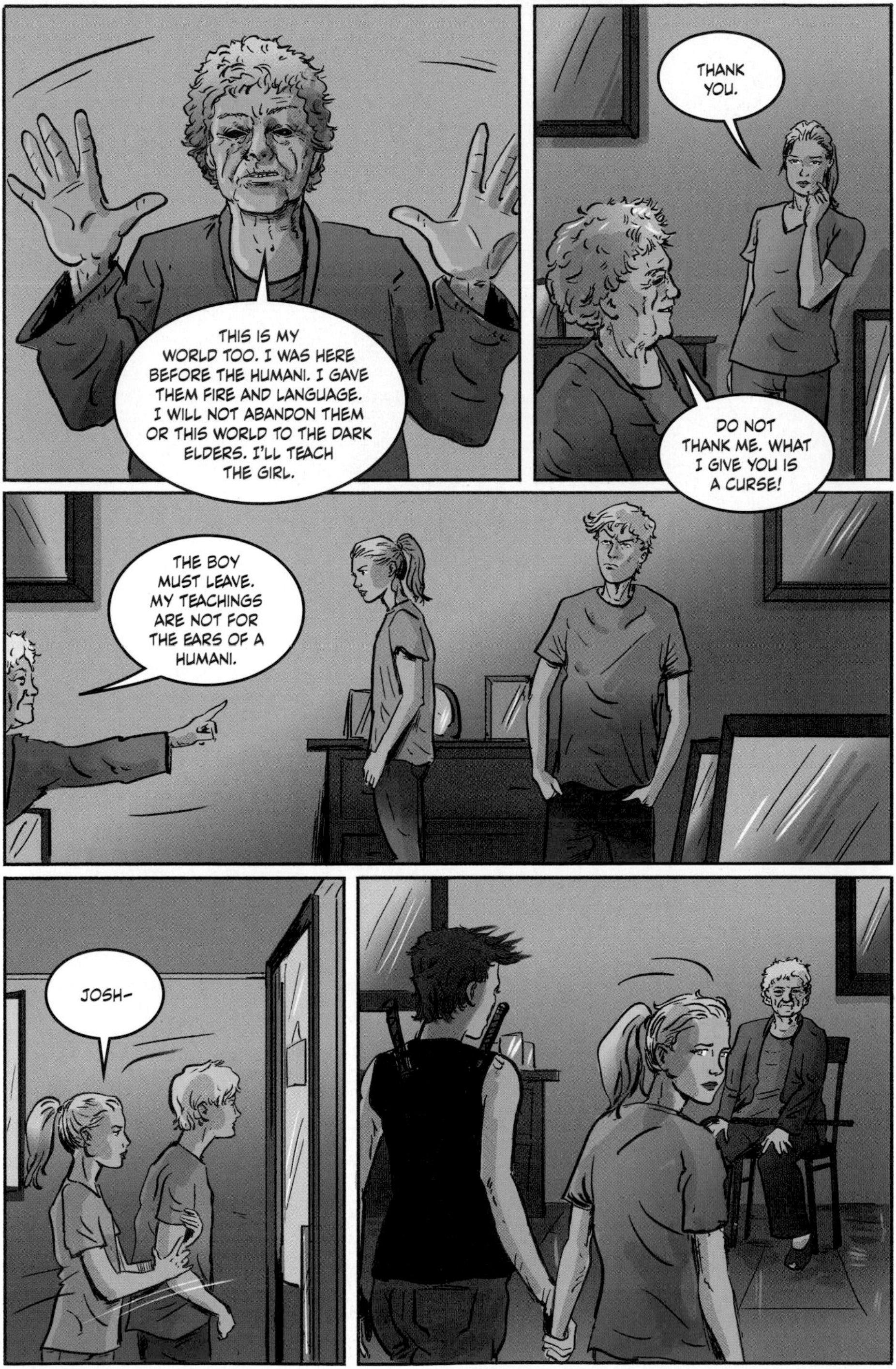
THIS IS MY WORLD TOO. I WAS HERE BEFORE THE HUMANI. I GAVE THEM FIRE AND LANGUAGE. I WILL NOT ABANDON THEM OR THIS WORLD TO THE DARK ELDERS. I'LL TEACH THE GIRL.
THANK YOU.
DO NOT THANK ME. WHAT I GIVE YOU IS A CURSE!
THE BOY MUST LEAVE. MY TEACHINGS ARE NOT FOR THE EARS OF A HUMANI.
JOSH-

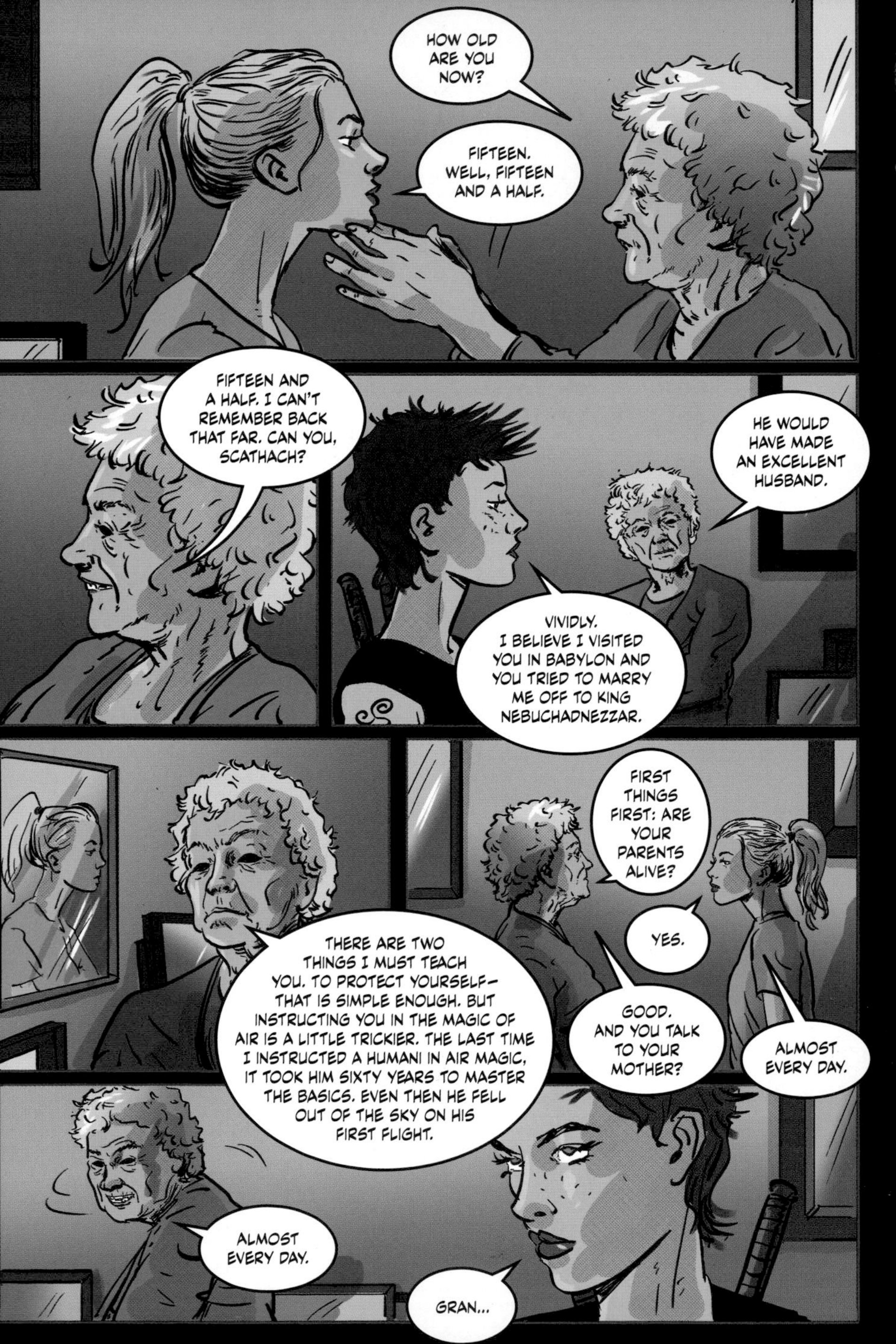
HOW OLD ARE YOU NOW?
FIFTEEN. WELL, FIFTEEN AND A HALF.
FIFTEEN AND A HALF. I CAN'T REMEMBER BACK THAT FAR. CAN YOU, SCATHACH?
VIVIDLY. I BELIEVE I VISITED YOU IN BABYLON AND YOU TRIED TO MARRY ME OFF TO KING NEBUCHADNEZZAR.
HE WOULD HAVE MADE AN EXCELLENT HUSBAND.
THERE ARE TWO THINGS I MUST TEACH YOU. TO PROTECT YOURSELF—THAT IS SIMPLE ENOUGH. BUT INSTRUCTING YOU IN THE MAGIC OF AIR IS A LITTLE TRICKIER. THE LAST TIME I INSTRUCTED A HUMANI IN AIR MAGIC, IT TOOK HIM SIXTY YEARS TO MASTER THE BASICS. EVEN THEN HE FELL OUT OF THE SKY ON HIS FIRST FLIGHT.
FIRST THINGS FIRST: ARE YOUR PARENTS ALIVE?
YES.
GOOD. AND YOU TALK TO YOUR MOTHER?
ALMOST EVERY DAY.
ALMOST EVERY DAY.
GRAN...

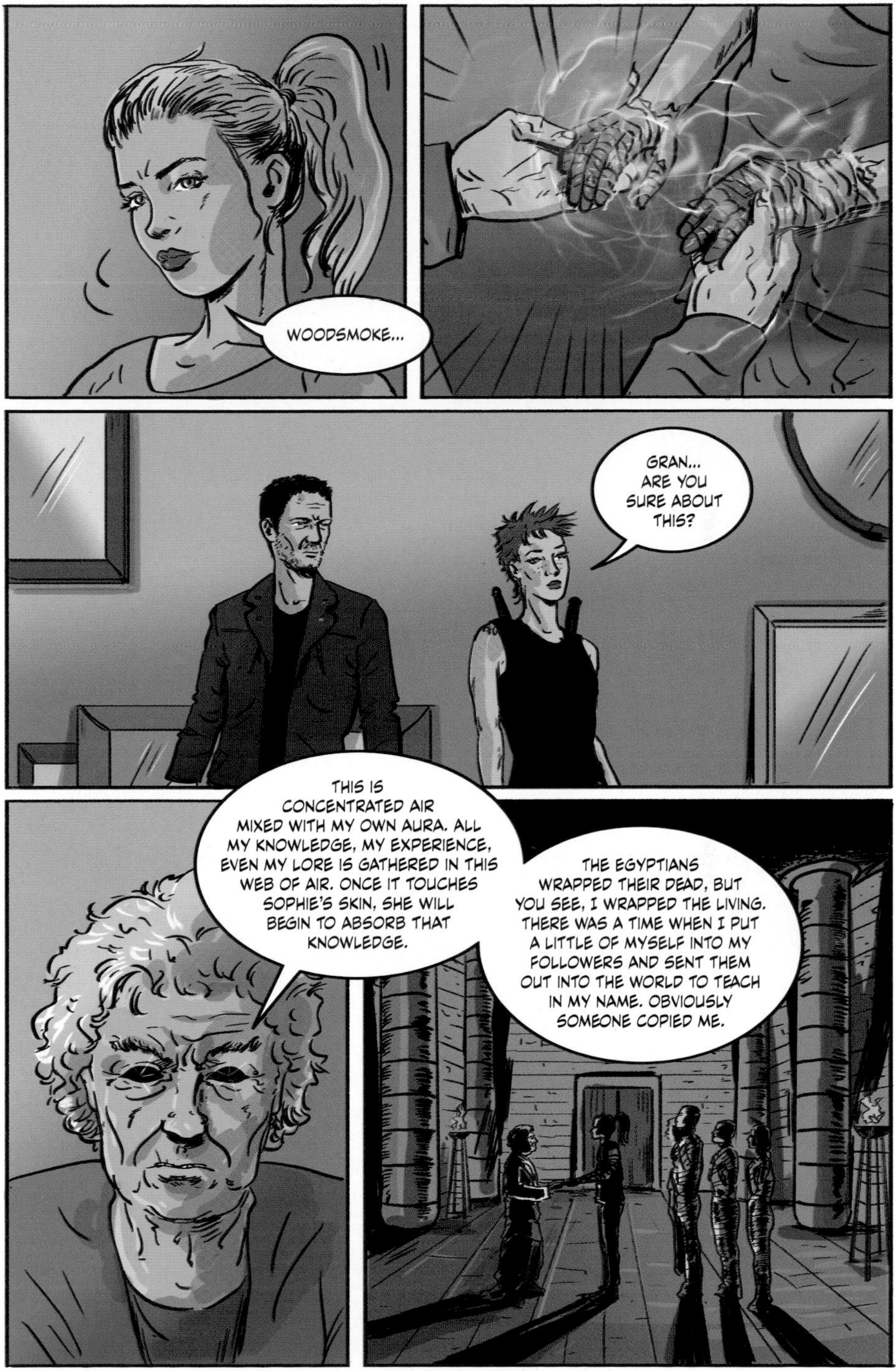
WOODSMOKE...
GRAN... ARE YOU SURE ABOUT THIS?
THIS IS CONCENTRATED AIR MIXED WITH MY OWN AURA. ALL MY KNOWLEDGE, MY EXPERIENCE, EVEN MY LORE IS GATHERED IN THIS WEB OF AIR. ONCE IT TOUCHES SOPHIE'S SKIN, SHE WILL BEGIN TO ABSORB THAT KNOWLEDGE.
THE EGYPTIANS WRAPPED THEIR DEAD, BUT YOU SEE, I WRAPPED THE LIVING. THERE WAS A TIME WHEN I PUT A LITTLE OF MYSELF INTO MY FOLLOWERS AND SENT THEM OUT INTO THE WORLD TO TEACH IN MY NAME. OBVIOUSLY SOMEONE COPIED ME.

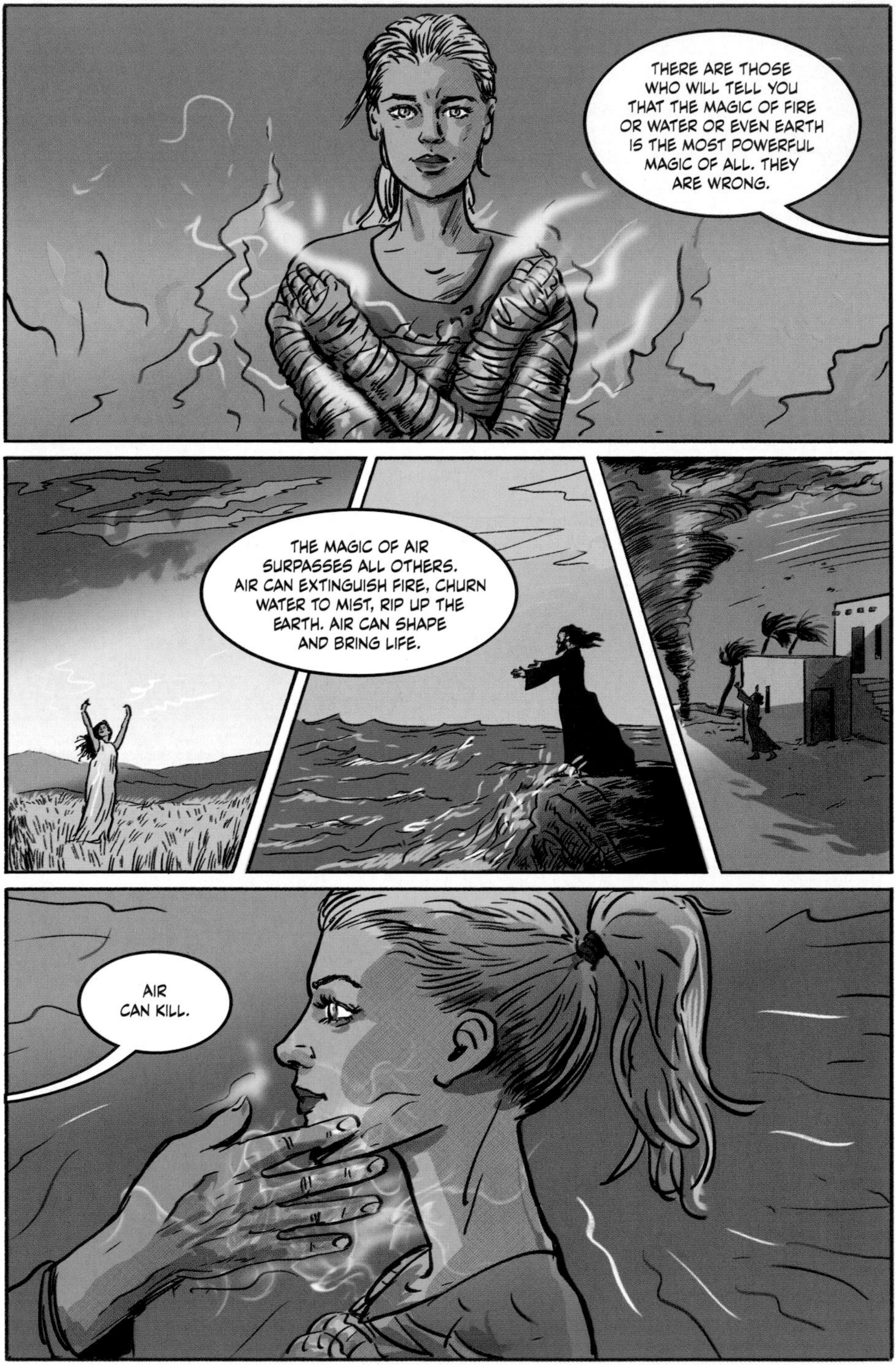
THERE ARE THOSE WHO WILL TELL YOU THAT THE MAGIC OF FIRE OR WATER OR EVEN EARTH IS THE MOST POWERFUL MAGIC OF ALL. THEY ARE WRONG.
THE MAGIC OF AIR SURPASSES ALL OTHERS. AIR CAN EXTINGUISH FIRE, CHURN WATER TO MIST, RIP UP THE EARTH. AIR CAN SHAPE AND BRING LIFE.
AIR CAN KILL.

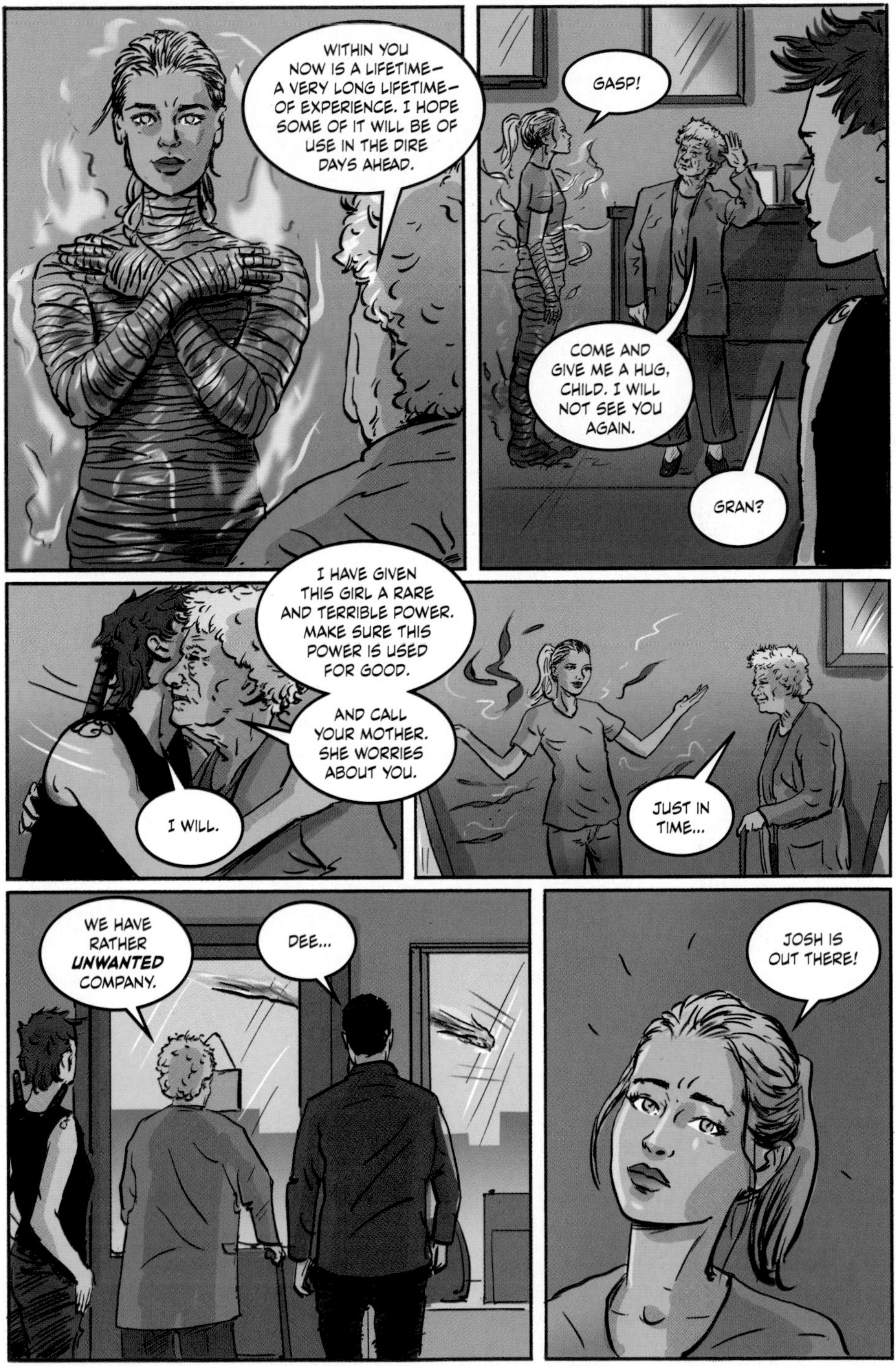
WITHIN YOU NOW IS A LIFETIME— A VERY LONG LIFETIME— OF EXPERIENCE. I HOPE SOME OF IT WILL BE OF USE IN THE DIRE DAYS AHEAD.
GASP!
COME AND GIVE ME A HUG, CHILD. I WILL NOT SEE YOU AGAIN.
GRAN?
I HAVE GIVEN THIS GIRL A RARE AND TERRIBLE POWER. MAKE SURE THIS POWER IS USED FOR GOOD.
AND CALL YOUR MOTHER. SHE WORRIES ABOUT YOU.
I WILL.
JUST IN TIME...
WE HAVE RATHER ***UNWANTED*** COMPANY.
DEE...
JOSH IS OUT THERE!

CHAPTER 37

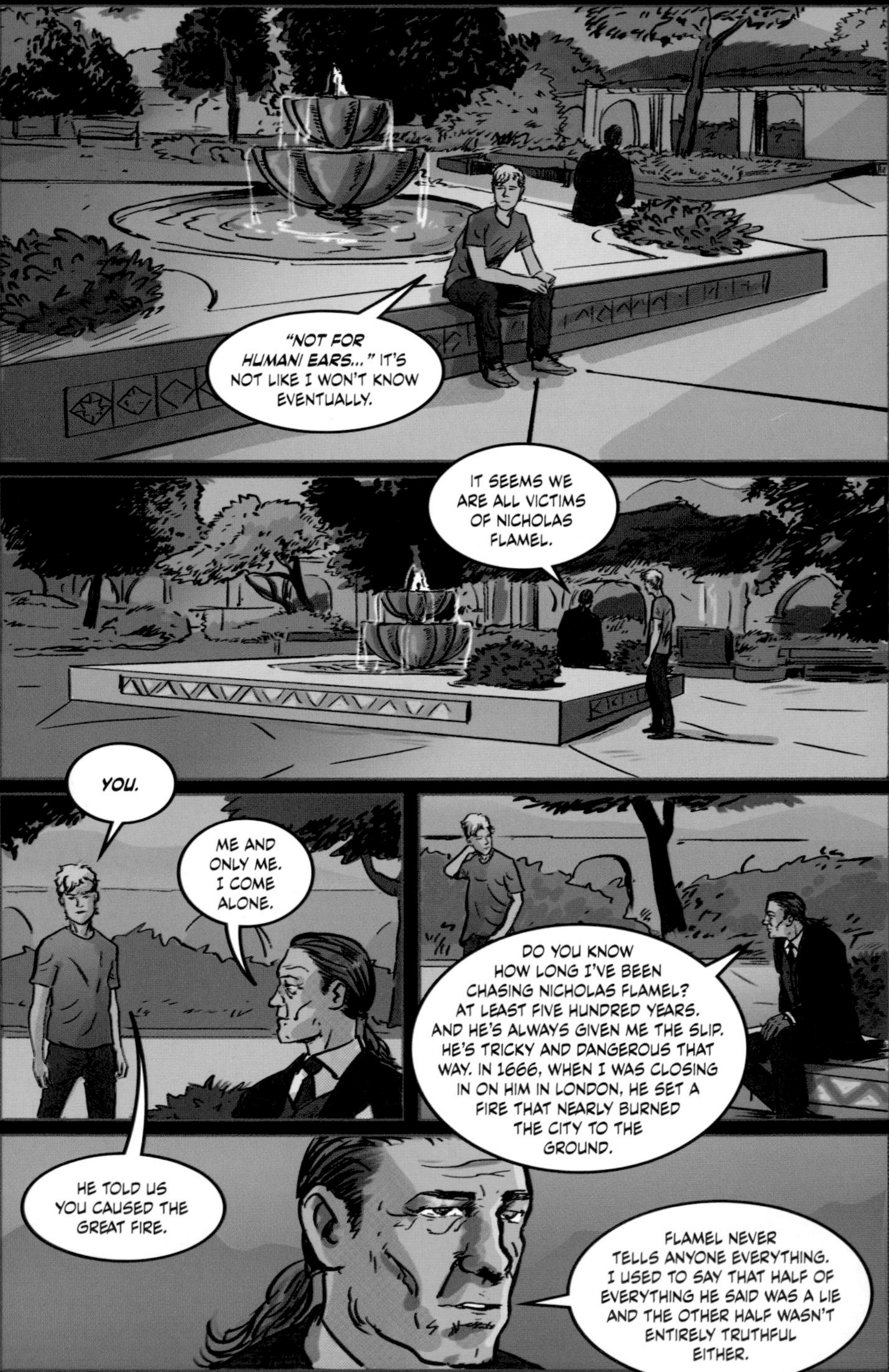
"NOT FOR HUMANI EARS..." IT'S NOT LIKE I WON'T KNOW EVENTUALLY.
IT SEEMS WE ARE ALL VICTIMS OF NICHOLAS FLAMEL.
YOU.
ME AND ONLY ME. I COME ALONE.
DO YOU KNOW HOW LONG I'VE BEEN CHASING NICHOLAS FLAMEL? AT LEAST FIVE HUNDRED YEARS. AND HE'S ALWAYS GIVEN ME THE SLIP. HE'S TRICKY AND DANGEROUS THAT WAY. IN 1666, WHEN I WAS CLOSING IN ON HIM IN LONDON, HE SET A FIRE THAT NEARLY BURNED THE CITY TO THE GROUND.
HE TOLD US YOU CAUSED THE GREAT FIRE.
FLAMEL NEVER TELLS ANYONE EVERYTHING. I USED TO SAY THAT HALF OF EVERYTHING HE SAID WAS A LIE AND THE OTHER HALF WASN'T ENTIRELY TRUTHFUL EITHER.

NICHOLAS SAYS YOU'RE WORKING WITH THE DARK ELDERS. ONCE YOU HAVE THE COMPLETE CODEX, YOU WILL BRING THEM BACK INTO THIS WORLD.

CORRECT IN EVERY DETAIL. THOUGH NO DOUBT NICHOLAS HAS TWISTED THE STORY SOMEWHAT.

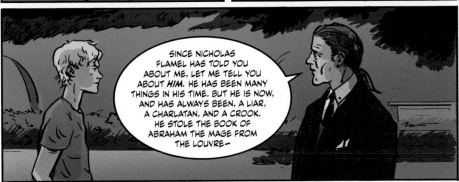

SINCE NICHOLAS FLAMEL HAS TOLD YOU ABOUT ME, LET ME TELL YOU ABOUT *HIM.* HE HAS BEEN MANY THINGS IN HIS TIME. BUT HE IS NOW, AND HAS ALWAYS BEEN, A LIAR, A CHARLATAN, AND A CROOK. HE STOLE THE BOOK OF ABRAHAM THE MAGE FROM THE LOUVRE—

HE *STOLE* IT?

OH YES. WHEN HE DISCOVERED THAT IT CONTAINED NOT ONLY THE IMMORTALITY POTION BUT ALSO THE PHILOSOPHER'S STONE RECIPE, HE STOLE IT AND USED IT FOR HIS OWN GAIN FOR CENTURIES.

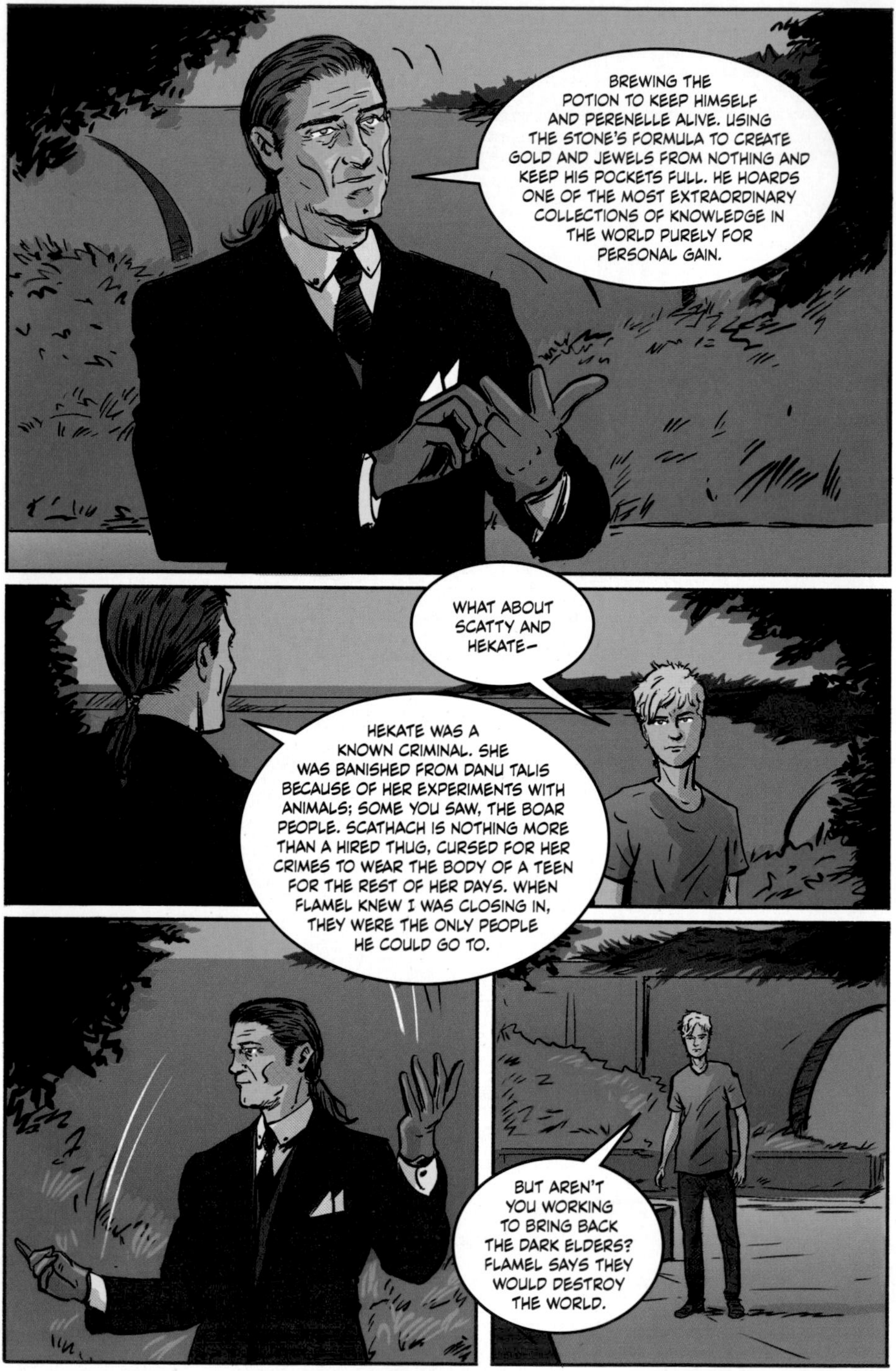
BREWING THE POTION TO KEEP HIMSELF AND PERENELLE ALIVE. USING THE STONE'S FORMULA TO CREATE GOLD AND JEWELS FROM NOTHING AND KEEP HIS POCKETS FULL. HE HOARDS ONE OF THE MOST EXTRAORDINARY COLLECTIONS OF KNOWLEDGE IN THE WORLD PURELY FOR PERSONAL GAIN.
WHAT ABOUT SCATTY AND HEKATE—
HEKATE WAS A KNOWN CRIMINAL. SHE WAS BANISHED FROM DANU TALIS BECAUSE OF HER EXPERIMENTS WITH ANIMALS; SOME YOU SAW, THE BOAR PEOPLE. SCATHACH IS NOTHING MORE THAN A HIRED THUG, CURSED FOR HER CRIMES TO WEAR THE BODY OF A TEEN FOR THE REST OF HER DAYS. WHEN FLAMEL KNEW I WAS CLOSING IN, THEY WERE THE ONLY PEOPLE HE COULD GO TO.
BUT AREN'T YOU WORKING TO BRING BACK THE DARK ELDERS? FLAMEL SAYS THEY WOULD DESTROY THE WORLD.

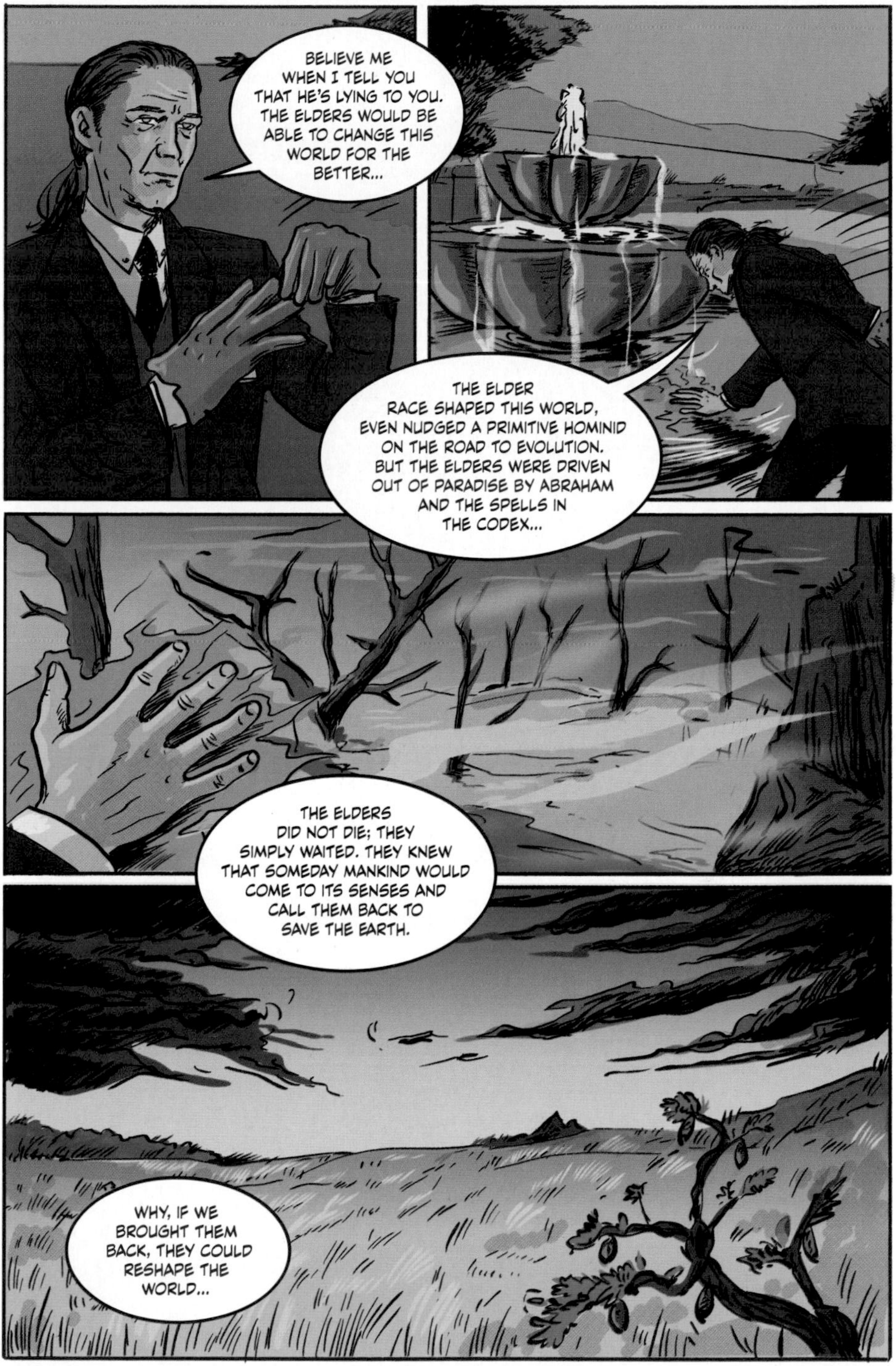
BELIEVE ME WHEN I TELL YOU THAT HE'S LYING TO YOU. THE ELDERS WOULD BE ABLE TO CHANGE THIS WORLD FOR THE BETTER...
THE ELDER RACE SHAPED THIS WORLD, EVEN NUDGED A PRIMITIVE HOMINID ON THE ROAD TO EVOLUTION. BUT THE ELDERS WERE DRIVEN OUT OF PARADISE BY ABRAHAM AND THE SPELLS IN THE CODEX...
THE ELDERS DID NOT DIE; THEY SIMPLY WAITED. THEY KNEW THAT SOMEDAY MANKIND WOULD COME TO ITS SENSES AND CALL THEM BACK TO SAVE THE EARTH.
WHY, IF WE BROUGHT THEM BACK, THEY COULD RESHAPE THE WORLD...

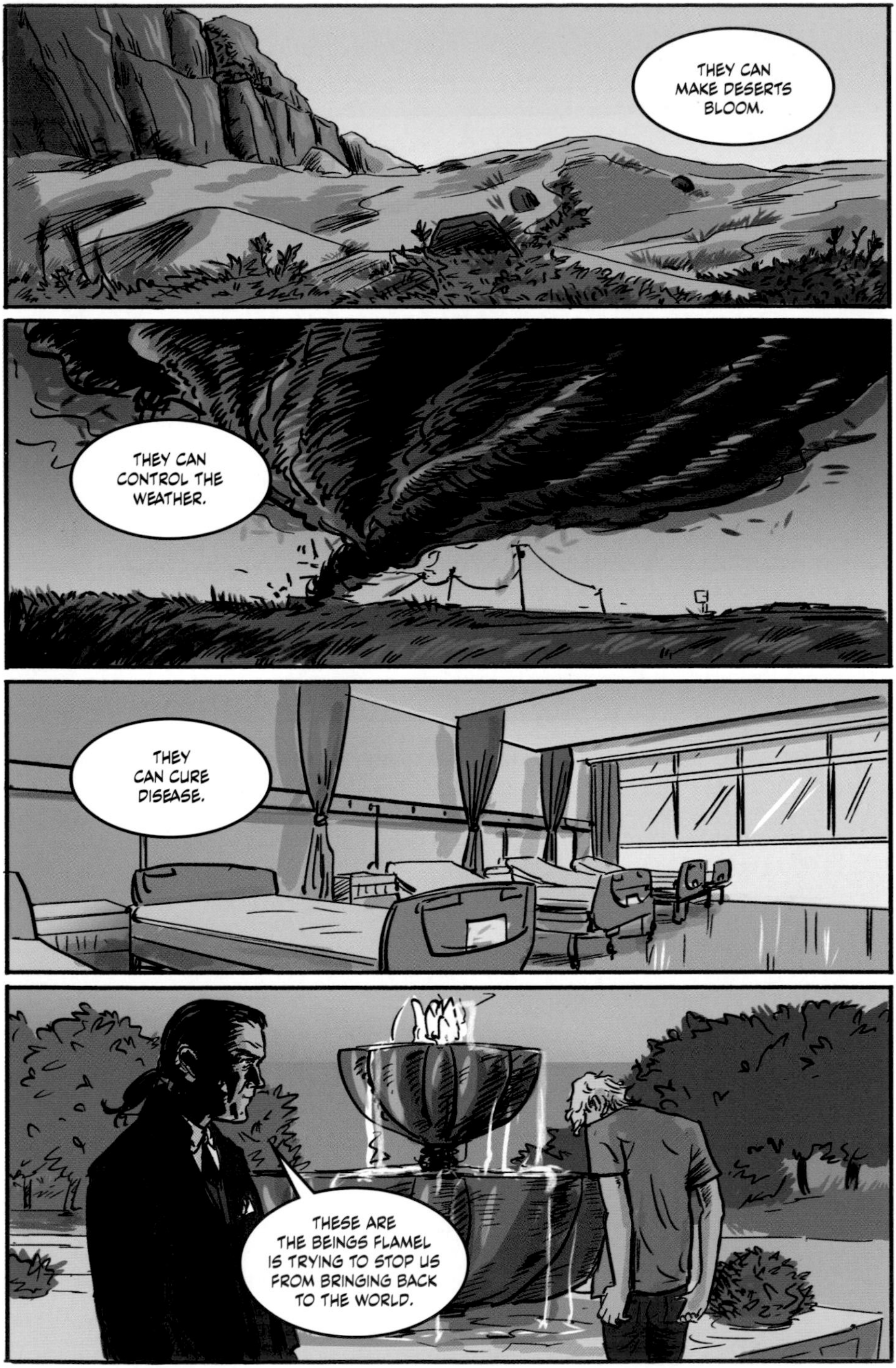
THEY CAN MAKE DESERTS BLOOM.
THEY CAN CONTROL THE WEATHER.
THEY CAN CURE DISEASE.
THESE ARE THE BEINGS FLAMEL IS TRYING TO STOP US FROM BRINGING BACK TO THE WORLD.

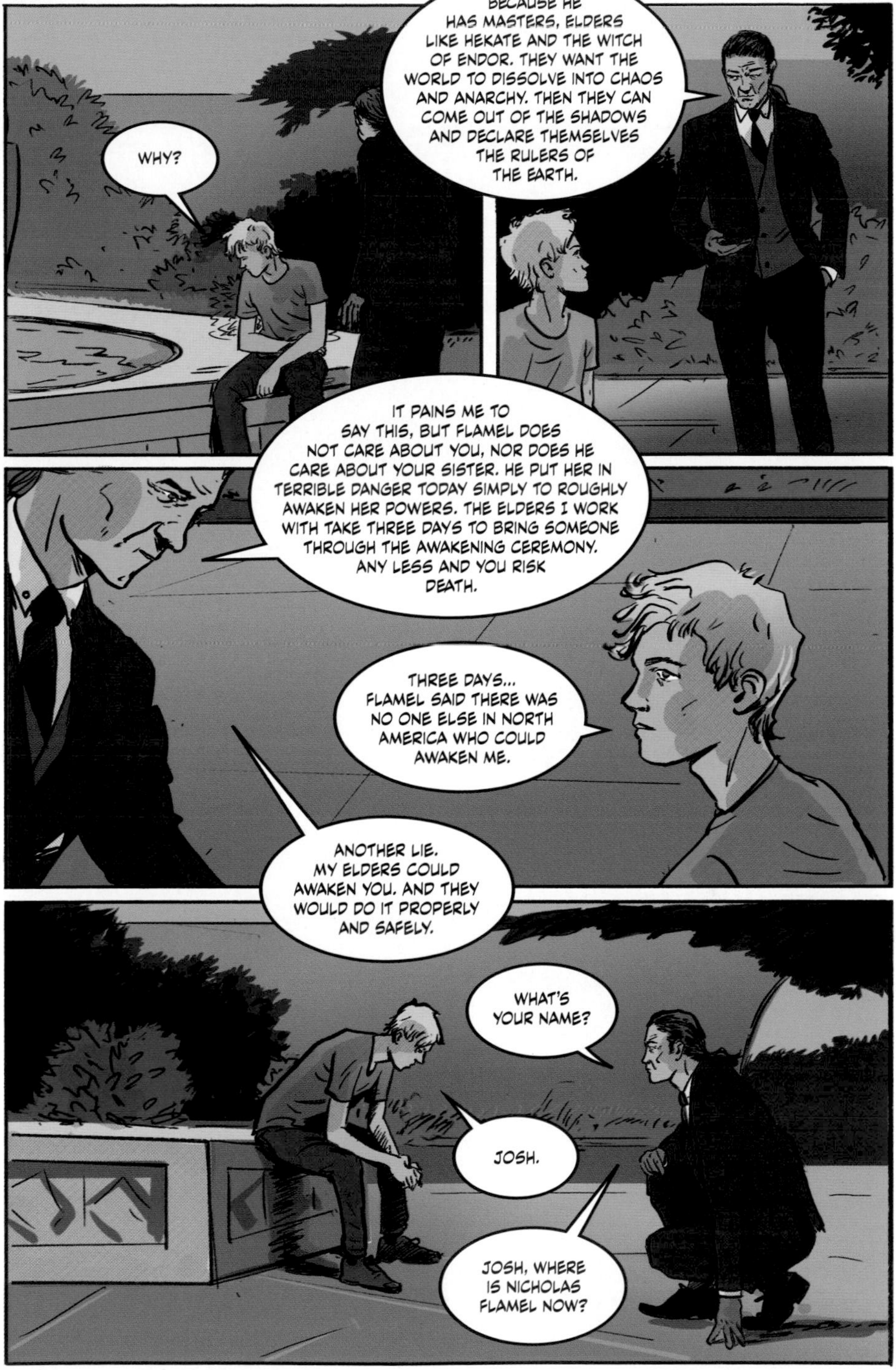
WHY?
BECAUSE HE HAS MASTERS, ELDERS LIKE HEKATE AND THE WITCH OF ENDOR. THEY WANT THE WORLD TO DISSOLVE INTO CHAOS AND ANARCHY. THEN THEY CAN COME OUT OF THE SHADOWS AND DECLARE THEMSELVES THE RULERS OF THE EARTH.
IT PAINS ME TO SAY THIS, BUT FLAMEL DOES NOT CARE ABOUT YOU, NOR DOES HE CARE ABOUT YOUR SISTER. HE PUT HER IN TERRIBLE DANGER TODAY SIMPLY TO ROUGHLY AWAKEN HER POWERS. THE ELDERS I WORK WITH TAKE THREE DAYS TO BRING SOMEONE THROUGH THE AWAKENING CEREMONY. ANY LESS AND YOU RISK DEATH.
THREE DAYS... FLAMEL SAID THERE WAS NO ONE ELSE IN NORTH AMERICA WHO COULD AWAKEN ME.
ANOTHER LIE. MY ELDERS COULD AWAKEN YOU. AND THEY WOULD DO IT PROPERLY AND SAFELY.
WHAT'S YOUR NAME?
JOSH.
JOSH, WHERE IS NICHOLAS FLAMEL NOW?

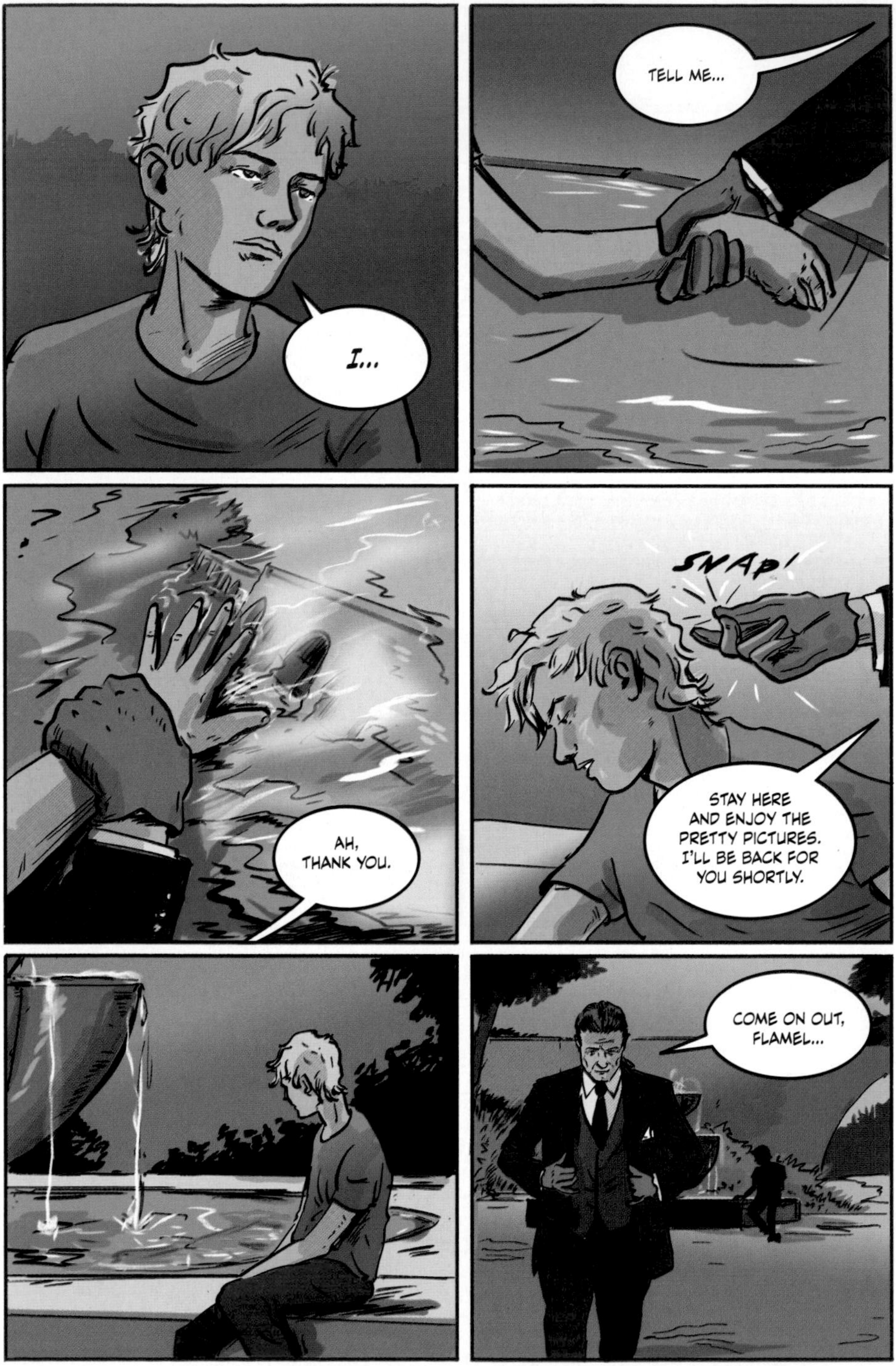
I...
TELL ME...
AH, THANK YOU.
SNAP!
STAY HERE AND ENJOY THE PRETTY PICTURES. I'LL BE BACK FOR YOU SHORTLY.
COME ON OUT, FLAMEL...

CHAPTER 38

JINGLE
SMELL THAT? IT'S STRONGER OUT HERE.
DEE'S CLOSE.
CRUNCH! CRUSH!
BEEP BEEP BEEP BEEP!
WE'VE OVERSTAYED OUR WELCOME.
WE DON'T WANT TO BE TRAPPED HERE. LET'S FIND JOSH AND GET BACK TO THE CAR.
I UNDERSTAND.
GO ON, AND CLOSE THE DOOR BEHIND YOU.

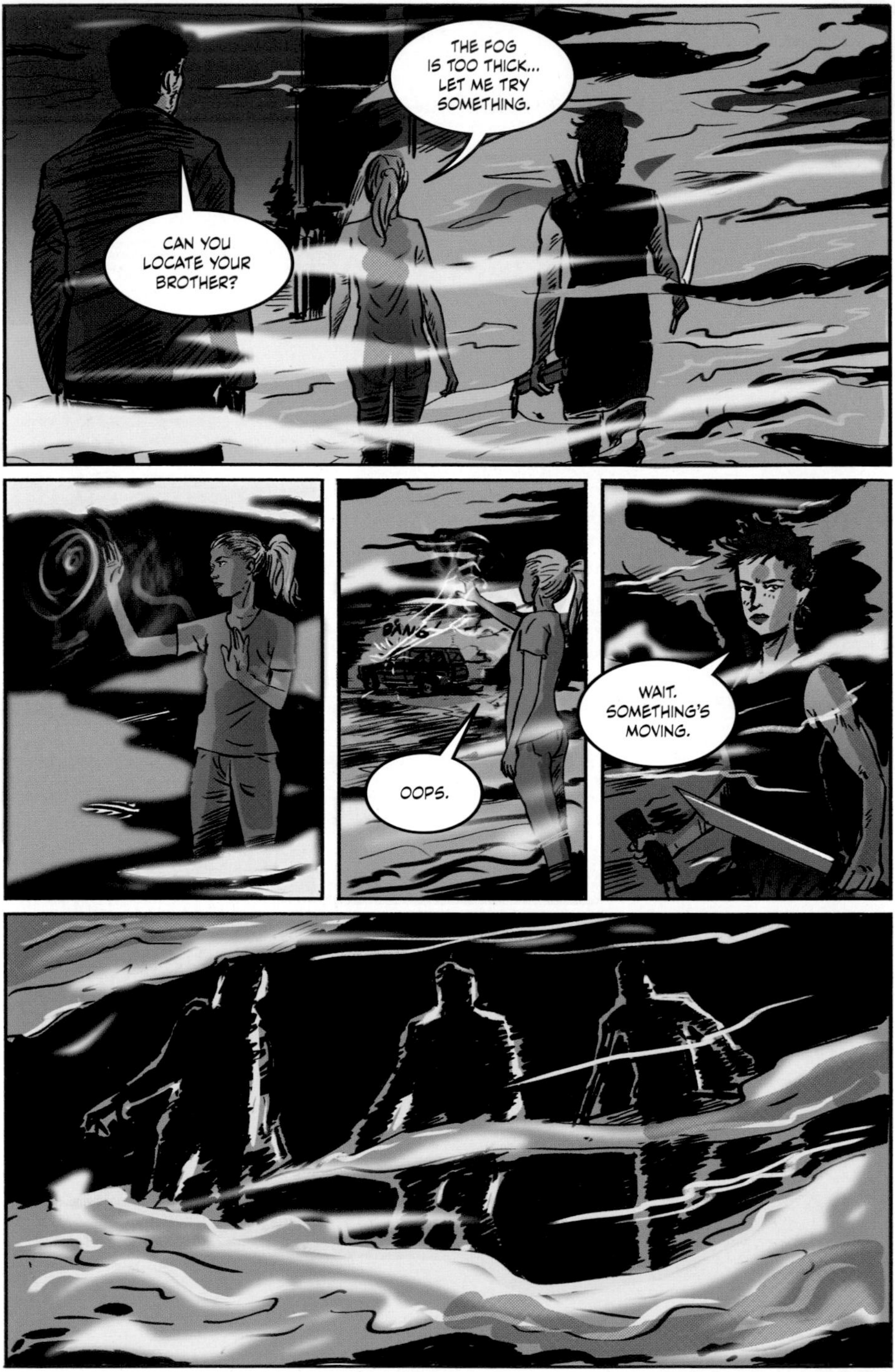
THE FOG IS TOO THICK... LET ME TRY SOMETHING.
CAN YOU LOCATE YOUR BROTHER?
BANG!
OOPS.
WAIT. SOMETHING'S MOVING.

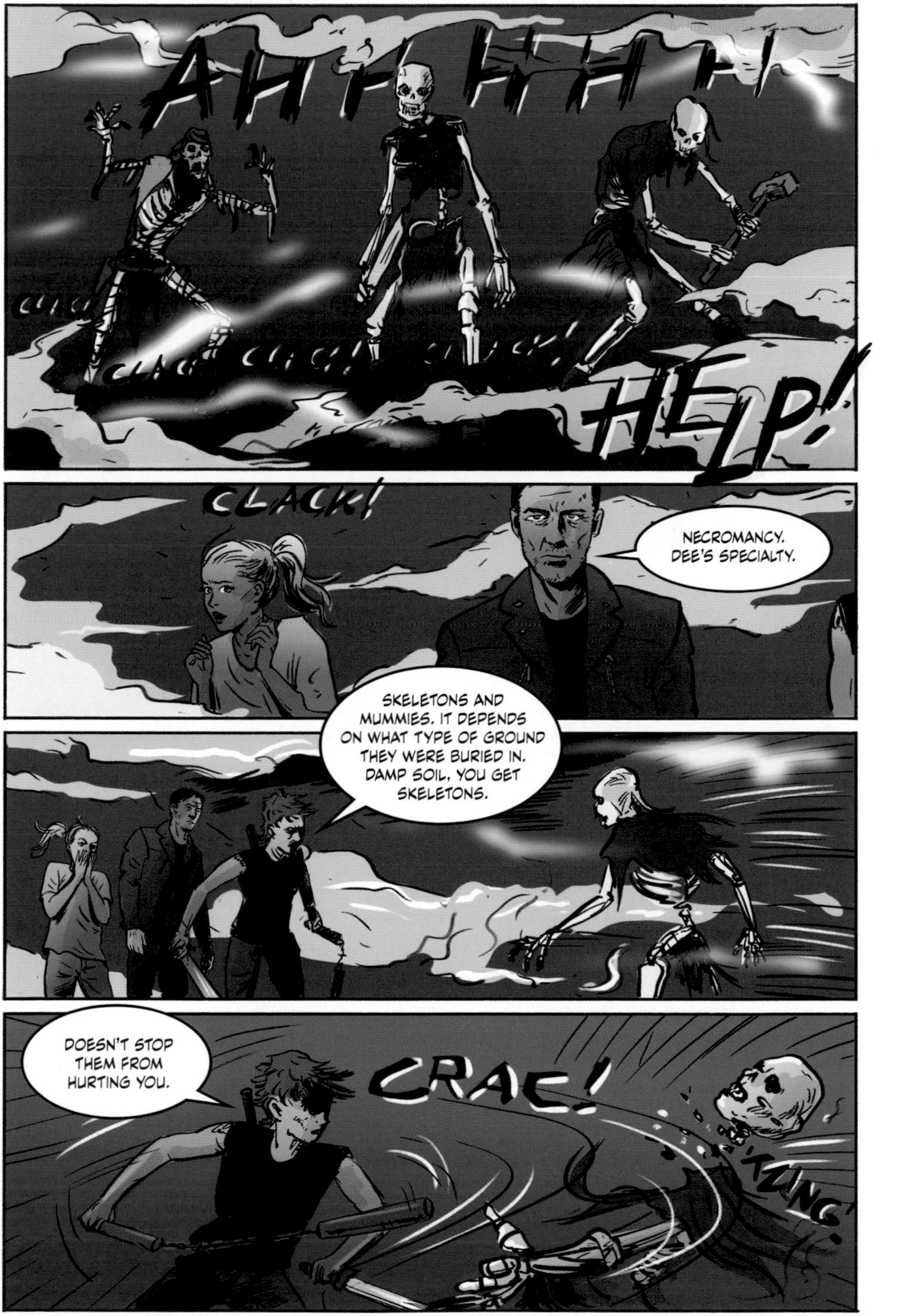
AHHHHHH!
CLACK
CLACK CLACK CLACK
HELP!
CLACK!
NECROMANCY. DEE'S SPECIALTY.
SKELETONS AND MUMMIES. IT DEPENDS ON WHAT TYPE OF GROUND THEY WERE BURIED IN. DAMP SOIL, YOU GET SKELETONS.
DOESN'T STOP THEM FROM HURTING YOU.
CRAC!
KLING!

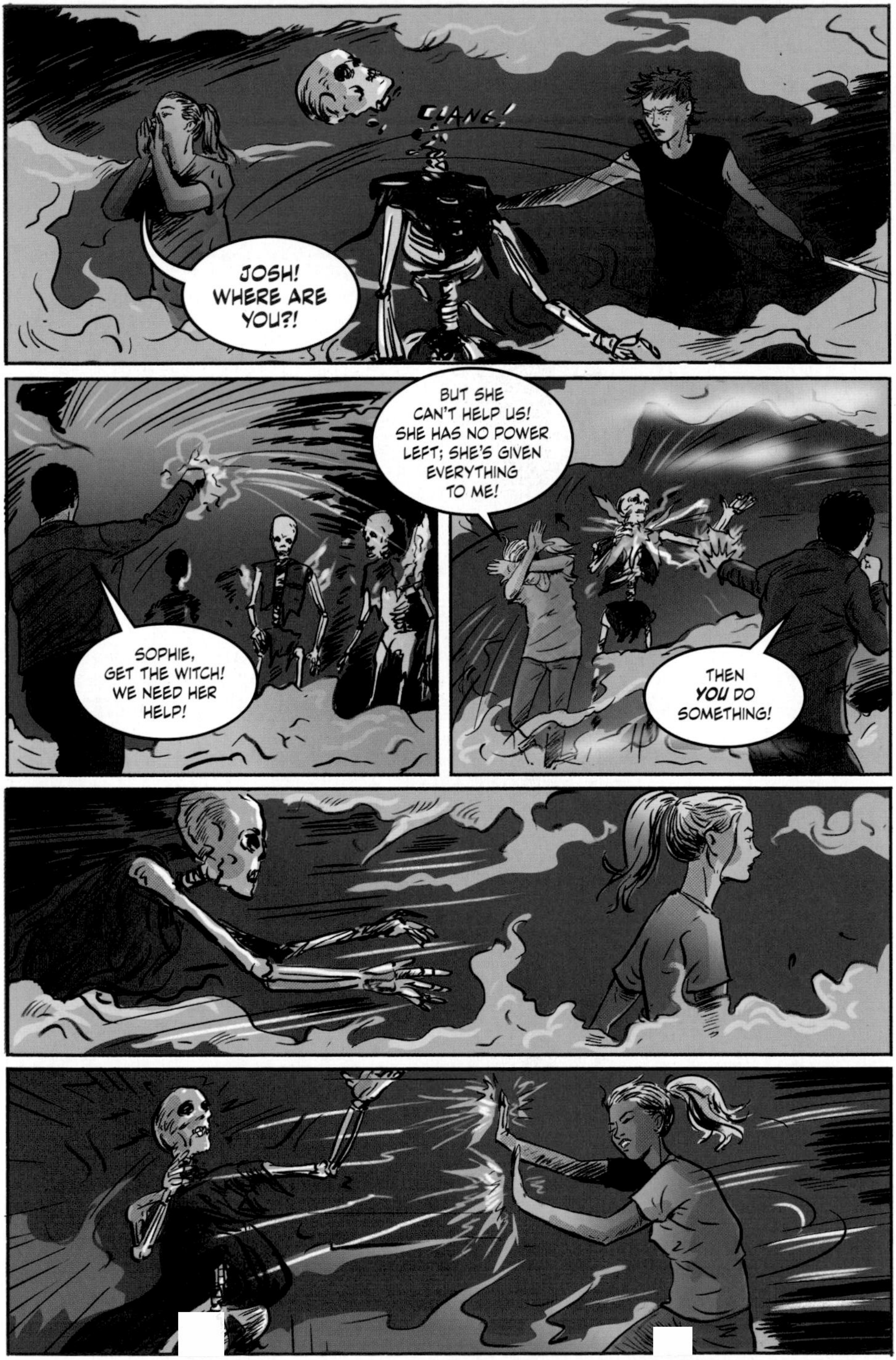
CLANG!
JOSH! WHERE ARE YOU?!
SOPHIE, GET THE WITCH! WE NEED HER HELP!
BUT SHE CAN'T HELP US! SHE HAS NO POWER LEFT; SHE'S GIVEN EVERYTHING TO ME!
THEN *YOU* DO SOMETHING!

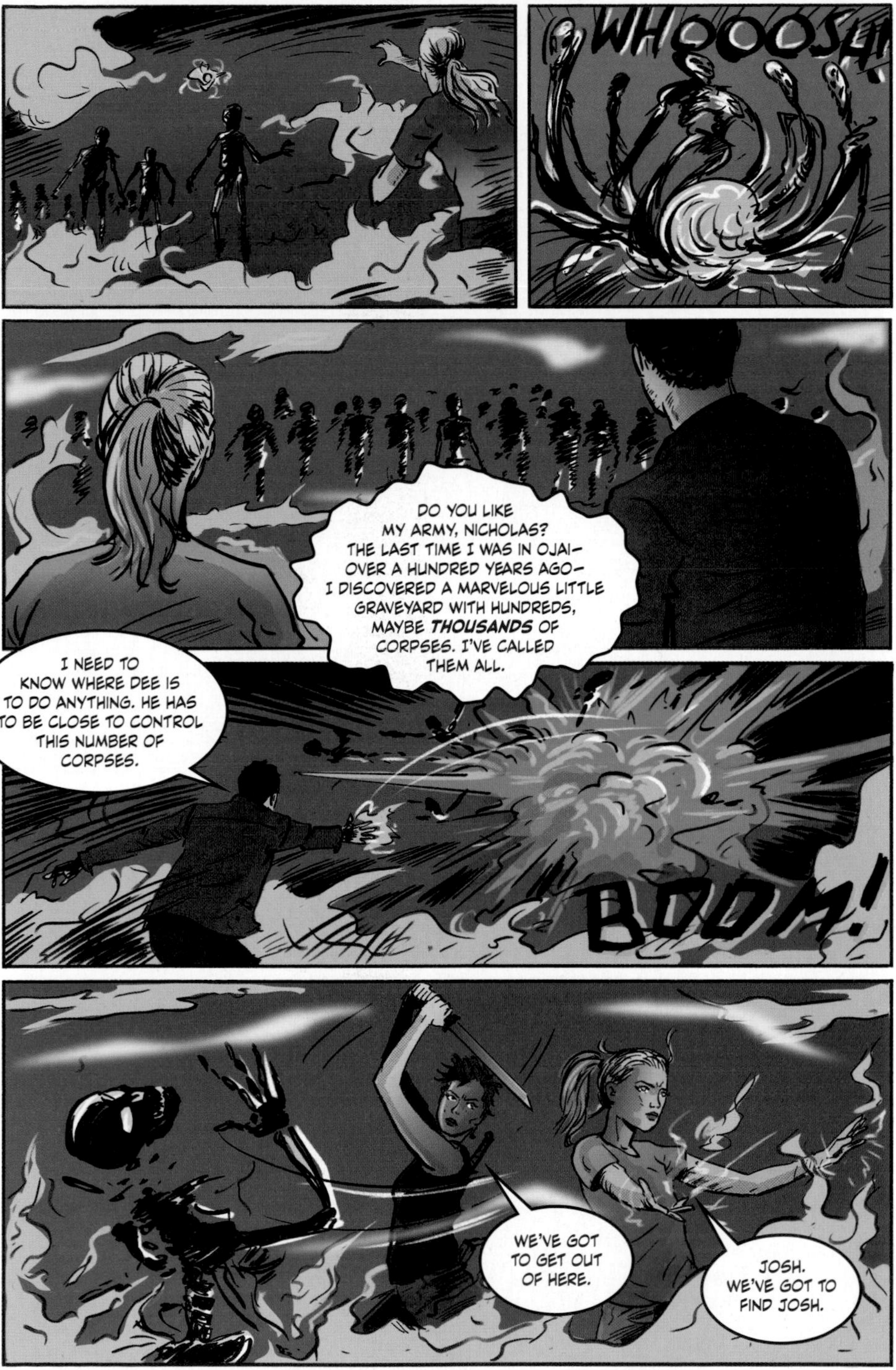
WHOOOSH!
DO YOU LIKE MY ARMY, NICHOLAS? THE LAST TIME I WAS IN OJAI— OVER A HUNDRED YEARS AGO— I DISCOVERED A MARVELOUS LITTLE GRAVEYARD WITH HUNDREDS, MAYBE ***THOUSANDS*** OF CORPSES. I'VE CALLED THEM ALL.
I NEED TO KNOW WHERE DEE IS TO DO ANYTHING. HE HAS TO BE CLOSE TO CONTROL THIS NUMBER OF CORPSES.
BOOM!
WE'VE GOT TO GET OUT OF HERE.
JOSH. WE'VE GOT TO FIND JOSH.

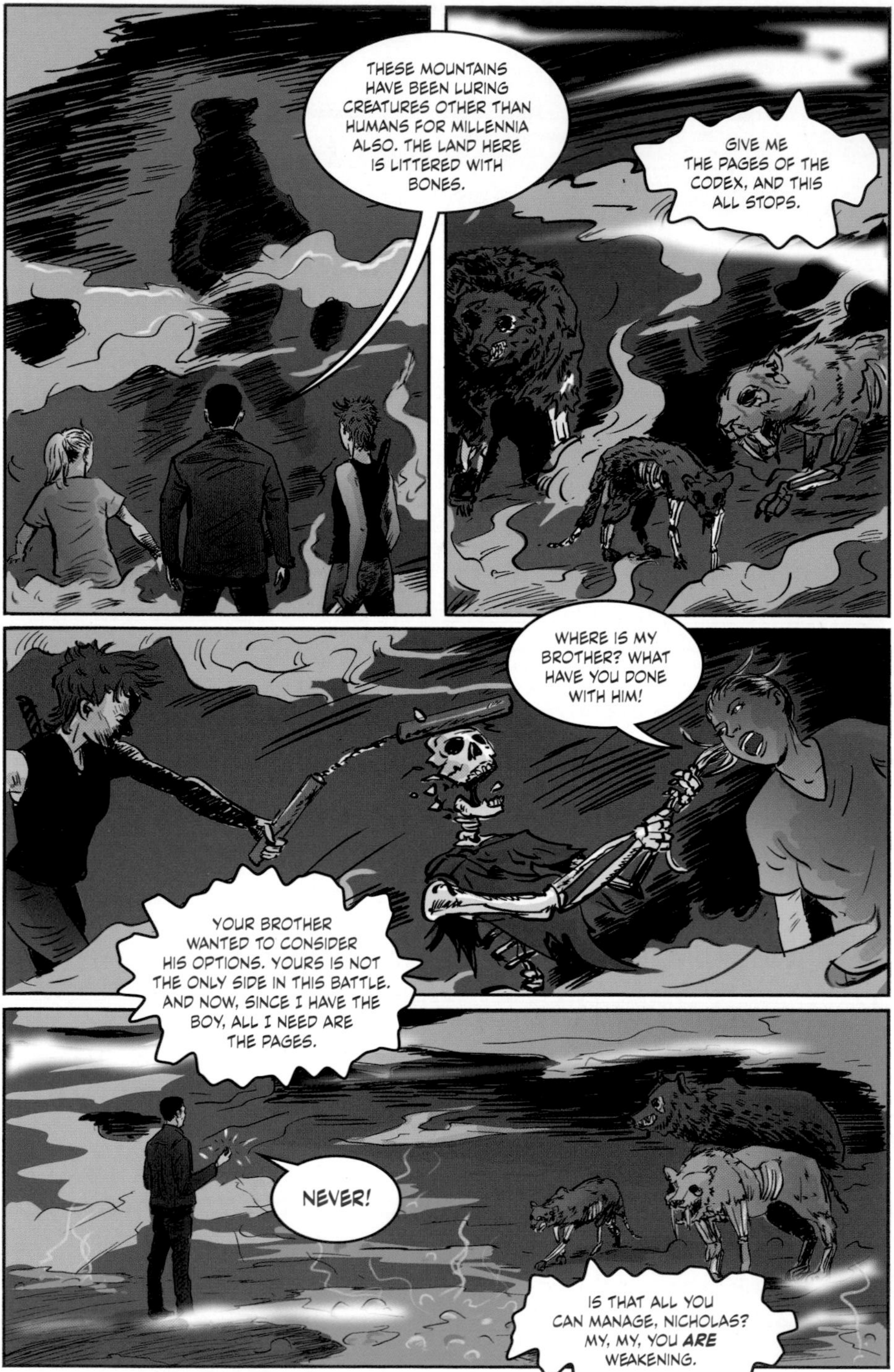
THESE MOUNTAINS HAVE BEEN LURING CREATURES OTHER THAN HUMANS FOR MILLENNIA ALSO. THE LAND HERE IS LITTERED WITH BONES.
GIVE ME THE PAGES OF THE CODEX, AND THIS ALL STOPS.
WHERE IS MY BROTHER? WHAT HAVE YOU DONE WITH HIM!
YOUR BROTHER WANTED TO CONSIDER HIS OPTIONS. YOURS IS NOT THE ONLY SIDE IN THIS BATTLE. AND NOW, SINCE I HAVE THE BOY, ALL I NEED ARE THE PAGES.
NEVER!
IS THAT ALL YOU CAN MANAGE, NICHOLAS? MY, MY, YOU *ARE* WEAKENING.

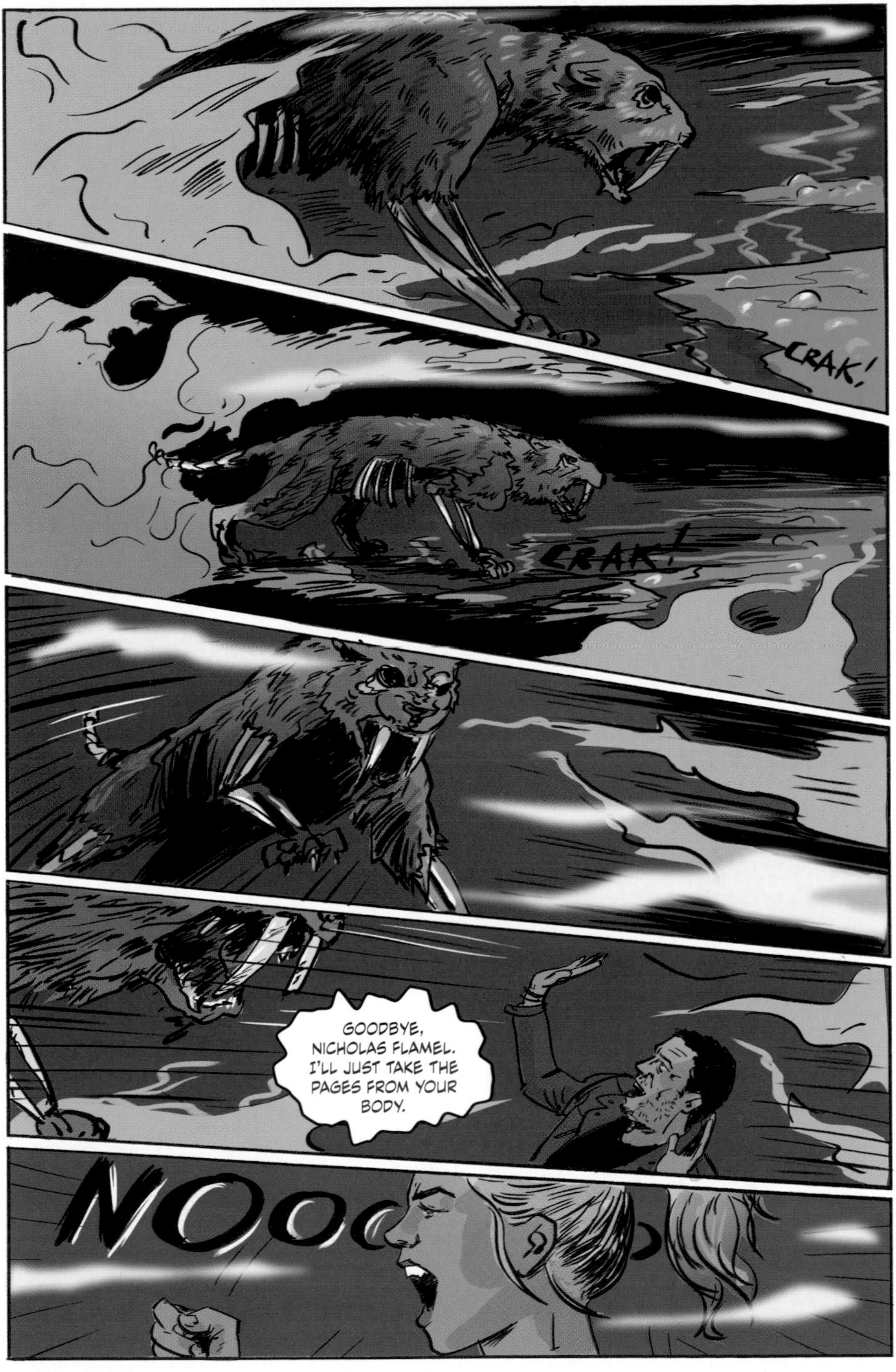
CRAK!
CRAK!
GOODBYE, NICHOLAS FLAMEL. I'LL JUST TAKE THE PAGES FROM YOUR BODY.
NOOO

CHAPTER 39

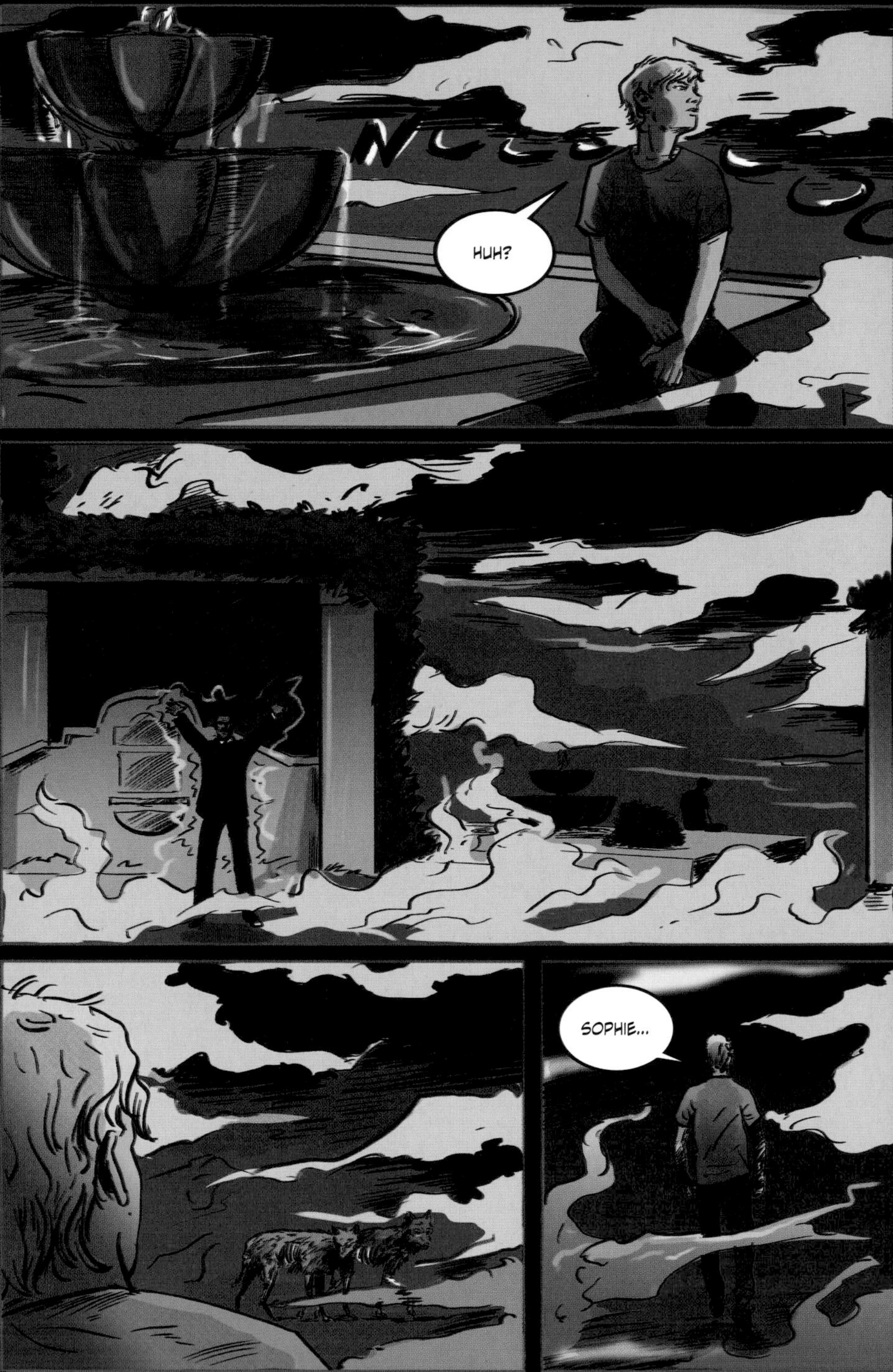
HUH?
SOPHIE...

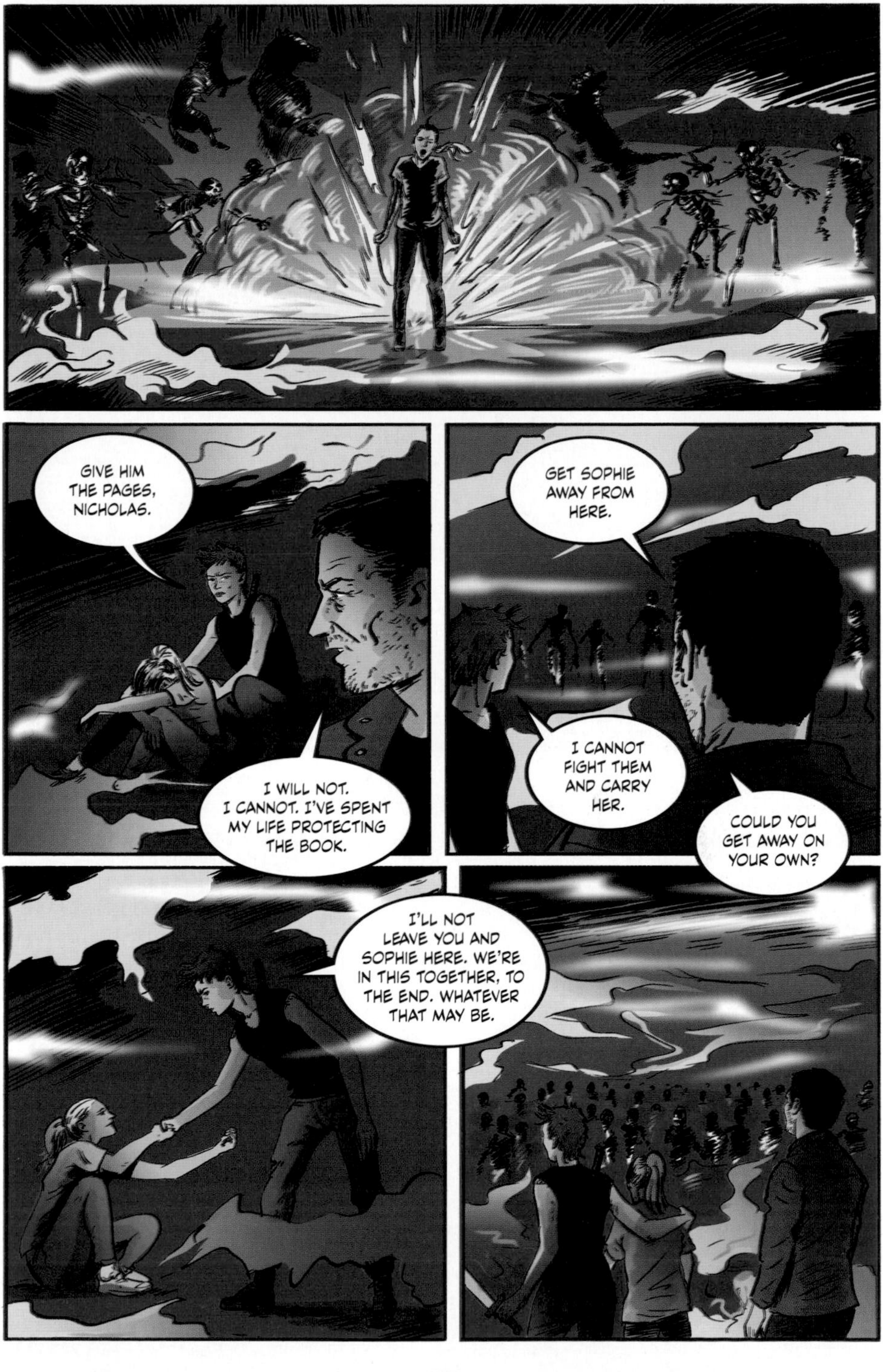
GIVE HIM THE PAGES, NICHOLAS.
I WILL NOT. I CANNOT. I'VE SPENT MY LIFE PROTECTING THE BOOK.
GET SOPHIE AWAY FROM HERE.
I CANNOT FIGHT THEM AND CARRY HER.
COULD YOU GET AWAY ON YOUR OWN?
I'LL NOT LEAVE YOU AND SOPHIE HERE. WE'RE IN THIS TOGETHER, TO THE END. WHATEVER THAT MAY BE.

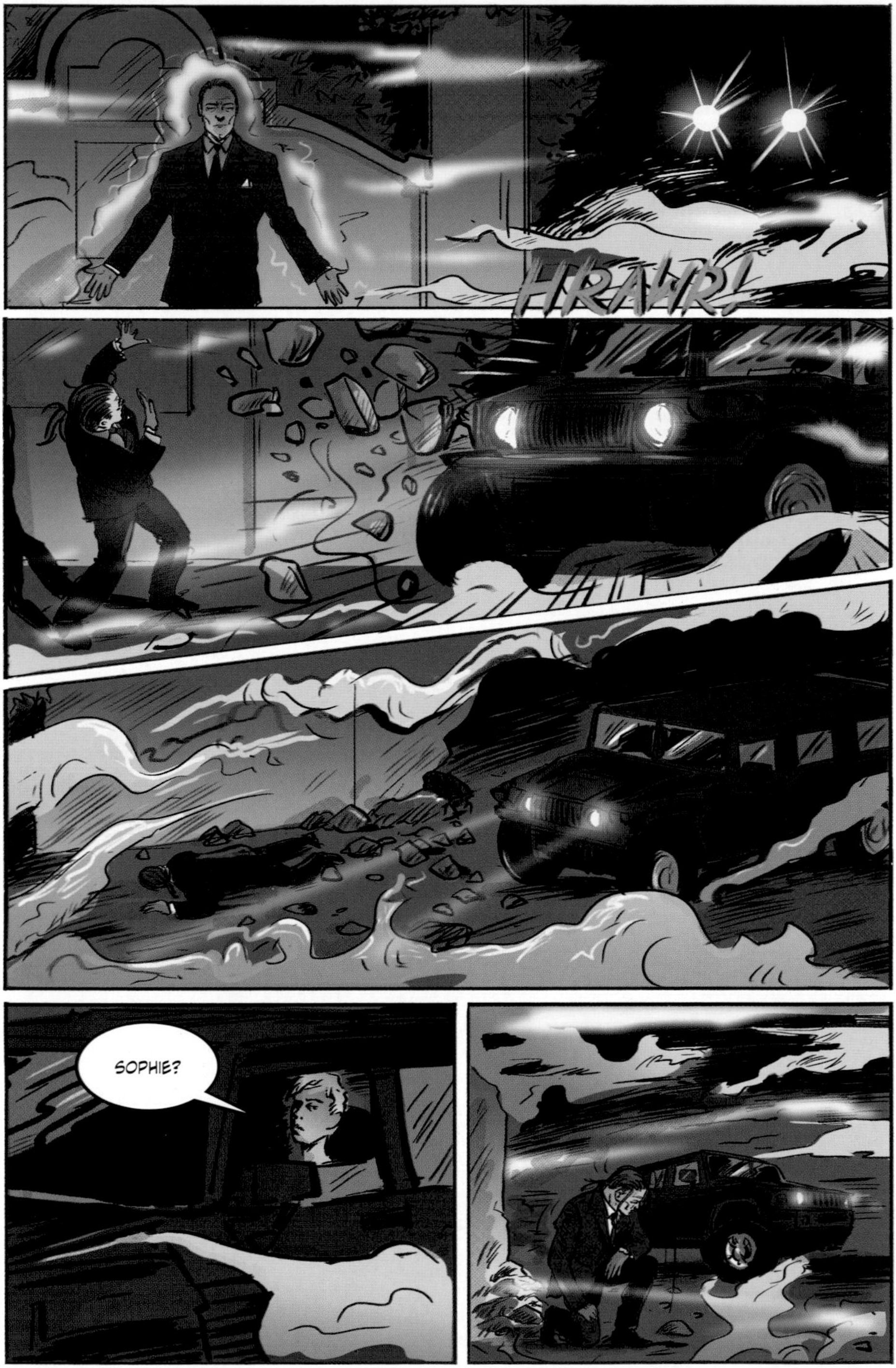
HRAWR!
SOPHIE?

I'VE WRECKED THE CAR.

JOSH!

WATCH OUT!

OOF!

SLICE!

THIS WAY! IN HERE!

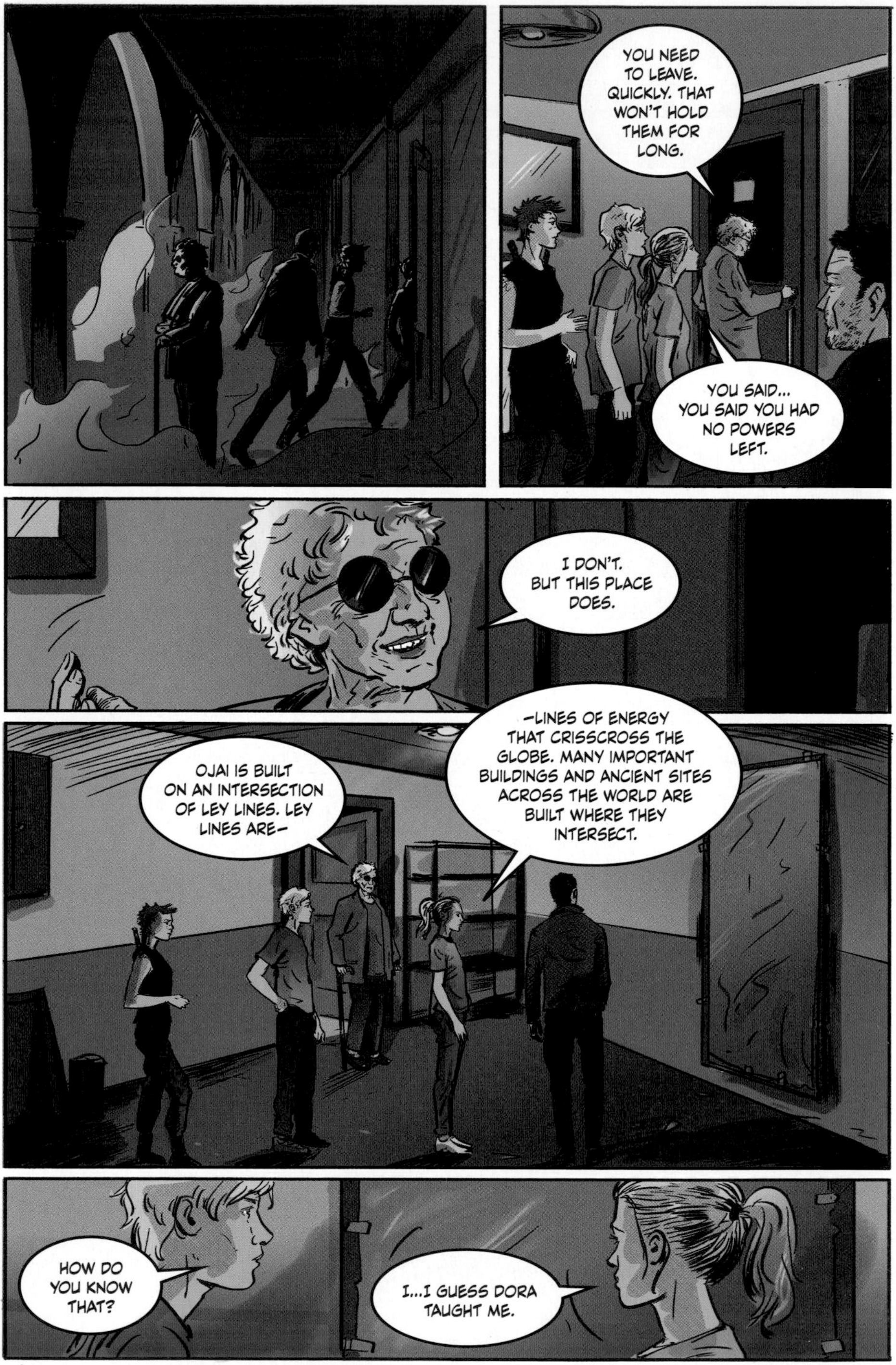
YOU NEED TO LEAVE. QUICKLY. THAT WON'T HOLD THEM FOR LONG.
YOU SAID... YOU SAID YOU HAD NO POWERS LEFT.
I DON'T. BUT THIS PLACE DOES.
OJAI IS BUILT ON AN INTERSECTION OF LEY LINES. LEY LINES ARE—
—LINES OF ENERGY THAT CRISSCROSS THE GLOBE. MANY IMPORTANT BUILDINGS AND ANCIENT SITES ACROSS THE WORLD ARE BUILT WHERE THEY INTERSECT.
HOW DO YOU KNOW THAT?
I...I GUESS DORA TAUGHT ME.

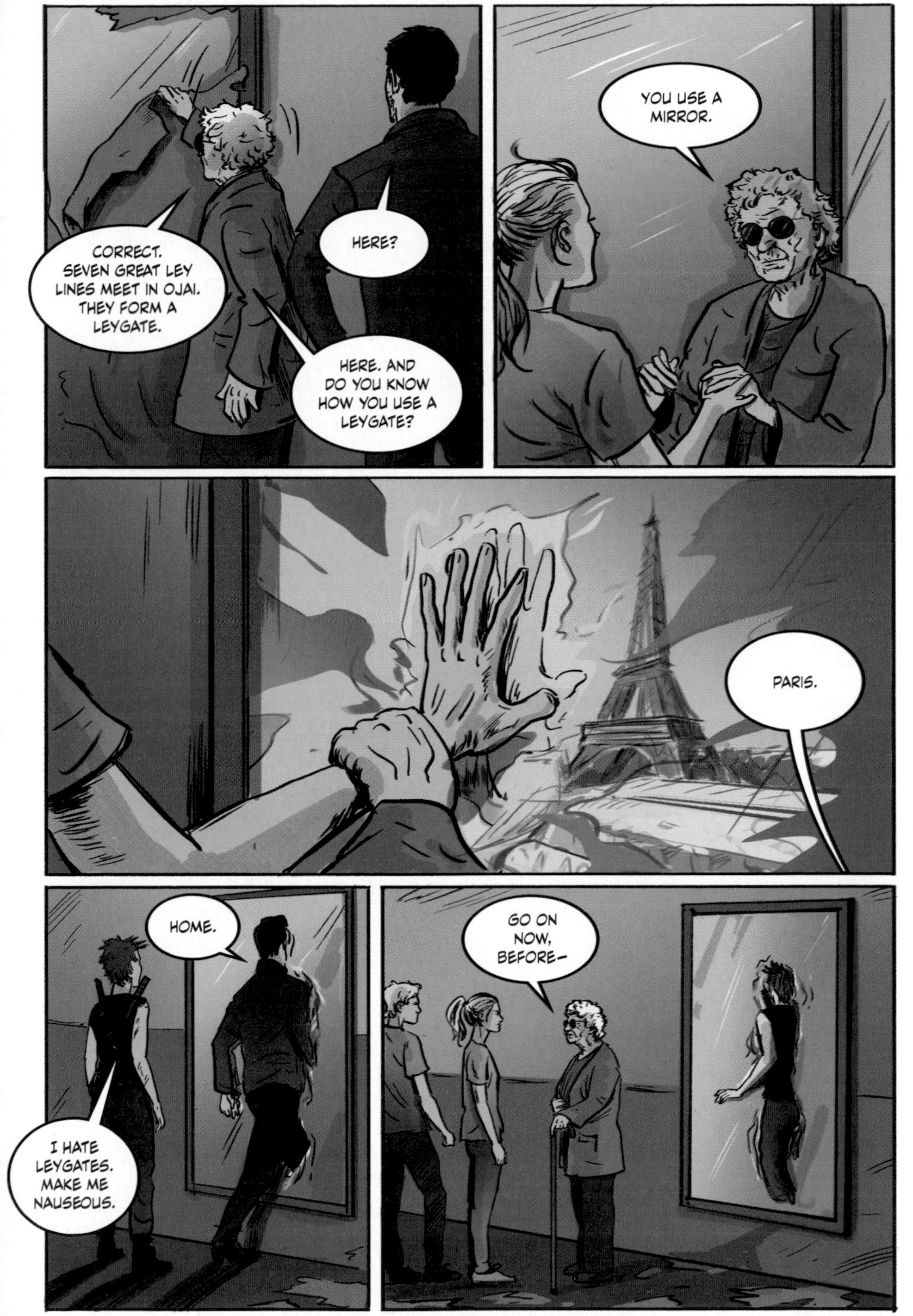
CORRECT. SEVEN GREAT LEY LINES MEET IN OJAI. THEY FORM A LEYGATE.
HERE?
HERE. AND DO YOU KNOW HOW YOU USE A LEYGATE?
YOU USE A MIRROR.
PARIS.
HOME.
I HATE LEYGATES. MAKE ME NAUSEOUS.
GO ON NOW, BEFORE–

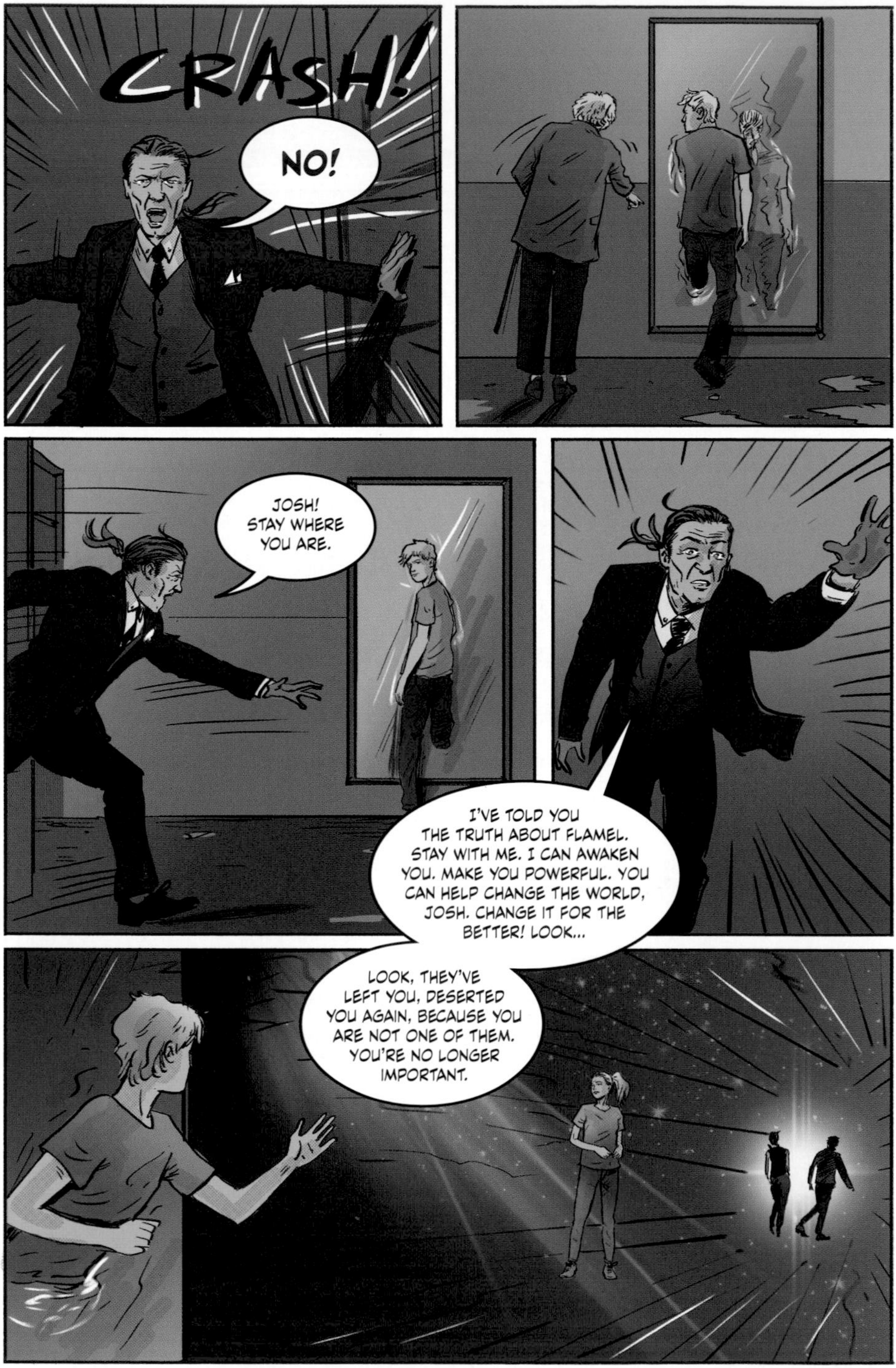
CRASH!
NO!
JOSH! STAY WHERE YOU ARE.
I'VE TOLD YOU THE TRUTH ABOUT FLAMEL. STAY WITH ME. I CAN AWAKEN YOU. MAKE YOU POWERFUL. YOU CAN HELP CHANGE THE WORLD, JOSH. CHANGE IT FOR THE BETTER! LOOK...
LOOK, THEY'VE LEFT YOU, DESERTED YOU AGAIN, BECAUSE YOU ARE NOT ONE OF THEM. YOU'RE NO LONGER IMPORTANT.

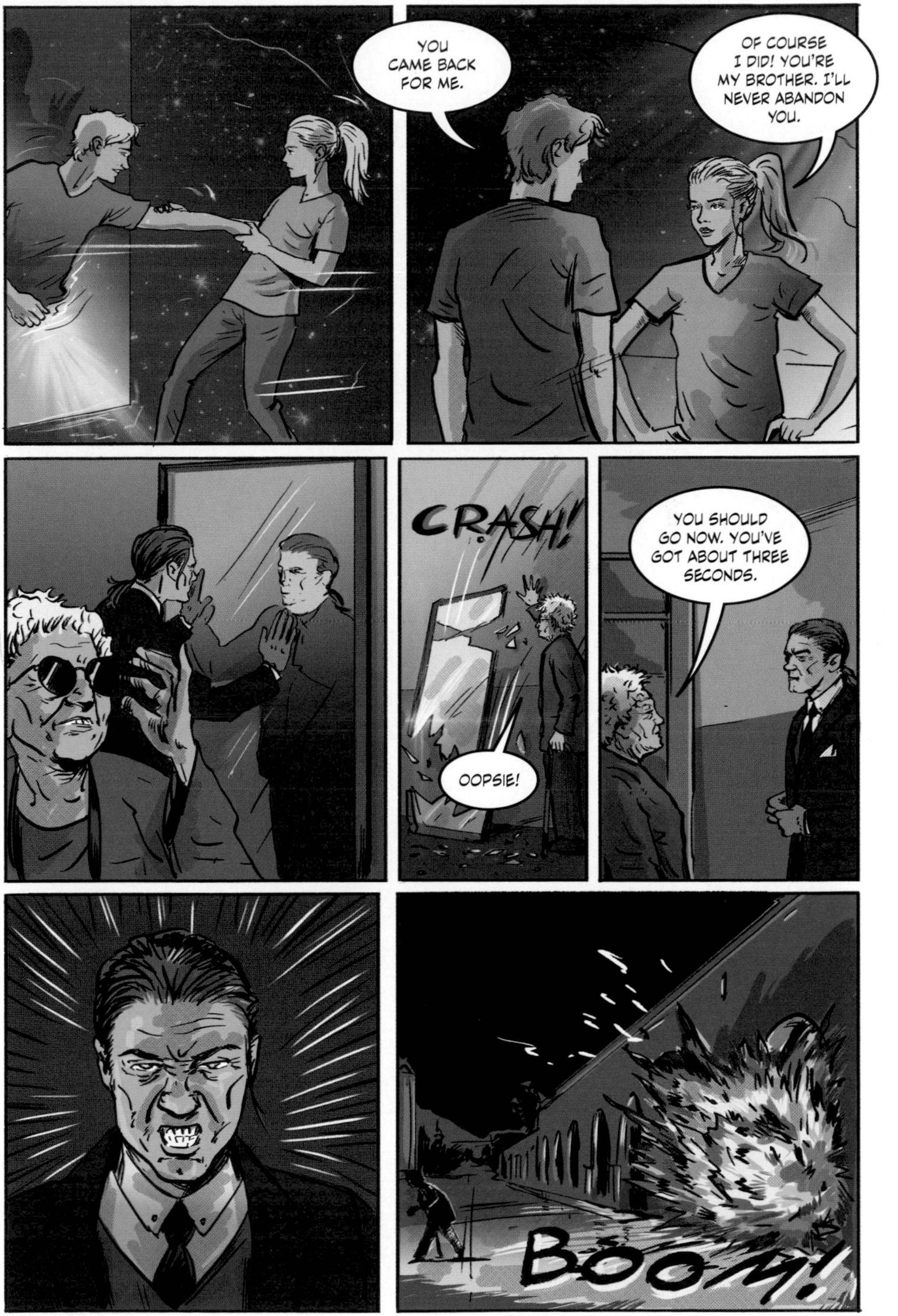
YOU CAME BACK FOR ME.
OF COURSE I DID! YOU'RE MY BROTHER. I'LL NEVER ABANDON YOU.
CRASH!
OOPSIE!
YOU SHOULD GO NOW. YOU'VE GOT ABOUT THREE SECONDS.
BOOM!

CHAPTER 40

OJAI VALLEY NEWS

═══ REPORTING FOR THE PEOPLE SINCE 1891 ═══

MOVIE COMPANY CAUSES MAYHEM IN SCENIC OJAI

The latest in a long line of horror movies from Enoch Studios caused traffic mayhem and more than a little confusion in downtown Ojai yesterday. The special effects were a bit too realistic for some locals, and emergency services were inundated with calls from people who claimed that the dead were walking the streets.

The spokesperson for John Dee, chairman of Enoch Films, a division of Enoch Enterprises, apologized profusely for the confusion, blaming it on a power outage and an unseasonable fog that swept in as they were about to shoot a scene from their new movie. "It certainly made the extras look *extra* scary," his rep said. In a related incident, a drunk driver smashed through the historic Libbey Park fountain and into the recently restored pergola. Enoch Enterprises has promised to restore the fountain and pergola to their former glory.

LOCAL ANTIQUES SHOP DEVASTATED BY EXPLOSION

A gas explosion destroyed the shop of longtime Ojai resident Dora Witcherly late last night. An electrical fault ignited solvents used by the owner to clean, polish, and restore her antiques. Miss Witcherly was in the shop's back room when the explosion occurred and was unharmed and apparently unconcerned by her brush with death. "When you've lived as long as I have, nothing much surprises you." She has promised to reopen the shop in time for the holidays.

CHAPTER 41

ALCATRAZ
FLAMEL. CHILDREN SAFE. OJAI. LEYGATE PARIS
IT IS ENDING. IMMORTAL.
ON THE CONTRARY, IT IS NOW ONLY JUST BEGINNING.

To be continued...

ABOUT THE AUTHOR

MICHAEL SCOTT is an authority on mythology and folklore, and one of Ireland's most successful authors. A master of fantasy, science fiction, horror, and folklore, he was hailed by the *Irish Times* as "the King of Fantasy in these isles." Look for the six books in his *New York Times* bestselling The Secrets of the Immortal Nicholas Flamel series: *The Alchemyst, The Magician, The Sorceress, The Necromancer, The Warlock,* and *The Enchantress,* as well as *The Lost Stories Collection,* a short story collection set in the Flamel universe.

dillonscott.com

NICOLE ANDELFINGER was crafting stories back when jelly shoes were cool. She continues to dwell in the realms of magic, monsters, and myth. When not changing her hair color or writing comics for some of her favorite franchises, such as Power Rangers, Jim Henson's Dark Crystal: Age of Resistance, The Dragon Prince, and others, she works a day job best described as "emails." She lives with her absolutely, most decidedly perfect cat in Los Angeles.

CHRIS CHALIK is a graphic novel artist, illustrator, and storyboard artist. Originally from Poland, he was born into a family with German and Russian roots. He has provided illustrations for Penguin Random House, Oxford University Press, Barrington Stoke, Benchmark Education, and many other publishers. Additionally, he has worked with multiple advertising agencies in Europe, contributing to storyboards for TV commercials. His work has been exhibited twice in Poland.

GRAPHIC NOVELS FOR EVERY YA READER

THE SECRETS OF THE IMMORTAL
NICHOLAS FLAMEL
THE ALCHEMYST
MICHAEL SCOTT

THE MAGIC FISH
TRUNG LE NGUYEN

NEW YORK TIMES BESTSELLING AUTHOR
david levithan
ILLUSTRATED BY dion mbd
every day
THE GRAPHIC NOVEL

BLUE DELLIQUANTI

TARA O'CONNOR
FLY BY NIGHT

THE MONTAGUE TWINS
THE WITCH'S HAND
BY NATHAN PAGE & DREW SHANNON

HIDDEN SYSTEMS
Water, Electricity, the Internet, and the Secrets Behind the Systems We Use Every Day
DAN NOTT

Jessi Zabarsky
Coming Back

SUNCATCHER
JOSÉ PIMIENTA

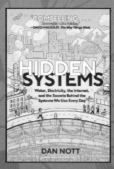

RH GRAPHIC

RHCBooks.com • A GRAPHIC NOVEL ON EVERY BOOKSHELF

1449E